Invocation

Complete *Invocation* Books I-VI
Published by Critical Documents May 2013
www.plantarchy.us

ISBN 978-1497562134

The cover photo is "First Forests in Space"
by Lorqiu Bilnxk, and includes artwork by Magda Boreysza.
The title font is Memory Lapses by Eduardo Recife.
Version 2.1. Printed by CreateSpace.

PROLOGUE

This is the story of—

Flip. I fibbed already.

I was going to say, "This is the story of how we got here."

Sounds like a safe opener, right?

"Here" could be anywhere. "Here" could be kissing Mr Darcy, having both finally got over ourselves.

Or "here" could be kneeling on the shore, dying with grief, because some dumb messenger forgot to switch black sails for white ones.

Or "here" could be out on that sea, rolling on darkness and foam, rowing ourselves towards some monstrous fish, and optimistically bouncing bits of pokey metal off his back.

Only the fib wasn't "here." The fib was "the."

This is — a *story, indefinite article — of how we all got here. A story of Veil, of Chancel, and everything else.*

I better warn you. It's a real story's story. When the stories go for a pyjama party, when the stories turn out the lights, this could be a story the stories would tell.

Oh, you'll see what I mean.

BTW, Moby Dick, or, The White Whale *is now one of my Top Ten "books with lots of out-of-date facts about whales." Can't remember how that story begins. "That damn whale would be the end of me, I could feel it!" — I think that's right?*

I'll do what I do best. I'll borrow someone else's. Someone who really knows how to start this off right. Dear Diary would do. "Dear Diary, I will never forget the wondrous events which transpired this morning . . ."

Or . . . I *know . . .*

"Sing, muse!"

Okay. I'll be back. For now, let's flip over to . . .

Book One

"You Can't Put Your Arms Around a Memory."

— Francoise Cactus

"Caaall me!"

Yeesh, Myfanwy mused. *Thought I just* did*!*

"Byebyebyebyeb—" Kitty's trilling voice vanished.

Myfanwy was only slightly cross. It was very Kitty to leave you four garbled voicemails then — when you phoned back half-panicked — to be so deep into some glam X with the Asians she had zero time to talk to you.

Myfanwy was used to it. She gave a sigh and gazed across her bed to her desk, where her powered-down tablet crowned a towering pyramid of Revulsion Notes.

Everyone was on edge nowadays. Next weekend the Tories were launching their newer, taller National Terror thermometer. Gold was at an all time high . . . or low, or whevs — either way, *terrifying*, right? Plus of course it was alleged strange gentlemen had been idling round the grounds of St Jerome's Senior School.

Revision.

With a yelp Myfanwy dove in under her duvet. The fabric felt cool on her cheeks. Through the tunnel of covers, illuminated by eldritch phone light, she wriggled on her tummy and elbows. Images danced in her hands. She scrolled to Paddy's glowing icon and gave him a good old tap.

Two rings. "Myffed!" Paddy obliged. "How's skiving, cuz? Enjoying the snow?"

Myfanwy poked her head into the light, mildly surprised at the angle at which she'd emerged.

"It's like snow in *here,*" she hazarded.

"Hmm?"

"Tissues!"

"Eww. You feeling a bit better yet?"

Myfanwy sniffed pitifully, just for Paddy's benefit. "I just can't *focus.* You know when you've read a whole page and suddenly you're like, 'What have I just read?'"

"Welcome to my world, cuz."

"So how's school anyway?"

"Uh, Myffed? An historic snowball fight has broken out in every east London borough. How could I *possibly* —"

"You're such a wasteman, Pad! God, is *anyone* actually in school today?"

"No A-Levels this year, trust. Down some Lemsips, help me run this crew off this corner?"

"Be careful, Dappy. Getting dark. They're almost certainly bigger than you."

"They may sling more than Lemsip too."

In one corner of Myfanwy's full-length mirror — over which her stuffed mouse, Object Petite A, precariously roosted — there hovered a curved fragment of a normal-looking girl, with a normal tangle of dark curls, and an abnormally rosy red nose. This fragment remonstrated her with tear-filled eyes.

"See ya Myffed," Paddy said. He added, "Feel better, yeah?"

"Yup. See you Pad. Make that — alas, *goodbye forever*!"

Myfanwy shifted angle. Lamplight filled the tears like engulfing flame.

She was alone in the house.

Everyone was on edge nowadays. Paddy had picked up on the third ring — it was good when people did stuff like that.

Myfanwy puffed out her already prodigiously plump cheeks. Then she pumped out her flat chest. Then she jutted out her jaw, smoothing away her waddle.

What a vision, she thought.

Shifting her gaze from her image, she sought some equally dangerous distraction. There was none. On the edges of shelves and stuff, threadbare and ancient stuffed toys regarded her quest with skepticism.

Object Petite A, one of her parliament's most venerable members, seemed almost to shake his whiskerless snout in gentle admonishment.

Austria, thought Myfanwy, reaching for her History Revulsion and snuggling deep.

World War I was over.

*

Achoo!

Snow splashed from elms. Watery sun flickered in wrought-iron railings. Snow had made Myfanwy late. St Jerome's Junior School play-time was well underway as she scuttled, sniffing and skidding, up towards the Womyn's Castle at the crest of the hill.

How did the snow slow down the Tube? The Tube was tucked away underground and quite proud of the fact. It went to show, snow was sneaky. *Sneakier than you might think.*

Myfanwy groped for a tissue without success.

"Sugar," she muttered.

Behind the railings, little working groups of girls gathered at the margins, talking, speechifying, demonstrating the sacred Handstand, holding hands and showing each other precious things with cupped palms. Whereas everywhere else, mankind's tiniest conscripts were pushing one another over, brain-damaging each other with grim winter weaponry — emanating as brazenly as ever its ill-deserved aura of innocence and virtue — and improving details of four stately snow castles, the least of which already put Catherine the Great's ice palace in the shade.

Gaining the black run's summit, Myfanwy caught her breath and glowered at the distant coven comprising St Jerome Junior's three cowardly play-workers. The three of them were camped on the high East Stairway, by the entrance to the Junior School, whilst spread below them, the future generation progressively dwindled into two divided and futile genders, surveilled but unattended. Meh! No doubt wringing their hands, Myfanwy imagined, like three impotent wimpled princesses.

Thinking of wimples, Myfanwy lost her footing for one final wobble, one which could quite easily have dropped her off back at the foot of the hill, and then was safely through the doors of the Womyn's Castle.

As soon as she entered the warmth, the tap in her nose sprang open. She wasn't quite well yet. She groped about for a tissue. Gross. She was alone again, at least. Never mind, there would be tissues in the kitchen — oh yes there would! Ha ha ha ha ha ha!

For the gendering of the Womyn's Castle — that sweet fortress formerly known as the St Jerome's Senior School Sixth Form Centre — was something else altogether.

When, towards the end of last August, the odious (literally) Freelance Nemesis, Kevin Thomas, had devoted one of his perpetual elective double free periods to boiling his own wee over and over again in the Communal Kettle, in some mystifying but apparently gleefully malign attempt to permeate the Sixth Form Centre atmosphere with a miasma of his own metabolising, it became clear that Now Something Would Have To Be Done.

Myfanwy had been a member (a soft-spoken member, true, rather secretarial in aspect, but nonetheless her heart swelled as she remembered it, and after all hadn't Stalin just been the secretary, or something?) of the cross-clique vanguard of women and trans revolutionaries who had liberated the Sixth Form Centre from Kev, his wee, his mates, and Things Like That. One day boys would be allowed back in unaccompanied and without extensive paperwork. For now, the girls had stewardship, and a governmental regime of Transitional Gynocracy was in place.

The Womyn's Castle was now quite the Safe Space, thoroughly aired and given a decorously amateurish lick of paint in luminous pastel hues. There was a little library of magazines and books and a droll purple recommendations booklet. "If you liked . . . Beyoncé Knowles, Michelle Williams and Kelly Rowland, *Soul Survivors*, why not try? . . . Mary Wollstonecraft, *The Rights of Woman*." There were cushions and hangings. There was for instance a print of Pieter Bruegel's *Jagers in de Sneeuw* — Myfanwy didn't know how she'd ever lived without it.

Obv the nastier boys claimed victory too — the Womyn's Castle supposedly was their scorched earth, a realm of piss and chaos where only scags and puta would now venture.

Myfanwy looked about with satisfaction. Most people, when they think "scorched earth," don't think "cosy and well-appointed." Through in the kitchen there would also be soft, strong "myn-sized" (actually max-sized), Kleenex tissues in the far left cupboard, procured with petty cash from the Communal Kitty. There would be a Colourful Little Sign up beside it saying who was responsible for stocking what and with what funds, a highly democratically accountable and transparent Colourful Little Sign. Two collection jars by the draining rack completed the domestic economy of the Sixth Form Centre, one (coming along gradually) to recarpet the pool table, possibly in paisley, though it wasn't clear yet if that would be extra, and the other (fantastically successful, outstripping all expectations — last Myfanwy checked, only £11.13 to go) for a giant replica tapestry of Europa depicted as a grand medieval beauty, bearing an orb and sceptre, with England for her head and the Urals for ruffles of her robe, and so on, a tapestry which Myfanwy's BBF Kitty — Myfanwy's v. AWOL BFF, these days — had found for everyone on Etsy.

Not all the clientele of the Womyn's Castle seemed to fully appreciate the feminist rationale of the rebranding. Many of them, Myfanwy noted dubiously, understood the spelling of "Womyn" in the spirit of "Ye Olde Pubbe Luynche, £18.99" without noticing, let alone pondering, the removal of the syllable "men." But at least everyone cheerfully consented to it. That was politics for you — everyone had their own reasons for subscribing to the Overlapping Consensus, whether they thought it was wholly fair, or just Wholesome Fayre. It was only a pity Myfanwy's boypal Paddy wasn't allowed in.

"It's like mice," Kitty had reasoned. "They're lovely but if you don't put down traps for them, rats will come. Patrick Akifemwe is a mouse, and Kevin Thomas is, well, some kind of monstrous scorpion pig."

"Can we at least put down humane traps for Paddy?" Myfanwy had asked.

"At first," Kitty had said firmly.

Oh, I was so sure *I had a tissue*, thought Myfanwy. *Right. Nose, then cup of tea. Then bell will go. Oh God, oh God —*

Myfanwy sneezed.

"Bless you," said a boy.

*

"Kitty?"

"Hon?"

"Scare me half to death?"

"Hon, I thought you'd never ask! Are you all tucked up? Good, me too. Lie still now, and listen. Once there was a young girl called Myfanwy. She was true of heart and tremendously kind. Her long glossy curls fell in cascades like the massed triggers of sniper rifles."

"Ooh, thank you!"

"Myfanwy was a Junior Partner at an International Financial Services firm called Delight and Touch."

"I see. We are in the realms of pure fantasy. Explains my cool hair at least."

"You must be asking yourself — why wasn't a girl as kind and brave and sensible as Myfanwy already a full Equity Partner?"

"Because she was a woman?"

"Well, obv. But also, Myfanwy had two flaws! First, she was a daydreamer. Myfanwy's brain would meander far abroad, and when reality flooded in, she found herself making a vital presentation to the board!"

"Gasp."

"Two long rows of expectant executives stretched off into the distance. Everyone nodded gently at Myfanwy, rather like foam moving in the wake of a luxury cruise liner. Of course, Myfanwy was completely at sea!"

"Ooh, that is *good."*

"But Myfanwy's real weak point was her puppy fat. Myfanwy had the rosiest, chubbiest cheeks in the entire Financial Services sector."

"Wait, not sure I like this anymore."

"Have you heard of corporate headhunters? Well, when Delight and Touch recruited Myfanwy, they had to use a team of three *headhunters, two more than usual just to handle her cheeks."*

"Okay. Now you're just taking cheap shots."

"Myfanwy is a fictional character, Myfanwy. It's not my fault if you are over-identifying with the protagonist of my scarytale, whose chubby cheeks I shall now continue to chronicle."

"By all means. Continue your cheek shots."

"Thank you. Telephone touchscreens obviously were the bane of Myfanwy's existence. She had but to chuckle with merriment whilst closing a deal, or whilst begging guidance from her tall, glamorous, blonde BFF Kitty —"

"Here we go."

"— a young Senior Tax Partner, who worked for a rival and slightly larger firm — larger both in terms of staff and turnover and, in a way, vision —"

"And who had incredibly chiselled cheekbones?"

"Interestingly enough, that is true. Kitty was what you might call conventionally beautiful on that kind of scale of conventions where Scandinavians and Barbie dolls

dominate the upper reaches, though she was saved from sheer basic blandness by the detailing of her throat —"

"You promised not to fret. You can barely see it, Kitsy."

"— which held, for those with careful stares, a delicate plump point of adam's apple — an unusual throat, therefore, for a woman — a fragment of proverbial fruit which lent Kitty a disconcerting air, particularly if you weren't aware of it, gently bobbing to the rhythm of her wit. But we're talking about Myfanwy trying to use touchscreen phones, in a corporate context. She had but to chuckle merrily and her chubby cheeks were liable to hang up on her behalf! She screwed up a lot of stuff that way. In fact Myfanwy's cheeks were so epically chubby —'"

"Veto any more cheek stuff. Seriously, Kitty."

"As you wish. Myfanwy's character having been fleshed out —"

"'Flesh' being the operative word."

"— we may continue our scarytale! Ahem. Now, the house where Myfanwy lived had once been a small, private, and very exclusive mental asylum. Earlier I said Kitty was her BFF, but I meant to say husband *as well. Myfanwy and Kitty lived together with their mildly attractive and deeply autistic son, Simon Buckerton."*

"Oh, does Simon have *to be my son in this one?"*

"Hush, hon, I'm telling a story. I should have mentioned Myfanwy's third weakness, which really told in her Annual 360° Reviews *— Myfanwy always heard voices whispering to her in the night . . . and she was haunted by the noise of someone sawing something, back and forth, back and forth . . . by sounds of heavy splashes . . . and soft sobbing. Many times Myfanwy had been on the verge of promotion, when she had slammed her palms on the boardroom table and shrieked at the top of her voice, 'Can't you hear it? Can't you hear the terrible sawing? MAKE IT STOP! MAKE IT STOP!' A few coughs. 'Thank you, Myfanwy, for that most enlightening presentation on —' 'MAKE IT STOP!' She made people uncomfortable. Her wise and beautiful wife Kitty —"*

"Hubby."

"— hubby, soz — decided it was time they moved out of that spooky old asylum once and for all. As Kitty pointed out, the couple were now in a position to downscale slightly and go more central."

"And? Did they?"

"If only Myfanwy had listened! Myfanwy could have walked to work along the canal, and Simon Buckerton could have fallen into the catchment area for the extremely technical specialist care he by now needed, or, even better, into the canal. Idyllic!"

"What about Myfanwy's husband, Kitty? Was it handy for Kitty to get to work? It doesn't sound like Kitty to ignore her own interests."

"I'm v. glad you asked, because the rival firms where Myfanwy and Kitty worked happened to face each other across a picturesque courtyard —'"

"Can it have a cute little well in it?"

"— where stood a cute little well. So yes, it would have been handy for Kitty too. What

mixture of selflessness and self-interest moved her, we never shall never know! The corporate buildings had expanded backwards and sideways as much as they could. The well was a listed building, so the firms had never been able to expand forwards. Now they just grew up and up, adding more and more loftly pinnacles and turrets every day."

"Every day?"

"Well, every week. And yes, 'loftly.' Highly specialised construction workers had to clear nests of angels with flamethrowers."

"Bit cruel."

"Honestly, hon? A few singed tailfeathers. You should be more alive to the realities of Big Smoke real estate. Let's stay on-message though. Poor, foolish Myffy! Her ears resounding with sawing and sobs! Poor, weak, foolish, lowly, maggot-like Myffy! Imagine had she but heeded her hubby Kitty, and taken the property! Every morning they could have walked along the canal together. Then, just as their rival skyscrapers emerged from the jumbled skyline, Myfanwy could have crossed a picturesque humpbacked bridge, Then they could have continued to their offices along different banks, gradually getting lost in different commuter crowds. At about two o' clock they could have met for lunch, eating their wraps or salads on the low stone benches by the well. Idyllic!"

"I'd just eat the nuts stashed in my chubby cheeks."

"I'm not sure I follow, but alas, it was not meant to be, plus I should have mentioned Myfanwy's fourth and fifth weaknesses. Her fourth weakness was that she hallucinated strange mutilated figures begging for their lives. They phased in and out. 'Please. No. Please. Stop. Why are you doing this?' Myfanwy heard footsteps upstairs when she was downstairs in the kitchen, and when she was upstairs investigating, she heard water running downstairs . . . doors slamming when no one was home . . . and always the dreadful, awful sawing. Saw, saw, saw."

"Saw, saw, saw."

"Saw, saw, saw. Her fifth weakness was her temper and terrible stubbornness. She treated all these frightening apparitions as just another Career Challenge. The sort of thing women have to deal with all the time. She never wanted to leave the old asylum, never, no, never, *not even after digging up a Waitrose bag full of bloodied DIY tools at the foot of the garden."*

"She had thought to make a kale patch."

"Exactly. Kitty appealed to the interests of their tiny disturbed son, Simon Buckerton. Myfanwy and Kitty quarrelled terribly. Stress at work didn't help. Eventually they arose from the maelstrom, kissed and made up. They compromised on renovating. After a fresh lick of paint, and one or two other adjustments, they could turn over a new leaf."

"What? What happened? Kitty? Kitty! What happened when they tried to renovate the old asylum? I'm nervous, all right? Are you happy? I'm scared! Just tell me what happened, please!"

"Myfanwy was very, very tired. Decorators and handymen —"

"Handypersons."

*"— and suchlike swarmed upstairs and downstairs. They turned up the floorboards in Simon Buckerton's room, and reaching into the dark corners, drew out bags, from Waitrose, Sainsbury's, Pret. Inside were bones, all broken up and notched with signs of sawing, the notches filled with soft brown scabs. 'Don't be afraid, Kitty,' murmured Myfanwy. 'Don't be afraid, Simon. The former owner must simply have killed herself, and hid her own body under the floorboards! I bet now she wishes she'd thrown it in the canal!' The chief decorator, who for some reason was dressed in a police uniform, looked very pale, and told Myfanwy what she had just said didn't make any sense. 'Of course it makes sense,' snapped Myfanwy. Turning to Kitty, she implored, 'Tell him, Kitty. Tell him it makes sense.' The chief decorator asked Myfanwy who she was talking to. Myfanwy looked uncertainly to her loving husband, Kitty. 'It's okay, darling,' Kitty said quietly. 'You're doing fine.' She squeezed her hand supportively. Meanwhile, their idiot savant son was piecing together the bones. Myfanwy saw that it was a small skeleton, the skeleton of a child, about the same size as Simon Buckerton himself! For a moment Myfanwy was unsure of herself. For some reason Kitty looked a little tearful. But Kitty smiled encouragingly. Myfanwy flew into a rage at the decorators! '*You *put those remains there!' she accused three junior decorators. '*You *put them there to make me feel my intolerable shame! You hid my son's bones in his own room, to make him afraid of his own mother!' The chief decorator had left now — perhaps gone to a 'feds 'n' felons' fancy dress party? The three junior decorators all wore long white coats and carried clipboards. 'You tell 'em, mammy,' droned Simon Buckerton."*

"Not sure, Kitsy."

*"'It was all you!' Myfanwy fumed at them, by now an unstoppable juggernaut! 'You buried those bloodstained bones, then you hid all my son's things, and decorated his bedroom with this ridiculous white padding! Now get this thing *off *me!' Myfanwy, by the way, was trussed up in a straitjacket — like the stumpiest, saddest Maypole ever. The first junior decorator sadly asked Myfanwy if she still believed she was standing in her son's room. Tears were streaming down Kitty and Simon Buckerton's normal-sized cheeks. 'Please, please be kind to Myfanwy,' implored Kitty. 'It's *my *fault, not hers. I knew how stressed she was. Then whilst she was busy with moving house for us — it was my idea for us to move — my team beat her team in an important bid. She just flipped!' But the junior interior decorators ignored Kitty. It was like she wasn't even there."*

"Can we wrap this up? I think —"

*"They weren't junior interior decorators, they were *psychiatrists! *Do you get it?!"*

"I see the way it's going, I must admit."

"Don't be so sure. 'Where did you hide Kitty's body, still beautiful in death?' the second junior decorator snapped. 'The feds have searched your old house and your new one,' cried the third junior decorator. 'Is it time to dredge the canal? Or did you stuff her down the well?' 'You're all crazy!' muttered Myfanwy wildly. 'How could I have murdered them? I love them so much, and besides, they're standing right there!' 'Do you still see them?' said the first junior interior decorator softly. She was a beautiful hilarious artistic Scottish stroke

East Asian girl who was new to the asylum, by the way. That's by the by. 'You have to let them go, Myfanwy, pal,' said this junior decorator, 'or you'll never get better.' The three junior decorators left, closing and locking the padded door behind them. All around her, Myfanwy heard murmuring voices, running water, sobbing and sawing. 'I'm not crazy, am I?' she asked Kitty and Simon Buckerton. Kitty stood on her right and took her left hand, and Simon Buckerton stood on her left and took her right —"

"Don't get it."

"Straightjacket, hon."

"Right, soz."

"Simon Buckerton took her right as best he could, since he was rearranging chunks of his body like a Rubick's cube. Kitty's hair floated around her, as if underwater. 'It's alright,' Kitty soothed her. 'Hush my darling. Don't listen to the pesky decorators. We'll make the best of it. We'll turn over a new leaf.' There they stood. There they stand still. The end."

". . . I'm not sure about the representation of —"

"Except that was the fake *end, because social media changes everything! Next, Myfanwy immediately whapped out her phone and went on Twitter, Weibo, Hexxus Nexus, Cynical April, etc. The next time the three junior decorators rolled through the door, there were* four *of them standing there — Myfanwy, Kitty, Simon Buckerton, plus Simon Buckerton's intriguing somewhat corsair-ish BFF Lewis Porteous. 'Let me introduce Lewis Porteous,' said Myfanwy breezily. Lewis grinned and waved. He smiled wolfishly at Kitty too. He had a pickaxe in his neck. 'But there's no one there,' said the first junior decorator sadly and patronisingly, ticking random boxes on her clipboard. They all ticked their boxes. 'We'll see about that,' said Myfanwy through slit eyes. That was just a hint of things to come. The next time the three junior decorators trooped in, there was an enormous house party underway. The whole gang was there — Myffy, Kitty, Simon, Lewis, Kevin Thomas, Sid Fairfax, Adika, Anu, Dora JayJay, Namond, Sean, Frances, Toal, Esi, Kojo —"*

"St Jerome's Senior School's finest. The good, the bad and the Muggles."

"— even like those new chiquitas, Lucia and Jemima —"

"Not sure about them to be honest."

"— anyway, they *were there too! It was a totally amazing party! The three junior decorators looked smug and softly intoned stuff like 'uhh . . . but there's nobody there' but nobody was really listening. They were just partying. Woo! Everyone had like guts pouring out and slit throats and axes in their heads and stuff, but all really tastefully done and not at all Halloweeny or Gothy."*

"Not sure I can picture that."

"Like for instance Adika's entrails might be piled up in a sort of beautiful low-cut ruff."

"Okay, no, yeah, I can picture that."

"Even though the three junior decorators claimed they couldn't see anyone, everyone at

the party thought they looked very awkward and out of place. They ended up just talking to themselves in a little huddle the whole evening. Myfanwy didn't feel triumphant or anything, just a bit sorry for them. Later on, as the sun rose over London, the party actually left Simon Buckerton's room and ran through the streets. They ended up in a conga line — not literally obv. — meandering along the canal, and climbing over the humpbacked bridge. This proud curve of hurt, partying bods flowed and popped pills and snogged and laughed and felt that special energy and threw shapes and had crazy deranged conversations that made them feel truly alive. The three interior decorators, or psychiatrists or whatever they were, sort of tagged along next to Myfanwy, faces red as bricks, saying really lame petty things like, 'You don't believe you've left your padded cell, do you? You'll never get better unless you face the truth!' But Myfanwy cried, 'Let's put it to the vote! See what these *guys say!' and all her many thousands upon thousands of partying dead friends cheered. After that she more or less ignored those three puffing naysayers. Basically sappers and buzz-killers, you know? Clipboards, you know? What's the moral?"*

"Since when do ghost stories have morals?"

"Ghost stories so *do have morals. 'Don't get out of your car under any circumstances. The person licking you under your bed is not your dog.'"*

"Um, okay."

"Besides, these are scarytales! They're different to ghost stories."

"Let's not split scares."

"And the moral here is . . ."

"You haven't thought of one, have you?"

"I so have! The moral is that, 'Sometimes . . . stuff is really annoying . . . and you, like, just have to let annoying things about your past drift away . . . and just like forget about them, and go wherever the next big warehouse party is . . . and stuff like that.' Also the other moral is, 'You can't just bolt social media onto your business model and expect everything to be okay and run itself. You have to have a proper strategy in place, and maybe that's something that, like, administrative entities charged with differentiating the sane from the insane should take into account a bit more, or they'll find they're playing catch-up.' The real *end."*

"Um . . . okay. Kitty you are my BFF and I love you to bits, but I don't think I get it. Did I kill Lewis and Adika and all them too?"

"I'm so glad you asked! It's left deliberately ambiguous, hon. The ending is more just an ecstatic image of liberation. For too long people have focused on the 'death' part of the so-called 'Danse Macabre' *or 'Dance With Death'. What about the actual* dancing *part? Winding and throwing shapes and just generally partying? Memento move-your-body, memento move-your-body —"*

"Sugar. Your stories used to be so funny. Then they were so scary. Now they're just so strange. *Yeesh, what was* that*?"*

"Me yawning."

"Scariest part so far."

"No, scariest part is that you have to sleep in the same bed as the dark and seething genius who germinated that deranged tale. Starting now, BTW."

"Thank you, hon. It hurt but it hurt good."

"My pleasure. Sleep now."

"Night then. Um, Kitty?"

"What?"

"Do you think Simon fancies me, or Sarah Cameron, or Anu, or Moo? It wasn't actually clear in the tale."

"God, sweetie, he's a boy*! He probably fancies you all for different reasons, or at least in different positions."*

"Appreciate, but do you think —"

"Don't hype. I'm sure one day he'll kiss your mouth and neck and run his fingers through your lovely curly hair."

"Like fidgeting snipers."

"And whisper you sweet nothings. Emphasis on the nothing. Personally I think you can do better. But you know what I think. Goodnight, mate. The real *goodnight."*

"Yeah. Maybe. Goodnight, Kitsy. Love you."

"Likewise, babes. Sweet screams, Myfanwy Morris. Mwahahaha!"

"But in your considered opinion —"

"The witching hour is over, Myfanwy. All the widdle witches are tucked up in their cauldrons."

"Night Kit."

"Night hon." A moment's silence. Then, very softly, almost a snuffling sound of a sleeping person, one last evil laugh. "Mwahahahaha."

*

No no not a boy in the Womyn's Castle! — something more acute!

A man!

He was dressed in a shellsuit, basically — shimmering black Adidas jacket, zipped open over nondescript T-shirt, plus joggers — and he was just closing the kitchen door, revolving to face her on a pair of deeply pimping trainers.

Myfanwy's nose was running like crazy.

"Can I help you?" she said.

Myfanwy hoped the saturated tissue that she'd finally discovered and stuffed over her nose muffled that squeak somewhat. She'd meant to sound formidable and prim. Instead what hung in the air like frozen breath was unmistakably . . . *scared* . . .

Or a boy after all? Say a *young* man, early twenties — somewhat Irish? — no, elfin — no, *vampiric* — tall and dark-haired, pale, rosy-cheeked, with wide, bright green eyes. Wild eyes. She had to confess, as to those chiselled features shifting to admit that disquieting grin, there was — in a Naughties sort of way, mind you — something quite attractive intruding on the sanctity of the Womyn's Castle. Yet there was also another quality too, subtle yet rich, faded yet impossible to ignore once you caught it — something shrewd, vicious, and permanently unlikeable.

A slim gold chain circled the intruder's neck.

"I doubt it," he said. To the unsavoury aura Myfanwy had already detected, his voice an additional stratum of insulting self-congratulation. It wasn't just a Bad Council Estate sort of voice. It was an I-Swaggeringly-Rule-The-Bad-Council-Estate-And-Make-It-Bad sort of voice.

Perhaps a bit Midlands too.

Finally he turned away his hungry stare. He wandered across the room and peered through one of the high little windows, the ones that faced down the hill. Myfanwy felt her confidence return. "Obviously you're not enrolled here," she pointed out. "Do you know one of the pupils?"

Something was sticking out of his tracksuit pocket.

A ski mask?

"Not really," he muttered. "You just reminded me of someone I used to — look, I'm a bit busy here —"

"Only there aren't meant to be men in here at all," Myfanwy blurted nervously. This was getting less funny. She felt vulnerable. She should do the sensible thing and run. "Um, I don't suppose Transitional Gynocracy means anything to you?"

He was just staring intently out the window.

"No," Myfanwy sighed. "Well, think of it like 'the Girls' Locker Room.' You have inadvertently wandered into 'the Girls' Lock—'"

He grunted. "When's the striptease? Just let me know when you're done."

Myfanwy studied the back of his neck. The gold necklace lay against the vertebral ridges. No stubble, just soft, light down.

"Excuse me?"

"All those layers. We'll be here all day."

"Are you being deliberately provocative?"

Turning over his shoulder, he flicked his gaze over her in a way that made her skin crawl. "My mistake. You're an oil painting. Alright from afar, and all that."

"I'm not going to let you get me angry. But I may have to ask you to l—"

"Keep it in your knickers then," he growled angrily. "Forever, for all I care. Christ. You're really not a patch on her."

And he left.

That was unexpected. Did it count as victory? She hadn't pronounced the '—eave'.

"A patch on — what? Huh? Hey!" she called.

Stupid arse.

Myfanwy hesitated but a heartbeat, then bust through the door into the kitchen. The honour of the Castle was at stake! If this vile and potentially vampiric — no, *certainly Satanic* — trespasser hadn't had permission to enter, he would at least need permission to *leave.*

The kitchen was empty. She glanced at the new Communal Kettle, then busted out onto the ice.

*

Halfway down the hill, the car door slammed with a deep reassuring clunk, the kind of clunk that must have built artfully into its acoustics by a team of elfin engineers, because the natural tendency of its luxurious lightweight material would be to close like a teaspoon tinkling into a teacup.

This was a real Jill Bond ride. A luxury Lexus, with a risqué, road-hugging figure, armoured in incandescent, high-gloss Performance Grey, its cadaverous bower of designer leather and designer shadows vaguely visible within. Powerful — the moment it hit you, it'd take your breath away.

A nice car, driven by a nice lady, grinning, muscular, and walking straight for Myfanwy. She was pretty, square-faced, quite made-up, with big blue eyes, her brunette bob parted at the side. Mid-thirties, Myfanwy guessed. Still there was something girlish about her smile. It was a smile she'd seen round St Jerome's before. She wore a deep blue satin scarf, and her ample set of shoulders filled out a three-quarters-length jacket in crimson leather.

"Oh, excellent!" the woman purred, snapping her pair of John Lennon sunnies shut in one hand. "Wotcha! Just the person I need!"

"Did someone just scamper this way?" Myfanwy asked. "A man?"

The woman stopped, inclined her head with a wounded expression. One wing of her bob fell away from a big gold hoop. In the big sky behind birds wheeled.

Myfanwy babbled on. "He just wandered into our Castle — our Sixth Form Centre." This didn't seem like enough. "We have a visitors system. He seemed to be a rapist!"

Ooh, too much?

"Golly! What did he look like, this person? Early twenties, perchance?"

"Um, I guess. Pale, dark hair. Sportswear, gold chain. Sorry, I have a cold."

The smile was back, but uncertain. "Bit sexy?" she asked. "And v. tall?"

"*Ish,*" said Myfanwy, surprised. "And *noo!*"

The woman's focus was no longer on Myfanwy. She swept her gaze up the hill, then along the elms to the school-gate.

Myfanwy stared at the tracks her Lexus had left. "Wait," she said. "I think I meant '*noo!*' and '*ish.*'"

"Okay," said the woman. "You have to trust me. Get in the car!"

They eyed each other warily, then laughed simultaneously.

"Worth a try," the woman added. Now she was scribbling something. "Okay, take my card then. Let's hope he's not who I think he is. Because if he is, believe me, he's dangerous. So next time you see him, call me."

"You seem stressed."

"Or if you feel you're being followed, or . . ." A little furrow appeared in the woman's brow. "If you feel like you're . . . *losing yourself* . . ."

Suddenly Myfanwy was staring at the card and the car door was closing with its high-tech clunk. The engine ignited, quiet and heavy like a world full of snow, and woman slipped down her window.

"Hey — I ain't strictly relevant, when you report this. If you *do* mention me, I have certain, uh, ways of knowing that you have. In which case I may not answer your call. But it's all up to you. I can't make your decisions for you."

"Well, obviously. What are you talking about? This card doesn't even have a name on it!"

"My name is Mara Drago-Ferrante. And *you* don't even *have* a card on you, Myfanwy. Take care, girlfriend!"

The Lexus didn't wheelspin, but glid away over the packed ice as though it were asphalt.

*

Myfanwy bit her lower lip and wiped her nose with her sleeve. The woman — Mara? — had had one of those unplaceable accents, like a bad movie actor.

She walked a little way down the hill. She felt queasy from adrenaline. He was nowhere to be seen. It was still play-time. *They look more like muffins than children*, Myfanwy thought. It pleased her that none of the little ones could be pierced by a falling icicle. Any icicle would simply bounce back to the place it had broken off — and instantly reseal, no doubt, bound by the cold of the world.

Everyone was on edge nowadays. The Christmas spending spike had been quite unprecedented. Like a Christmas Shard. The green group *Spare Norwich!* had been excommunicated from the Climate Change Alliance. "They did not share our universalist ethos." So far, eight out of nine pupils in her Art class, Myfanwy had noted, featured human skulls in their Final Portfolios.

Some weren't even really grinning.

Why hadn't she told Mara the whole truth? About what happened when she'd confronted him outside the Womyn's Castle?

With her free hand Myfanwy rubbed her own bruised skull. Her hair there was wet. Frozen particles sparkled on her fingers. Apart from the frantically scribbled number, there were just nine letters on the card which Myfanwy gripped so tightly, nine letters spelling out — in a somewhat fanciful font — *Sing, Muse.*

No reason to trust her either.

She watched her white breath until the bell went.

*

Nerves all flaming . . . skin all frazil ice . . .

Gold was . . . at an all time high or low or whevs . . . either way, terrifying, right? . . . gold lies in the ground, no longer in veins, but in long nerves now . . . pimping trainers with naient *Nike swoosh, padding softly through the slush . . .*

What do girls lie in the ground as? As ice at the bottom of a Slush Puppy, with all the syrup sucked out of us . . .

Cauldron of Souls . . . cold cinders . . .

What was happening? Where was this place?

Gulls visit . . . they want to veil you with their wings . . . think sense, girl . . .

No, not gulls . . . snow . . . snow angels flapping nearby . . . like Negro Slaves in Gone with the Wind, *with palm fans raising and falling, apparently softly . . . ha ha . . . ha ha . . .*

Somewhere on the sea, perhaps, or near to it.

The city was becoming clearer now. Its fragmented outer walls within it . . .

Yes . . . she could almost tell . . . where the city lay . . .

*

"Why *lie* to her, Myffy? Why not *tell her* this guy attacked you?"

"Fam, 'attack' is *such* an exaggeration! All he did was let go my hand. That's normally what you *want* from strange prowly men."

Myfanwy stood in the Glass Room — what everyone except her and Dad called the conservatory — on the phone to Kitty. In the snowy garden below, the neighbour's tabby kept watch of a bird. Muffled rock music rose through the parquet. Dad was in chef mode downstairs.

"So why omit it?" said Kitty.

"I've thought about that. I guess it was her smile. She used one of the smiles the Asians use. I can't *trust* that."

"Um —"

"Yeah, that's what everyone calls you and your new friends, BTW? The Asians, or the Cool Kids, which is even *more* ridiculous, and do *not* roll your eyes."

"How you tell on phone, I roll my eyes?"

"It's your long luscious lashes, my lovely. They stir freak whirlwinds. Woosh! Woosh! Woosh!"

"Cool. Gotta go. *Call* the chiquita, yeah?"

Myfanwy eyed the wicker bin, where the confetti she'd shredded of Mara Drago-Ferrante's calling card lay strewn on a soggy tissues cairn. "Exams in less than three months," she said. She swapped her phone to the opposite shoulder. "Then it's my eighteenth. Then a summer to remember, trust! You know, the one from the movies, where we go to the creek and cry?"

"Um, what? Is this all apposite, Myffy?"

"I don't want to get sucked into some weird adventure at this stage in my life. Seriously, it was like one of your scarytales or something. I mean, it's so good to talk to you though, Kitty. It's been so —"

"You're so on *edge* nowadays. Bye, hon. Call me? Byebyeby—"

"Byebyebyebyebye," mimicked Myfanwy to the dead line, making it like machine-gun fire. In her mind, a cardboard target of Kitty flipped over, riddled with openings.

Like Myfanwy had flipped over, that fateful day.

Oh, Woman! Your cause is just, but then you fall over!

For no sooner had Myfanwy left the Castle than she was sliding on her bum. And there *he* was, reaching out his hand. And she — in her instant of infinite disgrace — had reached for his blurry fingers. Linking, wrapping his gently, being steadied and lifted up. It was simple instinct. The instinct of a rapt, senseless creature.

Then he laughed at her and let go.

Had she hit her head *then*, or was it earlier? She wasn't sure. She'd lain her limbs down, utterly defeated, a soft Spring plant sprung too early.

Once, when she was quite little, Myfanwy had been taken to see *Swan Lake on Ice*. Mum had already been sick, even then, she remembered. And she remembered how one dancer, underestimating her own suppleness, had kicked herself in the back of the head with her skate blade, and blood had trickled on the ice. Myfanwy could still picture her just lying there, the dancer transfixed by her own body's betrayal. As though ambushed and abused by some new avant-garde Station of the Cross.

Now she thought she knew how that dancer felt.

Myfanwy, lain down where she belonged, listening to the intruder's mocking laughter wandering away down the hill.

Seconds passed, or centuries.

They were seconds, to be fair. She sat up. Frozen, but not solid. She got up. She had to get up. Life went on . . . ignominous, ginormous, insulted life.

She dragged her heels through the snow, like a divested bridezilla scuffing aside the crystalline chiffon of her innocence. And who was the first person she met?

Mara Drago-Ferrante.

This confident, intent, mature, mysterious woman, dismounting her magnificent technological steed.

No, it hadn't been distrust, which made her hold the whole truth back from Mara Drago-Ferrante, or made her shred up her card. It had been envy and shame.

How *could* she have told someone like that?

Whoever Mara Drago-Ferrante was, whatever she wanted, Myfanwy knew she never would have taken that hand and trusted it to hold hers.

*

Sphinxes. A high balcony.

Gently rocked side-to-side by something, Myfanwy was either dreaming or playing make-believe.

Away to the left, a dark and ornate tower. Down below, a nebulous hellmouth of iron and light. She was exultant. So happy. Flakes of snow. Floating in complex shapes, like flakes of gull. She smelled meat. Giddy with happiness.

Black pillars on a far hill. They danced for her. Snow floated more furiously lower down. Static gusted into functional caves which deepened and deepened, deepened perhaps forever . . . flurries of flakes across and along long sinuous lines, crossing and twisting . . . sinews of darkness . . . snakes, many millions of miles in length, flowing over each other's armoured backs . . .

Behind her, a presence. Hands on her hips. Cold, cold lips brushing her neck . . . she smiled . . . turned . . .

Oh, yes . . .

Myfanwy's eyes flicked open. A ridiculous dragon of the City of London was raspberrying her.

She breathed a sigh of relief.

Not yet her stop. She poked her tongue back at it.

Myfanwy had woken up that morning to the usual edgy news — a supermoon would soon grace the evening skies, Simon Cowell was now definitely dead, bees were attacking Indian paramilitaries.

She *had* planned to do something with Kitty. But it had been ages ago they'd made the date and Kitty, obvs, had forgot. Turned out Kitty had private tuition scheduled, *then* therapy with Professor MacAonghas, *then* parent stuff all afternoon. So, work then. It was defo time for Myfanwy to Get Her Head Down, re Art, but Get Her Head Down into which luminous sepia kinetoscope? Myfanwy had had a leisurely brekky with Dad and made a Tate date with Pad, ostensibly to get Portfolio ideas. The perfect synthesis of work and play!

Slowly the bus nosed into central London. Her seat was upstairs at the front. Gilded monuments glid by on her plane of existence. A black stone bayonet menaced her. Her jumper was pillowed against the juddering window. She lay her head against it again, enjoying late winter sun on her face.

January had been well mild.

All over the world February had been unseasonable — just like the one before, and the one before that. Myfanwy really had to wonder how many more such showings were necessary from February, before everyone gave in and ceded February its *very own season* — the People's Democratic Season of February, in which (as Dad put it) "everyone is to have everyone else's weather," and therefore a season when deep snow would cover all her beloved London (despite the best efforts of her boypal Paddy and several genuine postcode crews to throw it back into the sky), and snowdrifts on roads would be daily salted with dwindling municipal cellars, and snowdrifts would rise deep and vast in the Vs of London's plane trees, and layer day-by-day along their long arms, heavy enough to snap off their fingers, or, if those drifts froze and refused to slide loose, heavy enough even to break their arms down defeated by their sides.

Whereas in the Arctic, presumably, the Feb tulips would unfurl, and badgers go nosing about with teacups of Pimm's in bright little cotton jackets.

Anyways.

Now, first week of March, and the only snow now was clumped in zigzags on the clean wet roofs of bus shelters and parked cars.

The sun made Myfanwy sleepy. Traffic and bus became nurse and cradle. She drowsed again.

Sphinxes. A high balcony. Away to the left, an ornate tower, like a thorn on steroids.

Myfanwy startled awake just as the bus pulled past her stop. Grabbing her sketchbook, she bashed the bell button and spiralled down the stairwell. She had to admit, there was something quite nice about those cold lips upon her neck.

Weird stupid recurring dreams! — you may already have my nights, but you leave me my days! Do you hear me, dreams?

*

Paddy and Myfanwy stood outside Tate Modern by the strands and bridges and building sites of the Thames. Blue cranes rose into the white sky. A white helicopter moved over the Shard.

At Myfanwy's feet was a pigeon's wing, faded and trampled into almost a fresco. It should have been gross but it was gorgeous.

"It's weird," Myfanwy said. "After you leave a museum, for a while everything looks like you're still inside one."

Paddy nodded. "Yeah. Reverie and Stanchion exhibition especially. *Gris-gris* and *muti*, funded by extractive industries. I think the twist will be that we *never really left the museum*."

"Trust," said Myfanwy vaguely, not sure what Paddy was talking about now. "*Anyway*," she added sharply, breaking the pigeon wing's spell, "what shall —"

That was when she saw Kitty.

Kitty was about a hundred metres away, up on the far end of the Millennium Bridge, and she was with *them*. The Asians, AKA the Cool Kids. The Playboy Owsla, unmistakable even at this distance. One springbok-necked sidekick — Zara or Adrienne or Prunella or something — executed a truly spectacular hair-flick. She'd probably had had a neck job or something. Another — Chichi or Gris-Gris or Chloestantinople or something — delicately removed her thin cigarette — no, the cherry was at the wrong end, it was her fashion popsicle. Then *Kitty* flicked her hair, a gesture Myfanwy knew for a fact to be fake. Ha! So this was what Kitty had meant by *too busy!*

Myfanwy dragged her eyes back to earth. "Borough Market lunch?" she asked Paddy with insanely forced cheeriness. "We can go collect up all the free samples and sit at those pink tables. Like pigeons — where are you *going*?"

Paddy, typically oblivious to the subtleties of the situation, was trotting up the ramp. "I think that's totally Kitty and some Asians!" he called back excitedly. "Up on the bridge!"

"Oh my God." Myfanwy's eyes rolled — 360 degrees, it felt like. "Wait! They'll *see* you! Paddy, I *tried* to meet up with Kitty this morning? She said she'd forgot she had a *tutorial*."

"Okay, and —"

"*A tutorial in treachery*."

Paddy gazed at her a moment, then raised his shoulders. "Go say hi. You'll feel better."

He started strolling up the ramp and Myfanwy trailed reluctantly after him. Wise beyond his years, that boy.

"Besides," he mused. "Kitty's so distant at school. We all got another side to us though, yeah?"

"One-dimensionality implies not having even *one* side," Myfanwy grumped. "They're not *actually* cool, are they? The Cool Kids AKA Asians.

Are they, Paddy?"

"Public schools ain't actually public," replied Paddy thoughtfully. "Nor are public schoolgirls anymore. In a way."

There was something grotesquely public about the Asians though, something almost, like, *civic*. Their distant cheekbones became perfectly melded details of the bridge's Alien Sniper Rifle aesthetic. They weren't taking in the skyline — they were taking *on* the skyline, competing with the Big Smoke's skyscrapers to see who would be the more spectacular.

Then Myfanwy's blood froze.

*

A little way down, near the north end of the bridge, a statue strode briskly nearer.

And Myfanwy's blood thawed.

Just an off-duty riverbank performer, still covered with whatever that gunk was they used to make their skin, hair and clothes all gleam like granite. *Way* too easily spooked nowadays. A Living Statue — give him 50p, he'll stretch and smile.

For a moment, Myfanwy admired gentlestatue's lustrous stalking thews.

Ooh.

Then she focused on the clique again. A different sort of statuesque altogether. What was *their* going rate for a smile? A Grade One listed country house in the Lake District?

These days, Myfanwy felt she had way more in common with her boypal Paddy than she did with Kitty, her official BFF — even though she'd known Kitty nearly twelve years and Paddy only two.

The same wave of immigration which swept Kitty up into a high, inaccessible clique also left Paddy splayed on the shores of St Jerome's, like some oddly-shaped bit of driftwood. Nobody would ever mistake Paddy for a Cool Kid. He was slimly built, a lightie, about eight inches taller than Myfanwy if you counted his big Gnasheresque afro, which Myfanwy classified either as a form of dirigible or of chocolate cake — or about three inches taller than her if you didn't — with a downy squiggle on his upper lip, and nice boggly slate-grey eyes. Today he wore that incredibly stupid grey-and-green Stüssy hoodie with the built-in ruff, printed with fishes and floating weeds, plus only slightly stupid pale green *sans culottes* with enormous pockets and a prominent orange fly, boy slippers and mismatched socks, one of which displayed a little Dalek. Whereas the Cool Kids attended St Jerome's tactically — by swiftly slumming it in state schooling, they improved their chances of entering one of the Prestigious Universities with the Very Pointy

Tops (hence Paddy's comment — "public schoolgirls aren't public any more"), so they could stare for two or three years from lofty towers, suck up crusted port from the cellars' roots, then go work in Finance, Law, Policy or Public Affairs — Paddy had always just gone with the flow. His family were military and they moved round plenty. He probably had a different Glamorous Girl Who Didn't Even Know He Existed in every port. Wherever he was stationed, Paddy skived heinously. He never found friends easily, and hadn't ever expected to find one at St Jerome's.

Myfanwy narrowed her eyes as she and Paddy crossed the mid-point of the Millenium Bridge. Despite a mere scattering of the usual tourists for cover, the Cool Kids, self-obsessed as usual, still hadn't spotted them. She could hear the contemptuous carnality of their laughter now. The charnel committee, softly exuding its repugnant glamour, gradually expanded and sprouted details. Eight or nine of them, all female today. Heels by Jimmy Choo, hips by Louis Vitton, futures by Nappa, HiPC, Oxbridge, and Clifford Chance slash Essex One.

"I mean," Myfanwy added — quietly, just in case a freak zephyr gave her voice a nitro into their midst — "they're not actually Asians either. Not what I'd call Asian."

"The popsicle one —"

"Japonica or Rococo or something, yeah, she's sort of Japanese. And there's one other — and the *only* one, yeah, whose name I am even 100% sure of, and that was only because she's in Art with us —"

"And even *then* the name in question is 'Tallulah.'"

"Yeah, *ha ha ha!* —"

"She's Scottish, yeah?"

"Scottish but both her parents are Vietnamese. Isn't it only Americans who call East Asians 'Asians' anyway? — and there are no Americans at St Jerome's. Could the Asians have hired an American PR agency? Uh, *yes*."

"Myffed?"

"What?"

"*Chill out.*"

"What," Myfanwy teased him, "embarrassed to be seen with me?"

Paddy laughed pensively.

No, they weren't actually cool, when you broke it down. They just dressed like nobles and looked amazing and never had colds, and they had cheekbones, and their waists were all like snowflakes. Not cool. Just good-looking and snarky and bitchy and v. rich and sort of upsettingly *hale*.

Okay, okay, just *occasionally* one of them did something extreme and shocking or became involved in adventures of earth-shaking importance, which did suggest they *were* the true protagonists of life and everyone else just supporting cast. But even then these occasions were so very rare, and so covered with rumours! Besides, even if they were true, the Asians ate off them for months and months afterwards — as far as Myfanwy could tell, they ate nothing else — till even the most splendid ideas had become banal by repetition, and by constant association with these angular angelic shadows who *just didn't like you.* E.g. there was Lucinda or Lala or Logan or whatever, with the thing with the celeb and the snails, where supposedly she had —

Some bodies in the group had moved.

"Wait. Fam! Seriously! Pad!"

Myfanwy stopped dead.

"*What?*" said Paddy. "I just don't get it. You really don't want them to see us together?"

"It's not that. The *person* that's with them. Paddy, it's *her!*"

There, in their midst, easefully chatting to Kitty herself, was Mara Drago-Ferrante.

*

Myfanwy tried to remember Mara's exact words.

"Wotcha. Excellent. You're just the person to help."

Right. Help to find Kitty! Mara must somehow have Facestalked Kitty and seen Myfanwy in some of the older pictures. Maybe *that's* why they had two names. "Asians" was the local term, whereas the moniker "Cool Kids" represented membership in a pan-national, perhaps Galactic meta-clique, of which Mara was clearly an alumnus.

A big, grown-up Cool Kid.

"Let's get off this bridge and go buy some fags," Myfanwy muttered, not bothering to hide her bitterness.

"You don't want to talk with the nice lady again?" said Paddy uncertainly. "Besides, you said you were never gonna — *argh!* What was that for?"

He rubbed his arm where she'd hit him rather harder than she'd intended. "Come on, fam," she said. "The Cool Kids are just those snakes that just lie there boringly and now and then slip off and swallow a cow."

"Um, safe."

She glanced one more time along the bridge.

There was no time to react.

One moment ago the living statue's hands had been empty, but now he carried some white long thing. Mara was just starting to turn when the statue swung it with brutal, calculated, force into the side of her face.

The sickening sound of cheekbone crushing. Mara didn't even cry out. She just sagged against the side of the bridge, hands fluttering blindly like little birds on leashes. The Asians screamed all at once.

Only then did Myfanwy register how the statue had smoothly uncoupled a tourist's tablet from atop her tripod as he strode past and tossed the tablet over his shoulder, not turning to see where it went. One of the tourists caught it. She seemed to be filming whatever would happen next.

The tripod was in the statue's hands.

Mara swayed, started to look up — there was blood —

A second had passed —

Myfanwy realised he wasn't finished.

Her scream coincided with the second impact.

*

Mara must have tried to move her head this time, because the metal end of the tripod caught her chin. It tore it wide open. There was more blood, and Mara's head lolled at a grotesque angle. A blob of racing scarlet and paleness wormed its way deep into Myfanwy's memory.

The statue lifted Mara by her legs and dropped her over the railings. She sagged into space and vanished.

He advanced down the bridge towards Myfanwy.

"Paddy," she whispered.

Paddy was gone. She was alone.

The statue glanced at her as he passed — living stone, now moving forward fluently as a lion, everything stone, those chiselled features shifting to admit that disquieting grin, everything about him glittering deep granite except his deep glittering green eyes —

— eyes Myfanwy had met before.

The statue slowed momentarily, then seemed to change his mind. He rotated his head forward and continued down the bridge.

He's always bloody wandering off, Myfanwy thought grimly.

Down below on the north bank, figures were stripping their shirts and diving into the water. Myfanwy leant over the railing and saw Paddy's head in the river foam, his arms moving in rapid semi-circles. Clever little seal. She glanced back along the bridge.

None of the few tourists dared try stop the statue.

"Seize that statue!" she yelped.

They shuffled aside and gazed doggedly away, like they'd *finally* found that London skyline they'd been seeking all this time. Totes BridgeTrollFail, riverfront community. As the statue neared the south end, he turned and heaved the tripod in a high arc into the river. He disappeared down the ramp towards the Tate.

Mara still hadn't surfaced. Was that blood speckling the water?

By her foot Myfanwy saw Paddy's chaotically tangled T-shirt and hoodie and stooped to scoop it up. She hadn't even seen him dive. Did she dare to chase the statue alone? Where was —

Now Kitty was by Myfanwy's side, impossibly pale. Like a shivering chinaware doll. "Myfanwy, why are — who — did —"

"Sugar. Hon, come *on*. We have to *follow*." Kitty shrank back as Myfanwy made a grab for her hand. "We won't go *up* to him," Myfanwy promised hurriedly. "But I think he was the guy in the Castle. I need a closer look."

She thought of clunk of the Lexus door closing. She thought of the sickening crunch of bone.

"I feel I owe it to her."

"But he's vanished, hon. He's gone."

*

Myfanwy shook her head as relief flooded her blood. Kitty was right. The living statue had vanished. He was quite gone. The girls crossed slowly towards the south bank, both shaking, scanning the promenade.

"The woman was still conscious," Kitty mumbled. "Semi-conscious. She tried to hold onto me when he lifted her over. She — she touched my face . . . Myfanwy, I feel so strange . . ."

On the north side, apparently a German youth orchestra had waded into the Thames, leaving their black instrument cases strewn on the pale strand. From their shouts it was obvious Mara hadn't surfaced. By now it would be too late. Myfanwy still felt sick.

Kitty's grip tightened even more. "*There!*"

The statue was walking briskly towards Blackfriars. Some people on the south bank seemed interested in the searching swimmers, but none of them had seen what had happened. No one was looking twice at him.

"Just keep him in our sights," Myfanwy begged.

"Oh God. Oh God. Okay. Okay. And you wonder why we don't hang out anymore."

"*Nein!*" cried a half-naked boy straddling a yellow buoy. "*Nein! Nein!*" He seemed about to lose his balance and slide wildly into the grey water.

The bridge gently bounced up and down as the girls sprinted its length hand-in-hand.

*

Along the teeming riverfront they trailed the living statue, tense, terrified, seizing each other each time he seemed to turn. The embankment was shattered into a labyrinth of little building sites through which dense apparitions of tourists, joggers and construction workers swirled. They twisted through it, and if the stalking statue ever saw them, he gave no sign. Twice they almost lost him. Once they sighted him slipping through a building site, discarding a silver cloth into a spinning cement mixer. He'd cleaned his face and hair and hands. Cement mixers gave Myfanwy the creeps these days. All that cement!

"Closer," she urged. They threaded their fingers through the diamond mesh of the fence.

"Yes," she whispered tersely. "It's him."

"You're sure?"

"Oh flip. He's jogging! He's just drowned a woman and now he's pounding pavement. OMG he's got *headphones* in —"

"Myffed, once you break your routine," said Kitty emphatically, "that is *it.* You may as well eat every meal at Burger King. You may as well become their little Burger King mascot."

The Thames riverfront was one place where the very act of making a getaway was its own disguise. The statue had become just another slightly weird jogger now, and the breathless girls struggled to keep pace.

But the game changed at Skater's Cove.

They'd just lost him for the third time. A crowd of guys and one or two girls were gathered down in the half-pipe against the graffiti, fidgeting with their boards with their hands and feet, arguing heatedly. The foci were these two skater guys, the one about fifteenish with stupid pink hair, but a rather cute tribal neck tattoo, and the other guy maybe a couple of years older but shorter, stocky, skinheaded, with flesh tunnel earrings and lots of metal in his face. Both youths were in long white vests and sleeked with sweat. The Man in the Iron Mask seemed to be trying to press his board into Neck Tattoo's arms, but Neck Tattoo wasn't having it.

"Nah blud, nah, nah," Neck Tattoo said, wearing a tense, unhappy smile. "Allow it."

"Do you know him, bruv?" yelped Iron Mask, waving his head around like someone pretending to be a wizard, trying to force eye contact with Neck Tattoo. Neck Tattoo studied space. "Do you know him, bruv?" demanded Iron Mask.

Somehow Myfanwy knew they were talking about the statue. "Yo!" she called. "Anyone see a guy go past? Uh, tallish — not that tall, sort of —"

"March on," a random spokesboy told her. She ignored him, obv.

"With silver stuff on his clothes?" said Kitty.

Iron Mask rammed the curved end of the board right into Neck Tattoo's chest, the younger boy's fists instinctively curled closed. Everyone in the little crowd leaned in.

"You don't know him, *do* ya?" said Iron Mask. "He's just took it!"

"Back off, son," said Neck Tattoo quietly. "Back off. I'm not playing, yeah?"

A spotty girl with lovely eyes and masses of frizzy hair piled high was explaining the sitch to Kitty. "Man says he's a fed — undercover, yeah? Tries to 'commandeer' my bike." She was leaning on it. A sort of magic tractor. "He ain't no fed, besides which, no fed's jacking my bike. Then *this* mongo" — she indicated Neck Tattoo with a deferential little bow — "is all touching fists with him, bezzy mates, and he's taken his board —"

"He needs it to escape," Neck Tattoo pleaded.

"*You need to merk him,*" summarised Iron Mask.

"Nothing to *do* with you, cuz! Man is *safe*. Man *told* me —"

"Man told you *nothing*! You need to *merk* him! You need to merk him!"

For whatever reason, Neck Tattoo now turned a pair of hazel eyes to Myfanwy in silent, fraught appeal.

There was a pause as the circuit court considered its verdict.

"*You need to mer—*"

"For God's sake!" said Myfanwy, grabbing the board from the surprised little skinhead. "*I'll* go and merk him."

But Neck Tattoo seized her arm, hazel eyes narrowing.

An accomplice?

Then he shrugged. "Go for it, cuz. Best of luck, yeah?"

As she pushed, Myfanwy heard Iron Mask strike up again.

"Give me your deck! Give me your deck! Gyaaldem jacked my deck! I need to merk her, yeah? I need to merk her! *I need to merk her!*"

*

In mid-aerial Myfanwy sighted the murderous statue again. He was moving fast and dangerously now, startling and disarraying the riverfront crowd. Had he figured out someone was following? Or was he just making some miles between himself and Iron Mask's makeshift lynch mob?

"Cooey!"

Myfanwy noticed that none of the skater kids had rode out with her, whereas Kitty, in rather inappropriate footwear, was doing her best to keep up on a third hijacked deck.

"This is different than skiing!" Kitty yelled, dwindling.

Soon, inevitably, it was just Myfanwy and the statue.

What am I doing? Myfanwy thought. Then: *who knew riding on a skateboard was so terribly, terribly easy?*

Boom!

Encoded in the soft spring zephyrs was a tempest. Myfanwy rolled it open. The tempest flowed over her skin, filled her hair. Her ears were filled with fragmented curses, and the turning of her tiny tyres.

It wasn't chance, the statue pushed so hard.

It was *combat.* He knew now she followed him. She *knew* he knew.

The distance between them stayed constant. She carved through crowds, picking up speed. Faces were pastel from near-collisions, crossly tssking and shaking. *Maybe I have a slight edge,* Myfanwy wondered, *since the people come to me pre-scattered by his passing.* Precious toddlers were half-lifted to their pigeon chests.

"Watch ou—"

"—hat the—"

"—omes an—"

The air became her home . . . the skating statue took so many obstacles it was soon as if the ordinary hierarchy turned topsy-turvy . . . the sky was their rightful place, and the promenade concrete was some strange paradisiacal cosmos onto which they strivingly leapt . . .

"—nother o—"

"—ebastia—"

"—nts!"

At Golden Jubilee Bridges they carved sinuously then turned hard, climbing effortlessly onto the pedestrian bridge running parallel with the railway one. With a strange flick, the skating statue rose in the air, and somehow Myfanwy followed, and then she was nosegrinding the rail of the Golden Jubilee Bridge, the Thames foaming far below.

Oh God.

Please no.

Some gap, that. Mind the Hellmouth.

Some gap.

She felt herself teeter. She was going to go over. How far was the water foaming below? How deep?

At the same time, the skating statue was preparing for another yet more dangerous leap. The muscles of her legs mirrored his, taut, straining together, and almost at the same instant they rose again, a tiny, acutely endangered flock . . .

Mass . . . air . . .

Her chest slammed into the cold red wrought iron, and her deck fell away beneath her. With a gasp Myfanwy lifted herself through bars and onto the railway bridge.

A train was coming onto the bridge. Its brakes began to scream.

Myfanwy was screaming already. Not about the train. She was lying on the train tracks screaming, and the statue with the skinned face was standing over her, leaning forward. No playful, mocking hands outstretched this time. Panting mouth, murderous eyes. Knuckles white on the deck, half-raised, as behind him, the braking, sparking train spread like wings.

Myfanwy scrambled backwards over concrete slabs alternated with bands of huge lumps of gravel. The statue stalked forward and through his scissoring legs she glimpsed something. A uniformed figure, picking carefully and slowly along beside the train. Too far, too slow. No one to swoop in.

Fight him yourself!

She planted a palm behind her, but as she tried to wobble to her feet, the statue took three quick paces, transferring the deck to his right hand, and with his left grabbed her ankle. She shrieked and fell onto her back again, banging her tailbone on concrete.

The train had halted. "DESTINATION: HASTINGS" loomed. Myfanwy's free shoe kicked rocks without gaining traction.

"*Help!*" she screamed, trying to kick free, her forearm waving protectively over her face. "*Fucking help, help, help, help!*"

Tightening his grip on her ankle, the statue stole a look over his shoulder. "Bit harsh," he growled.

"*What?*"

"Hastings. Ain't *that* bad, is it?"

Buy time. "Depends where you stand on the sea."

He laughed mercilessly. "I suppose."

An old Tori Amos song was playing in Myfanwy's mind, with the added crackliness of vinyl. It was funny what you — no, that was how the song went. *Me, and a gun, and a man on my back . . . it's funny what you think of, at times like these . . .* God, the station guard was *right* behind the statue now! Why didn't he bloody grab him? PC gone mad! The statue grinned, breathing heavily. "Now," he said quietly, "take *that!*"

He released her heel, but with a strange gentle squeeze — like you might squeeze someone's hand before you let it go, just to let the person know that it was only *holding their hand* that was So Last Season, whilst *they* remained very much OTM. Funny what you think of at times like these.

The guard lunged. The statue became a whirling, tumbling, violent shape, all low, spinning muscle and shoulders. Suddenly Myfanwy saw the guard's terrified wide face, as if she were a camera angle and he was teetering into her. Then the guard's baldy, door-breaching type head slammed into her stomach.

"Oaf!" she yelled — pleased when she realised that she had. "Get off me! He's bloody getting away!"

The station guard grunted and flailed, snuggling into Myfanwy's tummy truffle-pig-like. Myfanwy saw the statue leap panther-like back onto the pedestrian bridge. He patted his sides apologetically as he passed a *Big Issue* seller at the far end, then vaulted the last section of the railing, to land lightly on the back of an open-top tourist bus. He was seating himself near the back as it swept out of view.

"Hello," sighed Myfanwy sweetly to the felled official on her stomach. "Single please."

For some reason the fact that *The Big Issue* is called *Z!* in Holland popped into her head. Better than Tori Amos — God!

The guard raised his panting face. "*You* are very, very lucky to be alive," he said, his tone composed of equal parts pain and pomposity.

"Not with *you* on top of me, I'm not. Honestly. I'm serious. I want to die. Death, take me!"

One skateboard lay beside her, a hairline crack where the statue caught the guard's shins.

And the other — lodged among the metal beams below, wheels still spinning.

*

By the time the feds were finished with Myfanwy — all a bit "Police Procedural" for her taste, she was more a Poirot person at heart — the sky had darkened, and although it was just gone three o' clock, it felt like evening.

"I didn't *fall off* it exactly," Kitty explained, gazing grimly over the Thames. "I sort of 'ghost rode' it. Also I had a board that wasn't my size."

She introduced Myfanwy to all the skater kids.

They all said hi.

Kitty had Myfanwy's sketchpad. Myfanwy didn't even remember at what point she'd lost it. The Asians had gone home (in tears! — clearly the *real* victims here?) and Paddy too (borderline hypothermic, idiot), though presumably not everyone together.

More worryingly, Neck Tattoo — his name was Marcus, apparently — had vanished, and Myfanwy still had his deck.

Iron Mask was relatively meek receiving his. "I heard it was a legendary push," he conciliated. "But *please* don't do that too often, yeah?"

The girl Myfanwy had met earlier, the one with the frizzy hair, popped up beside Iron Mask, took his arm and nodded. "It's what we have Boris Bikes for, fam."

"Sorry," said Myfanwy. "And cheers."

"No worries," said Iron Mask.

"Shall I take the other skateboard?" said Frizzy Hair.

"I'd rather return it myself, if that's okay. I took such terrible troubles retrieving it."

I should explain the crack, Myfanwy thought. *And . . . yes! I feel my little grey cells stirring! I wouldn't mind making some enquiries of my own!*

"So how can we touch base with him?" Kitty added. Six or so of the boys and one of the girls had their phones out.

"Sure, no probs —"

"I'll probably be seeing him tonight actually —"

"We'll text when we see him. Give us your number —"

"Yeah, give us your number —"

"I may go link him up *now* actually —"

"*Your* number as well," one doughnut-headed one nodded magnanimously to Myfanwy. "Although you're more threatening, and actually you're giving me mad evils right now."

"Does *anybody* have this Marcus's number?" Kitty demanded.

"Come to Wagamama's with me," recapped Iron Mask idly. Frizzy Hair stomped on his toe. "Aaah," he groaned dreamily.

Soon, *sans* skaters, the two girls walked through the afternoon twilight. The crescent moon stood over St Paul's. Feds were drifting to and fro. Mostly for their Thing, Myfanwy supposed, though perhaps a few for other Things.

"What was Mara saying to you?" said Myfanwy. "Up on the bridge?"

Kitty shook her head. "She wasn't on point yet. She asked about our uni plans. It was weird. She was acting like a web site that was trying to be relevant to us, you know? And it was almost like she was waiting for something. But she did know my name, and she mentioned your name too."

"She *did*, huh?"

"Uh-huh. Mega respect Myffy," said Kitty. "The guy barely got away."

"Sugar. More like *I* barely got away. What was I *thinking*." Then Myfanwy asked the question she had been dreading. "So darling didn't they — didn't they find her? In the river?"

Kitty puffed out her lower lip and shook her head mutely.

They were silent for a few moments. A white helicopter covered the crescent moon in a complicated inconstant eclipse. Kitty looked to one side and flapped her hand next to her head, as usual whenever she was trying not to cry. This time it worked.

"Hon," said Myfanwy. "Bredren."

"Look on the bright side," Kitty said eventually. "You got that neat skateboard!"

Myfanwy linked arms with her. "Did you think that Marcus guy was cute?"

"OMG, the Boy with the Druggie Tattoo?"

"I mean, I know he's a bit young —"

"You're kidding, right? Is *that* why you kept his board?"

"Maybe," laughed Myfanwy. "Like a massive business card, hard to confetti-ize?"

"Eww eww! Apparently he was all like, 'Blud, skaters be persecuted wherever we go! It is because we question conventional morality! Once this area designated to skating was a haven! I shall no longer skate here!' Paddy had to placate him, but Paddy was too dense to get his deets."

"Poor Pad, you leave him alone. He was probably frozen senseless. I love it when his 'fro gets wet."

"*Oh* yeah! *I* had to see his *nipples*."

"Lucky you."

"No, no, no! *That* boy could do with some gym time." Then Kitty added teasingly, "With *you* as his personal trainer."

"What's that supposed to mean?"

"Oh come *on* Myffed! *Everyone* assumes you're totally doing him."

"Kitty! You know I'm saving it for my wedding night or to celebrate Lords reform or something!"

"The only thing stopping you two," said Kitty perfunctorily, "is being joined at the hip. It makes it hard to navigate the relevant organ, the, uh, the Launch Pad into the Landing —"

"Gross! Whatever, everyone totally assumes *you're* doing all *your* new Cool Kids too."

"What did you just say?" said Kitty.

"Not really. But gyaaldem you is giving me *air*, cuz!"

"Whevs," said Kitty — suddenly very cool and composed. Almost bored. She got like that sometimes. Myfanwy could never work out what triggered it.

"I was just joking," said Myfanwy. "Nobody really says anything like that about you guys. And I don't think you're really abandoning me, or anything."

Kitty smiled tightly. They walked on for a bit.

Myfanwy noticed a dusting of blood on Kitty's new Whistles neo-kirtle. She didn't say anything about it. Instead she said, "What's the name of the your friend with the fashion popsicle again? Like a particularly crap Carmen. I don't think I've ever seen *Carmen*, but I know she works in a cigarette factory, and she's all covered with sweat and like, 'Come here!' It's weird, the stuff that's in your head. I kept thinking that song that's like, 'Me and a gun.'"

Kitty gave her a searching look.

They were walking back the other way, and now were passing the new bridge. Still nowhere near finished. Hadn't Myfanwy heard something about funding being suspended? Maybe the bridge would stay that way, unfinished, terminating in mid-air, a bridge to nowhere.

Or was she mixed up? Had she just heard it would be a *suspension* bridge?

Kitty seemed v. distant again. She wanted Kitty to laugh. Laugh with her, or laugh at her. Anything. God, why did she get like this?

Kitty sighed abruptly.

Myfanwy was thinking again of the cigarettes she'd been going to buy, earlier, when she'd first discovered Kitty's little betrayal. She had that vague longing again. Did they call them *bridging* drugs? No, *gateway*. Bridge would be better though — the way they jutted out of you, like they'd link you to something. But you ended up stuck on your own shore.

"It's a pity they used up the name Millennium Bridge," said Myfanwy. "They could have used it for the new one! You can only cross in the Millennium Falcon, and have to make sure you hit 88 miles per hour before you go off the tip."

"You're thinking of the DeLorean," said Kitty coldly. "And 99 miles per hour. It's like a percentage."

"Oh. I haven't actually seen it. Hey, you and me should have another film night at your *pied à terre* soon. Feels like it's been ages."

"I should call Looly and those guys," said Kitty. "Make sure they got home okay."

And they unlinked arms.

*

Nyam, nyam, nyam, moooo! Moooo!

Cows were grazing like goldfish, their hooves wavering against the blue like beautiful fins . . . their big lips kissing the grass . . .

They swam off through trees. Flourishing their pretty patchwork flanks.

Solidity. Clarity. She knew where she was now. The city was closer and clearer every day. It wasn't real exactly, but it had . . . solidarity with reality. Grass, mud. Blown by a sudden, unfair wind. Stunned her to the bone. To her right, a crooked avenue of trees. And the sense of a similar but more stately avenue behind.

She was in the city she called her Citadel, one of its vast gardens. Near home.

Bildungsroman Roads fanned out behind her.

On the distant bright grass, patches of snow were moving. No! — birds — gulls. Somewhere on the sea, perhaps, or near to it. All around, gentle, playful shouts. To her left —

a person —

holding her hand — a man — no,

a girl —

actually, it looked like her, *Myfanwy Morris — wait, then so who was* she? —

a squeeze of her hand and someone was turning, the world curling around them as someone leaned in to kiss someone's lips coming up . . .

*

Myfanwy awoke with a gasp and spent half the morning in bed, being a bit naughty. It was Saturday, so.

Mmmmmm.

Oh!

Myfanwy drowsed in her fever, tossing and turning.

If you feel you're . . . losing yourself . . .

How many ways could you lose yourself? What pieces could you lose? Your virginity. Ha ha.

Hmm. Your nerve.

Heart.

Your head, obvs.

Then there was that other kind of losing yourself — losing yourself among all the new things being born around you, forgetting which things were *you.* Myfanwy supposed that was what losing yourself to a demagogue was like. Dwindling, lagging behind some lolcat Hitler, some snazzy 21st century *Reichskanzler*, some cunning looter of a world already surfeited with content . . . for some reason, framing *yourself* for his weird crimes . . .

The sounds of Dad crashing around house cleaning entered Myfanwy's drowsy mind. When he drew close by her door, Myfanwy held still and bit her lip. Dad *claimed* he understood the concept of knocking, but he was usually standing sheepishly on the wrong side of her door when he made that claim.

Oh, yeesh.

Today was the day she would be visiting the feds.

Myfanwy's stuffed toys observed her with their abiding hope, shock and bumblyness. There were "Object Petite A," the stuffed mouse atop the mirror, "Other" the stuffed dinosaur, "Big Me" the stuffed sea-horse, and "Little Me" the weird thing — Mum had been big into Freud and Lacan and stuff. She must have guided Myfanwy's naming practices, though Myfanwy didn't remember it that way.

"Jasper," Myfanwy had decided to dub the living statue. Why? Because it was a kind of yellowish rock, and he reminded her of a preening, prowling, stalking Trafalgar lion . . .

Well, she didn't *need* a good reason. It was her own Personal Psychopath Naming System. She just had to make sure it didn't accidentally slip out when she was talking to the police.

Dad crashed along, singing wise Beefheart.

". . . with a *monkey* on his knee . . ."

Now their hoover started up. The hoover sucked loudly. Sun fell sweetly on her face. Myfanwy settled back, content.

Whenever Myfanwy was sleepy, her legs would jump by themselves. But recently they'd been going insane. Knees hopping and hopping like toast popping. Toes bouncing like Marios ascending platforms. Her dreams were very lovely and addictive nowadays. Too impatient to wait for her mind, Myfanwy's limbs would run out into her dreams before her mind had properly dropped off.

No wonder. Making out with yourself. Nice one, subconscious. Waking shmaking!

The only other times her dreams had ever given her similar vividness, similar insistence of theme, was when Myfanwy had been involved in some intense activity for the full length of a day. Then the imagery and energy of the activity, whatever it was, could accumulate a kind of mental momentum, and disconnect from source, and follow her forward into her sleep. The difference was, the source of these *new* dreams was a complete mystery to her. It wasn't like she had been learning to kayak all day, then learning to navigate her Sky Canoe all night. It wasn't like she'd been shyly stealing glances at Simon Buckerton all day, shyly stealing Simon Buckerton's ears and hiding them in her pencil case all night. Etc. If anything, the momentum ran in the opposite direction, the events of the night determining patterns of waking thought.

Finally Myfanwy leapt from her bed, turned on it and sort of made it, though not to her satisfaction, because her linen would never be truly disentangled or crisp and dry ever again. She wandered out to give Dad his good morning kiss.

"Good afternoon, sleepyhead."

"Good morning, Hoover Monster. Is the whole house satisfactorily inside your hoover?"

She hadn't told Dad about the statue or the woman, let alone the weird Citadel of rose-coloured stone which haunted her these days. Unless *she* haunted *it?*

Castles in the Sky. Isn't that a phrase meaning dreams and nonsense?

Or . . . it's Spain, isn't it?

Hmm, obviously a lot of ins and outs.

After brunch and a shower there was plenty Revulsion and plenty Portfolio to do before she visited DI Fontleroy, but she tried Kitty's mobile instead — because you just never know, right?

Straight to voicemail.

*

"Couldn't you just put them on Facebook?" Myfanwy said. "Then I could tag him. 'Lethal statue.'"

DI Fontleroy was leading Myfanwy through his police station to look at some photos.

"The issue with that," stated this Fed Who Led, very solemnly indeed, "is what if he untags himself?"

"Fair," admitted Myfanwy.

She wondered whether Fontleroy could be a master ironist. He hadn't shown any signs of it when he explained the frankly hilarious Issue with the photos — that the tourist who'd taken them with her tablet had neglected to adjust the auto filter settings on the app, and that they'd turned out, in DI Fontleroy's term, "funny." Myfanwy still wasn't quite clear what the filter had been — ("better just have a look") — but it had obviously proved difficult to reverse.

Soft-focus sepia stills, perhaps, to lend the assault that atmosphere of classy, nostalgic romance? Or worse, bridge and statue composited in vast crystalline splay of cubist facets? Her artistic temperament would prove invaluable to DI Fontelroy, she bet! Or else maybe one of those special filters, where it added period dress, or made you look naked, or gave everyone wobbly celebrity faces?

Oh, sugar — maybe even some terrible all-bungling combo? What if Fontleroy was about to get her to confirm for the record that what she witnessed on the Millennium Bridge was, like, a slightly puppety shemale Kate Windsor whacking an ewok over a parapet with a lacrosse stick? She'd better work out fast whether he *was* a master ironist, otherwise she might wind up jumping the wrong way and then you're in the dock for perverting the course of justice.

Two feds, a woman and a man, were coming down the corridor, chatting loudly about some obscure absent person. The woman was familiar. She was a bald and androgynous-looking woman, anywhere from fifty to seventy, her face a heavy stack of horizontal wrinkles. Myfanwy almost felt she knew her name. Fletcher? Philips? Merleau-Hastings?

As they passed, their shoulders brushed together lightly, and the name popped into her head.

"Police Constable Veitch," she said crossly, and the fed turned around.

"Inspector," said Fontleroy.

One deep crack in her skin ran across the fed's jaw and through her lower lip like a bridle. Her face was more like a stack of faces than any one face in particular. Myfanwy felt like she could shuffle them like cards.

"I *hate* you," Myfanwy said. She felt panicked, but she didn't know why. "You're crooked, Veitch. You're a bad cop. You did a bad thing."

Veitch — if that was her name — didn't respond directly. "Who's this young lady?" she demanded of Fontleroy.

Yes. Definitely her. Her voice was filled with little cracks, like her skin. But *who* was she?

"What's this about?" intoned Fontleroy ominously.

"I apologise," said Myfanwy quickly. "I'm feeling under the weather. I — won't be able to help you today. I remember the way out."

She walked past Veitch and down the long corridor. Three sets of footsteps followed.

*

Citadel. Somewhere on the sea, perhaps, or near to it.

The city was her home now.

Its sudden, unfair winds.

Its sphinxes.

Its labyrinth of bridges. No, not a labyrinth, precisely. More that you could be on a bridge and not know it, surrounded by buildings. And the stone of those stern bridge buildings! Some mornings, light reflecting from it held every quality in common with light which was boring through roses . . .

Its nerves all flaming . . . its snow-damasked tracks, sinuous for miles . . .

Its skies of clouds of rain and snow, shining with a grey more luminous than any golden . . .

*

Some particularly mangy pigeons, not willing to waste their wings on Myfanwy, swaggered begrudgingly aside.

It had taken ten more minutes of clamming up and borderline swooning before the feds stopped following her, but not before strongly implying that she was breaking a Special Secret Law which they all knew, but couldn't tell. Now she was weaving her way home through back-streets and alleyways.

She passed a tattered Yaris with "JUST MARRI" still faintly scarred into its paintwork by over-potent toothpaste or something.

A door opened and a waiter in a white blouse came out to smoke.

Had Fontleroy simply *implored* her, Myfanwy would have lingered to see the crime scene images. She was pretty sure she was just randomly freaking out. Fontleroy had just felt so manipulative and overbearing to her. Which just annoyed her and made her more resolute. And Veitch, saying nothing, just watching intently . . . *ew, ew, ew!* That was the worst part about murderers: the police.

Behind her, Myfanwy heard a strong beat of wings.

A song began to play somewhere — Beatles, "Paperback Writer."

Perhaps Myfanwy was being unfair to Fontleroy. Police were like a strange, dense poetry. You could never distinguish the bits they *really* meant from the bits you'd read into them. Their mere presence made necessary a special kind of paranoia, one which compressed and distorted that distinction out of all usefulness.

After just two drags the waiter stooped and stubbed her tab out. *That busy in the restaurant, at half three in the afternoon?* No cigarette on the ground, just a red-streaked chickenbone.

Myfanwy smiled nervously as she neared the waiter. The waiter nodded, returned her half-smoked tab to its box and went back inside. Not too busy to finish her fag, just poor and a bit gritty. Dragging out the drags — cigarettes were like Mother Nature's e-cigarettes.

Way too easily spooked these days. Oh dear. What if the fed had just resembled some actor from some cop show? Mortifying! Her face had been so distinctive though. Plus she *seemed* to respond to *Constable Veitch.* Fontleroy had said *Inspector* like it was a correction. Was he just correcting the rank, or could she have been completely wrong?

If you feel you're . . . losing yourself . . .

Mara's words.

After all, when people said *um* or *er* or paused for an ellipsis, it wasn't always because they were trying to find the right words. Sometimes they already knew they'd *never* find the right words. Because those words didn't exist.

Then again, sometimes it was just the opposite — people paused because they wanted you to know they had thought about it for a bit, and yes. They are *exactly* the right words.

The rest of the way Myfanwy stuck to main streets.

*

"Yo homegirl, wha gwaan."

"Yo bitch."

"Kitsy, I'm freaking out. First I go see the feds."

"God, how'd it go? Snitch, BTW."

"I stood tall, trust. I'm not actually joking — I freaked out, I was useless to them. Then to top it all, I got home and my dad was trying to enter his password into Google. I'm freaking out, Kitsy."

"I'm not *completely* sure I *understand.*"

"Like, Dad's normal homepage is his email logon, okay? I don't know why, but this time Google comes up instead. By the time I found him he was . . . oh God — slowly tapping in his password in with — uh, with two fingers. Sniff."

"Maybe you're freaking out, Myffy. Have you considered whether you're freaking out?"

"He just doesn't understand about *stuff*, you know?"

"Oh, hon. You're worried about him when you go to uni?"

"Kinda."

"So what? You gonna, like, leave him all his meals for the year, in little labeled plastic packages?"

"*Maybe*, Kitty — I mean, he can *cook* fine, save the caramelisation obsession obv. I just think he might forget to *eat* or something, you know? So I'll probably have to *take him with me!*"

"Eww."

"Then there's all this weirdness with Witness Protection. I just want to think about *one thing at a time.*"

Witness Protection Programme wasn't anything real, just Kitty's recent coinage for everything that freaked her out and/or put everyone on edge — basically mainly a euphemism for the murder on Millennium Bridge.

"Oh, hon," Kitty said kindly. "You're forgetting half of it. You don't know how *you're* gonna manage without *Petey* either! I know he looks after you too. Plus being his Sensible Daughter is an important part of *who you are*, and how you feel comfortable with yourself. In your heart you know that he *will* be okay next year and that you'll be okay . . ."

"Yeah . . ."

". . . but the *ways* you find to be okay mean you'll *both* have to change. You're a little scared of who you're going to become next, and a *lot* scared of your new Snitch Responsibilities in the Witness Protection Programme. You're anxious, and part of you just wants the same old responsibilities you've always been used to. But your dad wants you to grow, and *he* wants to grow too. The truth is, you two may *never* be this close again. But he's still your dad and you'll still be there when you need each other — *and* when you don't! Remember when it seemed like things could never get better? Well, they have, and they're going to *keep* getting better."

"That's what so incredibly hysterical about you. Over almost any normal thing you always get the weirdest, wrongest end of the stick. But then with certain family type stuff you are just *so bang on.*"

"OMG. It's so hysterical. I do the weirdest stuff, and then with certain stuff I'm just *so bang on.*"

"You totally flip out at teachers over nothing, you do the weirdest most nebulous stuff to boys."

"I'm constantly being massively paranoid and self-aggrandising, and viciously slandering myself and assaulting my own best interests."

They had hysterics.

"Plus his password is *my name and birthday*,' said Myfanwy. "Honestly Kitty I totally lost my shit."

"That is so sweet and sad, bitch. And I bet *your* password is 'DADDY69!'"

"You *know* my password."

"Oh yeah. Don't be talking 'bout no passwords an' shit on the *wire* yo. Look I'm totes too busy for you right now. Howsabout coffee tomorrow?"

"Totes. And we need to talk feds and Witness Prot. In a way, there's *developments*."

"Totes Wit hon. Can't wait, I'll call tonight, bye-bye-bye-bye-bye-bye—"

"That-is-so-annoying-bye-bye-bye-bye—"

"Bye-bye-b—"

Kitty flaked on the Sunday Costa by text when Myfanwy had already grabbed them a comfy corner sofa, but it was okay because they met in the evening for *booze*. Like coffee, only different.

"I need a large cocktail. So large it involves a complex system of locks," Kitty announced as they air-kissed.

"So evil on a school night," Myfanwy said appreciatively.

In the end they settled for weird beautiful vodkas, sitting, with their hair piled in buns, and big arty beads on their breastbones, on high swivelly stools at the long umbrageous obsidian bar of Zapomnieć, their favourite upmarket riverfront pan-Eastern European restaurant slash voddie bar.

The bartender turned his slender white-and-black back. "Zap could never ID us," Myfanwy murmured into her blouse's cuff-link (like a spy). "They'd have to admit the colossal extent of their error. The trick to getting served in most places when you're seventeen is to have been drinking there since you were fifteen."

"There's an infinite regress there," said Kitty. She checked her teeth in her compact. She'd had a seaweed snack-pack (without offering to share any of the six sheets).

"Not infinite," said Myfanwy. "Just important to start boozing as soon as you form limbs and lips."

"Myfanwy! It's highly irresponsible to drink when someone's pregnant with you." Kitty wore that wary look she sometimes got when mothers were mentioned, however obliquely. She needn't've worried, Myfanwy wasn't going to start going on about Mum.

"Lolz," she said.

"*Thank* you," gushed Kitty to the trim little bartender, and gathered every penny of change from the small silver plate. Between them they *never* had more than six vodkas here, and Myfanwy never paid for more than two.

"Especially in the first trimester," said Myfanwy.

"Anyway, you always forget I'm *actually* eighteen," Kitty whispered. "I'm through the threshold, hon. I'm an *olllld craaazy laaady*."

Myfanwy sipped her cucumber vodka. There were shards of ice in it. It tasted *amazing*. Kitty looked amazing. She wondered how *she* looked.

"So," said Kitty, snapping shut her purse, "developments?"

"Oh, dude, I *dunno*," Myfanwy sighed. "'Developments' may have been bold. It's more me being mental again."

"What was a non-'no comment' interview like? Was it weird?"

"I think the statue guy is controlling my mind."

Kitty tasted her cardamom vodka with the tip of her tongue and nodded sympathetically. "People You Think About Too Much."

Myfanwy shook her head.

People You Think About Too Much was one of Kitty's many Things, not relevant at this point.

"Not exactly," Myfanwy said. "I freaked out just before my police interview. I went nuts. I thought I recognised one of the lady cops. I was all like, 'I *know* you. You're crooked. I cannot continue this interview.'"

Kitty giggled. "That's awesome! '*I ain't no supergrass, guv'nor! Not for a pony of knickers, not for nuffink!*'" Kitty frowned and her persona fell off its platform. "And reflects badly on me. I wonder if this means I have a Record?"

"It gets *worse*, Kitty . . . I couldn't remember where she was crooked from! Which was so embarrassing. I was so *sure* she was famous! I mean, notorious. *Then* I got confused."

"To speak Truth to Power," said Kitty, "you've got to be so *on* it. You need to prep for it like it's admissions for a uni or a Spring Week or whevs. You know, hon? You know?"

Myfanwy wasn't properly listening. "It was some protest or something . . . racism, harassment . . . falsifying evidence . . . testifying in a trial or an inquest or something . . . accepting free stuff? Did the statue tell me, though?"

Kitty looked skeptical. Myfanwy's charges multiplied. "Telling people off and making them change their behaviour, even when they're within the law . . . using laws for purposes they were never designed for . . . applying laws unevenly . . . applying collective responsibility . . . wading in with batons, bish bash bosh . . . putting their horse where it was blatantly going to get nicked . . . provoking people to commit crimes, if not fully-fledged entrapment . . . starting riots . . . cuffing peace activists so it, like, cuts their wrists, then chucking them in the van like binbags . . . um, lying under oath."

"Myfanwy," Kitty sighed. "That's her *job!* It sounds like you really *embarrassed* us in there." She took a sip. "The state justice system," Kitty added perfunctorily, "solves crimes and loves doughnuts. I *really* don't see the problem."

"I'm sorry, hon. I guess even after the revolution we'll still need bent coppers. Basically, my point is, it was a facet of my *general* freaking out."

"Okay," Kitty nodded, scrunching up her brow.

"I hadn't figured it out then, but now I have. It's like the statue guy is putting images in my head. I keep having these Episodes. Visions, memories, whatever. They get in when my guard is down. Imagining myself in these situations, or really thinking I've been there, when I never have. I have to think, 'Whoa! *Is* this copper bent? Uh, *no!* Was I at a *carnival*, the day of the murder? Uh, *no!*'"

"Maybe you're thinking of something you and Paddy saw at the Tate," Kitty said thoughtfully. "Reverie and Stanchion exhibition, right?"

"Well remembered, but nay. This thing I'm remembering is half a protest, half a carnival. But it's *made up*, that's the point, Kitty! I was never there. *He* put it there."

"Like he's trying to erase what you saw? Cover it up?"

"And like, make me believe in stuff that never happened?"

"Sounds like a *man.*"

"I'm serious! Mostly it's this one creepy medieval city. I've nicknamed it the Citadel. I keep thinking, 'Oh, that reminds me of my *bildungromans* back when my home was in the Citadel.' Uh, what? *When was that?*'

"Never."

"Never! Trust! You've known me almost my whole —"

"The creepy medieval bit could be Oxford," Kitty interjected. Kitty had an offer to do Oxford. English and Economics. A, A, A, A. As in, "Aaaah!" Her brow furrowed with intense focus. "Or . . . or Cambridge!"

Myfanwy frowned. "I don't think so. There are travellers and scholars and beggars. And rickshaws. But it's bigger, a proper city. Filled with songs and weird wailing. And sometimes the stones in the morning glow with a kind of . . . a kind of rose light. The whole city shining and shy."

"Like the city hooked up the night before, and now it's blushing."

"Darling, you don't even *know* how apt that is! But also somewhere *inside* it, there are green meadows, filled with avenues of trees. And there are black towers. And Fingers of Ignominy. And white gulls."

"Near a landfill, then?"

"No, because there are sea-shells too — I mean, *God*, Kitty. Whatever. I was just *joking* anyway."

Myfanwy took a big swig. She felt embarrassed.

"Really?" said Kitty, intensely.

There were moments of terrible vexual silence. Myfanwy played with her glass. At the end of the bar, a thirtysomething with white sideburns kept staring at them.

"Um," said Myfanwy. "No. I just thought if I told you I'd realise it was ridiculous. But unexpectedly hon, you're giving me Serious Face."

"It's just . . . I have felt *bare* peculiar since the bridge, Myffed." Kitty took a last gulp of cardamom vodka and winced. "Seagulls, yeah? What about Venice? I mean, is it defo English?"

"Yes and no," said Myfanwy quietly. "I'm not sure it's a real place, exactly. There could be a distillery or brewery up on the cliffs. Or that could be someplace else. I'm not sure yet. I'm going crazy, Kitty."

Myfanwy finished her cucumber vodka. They ordered a rose vodka and a Pink Lady vodka.

"In other news," Kitty said, "skater boy number four texts me. I meet him at Pizza Express tomorrow night, I get the first digit of Marcus's number. Believe."

"Resourceful," said Myfanwy. "I don't know what's weirder, that you gave them all your phone number, or that you've assigned them integers. And that reminds me, I've gathered all but one scraps of Mara's card."

"Darling, you're gonna make a great networker one day."

"I practically had to de-weave the wicker. There was one that was *inside* the tissue that had —"

"Too much information, too much information, too much information —"

"Point *is*, we're only missing one digit! We can just call all ten possibilities, right?"

Kitty looked unhappy. "The possibility we want is at the bottom of the river. Full fathom five, thy Mara lies. Her vital spark has fled, alas, innit."

"You never know," said Myfanwy quietly.

They said nothing for a moment. A party of pinstripe suits was ushered through the swishing hanging beads.

"The one thing about Zap," said Kitty, "is the anal beads."

The curtains spindled and flowed across their suits. Some threads stayed between the lines. The bar part of Zapomnieć was pretty empty tonight, but the restaurant was filling up. Myfanwy was feeling the booze now. She was enjoying opening up to Kitty.

White Sideburns had vanished from his bar perch.

"There's more," Myfanwy admitted. "During these Episodes. I feel *his* presence. You know? I keep thinking about how *he* sees *me*. Like myself, only different. Prettier. More confident. More . . . Midlandsy."

"Oh my God is that the art teacher?"

"Prettier and less awkward, anyway. Kitty, I keep remembering what it's like to *kiss* me."

"Oh my God that's the art teacher's bun poking over that menu. OMG. Who else could it be? Don't look!"

"Madame MP? OMG it is her."

"It's more baguette than bun."

"Chax, Kitty. MP's safe. I want to tell you about —"

"That's not the point. *Shot* it, hon."

"Hon, I'm not downing a drink you just paid —"

"Hon, in *one*. We're outtie. I am never coming to this *staff room* again." Kitty was gathering up her many things.

Myfanwy watched her, wondering if she could in fact comfortably order another.

"Anyway," said Kitty. "I've just had an idea. I think I know how you can beat *him*, babe. Something *you* can do . . . that *I* could never do."

*

Citadel! City of splendid night, city of soft obscurities . . . arches and closes, bridges and death-plummets . . . short-cuts like serried Chess sets . . . city of swaddled obscenities . . .

Running, hand-in-hand . . .

City of meadows of mist . . . streetlamps haloed with mist, like hanging lanterns of strangest papers . . . skins of insect saints . . . distant figures moving . . . miles of drunkards . . . haloes . . . deeper darkness twisted into tree-tops like roosting bats . . .

And bats . . .

Apple. Rose. Cucumber. Cardamom.

Gasps. Kisses. Skin. Fingers under clothes.

She was way drunker than she thought. Why else would she be lost in this city of balconies and locked gardens, searching up and down its stone stairs with this girl . . . she tried to focus . . . remember herself . . . yes, with this girl, uh, Myfanwy Morris?

Throwing themselves into every shadow, behind every pillar, shoving themselves hard in every alcove. Too hard, try not to break her every bone. Urgent against her little body, feeling her hips, her breasts.

Myfanwy wanted her. Her full, hard breasts. She wanted Myfanwy too. Her hands pulling her neck, down into her hungry kisses. Her hands shaping her waist.

Kissing her neck, her hips gently bucking, feeling . . .

Moaning . . . "Not here," she whispered. She had to stop. She didn't want to stop. "Wait! Not here!"

"Okay," she gasped. She kissed spit from the girl's lip. She had to stop, dragging herself back from her warm and writhing frontispiece, but reaching to play with her ear and hair. "Okay."

The girl grabbed her finger and sucked it.

"Climb up," she instructed. The girl stepped into the well of her hands, her dress tight on her ass, beckoning just in front of her face. And now they were in the garden, laying under the tree, her hands undoing her buttons, undoing her belt, her mouth kissing her stomach, her fingers running along the edge of bra lace, brushing her hard, moving nipple. She —

"Myffy! Myffy what is it? You're dreaming, Myffy." He stood at the door, the corridor light spilling over his shoulders. "Have you been drinking, Myfanwy?"

"Daddy!" moaned Myfanwy. "Daddy! *Oh, Daddy, help me!*"

*

A column of warm sun, deranged by window smears and dust, fell through the skylight directly onto her canvas. Myfanwy inked in a last curl of water into her lake. Now it looked like all the dark little lilies were moving. Where did they want to go?

"Lilypad, Lilypad, fly away home. Your house is all burned, your children are gone."

Didn't work. *Again.*

It was Thursday afternoon, the last day of the three-day Controlled Composition in the St Jerome's Art Department. Myfanwy's canvases were almost completely full, full of things, and full of little wiggles of water and wind, suggesting the things wanted to go elsewhere. Away from their dragonfly admirals, deep into the sea.

Or at least into the C, which was all Myfanwy needed in Art to get her loan to do History and Business Studies at Bristol.

A, A, A, C.

The Controlled Composition was the first exam, but it wasn't really a real exam. People chatted, ate chocolate raisins. A few pupils who didn't want to overwork their comps had brought Portfolio pieces to work on while the clock ran down. So it was quite the gallery today in the Art Department.

Under Madame Valerie Merely-Pointy's questionable leadership, the St Jerome's Senior School Art Department had earned its reputation as the preeminent hub for secondary school conceptual artists. One of their first written assignments had been, "Class, produce an aesthetic manifesto *for which it would be right to DIE!*"

Now Merely-Pointy flitted agitatedly among the artworks, clucking, fretting, clutching her heart, while her towering bun — surely the boldest concept in the room? — wobbled with emotion.

Art classes gave Myfanwy her sole chance to inspect a Cool Kid — other than Kitty obv — up close and impersonal.

Myfanwy had to admit she quite liked Tallulah's piece. The intimidatingly other-worldly Scotch-Vietnamese-or-whatever Cool Kid had created a streaming film called *A History of Pointlessness*, which took the Art Lover (i.e. Examiner) through the booting-up of archaic plug-into-your-TV computers, then pixels turned like sand in hourglass icons, scored by dial-up modem sounds — which seemed to Myfanwy almost like birdsong — then images of landscapes and annoyed faces in certain formats coming slowly into focus, whereas images in *other* formats were gently being *rolled* into being, like the slowest blinds, and still *other* formats labouriously interlacing into existence like gates closing, then on to newer technologies, complex attempts to retrieve email on a Kindle, through to smartphones and tablets timing out, and myriad feeds waiting for one another, and myriad incommensurable apps obscuring vital info with the unfading ghosts of their windows, etc. Cunningly (well, smugly, actually) the last five minutes of the film were a faked-up "Please Wait . . . Streaming" insignia, so the film itself (in Myfanwy's reading of it, anyway) had become the most recent annoying and pointless application of technology.

Tallulah stood on the bridge that day. They'd never talked about it.

They never talked about anything.

Myfanwy added some particularly agitated tiny little ink marks. Well, Tallulah was just a flaky Cool Kid anyway. Those guys were all stories, no substance. Or only illicit substances. One of them, Lucy or Cecil or Samphire or something, had taken an MD bomb and wound up wearing nothing but heels and a turquoise tutu in the garden of a certain celeb — a douchebag whose main fame to date was playing the shy handsome underbutler in a popular TV *fin de siècle* soap opera who kept getting in entanglements above his station (*loins*, Myfanwy thought thoughtfully, and filled in a lily) — yeah, so the Cool Kid was in this guy's garden, hunting for the snails of the night, and thence in the celeb's bed, or at least draped over his sofa, wearing nothing but said heels and muddy tutu and said snails themselves on her outstretched windmilling arms, as jewels, and also for modesty as a disobliging, awkward, and slowly dislodging "snail bra," and thence repaired the Cool Kid to Business Studies the next morning, only ten minutes late, without the snails *or* the tutu *or* the celeb (whose number apparently she had to *block* in the end), looking *gorgeous as usual* and toying with some sort of annoying, poignant sense-rich memento or talisman, which she didn't draw any attention to, but which totally proved it was all true, every bit of it.

But was this Cool Kid's conduct commendable?

Even if you couldn't help but quite liking her for the snails, Myfanwy thought, she never really *said* anything, and it would probably be ten years before she ever *did* anything again.

Or when she did say things, they were like words of a page you only thought you'd been reading.

Myfanwy had hung out with these Asians for hours on Kitty's eighteenth birthday, convinced they would finally, like, *get* each other. No such luck. It was like being at the court in Versailles (or at least Myfanwy assumed it was).

So vapid. She honestly couldn't remember a word they had said.

She still didn't even know all their names.

So, yeah. Tallulah would have seen what Kitty saw, only *less*. No point in dredging up what was no doubt for Tallulah a, like, really painful, difficult time for her, which completely changed her life, although she'd probably already forgotten . . .

Dredging, thought Myfanwy, shivered, and searched for a chink to ink in one more lily. The lake looked like chainmail. What a mesh!

As for Sid Fairfax's conceptual work "Angels vs. Evil Angels: The War in Kevin," dedicated to his BFF Kevin Thomas, Stacy Lake's "High Street vs. High Art?" or Paddy's "Unspoilt Canvas No. 7," bless him, oh dear oh dear . . . well, Myfanwy was much less sure about those. In past years Madame Merely-Pointy had seemed just as thrilled by the F marks as by the A-stars. "For you, ze examination board are not ready," she would declare firmly. "Philistinism is zer only principle."

In her own marking practice, Merely-Pointy had run into trouble with the Head Teacher after giving a girl a 110%.

There were more tears in Merely-Pointy's final year classes than paint.

Myfanwy knew that she personally was one of Madame Merely-Pointy's few disappointments. She *had* piqued Merely-Pointy's interest during the printmaking module, producing a set of rather elegant index cards featuring decontextualised text messages (basically wouldn't have worked if Kitty wasn't so weird) — and there was the whole thing with Paddy in the giant envelope (probably wouldn't have worked with anyone else's hair) — but her heart wasn't in it. She just liked doing detailed ink landscapes with millions of tiny marks. She'd done such landscapes since she was little.

Merely-Pointy had difficulty focusing on these artworks, let alone remarking on them. Myfanwy shrugged and carried on. She only needed that damn C anyway. If ginormous ink landscapes weren't worth that much . . . then maybe for her, ze universities were not ready.

The task at hand was a little different though.

For the past three days, following Kitty's suggestion, Myfanwy had been drawing the Citadel. It was flowing straight out her arteries onto her canvas. It was so simple.

If the statue guy really *was* somehow sending her there, then she would go willingly. She would walk its spaces, count its flagstones. Solidify its barrels of flowers and its parks of woods, slowly petrify their reaching-up branches with her flowing-down brooks of ink.

It was *her* mind. And she would make the Citadel *her* place, not *his*.

It seemed to be working. The daydreams were less vivid. At night, asleep, sometimes she could determine the course of events.

Myfanwy knew there was more inside her than the Citadel. There was also a place called the Settlement, somewhere outside it. A vaguer, even more dangerous place, like stained glass clockwork, where beasts spoke, and tall paper golems stooped to watch the work of bright machines. A place of glittering dust, and tragic high nests, and long, snatching arms. Would *he* send her there next?

Then she'd draw that too.

And beyond the Settlement, even shapelesser, the shadow of some third place, legislative and cthuluic . . . people lurking like crows or like snipers . . . and in some dreams, a wheeled coffin tipped up and down atop a crag, then flung open . . . only concrete inside . . .

Tallulah glid by Myfanwy's desk.

Myfanwy blurted, "*GOD I LOVE YOUR WORK.*"

Left and right tilted Myfanwy's eyes, to see who was responsible for this statement.

Tallulah paused, just as stunned, and wheeled about her withering Cool Kid audit. Myfanwy blushed, feeling momentarily like one of her own landscapes under Merely-Pointy's grudgingly-appraising gaze.

"You're thin," Myfanwy squeaked.

Then Tallulah burst out laughing. "Is it good? I've never watched it through. It's so annoying." She tilted her svelte neck. "How's your one going?"

Tallulah studied Myfanwy's three-quarters filled canvas.

"It's my, uh," said Myfanwy. "It's my Ci—"

"Oh, brilliant!" Tallulah jumped in. "Edinburgh."

*

Myfanwy stood in the car park of Edinburgh Castle, imagining large siege engines reversing, ringing out like lorries. The wind whipped her hair onto her lips. She leaned on a parapet. She could see the sea, curving deep inland as the Firth of Forth. The city burst out in all directions below her, pocked by drifting pockets of mist.

Hmm.

Myfanwy turned away and regarded her flapping paper map for the umpteenth time.

It had not been a successful day. She'd been just about everywhere in the north, east and west parts of the city. Where did that leave? Nowhere!

So far Edinburgh felt familiar, uncanny . . . but also plain alien. The light was wrong. Nowhere fit with the place she sought, the intensest spot of the Citadel, from where it sprung like springwater, a place of fields and trees, which she obscurely felt lay on her way *home*, in this city she had never before visited . . .

Worst of all, she had a nagging feeling the towers weren't tall enough. What if Edinburgh wasn't the Citadel at all?

And yet Tallulah had been *so certain!*

"Why're you drawing *Edinburgh*? I have family there."

"I've never been," said Myfanwy shyly. "I mean — I *think* I went once, when I was really small. Hey, weird question, are there like — *sphinxes* anywhere near all this?"

"Near Waverley? Aye, defo, stone guys up on the museum. Is this landscape supposed to be through their eyes? *Loving* your train tracks by the way. Like snakes. *Scary*."

Endless dark snakes. Train tracks. To the left, a glowing line, blasted by a thorn-like tower. The Wilted Scar.

"What's this?"

"Scott Monument, eh? I was, like, Orphan Fifty in a production of *Oliver!* there once, which was pointless."

On the horizon, to the left, what were dubbed the Fingers of Ignominy. A little closer, a bright line, the Cauldron of Souls . . .

Tallulah's wandlike finger swept across the canvas. "Calton Hill. That used to be Clinton Cards. That used to be BHS," she showed off. She laughed. She sounded more Scottish than usual.

"But that's the Cauldron of Souls!"

"Clinton Cards? You're *so* right!"

"I was maybe going up there this weekend. Um, Edinburgh, not a card shop."

"Serious? You could probably stay with my dad and step-mum if you needed."

"Wow. Um. Maybe. I mean, I want to visit the same places I remember."

"Um. I mean, you're probably visiting friends."

"Bill's Used Tuck Shop. Is that a place in Edinburgh?"

"Possibly," said Tallulah apprehensively. "I don't think I've been in."

"Is there, like, an old Roman road?"

"Not that I know of —"

"And, uh, Sex Café?"

"Oh, there's loads of places like *that!*" Tallulah said, obviously now on firmer ground. "Possibly in the Pubic Triangle? You'd think that'd be near the Mound, but *actually* —"

"Ladies," trilled Madame Merely-Pointy. "Zis is an *examination!*"

"*MP*," Tallulah answered haughtily. "With mild alacrity, I've finished my Portfolio *and* my Controlled Composition. The only thing that keeps me in this classroom is the Geneva Convention's lamentable lack of clarity on my case. My *classmate* here is pure asking me about Scottish sex tourism."

Myfanwy nodded, a little confused. "I'm a fellow Cool Kid," she hazarded. Tallulah gazed at her thoughtfully.

Madame Merely-Pointy sniffed. Clearly anything an artiste like Tallulah cared to say to a wannabe like Myfanwy counted as a masterclass. "I zuppose it cannot do er any arm. Quietly, girls."

"So what are you into?" said Tallulah.

"Actually," Myfanwy whispered, blushing. "Sorry, Tallulah — can you tell me about um *green spaces* in Edinburgh? There's just this one specific forest or field or something, I can remember what it's *like*, but I can't . . ."

"They sphinxes are where the German Christmas Market goes, overlooking Princes Street Gardens. Do you remember any trams? Actually no, forgot that, they're unbelievably recent. Or Arthur's Seat, maybe? Can you remember rabbits and crows? Or an observatory? Blackford Hill, maybe? Or avenues of trees?"

"I *do* remember rabbits," Myfanwy admitted slowly. "But I think that was another time. Where are the trees? I remember . . . long rows of trees, lining the . . . at first I remembered Roman Roads, but now I think just pathways. Some were fallen. There'd been a storm."

"Um. There's the Meadows, which is all playgrounds, Ultimate Frisbee? Women exercising with prams. Melon and prawn barbecues? Ringing anything? Nooo. Hmm." Tallulah's gorgeous waist-length chestnut hair pooled on Myfanwy's canvas as she swooped to make her close examination. "*This* looks a lot like that loch at the end of the Innocent Railway. I can't mind what it's called. Fewer lily-pads than that anyway, an' mair jakies."

"No, I don't think it's any of those."

"Or the art galleries near Stockbridge. There was a big neon sign that said 'Everything Is Going To Be Okay' for ages, till they realised, and took it down. And the Botanical Gardens. There's *loads* of green spaces really."

"Oh."

"Right, well, I'm bored. I guess I'll go start revising History. It's more like 'vising' in my case."

"I call them my Revulsion Notes," Myfanwy said, feeling immediately like a moron.

"Cute. Enjoy Edinburgh though, it's the best city. It's no even really

Scottish. It's pointless that it's in Scotland."

That was Thursday.

Today was Saturday and here she was.

For some minutes Myfanwy had been staring numbly at the Saltire snapping over Edinburgh Castle. Her phone honked with a text from Kitty: Meet Costa 1pm no joke Kxx

Hmm.

Text to Kitty: Love to m8, in EDINBURGH today! I KNOW, right? ABROAD! Could do Sunday drunkenness again? Straight off Flying Scotsman (train)?x

Two seconds later, *honk honk*. No to sun m8 o m9.Obv ed Im there too.Costa royal mile TEN MIN Kxxxx

*

"Oh my days," Myfanwy murmured. "As I live and breathe."

It was ten past one and Kitty was trying to worm free of the fortress of bulging shopping she had just unintentionally constructed around herself on the Costa tile-work. "Myffed! Aren't I amazing? Looly told me you were like bugging her with weird questions. And *then* you were v. evasive about your plans this weekend. *Mwa! Mwa! So* I checked your emails and saw your stupid early East Coast train — I was actually on the same one as you, except —"

"On the same *train* as me?" Myfanwy eyed up Kitty's bags. Hot pink chiffon poked out of the little battlements.

"I've never *been* to Edinburgh, fam!" bleated the BFF. "I *had* to go see Greyfriars Bobby. So loyal and statuesque! Literally favourite Edinburgh dog? And the café where Francis Croque wrote *Melée dans La Sperme* when he was penniless and couldn't even afford a candle to unfreeze his ink. Very romantic but also very real. And Looly told me about some great vintage spots dotted about —"

"OMG she told me too," said Myfanwy. "Only I'm *on a massive quest*!"

"I'm so sorry hon. I *really* didn't think it would take that long? I didn't see the Castle of Edinburgh if that helps. The Womyn's Castle is obv way better. Look, how long do you think you'll be confronting your nemesis etc.? My train is at two tomorrow. I was thinking maybe in the morning —"

Myfanwy knocked the breath out of her with a massive hug. "Shut up, shut up, shut up. I love you, I love you, I love you. I'm changing my password."

"Ain't *nobody* breaking up this bromance again," said Kitty.

"*Edinbrothers*, yeah? Leggo. Let — go."

"I hope people are staring," said Myfanwy. "Because I want them to *know*."

*

Late afternoon. A hippie girl went by on a bike, no hands, talking in Portuguese, pedalling laconically. She wore a Prodigy-era Dual Mohawk.

Thoroughly sodden, the girls sat shivering side-by-side on a black bench. Now and then an awful gust reminded Myfanwy of the icy wetness of her garms. On the ground beside them, hopeful clumps of purple, white and yellow crocuses poked up their heads in little bouquets, as if Mother Natura herself macked on Interflora's market share.

At least the rain had stopped now. But then, the rain also somehow remained *in the air*. It was like being *inside* a rain cloud — the rain didn't *need* to fall. Myfanwy understood thc Saltirc now. It was a blue sky, crossed out.

Blue Skies Are Forbidden!

In the playground to the east, delighted children were swarming. On the horizon, hillwalking specks inspected Arthur's Seat. Lights changed, oblivious. Traffic came and went. Bollards sank, and the crocuses by the bench and in barrels by the traffic lights, presumably, all grew a little taller. And a buff boy wandered past shirtless, the band of his Jack Willis pants on prominent display.

Kitty shook her head in total despair. "Scottish people are insane."

Myfanwy nodded microscopically. "They talk constantly about the weather and then behave as if it's completely different to what it is. Isn't it terrible," she added, "the way those drunks congregate there right near all the kids?"

"Yes darling. The last thing I want to look at when I'm binge drinking is some child on a swing."

Myfanwy laughed, miserable in her skin, but euphoric in her heart. She knew now they were close!

On Kitty's suggestion again, Myfanwy had forgone her map, and spent the afternoon just drifting through the Citadel, letting her feet guide her. They had danced her south, through the Deluge of George Square, seen several brolly ribs bust open — they didn't even have an umbrella to sacrifice to the squall — then past a merry little joint called Snax Café — where she thought perhaps she'd once purchased a turkey and cranberry sandwich, which came with a free can of "juice," which in Scotland meant Coke or Irn Bru (careful, it's pronounced "Iron Brew") or something (but wait a minute, she'd never *been* here! She'd never *been* here!) — and past the jolly green frontage of Till's Second Hand Book Shop where she thought perhaps she'd considered and rejected a copy of Mary and Jane Findlater's *The Green Graves of Balgowrie* (now *that* didn't sound like her either, the rejection bit anyway) — to *this* spot, on the south edge of the Meadows.

Across the road, bare serried trees flourished their many twigs, massing them through the mists towards the sky, as proudly as if they were leaves. Further still towards town centre, old stone towers rose in a mingle with the glass and mirrors of the Quartermile flats and office complex. Gulls and crows hopped to and fro. One or two massive trees, uprooted by recent storms, showed their intimate inner wood, white as any snow. These fields seemed smaller by day too. And, Myfanwy had to remind herself, by the light of real life.

An ambulance klaxoned past.

"Fucking pigs," said Kitty abstractedly. "Oh, *Myffy*, I've had *enough* of this. I really am *soaking*."

"You're kidding, right? Come on, we'll try up the next one."

Kitty's mouth made the smallest possible sound available to mouths.

Myfanwy studied the skyline. "Hey Kitty," she said, "you know earlier I said the buildings weren't tall enough? Here's a theory. My main memory of the towers was looking up whilst wearing a *hood*."

Kitty held up a finger. She was to speak. Myfanwy waited patiently. "Is there," Kitty whispered, "*no* abatement in the ferociousness of this tempest?"

Myfanwy tutted.

Not far off, workers in yellow jackets were taking down an archway which a sign had helpfully informed Myfanwy was constructed of a whale's jawbone. Condemned, perhaps, or else just off for its centenary polishing or flossing or whatever, ready to be gleamingly reinstalled for the summer.

"Listen, fam," Myfanwy said patiently. "If I'm right at the foot of the building, and the rim of my hood coincides with the roof of the building . . . it could seem way taller than it actually is, right?"

"Yeah," said Kitty, now glancing around rather wildly. "Great." If any teeth would chatter on command, Kitty's would be all a-chatter now. "Do you think we could get a taxi to pull up right up to this bench? I mean *right up*. I'm afraid of moving anything."

Myfanwy's phone also showed a B&Q nearby, promising under any circumstances, but especially now. She thought she remembered a sign for B&Q. No sign here now, but who knew, maybe the sign vanished just last week, whereas the B&Q endured. Myfanwy rose. Kitty too, a moment later, moaning "I hate, hate, hate this stupid goldfish tank town."

Myfanwy sweetly offered to carry some of Kitty's shopping — by now she had already been carrying everything except Kitty's handbag for the last hour. As Kitty had pointed out several times, it was quite a large and expensive handbag.

"Sarky cow," sniffed Kitty. "You *did* offer. And *I* came all the way to *Scotland* for you —"

"For me to carry *your*—"

Hmm. Cow. Goldfish. Why so familiar?

This feels *like the right place. A place near home, no near . . . not B&Q! Near* H*Q!*

Technically the Meadows ended at this junction. Then the mini Links course led away to their left.

And goldfish. Golf?

Well, you never knew. "This way, Kitty!"

And thus they resumed their hunt, peering in front gardens and ground floor windows. Kitty cheered herself up a little by critiquing fragments of glimpsed decor. Myfanwy however was only half-listening. "Not these ones, not these ones," she muttered. "Too much garden. Too many plants. It has something *like* gravel, except —"

"Getting dark so *early*," said Kitty, distracted.

Soon they came upon a little district of charity shops and greengrocers. They paused in front of Peter Green & Co Wine Merchants. "I gotta admit Myffed," Kitty said, "until quite recently I just thought you were looking for your B&B. I mean, if we *are* that close, is it maybe time to call the feds? Send up the balloon? Choppers and hounds and bare snipers and ting?"

"What would I *tell* them though? That I have visions of a house, and I think that's where the man lives who's sexually assaulting me with his mind?"

Shaolin Traditional Kung Fu. Belly Babies.

"I see your point," said Kitty. "To be fair though, you *are* crazy."

Posters plastered the shop window, a Cubist rainbow of liquers flowing in the gutters between them.

Renaissance Music Choir. Zumba. Pilates at the Gillis Centre.

Myfanwy watched the overlapping varicoloured glasses intensify their glow, then, suddenly, searing white lines shot among parts of texts, connecting words in glittering clusters.

Kung Fu Music . . . Renault Clio . . .

Kitty followed Myfanwy's gaze. "'*Nemesis seeks showdown*,'" she said archly. "Only, pity hon, all the little phone number taggies have been taken."

Zeus . . . Pirates at the Gills Centre . . . B&B . . . B&Q . . . H&Q . . . H&M . . . !

Nope, just thinking random letters now.

Myfanwy shrugged. "At first I thought it had to be a street directly off the Meadows. Maybe it's just farther back." She stared up at the chimneys and widows' walkways. "Come on. This one is too straight. The street we're looking for," she added, "is wide, and long, but *curved* . . ."

A grey cat, who looked a lot like Flux, ran away under a red car. Taxis swished past, sloshing the puddles, sporting the faces of dead princes — the National Portrait Gallery was on a marketing offensive. The girls skirted an unpleasant altercation between two men, one in a motorcycle helmet. They snooped and declined garden after garden. They climbed up onto piles of bricks, and recycling boxes upturned, looked in chinks in drawn curtains, saw fragments of book shelves, cushions, beds — they investigated and declined them.

Forms moving past, fragments of human figures, moving and mangled as if hounded by dogs. Telly light. Rejected. Not right.

Children's plastic filled this front garden.

"Could *that* be the killer's little tractor?" Kitty inquired.

"Next one," Myfanwy muttered. "Next. Next. Not this one. Not —"

She stopped dead.

"What? What?"

Another brown wheelie bin. *Make Our City EDEN-burgh.*

"What? Have you only just got that? What?"

Myfanwy shivered, raised her eyes. Just an ordinary terraced house. Was it HQ? Was it the house from her head? How could she know?

The little iron gate left open, more derelict than welcoming. Some ivy. A blue crisp packet in the hedge. The door green and white, painted in a pattern. Not too forbidding.

In the garden, no plants but a few weeds. And sea-shells.

A column of buzzers, with labels in different handwritings.

"Is this *it*, Myffed? Jesus, *talk!*"

She became aware of a presence a few feet behind her.

She started turning, but an unfamiliar voice spoke. And what it said made her freeze mid-turn.

"Myfanwy, Kitty. Welcome to Chancelhouse. Shall we go in?"

Book Two

"FINE: Whoa. Think Blake was a spook? Government or black ops?
GALLAGHER: I think . . . this is way bigger than both of us."

— Alan Moore, *The Watchmen*

He had a subtly plummy Brummie accent. He wore tweeds. In one hand he carried a light blue carrier bag, fresh from the corner shop, and in the other a set of keys softly jangled. He was small and oldish — the first impression Myfanwy formed of him was of a sort of living garden gnome. Only, whatever spell had brought him to life had been overly potent, and filled him with superfluous, overflowing vitality. There was also something endlessly elusive about him too, like a series of insufficient CCTV images, temporally serried together into a little magus. Right now he was sizing up the tall, grand and generously chimney-potted tenement house like he'd never seen it before.

"Could this be the place?" he breathed with mock awe. "But what's *in* there? Which shall we ring? Let's ring them *all!* No, wait! I'm *afraid*, girls!" He sobbed and shielded his gaze in charlatan lament. "I — I can't do it! We'll come back later. We'll —"

The little guy's keys now hung over his nose. He jingle-jangled them. Myfanwy giggled.

"And *how* do you know our —" Kitty began.

He was examining her sharply through the key ring, as though it were a jeweller's loupes. "I believe the phrase is, '*Ah. Kitty*. We have been *expecting* you.' Except clearly we *have not*, I'm afraid. Not at any particular time anyway. For goodness sake, I was out *shopping*."

The gentleman now opened his blue carrier bag, demonstrating the presence of two cartons of milk — both girls raised their eyebrows in congratulation — and looped it over his keys-jangling hand, so he could stick the other one out for shaking.

"'In milky fondness, then on them he fixed his humble eye.' Blake. Haduken Blake. How do you do. How do you do. Do wah do wah do wah —"

The arm was swinging around like an unmanned oar. Myfanwy finally took pity, took aim, grabbed it and held on grimly. "Myfanwy, as you apparently know. Pleased to meet you."

"How do you do, Myfanwy! Then you must be Catherine — Kitty, is it?"

He doesn't know everything, Myfanwy thought. *He wasn't sure which of us was which.*

Myfanwy handed Blake's hand to Kitty — carefully, as though it might start veering off again — and looked to and fro between them, trying to judge her BFF's feeling. Later, Myfanwy would discover people often disagreed how best to describe Haduken Blake. His basic traits were plain enough — shrunken, a spry seventyish-plus. Neat white beard and neat white ponytail, on top his tonsure nearly balded to nowt. Floweringly rosy-cheeked, and somewhat burgundy and bulbous about the snout. Terrible teeth. But it was Blake's hard-to-pin-down aura that divided folks into those who mysteriously warmed to him and those whom he mysteriously freaked out. Though Kitty wore not a trace of smile, Myfanwy felt she was swiftly falling into the former category.

"My name is Sherlock Holmes," said Kitty, shaking Blake's hand with an exaggeratedly vast SINE.

"My mistake," said Blake solemnly. "I am a great venerator of your wildly uncorroborated inductions, Dr Holmes. Now shall we be brave, re this upstairs business? Would you like a cuppa?"

Myfanwy and Kitty looked at each other quizzically.

Blake was already scooching between them sideways. "In consequence of my latest triumph," he said, traipsing up the garden step and fussing with his keys, "we'll be equipped with the milk with the red top, the milk with the green top, and the milk with the blue top. No use crying over split milk, as they should say." He paused with the key in the lock, as if something infinitely terrible had just struck him. "I believe there is also a milk with a purple top," he said quietly, slightly bowing his head.

"I take my tea black!" Kitty chipped in.

"Wonderful, marvellous!" Blake said, his head boinging up just as the white and green door banged open, giving Myfanwy a small start. "Oh, marvellous! You can stay!"

The girls leaned forward. Deep shadows lay within.

"With lemon," Kitty added, with frills of friendly malice.

"Ah," Blake said, crestfallen once more, started to enter, straightened abruptly and whirled round so that both girls — on the verge of trotting dutifully behind — very nearly fell tumbling off the step and into the squashed sea-shells. "I do mean what I say, you know! Only you're not to breathe a word to friends or family. Unseasonable March, isn't it? I think it might snow. Now, why are we still out here? Oh yes! I wanted to point out to you — before we get too smug about detecting the correct door — that the whole street is ours, girls! Yes, yes! Any buzzer at all would have done!"

"Some might be broken," Myfanwy pointed out.

"So it's still a quest," Kitty added.

"Every buzzer the sun's light touches, my somber little Simbas!"

"With you," agreed Kitty.

"Including all those houses across on the west side, though you'd need my keycard for those, plus the deli on the corner you'll have passed. Ha, didn't expect that, did you? — yes we run a deli — and also two wee stores at the top end, which maybe you haven't seen, you'd have come to eventually — one is computer 'repairs,' although *actually* we make them worse, plus 3D printing, we probably make a cat's supper of that too, print things in the wrong three dimensions I'll warrant, plus God-knows-what. And the other is a media production company, plus, well, the Other Chap-knows-what."

Kitty homed in on the useful info. "Who's 'we'?" she asked carefully.

"Don't gallylaggle on the step like a pair of — euhh — giggly gargoyles — in you go, march on, ladies! Who's 'we'? Well Holmes, can't you guess? Didn't I mention? We're *Chancelhouse!* That's what we call ourselves, anyway. Why is it that? I have no idea. To be mysterious, I expect. What's *more* mysterious, all the locals up here call groceries 'the messages' — why is *that? What do they know that we don't?* Well, the world is full of terrifying secrets, ladies — I'm afraid — at any rate, no more lollygiggling. One or two of those secrets may lie inside, ladies. *So inside we go! Quick step! Unreasonable march!* I'll give you a tour. *Inside! Inside!*"

*

"Ah, now *that* door, aha, what a door," Haduken Blake announced, spinning up the stairwell at a terrible tempo. "Yes, yes. The houses all interconnect on the first and third floors, more-or-less. Had I slipped into our deli that way, I may never even have found you lamentable strays lily-goggling on our step! Chancelhouse runs them as legit enterprises, you see, our deli and our shops — makes it easier to take deliveries for the whole Chancelhouse HQ compound."

"Won't that mean more people snooping around?" said Kitty.

"Especially the deli?" said Myfanwy. "I mean, yum. Right? Yum."

Snooping around what? she wondered. So far it just seemed a posh if in places rather shabby old house.

"The deli does mean more snoopers, yes, but it also lends an aura of naturalness to the area. What could be more natural than paying through the nose for manchego!"

"Ingenious," said Kitty.

"Anyway, delis are for posh people, and by definition posh people don't pay attention — quick step, do keep up! Did I mention that rule? Offices, libraries, armoury, study rooms, kitchens, Valhalla — what we call our buttery — buttery is what we call our canteen — a roof terrace, a gym, more specialist research labs than you can shake a white coat out at — but absolutely *no lemons!* Budget cuts, you know — terrible times, everybody on edge. Duke's Deli's always something to fall back on, if the whole mystic agency angle goes pear-shaped, I suppose."

"The whole —" Kitty began.

"Now, the milk with the purple top, strictly speaking, lies *between* that with the red top and that with the green top, though purple does *not* lie between red and green. Yes, yes, keep up now! — have I mentioned that rule? More of a guideline, really, but a good one — funnily enough I've never been through *that* door, one of Aoide's offices and she keeps it locked — some odd chaps prowl from chamber to chamber, you see, though of course we're on a skeleton crew just now — very hush-hush — senior class, as it were, away on manouevres — insane, risky stuff, the sensible ones stay behind — as I was saying, no doubt the real rationale for the Chancelhouse deli is that I dabble in cheffery myself — versatile with a beetroot, I'm told, though on the other hand . . ."

Up and down staircases they flew, round and round stairwells, along short and long corridors, to and fro through the rambling honeycomb of chambers, mostly blurring past too swiftly to take measure of any of their specific purposes. Blake lapsed into a mostly incomprehensible soliloquy, touching upon tea and arcana, and woven with obscure allusions to alchemists and occultists. The impressions Myfanwy did catch were of plush rugs, tall Hellenic black-figured water pitchers empty in corners, cut-glass vases stuffed with browning azaleas on sills, slightly threadbare *chaise-longues*, expensive saddlebag chairs done in crimson or butterscotch leather, many dozens of neo-pre-Raphaelite paintings, the occasional gleaming claymore or halberd, and, *vis-à-vis* statuary, a marked stylistic over-reliance on carved heads of unicorns, hornéd hummingbirds and hornéd lions. A few doors had ornate engraved devices over them, and/or strange handwritten signs upon them, in many different handwritings — *Thorn, Ouzo, Golem; Meletē (Office C); Aoide (Office B); Merlin, Tase, Static.* One or two doors were ceremonially blocked off with ebony stanchions suspending between them the sly smiles of delicate silver chains.

"Excuse me!" Kitty eventually exclaimed, as she glanced through a tall narrow window between two bookshelves. "Excuse me — Mr White Rabbit? Is it possible we have double-backed on ourselves? Only I see this window commands the scene of a slightly familiar wheelie bin."

Blake waddled back with a wounded look. "Why, *yes*. But I'm giving you the tour."

"You're not actually saying anything sensible though," Kitty pointed out. "You're still talking about milk quite a lot."

Myfanwy nodded vigorously. "We have hard-hitting, investigative journalist type questions for you."

"No," Blake agreed with them. "I'm sort of *used* to these digs, I s'pose. You know what it's like — I never really know what to say to new people." He cast about desolately — every wall of the chamber was lined with antique books' gold-leafed spines. "This is a library!" he exclaimed, inspired.

"Oh *really*," said Kitty. "I thought it was the swimming pool."

"No. That's on Cellar Level Two," Blake added, puzzled. "By the

Myometrium. Do you fancy a quick dip then?" He sounded worried.

Myfanwy, meanwhile, had become mesmerised by one of the library's smaller paintings. "*This* looks familiar," she said. She ran her finger along the frame.

"Ah," Blake said softly, drawing up beside Myfanwy. "Genevieve Quaker. AKA Mnemosyne. Also known as — yes, there are several of Miss Quaker dotted about. Our patroness saint, you could say."

"Patron," Myfanwy automatically corrected her new companion.

"Patron saintess then," Blake rejoined mildly. "How do you stand on 'heroine' by the way?"

"I'm not familiar with the term," said Myfanwy.

It was funny, Myfanwy thought, how fashions came round again. The painter had put Genevieve Quaker in a woad blue bodice, cut in a low square window over a white chemise, which was fastened at her throat with a single pearl, plus a plain white coif and a simple, jagged little ruff round her neck. She had chubby cheeks without looking well-fed, exactly — "pauper fat," if you will. She bore that mixed expression you sometimes got upon imagery of putti or the Infant Christ, of almost impossibly tender and sweet yearning on one hand, and on the other hand — or rather, shoulder — apparently just needing a good burping.

"Of course," Blake said, "Genevieve Quaker was more than two hundred years dead when this likeness was done. Depending, that is, on how you reckon it, a rather intricate question actually. But she may have looked nothing like that."

"Oh. How sad."

"Yes. Well anything that is unlike anything else is sad, in at least one respect," said Blake obscurely. "And certainly, poor Miss Quaker looked nothing like herself when her . . . questioning was concluded."

"God. What *happened* to her?"

"Lynched," Blake said softly. "Oh yes. 'Confess! Confess!' She never did. Many more have been hanged than burnt at the stake, you see. Only the hangings aren't so well remembered."

"Witchcraft?"

"Ah. Quite right. The rope never sets the public imagination aflame, as it were, in quite the same way as the pyre. Folk like to think of us going up in smoke, I suppose! But we were strung up in our hundreds, you bet your life. We were the bunting of the medieval world. Never mind the stonings, the drownings, the crushings and suffocations. Well, we *did* mind, actually. The witch's family would be billed for the cost of it, whatever it was — monies so that the judges and priests could feast and be entertained. Then there's fee for the brodding, that means pricking the skin, and for the shaving — the shaver of the witch has mouths to feed, my dear! — for the cutting of tongue, and for mercy-strangling for any poor wretches who could convincingly confess and repent —*fuego resuelto!*— yes, yes, and of course firewood ain't cheap! All neatly itemised. In Antiquity we gulped hemlock. Though the Greeks liked cooking us too — they invented Reason, so I'm sure they knew what they were doing! I dabble in Reason myself. Do you know much about Perilaus's Brazen Bull, perchance? A sort of syrinx, foreshadowing of the fatal syringe, to be placed on hot coals. The innocent's screams were amplified by a series of tubes and stops, and were said to resemble the roaring breath of an enraged or ebullient bu—"

BANG!

Myfanwy yelped. Kitty had loudly slammed shut some volume she'd earlier seized at random — an ornate and obviously venerable folio, that looked like it might fetch more than Facebook on the open market — and through which she had been idly flicking, whilst Myfanwy and Blake wittered wildly beneath the painting.

"*Marvellous*," Kitty said. For a spell the pair span free of the Most Lamentable Tragedy of Genevieve Quaker. "Wicked," Kitty sighed. "Look sir, I'm sorry to cut short this, uh, Olympus moment, but I'm gonna need some info. What *is* this place? You called it . . . Chancelhouse?"

"'Chancelhouse' is the name of the agency," Blake elucidated. "These digs we just call 'HQ' or 'the compound' or 'the houses' — or 'the east houses,' seeing as no one goes in houses on the west side at present."

Kitty nodded pensively. "Right you are."

"The younger generation will say 'gaff' and 'enz' and so forth obviously," Blake added. "Along with 'safe' and 'cuz' and many an intolerable novelty. Better not to mention addresses, basically, is the point I'm making!"

"How did you know *our* names?" Myfanwy demanded. "Like, a database? Is 'chancel' some legal thing?"

"Ecclesiastical, cuz," said Kitty. "Myfanwy's thinking of 'chancery.'"

"Excellent!" warbled Blake, his Jazz Hands ardently a-flutter. "Excellent! Quite wrong, quite wrong. 'Chancel' was legal before it was ecclesiastical, though it may have been ecclesiastical before it was legal, I forget, and anyway, far enough back the two things are thoroughly mixed up! Speaking of getting thoroughly mixed up, you'll need callsongs soon, won't you?"

"We'll need what?" said Kitty.

"Is this a school for witches?" gasped Myfanwy.

"One thing at a time, my dears. The take-home points re *chancel*, from the Latin *cancelli*, are as follows: separation, security, restricted visibility. Got it? All a 'chancel' is, ladies, is a sort of tracery or latticework. Originally used in the courts of the Latins, as Myfanwy may have divined, and later in Christian churches, as Kitty so justly alludes, to separate clergy and choir from the uninitiated *hoi polloi* in the nave. I suppose our illustrious founders thought 'trellis' wasn't quite forbidding enough a name for secret mystic agency — they obviously hadn't attended quite the same barbeques in the Brum suburbia as I have! Now, Chancelhouse doesn't go back *quite* as far as Rome, I don't believe. My personal best guess is 1482, but it's difficult, you'll appreciate, to set an exact date, because we were founded with a sort of *false history* already in place. A false history, precisely to obscure our origins — you follow me?"

He regarded them quite carefully.

"Yes sir," said Kitty. "Like positioning a brand."

"I think so," said Myfanwy. "Like, did God make the world with dino fossil Readymades, just to test our faith?"

Blake nodded slowly. "You've both got it exactly, girls. Did God build the universe mere millenia hence, with her cellars full of dragon bone? Or perhaps the old dear was created in 1990, for instance — 'And on the seventh day Our Lord made the archives and news-reels' — and the memories for that matter — 'of the moon landings, of the Wall falling, of Bon Jovi, of Madonna . . . of big hair, and short little T-shirts on men'? — all *that*, just to test our faith? How old is the universe? How old *is* Chancelhouse? Well! Yes, the Eighties in particular certainly tested *my* faith, and I shouldn't be surprised if —"

"The Eighties?" said Myfanwy. "Really?"

"Is this a school for witches?" said Kitty.

"I'm just guessing here," Myfanwy added, "but did you have a witch called Mara Drago-Ferrante?"

"Ah." Blake's eyes crinkled, and his chin fell to his chest.

Oops. Shouldn't have sounded so chirpy, thought Myfanwy. *He really knew her.*

"Yes, she was an agent here once," he brooded. "But no more." Something fierce and bright lit inside Blake. His eyes lifted once more to the portrait of Genevieve Quaker. "No more," he said again gently.

The three stood in silence in the library. Myfanwy thought of ropes and flames, and rivers and stones.

"Way to kill a mood, Myfanwy," said Kitty softly. "Sir?" she cooed. "How about that cuppa you hyped? And then you can spill some beans. You can start — for example — why the key points are separation, security, and invisibility . . . and why it's better not to mention addresses . . ."

*

Somewhere along the south edge of Edinburgh Meadows, carefully concealed within two rows of Victorian tenement houses, gently curving uphill — along such a vector as might remind one of the long sinuous carves of a certain escaping skater, if one were inclined to make such strange connections — facing one another east-to-west across a quiet, although not unusually or suspiciously quiet, urb-suburban street, up from a pricey deli with signage reading "Duke's Deli" — rather than, say, "Chancelhouse Café – witches eat half-price on Tuesdays" which all agreed might well have given the game away — down from some shabby and unremarkable tecchy and media shops, where you probably really shouldn't take your computer, lie the secret headquarters of a venerable and clandestine mystic agency which is known, in this world and era, as Chancelhouse.

At that very moment Myfanwy and Kitty were sharing a single voluminous armchair in one of the libraries of Chancelhouse HQ — a different library from before, though except for the paintings Myfanwy probably never could have told them apart — blowing on two cups of tea, skimmed-milked and black respectively, whilst opposite them, Haduken Blake, Director of Chancelhouse, sat grinning and ignoring his own foaming full fat milked cuppa, and nodding with his chin in his hands and his elbows on his knees, which were jiggling.

For him, Myfanwy knew by now, all this counted as "calm."

A white and orange china plate of ginger snaps sat untouched on a little chestnut table between them. Myfanwy had decided the word for what surrounded them on the shelves was not *books* or even *volumes* so much as *grimoires*. This library was not the sort of place the Local Community could feel comfortable coming to regardless of levels of literacy. It was more the sort of place where you read the wrong paragraph aloud and suddenly your gargoyles start laughing and sneezing, and your garden gnome hops off his polka dot toadstool and gets all up in your grill.

"One more thing, before I tell you any more re Chancelhouse," Blake said. "I must check my intelligence re *you*. I'm Chancelhouse Director after all, what used to be called — rather more majestically, alas! — *Mousagetēs*. Now, if it turns out you're just here to read the gas meter, I'll be mortified. You girls have known each other for years, correct?"

They nodded in synch. "Since we were six," said Myfanwy.

"If our hips weren't such gifts to mankind," Kitty added dryly, "we'd have joined them."

"Humankind," Myfanwy autocorrected. "Edinbrothers," she footnoted.

Blake's brow furrowed. "Uh, hips? Edin—?"

"Oh, *nothing*," said Kitty.

"BFFs," said Myfanwy.

"Oh dear, I'm sorry. B . . . F —?"

"*Finishing* each other's sentences," Kitty butted in. "Plaiting each other's damn hair, knowing exactly what the other one's thinking, that kind of thing. 'Oh, but Kitty, Simon doesn't *know* I don't know how to kiss a boy yet!' 'Oh, Myffy!' V. boring. Look, what does any of this have to do with Myfanwy's pyscho stalker? Or the whole Witness Protection Programme?"

"I'm sorry. Kiss? The, ah, Witches Protec—?"

"*This is intolerable!*" bellowed Kitty.

"Excuse me," announced Myfanwy primly. "None of this will be necessary, Kitty. I believe I've worked it out. It's not witches at all, is it Blake? That statue guy. His speed, his strength. The mesmeric thing he's done to me." She turned to Blake, intensifying her focus. "This whole secret operation you've got here."

"Yes?" inquired Blake.

Kitty looked on eagerly.

Myfanwy took a deep breath. "*Vampires are real.*"

They both looked at Myfanwy thoughtfully.

The room was darker than before. It had started to sleet outside. Snakelike shadows began to wriggle across Blake's face. He turned his face down and away.

Then he was lurching from his chair towards her neck with a head of hissing teeth.

"Blood," he panted, "*blooood!*"

Myfanwy squealed with pleasure, not fooled for a second.

Kitty was unimpressed. "Hmmph."

Blake leant back chuckling. "Yes, yes. Excellent! Excellent!" He frowned. "Though come to think of it, it probably *would* fall to Chancelhouse to defend the planet from vampires, if such things do exist, and extra-dimensional demons, which probably *do*, come to think of it, and so forth. Large crabs. Oh dear. Perhaps I'll have Meletē start a working group, he's fond of pyrotechnics. And seafood, for that matter. Hope we're not too late. So far our luck has held, touch wood!"

"Torchwood?" cried Myfanwy. "Do you mean —"

"Vampires! Witches! Honestly! Now *tell* me something, ladies. *Why* is it — why is it — whenever anyone discovers that the world is not quite as they thought, that the world is actually a little stranger, a little more enchanted — *why* do they insist on seeing that difference in terms of *existing* categories of error? By definition, should not whatever is *fresh* and *weird* have few if any familiar words to express it? *No* name a perfect fit, and *no* concept a perfect fit either? *Why* must we always arrogate unfamiliar experience into werewolves, and satyrs and griffins and dragons and talking badgers and palfreys and suchlike? Is it a kind of arrogance?"

"Unicorns!" Myfanwy pointed out. Kitty's attempt to slurp tea was sabotaged by her own giggle.

"Quite," Blake agreed. "Unable to accept our profound ignorance, we relegate the truly new to the profoundly forgotten?"

"I'm not sure I follow," Kitty said, now setting down her cup and trying to mean business. "If he's not a vamp, can *I* guess what statue guy is?"

"Give it your best shot, my dear. I'm assuming 'statue guy' is some teenage girl term or hashtag or what-have-you for Jasper Robin?"

"That's his name?" said Myfanwy, startled. "He never exactly introduced himself. Or maybe he did." She tried it out in a whisper. "*Jasper Robin.*"

"Yes yes, the antagonist so keen on killing Chancelhouse agents. 'The one wiff a bi' o' the ol' attitude'."

Blake's imitation was overblown but sufficiently recogniseable to give Myfanwy a shiver.

"Well," Blake added softly. "No longer with Chancelhouse, obviously. Chosen rather a different career path."

"*My* guess," said Kitty smugly, "is this Jasper character is a rogue 'hyborg.' Chancelhouse is actually a secret agency of 'hyborgs.' What is a 'hyborg,' you ask, sir? It is *half* cyborg, *half* hybrid."

Gradually Myfanwy became conscious of the wagging of a wall — a pendulum clock ticked and tocked. Outside the weather was worsening. Freckles and pearls of rain fell down the pane.

"Well, that could be correct," admitted Blake. "If it made any sense."

"Well, whatever you guys are," Kitty sniffed, "you should consider rebranding yourselves 'hyborgs.'"

"He's *not* quite human though, *is* he?" Myfanwy said. "Call it what you like, they're just names. A *unicorn* could be a special . . . uh, form of light. Or a *vampire* could be a season of dreams. Or the ferryman to the Citadel in the Sky. That person, Jasper, he's not . . . I mean, he's not normal."

"Just *names*, eh? Hmm," Blake brooded. "Not *normal*, eh? Let's see. I didn't mean to suggest, Kitty, that we should invent a new word, and a new idea, for every new thing. Though there's much to admire in that approach, I must admit! I meant simply this. Old words and old ideas have a hold on new things, a grip which few are capable of loosening. Indeed, they have this hold on *all* things, not merely new ones! So perhaps we prefer words like *unicorn*, like *vampire*, because when applied to any truly new thing, to any deeply new thing, they remind us how imperfectly *all* words are welded to the world. Yes, yes! Such fanciful terminology, in its ostentatious meagerness, lets us glimpse the fact that forgetfulness is not something intermittent, and something only connected with the past. No, forgetfulness is a permanent feature, verily, a *prerequisite* of all present experience! It is our very medium and substrate! Every instant, our eyes must relinquish the richness and depths with have flown before them, or no inhabitable apparition could ever form! And what if! What if you *could* preserve all those countless details, all those concrete data for which human experience has no carrying capacity? Would one experience the most profound solitude, as phenomena without mortal equivalents swiftly accrued, as they were incorporated into one's individual life history? As someone sculpted from an utterly strange and incommensurable stuff, would one attain godhead? Or, in aromatic pain, die of a rose? Or, dear ladies, of a ginger snap? Well, I'm asking a silly question, because it's *not* possible. The rosy-fingered dawn won't flash so much as a false nail over the horizon, till she be assured she may let off another obnoxious, obliterative nova. And I refer, my dears, not to the dawn of a new day, but to the dawning of every fleeting new moment. Forgetting, letting go, disregarding — *these* are things we may practice through the lattice, ladies, and what allow data to flow as experience. It is what makes us normal, if that is what we are. It is what makes us human, if that is what we are. On the paths *we* must walk, it is not so much the mountain face which holds us up, as it is the mists. Following?"

"No," said Kitty. "Unfollow."

"No," said Myfanwy. "Whoosh!"

"Intense though," Kitty said kindly. "Great atmosphere."

"No," laughed Blake softly, leaning back. "Perhaps not. All a bit much for your first day. Well, I am over the hill *myself*, rather like those mists, and my mind is getting hazy. Great-great-great atmosphere. *Senex* is a good word. Scraps may serendipitously be wiser than the sum total would have been . . . no, no, to stay on message, where Kitty so loves to stay, and to answer your question, Myfanwy — I suppose Jasper Robin *is* as *human*, or as *normal*, as you or I. Which is as good as it gets, these days. But yes, he's one in a million at least. My dears, Jasper Robin is a muse."

*

The girls gasped in unison.

The library's pendulum clock wagged away the tense silence. On the pane, small droplets hopped into bigger drops zig-zagging past like hitchhikers.

From the corner of her mouth Myfanwy murmured, "Mean anything to you, Kitty?"

"As his mystic power," murmured Kitty from of the corner of hers, "he can magically fund community outreach writer-in-residency posts. We're doomed! We're doomed!"

"Very funny, ladies," said Blake, a bit put out. "Jasper's talent lies in inspiring the minds of men. Casting things into those minds — or *flipping* things into them, as many younger muses aptly put it nowadays."

"It makes sense, Kitty," said Myfanwy. "He's *given* me things."

"It is not a talent to be taken lightly, for whoever accepts such gifts pays a corresponding price, as you'll discover in time. Aha, looky looky! It *is* snowing again, sleeting, at any rate! — do you know, there ain't nearly enough words in English for what water and air do together . . . one winter in Edinburgh would teach you that, ladies . . . I ought to brush up on my Scots. Oh, my aching bones! My snowflake knees! More likely to die of a cold snap than a ginger snap, I am! Perhaps I'll attempt to invoke us a merry little fire, shall I?"

"With respect, sir," said Kitty, "I sort of suspect you'd escape up the chimney. Why doesn't Myfanwy do it?"

But there then came a knock. A girl of about the same age as Myfanwy and Kitty entered the library.

"Oh," said Blake sternly. "Bee."

Bee was short and small of head. She wore her hair in a dark feathery bundle with blue highlights and two bits shaved at the sides. She had very pale lovely skin, smoky eyeshadow, heavy eyeliner, and black lipstick which actually really suited her and somehow looked really natural on her. She wore an unobtrusively gothy jumpsuit with many safety pins in it.

She had the throaty voice of a Disney prawn. "Meletē called," she drawled. "Or some other dude. Says it's good news about Terpsichore. Or bad news, I can't remember. Um," she added, her eyes flicking warily over Kitty and Myfanwy. "And I think we have, like, another security breach?"

"Eh? Oh, *them*. I *do* know they're there, Bee." Myfanwy wasn't sure if it was her imagination, or if Blake betrayed a certain nervousness when he addressed this newcomer. "That's why I put the ginger snaps so near them. Afraid I can't introduce them because they haven't been assigned their callsongs — indeed, we *are* rather busy, Bee — that is to say, if you'd like to *sit in* —"

"Fine," said Bee. "Nope." After a beat, she spread Myfanwy and Kitty a huge rictus — a kind of Cheshire Bat thingy. It was fake, Myfanwy thought, but not "bitchy" fake . . . more just the fake smile of someone who *often* had to just make do with fake smile, someone who one day had given up caring if people knew they were fake. "I'm Bee," said Bee. "I'm *sure* we'll be *friends*, and everything. Come visit my room. You can come *any time*. I don't mind but I may not answer. Did your guys's shrinks headhunt you too?"

"No," said Kitty, and then looked quizzically at Blake. "Well, I mean, I don't —"

"Ah," Blake said. "We'll need to speak about Professor MacAonghas in fact. I mean to say, in terms of confidentiality —"

"*Professor MacAonghas!*" Kitty trilled, clapping her hands together. "I *knew* there was more between us than just a legitimate analyst-analysand relationship!"

Blake looked exasperated, but before he could reply there came from behind Bee a soft tickly cough.

"Is that . . . *Marinade*, lurking in the corridor?" Blake enquired instead. The prospect seemed to please him.

A second tiny figure shuffled forward beside Bee, a fragile-looking boy with a strawberry-blond Page Boy bob, a pale evenly-freckled face, and round, heavy-rimmed spectacles. He wore red trousers and a large T-shirt, featuring an incongruously cheerful cigar-chewing Bugs Bunny. He looked rather like an embarrassing photograph of someone from when they were younger, pointed to in an album by a tactless, fat-fingered parent.

By way of greeting, he hung his head.

"This," announced Blake happily, "is Marinade. Say hello, Marinade."

"Yuri," said Marinade.

Myfanwy and Kitty smiled uncomprehendingly at Marinade and then at each other. "Yuri to you too, sirrah?" suggested Myfanwy.

"Yuri up?" said Kitty. "Yuriba, yuriba!"

"*Yuri*!" insisted Marinade.

Moments of extraordinary awkwardness ticked past. Marinade removed his spectacles and polished them with a corner of his vast tablecloth-like Bugs Bunny T-shirt.

"W-e-e-ll," Bee said flatly. "You guys probably have so much ground to cover and all . . . it's so cool the way you both fit in one big chair . . . bye."

When Bee said goodbye, Marinade shuffled back into the gloom, but then Bee herself hesitated at the threshold. She looked at Blake and seemed to forget about anyone else. Suddenly it was like it was just her and him, set among the stars. "I'm real angry about some stuff," she said hotly. "Real angry, Blake. Only I don't — I mean like, I —"

"We'll talk, Bee," Blake soothed. "We'll talk. Come to my rooms this evening."

Then Bee remembered Chancelhouse's two newest guests, shot them another strange, sad grin, and buzzed off.

And Blake's gaze lingered after her.

*

The hearth remained cold.

"Are those guys muses too?" said Kitty. "Is Chancelhouse a sort of school for muses? Are those two a couple? I mean is that gorgeous hunk taken?"

"Perhaps a 'school' in the American sense," said Blake thoughtfully. "And an Ivy League one at that! Yes, yes! You could say Bee and Marinade are our Junior class, and soon you'll meet the Sophomores, Moth and Triffid. All the Senior muses are however away on a— well, it's rather hush-hush! Our hearts go with them. For perhaps another week. Then we can have our hearts back for the usual hearts nonsense . . . I'm not sure if the 'hunk' is taken, *you cruel girl!?*' He laughed. "I'm happy to make enquiries. 'My friend fancies your friend,' I believe is *modus operandi*?"

"No," explained Kitty.

"But how come nobody is called, like, Bill or Oscar?" asked Myfanwy. "Why is everyone, like, 'The Mothman!' and 'Princess Pollen!' and stuff?"

"Ah, those are what we call our callsongs, Myfanwy. A sort of soubriquet or moniker, contrived for security augmentation. *You'll* need them too."

"Like codenames?" said Kitty. "Wicked."

"More-or-less codenames, yes," said Blake, with a slightly pained expression. "When Chancelhouse agents are in the field, we exclusively call each other by our callsongs. Let me give you an example. 'Hello, Marinade!' Do you see how it goes? The rest of the time . . . well, it's up to the individual. You can reveal your civilian names, or not! Some do, some don't!"

"So is 'Blake' *your* callsong?" Myfanwy asked.

"Aha! Haduken Blake is my *real* name," he said — though Myfanwy decided to translate the twinkle in his eye into a pinch of salt. He stroked his ponytail, a gesture she had not seen yet from him. "My *callsong* . . . hmm, now, that's *Seuss*."

"Mine is Nessus," Kitty informed him. "From *The Inferno*."

"Ah," said Blake dubiously. "I mean, no need to be hasty. Actually, I'm trying to bring in some systematicity with callsongs. That's the difficulty with folksonomy. People have picked whatever is 'cool' or 'wicked' or 'safe' in the past and it's led to . . ."

"So what's a good example of a callsong?" asked Myfanwy.

"Well, the first nine muses, of course, were callsonged according to their classical forebears. Polyhymnia . . . Terpsichore . . . Undine and so on."

"*I* see," said Kitty brightly. "Chavvy names."

Myfanwy glared at her.

"In more recent times," Blake continued, "we've realised the muse talent divides into different families and specialisms. Rook is what's known as a doolittle muse, a sub-form of caster. Thorn is a driver muse, and so on. A good callsong gives a nod towards taxonomy, without giving away too much. So perhaps, Kitty, if you and I have a one-to-one later, we can —"

"Nessus." Kitty shook her head firmly. "Monstrous centaur tutor to Achilles. '*He who, using an arrow, scooped his great beard backwards upon his jaws, exposing his mouth, and then addressed his companions thus.*'"

Kitty waited expectantly.

"And then all the stuff he says," she added.

Blake sighed. "Nessus? Really? Cards on the table, Kitty. I know nowadays they string you up for saying this, but —"

"Hold up," Myfanwy blurted. "I'm not . . . I mean . . . um, if you only really need callsongs for going on, like, missions . . . and you want *me and Kitty* to have callsongs . . ."

"Plus Bee just mentioned headhunting!" said Kitty. "Are you trying to like *recruit* us?"

Blake looked puzzled, then amused. "Ha! Well, if you'd asked me this morning, I'd have said *of course not*, deary me, given the apparent disaster of our agent's last approach . . . entirely unsanctioned, by the way — Merlin's own initiative . . . but seeing as now you've come up on your own steam . . ."

"Oh God," Kitty muttered. "You *are* recruiting us! Bloody brilliant. Oh, *tell* me we all wear shiny silver jumpsuits!"

Blake looked momentarily wounded, and both girls burst out laughing. "We are exploring," he confessed airily, "a uniform for certain official occasions. We also have standard gym kit for physical training. That's more to do with sponsorship than anything else."

"Who would sponsor outfits for a *top secret* mystic taskforce?" said Myfanwy.

"Nike," said Blake simply.

"Oh," said Myfanwy.

"I know, I take a similar view. People sponsor strange stuff. I mean, *art?* Really?"

"I probably have an ethical objection to wearing these lamé onesies," said Kitty.

"We'll check them out first though," said Myfanwy.

"Obviously," said Kitty.

"So what do you want us for? Do you really want *both* of us?"

"Am I going to have to slice ham?" Kitty added darkly. "You want me for your deli, *don't* you? To slice *ham*. Unless I'm . . . I'm not a . . ."

"Wafer thin, for yummy mummies," Blake confirmed. "Well, we *do* all muck in, as it happens, at Duke's, and all round. But I rather thought training with Aoide might start first thing tomorrow. Aoide is Master Mystagogue — nothing less for our bright new recruits!"

"Aoide?" said Myfanwy, rapidly. "Recruits?"

"Recruits?" cried Kitty, overlapping. "Training?"

"Your muse training, of course, my dears! There aren't vampires and things, there are only muses like you, and me, and Jasper. But by God, that's all we'll need. Under the tutelage of the feared —"

"Me or Myfanwy?" whispered Kitty sternly. "*Who* has the muse talent?"

"Don't leave us in suspense," said Myfanwy. "Which?"

"Funnily enough, Merlin was only sure about one of you. But apparently you're two in two million. Because, oh yes! You *both* have it, my dears! *Both* of you are muses!"

*

"I don't get what this talent is we're supposed to have," Kitty whispered to Myfanwy, as Blake led them, at his usual thunderous waddle, through Chancelhouse HQ's many-levelled labyrinth to their quarters. "But I'm not sure I want to share it with those dorks. Marinade looks like he lives off those flavoured syrups that are supposed to go in lattés and nothing else, and as for *Bee* —"

"Bee is a wonderful girl!" called Blake abruptly.

Kitty looked abashed.

He couldn't have heard Kitty, could he?

"Marinade is a quite quiet chap," Blake continued loudly, "but if you ever get him on the topic of co-sleeping — that is, whether it's better for babies to sleep with their *mothers* in their beds, or in a *cot* — then you'll see another side to him."

"Um, Marinade seems v. young to have children," Myfanwy commented. "Not *judging*, but —"

"No no, nothing like that. He just has a strong technical interest in the subject! He also likes bananas sliced on toast and he has an album in which he's photographed every single bananas-on-toast he's had since he arrived at Chancelhouse. He thinks it was a mistake, but he's started now, so he has to go on. Are you getting a feel for him? He won't mind me telling you, you know."

"He sounds annoying," said Kitty.

"*We're* quite annoying," said Myfanwy. "Well, *I* am. Annoying people are very on-trend."

"If you think about how many films and books and media with you in there are," said Kitty thoughtfully, "that's true. Whereas I," she added solemnly, with slitty eyes, "have often *suspected* I may have a Power. When I eat small citrus fruits, I can tell where the pips are in my mouth without biting into them."

"Are you feeling them with your tongue?" said Blake.

"No."

"Worth looking into," Myfanwy confirmed. "You may be at the wrong secret mystic agency."

"Nearly there!" said Blake. "I hope you've been remembering the way."

"So how about Bee?" Myfanwy enquired. "What's her story?"

"And who are these others?" said Kitty. "You said odd chaps prowl these chambers."

"Well, here we are!" Blake announced. "This is your corridor. Your room is the last on the right. I'm sure you'll enjoy being tucked up all safe for a change! Unless of course someone accidentally eBays 'musepad,' I suppose. And so for now, my Freshman class . . . !"

"Freshpeople," Myfanwy autocorrected.

"Freshmuse," Blake happily assented. He gave Kitty a flourishing bow. "Nessus! And, Myfanwy, *you* I suppose have your heart set on —"

"My callsong?" Myfanwy only felt blank and a little tired now. "I don't know. Wall? Face? Um, Wollstonecraft?"

"Aha!" said Blake, evidently cheered by her indecision. "Then we'll have a one-to-one chat soon about what might be appropriate —"

"I'll think of something cool for you," said Kitty, giving her a bit of a rub. "'Wall' *is* cool. '*My Name Is The Wall.*'"

"I have a train tomorrow," said Myfanwy. "And I have exams coming up. One night only, okay?"

But Blake was already halfway down the corridor. "Adieu, Nessus! TBC, to you too, adieu!"

And he was gone.

"Bye bye, White Rabbit," said Kitty. "Hope you make it to the tea party on time. Oh God, what about my shopping?"

"Wow," Myfanwy sighed, rubbing her eyes. "Okay, last room on the right."

They passed by two doors. There was a sign on each in different hands. The first read "Grimalkin" and the second "Eft."

"I can't *believe* I'm going to have to remember everyone's names *and* their callsongs," said Kitty.

"Same," said Myfanwy. "Whenever anyone introduces themself my mind goes totally blank. Like, 'Why are you telling *me* this? I don't even *know* you!'"

"Yeah. And when they give you their business card," said Kitty, "you have a massive crisis and rip it into a million pieces."

"Yeah. 'Sing, Muse!' I'm still not exactly clear what a muse *does*," admitted Myfanwy. "Inspire people?"

The third door had no sign, but their key turned in its lock. All their luggage and Kitty's vintage shopping sat in wait. A large window, overlooking scraggly green gardens, received the early evening sun and a gentle evening breeze. Twin beds were dressed in white linens, with bountiful bright pillows and embroidered cushions piled at each head, and a set of towels, one violet and one black, folded neatly at each foot. There was a large-ish wardrobe built into one wall, which contained nothing but a few padded hangers — and, for the moment, Myfanwy's BFF Kitty, acting like a total four-year-old. In one corner stood a small sink and an oval mirror — the bathroom and separate shower room were down the corridor, shared with the two other rooms. The only other furniture was a small bedside unit done in deep chestnut, where sat a large frilly lamp, whose head Myfanwy had to angle till the frills hung just so, before she could attend to any other business. Framing the large sash window were a pair of slightly sorcerous pale violet curtains, tremoring on the light breeze. Mild floral wallpaper, mostly lavender and ash, and nothing else on the walls except empty picture-hooks.

All in all the room felt anonymous, but less like a hotel than some sort of seldom-used guest room, or place from which had been recently erased — out of grief, anger or pragmatism — any sign of earlier tenancy.

"Sweeeeet!" said Kitty, manifesting herself from within the wardrobe and *floomping* onto the bed of the pink towels — the one nearer the window and sink. "Check my crib *out.* You'll have to go in the wardrobe, Myffy when I bring back my mandem Marinade. If you peek, I'll *dead* you."

"He's so adorable," said Myfanwy, sitting on the other bed. "He's like Bee's bungled tattoo from ages ago, that she's not even embarrassed about anymore and doesn't mind showing you. God, I should call Dad!"

"Oh mate, don't *bother.* He thinks you're staying at mine, right?"

This was true. Kitty basically had her own flat — she went to her castle at the end of the Metropolitan Line on weekends, but during the week her folks let her stay in their *pied à terre* near St Jerome's. Myfanwy often questioned the wisdom of Kitty's folks. Snaffling that property had been the loophole which allowed the fruit of their loins to attend a Good State School. But over the years, said fruit and said fruit's BFF had adapted the loophole for many nefarious purposes of their own . . .

Kitty shrugged and lay back briefly on her bed. "Just say you're staying at mine all week to revise."

"Flip, revision," said Myfanwy. "If only all this had happened in the summer! I don't know, Kitty. I think I should go home soon. Maybe first thing. I don't like to think of Dad knocking around all alone."

Now Kitty was at the window, not listening. "So we get to look at the gardens," she said. "Nice. *Not* the houses across the street. I wonder what's in the west side of the compound, Myfanwy. I wonder what's in those other houses. Do you?"

*

A high arc of sparks leapt against the vivid cloudless blue, as flowingly rich as pumping blood. The saw screamed, and the lion screamed, but only in fear. The masked policewoman cut down tensely into the concrete.

Now her eye wandered farther.

Everyone got up as sorcerers, beasts, monsters, clowns. Giants gathered. The face of the lion was running free in his tears. Soon there would be a sacrifice.

A giant screamed.

A giant screamed. Myfanwy awoke in complete darkness. Where was she? What bed was this?

So dark.

Edinburgh, Myfanwy remembered, with a sort of relief. *Auld Reekie. Chancelhouse. Kitty.*

She was with Kitty. "Kitty," Myfanwy said. "Did you hear it?"

Kitty lay quietly. Myfanwy knew she was awake though — when Kitty slept, she snored without exception. Like a blazing bull with a witch inside and nostrils clogged with cinders. But Myfanwy, taking the hint, lay in her bed in the void, ears pricked.

It was pitch dark. No, not pitch. A very faint arch of light around the curtain's edges. But no other shapes. A faint smell of the Dim Sum they'd feasted on earlier.

On the unspecifiable frontier of sleep, a giant had screamed. Now there was only silent alertness.

A distant door slamming.

"Did you —"

"*Shh*," murmured Kitty's voice in the void.

Myfanwy bit her lip.

Wind, coiling in the trees.

Running footsteps, elsewhere in the compound.

A door slamming, closer.

More footsteps, starting off close, but drifting farther away.

Just now a giant screamed — didn't she?

"Kitty? I'm *freaking*. What's going on?"

"*Shh.*"

Wind.

"An alarm went, Myffy," Kitty then said sleepily. "But I think it's okay now. Let's be brave and sleep, okay?"

"An alarm? I was dreaming."

"Me too, hon. It's night."

"The alarm was a giant that screamed. In my dream. It could be the fire alarm."

"Mmph. It's stopped now."

Myfawny shivered and drew her duvet around her. "A giantess," she murmured. "A dreameress. A fire giantess. A burglaress alarm."

She wanted a Wee Hours Conversation, but she knew Kitty wasn't going to give her one.

It was *him*, wasn't it?

She knew it was him.

Maybe Jasper Robin knew she had come to Chancelhouse. Or maybe he didn't. Either way, minutes ago, he had tried to get inside — and, this time anyway, he had failed. And yet . . . Myfanwy would rather be *here* than anywhere else. However unsettling it was, she was *glad* to be here in the Chancelhouse compound, among her strange new allies, buried deep behind secure concentric walls, behind so many heavy, locked doors affixed with the yawning jaws of unicorns, and stupid horny hummingbirds, and all the mystic lions.

Not out there naked to the cold night, with the same moon on her face as on *his*.

"Goodnight, Kitty."

Even as she said it clattering footfalls strafed along the wall, and a sudden pounding came — so violent, so loud that Myfanwy sprung up without volition — and it wasn't the door to the *corridor* someone was banging on, but it was the door to their *room*.

Banging as if they wanted to break it apart. Her fingers tangled with Kitty's about the neck of their lamp and the room filled with soft light.

*

"It's him!"

"It's locked hon," said Kitty in a soft voice. "Shh."

Bang! bang! bang! bang! bang!

"Maybe we shouldn't have put on the light," Myfanwy whispered as the bulb brightened. Shadows shifted under the door.

Then came a muffled but vaguely familiar voice. "Open up! It's only me!"

"Defo not Blake, is it?" Myfanwy whispered. "Is it Jasper?"

Kitty was out of bed, shaking her head as she stalked softly towards the door. "Sounds female."

"What are you doing?" Myfanwy's bare feet gently touched down too.

"There's a peephole. What are *you* doing?"

Myfanwy was rummaging in Kitty's completely unsystematic side of the wardrobe. "Um, did you bring your belt with the massive buckle? You know, the massive one?"

"Like to use as a flail? I only have the relatively massive one." Kitty pressed her eye to the peephole. She leapt back as it banged and shook once more.

"It's just some woman with a sword," she said softly.

"Well, why didn't you bring the absolutely massive one?"

"Please forget about the belt, Myffy. Stand behind the door when I open it. I'll step back, and you brain her with the lamp. Then we'll both stomp on her."

"Okay. Turn on the main light so I can unplug it."

"Are you alright in there?" came the woman's voice.

"Bollocks," said Kitty gently. "The main light doesn't work. Um, can maybe the cord reach?"

"Um, oh geez," said Myfanwy. "I really wish rooms had more sockets."

"Well, why can't you brain her in the dark? Is that so difficult a task for you?"

"What if I brain you?"

"Either way, I can stop stressing. Wait a moment," said Kitty. She looked through the peephole. "That girl Bee's with her. I'm actually going to let them in instead."

"Hi," said Bee. She came in and sat on Myfanwy's bed. "You have a nice room. This is my friend Simidelay. She's brought along a sword. It's astonishing she of all people is trusted with its sharp edge and point."

The woman — Simidelay — stood on the threshold. She was very tall. If it weren't for the dark, 90% cocoa blemishes dappling her cheekbones and chin in a somewhat unfortunate muttonchops effect, she might have looked like a sort of loftier and slightly more pinched and angular Lenora Crichlow. She wore her hair in tight corn rows, woven with blonde, set off by scabbard at her side, which was richly decorated in gold damask. She was perhaps in her early forties. Her nightie was La Senza and somewhat kimono-esque.

She tilted her head to one side, wearing a look of heavily dramatised sympathy. "My darlings," she said, nodding ceaselessly. "Hello, hello. I'm Simi. You must be —"

"Myfanwy," said Myfanwy.

"Nessus," said Kitty gravely.

"Is this the woman with the sword you mentioned earlier?" said Myfanwy.

Simi continued her canted sympathetic nods for ages, then sheathed her sword. Somehow Myfanwy expected long colourful fingernails, but they were trimmed and bare. Simi had to stoop as she stepped through the door. "We had a breach tonight, loves. Everyone's now accounted for. This is a funny way to meet, isn't it!" She threw her head back and laughed a full-throated laugh. "'Ooh! Hello! You're alive! I'm alive! My name's Simi!' Well babes, have a good night. I mean a good sleep. We'll meet properly in the morning, yeah?"

Myfanwy glanced at Kitty, who shrugged and said, "Thanks. We weren't sure if it was a fire alarm."

"Fire alarm's more like *wee-aa-wee-aa-wee-aa*," Simi supplied helpfully. "Burglar alarm's *boooooooooooooo.* I say 'burglar,' my loves, but I don't suppose it was a burglar. Night, babes!"

"Murderer alarm?" suggested Kitty.

"Murderess," said Myfanwy. "Sorry. I'm still dreaming."

Bee made a noise which turned out to be a huge yawn, full of vocal fry. "There's a chrysanthemum design on the blade itself," she commented. "It's the best part. It's not etched on there, as far as I can tell. I wonder what manner of swordsmith melded it so subtly with Simidelay's deadly blade. Bye, Simidelay!"

"Wait," said Myfanwy, a tad wildly. She wanted to make darn sure Simi took Bee with her. "Um, was it Jasper Robin? Trying to get in, just now?"

"Funny you should say that, babes. All I saw was a shadow going over a wall."

Stupidly, Myfanwy looked to her own shadow, then back to Simi.

"But," said Simi, nodding grimly, "Jasper was who I thought of too."

"Who *is* this guy?" said Kitty. "What's his beef? We don't know anything. We don't even really know what a muse is, yet."

Something moved. Myfanwy jumped. "Jesus. Thought I saw a spider. Sorry."

"We do get them," Simi smiled reassuringly. "Little ones. Listen. Calm yourselves, my loves. Let's take five and I'll tell you a bedtime story, all about the muse Jasper Robin."

Book Three

"Κατθάνοισα δὲ κείσεαι πότα, κωὐ μναμοσύνα σέθεν
ἔσσετ' οὔτε τότ' οὔτ' ὔστερον· οὐ γὰρ πεδέχεις βρόδων
τῶν ἐκ Πιερίας, ἀλλ' ἀφάνης κὴν Ἀΐδα δόμοις
φοιτάσεις πεδ' ἀμαύρων νεκύων ἐκπεποταμένα . . ."

— Sappho, Fragment 68 (Bergk)

"Drown out my dreams! Keep me
from remembering whatever
wants me to remember it!"

— *The Last Unicorn*

Rather disconcertingly, Bee was fast asleep in Myfanwy's bed. Myfanwy and Kitty arranged themselves on Kitty's bed. Simi shut the door, put off the main light and perched on the corner of Myfanwy's bed. The atmosphere was tender. Simi's sheathed sword lay across her lap, like some strangely-scaled needlework. Myfanwy hugged her black-and-blue shins and leant her chin on her knees. The lamp threw shadows like ink into the crevices of the deeply wrought cornices.

"Jasper was once one of Chancelhouse's greatest caster class muses," Simi began. "He was our golden boy. And he's gone right off the rails, babes! Totally psychotic! Don't let him moping around in flash trainers fool you."

"We saw him beat a woman with a sort of stand and drown her in the Thames," said Kitty. "So."

"Yes, that's clear-cut," Simi admitted. "Back in the day, Jasper Robin was one of Chancelhouse's original nine Apollonian muses, before the whole Veil split. How much has Blake —"

Myfanwy gasped. "He's *immortal?*"

"You what, babes? Oh." Simi rolled her eyes. "One of the original cast of Chancelhouse in our most recent manifestation — I'm talking like six or seven years ago, when Chancelhouse started modernising."

"Oh. Still cool," said Myfanwy kindly.

"Rebooting the franchise," Kitty supplied. "Wicked."

Simi was counting under her breath. "Yep, six years. Christ alive! Around that time Chancelhouse became a registered charity — ten, forty, sixty-eight, three, as it happens!" She laughed. "Ten, forty, sixty-eight, three! Funny what you remember, innit? Anyway, for yonks, Chancelhouse had focused on concealment. Nurturing the muse talent, passing on the esoteric learning associated with it, and protecting our members and our secret. Now things were changing . . . a little. But most of the younger muses wanted faster, more drastic change."

"Going public?" asked Myfanwy.

"No, but they did want us to play more of a part in world affairs."

"Meddling," Kitty acknowledged sagely.

"Things got ugly, proper out of control. Of course there was a power struggle, and then a parting of ways. So now there are *two* organisations of muses, Chancelhouse and Veil."

"Monopolies are bad for business," Kitty alleged.

Simi shrugged. "If that's your bag, babes. May depend what business you're in."

"The *muse* business!" said Kitty severely.

"Veil," said Myfanwy in an undertone, "is an anagram of 'evil'!"

"They're not necessarily *evil*," said Simi with a smile. "Veil's not a registered uncharity or anything. But some of that lot still bear a grudge. Anyway, following the split, Chancelhouse has continued to adapt. We're exploring new directions, new ways of using the muse talent. Exciting times. The irony is, if only we'd done it at the start, the split never needed to happen!"

"What 'new directions' exactly?" asked Kitty.

"One area I'm quite involved with is post-traumatic stress counselling for black ops and spooks," said Simi, with an air of compassionate seriousness. "Operation Nepenthe."

"*Good* for you, Simi! That's such important and fulfilling work!"

Myfanwy felt confused. "How can muses help traumatised spies?"

Simi laughed. "Well, *us* three ain't much good, babes! We're caster muses, see? But I also mentor a *taker* muse. His muse talent is the reverse of ours — whereas we cast assets *into* minds, he can reel them *out*."

"So he can — excise the ordeal?"

"He will take a burden off someone's shoulders, until those shoulders are strong enough to bear it again."

Somehow, this seemed like a terrible idea to Myfanwy. But all she said was, "It sounds hard. For everyone."

"In this calling," said Simi softly, "there is sacrifice. Let's hope you lot don't find that out any sooner than you have to."

"Well," sniffed Kitty, "I'm sure Veil do Corporate Citizenship too. Veterans is a very OTM area."

Simi regarded Kitty carefully. "Veil don't have anything like Nepenthe, my love. Though they have many more takers than we do, and so they certainly could. Frankly they've got all the interesting classes. Touchlesses, shrouders, decrypts. Between you and I and these four walls, when the split occurred Meletē — he's another elder muse, you won't have met him yet — well, my loves, Meletē was *this* close to going with Veil! And between you and I — because who would trust these four walls? — *I* was this close as well! I'm joking, babes, I'm joking. But we did lose good young muses that day — it was Calliope and Urania, as they then were, who led the exodus. They have new callsongs now, obviously."

"Any excuse," said Kitty, a bit frostily.

"God," Simi murmured abstractedly, "never mind poor old Clio!" She glanced down at Bee with an affectionate frown. "Bloody hell, that girl's *sleeping*, isn't she?"

"Tell us more about Jasper," Myfanwy persisted. "I guess he didn't stick with Chancelhouse?"

"No, and in a funny way, my loves, we'd already lost him long before the split. Jasper was just never well in the head, you see. He had the loveliest girlfriend. This girl knew how to look after him. New Age type — chakras and that. Then one day — about the same time as all the trouble started — she only went and died!" Simi grimaced sorrowfully. "I know, innit? Died! Dead, dead, dead! Broke his heart *and* his brain."

"Oh," said Myfanwy softly. "So he lost someone."

"Now, I'll be honest, babes — I dunno if most of the Veil lot are *really* out for our blood. Gaga, Glass, Vertical, Undine — maybe they thirst for it on a bad day. We all have bad days! With Jasper, it's different. He's hunting us down, one by one. For whatever reason, with him, it's personal."

Kitty turned to Myfanwy. "And now he's up in *your* grill?"

"I guess Jasper cast me his memories of the Chancelhouse compound," Myfanwy reasoned. "Then he staked it out. Then when he saw us go in, he waited till night to slip in —"

"It's possible he has some master plan," Simi admitted. "But I wouldn't be too paranoid, babes!"

"Yeah," said Kitty. "Why lure you to like a high security compound? Makes no sense."

"I guess not," said Myfanwy reluctantly.

"Besides," said Simi, "when a memory — or some other aspect of one's self — leaves the muse's mind and enters another, that memory adjusts itself. It harmonises with what's already there, innit? Although to some extent that is a two-way process, it's an asymmetrically lossy one. In other words, a memory of a holiday you *didn't* have soon melds with a memory of a holiday you *did* have. D'you see what I mean, babes?"

"Partly," said Myfanwy.

"I s'pose," said Kitty.

"Put it this way. The fact that you managed to arrive here, having never visited before, and with only Jasper's memories from six years ago to guide you — you showed a bit of the old grit and ingenuity, my loves! Jasper *never* could have expected you would make it here."

"Okay, that makes me happy," said Kitty. "But then why *did* he do it? What's the whole beef between him and Myffy?"

"Oh gosh, it's a bit late for difficult questions! Maybe it was about what he got *out* of Myfanwy. Or maybe he's simply eager to forget about this place. Dump them painful memories anywhere he can, yeah?" Simi wore a strained look. "See, Jasper was even younger than you lot now, when it all kicked off. That's part of the reason none of us — I mean, *all* teenagers are — you're a troubled lot, ain't you?"

"Oh, we are troubled!" Kitty gushed euphorically. "We are troubled, Simi! Don't you worry! *Bee*, for instance!"

Bee was softly snoring now.

"I wish *I* was young and troubled, love!" Simi roared with laughter. Bee still did not stir. "There's some blokes I wouldn't mind being troubled about again! Anyway, that's why none of us realised poor Jasper was — *something special*, you know what I mean?"

"Bad news," said Kitty.

"Bad as they come, babes. Blake don't really talk about it. He's hard on himself." Laughing, Simi shook her head. "Well, enough for now! This is so funny, gabbling on here in our peejays!"

"Yes, with our sword!" said Kitty brightly.

"We do have super early training," Myfanwy admitted. "Somewhere called the Myometrium. With an elder muse called Aoide."

"Bloody hell," said Simi, wide-eyed.

"I'm already a bit scared," Myfanwy agreed. "I'm not really tired though."

"Me either," said Kitty. "But I guess we should —"

"I'd be tying some bed sheets together, if I was you."

"Yes. What?" said Myfanwy. "I don't understand."

"Not Aoide? You lot taking the mick?" Simi toyed with her scabbard distractedly. "In the Myometrium? Blake is throwing you in at the deep end, my loves. Sorry to have kept you up."

With this, Simi yawned, and Myfanwy and Kitty both found it to be contagious.

"What," Kitty yawned back, "is Aoide . . . like, *daunting* . . . ?"

"The Arch-Chancellor, Master Mystagogue, Head of Development, Chair of Senatus Academicus, High Balneator? You poor children. I'm just . . . glad it's not me," yawned Simi. "That's all I'm saying. Glad it's not me."

"'What sound do Bees make?'" said Myfanwy. "'*Zzzzzzzz*.'"

"Like it," chuckled Simi. "Like it. I'll have to watch you. You're a joker."

"Okay, but one last thing," said Kitty. "What did you mean when you said . . . what was it? Jasper was getting something out of it? What's he getting?"

"Oh my days! I *thought* I saw some blank faces. Has Blake not explained to you about memories shooting the other way?"

"I don't think so," said Kitty.

"Uh-uh," said Myfanwy.

Simi sighed. "Right babes. A fundamental fact, then to bed. You'll need your strength tomorrow."

"Fine," said Kitty.

"Your basic muse, a caster muse, can cast mental aspects of herself into another by touch. Yeah? Jasper selects what part he wants to put into *you*, Myfanwy, my love. A memory or whatever. But there's something else that's part and parcel with that. You see, casting works on a transaction principle. A compensatory transfer must take place. Every time he touched *you*, Myfanwy, my love, and put memories inside *you* —"

"So it works by touch? He has to *touch* me, to do it?"

"Yeah, yeah, but that's not the important part — listen now, because this *is* important —"

"I'm listening."

"We're listening, Simi."

"Every time he cast a memory into you, Myfanwy, my love, something knocked loose in *your* mind, span back out of *you*, and entered into *him*. And if I know Jasper Robin, he cares more about what he gets than what he gives."

"Are you saying — you mean he's — he's been —"

"Oh yeah," said Simi. "Oh *yeah* babes. He's taken a *liking* to you, my love. Feeling forgetful, recently? Jasper Robin has been stealing your memories."

*

The night was not through with them yet.

Simi had bade them dream sweetly, stroked Bee awake by her hair, and led her away like a groggy, grubby toddler. Myfanwy had locked their door, slipped into her covers, and was just about to ask to put out their lamp, when there came a light tap.

It was Marinade.

"It is not like English boarding school," he said airily. "We come and go as we please." Myfanwy was mildly surprised by an accent she'd missed earlier. Something East European, but not Polish. "We are civilised," sniffed Marinade. "We go and come. It is not too late?"

Kitty looked wary. It was nearly three in the morning. As she opened her mouth, Myfanwy blurted, "It's *fine*, Marinade. The first few days are weird. After all," she added dryly, eyes flicking to Kitty, "we may not *live* till dawn."

"Come in," said Kitty. "May I call you Mary?"

He nodded solemnly, and with a great sense of ceremony took precisely two steps forward. "But I prefer my name Yuri," he said. "I chose 'Marinade' from dictionary. Now sometimes I regret. Whereas 'Yuri,' my father and mother both discussed."

"Hi, Yuri!" they chimed together.

Myfanwy rubbed her face.

Yuri wasn't wearing his glasses. There were two little indentations where the nose pads normally pressed. He wore pale velvety spray-on jeans and a plum button-up shirt with fresh creases in it. He had probably changed into hilarious pyjamas, Myfanwy thought, then when woken by alarums, dressed himself up to the nines to come calling.

"There is mole in Chancelhouse," said Yuri né Marinade quietly. "*You*, I may tell this, because you are new here. Uncorrupted, I think."

"A spy?" cried Kitty — as though Yuri had brought her a thoughtful present, if still rather a trite one, carefully wrapped up in lovely wrapping paper. "Oh, Yuri! A spy!"

Yuri nodded once, decisively. "Yes. For now, only six live in HQ. Eight counting you. Nine if counting Flux. Soon many other muses return from mission, and the mole may be among them. So maybe soon *you* are compromised too."

"Oh, Yuri! Why, Yuri? For whom, Yuri? Veil?"

Yuri shrugged. "Who knows? Perhaps not so simple. Private sector, perhaps." Yuri was eyeing up the girls' few belongings arranged about the room, without much apparent interest. "My belief is that commercial interests must not controvert the muse capacity. I am idealist. However, you must decide to act or discount my advice. For following this communication, I will not collude again."

Myfanwy crossed her legs and adjusted her nightie. She wondered should she offer their envoy with the bad eye contact a cup of tea, and if so, where she would get it from.

"So," said Kitty. "Yuri."

"Yes. Goodnight."

He left — not bowing, but somehow conveying the impression he had. Myfanwy locked the door.

"I think it's you he fancies," Kitty said languidly. "I don't think he fancies me." She watched her paddling, cascading fingers with pure fascination.

"Safe," laughed Myfanwy. "Can we make a rule for the interesting inappropriate boys, from now on they have to fancy us *both*, or not at all?"

"We'll see. He *miaowed* at you Myfanwy."

"I didn't see the miaow."

"He definitely did a silent miaow."

Kitty raised a paw. "The tragic part," Kitty added thoughtfully, "is that *Jasper* is actually quite fit."

Myfanwy pulled a face. "A bit . . . a bit Naughties!" she said, really not quite sure what to say to that.

"Has there ever *been* any other decade?" said Kitty.

"The Eighties," Myfanwy pointed out.

"Please."

"Or the *1580s*. What did you think of Chancelhouse's founding mother, Kitsy? Do you know the portrait I mean?"

Kitty shot her a mysterious, sly look.

"*Do* you know the one?" Myfanwy laughed. "Genevieve Quaker, she was called. The Tudor muse. C'mon. There was something about her. I don't know. There was something so strange."

"Are you being serious?"

"What?"

"You don't know, do you? I mean, she's lush and all, hon . . ."

The portrait had stayed with Myfanwy. Genevieve Quaker the Tudor muse. It wasn't like a normal representation somehow. It was more like the image which rests on any living face. If that life were somehow reduced, so the image lying there could become clear as itself, without otherwise being changed. Like the skin of a girl in a coma from which she would never recover. Except, *this* expression was *awake*, just not alive. Delicately placed, as though deliberately, on the threshold of lifelessness . . .

"Lay it on me!" laughed Myfanwy. "Who is she? Where do we know her from?"

"Hon! She's *you*. Apart from the hair colour, and the funny last season lace. She looks *exactly* like you. Her cheeks follow you round the room. She looks more like you," said Kitty, starting to yawn another humungous, sleepy yawn, "than *you* do in half your photos of you . . ."

*

There came a tap on the door.

It was Yuri.

He looked totally mortified. "I heard you awake. I forgot. Ahem. Markets cannot allocate resources, when point of resource is to change people's preferences."

Kitty and Myfanwy nodded politely.

He was in yet another outfit.

"Say what?" said Myfanwy.

Yuri sighed. "Following this communication," he explained, "I will not collude again. So it is important I express my opinion fully. Journalism is example. Education is also example. Customer always is right, yes? But student sometimes must be wrong! Aoide was my sensei! She has been *more* than a service provider to me, and I to her, more than customer! A market could not have created this relationship!"

"So you guys are close," said Myfanwy.

"Why are you telling us this?" said Kitty.

"You will find out is same with muse. Muses change rationality, change desire. Muses must never be children of markets! Please if you are buttonholed ever, and hear this argument, that 'private sector knows best' — remember, *you* are responsible for critical mind."

"You've been very kind," said Kitty.

"Also there may be *two* moles. Perhaps Partnering Rule implies this."

"Partnering Rule?" said Myfanwy.

"Rule we all must follow. To avoid madness. Ask Aoide."

He left.

*

There was a tap on the door.

It was Yuri.

"Yuri!" cried Kitty.

"Yuri!" cried Myfanwy.

They were his biggest fans.

This time he didn't look embarrassed at all. "Do not discount *me*. This would not be consistent. Very easily I could now be doing double-bluff. Maybe mole is I! Goodnight."

He left.

They looked at each other.

"If he comes again,' said Myfanwy, "don't let him speak. Just open the door and be like, 'FURTHERMORE —'"

Only he didn't come again.

The darkness settled its form. There was the faintest arch of light about the curtains. Then even that faded, as perhaps clouds covered the moon.

Wind, in a world with many trees and few leaves.

In the morning, muses, moles and the mysterious . . . Aoide.

Kitty snoring.

Soon — and not a moment too soon — Myfanwy slept.

*

When Myfanwy awoke Kitty's bed was empty and neatly made. She found Kitty at breakfast talking to a girl with a long thin face, close-cropped pixie-platinum hair and a labret. The girl wore a big black headband, a red and white stripy top with a low back, a dark gauzy skirt and ballet pumps. She introduced herself as Moth.

Myfanwy rapidly ran through her list of acquaintances. *Blake AKA Seuss. The Director of Chancelhouse, what used to be known rather more majestically, alas, as the Chocolate Mousse. Simi the swordswoman. The mysterious Bee. The mysterious Marinade AKA Yuri, who sort of accuses himself of being a spy. And now Moth. And soon the Master Mystery Gonk, Aoide. Yikes.*

"Have you met Nessus?" Moth said, and Myfanwy had to laugh. Later she hoped it didn't come across bitchy. Moth had a lovely, gentle voice — Northumbrian or something.

"You were thrashing about last night," Kitty reprimanded Myfanwy. "Like a masculine person."

Myfanwy sat with them at a wobbly circular wooden table, sans tablecloth, at the foot of a wrought iron spiral staircase, apparently leading to a roof terrace.

Yuri and a tall boy called Triffid soon joined them.

Triffid. The mysterious Triffid. No wait, that's unfair. He just wants breakfast.

Chairlegs scraped tilework as the five muses squished round the one table, though every other table in the largish cafeteria space — "Valhalla," according to the device over the double doors Myfanwy had entered by — was empty.

"I wanted to come again," Yuri admitted. "I crept along corridor, and raised my hand like so."

"Very lifelike," Kitty agreed.

"But did not knock! But I wanted to say I — I am glad to see you. It is vague. I wanted to say, you know —"

"It's nice to meet you?" said Myfanwy.

"Yes."

"Yuri we're gonna have fun," said Kitty. "*Despite that of which we may never speak.*"

"Yes," said Yuri. "The mole." He ate his muesli.

"Normally this place is rammed," Triffid told them. He was lanky, floppy-lipped, with rimless designer glasses. Dark curls were sneaking from under an orange beanie. He wore a black-and-white stripy long-sleeved top, shiny white Bermuda shorts with two black vertical go-faster stripes, and very advanced Man Slippers. He had one of those posh accents which made his Rs sound a bit like Ws. "You won't be able to find a seat. Have you been to Edinburgh before, Nessus? It's no wonder everyone rams in here, it's carnage out there! Literally everyone's dad owns a small innovative graphic design company, and their mum is a sub-editor for *The Times*. You can't even *get* jeans south of Princes Street except in aerosol format. There will be like twenty or thirty agents of various classes and grades in here. Kermitcrab, Lego, Horae, Atë, Tar, Meletē, the whole gang."

"Did they tell you guys anything about the big mission?" Moth asked.

"Very hush-hush," said Myfanwy airily. "Probably against Veil."

At this Triffid gave a totally OTT snort, and Myfanwy turned on him, vexed and inspired. "Have *you* heard anything about the Chancelhouse Jumpsuits in development?" she grilled him. "Lamé onesies, most likely."

Triffid grinned. "I'm afraid not," he admitted.

"Can I point something out?" said Kitty. "Whenever my friends disappear on like a 'secret mission' which lasts weeks, it's normally just a nose job."

"Have I showed you *my* nose?" Moth squealed. "Look, from this side it's snub. From this side it's a bit *Rooman!*"

Indeed, some subtle sculptural principle — perhaps the flesh between the nostrils tugged at a slight angle where it joined the philtrum? — meant Moth's nose was just so.

"They're both lovely," Myfanwy reassured her.

"Me nose for adventure, and me nose for *peace!*" said Moth.

It was all very relieving. Myfanwy felt she might grow to feel at home in Chancelhouse. Triffid and Moth seemed a bit more normal to her than Yuri and Bee, but still not *intimidatingly* normal.

"Rumour has it," Kitty revealed, "that Blake has been in secret contact with a designer in Milano and a Parisian haberdasher —"

Triffid smiled. "Blake is *such* an Energizer Brummie! Nessus, you'll find he spends all his time organising entertainments and feats —"

"He's obsessed with having a five-a-side tournament," added Moth conspiratorially. "I actually can't wait!"

"We're also starting a new round of Tar and Blake's murder game," said Triffid. "And soon there's this Spring Feast. His heart's set on having it on the roof terrace." He chuckled. "He's developed his own weather models because the BBC ones won't tell him yet. He normally cooks for everyone on Tuesdays and Thursdays, BTW, if someone volunteers to sous chef."

"It all sounds marvellous!" cried Myfanwy.

Kitty cocked an eyebrow. "Jam your hype, fam," she murmured, as Myfanwy shoved down another spoonful of muesli. Myfanwy happily munched away, thinking of the St Jerome's Womyn's Castle. Perhaps this would be her Seventh Form Centre, where Transitional Gynocracy finally gave way to tolerably fair and free living for everyone!

"Are you guys all finished school?" said Myfanwy. "Me and Kitty still have exams."

"So who is *really* running this place?" Kitty meanwhile was asking Triffid. "Blake doesn't seem capable. Too public spirited."

Triffid roared with laughter.

"We were starting uni," Moth told Myfanwy. "Merlin nabbed me and Triffid during Fresher's Week. Uni's on hold now."

"You don't mind?"

Moth shrugged. "Never really wanted to do Classics and Tourism. This place is *amazing*."

"Blake should be careful," Triffid told Kitty. "Aoide's the real power behind the throne, you know. Meletē is her sidekick."

"And what about you, Yuri?" said Myfanwy. "You're the power behind the power behind, right?"

Yuri just shrugged slightly, and adjusted his spectacles. Kitty nodded sagely. "Yes, as Myffy mentioned, Blake will in fact be rolling out the new Chancelhouse look at the Spring Feast, which will take place atop the roof terrace. Initially it will only be for certain ceremonial occasions, but as time passes it will be required upon all missions. Have you done any missions yet, BTW?"

Moth shook her head. "We only arrived in November, and I was away over Christmas and most of Jan. But we were doing a deli shift yesterday —"

"I get you, fam," said Kitty sagely. "*Missions*."

Triffid took over. "Listen. We're on shift in the deli. Blake shamrocks up, tells us to buckle up for 'Operation Clover.' He demands milk, *then* reveals the first briefing won't be for another month! By which time me and Mothra have already synchronised our watches and are just all about to jump out of the chopper . . . "

"He's a dappy ho," admitted Moth. "I think that's why we get on, me and him. OMG, you should see his study!"

They chatted for a few more minutes. Myfanwy really liked Moth. Probably mole material — that's how it worked, right? The ones you like most? Moth wasn't a caster muse like her and Kitty. She was something called a haverer.

Whereas Triffid seemed quite clever and amusing in that kind of "oh God why won't you *shut up*?" kinda way. His eagerness to impress was touching, but his smoothy-oothy way of using your name all the time ("interesting you should say that, Nessus") was kinda gross. Maybe one day he'd calm down and notice the various receptacles for his wit and charm were actual human beings. Till then, Myfanwy decided she would adopt a policy of friendly scorn and occasionally running away. And maybe sometimes flap at him with both arms and sort of hit him a bit. Apparently he was a cloister muse, whatever that was. She didn't ask in case it was one of his jokes or tricks or something.

Moth and Triffid went off somewhere together, and it fell to Yuri to show them the kitchen and the dishwasher and then lead them downstairs.

"I don't think I'll ever get my bearings in this place," said Myfanwy. "Everything seems to *move*!"

They were headed for the Myometrium — the chamber on Cellar Level Two where they were fated to meet Aoide.

"Blake tells me you're into *co-sleeping*!" said Kitty, as though it were something incredibly kinky.

Yuri shrugged. "Very polarising topic. Class struggle. I believe it is unnecessarily polarising. It is simply parent's choice."

"I guess it's dangerous," said Myfanwy, "if you're likely to roll over and squish your baba. I mean, I thrash around a lot."

"No," said Yuri heatedly. "Is *parent's choice*. Bedsharing must be done correctly. For example, there can be a cot in the bed. For many who are fat, or very drunk, maybe it is not a good idea. Like any aspect of infancy, must be done correctly."

"I don't see why you'd want to," said Kitty. She sounded irritated. Well, what had she expected? "I don't think I'd have become truly independent," Kitty added, "if I'd always slept with mum and daddy. Besides, what about *their* sex life?"

"Ew," said Myfanwy.

"There are many myths," said Yuri. "Much misinformation and arcana. For me personally, I do not think it is cruel to allow a child to cry to sleep. Also, I do not think there is biological design to be near together with child."

"Till what age?" said Myfanwy.

"I do not know. For me, it is existential. It is parent's choice. In practice, many parents flee from such existential choice. Instead, allow their nation and class to decide for them. In Scotland, middle class woman prefers Attachment Parenting. Less structured, more flexible. Tendency to co-sleeping."

"What about where you're from, Yuri?"

But they had arrived. Yuri held open one of a set of swinging doors. Beyond was darkness and a soft drone.

"Careful," said Yuri. "Frigidarium. No running or horseplay."

Yuri put on the lights. They stood at the edge of a swimming pool, maybe ten by twenty-five metres in size. Mosaic tilework surrounded it, and slender pillars ribbed the chamber lengthwise, two in three of plain white stone, every third one a caryatid. And they were pretty good caryatids.

Yuri pointed to a door at the far end of the chamber.

"Have a nice day," he said ominously, and slipped away through the swinging doors.

They walked across the mosaic. The pool filter purred. Complexes of light played on the water's surface like time-lapse crystal.

"For some reason," murmured Myfanwy, "I expected it to be bigger."

As they neared the door Myfanwy observed the carved design which crowned it. It was like a mountain, its point hidden in clouds. On a sticker, in a somewhat childish hand, was written "Myometrium."

Kitty knocked firmly three times.

"Come in, girls!"

With great trepidation, they entered their training chamber.

*

The first thing Myfanwy saw was a door opening. The facing wall was one vast looking glass.

The Myometrium was a gymnasium.

It was a little larger than the chamber they'd just left, and floorboarded with pale smooth wood. At the far end two big tangerine balance balls and a little desk were pushed up against their own reflections. Over to the left were an adjustable bench, a sort of hat-stand thingy for hanging free weights, a water cooler, and another desk with stacks of paper cups shaped like dunces' caps, plus a flat-topped pyramid of rolled white towels. In the area to the right were a stack of cheery blue mats and three exercise machines. The treadmill and the power bike were switched off. On the display panel of the Cybex Arctrainer, a green heart oscillated in oversized pixels.

And there, right in the centre of the gym — her arms akimbo, the La Senza kimono she had sported in the wee hours exchanged now for a velvety lavender tracksuit, and her samurai sword exchanged for a grin every bit as gleamingly large and deadly — stood Simi.

"Waaait a minute," said Kitty.

"A joker," said Myfanwy. "I'll have to watch this one."

Her corn rows might as well have been flapping in the breeze, for all the appalling melodrama of her pose.

"Didn't expect *that*, did you babes?" said Simi. "'Ooh I am the great and powerful Aoide! Mwahahahahaha!' Right my loves, you're late! Let's go! Grab yourselves two of them and get comfy!"

"I stand by what I said last night," said Myfanwy, full of relief. "I'm *still* a bit scared."

Simi pointed to the blue mats. "Sorry we're late," said Kitty, as she slid one off the top. "Breakfast ran over. Yuri's fault. That guy! Yak yak yak!"

"Over here?" said Myfanwy.

"So 'Aoide' is your callsong, Simi?" said Kitty, plopping down.

"Yep my loves, there's great — and no kipping! You had your five hours last night! You're young, that should be enough!"

"I still haven't got a callsong," mused Myfanwy.

"We went clubbing after, actually," kidded Kitty.

"We're going to skip the theology and start with some very easy, simple visualisations. What I want you to do, babes, is close your eyes, and imagine a clear, vertical line, black against a white or pale backdrop."

"I see it!" cried Kitty excitedly. "I'm a *muse!*"

"Hush, babes."

"I'm sorry ma'am. From now on, I vow to put the interests of the recently-visualised vertical line *first.*"

Myfanwy watched the green pixels on the exercise machine pump in and out. At its lowest ebb, the shape was a lozenge, not a heart.

"Myfanwy? You with us, love?"

Myfanwy lay down and shut her eyes.

"A clear, vertical line. One day, this will be the spine of your muse's Altar. Focus on that beautiful, important line for a moment, babes . . . now I want you to . . . very gently . . . bring out six black buds, evenly spaced along this line . . . dividing it into five equal segments. Now you can get rid of the top bud, ladies . . . and the bottom four buds. Now on your remaining bud, bifurcate the top part of the line, opening it symmetrically like scissors, just swiveling it open on your bud. So you should just see a 'Y' babes, with a long skinny tail. That stands for the 'Yoga' in 'Muse Yoga,' which is what we're calling today. Now this next visualisation is a bit trickier. I want you to add *two curves . . .*"

*

Simi made them do peculiar things all morning, then allowed them — since it was their first day — a full hour for lunch. Kitty grazed on fruit and crackers as they walked to the Co-op, where Myfanwy got a hot vegetable lattice.

"*Scan,* damn you!"

Kitty eyed up the offending lattice. "Hon, I don't think barcodes were around when that thing was made."

They walked to the Meadows. It was sunny but chilly.

"What's going to happen when I don't show up tomorrow?" sighed Myfanwy. "Exams are *looming*, fam."

"Mmph."

"*Kitty!*"

"What? Oh. It's taken care of. Blake said it was all taken care of."

A siren. It was the blood transfusion van. Covered in hearts.

A mandem wandered past rocking an eight-pack of loo-roll like an old skool ghetto blaster.

Given their precious interval of privacy, the girls were saying very little. The scarce remarks Kitty did make were all vacuous grooming and effusive, coquettish compliments. "Your curls are *scandalous* today, Myfanwy,' she rebuked as they walked back down an avenue of trees they had just walked up. "Like bunches of black grapes."

In front of them, a woman pushing a buggy toe-banged a red football back into play.

By the time they returned to the houses, Kitty had lapsed into complete silence. Myfanwy had even resorted to Hexxus Nexus on her phone for some timewaste-while-you-traipse.

> *See 3931 photos of you and Kitty.*

Down in the Frigidarium, Triffid was doing Butterfly-stroke lengths in goggles and cap and a pair of speedos. Kitty waved pointlessly at him, then wore a smug look, as if all Triffid's thrashing in the water counted as him returning the wave. Maybe she was cheering up.

"Back for more, my loves?" said Simi, as they entered the Myometrium. "On your mats! Kitty, my love, you may start us off."

"What an honour."

"Warm up with some more word association."

"Cubicle," said Kitty.

"Mishap," said Myfanwy.

"*No,* Simi," snarled Kitty. "I'm *sick* of this. Show me how to flip a memory. Serious. Or I'm on the next plane home. I'm a damn muse. Show me how to *flip*."

*

Kitty rose to her feet. Myfanwy, uncertainly, joined her.

Six faint splashes elapsed.

Simi scoffed. "You don't even know how to *recognise* a memory, my love. Not in the way you need to. Words like *memory*, *thought*, *dream*, *idea* . . . how can I put this? They're, uh, folk psychology, in the lingo . . . they don't have stable neurocognitive correlates . . . now, why can't I think of a simple analogy?"

"Is this, like, what Blake was talking about?" said Myfanwy. "About words not welding properly to the world?"

"Possibly, my love. Um, my head is complete jelly! Oh yeah, *that's why* — because examples are *everywhere*, innit! Say you're having a nice glass of wine, babes, yeah? And this wine tastes, I dunno, woody, earthy, 'erbal, smoky, toasty, full-bodied, balsamic, them things. But if we distilled its constituents, we won't find a wooden stick, a peck of dirt —

"— a piece of toast," Kitty added, "a pack of fags —"

"— right, and some vinegar, etc. — mind you, I've had some dodgy plonks! — just joking, my loves, just joking! We'd find *chemicals*, wouldn't we? Which require a different vocabulary altogether. In the same way, mentality don't always decompose into intuitive particles — into thoughts, feelings, memories, at least not in the way we usually use those words. You *can* sculpt those things, but it takes skill. Take as another example, all these posh paintings we've got on all the walls. When the artist done a portrait of whoever it is, uh —"

"Genevieve Quaker," prompted Myfanwy.

"If you like, my love. That artist didn't dip their paintbrush in a pot full of cheek paint, then a pot full of eye paint, then a pot full of hair paint, did they?"

"Okay. We get the picture," said Kitty. "Examples are ubiquitous."

Myfanwy's mind flicked back to Madame Merely-Pointy's Art Department, and the gradually loading images in the Cool Kid Tallulah's "A History of Pointlessness."

"That artist has got their red and green," Simi was continuing, "and blue for the sky, pink for the skin and so on." Myfanwy looked at the soft brown skin of Simi's hand. Simi's fingers were drumming agitatedly. "Or then again, if you think of an orchestra playing a tune. They don't have *one* instrument for the sad bits, and *one* instrument for the loud bits and *one* —"

"So the . . . the *particles* that we muses flip," said Kitty, "aren't necessarily like passages of music, or whole integrated sections of paintings. They could be more like just the quavers, or just the violin part —"

"Or like the unintegrated brushstrokes," Myfanwy picked up. "If we're skilled, we can flip an entire memory or idea or emotion or whatever. But it's also possible to flip aspects of ourselves that are . . . more disordered."

"Hmm. Not necessarily more *disordered*, my love."

"Okay then, more difficult to name. In the same way, you can paint a cheek, and there is a name for a cheek, once it's been painted. But while it's still being painted, or if it's eroded after, it just becomes, like, a skein of colour with different strata phased out, and *that* doesn't have a name. But that structure also exists in the cheek all along, even when it's finished."

"Yeah," said Kitty suspiciously. "That's what I was going to say." She added, "Swot," in a low, angry murmur.

"Mnemosyne, that is beau'iful," said Simi. "Bloody beau'iful, babes. You have a very visual imagination, babes. And having said all that . . . it's still fine to think of it as swapping memories. Just don't forget the reality can get more intricate and subtle. In actually *doing* it, these subtleties will become clear."

"Wait," urged Myfanwy. "So could I flip someone the fact that I — love the sea, or find tiny dogs hilarious?"

"Potentially," said Simi, nodding vigorously. "Those are some of the exciting new directions we're exploring. The muse art is far-ranging and ever changing. Even better, babes, a muse might cast you the Arabic they've acquired the hard way. Our girl Tar speaks loads of funny languages. She'll loan them if you asks nicely, babes. Bloody hell, I didn't even speak loanwords before I come to this joint. Now I'm intercepting enemy communications, I'm reading the Bible in the original —"

"Same thing," said Myfanwy primly.

Kitty was brooding on something.

"Or someone could flip you how to operate a sniper rifle," Simi said, "or blow up a bridge. That's more Meletē's milieu, babes. It all depends how the individual muse learns to unlace themselves, to disintegrate themselves and give part of themselves away."

"That sounds . . . I mean, couldn't that be kinda dangerous?"

"Would it be possible in theory," asked Kitty, "to flip the muse talent itself?"

Simi grinned widely. "Just in theory?" She threw back her head and laughed. "Now you're learning, my loves! Now you are learning! That's a very advanced art, my love. Difficult and dangerous. Seldom attempted. You're nowhere near the stage of even flipping your first memory, let alone —"

"*Show* me then," said Kitty. "Don't be so patronising! Okay, I get your point, it takes time to learn. But *prove* it. You flip me a memory, Simi. Any damn memory."

Simi paused, contemplatively. "You can't quite believe it yet, can you?" she said in a soft, grim voice. "And now I know why. Myfanwy — Mnemosyne — she's *felt* it happen, but you never have! Do I detect a little jealousy, babes?"

"Envy," Kitty autocorrected. There was a little colour in her cheeks. Myfanwy glanced away.

"You're still half convinced these walls will come down with camera crews behind 'em. Ain't that so, Nessus?"

Kitty said nothing. She was just staring at Simi, her jaw set.

Myfanwy moved to give them space as Simi drew closer. Simi peered down. Kitty looked up blankly. "You know babes," said Simi, "that you'll lose a memory of your own?"

"Some next ting. I'm for real." Kitty nodded her head.

"Well then. If you think you're ready. You ever eaten scorpion, babes?"

"Scorpions?"

"I'll take that as a no."

Simi stalked across the Myometrium, went into her Louis Vitton handbag and produced a journal bound in snakeskin and a phone.

"Basic muse procedure. Before we cast any memory," Simi narrated, "we write it up with as much detail as we can remember. We keep an electronic *and* hard copy, just in case." She went on the phone, then over to a little door Myfanwy had only recently noticed. Today it was tucked behind two large tangerine-coloured balance balls. Rolling these aside like temple boulders, Simi revealed a closet where a small printer sat on a low desk.

In no time it had produced one double-sided page. Simi clipped it to the inside of the journal, which she returned to her bag, but kept out her phone.

"This particular memory I've had written up for a while — Blue Peter, innit? Never mind, before your time."

"He's a YouTube channel now," said Myfanwy uncertainly. "I think."

Simi was hooking Kitty's left hand into an arm wrestler's grip. "More procedure. Ordinarily there is a Partnering Rule. That means in training and practice, everyone is assigned a buddy whom they always cast with. Casting in pairs reduces the risk of Chimera Syndrome. You two are partners, so I'm breaking that rule now. And, Nessus?"

Yuri had mentioned the Partnering Rule. Myfanwy wanted to ask what Chimera Syndrome was, but the atmosphere had suddenly grown very tense. She held her tongue.

"Yes Simi?" said Kitty.

"When I take my hand away," Simi said, "*I want you to tell me what scorpion tastes like.*"

*

A flicker — no, not even a flicker. As though Myfanwy had blinked at them with transparent eyelids. Then Simi withdrew her hand, consulted her phone, and chuckled. Then Kitty was laughing too.

"Scorpion tastes crunchy and spicy!" she cried.

Simi made a face. "Oh! That's funny, babes! Because according to this, *I* thought he just tasted crunchy and 'orrible, 'orrible!"

Myfanwy felt a pang of jealousy, as they were excluding her from a private joke — even though she knew Simi now could no more remember the taste of scorpion than she could.

"I can't quite remember if I liked it or not," Kitty admitted. "I'm standing in a street in . . . like, *China*?"

"Ever *been* to China, my love?"

"No! Except for these few seconds . . . while a, a lady sells me this *critter* on a stick, it looks like a black crystal, all flaked with sugar and red bits."

"I'll take your word for it, my love! It's gone from *my* life!" Simi scrolled on her phone. "Good riddance, from the sounds."

"Someone, I think it's my Chinese friend, tell me only tourists eat those things. I say I *am* a tourist, babes . . . I bite, and it tastes . . ."

"Horrible!"

"Spicy!"

"I'm not much one for spicy foods, babes. That's your lesson number one from the demo. Memories change according to the contexts where they're introduced . . . lesson number two is more *simple.*" Simi's tone had changed abruptly. Myfanwy straightened. "I'm not just Simidelay," she said emphatically, "your mate who chats with you after lights out, when you've had a scare. I am also Aoide. I am Arch-Chancellor, Master Mystagogue, and

High Balneator. These are but titles, babes. This is their meaning, but nor is it a meaning which relies on such trappings. I am, no less than Haduken, an elder muse. He is but *primus inter parrus*. Do you know what *that* means?"

Kitty nodded awkwardly. "First among —"

"First among equals. Chancelhouse belongs to us, not him. And certainly not to *you*, Nessus, you brat. I have seen things, I have done things, you can't yet begin to imagine. You want to be able to do it, one day? To do what I just did, Nessus? To put a scorpion in someone's past, a place where it never belonged?"

She said nothing.

"Answer," she said.

"Yes, Aoide," Kitty said meekly.

"Then on yer back, as they say! And we'll warm up with word association. No need to look so pale, my loves! I'm only joking, my loves! I'm only joking! Word association, then chakra praxis exercise. Then some nanogenre goto runs, all Altar circulars."

"Impresario," said Kitty submissively, lying back.

"Depraved," said Myfanwy.

"Have I come at a bad time?" said Blake.

*

Standing at the doorway Blake clapped a japey namasker, then took one step closer, spread his arms and cried, "What a night! Everyone in one piece? Fewer than nine pieces, at least? — else it becomes tricky to work out what's what, let alone who's whom. Yes, yes, it's not always like this, I promise. Often it's worse."

Blake waddled across the gymnasium. Myfanwy felt incredibly relieved to see him. Through the open door, it sounded like Triffid had just dived into the water.

"I popped by," Blake said, "because I neglected to say yesterday, not a word to *psychoanalysts* either, ladies! Nada, zero, zilch! Not even so much as zilch — be like the Babylonians, who didn't even *have* zeros! Well, perhaps they did, without knowing it. The point is, don't even *repress* Chancelhouse in MacAonghas's presence — you know what that lot are like."

"Well!" said Kitty. "Professer MacAonghas is more like a *pet*. He's not a real psychotherapist and I'm *sure* he can't be a real professor."

"Yes," Blake said, with a worried look. "Well, a burrowing little ferret of a pet, no doubt. Kitty, I'm sure you're used to spilling every last bean to him, and rinsing out that funny sauce they come in too. Now, I plan eventually to bring MacAonghas into or at least nearby the Chancel fold, so that you may continue with such a practice."

Blake was sort of addressing the pair of them out of politeness, but Myfanwy knew this was really all about Kitty. She'd never been to any kind of counselling, other than the Seasons for Growth group after Mum died, and she'd stopped that a year ago. She'd sometimes wished Kitty would let her have a go on MacAonghas, though. Could it hurt? Kitty insisted you needed a lot of experience to use her psychotherapists and novices were liable to sustain severe psychic injuries.

Something else was puzzling Myfanwy though.

"Nevertheless," Blake said, "till MacAonghas is properly vetted, his standard level of professional confidentiality *will not do* for our purposes. So re Chancelhouse — not a word, Kitty?"

"Sir, I'm solid. Die, snitches."

"My other bit of news is that tomorrow afternoon a senior-ish civil servant arrives in your Head Teacher's office to wax eloquent about your enlistment in a prestigious national gifted and talented programme, a sort of last ditch effort to restore these isles to greatness before the ice caps thaw, and we all go the way of Atlantis. Give you deep cover before the deep covers us, if you like, though of course —"

"Wait a minute," said Myfanwy. "So it *wasn't* Professor MacAonghas who headhunted Kitty? Who then?"

"Aha! Who else but Merlin, Chancelhouse's last blazon muse! One positive ID, one potential — *you* lot!"

"A blazon?" said Kitty. "Refresh me?"

"Sort of a muse-detecting muse, my love," said Simi.

"If that's the case," Myfanwy persisted, "how does Chancelhouse even know about Professor MacAonghas?"

"Well, the dear chap is mentioned in Kitty's dossier," Blake said mildly. "Very meticulous wodge of bumf, compiled by Merlin. One on you too, Myfanwy. Frankly a bit of a waste of resources, given our current blazons dearth. Merlin's talent is liveried with me at the moment, and I've half a mind to keep it — oh yes! All this talk of talent-spotting reminds me! Most excellent! Aoide, could you possibly spare these chaps for ten? It's dreadfully crucial you do! *Sans* delay, Simidelay!"

"Yes, my love," said Simi, sounding less than happy. She gave them a little sock-puppet-yapping-type wave which they both immediately reciprocated.

"Ladies," cried Blake, "follow meee!"

Suddenly, oh no, it was happening again — Myfanwy and Kitty were being swept up and up through yet more Chancelhouse labyrinth, some of which Myfanwy was convinced she'd never seen, until they reached Blake's study ("Seuss (Office A)" said the sign) — which, Myfanwy thought sniffily, was where all the sweeping up really should have *started.* It was somehow much more pokey and crammed and chaotic than was really right for any clandestine mystic agency looking to inspire confidence in itself, especially as a forward-looking registered charity. There they stood, more-or-less on tip-toe, and more-or-less holding their breaths, lest they disturb some stack of paperwork and set off myriad chain reactions, while Blake swarmed through paperwork, like Scrooge McDuck through bullion, eventually rustling up a gargantuan, hand-scrawled chart of some sort, one panel of which he took pains to unfold, only to refold again to allow him to unfold some other — it couldn't have been unfolded all at once without knocking through a wall, which Myfanwy suddenly was worried he *might actually do* — and then, draping a panel awkwardly on a stack of grimoires, scribbling upon it a fairly mystifying network of arrows and lines and sigils and squiggles — two of the boldest of which, however, rather disconcertingly, Myfanwy recognised as her and Kitty's initials — and then one particularly long and complicated line.

What's all this about, eh?

When this line reached the edge of the chart, which lay on some other papers, Blake did not raise his stylus but continued the line onto some presumably unconnected documentation. Myfanwy giggled. Kitty was unimpressed. Blake seemed rapt, self-absorbed, but the performance had to be for their benefit. The pen nib continued wandering across half a dozen spilling piles, with Blake's nose not far behind, and then over the fore-edges of some rather ancient and precious looking grimoires, until, finally, it returned to the chart wherefrom it had set sail.

Meanwhile Myfanwy surreptitiously scanned the room for something resembling a pair of thick dossiers. Blake had seemed cheerful enough in mentioning Merlin, she thought. Perhaps Merlin wasn't Mara Drago-Ferrante. Perhaps they'd just been working together — Merlin the talent-spotter, Mara the recruiter. Anyone could have been the talent-spotter really, although hadn't Blake said something about "making an approach"? So didn't Mara *have* to be Merlin? Hmm. An image flashed through Myfanwy's mind, of pretty chestnut hair coiling on tiny inky lilies . . .

Satisfied, Blake folded up his chart, concluding, "Three miles as the crow files," then started, whirled around and peered at the pair with sudden suspicion and wonderment — as if they had just strong-armed their way into his study past numerous armed guardians. Perhaps they were former rainforest inhabitants who wanted it back, and were getting chippy about the state of it? "You *are* —" he began fearfully. "I mean, you *do* — you are competing in the Chancelhouse five-a-side all-ball tournament, aren't you? You'll be on the same team!" he appended pleadingly. "I've just seen to that!"

"Sports?" said Myfanwy, feeling flummoxed. "The sporting life?"

"I'm totally dyspraxic," Kitty said quickly. "Honestly sir, I'm a T35 at anything sports."

"All-ball," Blake explained. "Bit like footie, bit like Gaelic, bit like korfball, bit like kabaddi. There are certain rules by which the rules change. It's dreadfully easy to pick up. Bit like shinty. Not very widely played, for whatever reason."

"*That's* what this is about?" said Myfanwy. "Sports? *Confusing* sports*?*"

But Blake looked thunderously dark now. He shooed them from his study into the corridor then strode off down it. "Follow me! Keep up! Following certain necessary transfers, windows banging open and shut and so forth, and all conducted above board, in the interests of upholding the abundant bounty of the Bountiful Game, Miss Simidelay Bullock's team, *viz.* Aoide's All-Ball All-Stars, fell short of two players! If you'd been paying proper attention you would have observed that! More*over*, Chancelhouse's athletics programme is part of your heavily implied contract, ladies! No slack bobs to be tolerated, eh? Quick march! You are *already* late for Aoide!"

"Like that's our fault!" Kitty whispered. "Why bother asking us, if he's going to insist we play anyway?"

"Just fall over at the beginning," suggested Myfanwy kindly.

"Obv."

"Excuse me Blake," Myfanwy called, as they clattered down some stairs. "Will Veil be in the all-ball tournament?"

"Ha!" The idea amused Blake, and he momentarily slowed. "Alas! Perhaps one day, eh? More goodwill with Veil is highly desirable, of course. Not least because when Veil span off, they took certain rare muse classes with them. Chancel now limp on with, let me see . . . ten or so casters, one blazon and one skiller — though surely both the best in the business! — plus a skiller-taker, a pair of haverers and a trio of drivers. And among our five patterners, though cherish them we must, not one damn shrouder nor mirror! Oh, ladies!" he cried, reprising his patented sudden-stop-and-whirl-and-make-you-bump-into-your-friend move. "My kingdom for a mirror muse!"

"Get off me!" Kitty hissed at Myfanwy. "You're so *clumsy* nowadays!"

They were already off again — even Myfanwy's skate chase hadn't really prepared her for keeping up with Blake. She wouldn't be surprised if he slid down a banister next.

"Where are our touchlesses?" he lamented. "Where are our dryads? Keep up!"

"It's more clever to maintain a stopping distance," Myfanwy explained.

"Where our are mirrors? Alas!"

"Triffid says he's a cloister," said Kitty. "Did he make that up?"

"No, no. At least I certainly hope not, or he may have to leave! Cloister is a kind of patterner, Kitty. There are three main classes to my preferred taxonomy. You have us, your *casters*, your muses who write, who chuck selected stuff out and have random stuff hurtling back at us — ten-a-penny *we* are. Do I sense a pair of them dwindling in the distance behind me? No matter, plenty more where they come from — Aoide, myself, even our friend Jasper Robin — then you have your muses who *read*, who reel in what they fancy, in exchange for losing something at random. Perhaps something important! They're called takers. You've met Marinade, of course. *Then* there are your muses who *pattern* — cloisters, mirrors, cutters, decrypts, shrouders and so forth."

"They can read *and* write," Myfanwy guessed.

"Is this *really* the most direct route?" complained Kitty. Blake had just grabbed a door jamb to give himself more momentum going round a corner.

"Appalling guess, Myfanwy," he called from around the corner. "Patterners can do neither! Quite illiterate, from that perspective — that's why they're useless by themselves. No, what *patterners* do is shoogle things around inside. Now where are we? Keep up! Yes, patterners are wonks. Rearrange the old fridge, or the cognitive architecture, I should say. Cloisters, for instance, are crucial to eliminating stochastic effects from spellsongs. Down here, down here, my dears! Handy for duplicate stacking and Suture Reticula cleansing too. Is this making sense?"

"Spellsongs?" said Myfanwy feebly.

This time, at the crest of another vertiginous staircase, they *did* collide with the abruptly halting Haduken Blake, who wobbled, then cried, "'Forgive us our traipses, as we forgive those who traipse against us!'" He went toddling amicably downstairs. "Down we go! Keep up! Bit of congestion in the starting grid, eh? All-ball is quite a lot like Formula One, I should have mentioned. Has it ever occurred to you, ladies, that the line ought to read, 'lead us *only part the way* into temptation'? Quite an important plank of that particular deity's Free Will manifesto, along with apples, snakes and so forth, as presented pre-election — Election? — now I'm mixing up my metaphors! — the Science practiced behind the lattice, lady, embraces many other sciences, such as theology, and game practice, and tradecraft, and swordplay, and above all, teamwork! Bit like broomball, I should have said earlier. Bit like marn grook, I'd be prepared to argue. Bit like Chess, only without the White guilt. And a spellsong, my dear Myfanwy, is nothing but a spot of teamwork! A caster such as yourselves — or perhaps a skiller in a pinch — lends her talent to a cloister patterner. Then the cloister patterner lends both talents to a mirror patterner. *Then* what, eh? Gutenberg, is what! You more-or-less have a printing press for personal identity, is what!"

"You mean we can mass-produce memory?" demanded Kitty.

Miraculously they had emerged in the Frigidarium. "*We* can't, my dear! Veil have all the blasted mirror muses! Gutenberg was an overstatement. What you'd really have, frankly, is a very slow and perhaps slightly dizzy and pale scribe. Still, portentous, wouldn't you say?"

"How do they know Lewis?" Myfanwy whispered. They both knew a boy at St Jerome's called Lewis Porteous. "Is Lewis the mole?"

"Por*ten*tous, hon," said Kitty.

Triffid had gone from the pool but Moth had taken his place. She moved dark and gracefully, very close to the bottom.

Wow. She can hold her breath a long time.

"Perhaps you were right my dear," Blake pondered. "Perhaps I am a vamp. For I crave fresh blood to wash away the bad blood. What a terribly important time this is! Perhaps it will be *you* two charming casters who build bridges with Veil. Though I imagine pétanque, not all-ball, would be Veil's weapon of choice! Yes, yes! The *bonk*-full game! I can add *Mousagetēs* of caster-bridge to my CV." He paused by the Myometrium entrance. "Or perhaps Mahjong? But there we are. And, it seems, *here* you finally are."

"There should be a Colourful Little Sign put up," Myfanwy huffed. "'No Waddling-Weirdly-Fast So-It's-Like-Sprinting-By-The-Pool.'"

Moth surfaced with a gargantuan gasp. The door was ajar and Blake *rat-a-tat-tatted* it open for them.

"Aoide, I bring you back your charges! Actually I led them on a charge — were we more than ten minutes? Oh, my kingdom for a TARDIS muse! I'm teasing now, ah, Nessus, there's no such muse class. Myfanwy, we'll still need to chat about your callsong, don't forget. Don't look so worried."

"Cheers ears," said Simi. "Hello my loves."

"Hiya coach," said Kitty.

Myfanwy turned to Blake. "Um, actually, if you don't mind," she said shyly. "About my callsong? I've had an idea."

*

Myfanwy blushed. "I thought maybe I could be . . . Mnemosyne?" Her tongue tripped over the word a little. "You said it's the callsong Genevieve Quaker once used. The Tudor muse?"

"Mnemosyne! Funny what you remember, ain't it?"

For a moment it seemed tears had sprung to Blake's blinking eyes. But perhaps it was a trick of the light.

"Well," said Myfanwy. "Kitty says I look a bit like her. I mean, if it's not too presumptuous?"

"It *is* presumptuous. It is *just presumptuous enough*, my dear! Well then,

Mnemosyne it is. Very apt. And," said Blake, turning to Kitty with a pained expression. "Definitely still 'Nessus' for you? Or have you gone with 'Sherlock'? That at least might be Shirley for short —"

"Shirley not sir," said Kitty. "Sometimes I style myself 'Nessie,' in reference to the tranquil, yet chic, Celtic nation state in which Chancelhouse nestles. However in essence my namesake remains always the centaur Nessus, monstrous centaur tutor to Achilles."

"Um, when we were like thirteen or fourteen," Myfanwy apologised, "Kitty went through a massive 'Commedia' phase. Almost every homework assignment, she managed to get in how like Virgil had been her guide. She has these atavistic episodes every now and then."

"I don't know what you're talking about," sniffed Blake. "Obviously trivial teenage girl stuff. I *do* think the names of the ancients ought not rashly and promiscuously to be transferred to our new genera. I'm not talking about 'Mnemosyne,' Mnemosyne. I think that's a very touching choice. By the way, Aoide, there are a few tweaks to the tournie you should look at. No rush."

"Simi," Kitty supplicated. "He wants me to play *team sports*. I *know*, right?"

Simi gave a big sly laugh. "*Does* he? You poor thing. You poor thing."

"Aoide *invented* all-ball," Blake confided to them. "*I* think it's a ludicrous enterprise. When I was a lad, what sport do you think I represented my school in?"

"Cricket or rugger or tennis," Myfanwy said.

"All-ball!" gasped Kitty, with perfect conviction. She was sure she had spotted a very cunning trick.

"No, not all-ball! Cricket!"

"Or rowing," said Myfanwy.

"Cricket," complained Blake.

"We know," said Myfanwy kindly. "But we're still guessing."

"Wait," said Kitty. "Golf."

"Bowled like a damn centaur meself, back when."

"Babes," Simi cackled, "you'll get no sympathy here. Me and Blake are rival managers. More vital than the Veil rivalry, in my brain. The all-ball tournie is *looming*, my loves."

Now Blake was smiling craftily. "I must go find Yuri. One last thing. Kitty, it's *wonderful* you and Mnemosyne have been friends for so long —"

"Since we were six," said Myfanwy.

"Is that all it is?" frowned Kitty.

"And Chancelhouse regards that as an *asset* —"

"'*Chancelhouse regards that as an asset*,'" Kitty said in a stupid deep voice.

"Only I'm pretty certain now the centaur tutor to Achilles was called *Chiron*, and I wondered —"

"For the *normal* stuff," Kitty said, crinkling her nose. "For Latin and Greek and Peace Studies, it was Chiron. However, for his secret *Chancelhouse* work, it was *Nessus*. Read *between the lines*, sir."

"Well then, I am outgunned," moped Blake. "Aoide, my honoured rival, tell me this. Why does *no one* pick the callsongs I suggest? Ignoring me is rapidly becoming one of our best-loved Chancelhouse traditions! Names are so important! I just thought that 'Nessus' — well, I know nowadays they string you up for saying 'ladylike,' but —"

Simi and the girls gently edified him till he ran off.

"Adieu! Adieu!"

His adieus mingled with Moth's splashing. The gym door gradually stopped flapping.

*

For dinner they had salad in Valhalla, just the two of them. Quietly they plotted.

"I get the impression Bee is batcake crazy," said Myfanwy. "I doubt she can tell us anything useful."

"Bless! Triffo was telling me —"

"Triffo? Are you being serious, Kitty? Triffo?"

"Got a problem with that, Myfanwy? Me and Triffo have grown *very close* since we met at breakfast today. I also call him Trifling occasionally, although that is a sure sign I want something from him. Hmm. Anyway, he was telling me Bee is borderline Chimeric. It can happen to muses who flip too often and with too many different people. You kind of lose your sense of who you are."

"Really? Geeze. She seemed fine to me."

"Your standards were never especially high though, hon. We've discussed that in the context of Simon Buckerton, Paddy, *et al.*"

"Will Bee get better? If she stops flipping so much?"

"Triffo couldn't finish his explanation because she buzzed in out of nowhere and said all this crazy disconnected stuff. That kind of *did* conclude it though. I mean, he just had to add a pointed look, and that was us."

"The problem goes beyond that. And every other muse we meet now, there's some *reason* they've been left out of the secret mission. Bee and her dissociative order . . . Yuri has persecution delusions . . . Triffid blates just too smug . . . and Moth, I don't know yet, but I bet something will come up."

"Myffed, ain't *nothing* wrong with Riffs or Mo. Indeed, I even shared with them . . . my True Name!"

"Yeesh. I tell everyone that."

"So if anyone asks, I'm Anastasia von Enigmengera, okay? If you want to rather powerfully imply that I'm Ruratanian royalty in exile, that wouldn't exactly be rocking the boat either. Oh, Myffed, *why* must I lie? Why am I such a big weirdo?"

"But Anastasia, hon, being a big weirdo is what makes you so . . . weird. Well, how do you fancy splitting up?"

"My thoughts exactly. And it's von hon to you. I'll try Triffo. It's very honourable of you to only use un-smug informants, but it may really limit our options."

"The Oracle at Delphi was massively smug. '*Ooh there will be a battle that someone will lose, oh yeah it's you.*' I guess maybe I'll try Yuri?"

"Not Moth then?"

"What's *that* look for? Moth said she only arrived in November, and she's been home quite a lot. I don't think she knows much more than we do. I'll try Yuri, okay?"

"Beware. In his culture, when you visit a woman three times at night, it means you are wed."

"Let's say he visited us one-and-a-half times each."

"Whevs, hon. Roll out!"

"And don't roll your eyes!"

*

There was no answer at Yuri's door. Myfanwy knocked again super loud.

Ooh, I bet he's in there!

She resisted the urge to put her ear against the door, and wandered off in search of Kitty. She soon stumbled upon the correct corridor and the door marked "Triffdog & KCrab." No answer *there* either. Where was everyone? The sounds of water and someone singing — well, sort of MCing — emanated from the shower down the corridor.

She passed along to the next door. It was Bee's. She hesitated only a moment before knocking.

"Who is it?" Bee drawled behind the door, but didn't wait for an answer. "It's Bee! Are you after me? You have to be someone *after* B to come in! Like C can come in, D can come in, E can come in. But if you're that nasty old A —"

"It's me," said Myfanwy. "It's —"

She'd forgotten for a moment.

"Mnemosyne!"

There were some shuffles and clunks and the door opened. "I didn't even know the alphabet went that high," said Bee, obviously awe-struck.

"Mnemosyne must come after Elemenohpe. Come visit me in my room."

It was a dark, cluttered and pretty abode. Most of the light came from icy blue and cherry pink fairy lights. Some little bulbs curled themselves around bedposts, between fingers of a hand sculpture, and wreathed up the bow part of a cello case — but for the most part, they just lay in glowing clumps in corners, like some strange phosphorous fungus. The walls were covered in cartoons. These were mostly of horses, in thick black pen, on all kinds of scraps of paper and card. Bee was a doodler too.

"It's pretty where you live," said Myfanwy.

"You know what the prettiest part is?" said Bee. "Uh, *us?* Okay, can I do your make-up?"

Bee led Myfanwy to one of the gloomiest corners.

"You're pale," said Bee. "I'm pretty pale, but I wish I had your skin."

"I'm freckly," said Myfanwy. "It's worse in the summer."

"I'm gonna do each freckle a different colour except one. Blue!" Myfanwy felt a dab. "And green! I should really do the base first, then the powder, but maybe it will work anyway. And gold! Okay, I'm already bored of that fascinating practice. And purple! And now!"

Bee began work with a dark liquid eyeliner. Myfanwy suddenly remembered she was supposed to be gathering info, detective-style.

"So, Bee," she said craftily. She definitely hadn't blown her cover yet. "What's your view on the history of Chancelhouse? Blake implied it began in Tudor times. He gave us these long lists of like alchemists and occultists that were *maybe* Chancelhouse, and also some that defo weren't, only I can't remember which was which."

"Close your eyes," Bee instructed.

Myfanwy obeyed. She felt Bee's brush on her eyelids.

"During his tour, I think Blake said something about Rosicrucians," Myfanwy prattled on, "and I remember Hicks Templar, and John Milton's scribe, and John Howard of Bedford and, um, Marsilio Ficino, and lots of others. But Kitty, um, Nessus, said Triffid had traced us even earlier, maybe. Like to Orpheus's lyre, and the sorcerers of Thrace and Sparta, and the —"

"Unfortunately, Mnemosyne, there is a charge for that service. Open!"

Myfanwy laughed politely. But when she opened her eyes, Bee was bearing down on her very seriously. Myfanwy squirmed back a bit.

"Okay," Bee whispered huskily. "What do you wanna believe? About Chancelhouse or about *anything*. Just describe me something, okay? Because maybe I can remember believing something like that, and then I can sell it to you at, like, an unusually low price."

"*Sell* it to me? Well, I'd like the *truth*, Bee. But I don't know if —"

"I don't know if I can help you then," Bee said sadly. "We're going to be friends, so I don't mind selling you my memoirs. I have some very impressive past, Mnemosyne. It doesn't have to be, 'Oh, the architectural history of this archway is very interesting.' I mean, it doesn't have to be boring things like *you* like. Like this one time I got so drunk, with these two guys, who were like friends with my one friend, and they were like show us your —"

"Right," said Myfanwy. "I don't know if I want that."

"It gets luridly evocative," Bee pressed.

"I'm kind of new to all this, Bee. I guess I just need time."

"Okay, well, whatever. I mean, you know where my room is now. But for truth, seek elsewhere."

"I'll think about it. I'm just kind of confused. Maybe another time."

"Everybody's confused nowadays. Aoide spies on Simi and reports her to Seuss and then remembers she *is* Simi. So she reports her to Blake instead, who tells Zeus. He's Proust, except farther along the Möbius strip, he's Kobus and he wants that freaking arm. I'm Bee. I live here on my farm. Maybe another time, when you know what memories you wanna buy. Do you wanna go shopping online now? I don't have any money, as you can see by my humble abode, but I know where you can get amazing bargains, like 98% or 99% off. If I show you, we can get stuff we can both wear."

"Maybe another time. Did you draw these?" Myfanwy asked, indicating the walls.

The cartoons were kind of neither elegant nor crude, sort of Gary Larson crossed with Picasso scribbles.

"Everybody always thinks that the cosmonauts sent narrow dogs into space during the 1950s. It's not true. They were horses. This is Laika, the first earth-born creature to enter orbit. These are her friends Smelaya, Lise, Marfusha and Snezhinka." Bee pointed to each Soviet horse. "As you may see, only female horses were used on this programme. They were permitted to graze a nutritious grassy protein from a tube." Bee pointed to such a tube. "Here is Pchyolka. She's me. Pchyolka however was accompanied by dogs, rabbits, mice, rats, flies, flowers, fungus, plus the only stallion ever to orbit the earth to this day."

"I really like how simple your lines are, but how much movement they suggest."

"Pchyolka also took children's toys with her to test the effects of zero gravity on children's toys. I'm not, like, 100% okay about your information about the suggestions made by my outlines. Their movement was highly constrained in the cramped cabins."

Myfanwy was having difficulty judging Bee's tone. "Needless to say," she hazarded, "many beautiful mares participated unwillingly and paid with their lives."

Bee grabbed Myfanwy by the waist and raised her phone. "Let's take photos. I *love* photos."

They pouted and growled for a little photo shoot.

"I *love* photos," she kept repeating. Was she being sarcastic? She sounded very flat.

"Do you have old photos of Chancelhouse?" said Myfanwy, trying a new tactic.

"No. I love *deleting* even more than *taking*. Okay, now do a face like you're really innocent. Pout like you've never even had anyone in your mouth."

Myfanwy blushed under a mash of weird goth paint, and Bee snapped and snapped.

"Okay, now do this."

They opened their mouths as widely as they possibly could. Myfanwy could open her mouth really wide. She felt she'd finally earned Bee's respect and trust.

"I can't *wait* to delete those," said Bee.

"I should be getting back," said Myfanwy. She hesitated, blinked a few times. She'd be going back empty-handed. Her anxiety helped her go out on a limb. "I've heard that someone in Chancelhouse is like a leak," she blurted. "Like L-E-A-K?"

"You know what I think?" said Bee. "When Veil come in the night, they don't really want to seize us from our beds. They're linking with some of us. Some of us who are Veil."

"Geeze." Myfanwy remembered the frenetic nocturnes unhappily. "What's wrong with just doing it in 'Spoons? Some people have revision and things."

"Duh," said Bee. "If you're a double agent, and your Partner flips you, you might give away your memories of when you met your handlers. Clearly, Veil have learned to flip us stuff in our sleep, so that's no longer a problem. Veil swapped my breasts around once. Now the left one's bigger. Do you want to remember finding out your boobs are swapped over? It's pretty cool. It's actually on special this week. Do you have a job or anything? Do your parents give you money?"

It was the most lucid — well, apart from the last bit — Myfanwy had ever heard Bee sounding.

"So we can't do that? Flip stuff into dreamers, I mean?"

"No, Mnemosyne, we can't. Veil kick our ass at everything. We're in the wrong organisation but we're still a pretty cool pair of girls. You can use my sink to wash your stupid face."

"This? No way, mate. I'm rocking this look."

"Please leave now," said Bee coldly. "I'm Bee. This is my room. Your time is now up."

"See you round, hon," said Myfanwy.

But as she stepped into the corridor, Bee came out bearing a gift. "Take them for your room. I kind of hate them now."

It was a cartoon of two horses, done on some ragged-edged graph paper. One of the horses, more anthropomorphic, rode the other. They seemed surrounded by waves.

"Thanks. Are these also space horses?"

"No. They're called George and Horse." Bee pointed to each one. Horse was riding along in George's saddle. "They ran away to a river island where the wicked farmer can't get them."

"Thanks so much, hon. Do you want —"

"No, I don't sell my things, I just sell *myself*. My *things* are not for sale. Bye, Mnemosyne."

*

As Bee shut the door, another down the corridor swung open. Myfanwy rubbed her cheeks self-consciously. Triffid came out of the shower, a brightly spangled beach towel round his waist.

He was skinny but kinda hench.

"Mnemo! What's up?"

Myfanwy stared at Bee's door. "Soz," she said. "Just wandering, really. Trying to get this place figured out."

"A maze for muses," Triffid agreed. "Hey," he added very quietly. "I wanted to warn you about her. She'll try and sell you memories."

"She just did. I said I'd think about it."

"Bee's kind of nuts. But please don't mention it. Especially not to Blake or Aoide or Meletē. She's on her last warning, but she really can't afford to get kicked out. She needs to be among people who understand her. You know?"

"What's her story? Kitty said she was — Chimeric?"

Triffid shrugged. "I think she's just sold every beautiful experience she's ever had, and everything beautiful that's ever come her way. Plus she's going around with a dozen different people's memories inside her. It's kind of made her nuts. Okay, I'm making a massive puddle."

"God, sorry! Aha, you are the leak!"

"What?"

"Nothing. Just this stupid thing. I'll see you —"

Triffid was observing her with uncustomary intentness. "You and Anastasia come hang out some time when I have garms on, y'hear? Plus when Kermo gets back, we all need to hang out. He'll love you."

"Sick," said Myfanwy. As he was leaving she called after, "You have blood and shaving foam on your face."

"You have rainbows," said Triffid.

*

On the winding way back Myfanwy inspected various vintage swords and pikes and stuff. All securely bolted to the wall. Among them, a young stag, his antlers covered in adolescent velvet, a faraway look in his eyes. On either side of him, ornate sconces covered with cold candlewax.

This freaking place, thought Myfanwy, and went to her room.

"How was *Yuri*," said Kitty, lying on her front, browsing on her phones. She was dressed for bed.

"Hmm?" Myfanwy shut the door softly. "Oh, he didn't answer, so I went and saw Bee."

"*That* girl. God."

Then Kitty gave Myfanwy a most significant gaze.

"I'm going to brush my teeth," said Myfanwy.

She quietly and quickly readied herself for bed. She put out the lamp. Everything was invisible except the faint archway of light that limned the curtains' edges. Chancelhouse HQ was completely quiet. Softly Myfanwy called out Kitty's name.

"Yes, Myffy?" said Kitty woozily.

"'*Scare me half to death.*'"

*

For as many years as Myfanwy could remember, Kitty had told her scarytales. You pronounced the word with the same cadence as "fairytales." When they were still little, Kitty could get really cross if Myfanwy said "ghost story" or "fairytale" by mistake. Kitty might faux clam up, making Myfanwy beg and beg before she'd begin the next scarytale.

Those "make-up" scarytales could be extra good though.

In recent years Kitty still corrected her in this respect — "Besides, these are scarytales! They're different to ghost stories" — but now with arch sorrow and extravagant urbanity, as if rectifying the title of some fine wine, implying that while of course such snobbery was sheer pettiness of course, it was — alas! — important to some important people.

"Mmph," said Kitty. "I dunno —"

"Oh, *Kitty!*" wailed Myfanwy.

There was a ritual associated with the origin of each scarytale. Myfanwy would sense a certain agitation of Kitty's aura, some secret outcome of Kitty's expanded alchemical anatomy. Sometimes she'd sense it in broad daylight and some public place. Then she'd say nothing, but register the change with hungry pleasure, and whenever they were next alone in the darkness — whether they lay top-and-tail in Myfanwy's three-quarter bed in Brixton, or side-by-side in Kitty's king-sized in her *pied à terre* — even if one or both craved sleep more than anything in the world, Myfanwy would always speak the incantation, and Kitty would start the scarytale.

"Okay hon," Kitty relented. "It's a good one." She paused only a moment. "Once, not long ago — or was it? — there was a young girl called Myfanwy. She was clever and hardworking and had pale skin, a sprinkling of freckles on the bridge of her nose during the summers, and curly, beautiful dark hair. She was otherwise a very ordinary girl. Nothing too out-of-the-ordinary had ever happened to Myfanwy. She lived alone with her father in a little house with an upstairs and a downstairs and a cellar. The upstairs was above a hardware and home furnishings store. They had a green little garden out back, which strangers traipsed through day and night, because it appeared to those strangers like public access to some hairdressers and herbal remedy type shops. They could see the strangers from their conservatory, which was also their sitting room, though for some reason Myfanwy and her father always called it the Glass Room. But the two of them were kind and happy and never minded. One Bank Holiday weekend, her father went away to Edinburgh on some secret and dangerous business, and Myfanwy was left all alone in the house. Previously when her father had been away, Myfanwy would spend the weekend with her glamorous and frighteningly ambitious best friend. The friend had her own tiny flat near the school they both attended. On this occasion, however, for some reason the friend just didn't want her around. So poor Myfanwy was all by herself. All alone, all by herself, and to be frank she was a little afraid of the dark. So she gathered her toy rat and her toy dinosaur, and hoped sleep would come to take her soon. She couldn't find her toy scorpion. Perhaps he'd crawled off. How strange. How very, very strange. She couldn't sleep. Perhaps she nodded off for a bit, and a distant scream woke her. Or perhaps she dreamt it. Or imagined it. One way or another, instead of sleep, there gradually came a sound. At first Myfanwy supposed it to be the steady patter of rain on some iron pipe. But that wasn't right. She knew this house well, and she knew the sounds it could make. The sound in her room right now wasn't rain on a pipe. It was almost like the soft pop of a distant firework. But she knew it was closer than that. It was somewhere in the house, deep down in the house. Myfanwy held her rat and her dinosaur and hoped it would go away. Then Myfanwy thought she did recognise the sound. It was a scratching. Scratch, scratch. Yes. Scratch, scratch. By listening over and over again, she could almost separate out the ingredients of the sound, the part where a fingernail ticked on something resonant, where it dragged momentarily against it, then bent, so that the soft fingertip was drawn along after it. Oh — nonsense! Sugar! There was no fingertip! There was no fingernail! What if it was a trapped bird? What if it was something to do with the gas or the water? Myfanwy was sensible and knew out-of-the-ordinary things never happen. So she rose primly from her bed. Her phone said it was . . . let's say, fifty-four minutes past three. The overhead light wasn't working. Nor was the grandmother clock in the corridor. Nor were the lights or the clocks in the Glass Room. There was a little moonlight there however, and Myfanwy felt better by it. Whatever the sound was, it no doubt related to all the malfunctioning electrical equipment. Myfanwy went carefully down the stairs. In the complete darkness of the kitchen, the scratching was loud. Perhaps beneath her feet, communicated upwards by pipes. In pitch blackness, where she could not see her own arms, Myfanwy felt her way through the kitchen she knew so well, to a particular drawer, from which she drew out a long candle, which she knew to be white, and a box of matches. She thought perhaps she discerned other noises muffled with the scratching. Like the splintering of wet wood, and a gasp cut short, again and again. She felt only three matches. The first broke without flaming. The second flamed and then her candle was lit. So equipped, Myfanwy moved onto the landing, and raised her candle to look at one last clock face, stopped at fifty-four minutes past three. And she moved the candle to illuminate the doorknob, and she opened the door into the hole under the stairs, where there began a second flight of stairs, the flight down into the cellar. They were old and rotten and Myfanwy took a tumble that snapped the bones in both her legs. The light from her candle was snuffed as she landed, but she had just enough time to glimpse rather a lot of people down there with her. Although it was great, her pain by no means approached in magnitude her terror. So she screamed and screamed until she could scream no more. Then she remembered the last match. Her hand shook in the darkness, but she managed to light it. And by its little light, what did she see? What but herself, a whole pit of herselves, Myfanwy, in every degree of thirst and decay, famishing, thinning and wasting, flesh drawing back from bones, and at the bottom of the pits, infinite skeletons, and they all reached up. And she too reached up, and with her last remaining strength, she scratched upon a metal pipe which ran up the cellar wall. And what was the last thing she heard before the match burned down and the darkness swallowed her? Two stories above her, Myfanwy, who was sensible and knew out-of-the-ordinary things didn't happen, was rising from her bed, and coming to see what the disturbance was. Two stories above her, Myfanwy was telling herself, oh, nonsense. Sugar. What if these were the claws and the feathers of some trapped bird, who would be dead by morning? What if it was something to do with the gas, with the water?"

Silence.

Myfanwy shivered and almost sneezed. "Don't get it."

"*She's caught in a time loop.*"

"What causes it?"

"*Star Trek.*"

"Really scary, mate. Thanks."

"You're welcome, hon."

"Why didn't the screaming wake her?"

"That's neither here nor there. Your wits are deranged. You have gazed into an abyss of irrationality."

"Maybe the screams weren't part of the loop."

"Whevs, Myffy. Sleep, fam. God. I just have that horrible feeling of exhaustion and insomnia."

"Night, Kitty. Just let yourself drift, hey?"

"Yeah obviously," said Kitty irritably. "I'll drift half to death. Sweet screams, Myffy."

They lay in the dark till Myfanwy said, "What does scorpion taste like?"

"Spicy," said Kitty. "Not that nice."

"It's been ages since the last scarytale."

"Sure has. Find anything out from Yuri, by the way?"

"Oh, I totally forgot!" Myfanwy laughed. "Well, did *you* find anything out from Triffo?" she asked innocently. She was just about to add, "*I* did," when Kitty chirped up in the darkness.

"Oh, not much," Kitty said. Bedclothes slid and rustled. "We just got chatting."

Myfanwy's breath caught. She studied the darkness. She'd never been afraid of the dark.

Just some of the things in it. Kitty *couldn't* have seen Triffid. There wasn't time. Not without being in the damn shower with him.

So why lie?

Just to make Myfanwy weirdly jealous?

She listened to Kitty's breathing.

She felt scared half to death.

Should she say something?

"So I take it Yuri said nothing?" Kitty asked eventually. She'd rolled over. Her voice was much clearer and nearer.

Where had Kitty really been?

"He wasn't in. Night, hon. Sweet screams."

"Sweet screams."

*

The saw screamed, and the lion screamed, but only in fear. A high arc of sparks leapt against the vivid cloudless blue, as flowingly rich as pumping blood. The masked policewoman cut down tensely into the concrete.

Her eye wandered farther.

Everyone got up as sorcerers, beasts, monsters, clowns. Giants gathered. Their legs were thin. The face of the lion was running free in his tears. Soon there would be a sacrifice. Beings were woven into the buildings.

Now guns.

Guns. Guns.

The room was pitch dark. Myfanwy took a moment to remember what bed she was in, and relief returned to her heart.

Two short bursts in the distance, hadn't there been?

Then another, different — returning fire.

"Kitty!" she hissed. "Did you *hear* that?"

Kitty was defo awake. Myfanwy took the hint and lay in the darkness with ears pricked. Myfanwy was sure the guns had been real — they were what woke her, not the last thing she dreamt — right?

Wind, coiling in the trees.

Running footsteps, elsewhere in the compound.

A door slamming.

Then a piercing wailing, the alarm possessing her like a physical pain. Myfanwy clapped her hands over her ears, cursing. Seconds later the sound cut out. Next nothing but wind. The giant silent.

Myfanwy shivered.

Veil, surely. Perhaps Jasper himself.

She felt it was him. However unsettling it was, however baffling the behaviours of her new allies and her BFF, she was glad she was here in the Chancelhouse compound, and not . . .

"Hon," she said. "I'm freaking again." She fumbled for the neck of the lamp.

Their room was filled with light — and Kitty's bed was empty.

*

Along the starlit streets Myfanwy pounded in her pyjamas. Coming to a line of shut-up greengrocer shops she stopped dead.

"Kitty!" she yelled.

She figured she'd follow the gunfire or whatever, but now there was nothing to guide her.

Surely she should go back to HQ. Rouse Blake and the rest, and work out what the heck was happening. They probably had a secret team of griffins or something for just such an occasion . . .

Put some shoes on.

"Kitty!"

The wind from the Meadows whipped up a faint scream and Myfanwy once more was running alone into the mist.

She stopped again near traffic lights, by the bench where she'd shivered with Kitty on the day they'd uncovered Chancelhouse. The world was steeped in mist. Myfanwy walked briskly along the edge of the Meadows, massaging the stitch in her side, trying to breathe evenly, listening intently to the night.

"Kitty?" she called. "Kitty? Where are you? Kitty? Kitty?"

As she approached the playground at the south-eastern edge, the cries she had heard came again — from among the climbing frames, the sovereign territory of any midnight children in possession of White Lightning, Malibu, So Co and Coke.

Myfanwy cursed.

Not Kitty. Just some random drunk lads and lassies.

The lanterns stretched away across the Meadows, lighting the undersides of the leafless cherries, transforming them into ghastly sepia fountains and columns, shrinking to vanishing point.

She heard laughter. A bottle smashed. Her body shaking, Myfanwy turned back up the road. On the ground was a fraction of her foot printed in dark fresh blood. Her heel was still flowing — when had *that* happened? *God.*

Then long hard arms reached from the mist and gathered her up.

Book Four

"The women of Helium are taught to frown with displeasure upon the tongue of the flatterer . . ."

— Edgar Rice Burroughs, *The Chessmen of Mars*

"What are you doing out here, sweetheart?" spoke the voice in her ear. "It's *winter*, sweetheart. Where are your *shoes* and *coat?*"

Very unfair! Myfanwy couldn't reply — he'd slid both hands hard across her jaw, and she could barely *breathe.*

It wasn't Jasper though — this guy's body was just as strong as Jasper's, but his voice was too polished and high-pitched. Some accomplice, silent so far, was gripping her wrists, twisting them — maybe *this* was Jasper? Who were they?

Did they have Kitty too?

Myfanwy's lungs felt as though aflame, and her left shoulder half-dislocated. She stopped struggling, lay limp in the gathering arms. *The secret to munching any man who is all "muzzly" with his hands*, Myfanwy hypothesised on the fly, *must be making sure you pick the right moment* . . .

"Chancelhouse larvae," gloated the accomplice. "Yum yum."

"Oni is just taking the piss, love. Just taking the piss."

Right. So the man holding my wrists is called Oni. Sounds like a callsong — Veil agents?

"One of theirs for one of ours, eh?" Oni grunted.

"Calm now, sweetheart. Stressful night for us all. We're just going to have a chat about your behaviour."

"Uh, Vertical?" said Oni. "Wee problem."

Out of the teeming mist around the playground, teenagers were emerging drunkenly. All held bottles and one lad hefted his drained voddie bottle — Myfanwy noted with mixed feelings — by its neck, like a club.

"There a difficulty here, chief?" this lad called.

"No difficulty," Vertical told the silhouette. "We're just pished! On our way home!"

"Aye, us an aw, chief!" the lad called. "Gonny let the *wifey* speak though, eh!"

Wifey!

Both Myfanwy's captors swore under their breaths.

"Tell these wee neds we're your friends," Vertical murmured in her ear. "And *we* won't have to hurt them. *Capische?*"

Myfanwy thought about it a bit, then bit as hard as she could into the pulp of his palm.

*

Her plan didn't have the desired effect. Vertical didn't yelp or flinch. As Myfanwy's teeth sank deeper, he tranquilly withdrew the last of her breathing privileges. Myfanwy wondered dizzily whether she might survive on the oxygen in his blood alone. Well, she'd damn well try, and at least dwindle into the dark in an Enlightenment Spirit of enquiry — rather than just cotching — dwindle just as Mary Wollstonecraft would have done.

Or Jane Findlater. Or any number of . . .

In the flowing void which contained her, the voices were continuing, but Myfanwy couldn't follow their content . . .

Goodness, was she *dying?*

A strange dawn of white glass drew up through the darkness. It shattered somewhere behind her to the right, and suddenly sweet misty air was flowing in her chest again.

Myfanwy gasped and dry-heaved.

"I'm sick of you scum," Vertical's voice hissed ahead of her like the sweep of a firework's fuse.

Myfanwy twisted her wrists. They were like stripped screws. Behind her, Oni still held on hard.

"Help!" she yelped with a mouthful of grass, then raised her face. Vertical easefully ducked a second speculative glass missile and dropped into a measured sprint, pregnant with danger.

"Watch out!" she yelled. "He's not normal!"

Against the mist-filled rigging and loops and poles of the playground, a ragged vision wavered, of six lads and lassies all locking lips with uplifted glass vessels. Presumably to waste the less precious ambrosia when, inevitably, they smashed them apart on the skull of this person, who — tall, all in black, bearded, and generally rather dashingly ninja in aspect — was now sprinting towards them in warlike display.

Vertical.

"Help!" Myfanwy screamed. "Feds! Neds! *Anybody!*"

Through the mist the lads and lassies seemed like six infant swine suckling at the underbelly of their glass mother-sow machine, sprung from some unsung steampunk modernity. But Vertical was already among them, tricking, kicking, leaping, striking. They scattered, regrouped, swarmed, were cut down, rose again. Yowls and curses filled the night. A butterfly kick foot caught a green bottle and sent it flying into the playground, where it smashed against one of the zip-wire's towers.

"That's actually a good effort," someone said.

As if all *that* wasn't weird enough, *Kitty* had joined the fray, mostly naked — a towel or something? v. bold non-outfit anyway — and was poking ineffectually at Vertical with a big jagged tree branch. Kitty wasn't actually *saying,* "Brute! Brute!" — but that was the basic combat style she was alluding to.

More glass exploded.

Oni violently frogmarched her forward into the fray. It was all Myfanwy could do to steer giddily between big shards. They were at playground's gate now.

He was unbeatable, grabbing everything, moving everything, aware of every process and momentum, whizzing among the play equipment like viruses infiltrating killer mecha. The lads and lassies who weren't being directly ass-whipped were appreciatively whooping his agility.

Their honoured adversary now drove them back through the climbing frames and, seizing a spot among the swings, whirled the chains to and fro with his hands and feet, smacking and entangling his young foes. Flying wood cracked bone — two lads scrambled away whimpering, including the silhouette who had first spoken.

Now it was just two lads, two lassies, plus Kitty, who stood against Vertical.

"Let go!" Myfanwy gasped pointlessly.

Oni tightened his grip on her wrists and twisted the skin back and forth. She glimpsed other shadowy figures on the margins. Allies? Rivals? Or both?

One small spotty lassie took advantage of Kitty's Branch Attack and breached Vertical's perimeter of rattling tentacles, finally bringing brittle Lambrini justice thumping down on the Veil thug's back — but with little force. Now Vertical was dragging this agile wee lassie towards the seesaw for some sort of horrible reprisal.

"It's Meletē!" came a woman's voice from a zip-wire tower. "He's got a bloody flamethrower!"

There came a *woosh* and a tall arm of smoke and flame licked through a kiddies roundabout's spinning rails, filling the world with warmth and colour and linking its contending figures in one dazzling frame. Vertical cursed. The lassie scampered free and away.

Then another new voice emerged from the same place as the flame, and somehow no less terrifying than that flame — "Was that you, Germ? I guess *all* this equipment needs sterilising!"

"Give Vert a 'and then, Germ!" Oni growled. "I've got me 'ands full!" He yanked Myfanwy's arms higher and she yowled in pain. Again a *woosh*, and yellow flames licked along the base of the playground's crawling tube.

"This's *amazing*!" one of the remaining lads kept shouting. "This's *amazing*!"

Vertical was flying to and fro, from the geodesic monkey bars to the roundabout to the boingy-y horse to the twisting, flapping swings — every surface apparently as stable to his flying, whirling legs as every other. On the plus side, Myfanwy elbowed this Oni fellow square in the nose, with the force of a mailed fist — *Special Delivery*.

She collapsed together with her attacker into an amorphous wrestle, punching and squeezing, rolling around in the damp clumps of grass, absorbing splinters of glass like dough absorbing flour.

She caught glimpses of him, another ninja-like beardy-weirdy. As the grass whirled into sky and stars, Myfanwy caught snatches of arms grabbing at Kitty and disabusing her of her branch. Now new arms were helping Myfanwy, dragging at Oni, grabbing his throat — it was Simi, Simi and Yuri!

"You alright, love?" Simi said cheerfully.

— but Yuri gave a high, clear cry and Oni bust free of them. With a gurgle Oni darted deeper into the playground. Yuri helped Myfanwy to her knees. His glasses hung squiff.

"It is nice to see you," he said.

"Kit!" cried Myfanwy.

"Myff!" cried Kitty from the sky. Vertical was carrying Kitty's kicking legs high into the boughs of a towering cherry. They were at least three storeys up. Kitty's towel drifted down till it intersected a torrent of burning liquid and was incinerated. Oni lunged for the figure wielding the flamethrower just as that figure discarded it to catch Kitty falling, naked, from the flaming tree. The flamethrower went skidding away from the grappling trio. The lads who'd fled earlier were back with reinforcements. Two of them shoved a third along the street in a shopping trolley. Stones and bottles rained upwards from the drive-by shooting while Vertical, screeching, flipped around among the burning boughs like a tiny insect blurring inside a jar. Sirens wailed. Above them the firestorm in the cherry crackled and spat. Kitty crawled on her hands and knees towards the flickering six-inch pilot flame just as, dangling from the zip-wire, a dark squat figure buzzed down diagonally from the far tower.

"Stressful night all round!" Vert screeched from his up-side-down perch. "A lot of *feelings* just now!"

Kitty and the zip-wire rider collided and contended.

"Go-ball, Germ!" Oni yelled to the zip-wire assailant. "Go-ball! Go-ball!"

Somehow emerging successful from her wrestle with Germ, Kitty lit up the night with a ten-foot flare. "I am *woman!*" she bellowed. "And I am *Phoenix!*" Screaming murderously, Kitty poured molten arcs of pressurised liquid willy-nilly. In the intense light Myfanwy registered Germ's red hair and red-lipsticked rictus of fear and elation. Germ scuttled retreat to Myfanwy's right, running over the road into some daffodils.

Kitty was clearly out of control. Flame on max, she charged shrieking towards Myfanwy, and Myfanwy felt the intolerable heat of the hellmouth's yawn.

Then the fuel ran dry.

Intense pulses of blue harrowed the nightscape. A geodesic rope system was in flames, searing Myfanwy's iris with afterimages of its network. The first Borders and Lothian fire truck was nosing around the corner of the intersection.

"Babes," muttered Simi. "Maybe it's time we made a move. Yuri, you get back to HQ. Mnemosyne, have you met Meletē yet?"

Among the mingled sirens, jeers, moans and cat-calls, a consensus was emerging that the skirmish had ended in a draw.

*

Meletē was a stocky, muscular man, Sri Lankan-looking, in his early to mid forties. He had his hair in a buzz-cut with a prominent widow's peak, and his sideburns shaved very narrow then neatly tapered along his jaw. He spoke with a Brummie twang, thicker than Blake's. He wore a white muscle vest, faded blue jeans and Nike trainers.

The navy chunky-knit hoodie with tartan interiors which Meletē had until recently also worn was now on Kitty, zipped up and with the hood up. The hoodie came just low enough to cover Kitty's v. minimalist "topiary," about which Myfanwy felt she would soon need to have a Conversation.

"Chancelhouse respects no boundary," Kitty flirted, as Meletē swiped his Chancelhouse keycard and punched in a code. "We're right up there with fun, or sex, or fashion. We respect no boundary."

Together Meletē, Myfanwy, Kitty and Simi entered the houses on the west side of the street.

The decor inside was contemporary — like cold, classy offices. Some doors were crested with devices Myfanwy recognised, but these were done as spray-paint stencilled icons, rather than ebony carvings or counter-embossed gilts over the street. East houses were about the past. West houses were about the future.

They stopped at a second door requiring keycard and PIN. "The Cache, my loves," Simi said.

"What's the big Cache?" said Myfanwy, and giggled.

Simi bit her lip. "You sure about this, Melee babes?"

"On my head," Meletē said. "Blake won't like it, but I can't trust him on security anymore. Pure luck I was back tonight. If I *hadn't* been —" He gave a gruff laugh checked his wristwatch. "Come on, he'll be back on the grid any minute. Let's tool up."

Had it just been pure luck? Nervousness crept into Myfanwy's excitement. The last thing she wanted was to get swept up into some sort of Chancel leadership dispute.

The doors opened. Bluish light and a hum swept into the long room. Swords, rifles, and light machine guns adorned both long walls in chevrons and crosses. Meletē entered and they trooped after, exhilarated. Running along one wall was a low broad counter, on which long-barrelled rifles posed on tripods and bipods. Cartridges, and other miscellaneous military paraphernalia, were tucked overflowingly into cubby holes under the counter.

At the far end of the Cache were four armoured green crates. A ruggedized Sony tablet sat atop one. Meletē approached it purposefully.

"Bare shanks, bare shooters," Kitty summarised. "Still no lycra."

"Why this medieval stuff?" Myfanwy asked Simi, examining a sword. "Because of honour?"

"A typical insertion op involves only civilians," Simi explained. "Blades are usually sufficient, babes. Shooters can get . . . out of hand, innit? Like tonight."

"What's an insertion op?" said Kitty.

"Swordsman to intimidate and contain the subject," Meletē amplified. "Caster to insert the asset into the subject. A taker to clear all trace of the insertion and steal away unnoticed."

"That's what we do?" said Myfanwy, giddy.

"What we *do*," said Simi darkly, "is inspire the minds of men."

Meletē smiled grimly. "If you ever find yourself feeling *déjà vu*, standing in the snow, staring at a second set of footprints, with a little scratch under your chin . . . chances are *you've* just had a visit from Chancel."

Myfanwy sort of liked Meletē. She felt a few of his curt grunts and battlecries would yield more info than a lifetime of baffled jogging beside the waffling Haduken Blake.

"Or a visit from Veil," Simi jumped in, sounding stressed. "If you've been jostled in the street. If you're in your yard, staring at a wall. 'Now why did I come in here for? I forget!' Or a warm cushion. A cracked window. A smoking ashtray. It's enough to make you paranoid, babes."

"But why?" Myfanwy asked. "Why play people like that?"

"Wisely though," said Simi. "We play 'em *wisely*."

"To protect our kind," Meletē said, activating the tablet.

Simi nodded. "We can't allow Chancelhouse's existence to be known. Them new pals you made in the park today? We'll reward their bravery with a brainwash." She shared a glance with Meletē. "Assuming we can round them up."

"The more basic reason for the cutlery," Meletē added, "is because firearms are illegal on civvy street. Elder muses are registered as special constables, scattered across various Deadly Force police forces. Technically, Simi's Civil Nuclear Constabulary, I'm Royal Protection Unit."

"That is one saved King," said Kitty. "So why *this* puppy tonight?" she asked, jiggling the flamethrower like a grizzly infant.

"And you can pop it down now, babes," said Simi.

"*Aww.*"

"Least lethal thing I could grab at short notice," Meletē explained. "Mini-flamethrower — South African make. No external fuel tank, lucky for your mate Mnemosyne, as it turns out."

Meletē made some changes on the tablet and powered it down again. Someone was speaking behind a wall. Chinese? No — Myfanwy strained to locate it but the voice stopped abruptly.

She shivered.

She looked down on an unzipped camo carrybag marked "M72 LAW." Did the empty bag mean the bazooka, or whatever it was, was out in the field?

"Whereas a *real* man," said Myfanwy solemnly, "cannot lay his hands on anything less than a nuclear warhead without at least one full week's notice."

Myfanwy pulled on a sash of spare cartridges. She gave them a twirl. She wondered if there was a small fine if you were late returning your M72 LAW. That would be a good system.

"I never even *realised* those were bears on those pyjamas!" said Kitty.

"Sloths," said Myfanwy. "Supposedly."

"Oi. Quit screwing around," said Meletē. "You. Nessus." He thrust his jaw at Kitty. "Here." He pointed to his feet.

She drew near.

"I'm a skiller, Nessus. You know what that is?"

"A muse class," said Kitty nervously. "Which is perfectly fine. I don't have a problem with it."

"Skillers are similar to you casters. But we specialise in procedural memory. Memory *how to* such-and-such, not memory *that* such-and-such. There's something you need to take on board, Nessus. Take down your hood. Good. Now stay very still."

Kitty flinched as Meletē raised his hand.

Myfanwy wasn't sure, but for a moment she thought she caught a flicker of empty light pass over them. As if they'd both been teleported to exactly the spot they'd started from, or something.

Meletē gently drew his hand back from Kitty's cheek. "You had an eyelash. Make a wish," he instructed.

Kitty smiled and blew for a long time on Meletē's fingertips. Myfanwy didn't see any lash or anything fly up.

"Did you wish you could kick ass?" said Meletē. "Because you can now kick ass, Nessus."

"If I *tell* you my wish," said Kitty, "then *duh*."

Meletē nodded to a rack where gleaming swords clustered thickly. "Take one of the lighter rapiers down off the wall. I've skilled you in swordplay. Be careful not to overdo it. You have the muscle memories, without the muscles."

Kitty did as she was told. The blade glowed with a deep, almost bluish sheen. She paced back and began whipping it about her body in swift, guarded arabesques.

"Oh, yes," she murmured. "Oh, *yes!*"

"It's only a loan, Nessus. Till such time as Operation Terpsichore is terminated and I'm back in town to handle security. In the meanwhile, you are my unofficial army in Chancel HQ."

Suddenly Myfanwy was wondering if *she* had any lashes left *at all* after her cozy intro to the mini-flamethrower.

"Don't you *dare*," Meletē added, "get killed while my swordplay is in you. Or I'll dig you up and kill you again."

The blade flew so fast, Kitty seemed cocooned in an aria of iridescent steel. The room even *smelled* of metal.

"This Vertical guy," Myfanwy reasoned. "He's absorbed some serious acrobatics, hasn't he? Endurance stuff too. I bit him, he didn't flinch."

Meletē looked at Myfanwy and nodded curtly. "Vertical. FKA Thalia, civvy name Abbas Macleod. One of the first nine. My hunch is somewhere in Veil HQ there's a family of flying foxes with some very confused recollections of Vert's childhood holidays in Bognor. All them big bullies who bog-washed and wedgied him and made him the muse he is today."

"Do you mean that? Vertical has absorbed animal aptitudes?"

"Technically possible," Simi admitted glumly. "It's an exciting time to be a Veil muse too."

"But *how?*"

"A spellsong," said Simi. "Different muse classes working together."

"When you arrange muses like modules in a computer program," said Meletē, "the combinatorial possibilities are tremendous. Veil have skillers, they have doolittle muses, they have mirrors aplenty, they have patterners. Why not hack beast agility?"

"Teamwork, my loves," said Simi. "It's the most important thing in the world."

"Yeah," said Kitty. "And always believe in yourself, babes?"

"And," added Myfanwy, "like, always follow through?"

"Oi," protested Simi.

"Babes!" cried Kitty. "Never let someone who gave up on their dreams, like, talk you out of yours!"

"Your tutor is correct," said Meletē. "Tell your tutor *damn straight.*"

"*Damn straight,*" barked Kitty.

"Tonight was an example," Meletē elaborated, "of Veil totally outstripping us in terms of teamwork. Nessus, why did you lose control of the mini-flamethrower?"

"Didn't lose control, Meals on Wheels. The Germ chiquita had grabbed me, so I used intimidation tactics on the enemy, sir! I attacked Myffy because I knew the fuel would run out."

Meletē shook his head. "Uh-uh. Wrong. Confabulation, Nessus."

"Mutually Assured Destruction, sir?"

"Ness, here's the truth. Germ influenced you. Our intel *did* suggest Germ was still mirror class. But she cast something special tonight." He and Simi shared a glance. "Now Veil have perfected Go-Ball, I'd say that counts as new class — mesmer."

"Go-Ball, babes," Simi explained gloomily, "was something in dev at the time of the Veil split. Germ's ex-Chancel too, you see. *We've* made zilch progress since. The idea was to harvest and prepare, uh, shavings of various affective states. Little scraps of anger, say, or of fear. Then these primitives would be lathed by cutters and cloisters working together and woven together into a sort of . . . *motives sphere*, babes. Germ cast it into Kitty. A shifting, complex, contextually-robust cue to behave in a specific way —"

"What?" said Myfanwy.

"Temporary mind control," Meletē summarised. "Enchantment."

Kitty raised her eyebrows and looked to Myfanwy.

"Um, to be honest," said Myfanwy, "it doesn't take that much, with Kitty?"

"Yeah," Kitty readily agreed. "That wasn't *just* the Go-Ball talking, you know what I mean?"

Meletē smiled wearily. "Well, sheath your blade, Nessus. Go easy on Aoide in the morning — I'm afraid I'm going to be keeping her up late tonight. Mnemosyne, over the next week, *you* stay near Nessus, you hear? If there's a breach, buddy up on patrol. We can't have a repeat of tonight. Nessus, when the time is ripe, you, me and Ouzo will configure a spellsong to repatriate my swordplay."

"Fight you for it," Kitty teased.

"Goodnight troops," Meletē said. "I won't bother walking you back. Trust me, you'll be fine."

"Night Simi," said Myfanwy. "Goodnight Meletē, it was nice to meet you."

"What about all the guns?" said Kitty. "Or is that maybe greedy."

"I've given you swordplay," said Meletē. "Where *I'm* going, I may need gunplay."

*

Back in their room, Myfanwy marveled sleepily at the alacrity of Kitty's dancing sword-point. "'*Where I'm going, I may need gunplay*,'" Kitty laughed. "'*To shoot people*.' God. The *whole* time I was in the Cache I was imagining Wu Tang hippity-hop in my head. Were you?"

"Mmph. Why you be in towel, Kit?"

Early birds sang. Kitty saluted the Clarins-heaped sink and whirled her blue steel and her Blue Steel. "If we ever go back in there," she said, "I'm *so* bringing my speakers!"

"Kitty, what the flip just *happened*? Why weren't you in your bed? Why towel?"

"Oh, safe fam. Isn't it obv? I went *swimming*. I couldn't sleep, *you* were doing your Myfanwy vs. Myfanwy snoozy Sumo routine. So I just figured I'd swim. Then after the Murderer Alarm went, I kinda knew you'd freak out like a moron and run outside, so I ran outside too — I didn't think I'd end up, like, half a mile away —"

"I get it, story-topper. *I* courageously run out in my jammies, *you* courageously run out in your cozzie, see me disappearing round the corner. I can't believe you even packed a cozzie to come to Scotland."

"What did *you* pack?"

"History Revulsion."

"Uh, Venus to Myfanwy? I *didn't* pack a cozzie? That's why I was skinny-dipping at like two in the morning? I ran out in my *coochie*."

"Ho."

"Master swords-ho, to *you*. You'll thank me when Veil walk through that door. I wonder what they want?"

"Oh yeah," remembered Myfanwy. "Earlier tonight. Yuri wasn't in, but I saw Bee. *She* intimated the Veil incursions could be live drops with the mole! You know, to brief and debrief?"

"You been kicking it with Bee?"

Myfanwy picked up Bee's cartoon offering uncertainly. Without quite knowing why, she formed a small, indignant lie. "Yes. I just bumped into her in the stairwell. You know. Bumbling. She gave us this."

"Oh, nang," said Kitty vaguely. "Is that meant to be you and me?"

"Horses." Myfanwy shook her head, stupefied.

"Why would Veil break in just to chat? Why not meet the mole somewhere, or use a dead letter box?"

"Bee believes Veil retrieve the intelligence from the mole while the mole is sleeping. That way, whoever they are, they don't form lots of incriminating memories of *being* the mole. Less risk of letting something slip to their casting partner, right? But God. It was only Bee."

"Fam, I doubt there even *is* a mole. Veil just have a death wish! Did you get a load of Meletē's guns?"

"A real Cache."

"OMG, you know those Daddy Dolls American kids get made when their real dads are fighting in wars? He's like one of those!"

"Sugar. Just glad he's on our side. That was a flirty-type flip he did you, Kit."

"'*I'm a-keep Aoide up to the break of dawn. Freak me!*' Oh come on, he's *cute!* You're still Paddy-obsessed, is your problem. That's the *old* world, Myfanwy! Get yourself a *muse* man! Miceginator! *Muse*-ceginator!"

It all went over Myfanwy's head. She yawned hugely. "Can't believe you're still so hyper. It's four AM. Hey," Myfanwy added, as Kitty's swordplay exercises drew closer. "Did you *really* go to see Triffid, Kitty? Or did you just say tha— *ehr maw Gahd!* Don't *point* that thing at me!"

"I can't really remember when you're talking about," said Kitty, staring down her path of steel. "I'm a *God of War!*"

Myfanwy slipped into bed. It felt amazing. "The nap is mightier than the sword, hon."

"We'll be up in three point five zero hours. Wanna just play through?"

"Blade maiden, if you *must* whirl your deadly blade so wildly," said Myfanwy — as she reached for the neck of the lamp — "do it in the dark."

*

But the girls saw no more of Meletē, and precious little of Blake.

Simi, on the other hand, was all up in their grill, showing no mercy, drilling them hard.

Control Your Muse Talent, Step One: *visualise* your talent as a kind of command centre. Every new muse needed to invent a virtual space, an intimate yet alien topology, known as their Dwelling. A newbuild Dwelling, the girls soon discovered, overflowed with intricate, inscrutable objects, associated with equally inscrutable sets of possible statuses.

"We're just making up images," Myfanwy complained quietly.

"So was Michelangelo," remarked Kitty.

"So was *Hitler*," Myfanwy pouted.

Their Dwellings might look like anything. Although Myfanwy and Kitty memorised the same ontology and used the same names — Dove, Hoard, Sealant, Radix, Wake, etc. — each developed her own precise imagery and décor.

For instance, when Kitty described her Dove, it was an actual gleaming bird-faced homunculus, versus Myfanwy's Dove, which was more of a simple dais with just a hint of wings.

Kitty was developing a Dwelling filled with clouds of deep, inward light, a Dwelling whose surfaces — mostly done in fluted marbles, mined out of many pale unvisited heavenly bodies — flickered with delicate, twisting shadows, shimmered with glints, twinkles and flashing reflections. Kitty's thriving diaphanous auras, secondary to her Dwelling's solidity, hoovered up the promise of pending functionality.

Whereas any light and darkness Myfanwy introduced into *her* Dwelling —a somewhat frail and shabby grotto, loosely based on the Glass Room at home — became false baubles and bad special effects. Shadows got stranded embarrassingly far from their sources. Amber glows, incorrectly arrayed as if by drunkard calculation, darkened what drew near them. Soon Myfanwy, desparate to keep up with Kitty, had to try a different tactic. She laid down and strung up alternative forms of translucence and iridescence — frumpy, frowzy things resembling cloth, ribbons, and lace — to do artificially, and with awful fuss, the things Kitty did with ease using native lines of glamour and the darkling nets they cast.

The days flew by. Myfanwy's Dwelling seemed to get more and more clogged and crowded. Each item Kitty introduced into *her* Dwelling somehow *increased* her inward scope and liberty.

"Aoide," said Kitty crossly. "These bags under my eyes are *not* Gucci. You don't seem to appreciate that I am undertaking a *fully rounded* education! In less than a month I have exams in Econ, English, History and German. All very venerable and advanced fields, you will appreciate!"

"Babes. Are you a muse, or a mouse?"

"Technically," frowned Kitty, "I'm a kitty . . ."

Myfanwy felt frayed, full of buzzes. The only times she could really keep up with Kitty was when they emerged from their Dwellings to do physical training. There seemed to be a terrible lot of that — endurance, agility, stick waving, ball control (which Simi insisted was a *highly transferrable skill*) — but it scarcely made up for being Dunce Muse the rest of the time.

By the end of the first week, Kitty was effortlessly executing graceful Multiple Simultaneous Apophantic Uncastles both sides of her Grand Turn — scored by Simi's rapturous chortles — whereas Myfanwy was still stuck on the Homo Faber Forward Rolls, supposedly the move which would reveal the contour of her Grand Turn in the first place.

"Can't I just use Hogarth's line of beauty?" Myfanwy fumed, after her whole Dwelling crumbled in shards for the umpteenth time in ten minutes. "I mean the Turn's basically a stretchy S, right?"

Kitty, meanwhile, was splayed on her balance ball, ignoring Simi's advice to take it easy, her eyelids flickering with bliss, as she no doubt embroidered her Dwelling with trillions more tiny pearlescent demonic countenances with dancing eyes and tongues.

Kitty had privately confessed to Myfanwy that, *as well* as the supposedly soon-to-be functional patterns which Simi had so relentlessly imposed, she was *also* unfurling day-by-day thousands of twirling *extra* minor seams — just for the sheer delight of it, swirling her structures' surfaces with an incidental celestial sub-structure of sorcerous marbles and white ink-like crystals, orreries of delicate allusions to faces, all sprawling impeccably and trivially into every unused interstice, all virtuoso, unnecessary, impertinent and perhaps permanent.

She couldn't help it, she'd giggled to Myfanwy. She was *obsessed.*

"Mnemosyne," Simi soothed, with quiet merriment. "The stretchy S that's *right for you*, love. The stretchy S you know you can *rely* on."

"Yeesh. How can you be so patient with me, Aoide?"

"Stop vexing," Simi reassured her. "You're doing fine. What matters is that the relationships feel concrete, not the details of their concretisation. Getting too attached to visual can even become a disadvantage at a more advanced level."

Simi glanced over at Kitty on the balance ball.

Kitty emitted a low gurgle.

Myfanwy sighed. "Sorry, Coax. Gotcha, Coax. On the level and solid as concrete, Coax. The stretchy S that's *right for me.*"

Only no relationship *did* feel concrete to Myfanwy.

She doubted she'd ever reach the "more advanced level" Simi spoke of.

She was unsure of the appearance of her most basic arrangements. Her Dwelling mutated every morning, its decor shifting and refusing to settle, as though rival factions of helpful elves haunted it with their myriad trivial edit wars. Everything trembled, felt frail. No stretchy S shapes seemed more safe than any other. Myfanwy's Dove and Altar, the most solid pieces of her Dwelling, looked v. v. Naughties Ikea.

"Take five," said Simi. "Then we'll take it from the top."

*

A few technical terms Simi taught them hinted tantalisingly at purposes. But by-and-large the terminology felt deliberately enigmatic, and all learning was rote, simply establishing and transforming mental structures — no higher theory, and no attempt to flip any memory of their own.

There were a few quirky perks. Myfanwy eventually learned how to think a thought so that even *one second later* she would have forgotten it, try as she might to get it back. Like keeping secrets from yourself. Like writing a sentence without quite putting the nib all the way to the paper.

After a lot of bother, learned how to think *two sentences at once*, either side of her Altar, one speech and one song, and how to castle them like in Chess.

She learned what it would be like to have synaesthesia.

Kitty, of course, could switch synaesthesiac experience on and off at will. But never mind.

She learned about that terrible thought she used to have, after Mum died. *Your love kills people.* She learned what made it different from other thoughts.

She learned the *real* difference between ideas and dreams.

Or perhaps she did — she couldn't have explained it to anyone who didn't already know, except to advise they develop a Dwelling for themselves. But she felt she knew.

Myfanwy tried to focus on these little triumphs, but her heart felt heavy. As if everything else weren't already enough, Simi expected them to spend their "spare" time writing their autobiographies. These memoirs, suitably segmented and tagged with metadata, would one day help them keep on top of their lives, once they started casting memories willy-nilly.

Kitty's accounts were elaborately embellished and a wee bit Upanishad-ish.

"One day," said Myfanwy, "you may actually believe it happened like that."

"So what?" said Kitty languidly. "It's *better* that way! Besides," she added more softly. "You've only seen the ones I've shown you."

Not strictly true, Myfanwy thought.

In the early hours of Thursday morning, the girls floated on their backs in the pool in the Frigidarium, head-to-head with their hair spread out and mixing. The ceiling crawled with the snakeskin light reflected off the water's surface.

"One thing's for sure," Myfanwy sighed. "Remember when Blake talked about our dossiers? How one was pure muse, and the other only a maybe?"

"And?" said Kitty.

"I guess now we know which was which."

"Oh, *poor* you," Kitty said sardonically. Her reserves of patience were not so ample as Simi's.

Spread across the ceiling of Cellar Level Two, ghosts of pool water flamed. A small part of Myfanwy *wanted* to fail. The thought of switching memories with Kitty filled her with dread. What if she learned something really personal or weird? Like how Dad still tucked her in, a seventeen year old woman, tucked her in every night and stroked her hair, perfunctorily but tenderly, or else she couldn't sleep?

How sometimes, when it was a really bad night, she even still crept into his bed and wrapped herself shivering in his arms?

She'd just have to say they were memories from a long time ago, altered in the casting. Apparently that could happen. Anyway, didn't everyone have their own weird stuff that other people could never really understand? That was the *whole point* of Ludwig Wittgenstein.

There was something else though. If she became a caster, what excuse was there to hold onto Jasper Robin's memories?

Lanterns on the meadows . . .

Flurries of flakes across and along long sinuous lines, crossing and twisting . . . sinews of darkness . . . Waverley's reaching arms, many millions of miles in length, flowing over each other's armoured joints . . .

Behind her, a presence. Hands on her hips. Cold, cold lips brushing her neck . . . she smiled . . . turned . . .

There was some soft splashing. Her skull gently bumped with Kitty's.

"I have the talent," said Myfanwy. "I just dunno if I have what it takes to develop it."

Getting chilly. Time to get out.

"It's all basically daydreaming and doodling," Kitty sniffed. "You've done it in every single class since Year One and now it has its own class. God, you should be amazing at it."

Myfanwy heard a deep gasp of breath, then a splash as Kitty went under. She twisted round.

"But I'm not," she told bubbles of BFF breath. "I'm just *not.*"

She inhaled and immersed herself.

Submerged, the girls stared at each other.

*

Concrete . . .

"Myfanwy," Kitty purred. "Are you awake?"

"Mmph?"

"Yes, Myfanwy. *Somebody* is having *sex*. Listen."

"Oh my God."

They listened to the sighs and creaks. Every now and then she made out a word. "Eww," Myfanwy laughed. "Gross!"

"Night then, Myfanwy," said Kitty.

From Kitty's tone, she felt like she'd said the wrong thing. It didn't feel fair.

In the dream she'd just left, she'd been wandering in a house rather like this one. Finding a suit of armour, she'd lifted the visor, to be met by the bludgeoned gaze of a crude concrete statue.

"Night, Kitty," she said.

If she tried to tell her how she felt, about the darkness she felt herself edging towards, she knew how Kitty would take it. She'd make it *all* about the two of them. She'd make it worse.

Every bit of her body ached.

She buried her head under the pillow.

All the vibrant blue above and around. Every bit of her body ached. Around and down, masses of gorse flowering yellow, either side of the rocky red downhill path. Forest line below them . . . Genevieve Quaker, the Tudor muse in front . . . crows, wood pigeons and doves . . .

the hills . . .

and far below them . . . the Settlement . . .

Breakfast the next morning was a quiet affair. Kitty had headphones in and wasn't making eye contact.

Slowly Myfanwy became aware of a presence at her shoulder. Bee had come bearing a new cartoon.

"For you, Mnemosyne," said Bee. "I hate this one too. Hate, hate."

Myfanwy felt plum tuckered out. "Cheers, Bee. More horses, I see?"

"Yes. However, they are not horses. You have failed closely to observe the latest addition to my unstable."

"Not horses? Oh, unicorns!"

"A common error. Mnemosyne they're called *borses*. They're crosses between horses and bees. This one's a *bumble borse*." Bee pointed. "She can gore you as much as she likes. Gore, gore, gore, gore, gore, for instance. This one however is a *honey borse*." Bee pointed.

Myfanwy smiled politely. She was feeling slightly threatened and intruded upon by this latest gift, coming so swift on the hooves of the last. Frankly, she was worried that she was making one of those deranged, Follow-You-Around-Cuz-I'm-Damaged kind of friends.

"How kind," she murmured, with Contessa-esque grace.

"When the honey borse stabs you," Bee instructed, "sadly, she leaves her head behind buried in your chest. Needless to say, with her head ripped off, the honey borse will soon perish. Such a kamikaze attack is for the greater good of the collective, which, as you will have guessed, is known as the *uniswarm*."

Myfanwy smiled grudgingly and sighed. "You *shouldn't have*, Bee!"

She knew she sometimes radiated an aura of competence, assurance and calm, and she just didn't want to give Bee the wrong idea. Okay, Bee could be her little buddy. But Myfanwy needed to warn her, somehow, that the competence was partly a fragile act, that the assurance and calm were a kind of overcompensation. Myfanwy had her own deep damage, pieced together for now, but frail, capable of fragmenting at any moment. Especially these days, traumatised by Mara's murder, terrified by Jasper's vendetta, gripped by the irresistible pull of his Citadel and his Settlement — perhaps the gravity that kept tearing her Dwelling apart — cast deep inside her, tantalised by Yuri's mole paranoia, freaked out by Veil's incursions, homesick and Dadsick, petrified by St Jerome's secular exams looming, plus on top of all that, brutalised by Simi's punishing training schedule, mind and body, day after day, and *still* being in the bottom set here at Chancelhouse, *still* holding Kitty back, no matter how hard she tried, *still* making Kitty angry with her, making Kitty *hate* her . . . God!

Stress!

Did Bee *really* want to know her?

Ten minutes later, as Myfanwy and Bee stuck their spoons in the dishwasher basket, like a pair of swashbucklers — ooh, or like *muse*-keteers! — a pleasant doubt crept into Myfanwy's heart. She laughed quietly at herself.

Maybe she *wasn't* as frail as all that any more. Maybe she wasn't as prone to the fits of temper, to the days and nights of fretful paralysis. Maybe she just liked to *tell* herself she was, so she never needed to be brave or selfless. And maybe Kitty treated her with a combo of irritation and kid gloves out of basic BFF habit, not because Myfanwy really called for it anymore . . .

"Thanks again, Bee. I know just the place for it."

Whevs.

Either way, maybe she could use every friend she could get.

*

Presently Blake popped by the Myometrium.

"Aoide!" he cried. "Is that you? Feels like years!"

"Has to be Paris, mid-Nineties," Simi teased. "Wouldn't have known you, but it's the same suit."

Blake flourished a little tupperware. "I've brought you fresh baking. Simnel cakes! Am I forgiven?"

"Always," said Simi, with a twinkle in her eye. "And don't call me Simi Cakes."

"That settles it Myfanwy," Kitty whispered. "They *are* doing it."

The girls were wobbling side-by-side on two gigantic tangerine balance balls. Simi always called them "stress balls," making Myfanwy think more on the topic of giants.

Myfanwy pushed sweaty hair from her eyes. "Hi Blake." She noticed faint floury fingerprints all over his shirt.

"No *thank you*, sir," Kitty said brightly. "Starvation is the sixth food group."

Myfanwy gazed at Kitty in surprise. There had been a real edge to her voice. Kitty was slicked with sweat — once more, it was a very Phys Ed type morning so far — and she wore a sharp, brittle little smile.

Myfanwy breathed in the sharp scent of their own bodies.

Something was up, but Simi and Blake were oblivious. Simi selected a Simnel cake and bit into it. "Seuss is my assigned Partner under the Rule," she said, through munches, "an' yet I never even see him! S'posed to be *teaching* you chaps to cast . . . 'm rusty m'self!"

Kitty had been surreptitiously bobbing towards Blake on her tangerine ball. Now she pounced, tangling her arms round the little Executive Director's neck.

"Time," she said, "for a little chat?"

*

Blake eyes widened. "Ah, and how are our two young blossoms?" he said. "*Pseudo-narcissus hostile hostile*, if I'm not mistaken? Fine specimens of womanhood! Sure you won't try a Simnel — *ack!*"

Kitty bounced deep into her tangerine balance ball, a kind of rebellious Praxis Curtsey, asphyxiating Blake with her ambiguously-affectionate grasp.

"A *quasi-Nessus hostile hostile*?" she interrogated sweetly. "And what kind of blossom is *that*, sir?"

Blake patted Kitty's forearm awkwardly and coughed. "A kind of daffodilly thing, I think. I am not as florally-minded as I should be. And speaking of stems, the old trachea could do with a bit of —"

"Well that's fine, sir," said Kitty. She shook him rather hard. Her balance ball wobbled. "Fine, fine, fine."

"Ah . . . gently, my dear," chuckled Blake weakly. "I'm not as firmly rooted as you are! The crystalline ravages of gout are far advanced in the left knee in particular —"

"I think we can tolerate a certain low level of sexism in the older generation," said Kitty, "provided it's chivalric, and you are actually literally dying off before our very eyes. What do you reckon, Myffy?"

"Provided it helps them die off faster," said Myfanwy quietly. "All for it."

"*Finey finey finey!*" Kitty shook Blake rather wildly indeed, her ball now bucking beneath her.

Simi cocked her head. Myfanwy, very interested to see where this was going, did a deep bounce into her own ball.

Blake, looking rather — well, looking rather choked up and shaken — firmly pried away Kitty's arms. "Well, Nessus, your solicitousness is terribly affecting of course, however —"

"Haduken!" Kitty thundered.

She leapt from her spherical steed with as much extra springiness at it would spare her, landed lightly on her feet and glowered down at Blake. He now wore the exactly expression chosen by the bellhop Rudolph in *The Lady Vanishes* as he helps the glam Matilda Henderson hop over the chicken and magnum of champagne.

Whereas Kitty wore her War God face.

"My dear Nessus," Blake began weakly, wiping the corners of his eyes.

"Just be quiet, sir. Three words for you: WTF. I may be but a noob muse, but are you aware but I carry in me the swordplay of the elder Meletē?"

"I had heard, yes," Blake babbled. "Very grateful indeed. Temp arrangements."

"*I* pack security for this yard, not you —"

"Special circumstances — yes —"

"I think *that* deserves some respect —"

"Contingencies. Not my decision. Oh dear."

"And *let me tell you*, Haduken, I — by which I mean me, and fragments of Meletē — feel *ill-used* in all of this. *And do you know why?*"

"Babes," Simi reasoned soothingly, stepping forward with a rather smug smile.

"Because of *that venomous woman*!" Kitty snarled, jabbing a finger in Simi's face without looking at her. Simi froze.

"Not long ago," Kitty continued. "I ask her very nicely, 'Simi, may I do my first flip now? Just to prove that it's possible, that I'm not wasting my time here, while my friends miss me and my school studies suffer.' Okay, I got a demo, but you know what else I got? Just the most totally *conceited*, self-centred *torrent* of irrelevant line managerial information! 'I am Aoide the elder, *wooooo*, *WOOOOOO,* I answer to no one, *blah blah blah*. Do what I say or I'll strop.' Then we're back to work, *twice as hard*, poor wee Myfanwy made to suffer also for my supposed impertinence! I just don't understand these absurd hours. We're not merchant bankers, we're just muses! You're asking us to neglect our real education, and *Myfanwy*," she finished, in a very deep voice, whilst gathering herself to her full, righteous height, "is an *orphan*."

"There is Dad," Myfanwy pointed out quietly.

"You can't count Pete," Kitty snapped as an aside. Then she glanced quickly at Myfanwy. "And I'm not being mean, hon. *I* wouldn't count *Daddy* either."

"It's fine, dude," said Myfanwy. "Sorry for the inconvenience. Tight outburst."

"I'm not through! I am *exhausted*, Haduken! I am exhausted, and I don't even know why I'm doing it. Literally, I feel like I'm being fast-tracked in the Hitler Youth. *Why* are you so anxious to take over every aspect of our lives? What, pray tell, is the big crisis that can't wait a few weeks?"

It was fading now, but Myfanwy realised what had been so frightening about Kitty's movements over the last few minutes. Her Wiles were weaponised. Kitty's familiar, characteristic friskiness, her whole ensemble of trifling, teasing, playful flamboyance — the gestural patterns which Myfanwy had lived among, and felt evolve from girlhood to womanhood — was now melded with an exotic, brilliant violence . . . *Meletē's* violence . . . and the two worked without disharmony, slipping together in perfect synthesis, even synergy.

Blake waddled despondently up and down the gym. "Oh, Nessus," he cried, "the truth is, I just don't know! Everything is so dark and clouded! I see . . . splinters on the horizon . . . something is coming . . . that I feel to be significant. Only . . . I can't piece the fragments together. Mists and mazes! What if a few weeks is too late?"

"It will be too late for our secular education," said Kitty, calmer now, but still righteous. "That's for sure. My muse friend, Myfanwy, *has worked very hard studying for her A-Levels. She has her heart set on university or maybe art college*! How *dare* you leave us, at this crucial point in our studies, in the so-called care of this Insane Coachy Person?"

The Insane Coachy Person gave a throaty chuckle.

"If you so dislike Aoide's style," Blake said with a cross frown, "you're free to seek your muse tuition elsewhere. Fancy a flexi-time Masters in Musing from Birkbeck University, maybe?"

"My sides *ache*, Haduken. But there's always Veil! I wonder how *they* treat their noobs? Do they get told to memorise things, but never why those things matter? Fam, it's frankly Neolithic pedagogy. You'll end up with shamans, *gaga gaga gaga, goop goop goop*. I have half a mind not even to argue, just to head to London right now."

"Defo not art school anymore BTW," murmured Myfanwy.

"You have a *beautiful talent*!" Kitty wailed. "Besides, when it's not bloody Dwelling, Grand Turn, Radix, Sealant, Dove, it's 'run there!' 'kick this!' 'catch that!' 'shinny up that!' 'hit the ball into your head!' I mean, *really*?"

Blake stopped pacing and looked up sharply. "Wait a minute. *What* did you just say?"

*

Blake eyed up Simi slyly. Full of thought, he stroked his silver ponytail.

Simi was, in fact, looking a bit abashed.

"I mean, *really?*" Kitty flounced. "It's against nature!"

Blake gave an exasperated sigh, and gazed at the four figures in the mirror, as if he might have better luck talking to them.

Mirror muses, thought Myfanwy.

Eventually, he waddled over to Simi and gently took hold of the crook of her arm. Myfanwy, despite herself, smiled at the height difference.

"Technically," said Blake airily, "the early curriculum is entirely up to Aoide, wearing her Master Mystagogue hat." He looked up vaguely, as if expecting to see such a hat. "However, from the sounds, Aoide has rather significantly upped the Phys Ed constituent compared with previous years. *Yes*, Aoide?"

Staring fixedly at nothing, Simi groped around for Blake's tupperware and popped a second Simnel.

"From a baseline," Blake added, "of approximately zero? Yes, Aoide?"

"Wasn't right of you to dump both on me," she muttered, chewing ferociously. "With such little time left."

"*Zero?*" Kitty shook her head, exasperated. Myfanwy took it as her cue to roll the balance ball so it knocked against Kitty legs, and was satisfied when she settled back down on it.

"Well, yes," muttered Blake. "Meletē handles that side of things, *obviously*. Once you've founded your Dwellings and learnt to control your talents. Aoide, perhaps it's time to explain?"

Simi was on her third and fourth Simnel cakes simultaneously. She chewed and swallowed. "Babes," she said, addressing Kitty. "I want to make something clear. Chancelhouse ain't some kind of public school for witches — full of cute analogies and audited by Owlsted, yeah? What you get here is the masterclass, babes. You get the element of education that can't be comprehended in curricula, the part that's irreducible to policy. So put up with the demanding nature and other eccentricities of your beloved tutor, innit? In general, my classroom is not the place for tantrums, Nessus."

"However!" said Blake.

"However," Simi added reluctantly. "Babes, I may have allowed a healthy competitive spirit cloud my judgement just a bit, and for that I apologise. I really do. I really do."

"The all-ball tournament," gasped Kitty. "Oh my God. You've had us on two training programmes at once! Guys, there is *no way* we want to participate in that. It's not why we're here. And that's *final*, okay?"

Simi nodded sheepishly. "I don't blame you, Nessus. We could focus more on core Dwelling work going forward, and backburner the old . . . all the sports stuff."

"That's not enough," said Myfanwy quietly. "What about our lives back at home? What about —"

"*And* back at St Jerome's!" said Kitty. "You *say* it's all taken care of. Frankly, I question your competence! I can't trust you to handle the —" She frowned. "Hold on. Unless that's just the Meletē talking."

Blake looked sorrowful. "Cover stories were delivered to your Head of Teacher and Head of Year, as I've trumpeted before. Even a little insertion op re the latter, for a deeper ambience of veracity. You've both been good at creating a consistent social media trail. So unless you want us to arrange a visitation by St Jerome himself, what more can be done?"

"But did it *work?*" demanded Kitty. "Looly *et al.* are sure to assume I'm receiving contra-trending labioplasty, whereof I often spake, so it's more the faculty I'm worried about."

"Oh, it's *working*, Nessus. St Jerome won't expect you back in his niche till your first exam — History, I believe. Does that meet with your approval, my dear? This talk of running away to London breaks my heart! Mnemosyne, can't *you* talk to her?"

"There's more," Kitty pointed out. "Because we need time to *study* for those exams."

"Absolutely," said Blake. "Whatever you need. Whatever you say! What *do* you say then, Nessus? I mean in the sense of, 'Whaddayasay?' Give Chancelhouse a chance, eh? I can see you want to!"

"And," said Kitty, sensing crushing victory, "we *also* need more time off to just *chax*, you know? Kick back. Defrag our chakras. Cotch with swag muses. I think . . . until our exams, a maximum of four hours muse school per weekday is reasonable. Moreover, we'll go down to London a week before the first exam."

Blake and Simi glanced at each other. Simi shrugged.

"Agreed," said Blake.

"Then we'll stay," said Kitty, sweetly. "Now. *What* was it you wanted, sir?"

*

"Eh? Oh! It was nothing. Nothing at all." Blake hesitated. "Only, after you two so kindly volunteered to sous the Spring Feast, I *did* wonder if you might be able to turn a few extra shifts re housework and/or in Duke's? Moth, you see, has been rather rushed off her wings by recent —"

"*Aaaargh!*"

Once again Kitty careened from her balance ball, eyes blazing and teeth bared, like a cannonball ejecting a cannon.

"As I said," Blake added brightly, backing away rapidly, "nothing whatsoever! Ta-ra!"

The Myometrium door was swinging.

Simi was looking thoughtfully at Myfanwy.

Myfanwy realised she must be looking quite thoughtful herself. She managed a weak smile and, out of politeness, boinged on her ball a bit.

"Five minutes, babes," said Simi softly. "Composure, both of you."

"Oh, I'm *fine*," purred Kitty. "I'm back on my ball, babes. You and I played Blake rather well I thought, Aoide. Couldn't have done it better if we'd planned it, eh?"

"*Hmm.* You're always on the ball, you lot! Only joking, my loves. I have been naughty. I'll put my hand up. But five minutes, yeah? Then we'll practice the No-Dollies Hoard Sift again. You were doing those well, Mnemosyne. Five minutes, my loves!"

"I'll be right back," said Myfanwy.

"Back down to No-Dollies?" moaned Kitty. "Are you *serious,* fam?"

Myfanwy went to her room by the straightest route she knew. Nonetheless her five minute head start was gone by the time she arrived. She packed her bag quickly, left no note, but simply slipped back downstairs and headed, under the soft iron of an overcast sky, for the centre of town. No one saw her, no one tried to stop her.

It had been raining earlier. As she passed the soggy blackened playground she dug about in her coat pocket.

Aha! Old friend.

With deep satisfaction, Myfanwy tore apart her orange. Her mittens swung on their strings. The wind cut into her skin, fragrant and wet with juice, in a self-harmy kinda way.

My loves, she thought.

Fam, she thought.

On the saddle of a swingset, separated from its chains, she read the lettering WICKSTEED. A wet paper poppy was plastered to it.

Yum.

You weren't really supposed to eat oranges like this. This was how you ate clementines. Oranges were all cut up on a little breakfast plate or on a tray at half time during netball.

Myfanwy thought of eating cucumbers like apples.

A tabby cat with a terrifyingly human-looking face lay curled under a bench. Not just any human-looking face, Myfanwy realised. Whoopie Goldberg.

Myfanwy hustled through the squares and streets. It was the first time she had been alone in Edinburgh since the morning she'd arrived. She'd almost forgotten that it wasn't only Edinburgh — it was also the Citadel, planted deep in her past by her antagonist.

Today the Citadel seemed *filled* with Jasper. Underneath every pointy hoodie, round the corner of every twisting muscled shoulder. Most of these false scares looked nothing like him. Myfanwy decided she was a new and futile muse class whose talent was they could mistake anyone for Jasper. A Scottie dog trotted across the road on a lead. Myfanwy furrowed her brow at him resolutely.

A stripy boy bounced a ball once.

A long bus rounded a corner.

Myfanwy checked her phone and popped a nitro in her step.

Sunlight dazzled off the rain-slicked street. A woman on crutches tolled across cobbles into the stargate.

A Jasper impressionist shrieked, "Where the Christ is Angela?" so loudly that the little automaton in Myfanwy's phone awoke and said, "Okay. I'll suggest a route for you."

Myfanwy giggled.

Two Jasper impressionists wrestled up against a monument. Was it serious? She hesitated. Now they were kissing. Maybe it *was* serious!

Daddy. Oh, Daddy. What have I been thinking?

Trains to London left on the half hour. If she got a fast service, she could meet her tiny family just as he knocked off work.

*

Myfanwy half-suspected colours were seen differently when manifest on the surface of your own skin. It was a hypothesis worth pursuing. Perhaps it could end global conflict?

Myfanwy's Jubilee Bridges bruises, for instance, were mad swag. She could see hematomas through her darkest tights — like skins of tinned tomatoes slowly rolling in softly boiling water. For weeks Myfanwy had walked around shin-padded in these dirty rainbows. Swaddled in soap bubbles, down-shifted to an appalling dark palette.

Worse, the leg hematomas began "healing" by proliferating vegetably. Florid mists, burgundy-dappled viridian, welled up in her legs. Certain bruise-strokes were so delicate, Myfanwy coveted them for tattoo ink, though the thought of a needle near her fragile, reknitting skin made her want to retch. Sometimes the discolourations seemed like zoomed-in fingerprints — CSI-style, except the pigments were pointlessly, frighteningly gaudy, and the murderer's whorls were still spasming, trembling, tapping a silent tune in slow motion. Smoke of blood billowing on the shin bone. That skate gale was locked up safe again, in memories incapable of fanning it free. Blood billowed blown only by the initial monstrous ictus.

But slowly that was settling.

Except that was nothing — because far worse than damage to Myfanwy's legs was the damage to her *ribs*. All up her right side, pinned to an anguishing, billowing whalebone Rorschach of shifting black and purple, there splayed a lurid ictirene yellow tracework, like pus in sunlight, threaded with raw deep crimson courses, the uncontained capillaries, effervescent filament caterpillars crawling in her flesh, horrific little rivers with heads but no mouths, pooling and clotting, promiscuously dyeing her aching tissue sienna, plum, persian indigo, umber, lava brown, auburn, jale, fuligin, even dressing her in vivid little splashes of ultramarine.

Then Oni gave her her new bracelets.

Then, finally, one day, no sooner had the last traces of colour completely slipped from her wrists and from her ribs, no sooner had her virtual corset unfastened, so Myfanwy could finally breathe as deep or laugh as hard as she liked, or throw at least basic Euclidian shapes, without automatic chastisement, and no sooner were her knees and shins as clean as they ever had been, except maybe for a last blue freckle or two, than Myfanwy ran once more straight into the arms of Jasper Robin.

*

Jasper hopped lightly as his redbreasted namesake onto Waverley Platform Eleven.

Myfanwy turned immediately and started walking.

She was proud of her calm.

"The train at Platform Eleven is the delayed twelve o' clock service to London Kings Cross. Calling at Berwick-upon-Tweed, Newcastle, York, Darlington, and London Kings Cross."

He didn't see me. Don't run.

Walk calmly.

She moved through the Waverley crowds. Hairs on the nape of her neck rose up.

"First class carriages are situated towards the rear of the train."

Near the taxi rank was a mini-roundabout. A circle of clouds had been cut into roof over it, a sort of light well, where the rain fell solidly. It looked like an eviscerated water tower. Through the water she saw Jasper's wavering outline join the taxi queue.

Jesus! Which way did he go?

Veering abruptly, she almost crashed into a man in a chequered shirt.

"Oh bugger this!" Myfanwy inspected the man's brawnful and vacant nature with expert approval. "Sorry. Could you quickly pretend to be my boyfriend?"

The victim was inauspiciously alarmed by this offer.

Myfanwy sighed. "You just have to stand there," she clarified. "Manly protective arms more or less kosher, if tactically necessary, but *no* snuggling, or honestly I'll *dead* you."

"Uh — sorry, I don't — I'm getting a train to Norfolk in just under twenty minutes, you see."

"Ah, poor, naïve Passenger for Norfolk!" Myfanwy chided. "I have had *far* shorter relationships than that which I count as splendid successes to this day. Now take my hand — e.g. in Year Eight me and Sid Fairfax once broke up *twice* in one Art lesson. So you know the score, yeah? — mandem in that there taxi rank is my Psychotic Ex, *I* have gotta have closure with him, but I need *you* to stand there just in case — oh *sugar*, he's hailing a cab — make haste, Passenger for Norfolk! Make haste, but alas for you, not for Norfolk!"

For a bad moment, she had a bollard on a lead, but then Passenger for Norfolk reckoned he was game for *anything*.

"My name's Kenneth!" he cried, as though he'd never truly Lived before.

"That's interesting and a lovely name," Myfanwy told him. "Please try to stay on-message, Passenger for Norfolk. *Jasper!*" She shrieked his name at the silo of thickly sloshing rain. It hissed in the air and sparkled and rattled on the black cab's hoods. "*Jasper!* Hush now, you, Passenger for Norfolk. No 'getting into the role.' And don't *escalate* — I didn't select you for your masculinity, yeah? This is about teamwork. *Jasper!* I'm team captain, that's why I picked you."

Myfanwy strode towards Jasper's cab unwaveringly vividly. The sheer glamour of her approach would fill every taxi's fuel tank with sugar.

His black cab was curving slowly round the mini-roundabout in the rain. Myfanwy stepped into the downpour, off the kerb and into the cab's path.

His horn blared. A chorus blared. She put her hands down on the hood.

Jasper got out. "You."

"Us," said Myfanwy.

Jasper stepped closer and she circled away, hands still on the hood. The cab was between them, the rain beating down like blows. The cabbie leaned on his horn. They lifted their palms and let him pull away. Nothing between them now but rain.

Jasper's face a mask of rain.

He spoke first. "I don't expect to be let off. But I am sorry."

Jasper had spoken with a certain kind of gravelly, exacting ponderousness — of a kind Myfanwy realised she associated with self-educated people. Like he'd superglued the chip back onto his shoulder. But the little *cracks* around the chip were still visible.

It was *like* that, but it wasn't *quite* that.

She didn't need to reply yet — another cab nosed between them. She glimpsed Jasper's body through the windows, his posture subtly strange compared to what she'd just seen. As if he was using the cab's passing between them as privacy, time to compose himself. But she'd seen him! She'd given him no privacy. With that one glimpse through the window, she was already winning the encounter.

His signature terrible dress sense. Soaked, through his sports silks, to his skin.

Where had her bodyguard got to? — good, sort of noodling around getting soaked. *Doesn't mind a bit of wet. Still a little while till his train. I am a* brilliant *judge of character!*

The cab left and she lifted her chin. "'Sorry?' Are you being deliberately provocative? I'm talking to you for one reason, Jasper. You're going to tell me everything you've stolen. Anything I want to keep, you're flipping me back now. And we can go round and round until I'm satisfied, Jasper, or you're *drowned.*"

"Me and ditzy BFF," said Jasper. Deadpan, no hesitation. She felt her confidence sink. She beckoned Passenger close. "Watching pretentious vintage DVDs," Jasper continued, deadpan in the rain. "BFF has a little Christmas tree decorated with her jewellery. Chocolate. I'm talking about a whole reindeer here."

Myfanwy crossed to him. Two paces away now. Passenger for Norfolk's hand in hers again. Cabs swished by more swiftly.

"And much earlier," Jasper said. "I had jammy hands. I wiped them on the table side. A mad little thing running into the world, heedless of that pair behind me. 'No, Myfanwy. Stop, Myfanwy. Come out of there, Myfanwy. Put it down, Myfanwy. Leave him alone, Myfanwy. Where are you? Please, Myfanwy! Please, Myfanwy!' And that's all. Guilt about it much later. When does your mum die?"

"No. Spill the mnemes, hon."

"I know there's more. But that's all I recognise."

Myfanwy shook her head. "Not nearly enough."

"Illegal immigrants swamp my soul. No papers, impossible to trace. Paying tax though, contributing to the whole country. I'm happy to go talk. I want to. I mean it. Be my guest."

"No, Jasper. *Now.*" She shook her head, and drops fell from her hair, while new drops filled it. "I'm not your guest. You are my intruder. You've given me so much *more* than that. So many unreal memories."

Jasper hesitated shrewdly. "No such thing."

Myfanwy rolled her eyes. She bounced from one foot to the other. "You *know* what I mean."

"I've given you her, haven't I? I've lost so much of her."

"A lot of *sex* with her," snarled Myfanwy. She stared at him. "And I'm a *virgin*," she blurted.

"Damn." Jasper looked like he was trying not to smile. "I'm trying to say I'm sorry. Let's just go somewhere where we can work this out. What's mine is yours."

"And the only reason you did it," said Myfanwy, "is because I *look* a bit like her. You haven't *got* a fucking soul."

"I couldn't help myself. I really couldn't."

"You said I wasn't a patch on her."

"Now she's a patch on you. Look, I — I admit acted like an ass the first time. Not just the flip —"

"The crude, 'I'm-still-obsessed-with-my-ex' come-on? OMG. Whereas the *second* time we met —"

"Leaving you on ice, that was wrong. This man you're with is *hilarious*, by the way. Look at him."

"The *second* time, you brutally murdered that woman!"

"*That?* But Myffy, that was no reflection on *you*."

"I shouldn't say that," Myfanwy sniffed. "She gave me her card, actually."

Jasper looked startled. "Then it was quite wrong of me," he nodded, seeming to supress a smile. "I shan't brutally murder her again. Your teeth are chattering, Myffy."

This wasn't going how she'd intended. "Look, *Jazz*. First of all, don't call me *Myffy*. Second, don't bother vibing civil no more, okay? I just realised why you're doing it, but I'm not coming to work for — you know."

Myfanwy waggled her head at the Passenger for Norfolk.

"The *VVV* thing," she said, out of the corner of her mouth.

"Sorry?" said Jasper, acting puzzled.

"The *VVVVV* thing. And I shan't work for the *Ch Ch Ch* thing either."

"Still chattering."

"I am through with all these *amusements*."

"Oh, Veil?" Jasper laughed. "Is *that* what you think I am? I've no allegiance to them, Myffed. I'll rid us of Poly and Calli, and Thalia and Urania, and Zeus and Aoide and Meletē — I'm equal opportunities."

"Don't," said Myfanwy, in a voice she hardly recognised.

He seemed taken aback by her rawness. Neither spoke.

"Um," said the Passenger for Norfolk.

"I *have* to," Jasper hissed. "You don't understand what they are. Listen to me, Myffy —"

"I told you!"

"Chancelhouse is built on *lies*, okay? It's only a few years old."

"Aoide told us about the relaunch. So what?"

"No. It wasn't relaunched. It was founded. Blake was the first muse. Do you get it? The *first muse ever*."

"There's plenty doesn't add up about that place," Myfanwy retorted hotly. "Doesn't mean I'll trust *you*. Some myths are necessary!"

"For all *you* know," said Jasper, moving closer, "I just flipped the whole damn thing in your head just now. Maybe this whole last *week* never happened."

She didn't know where to look. "Shut up. I know you didn't, because you haven't *touched* me."

"Well I'm *about* to touch you. Is that okay?"

"Don't you *dare*. I will *dead* you."

As Jasper beetled over her, she drew Passenger for Norfolk's arm across her chest like a sash. Jasper paused, seeming to have completely forgotten about him.

"Ah," he said, and then seemed to disregard him.

"Indeed," she said, with a careless hair-toss, "it would profit me nothing to slay you now. Me and Norf are *leaving* your stupid Citadel."

They looked at each other. He lowered his face and he —

And for a second — or for two — just long enough for the Passenger for Norfolk to reiterate an "um" all forlorn — her lips, startled, kissed Jasper's lips. There wasn't a thought in her head. There couldn't have been. No thought on earth could correspond to this. To Jasper Robin kissing you, and you leaning back, and opening your lips.

Then Passenger for Norfolk's arm, extricating tactfully from between their bodies, brought Myfanwy to — she made the best of a bad situation by headbutting the weird bastard.

"*Aargh!*"

"Edinburgh Kiss!" she bellowed triumphantly. "Forcefeeder! Cat and Mouse Act! Bitch!"

These weren't meaningful proclamations. They were guttural battle cries.

There was something strangely prim about Jasper's pose — his hand clapped over his nose — as though in a flap over some matronly innuendo, or flustered about whether he'd left his iron on.

"Why did you kiss me? Why did you kill Mara?"

"Because," said Jasper. Gingerly he removed his hand. No blood, or else cleansed already in rainwater. "She murdered someone I love."

"That doesn't make it right."

"I think you know it does. I think you do . . . because I think now you loved her too."

"It's not *real.*"

"They all murdered her, Myfanwy. All the original nine. You know what that means, don't you?"

"*No one* can know what that means, Jasper. And Gen—" She'd almost said "Genevieve." But that was *ridiculous.* "Your girlfriend — your beloved — *can't* have nine murderers."

Jasper growled with frustration. "They stood by and let it happen, what's the difference? I don't *know* exactly who —"

"Girlfriend," thought Myfanwy, *doesn't seem right when you're avenging her death. "Partner"?*

"Face rapist!" Myfanwy spat. "Soul rapist!"

"Hey now," said Passenger for Norfolk, rolling into action. "You ought not to say things you don't mean."

She stepped forward and slapped Jasper as hard as she could. Her hand stung.

He turned back. She saw the rosy shape of the slap.

"*Hey! That's* out of order!" said Passenger for Norfolk.

"And it's not true," said Myfanwy, "about being a mad little thing. I was well-behaved. Mum had to *yell* at me in Tesco or on the train to have the odd tantrum so I could grow up *normal.* 'Kick the nice gentleman, Myfanwy.' You don't know *shit.*"

"Watch your mouth," snapped the Passenger for Norfolk, and addressing himself to Jasper, "Sir, shall we restrain her? Shall I telephone the police?"

Myfanwy shoved him hard in the chest. "*You are a terrible judge of character, Passenger from Norfolk!*" she shrieked.

She barely noticed Jasper getting into another cab.

"Passenger from Norfolk, you and me are finished!"

Oh, flip. Passenger for Norfolk was one of those men who could hold both your hands still with just *one* of his. Ugh! What was he going to do with his free hand . . . Teach Her A Lesson?

He raised it like a preacher. "You're very lucky, ma'am, that I have a train to catch!"

"Aaargh!"

*

She was sheltering under a striped green-and-white shop canopy, on a pedestrianised balcony not far from Waverley. The basic constituent of Edinburgh, Myfanwy decided, was lovely views of Edinburgh.

She had, in the courtyard below her, a bird's eye view of a stiffly-moving old man, his face fully hidden by his black brimmed hat, from which he shook the rain every few tentative steps. A little boy and girl, perhaps grandchildren, played at chasing each other around him. All three dressed perhaps for a funeral, and all three drenched.

In the distance the Castle loomed.

"Scottish people are insane," Myfanwy murmured.

Turning, each chased child then became the huntschild. Clockwise, counterclockwise, swapping back and forth, drifting slowly down the slope of the courtyard with the rainwater. Soaking braids bright and high in the girl's hair.

Myfanwy held her phone to her ear and pictured her landline ringing inside her little London house, Dad grunting and observing some vital rugby kick or throw or esteemed cisgender grope before pausing their telly . . . or else emerging from their kitchen, grunting and wiping flour onto his trousers — or else, Myfanwy then chose charitably, grunting and wiping his floury, hairy hands on that little hammer-and-sickle floral pinny that she'd nabbed for him at the Tate Modern shop last summer . . .

Myfanwy bobbled her head side-to-side, bored with the ringing. Big blobs of rain flopped off the canopy onto the balustrade.

She imagined Dad yelling at the telly, or singing loudly along to Zappa or Dylan, oblivious to the ringing.

She held out her hand. Not shaking too much anymore. A big blob splashed on her wrist.

She really needed to hear a friendly voice.

Paddy?

But what could she tell *Paddy*, of the things that mattered to her now?

The mourner-orrery moved out of sight.

Simon? Sarah? Gareth? Seasons for Growth peops? Same thing applied! Mara's ten numbers once more? And same thing applied, for that matter, to *Dad*. Myfanwy realised she couldn't share *anything* important to her with *anyone* important to her. Even supposing Dad did pick up, she could hardly tell *him* —

"Uh. Hello, Peter Morris speaking?"

But after the initial wave of relief, there followed a heartbreaking and bewildering conversation, like a short and deeply sorrowful dream. First Myfanwy announced she was at "the train station" and got told off for talking American again. Then Dad asked sharply *what* rail station and she said oops, she'd meant the Tube — the Tube at Stratford — and she was about to go underground. In retrospect, that was speedy thinking of the stupido variety, because why would she be leaving St Jerome's early afternoon except to skive? But Dad, no Taggart, let alone a Ms Marple, wasn't paying much attention, then was obviously about to wrap up the call, and suddenly Myfanwy was blurting out about how she'd be back that very evening and how much she missed him . . . and Dad seemed really, like . . . *lukewarm* about it. He said not to rush home on his account. Then the reception went funny.

Then he was gone.

The light was really filling the rain. It looked like telly noise or like a sandstorm.

Myfanwy choked back tears.

Could Dad be *seeing* someone? She could think of nothing else that would explain this attitude. Perhaps his reception was crap because he was whirling round the Teacups ride, whilst across from him there vamped some smouldering, rouged and scarlet-lipsticked cougar, with three hubbies under her Gucci belt already and a holster for one more, or else Dad's arm nervously draped, maybe even via a yawn, around some slim anonymous thing's shoulder, someone young enough to be his daughter, for heaven's sake, her head in shadow, save for her youthful cheek and neck, as their car glided into the Love Tunnel . . .

Damn it. Myfanwy dialed Kitty. Straight to answerphone — HQ did have some old school bad reception. You'd do better in a teacup.

Or perhaps Dad had just texted all his bredren, "Daughter away, free house this weekend, gonna be wicked" etc.? In a daze, Myfanwy texted him that maybe she wouldn't be home for the weekend after all.

She walked off into rain and her phone honked.

My darling that is ok if that is where you work best. Am busy tomorrow in garden see about downstairs shower curtain. I love you. X x x x daddy Say hi to Kitty, where has she been, is she still with Lewis

Oh sugar. Still plenty of time to make the next train.

She couldn't decide.

Chancelhouse? My house?

Chancelhouse? My house?

Daddy, or—

Then there was Blake.

There he was.

There he was, of course, wet of course, wearing cycling gloves, winding up his bicycle lock. A silly floppy hat with the brim turned up at the front, and a fluorescent vest and knee and elbow pads. Myfanwy saw, as he raised his gaze, in big silly glasses she'd never ever seen him in before, an expression of enormous relief — edged with just a tinge of anger.

"There you are," he murmured. "Oh, there you are."

She felt quite the wrong word about to drop from her lips. She remembered Kitty calling the teacher "mummy" in Year Eight. Cringe!

"There *you* are," she said. "There *you* are."

*

In his panniers Blake had brought along two brollies. They thought they'd wheel the bike between them, with a brolly in her left hand and the bicycle in her right, and the bicycle in Blake's left hand and a brolly in his right, but no sooner had they arranged themselves in this sensible fashion than the clouds parted and glorious sun began to shine.

"My poor bedraggled Myfanwy! Miss your rail service, did you? Lucky! Say what you like about the trains running on time, there is a certain superficial association with *fascismo* and the bellicose expansion into *Italia Irredenta* and *Mare Nostrum . . .*"

What was he on about? Should she tell him about Jasper?

She wasn't sure.

"*That's* better," Blake sang. "The breezes have a bit of colour to them again. You'll enjoy an Edinburgh spring, my dear. Why, this time last year I saw a zephyr that was quite indigo. You must be frozen. I've been very foolish. Of course Aoide and I worked you too hard, making no allowances for your secular studies, giving you no stake in your studies. Bad pedagogy and bad pastoral care. I coveted you pair as feathers in my cap for the Spring Feast on the roof, you see. Too zealous to be proud of you! But how selfish, when there's no real rush. Study, sit your exams. And, at your own pace, learn what we're really like! Find your path, Mnemosyne! Alas, when Nessus piped up, I acted like she was your elected representative. How foolish! Of course, Myfanwy, your path at Chancelhouse may be quite different from Kitty's. Chancel in the field ain't all Dwelling and spellsongs, you know! There's how to froach an egg. There is the fine science of diplomacy. There is Counselling, Soresu, Shien, Djem So, and of course Copia! Indeed, you might like to spend some time with Rook, when he returns. We'll call it Shadow-a-Wannabe-Doolittle Day! Or Eft would love to show off her research, casting into non-cognitive complex systems. The wind, the weather, the woods — perhaps we'll cast into plants some day! Veil are probably already at it, tree-hugging upstarts, just as they're doolittling while we're doolallying! At least I think it was indigo. They zip by, you know, breezes. At a rate of knots, I think by definition actually they don't. At any rate, I'm so sorry. This is what I really mean to say. I'm so sorry, Myfanwy Mnemosyne Morris, and so glad you've decided to come back, decided to take a chance on Chancel once more."

"Thank you Blake," said Myfanwy. His emotion and formality embarrassed her. "I'm sorry I ran off without talking to you. I don't want you to think that I — you know. Thank you for being understanding about the tournament, and A-Levels, and about me not being as talented as Nessus and everything. I don't mind playing in the all-ball tournament, so long as we don't have to train all the time."

"Oh, it will be such fun! Could you convince Nessus?"

"I can try. I have another favour to ask though. Even though I've been so rotten. Could I have a room of my own? I thought . . . maybe I could ask Moth if she'd mind swapping. Um. Rooms, I mean."

"Of course!" cried Blake. "Easy-peasy, lemon squeezy. Which is to say, Chancelhouse is a bit of a squeeze these days, and still no lemons, but of course, my dear, of course! Oh! You and Kitty haven't *fallen out*, have you?"

"Not exactly. Sometimes I just need privacy for sniffling into my pillow, you know? If Kitty's there it escalates, and I end up, like, howling at the moon."

Then they chatted complete nonsense.

"Can you paint with all the colours of the wind?" said Blake.

"It might be like painting with milk."

"Only what gets twisted away contains the colour, eh? Of course all that bottletop malarkey encodes fat content. But then, wind stirs dust, and flakes of skin make up the best part of dust. So who is to say whether different breezes *don't* have different fat contents? When I was much younger, I went to something called a Traffic Light Disco."

"Too much information, too much information, too much infor— did you pull?"

"No, I *pushed,* I shoved my way out of there, my dear. People had on red, amber or green tops according to their fat contents. Well, according to their loneliness and despair, but there was a statistically significant correlation —"

Myfanwy made a decision. "Plus I just saw Jasper," she said nonchalantly. "At Waverley."

"Ha! How *very* interesting! You're sure it was he?"

"I confronted him. Blake, could I see some photos some time? Of Chancelhouse in the old days? Before the Veil spin-off?"

Myfanwy had found one photo album in all the bookshelves – strange allegorical daguerreotypes, bound in gorgeous sun-bleached cedarwood. But it was just another mysterious artefact of the houses, its connection with Chancelhouse heritage obscure.

Blake shrugged. "I'll dig around. What's this to do with Jasper? What happened? Did you confront him?"

"He told me — he said Chancelhouse isn't hundreds of years old at all."

"Ah," Blake chuckled thoughtfully. "Well, perhaps our lugubrious antagonist is right about one thing. It's a funny thing these days . . . the *age* of things. Every man jack of us playing at Divinity with our dino bones. You know, sometimes I wonder whether there weren't muses long before even Chancelhouse. There are trees in Canada over ten thousand years old. I do wonder what might be remembered there, if one had the courage to place both palms on the right trunk, and cast past the bark. Yes, perhaps in a way Chancelhouse isn't that old. With such licentious intersection of mental materials, more and more the true questions are things like, 'When is so-and-so's story set? Oh yes? And who is telling it now? Oh really? How many have told it before he?' . . . rather than, you know, how long so-and-so has endured, and if he can produce papers to prove it. Courage, by the way, is something Aoide has been testing, this past week. It hasn't just been about development, you know. Or about her rather insane novelty team sports obsession. Last night Aoide delivered the due diligence on you girls. We've agreed you're Chancel material."

"Only last night?" Myfanwy was shocked.

"The one negative was Nessus skiving some duties. She cons Moth and Triffid to do them, you know, and it's not fair. Aye, my dear, that's really what I was popping in to tell you about this morning. You've breezed through with flying colours!"

"I don't understand. What if I'd failed? Would you have just kicked me out, and trusted me not to blab?"

Blake looked at her steadily. "Think," he said.

"Oh," Myfanwy said. "You would have wiped me. Everything. The whole week."

Blake gave a slight, sad nod. "From our perspective, a difficult and extremely costly procedure. Your recruiter will be particularly relieved you've cut the mustard. If you ever required a wipe, from Merlin's head be it!"

"Merlin's memories, you mean? In exchange for mine?"

"Indeed, my dear. Via various intermediaries, of course. Consultant patterners on the spellsong. Pared and fit-for-purpose. Merlin's memories may not match up very well with the life of such a wonderful seventeen-year-old girl, but one can . . . chop and change within a pool of agents, get some patterners slicing and fusing, conflating and confusing . . ."

"You could have said 'cut the *muse*-tard.' No, wait. Maybe you couldn't."

"All much easier if you have a proper mirror, of course. We have none, and Veil seem to have a whole barbershop's worth . . ."

Now strolling through Bristo Square, they skirted a bald guy getting clumsily off his bike with a skinless bass drum strapped on his back. Myfawny felt sorry she hadn't any litter to pop in it.

Student chalk was everywhere. Posters for student elections ivied up every streetlamp. *Free Universal Education. Off With Their Heads. More Club Nights in*

Potterrow. Tories Drink Blood.

They passed a middle-aged woman in a purple chunky-knit beanie, wearing round John Lennon glasses with purple lenses and an awesome blue leather coat and yellow tights.

Ooh, must remember that look, for roughly thirty years' time, thought Myfanwy. *Remember remember remember.*

"Is that why you've been so evasive?" Myfanwy said suddenly. "Not giving away too much, in case it all had to be wiped?"

"Well now," chuckled Blake. "I'm afraid caginess has become second nature to me. But yes, I confess that may have entered my calculations. You've been rather cagey yourself, my dear."

"Oh — holding out about Jasper, you mean? Yeah. I'm sorry."

"It's rather fascinating. Meletē is in the north of England at this moment, Mnemosyne. Staking out a rather dramatic clifftop distillery, all dressed in a ghillie suit, and upset he's scratched some rather fancy binoculars. So he'll be *very* dismayed if you really *did* spot Jasper here in Edinburgh just twenty minutes ago. Which is why I must ask, my dear — is there *any* possibility that that evidence has been tampered with? Or is its seal not only unbroken, but unbreakable? Give the word, and I'll trust it implicitly!"

"Well of cour—"

But Myfanwy stopped.

Motown Idol Tonight, said the pale purple chalk.

Off With Their Heads, said the posters all up the lamps. *Free Universal Education. Every Tutorial Reading Online — EVER.*

Someone called *ALEX* had had the vision to turn the terminal *X* of his name into a cross in a ballot box, whereas *MAX* had missed this trick — surely Max and his ideology of *More Club Nights in Potterrow* would be consigned to the margins of history?

Not very many women running.

An abundantly burlful fire officer. *Make Sure He Only Appears As A Kissogram.*

She felt weirdly similar to how she'd felt that day with Kitty, strolling along the Thames. Just after Jasper had just flipped her for the second time.

Blake was chuckling merrily. "What's going on in those heads of yours, my dear? Do they still teach Caledonian Antisyzygy in schools these days? The Russian is a riddle, wrapped in a mystery, inside an enigma, is the gist of it, and the Scotsperson the same, but then wrapped in another inscrutability, a layer of breadcrumbs, and deep fried . . ."

"I'm almost positive it *was* Jasper," Myfanwy said slowly. Then, more rapidly, "BTW congrats on 'Scotsperson' but that's still either rather weightist of you *or* rather ethno-prejudicial, but I haven't got the time to work out which, because —"

Who could have flipped me? Who was the last person to touch me? The Passenger for Norfolk? Not Veil? But I *chose* him!

. . . didn't I?

And when the Passenger for Norfolk let go of my wrist, Jasper was nowhere in sight . . .

"There *was* someone else involved though," Myfanwy admitted with a sigh. "At Waverley. Am I being paranoid?"

"Well, let's stay on the safe side," brooded Blake. "Any idea where that is? No . . . no, me neither."

"Let's get back anyway," said Myfanwy. "And I'll tell you all about it."

*

"Kitty, check these out!"

"Sure! Only I cannot think of anything more boring and tacky!"

Myfanwy was turning the pages of a photo album. Here was Chancelhouse circa six years ago, courtesy of Blake. But many empty plastic envelopes suggested that the exciting images had already been deleted.

Myfanwy paused over an image of the murdered muse Tamara Drago-Ferrante. The sticky label carried her callsong — Polyhymnia.

Sing, muse!

Kitty wandered off without saying where she was going.

As she leafed the images, Myfanwy was trying to figure out exactly how much of her life was now drawn from Jasper's life. She wanted to draw clear lines between her memories and his. That was Reason A for studying the album, and the one she emphasised to Blake.

"A bold endeavour," Blake had told her dubiously, as he handed her the album. "But, seeing as you did so well in following the trail of Jasper's memories, we may as well press your accomplishments a little further . . ."

No images of Jasper at all.

An image of Blake gurning in a Hawaiian shirt undone to the third button.

And he left that *in?*

Myfanwy leafed on, mystified.

"'Aoide delivered the due diligence,'" Myfanwy mimicked, "'on you fillies ten minutes ago. We think you're Griffinhouse material. We have detected you have . . . courage!'"

C-ringe!

A-ha!

It was a photograph of the Chancelhouse street, or perhaps of the gorgeous sky over it. BUILDING SERVICES was painted on a corrugated surface, near the newly-opened computer repairs shop, letters removed by the ridges' angles — BULDNGSRICES.

Bildungromans?

Reason B, of course, was to see if she could find anything to support Jasper's accusations. She felt obscurely as though Blake knew she was doing this, and approved. It wasn't just that Blake wanted her to debunk Jasper's claims. It was a more subtle, a more intricate puzzle than that . . . and perhaps even Blake hadn't yet mastered its construction . . .

She pulled a photo of a picnic out of its sleeve. There was a cement tile visible in the grass behind the picnickers — who included a rather risqué and skimpified Simi, Myfanwy saw with a smile! — and on the cement were stencilled the letters *BBQ BBQ BBQ*.

B&Q? A-ha!

Almost too easy.

A second image was printed on the reverse of the picnic. An early sketch of a device Myfanwy recognised from somewhere in the compound — a cornucopia of gems, fruit, hooves and bones.

Hmm.

After she found that, she made sure to slide every photo from its sleeve. Several were printed double-sided.

Eventually slipping a photo of a rose bush, perhaps, although one without blossoms, from its sleeve and flipping it over, Myfanwy found an image of the "Tudor" muse Genevieve Quaker.

Indeed, with frills substituted for the Topshop top, it could even have been the very image the painting in the library was based on. Unless the girl, whoever she was, *always* made that face in photos?

I look nothing *like that,* Myfanwy thought sniffily. *Still. V. interesting.*

*

All the vibrant blue above and around. Around and down, masses of gorse flowering yellow, either side of the rocky red downhill path. Forest line below them . . . Genevieve Quaker in front . . . crows, wood pigeons and doves, the hills . . . aroma of the oils of Genevieve's hair, mingled with sweet gorse smell, honey, cinnamon, mingled with both their sweats . . . lacing her arms, hot from the climb, round Genevieve's slim waist, and Genevieve not turning . . . and then she kissed the back of Genevieve's ear, and her not turning, and then following Genevieve's gaze . . . on the far hill face, veils of dust floating up, and pinpricks of dazzling sun . . . a tiny convoy of many more police vehicles, trickling down towards the camp . . . preposterous twinkling. . .

"Guess we better go."

"Mm-hmm?"

Genevieve leaning then back to kiss — and rabble of slurred voices, as if the hill surrounded — horrific song . . . !

"Something something!

Something something!"

Light laughter, because she did not hear them . . .

"We're in your house!"

And then taking Genevieve's hand in her left, helping each other down the steep shattered path . . .

"We'll fuck on you!"

Awake.

Drunk laughter of the lads and lassies processing past. Had been singing something. In the centre of the curtains, a little column of soft light, falling only on the bedside table.

No snoring —

"Kitty, answer instantaneously."

Kitty's hand appeared on the bedside table. "*Awake*, obviously," she sighed. Kitty's hand felt around for the ten-pack of menthols then vanished. The menthols fell back into the pool of moonlight.

A match flared, in the darkness showing Kitty's features floating orange, then shrank, then swung to and fro to nothing. The menthol's cherry lit up her mouth and nose when she breathed in.

Kitty pushed open the window without parting the curtains any wider.

The voices were a little clearer.

"We are black!

We are blue!

We're the House

Who'll fuck on you!"

"Oh my God," Myfanwy moaned. "Do they have to do that *right* outside?"

"Imagine what it's like in Triffid's room," murmured Kitty. Doors elsewhere in the compound were indeed opening and closing. Soon the noise from the street stopped. Myfanwy saw the cherry do small arcs to and fro near Kitty's lips and listened to the slight pop, like a soft kiss, as the cigarette left them.

Myfanwy hesitated. Had she perhaps detected, earlier —

"Scare me half to death."

"'Once upon a time, there was a girl called Myfanwy. There was a big horrible spider in her shoe. The end.'"

"Eek. You know who's a big horrible spider? Vertical."

"He is. He's Spiderspy."

"I'd like to pop a vast jar over him and stick a big bit of junk mail under him, approximately five metres across, and pop him outside. I'd like to —"

And quite suddenly the same loutish voices started up again, and this time, they quite clearly came from *inside* the compound.

"I *knew* it!" Kitty hissed loudly. "They're *us!* They're the other muses! They're ba-a-a-ack!"

"And it sounds like they're in a good mood."

Noises spread through the compound, opening and shutting doors, singing and laughing.

"I'm gonna go say hi," Kitty determined. "See what happened."

"Mmph? I'm so tired. I may wait till morning." Myfanwy hid her head under the pillow and scrunched up her eyes. "You can put on the lamp."

A pause. "Don't worry hon, I can go like this. I won't be long."

Myfanwy emerged from the pillow. The sound of Kitty exhaling smoke.

"You are so *femme fatale* these days," said Myfanwy. "So Morgan le Fay."

Kitty didn't appear to be listening. Footsteps were coming up their corridor.

Then the giant screamed.

*

Myfanwy heard Triffid's muffled voice. "Nessus and Mnemo, you okay?"

Kitty took a hurried puff and drew the curtains wide. "Dandy, Triffo! Yourself?" She flicked the cherry in a high arc over the garden.

"Is Myfanwy in there?"

"Fine," called Myfanwy. "Thanks."

Kitty was by the sink, leaning over and giving her hair a quick seismic ruffle. Upside-down she called, "False alarm, right? Just senior class back on campus? Ready to rumpus?"

Myfanwy slipped out of bed and drew the door slightly ajar. She gave what she hoped was an expressive sigh.

She squinted into the bright corridor light. There was another boy with Triffid, looking sleepy and bored. Triffid looked sleepy and nervous.

"*Hey*," said the new wing-man, in a ridiculously deep voice. He had a muscly face and spiky peroxided hair, shaved at the sides.

Myfanwy addressed herself to Triffid. "Someone probably just put in the wrong code," she said frostily. "Everyone's obviously off their faces."

"You're the new casters," the newcomer rumbled. "Nessus and Mnemosyne, huh? Cute callsongs. I'm Kermitcrab."

"Our heroes have returned," Triffid confirmed. "Witness!"

"We've heard," said Myfanwy. "They're loud."

"Achievement unlocked," Kermitcrab added. "Woo."

Kitty came and leant against Myfanwy, chin on her shoulder. "That's *thrilling* news, Kermitcrab! I'm seriously so proud of you *all!*"

"It was a team effort," boomed Kermitcrab. He scratched the shaved side of his head. "In fact, I had nothing to do with it. Actually, I almost wrecked it for us."

For a moment, all four faces clustered in silence around the crack Myfanwy held open. Myfanwy smiled.

"I smell boo-*ooze*," said Kitty brightly.

"But I didn't," Kermitcrab said. "Level complete. Achievement unlocked. Woo."

Suddenly everything came together in Myfanwy's mind. "Come to sponge off our loofah, Señor Subwoofer?" she said.

Kitty giggled but Triffid heaved a big sigh. "There's still this possible breach," he said. "So shut it, lock it, and stay put till we sort it."

He moved away, and Myfanwy shut the door on Kermitcrab's affable but slightly swaying smirk.

Kitty had something hid behind her back.

"Oh my God," said Myfanwy. "Is that the —"

Kitty flourished the sword, and pressed the bare blade to her lips. "Shhh."

They listened as Triffid and Kermitcrab rumbled up and down their corridor. When Kermitcrab's shaking bass finally withdrew, the line that Kitty had had all the time in the world to prepare turned out to be:

"I'm *going* to the *prom.*"

*

So saying, Kitty slipped away down the corridor. Myfanwy, hands feeling very empty, crept after her. "I feel this is gonna end in tears after bed time, you know? Plus I've been thinking about it, Kitsy, and I really think a big part of that particular vibe is because of that stupid like ninja or samurai way of walking you're doing right now. Did Meletē cast you that or is that Model's Own?"

"Ain't sure," Kitty admitted. "I think I *am* crouched like the tensed panther though. Do you know what a ronin is?"

"Baby horse, right?"

"A samurai without a master."

She swirled around a corner.

They encountered no one around that corner.

Nor the next.

"I'm feeling a bit dizzy," admitted Kitty, after several corners. "Or *no*, I'm feeling —"

The giant's scream gave another brief burst and shut off. Kitty swore.

Myfanwy felt tense again. Her heart was going too fast. She breathed deeply and regularly.

Kitty too, she noticed, was breathing strangely. "Epi," Kitty muttered. "I'm feeling a bit epileptic maybe."

"Did you take your meds?"

"I think so."

No laughter nor voices could be heard elsewhere in the compound. They strained to hear anything. Pipes groaning. Water moving in the walls. Myfanwy thought maybe she heard footsteps.

Kitty started moving less melodramatically. She stopped. "Maybe we should go back," she admitted. "If you're scared."

"Oh as *if*," Myfanwy said. "When you kick off, I just give your sword to bite down on, right?"

"Yup. Joking though, yeah?"

They entered an accommodation corridor. This one had a kitchenette at one end, empty.

Kitty checked the cupboard under the sink. An orange rag fell out.

"Thorough," Myfanwy whispered.

Kitty shrugged. Her eyes were glazed. Her knuckles were white on the sword hilt.

There were five more doors. Three bedrooms, a bathroom and shower cubicle. The farthest bedroom door was slightly ajar.

"We'll check these and go back," Myfanwy whispered.

The first room was Ouzo's.

Kitty jiggled the handle. *Locked*, she mouthed.

Myfanwy nodded and they glid down to the second door. It was Thorn's. Kitty tried the handle and it turned. With their eyes they agreed what they would do next.

Kitty gently kicked open the door and stepped slowly into the darkness. It seemed empty. Myfanwy groped for the light switch, while keeping her gaze trained on the third door that stood ajar a few feet down the corridor.

Kitty moved quickly around in the room.

"Clear," she said.

The third room was Golem's. It seemed empty. The overhead light didn't work. Kitty moved in and turned on the lamp. There was a tall bottle of vodka on a writing desk. It had lipstick round its rim. Myfanwy stared at the red ring while Kitty checked the wardrobe and under the bed. She checked the window. "It was unlocked," she said, and locked it.

They went down the corridor and checked the bathroom.

"Clear."

Myfanwy pulled back the shower curtain.

"Clear," said Kitty.

"Back?" said Myfanwy. "Hon? Please?"

Kitty shook her head.

"One more corridor," she said.

"You don't look that well."

"One more. Then back."

Footsteps on the level above them, and perhaps low voices. They stepped into another accommodation corridor. All three doors were ajar.

The first room was Static's. It seemed empty. Kitty opened the wardrobe. Myfanwy stayed near the door. She looked along the corridor then back into the room. Kitty checked under the bed. She checked the window.

The next room was Tase's. It was messier. The overhead light didn't work. Lit only from the corridor, Kitty glid towards the bed. She crouched, and with her sword-point lifted the valence.

"Clear," she said. She put on the lamp. She opened the wardrobe. It was full of clothes. She thrust her sword in a couple of times.

"Christ," said Myfanwy.

Kitty checked the window. "It was unlocked," she said, and locked it.

"Shh!" said Myfanwy sharply.

They stayed quiet a second, Kitty in her ronin stance.

Myfanwy tilted her head to the third room, and Kitty nodded softly.

The corridor was empty.

The final room on the corridor was Merlin's. The overhead light didn't work. The curtains were drawn, but waving gently. The lamp was unplugged, the socket near to the bed.

Kitty opened the wardrobe.

"Clear," she said.

Kitty turned towards the bed. When she turned away something horrific flipped down between them, his back to Myfanwy.

"Behind!" screamed Myfanwy but too late — Kitty was turning already, leaning even as she span, evading the swinging out arms and nipping their flesh twice with her sword-tip. There was a howl and two bright bursts of blood.

The dark figure was thrashing at the curtains. It was gone, and half of Kitty vanished behind the curtains after him. Myfanwy heard a grunt and then a guttural scream, and then sideways scampering, along the outside of the compound.

Kitty shut and bolted the window and turned. "He was on the ceiling," said Myfanwy. There were footsteps in the corridor.

The shadows above them were empty.

"Vertical," said Kitty. "I cut him three times."

Myfanwy saw the sword was three inches wet with blood. She felt pale and sick. The door was opening.

"There's one under the bed!" Myfanwy shrieked.

A small dark bundle was rolling across the floor, but Kitty's sword-point was by his throat.

Meletē shoulder-checked Myfanwy. "Nessus! Stand down!"

"It's me! It's me!"

"It's only Merlin!" someone else cried. Bodies were jamming the doorway. "Nessus, babes, he's one of ours!" — Simi's voice.

"Simi," gasped Myfanwy, whirling. "He was *in* here. Vertical was *in* here."

"*You?*" Kitty cried. She was shaking. "*You?*"

"I heard him come in," said the figure on the floor. Myfanwy, stunned, drew away from Simi. "And I couldn't make the door, so I rolled under the bed. I didn't know how many there were, yeah?"

Kitty gradually let her sword-tip drift away from his throat, and started to giggle.

That's when Myfanwy decided to start believing her eyes, and joy flooded her heart.

"Stop and search, stop and search," Paddy complained, wearing a massive grin. "Can't a man cotch under his own bed no more?"

"Wha gwaan, Paddy," said Myfanwy. "I hear we're on the same team."

"Alright, Myfanwy," said Paddy. "Wha gwaan? Or should I say, Mnemosyne? Help me up, fam!"

Myfanwy burst out laughing. "I'm sorry! I'm sorry. Oh my little lily Pad," she said tenderly, and reached out her hand. "No power on *earth* can make me call you Merlin!"

*

Paddy and Myfanwy were locked in a ferocious hug.

"Nessus, your sword's wet!" marvelled Meletē. "I guess I got one."

"*I* got one," said Kitty. "Vertical. Two nips on the arm in here, and a nice cut of shoulder through the window. Okay sir. It's the moment you tell me you never flipped me any swordplay — I *had it in me all along!*"

"Well," Meletē smiled. "You added some value, kid."

"My mother tried to teach me to ride a bike like that," Kitty added. "You know, with deception and stuff? Futile. In the end I went to a bike tutor."

Myfanwy finally let go of Paddy. "Mara Drago-Ferrante didn't headhunt us." She sized him up. "It was *you*!"

"I'm a blazon class," Paddy confirmed. "So I specialise in sensing the muse talent. That's the real reason I change schools so much."

"Your family's not military?"

Paddy cocked his afro at Meletē and Kitty. "Depends which family you mean. Myfanwy, I knew you had the muse talent the moment I met you. But Nessus, *you* I wasn't sure about."

Kitty shrugged. "The moment you met *me*, you knew I'd run around stabbing everyone with swords."

"That's probably true," laughed Paddy. "I mean, muse-wise, I sensed a faint *something*, but I couldn't get close enough for long enough."

"Yes," said Kitty happily.

"One day I saw this Veil guy, callsong Vertical, prowling St Jerome's. So I had to rush it, go with what I had. I let Blake and Aoide and Meletē know and hoped for the best — you know the rest. Since then my time's been taken up by Operation Terpsichore. Meanwhile *you* were the ones actually dealing with Jasper and finding your way here."

"And I thought you *fancied* us!" Kitty blurted. "But you were merely *spying* on us! I mean — thank God, right?"

"We'll clear the final two corridors," said Meletē. "Nessus, swordplay's due back in the morning."

"Kitty's got the muse talent alright," Myfanwy told Paddy. "She beats me in every exercise."

"Really?" Paddy laughed. "Safe, I'm so glad! I mean — you know what I mean. Just glad I was right about you both."

"So anyway Pad," said Kitty, "why the callsong 'Gandalf'? Never mind — Simi, Meletē, wait! Wait for me! If this is really due back in the morning," she added, flourishing her large sword, "I want to enjoy every last moment of it."

*

There was bare catching up to be done with Paddy, plus she had a stroke of genius on the way back to her bed, so it seemed like hours before she got back, and she was sure she would be met by Kitty's snores.

Darkness. Silence.

Waiting up?

"Kitty?" she called softly.

No, still not back. Don't be so possessive. Kitty's a big girl.

There came a knock. It was Kermitcrab. "Hey," he boomed. "Remember me? Triff's roomie? Triff and Nessie are using the room, so . . . I guess tonight it's you and me in here."

"Have you brought a toothbrush?" said Myfanwy crossly. "No, in fact. I'm sorry, Kermitcrab. I'd really rather you didn't."

"Where will I sleep?" he boomed sadly. "Where will I sleep?"

"You must have lots of friends here, Kermitcrab. Plus there are plenty *chaises longue* dotted about. Would you like to borrow some bedding?"

He shrugged and slouched off.

"You can tell Triffid what a mean bitch I was," she sang down the corridor after him. "And he'll owe you one. Um, bro."

She sort of missed him for about two seconds.

She lay on the bed.

The door handle rattled.

"Kermitcrab!" she chastised.

But it was Kitty, a bit chonged. She stared at Myfanwy with bloodshot eyes.

"How is Triffid?" Myfanwy enquired icily.

"Oh my *God.* Have you ever heard how he chose 'Triffid' because 'Triceratops' was taken? Well, he should have gone for Ptera*tactile.* Ha ha! Sorry," she admitted, "I'm a bit chonged."

"I'm glad you're back, hon. I thought I was going to have to live with Triffid's mashed roomie Kermitcrab."

"Oh, Kermitcrab?" said Kitty vaguely. "Don't be afraid, Myfanwy. I made sure he won't be bothering anyone with that thing for at least twenty minutes. Mate, in our gap years, we *have* to go to Peru. Tallulah was saying how they have cocaine there that's actually *good* for you? It's so pure and natural there are genuine health benefits. You don't have to pick up — it just blows around in the breezes all day? When some blows in your face, they call it being kissed by an angel. *El bisouz de loco angelicos.* Whereas what you get *here* is like some twisted evil anti-homeopathy."

"If only I could afford it," said Myfanwy. "Plus avoid glamourising drug use."

"I know, as if *drugs* need *people* to glamourise them, right? But fam, we should take Looly and Moth too, and maybe also the boys. Moth was telling me about all this crazy flipping stuff she and Bee have done whilst on all different stuffs . . . they did this thing where they broke the fourth wall of the K-hole . . ."

"And I can tag along and help you all find your hotels?"

"You *should* tag along," said Kitty curtly. "*If* you can afford it." She sighed and stretched out languidly. "OMG, fam. All the men here are *so dry.*"

"Yeah," Myfanwy laughed. "I haven't met anyone. But me and Pad did bare catching up. Um, Kitty, don't be freaked by this. Paddy is actually *nineteen.*"

"Serious? Like, kept back?"

"His folks aren't in the forces. He's been prowling for muses. He's been doing it for the past four years, since he was fourteen."

"That is so him," said Kitty scornfully. "Ick. He looks and acts about twelve. Perilous quality for a paedo to possess."

"Anyway," Myfanwy murmured, half to herself. "That means Chancelhouse is at least four years old. Plus the photographs probably push it back to at least six. But five hundred?"

She was . . . *bemused*, that was the word. Chancelhouse felt like something that had arrived, at its present point in time, from both future and past at once. It was a spectre inherited from ancients, of course, gone out of focus as it manifested down the corrupting centuries. But its outlines also were formed to some dimly foreseen spec, some curse or joyous prophecy wavering through many incorrect formations.

There came the sound of pillows being furiously rearranged. "I can't understand you, Myfanwy," said Kitty. "You're behind glass, these days. Night, blud."

"And all I'm *saying*," said Myfanwy primly, "is that attributing childlike qualities to a mixed-race man such as Paddy comes with a complex history of paternalistic colonial and post-colonial persecution."

"OMG, I'm not like some massive racist! I mean, okay, sometimes I have weird thoughts. But they're just goop, bolus, they never journey to the chine stage. Sorry, I'm a bit caned. I'm trying to say — those thoughts aren't *part* of me."

"Like when you said the black swan would only rap once, upon the day she died?"

"I wasn't even thinking like 'black' like 'black'! That shows how totally liberal and colour-blind I am, right? Doesn't it? Doesn't it? I was speaking as a rapper myself, and something of a black sheep."

"Well, all *I'm* saying," Myfanwy said primly, "is that sometimes the things you *say* aren't *just* about whatever you happen to *mean* by them." She paused. When she spoke again, it was much more quietly. "Kitty? Are you scared about what might . . . like . . . *come out*? When we flip each other for the first time. When you get flipped for the first time."

"Yeah," Kitty said. "I really wish . . . I really wish it wasn't random."

"It could be anything. I feel sure it's gonna be something terrible."

"Myfanwy, in the past . . . I mean . . . I've thought really terrible things about you. I really have, hon. But they never lasted."

"Me too, Kitty," whispered Myfanwy. "If something comes out and it doesn't seem like me . . . please just remember I don't mean it."

"I'm so glad you said that. I know you don't hon. I mean, you *did* mean it, but you don't. You just, like, *own* those thoughts. They're not *you*."

"And it's the same for you! You *did* mean those things, but now you don't. You just *own* those thoughts. They're not *you*."

"I mean really creatively brutal stuff," laughed Kitty. "Like really extended, vicious, detailed molestation and denouncement."

"Um."

"You'll see, hon. I'm hilarious. Just imagine if you get some of the weird stuff I think about Jasper."

"Oh my God Kitty," said Myfanwy, sitting up in the dark. "Do you fancy Jasper?"

Then she put on the light.

"Jesus!" said Kitty hotly. "Melodrama! Jam your hype, bitch. I don't *fancy* the guy except in an obvious 'death wish' way. Like, 'oh, kidnap me, tie me up, flip me full of all these depraved desires I thought were impossible, ooh,' you know, normal level of stuff. But in principle it's none of your business *who* I do *what* with, unless maybe it's Paddy."

"*Paddy?* Uh *no-mance!* — plus you're trying to distract me. Tell me if you genuinely fancy Jasper, and lemme me see your fingers."

One of Kitty's Things was that she always had to cross her fingers when she lied.

"Here. No I don't."

"They're crossed!" said Myfanwy.

"They are not crossed! That one is about *two millimetres* forward."

"Forward — *and to the side.*"

"That's just how I'm holding my fingers."

"*Spread* them."

"I'm *not* going to spread them just because you —"

"Fam — you *fancy* him!"

"Okay! I don't fancy him, it's just he's —"

"Yes?"

"He's —"

"*What?*"

"He's currently my Person I Think About Too Much."

"Really?"

"Yes!"

Kitty's forefinger gently moved back into line.

People Kitty Thought About Too Much were another of her Things. They were like a kind of elevated socio-emotio-cultural version of when you, like, put a hat on a hen, and it goes completely calm.

The girls had long ago agreed that they did *not* count as crushes — Kitty could have a crush completely independent of a Person She Thought About Too Much.

When Kitty did herself a quite serious disservice sometimes, for example, by missing something important or fun, afterwards she usually would usually be evasive at first, then eventually admit that she had spent the afternoon just lying curled up on the sofa of her *pied-à-terre* thinking about Slim Charles or Dale Winton or Captain Sam Vimes.

"That is *perfectly normal* darling," said Myfanwy, relieved.

Jasper and Kitty would look unearthly together, she thought.

"Your skin and bones," Myfanwy told her, "are like river water and crystals."

"Thank you very much," said Kitty politely. She put out the light.

"*Schlaf gut*," said Myfanwy, still sitting up in her bedclothes. "*Bis Morgen.* Love you."

"Mmph."

Silence.

"Kitty?" said Myfanwy. She hated how small her voice sounded.

"*Mmph?*"

"Scare me half to death?"

"OMG! Once there was an annoying girl called Myfanwy. Her stoned, sleep-deprived ex-BFF murdered her. The end."

But her tone was forgiving.

"Please? I know you've got one. I sensed it earlier."

Silence.

Kitty cleared her throat.

Silence.

"Once there was a kind, sensible girl called Myfanwy, with bold flashing eyes and pretty curly hair."

*

"Myfanwy was a Black Panther in a plantation penitentiary in Louisiana during the late 1960s. She was otherwise a very ordinary girl. Even an omniscient narrator like me doesn't really know if Myfanwy *really* did the armed house invasion she was accused of — she always claimed she was innocent. Myfanwy's BFF was a prison screw called Kitty. Now, Kitty was very much a man of her time. One day as Myfanwy was picking tobacco leaves, Kitty said to Myfanwy, 'The way I sees it, we get 'em white boys to look after you coloured boys, *I* can spend more time with my kids.' So saying, Kitty spat out a stream of baccy at Myfanwy's feet — rather rude, as Myfanwy may well have been the person who pulled it up out the ground in the first place! After that day, the white prisoners were issued with pistols and referred to as Overseers. You can imagine what they got up to, knowing they had the prison screws to back them up! Well, Myfanwy kicked up such a fuss, she was put in solitary confinement for forty years. She lived in a six-by-nine cell for twenty-three hours a day, until some well-meaning human rights solicitors secured her release in the Naughties — a little late, you'll agree! And you know what? When Myfanwy ventured outside, now an old woman, she wasn't familiar even with crossing the breadth of a road, let alone judging the speed of busy traffic, or remembering about blind spots! So the very same week as Myfanwy was released, she was smacked over by a motorcyclist. She had injuries on her legs and ribs and couldn't get to her feet. An hour later, bone pierced her heart and she died on a hospital gurney in a busy ER before a doctor could even get a look at her. But that's not the end, or it wouldn't be a proper scarytale. Myfanwy's mind, or whatever you want to call it, which she had felt dwindling over those forty years, *now* felt like it was expanding. She saw some peculiar sights, which we'll call the Pearly Gates. And she felt a peculiar presence, whom we'll call St Peter. 'There's someone here I want you to meet,' said St Peter in a rich, wonderful voice. Myfanwy's ectoplasm gasped. For the person St Peter introduced her to was none other than her old friend, the prison screw Kitty — feathered, refulgent. 'What we did back then was wrong,' she said. 'I ain't asking your forgiveness, exactly.' Then for a long time Myfanwy was silent. St Peter looked on with keen interest. 'Ain't nothing much to say,' Myfanwy replied eventually. 'It wa'n't right. You always knew dat. But you ben forgiven. Long way back. Any matters you still sorry for, I forgive 'em too. Man, I only wish, when I gots free for them four days, it was in the summer time, not in the winter time.' Myfanwy chuckled. Then she asked Kitty, 'But how 'bout you, Kitty? You dead too?' 'Yes, I took my own life,' said Kitty. 'I was real sick, and the pain got too much.' Myfanwy shook her head. 'Now how's that gonna look in the eyes of the Authorities?' she said. 'I don't rightly know how it will play,' Kitty replied. And thereupon St Peter raised his arms. Myfanwy said, 'I hope they look mercifully upon your case,' and as Kitty was led away in one direction, a choir of angels lifted Myfanwy and conducted her in another, to a box of clouds, which was six-by-nine feet in size, and from which she would be allowed one hour of exercise per day. The end. Although PS eternity has no end.'"

Silence.

"I don't get it. St Peter was a racist from 1970s Louisiana?"

"The system of persecution goes far deeper and higher than its victims perceive," said Kitty. "It's not just about conspiracy and collusion. It's tough to figure out, and it often replicates itself *even* though everybody involved is really nice and well-meaning. Geeze, I'm really playing to the galleries with this one Myffy — don't you like it?"

"I'm behind glass, darling. I'm like a painting."

*

"Hibermate! Hibermate! My li'l' Hibermate's awake!"

"Kitty . . . wha' . . ."

"Why so sleepy? In the dawn chorus," Kitty lectured, "each organism finds its own acoustic bandwidth. Perhaps you'd prefer my recycling truck noises? *Rrrrr! Chuck chuck chuck! Mawawawawawa! I'm going to recycle you Myffy* . . . "

A note was pinned to the Myometrium entrance.

NO LESSONS TODAY MY CHICKADEES – DEALING WITH LAST NIGHT'S INTRUSION / THEFT!!!

PPS KITTY PLS SEE MELETÉ TO DESKILL IMMEDIATELY

"Simi doesn't mess around," Kitty proofread with approval. "Goes straight for the PPS."

"Guess we better find Meletē."

"My secret conjecture," Kitty confessed, "is that his swordplay is too tangled up to be retrieved by normal methods. There will be a *sticky residue*, fam. He may have to *dive right in* to claim what's rightfully his, you get me?"

"You're so gross, fam."

"You go enjoy your day off, hon. Leave me to Meletē."

*

Soon Myfanwy stood staring at the lightened rectangle where Genevieve Quaker till so recently had hung.

Around her the library lay in disarray. It smelled of smoke, and its deep soft rug was accented with smudges and stars of ash. On the armchair, atop a high twisting stack of grimoires, there balanced a brimming pale blue cocktail with a clumsily-hacked wodge of lime drifting disconsolately down to its little cocktail sea-bed, whilst a pink bendy straw drifted out speculatively out like a white cane.

As Myfanwy drew in to make a closer inspection, Flux squeezed out from under the chair with a miaow. She massagingly arabesqued through Myfanwy's legs, vibrating with deep purrs, then formed her tail into an expressive question mark and aloofly trotted off.

"Oh, come *back*, puss! Come back, Flux! Petal?"

At the door, Flux gave her one guilty backward glance, miaowed evasively and vanished.

Whoever had taken the trouble of mixing the cocktail must have passed out, or hooked up, before they took a single sip.

Already the theft was rumoured — v. disconcertingly — to be an ill-judged prank. Amid last night's revelry and randomness, perhaps some returning muse simply re-parked the portrait of Chancel's patron saint. Of course, most muses believed Veil had stolen the portrait. Why? With what motive? All morning a befuddled and hungover Chancelhouse shrugged its collective shoulders. Like, a sort of default capture-the-flag mentality? Whevs . . .

A very Kitty-esque shriek sounded elsewhere in the compound. More Meletē flirtation, no doubt. She was shameless.

On detox-esque impulse, Myfanwy dove into her Dwelling. The disarray here was even worse . . . and here it was *all* her fault. To work! She would build a crystal houseboat of it. No, she would bloat this Glass Room pretender a hundredfold and reconfigure it as vast gothic castle bedecked with flying buttresses of rainbowcoloured bricks.

Myfanwy took one look at the state of the Suture Reticula surrounding her Altar and surrendered.

Resurfacing from herself — mildly surprised at the angle at which she'd emerged — Myfanwy pictured a fat fruit-fly alighting on the bendy bit of the pink straw, and toppling the whole precarious edifice.

She sighed. She was beginning to doubt if she'd ever be a muse. She gave the blank wall one last stare and turned to leave the library.

A broad-shouldered Arabic-looking guy with a strangely babyish face and designs shaved into his eyebrows was strolling silently towards her, holding up a tall red BBQ Pringles tube and a Starbucks cardboard cup almost equally as tall. Myfanwy yelped.

He stopped and slurped. "Mnemosyne, eh?"

She couldn't tell if his voice was affable or a bit sinister. It was definitely Scottish, which she supposed was technically automatically both.

"Yeesh, you startled me! Indeed I am. And you are?"

He slurped and giggled. He wore stupid fancy hip-hop type clothes, elaborate, glamorous and voluminous.

Myfanwy rolled her eyes. "I'm just being polite, I don't actually care. And you are?"

He just slurped and stared with his big, babyish eyes. Was he still drunk?

"Are you looking for your Pacific Island Ice Tea?" Myfanwy probed courteously. "Mm, *yum*, right? I mean, *yum!* It's *way* up there. A wise precaution for any Pacific Island these days, I agree! Oh dear, you may just have to suck from the straw, because I have serious ethical objections about holding that specific mocha for you, and as for *Pringles* — well!"

"So you're saying," grinned the stranger, "that you're a bletherer."

"Once you pop," Myfanwy explained, "you can't —"

"You're deid," he said hollowly.

He transferred the Pringles to the crook of his arm, fished a crumpled envelope from his jeans, and handed it to her.

She felt a little faint. "What are you doing?" she breathed.

The envelope was already open. She slipped out a blue, black-bordered card.

Her callsong written on it. And crossed out.

"You're deid." He slurped. "Rule sez if you're on your ain, an sumdy's goat your name card, that's you." The stranger pointed to the card with his chunky Pringley wand. "That you or no?"

"Yes," she squeaked. She cleared her throat. "Aye," she said, more firmly.

"Chancelhoose Annual Murder Game. You're oot, Mnemosyne. That's you."

"No. I didn't even know I was in the game."

"That's why you're no very guid at it. That's you. Ah've been Rook." Rook giggled. "See ya roond, nae doubt."

"Wait! Nobody told me about the game, Rook! How is the abrupt application of a lone, contextless rule going to improve community spirit?"

"Ah widnae worry, Mnemosyne. Loadsy brilliant fowk're deid. Wee Marinade, Neilo, Static, Eft. Pure goat awa wi thi loady it an aw." Rook slurped. "About ten minute ago Ah murdered Trice, come tae think of it. Hypnos, Frog, Sequin, Lap, Geist, Bit . . ."

"Oh, you're just *making up* muses now!"

"Naw, only they last wans are *proper deid.*" Rook giggled ecstatically and slurped the last dregs. He was turning to go now. "Mebbe see you next Chancelhoose Annual Murder Game, eh? Or mebbe *no*, eh?"

"Sugar! What manner of muse are you, Rook?"

"Dribble, Kaiou, Struct, deid, deid, deid. Asphyxia Noir, Aglet, Turturle, deid."

"Are you a dishonourable heel muse? Or are you —"

"Ameonna, Enenra. Loads, when a boy gets tae thinking."

"Or are you a 'it's-no-fun-to-play-that-way, give-a-girl-a-sporting-chance' muse? Rook! Think carefully! Your utility may depend on it!"

"Caddy, Cricetid." Rook paused at the doorway. He slurped. "No even counting Veil bodies, eh? Ah'm alive for jokes, *and!* Ah'm alive *for real.* An that's no through givin fowk second chances, Mnemosyne. But . . . Ah'm a doolittle muse, since you ask. Ah flip with the animals, Ah'm hip tae the animals." He sucked his straw, but there was nothing there. "Wee Flux, for example."

Rook giggled one last time and vanished.

Myfanwy went in search of that wicked, unsports-cat-like cat. No luck.

This isn't over, Flux!

She stormed back to her room for some R&D or R&R or D&D or something, whevs. But Triffid seemed to be standing guard.

"'Sup Mnemo," he said breezily. "Do you really have to go in? Be very quiet."

"Yeesh, Triffid! Last I checked I *lived* here."

"So does Nessus. Don't you know? The deskill spellsong really hit her hard, Mnemo. I thought everyone knew."

"What are you *talking* about? What's *happened*?"

"Whoa, whoa, whoa! Muzzle it, muse. Lost some vision and co-ordination, is all. It's temporary."

"Jesus! Why didn't you bloody *tell* me?"

"Mute it, muse! Moth's playing nursemaid. As per Nessus's specifications. It's typical Meletē," he added, with a pained attempt at a grin. "He'd rather dig out too much than too little."

She needed to strangle his smug neck.

Keeping her voice level, she told him, "I can tell you're upset. Don't you dare take it out on me."

"Nessus —"

"*Move* it, muse!"

The room was very dim. Kitty lay back on the bed, a flannel over her face. Moth was perched on the bed contentedly holding her hand. The curtains were drawn. Moth waved her free hand with exaggerated clumsiness.

Myfanwy softly shut the door on them.

*

Later as Myfanwy and supposed-BFF were getting dolled down, Moth popped by and Kitnapped Kitty again. They were *supposed* to be going for noodles — just her, Kitty and Paddy — then joining Moth and some other muses for cocktails, then afterwards to some cheesy club in New Town.

Change of plan, apparently. No apologies, explanation or even a goodbye. And was that a triumphant *pout* Moth poked her way as she left?

Myfanwy was going right off Moth! Moth had *ummed* and *ahhed* about swapping rooms, so now who knew if that was still happening? Yes she had a beautiful voice, but she also had this annoying way of sort of *pushing* her head forward when she said significant words, and then withdrawing it with delight, like she'd just breathed out a fairy. Plus without admitting it, Myfanwy had sort of hoped "Syn" would catch on as a shortening of "Mnemosyne," but Moth was adamently pushing "Mnemo," which someone said was a one-finned Disney fish. Which could be cool, to be fair, it was just — well, she felt like she and Moth both thought of each other as really shallow.

That pair of trashionistas were obviously up to something, but Myfanwy didn't care enough to feel left out.

She had Pad now.

And of course, Myfanwy thought, as she and Paddy made their way to Red Box noodle bar, and Paddy instinctively bent forward and cootchie-cooed at an oncoming empty push-chair, *I have my ongoing investigation . . .*

*

"I reckon I know how spoons were invented," Paddy said. Myfanwy slurped some noodles quizzically. "Lao Tzu lifts a piece of water chestnut with his chopsticks. *Voilà*!"

"Lucky it wasn't broccoli. Spoons would be so *weird*."

They'd shared wor teip dumplings. Now she was having ho fun noodles with chicken with carrots, sugar snap beans, baby sweetcorn with black pepper sauce. Paddy was having udon noodles with beef, bak choi, water chestnuts and shitaake mushrooms, with chillis and onions and stuff, in red Thai curry sauce.

"The ramifications could be huge," said Paddy.

"God, Kitty is my BFF but sometimes I feel like I can't say stupid stuff to her." Myfanwy slurped messily.

"How is Kitty anyway? After this morning an' ting?"

But Myfanwy had her own agenda. "I can't *believe* Veil went to all that effort," she pondered, "to get a muse who was already dead."

"Wha'? You change topics so suddenly, fam. We was just talking about Kitty."

"Genevieve Quaker, the Tudor muse. Her portrait got nicked last night."

The wall just a little paler, where she had hung . . . for how *many years . . . ? Time to find out!*

Paddy shrugged. "Or early this morning."

"Naaah," said Myfanwy, now concentrating on noodles.

"Serious, fam. How do you know it *was* Veil who jacked it?" Paddy insisted. "Oi Myffed, dare me to down this whole box?"

A tiny fragment of chili pepper fell from his chopsticks back into his box.

"Oh my days!" said Myfanwy. "There were *bare* Veil in your room last night!"

"*Yeah*, but Vert didn't go near the library."

"*One* of them must have. My money's on Germ using, like, Jedi mind tricks. Oh my God, that's pure oil! Oh you are disgusting, Paddy!"

"Mmm," he said, smacking his lips. "Yeah, and now my oil tank's full. Should we get going? Where is Kitty?"

"In a sec, but just while I have you alone, I wanted to ask you — don't look so scared!"

Paddy laughed and scratched his head.

"I wanted to ask about Chancelhouse," Myfanwy continued. "Sometimes Blake acts like it's hundreds of years old. Sometimes he implies it isn't. It's almost like he cultivates the uncertainty for a purpose. What do you think? How old is it really?"

Paddy shrugged and grinned. "I think you're right. The elder muses want us to think beyond those sorts of questions. I remember this thing Meletē said to me once. 'Merlin! Soldier!'"

"Is that meant to be Brummie? You musn't attempt accents, Paddy. It hurts people. People get badly hurt."

"'Merlin! My boy! Think of the modern city of Rome, yeah? Is *that* the same city as was once capital of the Roman Empire? Or two different cities? You can trace their continuity. At the same time, you're tracing discontinuity! Things are constantly replaced as you go from one city to the other. As a *counterexample*, yeah, think of a secret society, only founded six years ago, but with a forged history going back to the Roman Empire!' 'Whoa, sergeant Meletē, that's *amazing*!'"

"You're actually having difficulty doing your own accent now."

"'Imagine the homework was meticulous, Merlin, and the secret society really did replicate values and traditions which were current, like, back in the day. *Now* say the person who forged the history *dies*, so no one in the secret society even knows it's fake. *Is* it fake? Is it real?' 'Whoa!' 'Who are the true inheritors of Rome, Merlin? Is it the secret society, or is it the Laughing Yoga club that happens to meet in the Coliseum on Tuesdays?' 'Whoa! Whoa! Whoa!'"

"What do *you* think though?" Myfanwy demanded, amid self-amused Paddy's chuckles. "About Chancelhouse, I mean? Forget the elder muses, forget all their smoke and mirrors."

Paddy shrugged. He didn't meet her eye.

"Paddy! You *know* something, don't you?"

"No, I —"

"Don't hold back on me!"

"Me and Static were just talking." He hesitated. "It's just that —"

"You think you're standing tall for *Static?* This ain't just Merlin and Mnemosyne here, Pad! It's *you* and *me!* Mates before muses, yeah?"

"Fam, it's getting late — I guess you'll want to hit up the yard to dump that beast?" Paddy indicated Myfanwy's bag. "Maybe later —"

"Don't exploit gendered paraphenalia and don't change the damn subject! *Now*, Paddy! *Anything* you can share with Static, you can share with *me*."

Paddy bit his lip and sighed. "Me and Static made a theory. Under your hat, fam?"

"Safe."

"Chancelhouse could be old or young, or freakishly *both* like Ant and Dec."

"Sorry, Anton —"

"Never mind, *whatever*, yeah? But how old is the muse talent? What if Chancel has been a magical society since back in the day . . . but never had *magic* till now? Or what if we had the magic . . . but the magic wasn't *real* yet?"

"You mean the laws of this world changed?"

"In a sense. So that magic which never worked before suddenly did."

"Okay. In a certain sense that would be both old and young. But what's your evidence?"

"It's not exactly an 'evidence' kind of thing." Paddy laughed. "It sounds crazy, but when you start distrusting your senses . . . you try to use reason alone! See, when the elders talk about Genevieve Quaker, Chancelhouse, Hermes Trismegistus, Hieronymian arcana . . ."

"Hellfire Club, links with occultists, angelographers, blond shamans and bokors . . ."

"Exactly, Soviet military telepaths, Order of the Golden Dawn, Kabbalastic theosophers and cryptographers, all dem ting, down through the centuries. . . it all feels *solid*, you get me?"

"I guess. I'm not so sure."

Paddy laughed extravagantly and slapped his hands on the sides of his head. "These mandem sought esoteric wisdom, trust! But is there any evidence that they ever *used* it? Why do they remain in the shadows, never appearing on the world stage? Where is Faust? Where is Merlin?"

"Sitting in front of me."

"Sitting in front of you, fam."

"Safe," said Myfanwy. "So let's say Chancelhouse and its precedents developed some of the theory to use the muse talent. But none of them ever had the talent itself! The talent has to be inborn, inherent. Then finally one day someone innately blessed — probably Blake — stumbled upon some ancient grimoire . . . and *kapow* . . ."

Paddy looked briefly at the top of her head. "Yeah," he said.

"Paddy! That's not quite it, is it? There's more!"

"Well . . . okay. It's about that 'inborn' bit. How much do you know about the different muse classes?"

"Enough to be confused. There are three basic families, right? Caster, taker, patterner."

He nodded. "And there's this caster specialism called a touchless. Veil have a couple of 'em. Heptapora is one — she doesn't need to touch your skin to flip you. She just needs to *see* you."

Myfanwy shivered. "Does Chancelhouse have any touchlesses?"

"Nope. We've got pure casters out the kazoo, plus a couple of other specialist casters — drivers like Thorn and Golem and one big old skiller, Meletē. Rook and Eft are trying to specialise as doolittle or dryad casters, but they're not ready yet."

"I think Rook's getting close," said Myfanwy, thinking darkly on the snitch pussycat Flux.

"Haverers technically come into the caster family too," Paddy added. "You and Kitty know Moth, yeah? She's one. Haverers don't use the same access points, so they can't flip full memories, not without special patterner help. On their own, they just flip scraps — stuff we call hoverware and neverware. Anyway. That's not the important point."

"Wow. That clears that up."

"Okay, sorry. *This* is the important point. We blazons are part of *another* crew. Not casters, not patterners, but takers. Technically blazons are the taker version of haverers, get me? We take little scraps of hoverware that won't be missed, then inspect them for traces of the muse talent. But *some* takers are *way* more impressive than even me, fam. There's this one Chancel kid Marinade, he's a pure taker. He has the *reverse* of your caster talent —"

"I know Yuri," said Myfanwy. "He's our little mate."

"He can split you open, have a nose around and suck out whatever he likes. Of course he loses something of his own. Pretty precious class. Veil have some taker-skillers, taker-drivers and taker-doolittles but they only have two pure takers — go by Undine and Leech."

Myfanwy wrinkled up her nose. "Nice. So takers can read your mind? So they can choose which bit to take?"

"It ain't exactly like that. It's like they can't understand it properly till they've actually taken it. Marinade could explain it, if you really want to know. He's terrified to use it though. I've never seen him do it."

"Poor Yuri. I almost fancy him, you know. Lol! But I'm worried I might get two weeks into a relationship with him, then realise what I *really* wanted was to let him out of his cage for twenty minutes for a bit of a runaround in his ball. But listen, so what on earth does all this have to do with Chancelhouse's origins? With the muse talent?"

"I'm coming to that. The hypothesis is that there exists a place where muse talents are more common. It could be somewhere far away, or somewhere hidden in some way. Me and Static just call it the Other Place."

"Hypothetical, right?"

"So far it is. Now just suppose there was someone with a talent similar to Marinade's in the Other Place. A taker muse. Say they had something like Heptapora's touchless talent too, only a bit more advanced — this muse wouldn't even need to *see* you, they could just *find* your mind, anywhere in the cosmos. Even across whatever it is that separates *us* from *them*. Let's call this muse . . . master taker class!"

"Hypothetical too, right?"

"Hypothetical, but not far off what we already know exists. And imagine one day this someone — or *something* — is fishing around as usual, but this time when it takes, it doesn't just exchange some trivial aspect of itself." Paddy paused.

"What?"

"It loses its muse talent."

Myfanwy pondered, excitement growing in her chest. "Oh," she breathed. "Wow! If someone in our world suddenly became this, like, master vamp class, or whatever . . . they might be able to . . . to steal even more powers! Steal them right out of the Other Place! Then, as soon as they sucked up their first caster talent, they'd be able to distribute talents here. Paddy, you're a genius!"

"Well, maybe," he laughed. What a lovely laugh. She'd never noticed before. "It would explain why there were no muses for so long, and now a sudden proliferation."

"Why didn't the Other Place just suck the talents back?"

"Beats me. Maybe there was only ever one master taker."

Myfanwy glanced round the noodle bar. There'd been nearly a complete change of cast since they'd first arrived. "But it's all still speculation," she said. "And who? *Who* here is supposed to have done this? Blake? Aoide? Jasper?"

"You've got him on the mind, don't you? *If* it's true, then either it's someone who has never shown themselves . . . or else someone, whether Veil or Chancelhouse, has been hiding the full extent of their talent. My money's on Blake. Why is he so keen to complicate the past? To allude to these . . . grey areas of origin and provenance?"

"Because *he's* a thief too," said Myfanwy. "And perhaps a liar. So maybe the muse talent isn't inborn at all. Maybe *he* distributes it! That would explain why both Kitty and I have it. He gave it to us the day we showed up. He was eager to shake hands, I remember."

"Well . . . more likely he just wanted to blazon you. I lent him my talent while I was away. But I tell you what, fam. Whenever I see Blake work, I just have a funny feeling he's not just a pure caster. Remember, my funny feelings can be pretty valuable."

"But what —"

"Seriously, Myffed? Can we get *going* now? That's basically it. That's basically all we've come up with, me and Static."

"I'll think about it. You're right though. I need to get to that club."

"So back to dump bags?"

"Nah," said Myfanwy thoughtfully. "No time now, but they probably have a check in the club. Fingers Piano Bar, sounds classy, right?"

She hefted it onto her shoulder and they wove through the tables.

"Hell have you got *in* there anyway?" said Paddy. "Women are insane."

"Tonight," admitted Myfanwy, "I maybe *feel* a bit insane."

Or just uncharacteristically tolerant of casual gender essentialism.

"A'ight, it's gonna go off. Don't be winding up on me, make all dem piff honeys think you my girl, yeah?"

"There are *so* many things wrong with that statement."

"And give me Kitty's number so's I can text those guys?"

"*Those* losers? We see 'em or we don't. Wooh! Wooh! New Town, here we come! . . . why are you laughing at me?"

"Nothing," said Paddy. "Just so good to see you again."

*

Myfanwy never really believed she'd get into the club.

She was convinced the other muses would sail on with a good fair wind in their IDs, whilst her and maybe Static would BOINNNG back from the bouncer's weirdly friendly belly, WEEEEEEE, and roll all the way back to HQ and into bed, pointlessly pissed — a waste of getting wasted! But here she was, in da club, drinking it all in, and yeah, dancing! Clinking shot glasses now with these deliriously thrusting arms, downing some kinda spicy booze called "Unicum" — though apparently it wasn't the *real* Unicum you got wherever you were unfortunate enough to be getting the *real* Unicum — downing this fake spicy booze which was neither disgusting nor lovely exactly but sort of All Of The Above, and which was *just about* tipping her over the edge into the realms of Ba-Dunk-A-Drunk, and now she was, in additional to all this, wiggling her elbows and wrists in the air and making this sound: "Woooooooo! Woooooooo!"

Her eyes watered and her throat burned. Planet Unicum, *heyyy!* It was her, um, *third* Unicum? — totes unecessary because they'd all shared this bottle of voddie on the way, elegantly discarding the glass in a recycling bank conveniently and, for all she knew, *deliberately* located on the corner of the street where da club stood, but now Rook was buying her these Unicums, and it would be churlish not to impair her judgement further!

"THEY'RE GROWING ON ME!" she yelled to Rook.

"WHAT?"

"UNIYUM!"

"EH?"

Although she really better drink no more Uniyum, if she was to maintain her sense of higher purpose, and of questing for true knowledge, and of the Enlightenment as a Work in Progress, which was what this outing was all about.

"WOOOOOOO!"

The giddy, fragrant jostle of bodies bish-bash-boshed her, or she bish-bash-boshed them. But she *had* to keep madly dancing or she'd set into this stickiness! Bird lime *and* lad lime. She was totally mortified by her own massive bag, around which she and Bee and Static and Rook and Triffid were now worshipping ecstatically. The DJs had been playing chart stuff somehow woven wub-wubbier for the club, and they threw in some indie stuff, Killin' Kittenish and Bird Bird and False Flags and stuff. Next they danced to Too OK, Death of Pringle — during which a fourth Unicum! — Octet, Dig Oubliette, Eleven Days — Unicum! She went to the loo again during No Class. Next they danced to Blade Pitch Control Unit and Flash Bang and something she didn't know! But sugar, was it a banger or *what?* Time moved quickly, she kept forgetting exactly why she was here.

"Wooooo," that's your answer to everything, isn't *it Mnemosyne?*

Everyone kept calling her "Making-a-Scene" like it was her Party Callsong or something! At least from a distance her epic bag might look like a cairn of bags — result! Nearby danced Kitty, Moth, Kermitcrab, Atë, Sylph and Tar — at first she'd thought Tar was everyone's chaperone, but she was starting to worry everyone was *Tar's chaperones.* Tar would make, for example, lewd gestures!

Hmm!

Through the dancing Myfanwy glimpsed a shape thrown by Moth and surreptitiously incorporated it into her own system. They were dancing to a One Occasion song now. One day, she marvelled woozily, maybe she could borrow a piece of anyone she fancied, flip with anyone she fancied. Clubs, that was where you could just browse and pick and choose. Everyone just boshed into everyone, everyone brushed lingeringly past, dancing peremptorily, walking towards friends, sloshing around together, shrugging off fragrance and sweat. Clubbers don't question touch!

Ooh, that was close — they might question touch if Triffid punched them! A City Break Weekend song was playing now, and Triffo had a dangerously epi and kata-esque dance style, correlated to invisible assailants, not beats.

"TRIFFID, IS YOUR FAVOURITE MUSIC 'RHYTHM AND MUSE'?"

Clubs! The *best* place for wordplay!

"WHAT? YOU'RE SO DRUNK! ARE YOU OKAY?"

Had it been *that* bad a pun? She threw some Swing-style eggbeater shapes into the mix, almost dislocating a shoulder, and was abashed as Static, Bee and Triffid instantly alluded to them. Uh-oh, was *she* really calling the steps here? Was there no one more qualified in Cool Kid in this particular spinning discolet teacup than she was? Bad sign, Making-a-Scene! She shifted to a shy, conservative two-step and tiptoed up to Triffid's ear again.

"IS YOUR FAVOURITE MUSIC 'RHYTHMLESS BLOWS'? WOO."

Oh, God, she felt sick! Now some epic Failcore tune tore Triffo's attention off to the left and suddenly he and Kitty were bashing into Myfanwy's side then away into the jostle, jumping up and down and headbanging and holding each other's arms for dear life. Obviously the flannel had been effective. God, Bee had vanished too! It was just Myfanwy, Static and Rook! Aw-kward! She waved her arms sinuously like a virtuous peasant girl with traditional mores.

"ROOK? YOU'RE *DEID*!"

"WHAT?"

"I *SAID* . . . I AM A *MUSE-LIM* FROM AN *EXTREMELY* . . . CONSERVATIVE FAMILY!"

"WHAT?"

"UH . . . NOTHING! *WOOOOOOOOO!*"

*

She had some memory missing from that night.

In the days that followed, Chancelhouse seemed *infested* by its inhabitants. Names, classes, callsongs, voices, reputations, precedents, parallels, projections, qualities and apparitions packed Valhalla, swarmed the stairs and corridors, tore the pool water white and reverberated behind every suddenly very thin wall. They must have been attracted indoors by the warmth, the dry, the abundant food, and their names on the doors to their rooms. How dare they!

There was Lego and Tase, Triceratops and Thorn, Nova and Puck, Rook and Static, Kermitcrab and Golem, Ouzo and Tar, Sylph and Neilo, Atë and Horae. There were Grimalkin and Eft, who lived on Myfanwy and Kitty's corridor and lurked in their kitchenette without ever seeming to create anything in it, and moved the girls' snacks around without even stealing them. Grimalkin was a scarily-muscled caster covered in colourful Biblical tattoos, with biceps almost as big as his bald head, a big bald head around which a set of bright scarlet headphones were invariably snapped and blaring tinnily. These headphones, Myfanwy soon learned, were not to be disturbed on account of (for instance) a charming new neighbour making wittily friendly overtures, whilst carefully not mentioning any startling new geography re any boxes of Earl Grey teabags. The only person Grimalkin ever perturbed his perpetual blare for was Meletē, and even then he didn't actually *remove* his headphones, only sort of cock one can and nod gloomily without speaking.

Eft was altogether a more heartening presence, a middle-aged Latina-ish woman from New Orleans who basically looked like a twig with a large nose. Eft was a caster too, developing herself as a dryad subclass.

"I got two boys," she said, as if this explained absolutely everything.

"Oh. Um. So you were on Operation Terpsichore?"

"Oh, sure was! Are you kidding me? Then after Spring Feast it's over the pond for cosy old Operation Almar. I wanted to go on Clover, but Aoide was like, 'Uh-uh! You've had enough excitement for a while, lady!'"

"I'm not allowed on missions till I learn to flip," Myfanwy admitted. "What's Operation Almar? Is it top secret?"

"Well of *course*, honey! We're gonna be at the Michigan Caucuses shaking some important folks' hands. Pity we don't have a muse baby for 'em to kiss! But after Terpsi, it all sounds like a vacation."

"I bet Veil have a muse baby," Myfanwy smiled. "They've very advanced like that."

"Well, I like rumbling with Veil as much as the next guy. And it's kinda neat to be influencing world affairs too. When I was your age, I just knew I was special. I thought I'd be a big celeb. Now I'm a secret agent! Just the opposite!"

"Hey, you're a big celeb within Chancelhouse," said Myfanwy. "Blake's always talking about your research. Casting into vegetable matter, right?"

Eft laughed. "You make me sound like I wanna flip with an eggplant! Yeah, the elders say I got the potential, but I dunno. Feels more like homework than research. It's good they push me, I guess. I'll get there, or I won't."

"Hey," Myfanwy then added in a low voice, "What about our other neighbour, that Grimalkin guy? Is *he* going on this — Operation Almar?"

"*That* guy?" Eft didn't lower her voice. "Who *knows*, right? Well, I've been yakking your ear off! Must be the pits, yakking with an old broad like me . . ."

It was possible of course Grimalkin just didn't speak much English. Chancelhouse HQ now also rang out with Greek and Russian and Chechen, and Polish and Turkish and Tsotsitaal, and strange fuddled dialect and patois and mongrel macronics and abundant and profligate code-switches.

There were friendly faces and closed ones, young ones and old ones, attractive ones and scary ones. There were casters, who were furthermore skillers or drivers or whevs, and there were patterners, who were furthermore cutters or cloisters or whevs. It was too much. It was impossible to remember everything. Besides, the recent mutabilities to which Myfanwy had lately been introduced made her unusually reluctant to align the particulars into neat silhouettes, to commit them to her Dwelling or commend them to her heart.

"Ouzo seems a bit Lewis Porteous," Myfanwy commented to Kitty one day.

Lewis Porteous was this one boy they both knew from St Jerome's, whose Thing was he never gave anyone a straight answer, to the point that he was often found gleefully orating to enraged mobs, and in serious danger of life and limb.

"Tar seems a bit Sarah Cameron," said Kitty.

Sarah Cameron was this one girl they both knew from St Jerome's, whose Thing was she always attributed stuff that happened to her to her amazing looks. Like, when creepy men came up to her it wasn't because they were creepy, it was because she was just irresistibly amazingly hot, and when females hated her, it was "because they resented her." *The tragic thing,* Myfanwy thought, *is Sarah's not even that . . . but no point thinking like that.*

"Which one is Tar again?" she asked.

"The one that's a bit Sarah Cameron," said Kitty. "Oh, don't give me Blank Face. The yummy quasi-elder. The one that egged on Triffid and Kermitcrab to snog in Fingers. Like they needed it."

"Lol," said Myfanwy, pretending to remember.

Past midnight, descending barefoot the stairs to the Frigidarium, towel for a scarf, Myfanwy envisioned herself surfacing from her dive to hear someone's huge muscled body and addled brain crashing into the waters behind her, and shivered.

Kitty somehow had already firmly established a separate and glamorous existence among these hordes of homecoming heroes. She shared complex nth-iteration private jokes with muses Myfanwy had barely even *glimpsed* before. Where did she find the time?

Nor were the hallowed Chancelhouse corridors and chambers hers to storm around in any more, since round every corner lurked a collision to take the wind out of her sails. Nor could Myfanwy wander aimlessly to get her head straight, since every door might creak open to awkward encounters or accurate but unhelpful directions, which would put her head crooked again. Nor were these corridors and chambers any more her emporium of obscure artefacts, of sun-bleached cedarwood, say, or the mossy turns of a mounted antler — forms endlessly absorptive of her attention and elusively alchemical with her mood — since some muse was always liable to bustle by and destructively elucidate what this thingy meant to them, or worse, shoot her a funny look and breeze past.

She'd already been murdered.

It was as though the drunken Throwing of Shapes had not quite ended when they walked sweat-streaked out of Fingers into that cool night, as though the delirious dancing and glancing had lingered and transcended, snuck into the fabric of quotidian existence.

Some days, Myfanwy escaped the new oppressive bustle, into the chilly gardens behind the east houses, or into sports-addled grass of the Meadows. Accompanied by Kitty or Triffid or Moth, but mostly by Paddy, she gradually explored the city of Edinburgh, probing this way and that. In the Grassmarket, on the Royal Mile, down by the canal or all the way up to Lethe or to Stockbridge. She saw the people more vividly than the buildings. Perhaps it was because she so seldom could recapture the sense of dreamy, rose-like light which had seemed to fill this place when it was just the Citadel, before it had its everyday name printed on every world map. She realised that, as beautiful as Edinburgh could be, the memories Jasper gave her weren't just a memory of a place. It was a memory of a place at a time — a time of being in love.

*

A fragment of spring must have got lodged in winter, and for two or three days the hazy sun fell through dense leafless twigs.

One morning it all got too much for Myfanwy.

"It's not just being *inside*," she told Simi. "It's being *underground*. Honestly, I knew Chancelhouse had moles, but not like *this!*"

The Master Mystagogue relented, and the girls were allowed to defer studies for a few hours and escape into the sun. The deal was they'd make it up after supper.

Myfanwy briefly wondered if mentioning the mole hadn't been exactly a moment of genius. But, *meh*. By now the sunflower in her was calling all the shots, and the time for subtlety was way past — in her great soligenous haste, Myfanwy even forgot her bag, abandoning it dangling from an antler of the Myometrium arctrainer — dancing up out into the dazzling day.

Kitty made straight for the roof terrace, with a grim and warlike aspect, and a boutique tube of, like, Factor 0.3 sun paste in one hand, for some socially quasi-sanctioned self-harm. Myfanwy texted Paddy and pretty soon she was strolling out with him, plus Triffid and Static in tow, all out laden with Picnic Things.

On the Meadows, a hazed band blew out just below the horizon, of barbecue smoke sifting the angles of the still-leafless cherry boughs. In the long smoky swatch, hazed beings were chucking balls and soundlessly hallooing.

Static was a big, quiet muse. Her raw pumping arms kept mesmerising Myfanwy today — like the rosy, pulpy flesh of infants. Previously Myfanwy had always seen Static in doo-rags, but today the golden sunshine was allowed to fall upon full glory of her peach-fuzzed pate. She had a pretty face and slightly bucked teeth, and wore thick square glasses. Static was one of the ones who really flocked to Pad in his Merlin persona. There was a lot of kudos for the only active blazon, Myfanwy guessed.

Big man on campus. Little man on hippocampus.

Myfanwy fell behind for a bit, when she stopped to look at wares laid outside a bric-a-brac and antiques shop. On a mossy ledge stood a set of fireplace tools — hearth brush, poker, tongs and Strange Thing dangling from a kind of ornate menorah-type structure, all the silver handles done in the shape of frigates. And at the other end was a box of door handles, like pretty floral dumb-bells, with weird implied invisible doors. But the object which caught Myfanwy's attention was between them.

It was a little tripod, black, branded "SLIK" and bearing the words "Made in Japan." She stared carefully at the knobbly top of it, the packed landscape of bolts and corners, with one large adjustment handle jutting right out like a screwdriver slammed only a little way into a skull.

She shivered.

"Myffed!" — Paddy, noticing she'd fallen behind.

Not far from the Meadows, the foursome picked up the trail of the old Innocent Railway, following it through Holyrood Park to the edge of a wee loch. They were still well within Edinburgh, but if you stood in the right spots every creation of concrete or iron could be concealed, and you could imagine you were deep in the countryside, or perhaps deep in the past. Take a step or two, of course, and a tower block or a crane or crescent of A-road would glide from behind the tree-line.

They ate their Picnic Things and threw scraps for the ducks. Myfanwy didn't say much, but glowed with a sense of acceptance and comfort. The boys talked a lot, obviously. How odd it was. If you were the quiet one, you got to hear all the words — the ones inside your head, and the ones whizzing around it. But if you were the talking one, you only ever heard half the words.

On the boggy, daisy-stubbled bank of the loch, ducks mingled calmly with geese and the odd crow or gull or moorhen. Thuggish swans glid all around nearby, dunking their elegant throats and hating the English.

Myfanwy drifted in and out of Triffid's various soliloquys and Stand-Up Alpha Testing, and out and in of her own soporific fantasies. She watched a duck sit himself down. He took a very long time to get comfy, this duck. His tail wagged, his wings shuddered, again and again he summoned out a subalary webbed foot for One Last Mission of mad scratching, and many bad sequels. Finally he settled into a rhythm, and settled, softly pumping in and out.

Suddenly Myfanwy remembered she'd left her bag on the Arctrainer in the Myometrium.

All around them, ducks started quacking like frogs croaking.

Static was studying her through squinted lashes.

Was Static working for the ducks?

Myfanwy lay with her arm on her face, a smeared black pillar edged by blazes. Totally dorkily she had her History Revulsion with her. She hadn't got past the first page, but it was hardly her fault that interesting little friends kept falling from the sky to her text and doing different stuff.

A dog called Tiffin — called it often — kept confusing Triffid.

"Just go to them," said Static, the umpteenth time Triffid looked up, squintingly alert. "They'll give you a good home."

They walked round a bit, then the boys went in the loch in their boxers. She and Static took off their kicks and tights and splooshed about a bit. The water was chilly. Hundreds of enigmatic green motes were suspended there.

A big drowned bumblebee drifted by.

Myfanwy had a sudden powerful urge to look at news sites, but her phone was in her bag.

Heading back, smug and sun-kissed, they surprised four ducks looking incredibly guilty in some hedgerows.

They followed the path of the Innocent Railway in near silence. It was called Innocent, Triffid explained, because though there had been rails here, there had never been engines. The cars had been pulled along by horses.

"Thank you, Triffo," said Myfanwy. "You are like a little Information Sign." He looked sullen and she impulsively added, "Oh, I *love* little Information Signs!"

Horses meant innocence, and steam meant sin. Barbecue smoke was still billowing as they picked across the Meadows. The halo of a giant archangel, snapped like a glow stick, left to drift lazily to earth.

Thank you, angels!

Myfanwy breathed in the smell of cooking skewers and burgers, and coconut from behind her ears, and hashish from behind the hedge. Among the ordinary litter overflowing from the bins she spied one or two odd things — the peeled skin of a golf ball, a Christmas Tree bauble, and a tiny white fork of indeterminable purpose, like some sea monkey's trident.

As they turned into the road of facing Chancelhouse houses, Triffid asked for her number, in a casual "BTW" kind of way, but her phone was still in her bag. They all said "see yous later" in spontaneous imitation of the locals, and Myfanwy went in, not by her usual door, but one closer to the Myometrium, which happened to be the same green and white doorway where she had met Blake, not so very long ago, though it seemed it.

She went up the broad broken steps, bracketed by elegent wrought iron and surrounded by shattered sea-shell, through two now-familiar corridors — distances grew shorter, as you grew to know places — and down the stairs to Cellar Level Two.

*

There was no one in the pool. Approaching the Myometrium, Myfanwy thought she heard a voice, and paused.

Too muffled. Myfanwy couldn't make out the words. She glanced over the pool to the filter. The machinery groaned and the bubbles wooshed gently. If she could switch it off . . .

Then the voice — Simi's, she thought — rose as if in anger. ". . . *can't play darts in a pub without dunkin' 'em in curare!*" A pause. "*No, the new blood, Nessus and her pal.*" Pause, then something indistinct. Then, "*No, listen. . . . situation. At present, they're up front with me.*" Pause. "*Matter of time, yeah? It has . . . as a fait accompli, so Seuss sees he can't do nothing — no.*" Pause. "*No. No.*" The voice sounded less angry, but much clearer and closer now. "*Yeah. I appreciate that.*"

What had to be done as a *fait accompli*?

The Myometrium's door started to open. Acting on an inexplicable instinct, Myfanwy slipped back across the tiles and through the door. She spiralled up the stairwell.

Paranoia. The perfect end to a perfect day.

Well, she'd be back soon. The bag could wait. And just maybe it would be better for Simi — if it really *was* Simi — didn't know she'd been eavesdropping . . .

*

"Hon, come see," said Kitty, late that night. "I've made a list of the major emotions. I can only feel five of them."

Myfanwy had a look. "You left off 'overdressed.'"

"Ooh, six. That's respectable, yeah?"

News had been esp edgy today. Cannibalism rife in Detroit. MP for Barking and Dagenham hospitalised after getting tarred and feathered at her constituent surgery.

And, OMG, the pyramids had been blown up.

"Kitty, they've destroyed the pyramids."

"Who?"

"Doesn't say. I mean, whoever did it didn't say. Wow. Khufu's Horizon. Chephren, Mykerinos."

"A world without pyramids."

"I mean, definitely without the Giza Necropolis, fam. They were so *old.* OMG, the BBC coverage is *hilarious*. It's so UK-centric. You know how they'd report a genocide? 'British woman feared among 6,000,000 murdered European Jews.'"

Ten minutes in agreeable silence passed and Kitty squealed, "I *knew* my happiness was on the internet in pictoral cat form!"

"You know how this place is full of mysteries?" said Myfanwy. "Do you ever accidentally think, 'Oh, I'll Google that'?"

"I've stopped using Google," said Kitty. "I use BuzzFeed now."

Myfanwy switched from Egyptian rubble to browse old English tales. The bailiffs of Bridge Croft. Police brutality, though the news sites didn't put it that way. Protestors on stilts, burning dust.

Yes.

She'd been there. Bridge Croft could, perhaps, be her Settlement.

Soon she found an image of Molly Miller, the girl who died there. Pretty, square-jawed, with a birthmark swirled around one eye. Frizzy ginger hair.

Nothing like the portrait.

So Genevieve Quaker wasn't Molly Miller. And she wasn't some Tudor witch. So who was she?

"BTW hon," said Kitty breezily. "You know how Madame Merely-Pointy always criticises your ink landscapes for being conceptually vacuous? Why don't you put a tiny droplet, I mean like barely even a vapour, of colourful paint on one distant window or rooftop or something in each one, and retitle the whole sequence 'Homes'? Obv vom-ville but it's the kind of thing they love."

Myfanwy thought about it. "Could do. 'Home', hmm?"

"'Homes,' homey."

"Only Blake couriered my art to the exam board this morning."

"Oh really? Pity. I've been meaning to say for ages."

"It's crazy how bronzed you go in one day."

"Homey, that's just how I roast."

*

Leaves came day by day. The trees sang and let their tiny wings spree out. The girls both got sunburnt one day when Simi was persuaded to hold afternoon lessons in the garden.

"It's like being *branded*," Kitty moaned, as Myfanwy dabbed her back with Solace. This felt a very natural thing to do by the edge of the pool, even deep underground. "Ow! It's alright for *Aoide*. She can't burn."

"Black skin can burn," said Myfanwy. "Paddy burns. Paddy blushes even."

"Yeah? He's lighter than Aiode. Ow!"

"Pantone 71-4, I'd call Paddy."

"What a weird thing to know. Art geeks gross me out."

"That's not from Art. I don't remember how I know it."

"I bet even Paddy Smurf would blush bright red for you, Myfanwy."

"Shut it, yeah?"

"Shut your *legs*, bitch. Ow!"

They were dangling their legs in the pool. Kitty lay back on the tiles and stared upward. Myfanwy followed suit. Loops of reflected light moved on the raftered ceiling.

They were both in a kind of crazy mood. Myfanwy had made good progress in the garden, but it was still a total surprise when Simi announced, with grave solemnity, that the girls were ready for their first flip.

It was to take place first thing in the morning. Blake and Meletē were coming to watch.

Terror was giving way to excitement. *To finally be in control of myself!* thought Myfanwy. *Not to have some guy forcing myself into me . . .*

Kitty interrupted the reverie. "Merlin seems a bit Patrick Akifemwe to me," she said.

Myfanwy giggled. "You mean Paddy seems a bit Paddy to you? Whoa! Way to mind-blowingly toy with the nature of identity and personal continuity, fam!"

"Ta."

"Static seems a bit Kevin Thomas."

"Meany," said Kitty. "Static more reminds me of the boss in that helicopter game me and Lewis were obsessed with. You remember?"

"Do I *remember*? I nearly lost you to that thing, fam! Old school top-scroller, arcade vibe. Trick was to frontload all the risk and get massively powered up early on, then just sit in the middle of the screen and hold down space bar, making this, like, Flower of Death. Donations to my high score, in lieu of flowers in synanthy. I just made a clever joke but you'll have to take my word for it. Somehow the game was probably a metaphor for your abortive relationship, but I never really worked that out."

"Well, whevs. Static reminds me of the final boss on the first level, yeah? She's this Alien Bogie that takes up half the screen and just slowly follows her pre-arranged flight path arabesques. For once you actually do have to shoofty your Flower of Death to the bottom of the screen, because she would just crush you, dude. I mean, she just keeps coming."

"And *this* isn't mean?"

"Wait wait wait. She's also kind of weirdly elegant and she knows what she's about and she has all these extra turrets and attachments and things, which you have to defeat individually. Her and Merlin seem pretty close, BTW. I think one day he might be one of her little gun turrets. How do you feel about that, Mnemosyne?"

"Just fine, Nessus."

"So while we're on the topic, I have a suspect for the painting theft," Kitty added. "Paddy is an artful dodger like yourself. A soulful dude and so forth. I think Paddy pinched it."

"*Paddy?* I have serious cause to doubt that. Trust me."

"Only because of that massive bag he had with him last weekend? When we went clubbing? Think about it! Before Fingers, he arrived late to the bar, right? Don't worry, I'm not going to grass him in or anything."

Myfanwy stared incredulously at Kitty. This was *so* typical. "Kitty! You *know* where he was before Fingers!"

Kitty kept staring at the ceiling. "Eh? No, I don't know weird stuff like that, hon. C'mon, hear me out! Don't be blinded by your love horniness. What if, just before Fingers, Paddy went to get the portrait appraised? He found out it wasn't worth much. He flew into an incensed rage. He decided to take it back. Why else would he be schlepping that huge —"

"That was *my* bag," said Myfanwy, determined not to lose her temper. "Before the club, *I* was with Paddy *the whole time, you total idiot!* — we *went* to Red Box Noodle and we all up *invited* your ass! — and you even *said* you were coming! — and then you went off with *Moth* and anyway that was *my* bag which Paddy only carried on the way *back* from the club to be *sweet* to me! *Aaaaaargh!*"

"Okay," said Kitty calmly. "First of all, jam your hype. Picture a baby pangolin. Second, there goes that theory, but it was still great. Is it *my* fault Paddy's not an international art thief?"

"Oh, God! What *is* it you have against him, Kit? Seriously. Why are you always trying to *slander* him?"

"Fam, null."

Kitty hummed a passage of Scarletti, cut and pasted some Sugababes accidentally at one point.

Myfanwy's legs felt cold.

"I think I'm going up in a sec," she grumbled.

Myfanwy scooched back on the tiles. She sat up, cross-legged, staring blankly at her chlorine-pickled gooseflesh.

"If you *must* know," said Kitty. "Moth and I are part of an internal team who investigate instances of muse-conduct. We're completely deniable, we're accountable to no one."

"You mean you made yourselves up."

"At present, the team consists of me and Moth. As you will notice from our memberships roll, we are an elite taskforce. The Moth-Ness Monster Protection Programme, if you will. Now, we have been *considering* you and Triffid. The issue with Triffo is — would he try and bring in Kermitcrab? And the issue with *you* — would you bang on about bringing in Merlin and Marinade? You see our predicament."

"If Merlin and Marinade aren't good enough for you," said Myfanwy, "neither am I."

"I have a secret," said Kitty.

"What?"

Silence.

"*What?*"

"Now that you know of the taskforce's existence," Kitty began.

"You and Moth."

"Yes. Don't you want to know where it was headed the other night?"

"Um. Sushi? I'm sorry, hon. I just don't —"

"*Listen,*" hissed Kitty. "From time to time, Moth gets sent to fetch stuff from the deli. The door between the east houses and the deli locks automatically behind you. You return through the street . . . but when it's *raining*, Blake usually lends her his keycard."

Kitty paused, as if daring Myfanwy to butt in. Myfanwy kept her mouth shut. She was hooked.

"The west houses," Kitty continued, "requires a secret combination, different to the deli. Obviously, *I* know what that combination is."

"You're kidding. What?"

"The night when Meletē took us west side to tool up, I channeled dappy, leant over his shoulder, and checked out what numbers he keyed in. So me and Moth made our plan, that the next time Blake lent her his card —"

Myfanwy sprung up. "OMG! You guys snuck into the west houses?"

Kitty lay with her sunburnt legs waving under pool water, golden hair spread on the tiles like a halo. She grinned a proud, lazy grin. "Gimme those props, hon."

Myfanwy snapped fingers with her and shoogled round to sit cross-legged at the edge of the halo. "Oh, Kitty! You've *always* wanted to sneak into the west houses! Wait, *shh* — don't tell me what you found."

Kitty had hysterics, kicking up big fountains of pool water, splashing them both.

"Hey!" laughed Myfanwy. "Hey!"

"Oh, it's hilarious," said Kitty's upside-down face. "It's nothing bad. It's just —"

"I'm serious, Kitty. Shut up. You're my BFF. I love you. I have an idea."

Upside-down Kitty looked at her wide-eyed.

"Kitty, I want you to do something for me now. I want that memory. I don't want you to *tell* me. I want you to *give* it to me. Let's go back upstairs to our room, Kitty, and flip. You know we're ready. Let's *flip*."

*

Moth came by with the keycard. Myfanwy was acting zonked and dorky and there was zero point in taking her along.

"What about Mnemo?" Moth whispered as they left. "Don't you want to —"

She scoffed. "Cramp our style. Let me see the keycard, hon."

"Here," said Moth nervously. "Blake wants quorn mince. We got maybe fifteen minutes, then he may come looking."

"You can say you thought he said 'unicorn mince,' that's why you took so long."

Descending the stairwell, they met Tar hurrying the other way.

She studied Tar's smooth, deep Mediterannean complexion and vaguely Eastern European features, her large, heart-shaped face, long elegant eyes and thin lips — usually animated, given to lively clowning, hyperbolic gasps and grins, but this evening rather drawn and tired. A beauty spot of the sort that just bordered on Ordinary Gross Mole, in terms of camber and basic bulkiness, graced Tar's left cheek.

There was something scandalous about Tar's shimmery, spacious, shoulder-length hair. Like bunches of black grapes, ironed out under the heels of hicks.

God. If Myfanwy couldn't even do something with her hair, how could she hope to do something with her life?

Today Tar was rocking double denim with a beige tank top under her jacket, lol.

"Hello, hello, hello, hello," Tar said, as if incredibly busy, or addressing each riser. "Where you going?"

"Errands for Blake," Moth blurted.

She just nodded and kept quiet. She quite enjoyed Tar — especially that she looked amazing for her age — but no way did she trust her. Besides, Tar was old school bad ass, one of the nine original muses.

"Oh my God," Tar said. "Aren't we all doing errands for Blake?" She laughed hollowly as she passed.

"So shall we call it off?" Moth whispered. "We've been seen."

"Are you kidding*?"*

Outside it was gloomy and lightly spitting. Puddles dappled the pavement with reflected lamplight. No one about. Curtains were drawn in most of the east windows and of course all of the west.

The wind was rolling an empty milk carton around as they crossed the road. Organic Full Fat, she recognised, with a vague and inexplicable anger.

"Anyone watching?" said Moth.

Those few windows whose curtains weren't drawn were a little further up the street. "I don't think so," she said briskly. "We'll have to risk it."

They mounted the stairs.

For a moment her pounding heart sank as she grew sure the stolen keycard wouldn't work, or that the code would have changed or something, or that she'd misremembered it.

Now they were in, navigating the long gloomy corridors by the light of their phones.

Moth kept toying with her labrette. It was really, really stressing her out. She was about to say something, or possibly rip it out, *when —*

"Kitsy, shh!" said Moth, and touched her arm.

They paused.

She could hear a voice, behind one of the walls. Too low to make out words. Moth looked at her wide-eyed.

She ignored her gutless squire and on impulse swished her phone low over the formica floor, searching out specks of dried blood. Myfanwy had been totally trailing it everywhere from those two steaks she'd been using for feet, the night they met Meletē.

Pristine. Maybe someone had been scrubbing.

God, how awkward and embarrassing. She hoped nobody thought it had been her *blood. Anyway, she hadn't come here to be reminded how gauche and obvious Myfanwy was, particularly whilst wounded. Why* had *she come here?*

She wasn't sure. As they crept onwards the voice diminished. The floor beneath them did not creak.

"How long has it been?" said Moth.

"Since you met me, five minutes and thirty seconds," she said, totally making it up. "Let's try in here."

The device over the door was difficult to make out. She pressed her ear against the door. Nothing.

She tried the handle, and the door opened.

"I'm gonna risk the light," said Moth. "You think?"

"Do it, mate."

Light flooded along a spacious, messy technological workshop. There were four long tables, all covered with computer towers in various states of disassembly. Strewn among them were bezoars of cords and coloured wire, headphones, goggles, and clipboards and stray items of whimsical stationery. A set of floral, sawtoothed pinking shears seemed a bit out of place. Several ergonomic stools and pouffes, one pouffe fallen on its side. At the far end were a set of large double doors. A few tall rolls of cotton fabrics, like you might get in a haberdasher's, were leant together beside it. Next to them were some more spools, of the kind used by 3D printing machines.

Most of this stuff was probably just shop-related.

She looked at Moth probingly.

"Howay man!" Moth whispered obscurely. "One more an' then back."

The device atop the double doors, also done in black spraypaint stencil, seemed to show a big mask and bearded figure with long curly hair, his arm raised in ambiguous but vehement gesture, perhaps reaching for or fending off the mask. The mask was giant Zorro-type mask, almost as tall as he was.

The doors were already very slightly ajar. She put her palms against them and pushed.

The next space was . . . vast . . . it swept away into deep shadows, so its full dimensions impossible to judge, but she felt sure that the room ran the length of three or more houses. Her view was moreover blocked by a clutter of gloomy, insect-like furniture here by the entrance. Moth was hunting in vain for the light. But meanwhile, as her eyes adjusted a little . . .

OMG.

"What?" said Kitty. "What? What's so funny?" She snatched up her phone. "What did we find?"

In the harbour of soft light that shone about her and Moth's shoulders, there waited a small flotilla of easel-like structures, proudly displaying on-going designs.

And on tables beyond there lay . . . collars, hems, crotches, brims, elbow patches, coiled shiny sleeves crowned by fingerless gloves, the jewelled breasts of queens, an oval snipped from a bandit mask's canthus, a collar, a seam, a sole, all in a billowing tangle, draping over the edges of the tables, here and there spilling to the floor, and all seeming gradually to drain of colour as it flowed away into deepening shadow. There was brocade and brilliantine, cashmere and chiffon, cheesecloth and tweed, flannel and terrycloth, moleskin and taffeta, partridge feathers and skins of otters and lion and ass pelts, and in five or six parts of the scape she caught glimpses, like the fins and breaching backs of soft toys playing at sea monsters, of textures and blanched colours of fantastical syntheses — of tartan denim, and of paisley Goretex — and what were surely eddies of ectoplasm simulating kinks of sheer and light gauze, as if the inverse of a fin de siècle *séance. Impressive, industrial-seeming sewing machines rose at regular intervals, as if island cliff faces. One wore a yellow trilby.*

"Kitsy," said Moth reverently. "Where are we?"

She studied the closest sketch, which aspired to skimpiness suitable for both the town centre and the boudoir. More skin than cloth, and most of the cloth focused in the warlock-inspired shoulderpads. A few figures with little question marks after them. An empty call-out box. Still in progress, obv.

"I know exactly where we are," she said dryly. "Oh, you idiot."

"Don't be mean! I'm no ninny! I'm an explorer*!"*

"Not you, hon. Haduken Blake. He's an explorer too."

The next sketch was even less complete. It conveyed the impression of clothes themselves surprised in a state of partial undress. Despite the patchiness, its aspirations seemed less smouldering — there was a label in a crabbed hand. "Civil Servant Visiting Construction Site #2." In the bottom right corner, the designer was playing with constellations of paint splatter.

She thought back to Blake's wounded look when, just as a joke, she'd mentioned silver jumpsuits. Apparently every possibility was *under consideration.*

"Superheroes," she whispered. "He thinks we'll be superheroes."

"Why is this here?" *moaned Moth.*

"'We are exploring,'" she said, in a stupid, deep voice, "'options for formal attire . . .'"

*

Kitty was in bed, reading her memory on her phone and snickering.

"*That's* not what's interesting," said Myfanwy, pulling her covers up to her chin. "The really important bit's not even in your write-up. But it's in your memory."

"Eh?" Kitty glanced up with a frown. "What is?"

"The voice. You were so taken by the costume factory, the bathetic hilarious secret of the west houses, that you forgot about the *voice.*"

"Serious? What did it say? Are you sure it wasn't just copyright bumf? 'This memory belongs to Catherine Esterhase. Unauthorised copying or transfer prohibited.'"

"You never know. It was too faint to make out the words. But definitely coming from somewhere in the west houses."

"So what's your point?"

"Well, *I* thought I heard a voice before, when we were with Simi and Meletē, and suspected it might be Blake. But this time you had stolen Blake's keycard. So the voice couldn't have been Blake, nor Simi, nor Meletē — then who? A secret elder muse?"

"Meh, I dunno. Sounds like a clue searching for a mystery." Kitty fiddled with her phone then slid it onto the floor. "Could just be some neighbour, no connection with Chancelhouse."

"It sounded really close."

"Or a different voice each time. Blake the first time, Simi or Meletē the second."

Myfanwy was thoughtful. "Perhaps. I hadn't thought about that. Still, your write-up has some funny priorities. Mentioning me traipsing blood everywhere — BTW, I think it would be inappropriate and embarrassing for there *not* to be some blood in the Cache — but nothing about the voice. Don't you think the voice is *important?*"

Kitty groaned and put out the light. Myfanwy spent some moments in the darkness plumping pillows and trying to get comfortable. She thought about Moth for a few moments. Kitty seemed to find her kind of annoying too. Then why were they so bezzy-bezzy, hmm?

Then Myfanwy thought about how Kitty's memory seemed bang on about everybody's skin. Kitty had used anti-wrinkle products from age thirteen, against everybody's advice. They were probably pickling her. She should just take the leap and get herself stuffed and preserved in formaldehyde. What every woman wants.

Myfanwy's train of thought rumbled on into a deep cutting in the trees.

"Kitty," she said eventually. "Remember that shizzle re that rozzer? PC Veitch?"

Kitty sat up. "Oh God, oh God, oh God. Is this something I was meant to do? What? What? Just *tell* me, Myffy!"

"Relax, fam! I'm talking about London, when I freaked in the cop shop. 'You're crooked, PC Veitch. You're a bad cop. You did a bad thing.'"

"Oh yeah." Kitty lay back down. "Lol. Well done. What of it?"

"I remembered recently who PC Veitch is. When we were in about Year Seven, there was a protest in a place called Bridge Croft shown on telly. Afterwards there was a big enquiry, and Veitch gave the key testimony."

"Oh, I remember *that*. The anarchist chick that got splatted. The one with the weird thing on her face."

"Molly Miller."

"Yeah. And the feds merked in her wake. Riots across England! Lewisham Foot Lockers, unlock and unload! Gregg's — trick is, loot it, *then* light it up! Cause of death, smoke inhalation and/or snacks. Also, London gets a new Eye. Result!"

"Legacy, dog. There's more though. I'm pretty sure now Bridge Croft is my Settlement. Jasper must have been at the demo. So was the girl from the painting. Maybe they saw PC Veitch, or saw what she was supposed to have seen."

"So Jasper is a big greenie? Figures. Myffy, lemme play Devil's Advocate —"

"Not sure. Cases against His Satanic Majesty seldom come to court nowadays. The cost of litigation is prohibitive."

"No, that's actually a decent point. Let me play Devil's innovation and co-creation consultancy subcontractor. *Soo*, like, I know capitalism's *bait*, and everything —"

"There *can't* be a 'but,' can there be?"

"*But* what I don't get is what Travellers had to do with it. You know?"

"Does there have to be a direct link? Remember the dude that started the Arab Spring? Molly Miller's martyrdom was a spark for something bigger."

"*Martyr*, Myffed? Eww! This is England! Have you ever seen those awards for people who die in moronic ways, and thus raise the genetic stock of the human race?"

"'*I'm a greenie in a battle*,'" sang Myfanwy. "'*You gotta smear me the right way*.'"

"Well, they were designated green belt land, hon. I'm sure the residents said it was a different belt and everything, but any real greenie would go up against the gypsies. To a real greenie, *all* belts are green. So you have to wonder if some people are just attention-seekers."

"Hon, they were Irish Travellers, not Hexxus, last I checked? Yeah, okay, the council spin doctored the clearance as green policy. That's what alerted many climate activists, right? 'Not in my name.' You can understand that, right?"

"Wow, could you be a little bit more condescending? I'm having a hard time being respected so much. It's not as the council were like, 'Move it, tinkers! This site clearance was brought to you by Molly Miller, the weird thing on her face, and her hippie friends.' And hon, you *can't* say it wasn't a green policy. I'm sorry, you can't! Imagine it from a *leaf's* perspective!"

"Be leaf, fam," Myfanwy soothed. "Conservation was *never* a main driver. It was party politics, pure and simple. A civil disintegration deliverable, right? The MP won her seat by pandering to prejudice. She basically ran on a platform of, like, 'Let's Give Those Bleeding Gyppos What-For, Eh, Giles? That Kyle Chappie's With Us!'"

"You refer," Kitty protested smoothly, "to democracy."

"That's so *brave* of you, pampered metropole! But is it *liberal* democracy? Not sure."

"You split the hairs of democracy."

"They're already split. *You* just wanna airbrush them together again."

"Myffed! Britannia's barnet be unimpeachable, bitch!"

"This convo is outta control. My whole point was, *what* brought me and —"

"Look, I just *genuinely* don't think those sorts of protest are helpful! Pump the countryside with pamphlets, by all means. But get down off the pole before someone bulldozes you off."

"Is it inevitable? Dressed as a wizard?"

"Because wizards are annoying, you mean? I'd say it's up in the air."

"Lol. Only *not.* All I want to say, if you'd just let me, is what brought me and Jasper to Bridge Croft?"

"What brought — Jasper and *his girl* there, you mean."

"As I said. Jasper and Gen. That's what I call her."

Kitty sighed languidly. "So *that's* why you were so obsessed with that portrait, hmm? Bad-ass Jasper Robin and the innocent, wide-eyed ingénue. No wonder you fail so miserably to celebrate me and Moth in our hilarious triumphs."

"Not everything necessarily has to be about you, you know. I'm trying to run an investigation here."

"I'm serious. Don't make me put on this light. Can't you just stop being so paranoid and horny for just one moment? I mean, how can you even know what Jasper's memories all *mean?* My little maidenheaded one?"

"Sugar," said Myfanwy crossly. "At least *I* can *come*."

"That is so *low*," said Kitty. "Do not *ever* knock my loving. *Pervert*."

"Listen! Bridge Croft! There were bare Black Bloc anarchists, church groups, locals supporting their neighbours, some old school folk who were, like, veterans of Dale Farm, and Romany resistance to Sarkozy, and Occupy. I don't think Jasper and Gen fit those categories. There were also bare, bare climate activists at Bridge Croft, and that's more likely — they knew this one Oscar geezer, so they coulda tagged along with him. But I got the vibe they weren't that close before. He just worked for Gen's dad or something. They only really got to know each other *during*."

"Hon," said Kitty, somewhat aggro. "Is any of this going to be on the exam?"

"On the exam?"

"Is *now* the time? I don't just mean because it's late, I mean in general. Of course, it's *sad* the brightly-coloured caravans are put to pasture, it's sad what happened to Molly Miller, but can't you see —"

"Then there were the Bridge Croft residents themselves," Myfanwy continued frostily, "and their friends and families. What if that was it? There's probably a pretty good record of who was pushed off the land! If we could track down some of the families —"

"Oh, God! You're kidding! What could we possibly gain?"

"I'm just saying —"

"And I'm just saying, Myfanwy, that I couldn't possibly bring myself to care. Some girl who died six years ago that nobody remembers. Wow! Some ex boyf or girlf you never even *had*. OMG! It's not about policing tactics, it's not about the rights of your merry ramblers."

"That's not offensive, hon. It's just tasteless."

"You are so *dry* these days! Don't try to dress it up as some kind of political issue. Whenever you talk about politics, Myffy, it's really about *you*. What's your state of mind tonight? Are you dreaming and procrastinating and being socially paranoid and awkward and making yourself feel guilty? Or are you all up in whereinup you need to be? You're living in somebody else's past, Myffy, and it's time you start thinking about *your* future, okay? What you need to ask yourself is, is Chancelhouse really for you?"

"Don't be like that."

"*Is* it, Myffed? I don't mean to be harsh, hon, but all the memories you've tried to flip me have been pretty glitchy, and everything you say about your Dwelling sounds a little Global South to me. What if you never become a proper muse? *Then* what if you don't get the exam results you're looking for? So you lose your uni place as well? This is a crucial time in our lives."

It felt like an impressive pitch. "I guess you're right. At the very least, it can wait till after the exams."

"Whatever. Do what you want. I don't care."

Silence and darkness.

"Scare me half to death?" Myfanwy guessed, by way of a reconciliation.

"One night," intoned Kitty, "Kitty couldn't hear Myfanwy tossing and turning as usual. She put on the light but the other bed was empty. So she crept downstairs for a midnight swim. The water was lovely and warm. Oh, the lights in the pool area weren't working. She went upstairs where she met her friend Triffid. He looked at her in horror. 'Where have you been, Kitty?' 'I've been swimming, Triffid.' 'But the pool heating system has been broken for weeks.' 'It was still lovely and warm.' 'That's because . . . you're covered head to toe in blood!' The end."

"Not your best."

"Only because you don't *get* it," Kitty rejoined irritably. "Your *body* was chopped up and caught in the filtration system."

"Oh I see. You did have a scarytale to tell, didn't you? You just decided to spoil it."

"The blood went round and round. Like a big horrible open heart for everyone to splash in as much as they wanted. Pulse, pulse, pulse, pulse, pulse."

"Goodnight then, Kitty."

"Goodnight, Myfanwy. And they don't pay taxes."

"Neither does your daddy!"

"He doesn't pinch scrap metal though," Kitty pointed out.

"Yeah he does," snapped Myfanwy irritably. "Loads!"

"No, he doesn't."

"Actually he does."

"He doesn't actually. My dad doesn't steal scrap metal."

"True dat, but actually, he does?"

"Yeah, except actually he doesn't?"

"Yeah, your dad steals it, though?"

*

Myfanwy awoke with a start in the darkness, where Kitty was talking.

". . . upon a scary time, there was an ordinary woman of about seventeen or eighteen, Myfanwy Morris."

"I *knew* it!"

"Hush, hon. I'm scaring you half to death ASAP. She was kind and brave and totally erotic, but she was sometimes sad and angry and never trusted anyone, least of all herself, so she fell behind in her studies and soon enough, her life left her behind too. One night she was on Twitter and she looked up. She saw a ghost called Kitty Esterhase. The ghost stood just between the bookshelf and the millefleur curtain. That means 'millions of flowers,' Myfanwy. Myfanwy tried to talk to her. Kitty shook her translucent hair, and for a moment, it was as if the still millefleur were scattered by winds through her locks. Myfanwy could better read the expression of the portrait behind Kitty, than Kitty's own expression."

"Oh Kitty."

"I can't tell you what they talked about, because I don't know myself. But I can tell you this. The very last thing Myfanwy said to Kitty, before she turned through the wall and fled into the night sky, must have been *right*, because it caused Kitty to blush. And when Myfanwy rose and touched a new smudge on the curtain, she found it damp. Kitty had left a little of the blood that had leapt to her cheek. So if Myfanwy had brought a drop of her back, it was just possible she could, bit by bit, bring her back completely. The end."

"I don't —"

"Don't analyse it, hon. Night now."

"Night Kitsy. Thanks. I'm well scared."

"Night, mate . . . elephant chew."

"Yeah. *Gute Nacht. Dir auch.* Elephant YouTube, Kitty."

*

"So you're a taker?"

Myfanwy stood in Yuri's room. One wall was stacked almost to the ceiling with cutesy, multicoloured storage boxes, conveying a mixed vibe of Pride plus lumberjack plaid. The walls were barley white, the bed linen plain white, and the matching white curtains were open to the night. Slid behind the bed like a headboard was a flatpack Ikea bookshelf, taped up and probably never opened. There was a nice A2 piece of lime green paper stuck beside the window. On it was written a column of words like "Courage," "Conversation," "Sensitivity," "Charisma," "Strength," "Kindness," and "Husbandry." Each metric was associated with an axis from "0%" to "100%" but no scores were given. The bottom virtue, "Dancing," was crossed out. One or two were in a kind of Cyrillic script.

Yuri nodded.

"What is it like, looking at a . . . at a person, selecting what part to take?"

"Like social media."

"Oh."

"Very messy tags. Mislabels. Very time-consuming. Can take up day. Very annoying and hateful."

"Oh. Um, more like Twitter, or like Fuckbook?"

"Every eye sees differently. As the eye, so the subject. Every person is like a different social media network with solitary member. One person is maybe Vortex Nexus, next is Twitter, next is Fuckbook, next is Pinterest. It is difficult to describe."

Myfanwy giggled. Yuri had said "Fuckbook."

"I want you to do something for me," she said, very seriously.

Yuri nodded.

"I know we're not supposed to, what with Partnering Rule and everything. But Jasper Robin has given me feelings and memories I no longer want. Can you take them from me? I don't care what you do with them, just —"

He was shaking his little head.

"Oh *Yuri*, please! Why not?"

"If I take them away, I lose my memories to you. Probably," he said with a small bitter smile, "you like those even less."

Myfanwy was crestfallen. "Oh yeah. I forgot how it works. So dumb. Sorry."

"Unless he colludes. Unless I and you and Jasper and a cloister muse, together we create a spellsong to fix memories which now are jumble." Yuri shrugged. "Most memories, at least, we may still fix. My friend Lego or your friend Triffid maybe, could be cloister."

"Thank you Yuri. That makes me feel better."

Myfanwy felt she should say more. She looked at the wall of boxes. There were many fore-edges and spines blurred behind the coloured semi-translucent plastic. Like a library immured in jelly.

"I bet you have a lot of interests, Yuri. You should unpack."

Dude said nada. She hoped she hadn't offended.

She already knew the answer, but she asked anyway: "Another thing, Yuri. I have an important memory I want to show someone. But if I flip it to you, you can't flip it back, can you? And if you take it, I can't take it back."

Yuri nodded. "In this sense we are incompatible."

"And *only* this sense," she said, mystified why she would flirt with him. "Farewell, Yuri. I will see you anon. That's ungrammatical, isn't it? See you later, alligator."

"In a while crocodile," Yuri agreed solemnly.

Then she had an idea. "Wait a sec. Could you just peek at it, without actually fully taking it?"

"No. When choosing what to take, it is like looking at page written in Czech. Some words look similar in Macedonian, even in English. Some seem similar, but actually they are tricks. Also I can see layout and paragraphs and diagrams, and guess what it is about. But until I actually take the mentality, it is untranslated. It is . . . encrypted."

"You're not much use, are you?" she teased.

"It is like no talent at all," Yuri said, with strange intensity.

She wandered down the corridor and knocked on Kermitcrab and Triffid's door.

There was a sort of gasp, followed by Kermitcrab's unmistakeable bass line. "It's unlocked!"

She dithered — even emitting, much to her own amusement, a small moan — then she entered. An awful sight assailed her. He was shirtless on the floor doing stomach crunches, twisting his torso left then right. The sharp smell of his sweat swirled in her nostrils. His sharp breaths were like air puffed by an optometrist's fan gun.

"Nine thousand, nine hundred and ninety nine," Kermitcrab gasped. "Ten thousand!"

She smiled. "As if."

"Ay, Mnemosyne," he rumbled, lying back. "Whud up?"

"Can you give me a second opinion on this memory? I can't tell if I'm being paranoid."

Myfanwy perched down on the very edge of Kermitcrab's obviously long-term unmade bed. Kermitcrab and Triffid had a hilarious Line Down The Middle rule in their room. Kermitcrab's half-plus-diplomatic incident was a state.

"Huh. I dunno. Uh, I'd *like* to. There's this thing called the Partnering Rule —"

"I *know* about the Rule," said Myfanwy impatiently. "I don't want to flip it with Kitty though. We're becoming like —" Unexpectedly, tears stung Myfanwy's eyes. She swallowed, subtly composing herself. "Like one of those crap grown-up couples, who only love each other on the edge of sleep. I mean, the memory concerns Kitty, so I don't completely trust her. Not in this case. Kermitcrab, I overheard a bit of conversation. I think a faction within Chancel may be planning a coup d'état. Remain calm, Kermitcrab! There is also the possibility we have been controverted by outside interests. I think the person was talking about, like, driving a wedge between me and Kitty?"

"A wedge, huh?

Myfanwy glanced over to Triffid's 49% of the room. Over there it was all Feng Shui and OCD. She sighed and genuflected peaceably. "Basically I'm not sure. That's why I want your help."

Kermitcrab got up and closed the door. Then he shrugged. "I mean, *I* don't really care about the Partnering Rule if *you* don't. Just don't tell any of the elders we flipped, okay?"

"Thank you! Trust me, you're my totes last ditch. With Moth, I feel it might get back to Kitty? They're bezz-bezzy these days. And Yuri takes, Pad blazes, Triffid, uh, cloists, none of them *flip*."

Kermitcrab was putting on a stripy cotton hoodie. He slipped the hood on first then fumbled behind him for the sleeves. "So you want me to flip it back when I'm done? You remember the law of exchange, right? You flip it to me, you get some part of me. I flip it back to *you*, I don't necessarily get the same part back. I get a part of *you* instead. That could be anything. You're okay with that?"

"Totes. Aye. *Genau.* I'm okay with it."

"Uh, cool." Kermitcrab did the hoodie together at the bottom but didn't bother zipping it up. "How can I put this?" he said, with what passed for thoughtfulness. "What about Static instead of me? Some people think it's better if guys flip with guys and chicks flip with —"

"I don't know who these 'people' are, but they sound very out-of-touch with the realities of personal identity and gender performance and so on. Ooh, I sound stuck up! Look, I'm not one of those, like, 'the lady is not for Kerming' types, Kermitcrab. I just — I hardly *know* Static. To be perfectly frank I'm not sure I like the sound of her."

"Uh, okay. Cool."

Oh my God, thought Myfanwy. *I'm about to see into Beavis's soul.*

"Just before we do it," he said. "Like, whatever part of you comes out — I promise I won't tell anyone, so long as I *recognise* it."

"I understand. But if you mistake it for something that really happened to you, then some of my personal stuff might get out."

"So you can't be mad at me if one day I say something embarrassing."

Myfanwy shrugged. "So long as you tell it about you, not me, I don't really care."

"Wicked," said Kermitcrab. "Um, and obviously I have *no* embarrassing secrets, but it would be good —"

"Yeah, sure. Same thing applies. I won't tell. Boy Crab's honour, blah blah blah."

"Pinky promise!" Kermitcrab boomed.

"When I let go Kermitcrab!" instructed Myfanwy. "Tell me what you overheard Simi say in the Myometrium!"

They linked pinkies and flipped.

"Damn," said Myfanwy. "I didn't mean to say her name. I may have tampered with the witness. So what do you think . . . *is* it Simi? Or somebody else?"

"Whoa. No idea. That conversation could mean anything."

"I'm overreacting?"

Myfanwy got out her phone and checked the transcript she had made. Synonyms divided by slashes, question marks in parentheses.

"I guess it's kinda ambiguous," she admitted. "It could be like, '*we need to split those two up because they'll work better apart, but Blake wants them trained together.*'"

"Okay here, have it back."

They linked pinkies. There was something hungry about Kermitcrab's manner now.

She felt something faint as her past altered again, like when a nurse tells you something might hurt and then it doesn't.

"All done," rumbled Kermitcrab. "You feel like a swim or anything? I sometimes swim instead of showering."

"No thank you. I'm one of those people who sometimes shower instead of swimming. Thank you for your help."

"Man, I'm always *there* for this stuff, you feel?"

She went to the door.

"Oh yeah, Mnemosyne? If you *are* doing more banned flips, you might want to keep two different journal archives. One you can show the elders and one for your own use."

"Geeze. Subjectivity fraud."

"Huh? I mean that's what Static and them do. It's maybe what Bee should have done, right? So see you tomorrow at the briefing?"

Myfanwy blinked.

"You haven't heard yet? I could be wrong. I'm pretty sure all the newbloods are gonna be on Operation Clover. Yeah, that's what everyone calls your clique, by the way? You, Nessus, Triffid, Moth. Makes it doubly hilarious none of you guys trust each other, huh? Now that we're all gonna be relying on each other to have each other's backs? And if you change your mind about the swim you better make it fast — I'm only gonna do three thousand lengths this time. Maybe you're thinking about re-suturing your Altar filters tonight though. Seems like your workspace is shifting pretty sluggish and I don't much like being compared to Beavis. See ya soon, I guess."

He closed the door in her face.

Beavis? What was he even talking about?

*

They sat in an Ops Room in a circle of eight — Blake, Aoide, Paddy, her, Moth, Kitty, Triffid, Meletē, Blake again and so on.

Kermitcrab was late. Kitty and Triffid were giggling at something on his phone, and the elders were chatting, with an air of exasperation, about their portrait's mysterious repatriation.

Myfanwy tried not to seem too nosy.

"Operation Clover!" said Paddy. "Och, I'm so hype."

"Did you just say *och?*" said Myfanwy.

"I'm Mr Clover Man, Clover, Clover, Clover," sang Moth in a totally nebulous accent.

"I don't think I should even *be* here," Myfanwy sighed, then felt embarrassed for letting Moth see her so mopey. "I dunno. I just don't think I'm that ready!"

Paddy studied her discomfiture. "Mnemo's finding visualisation hard," he said quietly. "Ain't ya, matey? Keep finding the decorators in your Dwelling."

Myfanwy shrugged. "*Developers*, more like."

Moth wrinkled the subtly dual nose of which she was so proud. "You know Tar?" she said thoughtfully.

"Of course," said Myfanwy. "Well, I'm not sure we've actually *spoken* yet."

"Ask Tar about her Dwelling. It's not even a room any more! It's like a bloc of protoplasm! It's lit from within with different colours, cells rapidly dividing and merging according to a complex order, constantly rushing through a kind of dark tunnel." Moth blinked rapidly, totally stunned by her own eloquence. Then she laughed lightly. "Maybe you just need to find the right representation, Mnemo. Most of us have rooms and houses and stuff, but maybe that's not right for you."

"What then?"

"You have to work it out. Bee used to call her Dwelling her 'Unicornscious.' I think it's a bit like a celebrity talent show."

"But for monsters," added Paddy, nodding. "Just be flexible, fam. My Dwelling was some next ting till I found this old tome in one of the libraries — *Fortification Réduicte Art and Démonstrée.* For instance, how *big* would you say your Dwelling is?"

Now Blake clapped briskly. "Bien venu!" he cried. "Ciao! Hiya! Triffid, any idea of Kermitcrab's whereabouts?"

"Wicked," said Triffid, prompted by Blake, but still referring to whatever was on his phone. He and Kitty looked up dreamily.

"How big?" said Myfanwy, mystified. "I'm not sure. Standard Dwelling dimensions, say about six by twelve?"

"Let's start, Seuss," said Meletē.

"Six by twelve *nanometres*, Mnemo?"

"Metres!"

"Or miles, maybe? Just something to bear in mind."

The door slammed and suddenly Kermitcrab was trying to shove a chair in between Kitty and Triffid. "'pols," he said.

"The prodigal crab!" cried Blake. "Pincer a seat, my boy!"

Kitty's seating citadel was unconquerable. Kermitcrab managed to worm in between Triffid and Meletē instead.

"What's *your* Dwelling like?" Myfanwy whispered to Moth.

"A big elegant eatery with a lot of milky green glass in the ceiling!"

"Ooh," said Myfanwy. "Ceiling fans?"

"I tried to put some in once but they kept wobbling off and giving me bipolar disorder with paranoid delusions! Plus at first I got it wrong and thought I had to *be* a moth and I had these open-flame chandeliers —"

"Ladies," said Simi sharply.

A ninesome was swirled round the Ops Room now — Blake, Aoide, Paddy, her, Moth, Kitty, Triffid, Kermitcrab (already staring comatosely at some weird fidget-tangle he'd made in his lap with what she hoped were just his fingers), Meletē, Blake again and so on.

"Aloha! Ciao!" cried the latter and former. "Start with some mixed news for those who haven't heard — Miss Quaker has found her own way home! Yes, yes! 'Woot,' is that the phrase? Hung right back where she belongs, not even squiffy! I say *mixed* news because — glad as we are to see her safely home, little minx, dirty stop-out — does this imply a *second* security breach? A breach so subtle, alarums did not even sound? Alas! What does everyone think, eh? Oh, you look like a bunch of fraidy-cats! Well, well, I'll put that to one side, and welcome you to the inaugural brief for Operation Clover — named not in honour of our friend *trifid triffidus* here, but for our three new muses — our virgins and virginesses as it were —"

Myfanwy sat still.

"— and in hope of a lucky fourth! New muse, that is. We'll get to that in a minute — but lads, if you're wondering why we're so loaded on newbies, be at ease. The mixture of experience and fresh profile gathered in this room has been carefully calculated with input from all the elder muses, and from Tar too. Mnemosyne, Moth, and, uh, the lovely Nessus will be involved in various snoops and suasions. Running around with socks on your head, for the most part, will be left to you three lads —"

Myfanwy stuck up her hand. "This is a very *gendered* magical secret mission."

"Overruled," Meletē said.

"Hush love," said Simi. "Eyes front."

"So that's that," Myfanwy murmured bitterly.

"Aoide is Workstream A, Meletē Workstream B," said Blake. "As usual, I shall lurk in the shadows — I'll be steering Clover, meaning I'll ask these two silly questions whenever I remember to, and whenever I can find them. Those two things rarely happen at once, so they'll have a pretty free rein with you lot. Lucky you! Anything either of you want to —"

Simi shook her head.

"Just a wee mnemonic hand-out," said Meletē. "It's a memory which belonged to Veil agent Glass. Triffid, you good for this?"

Wearing a look of lofty forbearance, Triffid reached across Kermitcrab and bumped fists with Meletē.

"First time you met Ladybird," said Meletē.

Triffid was already scribbling notes on his phone. A curious Kermitcrab craned over his shoulder.

"Ladies," said Simi. "Technically this will be your first spellsong."

"Not mine," said Kitty darkly. "The deskill?"

"Mnemosyne," laughed Simi. "Don't look so worried! When it comes to your turn, just cast Triffid some charming little remembrance, and make a note of what takes its place. Then cast it back to him."

"Aoide," said Triffid, with a little smile. "You make it all sound so easy."

"So this isn't dangerous?" asked Myfanwy hesitantly. There were a few more smiles around the room.

"My love, it's safe," said Simi, "and simple as they come! Triffid is a cloister. He can pattern his mind to determine which part will switch out when you cast into him. He'll put the memory you give him to the front of the queue, so you'll get it back."

"'Queue'!" hooted Triffid. "Honestly, you people haven't a clue what I go through in here. Nessus, you're up."

"Maybe he should *keep* my memory," Kitty mulled. "I'm not sure I can look at it in the same light, once it's been inside Triffid."

"Don't answer such a low remark," Kermitcrab rumbled.

Triffid adopted a genteel, wounded expression. Kitty and Triffid held hands. There was an imperceptible adjustment in the air between them. Like the space around those tiny spiders, who cast out an invisible thread of silk to sail on the breeze.

"The only slightly tricky bit," Moth added, "is because I'm a haverer, Triffid has to shift the format for me. The first time we tried it, we did it wrong and Triffid fell asleep! He was snoozing!"

"*Snoo*-zing," Kitty echoed for some reason.

"I was suddenly feeling a bit asleep," admitted Triffid. "That was a while ago."

"Don't be embarrassed, my love," laughed Simi. "You've come a long way. It's all child's play."

Blake frowned pensively. "I'd prefer if we all made an effort to say 'easy-peasy, lemon-squeezy.' Any spellsong involving memories of playing as a child is certain to be bafflingly intricate! Cloistering Piagetian schema primifluously in particular —"

"Let's get started, Seuss," said Meletē.

"Well then. Ladies and gents! Veil callsongs don't *seem* to have pure systematicity. Some agents simply shoogle their civilian names a little. Dorothy *Farmer* became the muse *Foreigner*."

"It's a fine line," said Kitty, "between living off the land, and sponging off the state."

Myfanwy would have glared at her, but Kitty was holding Triffid's hand again, and a glare might be misconstrued. Instead Myfanwy congratulated herself on her social perspicacity.

"Whereas the civilian *Susan* Romanoff," said Blake, "soon became the muse *Season*."

"That muse is *so* last season," rumbled Kermitcrab.

"Eyes front, my loves," said Simi. "Don't speak ill of the dead, you lot."

Triffid gave Kermitcrab a swift bromantic back rub.

"Other callsongs," Blake continued breezily, "have oblique relationships with muse classes. The muse Scan — rest her soul also — was almost certainly a blazon. Haecceity was a haverer. Crypt is a confirmed shrouder. Cracks is likely a decrypt, and Cricket a doolittle — or perhaps taker-doolittle. A *third* set of callsongs seem to be inspired by existing agents. Down, for instance, class unknown, works with Vertical a lot. Cricket and Not Cricket got paired up over Christmas. And then we have Egg and Cracks, the two shrouders."

"Often yolked together," said Kitty. "Sorry! I'll shut up."

"Eyes front, love," repeated Simi.

"Only you *have* to, with —"

"Aha!" cried Blake rapturously. "There's a skillet to such yolks, my dear! Must pick the instant to crack them, emerging boiledly from one's shell! Can't be yell—"

"God!" cried Kitty. "What have I done?"

"He probably will forget about the mission now," Meletē confessed.

"Eyes, uh, *back*, Haduken," said Simi.

"Can I ask everyone a question?" said Moth. "Would Veil *really* be so open about their talent set?"

"Good," remarked Meletē.

"That's what *I* said," said Simi nodding.

"Aha!" said Blake. "Egg-zactly! Do Veil make it all too over-easy? Do they seek to scramble our senses, and one day feed us . . . a bad egg? Are we, in short, toast? Yes, yes!"

"Please don't give us any actually important information as egg puns," said Kitty coldly.

"Admirably paranoid, my dear Moth! Aoide also recommended Meletē and I apply pinch of salt. We, however, think it's at worth dipping in one or two soldiers —"

Triffid leaned across Kitty and high-fived Moth.

"Oh!" said Moth, wide-eyed. "What a *douchebag*!"

Triffid frowned at his notes. "I didn't put that," he said. "Can I see that again?"

"In a *minute*, you," said Moth. She pursed her lips and rumpled her brow. "Ooh."

"I miss 'take one copy and pass on,'" Kermitcrab rumbled.

Simi clucked appreciatively. "'Oops I got two,'" she recalled fondly. "Funny you should mention that, babes!"

Blake nodded. "Yes, yes! The mirror dearth is exactly why we're here today! Meletē?"

"Some callsongs for you," said Meletē, "all recent Veil recruits. Dopple, Copycat, Clone, Mimesis. Anything strike you?"

A pause. Paddy spoke first. "They're all mirror muses?"

"Maybe babes," said Simi. "Or callsonged to send that impression, as Moth was just saying. But, yeah. *Maybe.*"

"With Ladybird, and perhaps Germ," said Meletē, "that may make five or six mirrors."

"Six years ago," said Blake, "mirror was among the rarest of muse talents. Veil had only one — Germ, or Calliope as she was then. Have Veil *really* drafted mirrors at a rate of one a year? Is their blazon's stall the busiest at the career fair? Or . . ."

"Mnemo?" Triffid said softly.

The memory had been passed to and fro and was now with Triffid again. It was Myfanwy's turn.

She scooched her chair a little as Triffid reached across the circle. Myfanwy felt his light touch on her fingertips, and something in her past altered.

"Um, thanks Triffid," she muttered, in what she hoped was a blasé manner.

"Or!" Blake thundered, making Myfanwy jump. "Or indeed! Or has Germ perhaps developed her talent to the point where she can *clone the mirror talent itself?*"

Triffid and Kermitcrab glanced at each other with raised eyebrows.

"Can Germ *manufacture* mirror muses?" Blake continued.

"*What* am I supposed to be remembering again?" Myfanwy whispered to Paddy.

"Remember when you used to be Veil agent Glass," Paddy whispered.

"First time you met Ladybird?"

"I can't —"

"Could be a bit of a douche?"

"Oh yeah," said Myfanwy.

Yeah, that *had* been weird . . .

*

Distilling memory . . .

Some kind of barn . . .

By the sea . . .

Sitting on colourful cushions on top of straw, eating spicy porridge. Ladybird pulling up a pouffe. He was lanky, with a tight orange beanie with a nipple on top. He wore a black-and-white stripy top emblazoned, "Foe Ghast."

"You're the new mirrors, right? Cute callsongs."

"Thanks, although Blake — I mean, Germ — didn't think they were girly enough. Sorry, I mean evil enough. How did you choose yours, Ladybird? They live on aphids, don't they? I mean triffids?"

"You must mean orphans. Don't worry, I'm a mirror muse too. You know when you used to do those paintings, where you fold it in the middle, and it makes the image of a butterfly? A butterfly?"

"Yep," Myfanwy said. "Meant to do one for my Controlled Assessment! I'm joking but I don't think you get my humour. You refuse to process it with sophisticated apparatus!"

"Anyways, that's what I thought of first, that school of painting. The folder patterner class of painter. But I thought 'Butterfly' sounded a bit girly whirly."

"So you went for Ladybird?"

Ladybird nodded without irony.

"Ladybird," said Myfanwy kindly. "What's your real name? Behind my Veil, my real face is Glass."

"My real name is Ladybird," Ladybird said.

He looked at her frostily and flew away home.

Hmm. This couldn't be right.

Sunbeams fell from both halves of the roof at 45°, criss-crossing all the way down the barn . . . the dust in the sun was full of hay . . .

"You're the new mirrors, right? Cute callsongs."

Blake was waffling on. Myfanwy was racking her brains. She realised she was blushing.

"Aoide says she's not sure. Why are you and Meletē so keen to trust the Veil tells?"

Paddy had just asked that.

She was getting it wrong. She should just pass on the memory before she made it worse.

"Good question, Merlin!" said Myfanwy awkwardly. She grabbed his hand tightly and flipped. "Here, have some porridge."

Paddy's eyes widened. "Um, thanks," he whispered. "Should have gone through Triffid, really."

"Sugar," Myfanwy whispered back. "What have I done?"

Nobody seemed to have noticed.

"It's fine, fam. But can I have my hand back now?"

Myfanwy let go abruptly as if bitten.

"We don't *trust* Veil's callsongs, exactly," Blake was saying. "Consider this parallel, Merlin."

Myfanwy's mind was elsewhere.

*

"Normally this place is rammed," Triffid told them. He was lanky, floppy-lipped, with rimless designer glasses. "You won't be able to find a seat. Nessus, have you been to Edinburgh before? It's no wonder everyone rams in here, it's carnage out there! You can't even get jeans south of Princes Street except in aerosol format. Literally everyone puts on blue hoodies and organises their own *bloopcore gigs in beautiful church halls without* needing *the promo companies. There will be like twenty or thirty agents of various classes and grades in here. Kermitcrab, Tar, Meletē, Eft, Lego, Horae, Atë, the whole gang. The whole atmosphere will change. You're right to be scared."*

"I'm pretty new to this too," Moth added. "I probs don't know any more than you. But in terms of missions, me and Triffid were working in the deli the other day —"

"I get you, fam," said Kitty sagely. "Missions."

Triffid jumped in. "We're on shift in the deli. Blake shamrocks up, tells us to buckle up for 'Operation Clover.' It's big, it's dangerous, Veil are involved. He demands milk, then reveals the first briefing won't be for another month! By which time me and Mothra have already synchronised our watches and are just all about to jump out of the chopper . . . "

"He's a dappy ho," admitted Moth. "I think that's why we get on, me and him. OMG, you should see his study!"

"So why 'Moth'?" said Kitty. "Why 'Moth'"?

"They're like my second-favourite band!"

"Must already be a muse called One Direction," Triffid teased.

"Well, why 'Triffid' then?" Myfanwy interrogated. "They're those singing plants from Little Shop of Horrors, *right?"*

"Um, no. It's because I'm a patterner class. Cloister specialism. It's mainly an admin and defensive class, and I wanted Triceratops, and that was taken. So somehow, Triffid."

"No other dinosaur would do?"

"Some would say Steggy has a shield vibe. Truth is, she was just massively passive-aggressive."

"Hey," said Myfanwy. "Do you happen to know if Merlin once had a different callsong? Like Polyhymnia perhaps? Wait, could I be saying this to you yet?"

"Our blazon? Maybe," said Moth. "I've only been here since, like, November. I wish I *was a blazon! Look at my lovely nose!"*

They chatted pleasantly for some minutes. Maybe this, not St Veil's, was the place for Myfanwy after all!

She just hoped she wouldn't mess it all up . . .

*

"Consider this parallel, Merlin," Blake was saying. "Once upon a time, one would name one's military operations would after, oh, any old thing. One would hear the news that one's son laid down his life in service of Queen and country, but never fear! — his sacrifice was crucial to the success of Operation Lollipop. Then one day someone had the bright idea of titling missions with a bit more *oomph.* Good for the chaps' morale if you tell them they're dying on Operation Shockingly Just What What. Emotional salience etc. Thus began the long and profitable romance between marketing and military puissance, and I dare say —"

"Wait," Kitty objected. "That's not quite calling it, like, Operation Sneak Over The Western Wall At Midnight, uh, There Will Be Ten Of Us. Triffid's Leg Is Gammy. Just e.g."

"Indeed, Nessus," said Blake gravely. "And perhaps Veil *do* concoct some faux tells, as Moth and Aoide aptly wonder, in advance of some double-bluff. Even so, these many misdirecting mirrors may brook examination in their own right!"

"It's intel we *want,*" said Meletē. "Stream B to the mission. Objective: how many mirrors *do* Veil have, and who are they?"

"After all," said Blake placidly. "Copycat could be a doolittle, for instance. Glass could be a cutter. Moreover, mirror talents may be lent out. Germ was certainly a mirror at Chancelhouse, as Calliope. Yet the other night, there she was, casting a Go-Ball into poor old Nessus."

"Not 'poor old' Nessus," said Kitty. "Never 'poor old' Nessus."

"For all we know," Blake added, "those five or six muses could just be taking turns with one mirror talent — perhaps Germ's, if she's not using it these days! Poor old *them,* if they are. But let us *imagine* you find some mirrors. Stream A, brave friends, will be . . . to turn a mirror for Chancelhouse. Objective: *go get us a Veil mirror muse!* Yes, yes! For *too* long we've hunted high and low for one. Yet the *one place* we know where mirror talent must dwell, we've been too afraid to venture. Get us a mirror, my muses. Get us a mirror, that Chancelhouse may once more see ourselves clearly!"

"It is *awful* not having a mirror," said Kitty with incredible intensity.

"Righto! That's all folks! Now put it all from your minds for a night! Not literally, obviously. Tomorrow, detailed Clover briefings in your Partner pairs. But tonight — feasting and celebrating! Yes, yes! And never so well deserved! And orations in a less administrative vein! Never so eagerly anticipated, by the orator at least! Any other business, anyone?"

"Merlin," said Simi, "we'll need to pencil in a spellsong including Marinade to get that memory back."

"Um," Paddy said. "Is that really necessary? We've all remembered it now. You know how reluctant that guy can be."

"It *is* necessary," said Meletē.

Myfanwy suddenly realised that Meletē had been saying very little and focusing very intensely on her for some time now.

She looked at her leggings.

Ooh, they were ripped.

"Um, I'm really sorry," said Paddy. "Meletē, Seuss, uh, Aoide . . . I know that was our only copy . . . only, I think I've . . ."

"Christ," exhaled Meletē.

"What is it, my love?" said Simi, with an edge to her voice.

"I got distracted," said Paddy, "and I musta spilled . . ."

Meletē shut his eyes. When he opened them they stared hard into Myfanwy's. "Can we all *try* to be a little more careful?" he growled.

"Ready your hearts and your bellies," rhapsodized Blake, who either hadn't heard what was going on, or just hadn't been interested in it. "Oh, dear friends! It looks to be a fine evening, touch wood, so we'll be up on the terrace. Operation Clover, commence! Spring Feast, commence! Chancelhouse reborn! Yes, yes, yes!"

"Merlin," said Meletē menacingly. "Tomorrow I'll be flipping you my hangover, son."

But he still stared at Myfanwy as he said it.

*

Paddy fell in beside her as they were leaving. "I'm such an idiot," Myfanwy murmured quietly. "It was me who conflated the intel, wasn't it?"

Pad shrugged. "Whevs. '*Many rebel spies died bringing us this information.*' Young muses coming up in the world, seen. Elders can chax, seen?"

"Safe, but Meletē blates guessed it wasn't your fault — though thanks for trying to take the bullet. You are over-sweet. I guess I just about got —"

"You should relax as well, Myffed. It's no big —"

"Oh, and Mnemosyne?" came Blake's voice,.

Oh, geeze!

"Linger awhile, Mnemosyne." Blake nodded to Paddy. "Till tonight, Merlin."

But he only wanted to let her know that she was last sous chef standing for tonight's feast.

"Marinade and Static will help set up and *serve*," he explained. "And Eft and Moth will clear and *load*. But re the sous, Kermitcrab *plus* understudy Nessus *both* have begged, ah, subsequent engagements. I didn't *think* I extorted Kitty's offer, did I?"

Blake looked mystified.

"Voluntarism is a complex phenomenon," Myfanwy soothed. "Maybe if I sous'd *and* cleared, Moth could sous instead —"

"Well, it's not a complex menu, frankly. I think you and I *could* tackle it ourselves. That is if you're up for it?"

"Well, totes, fam! Too many chefs spoil the — what *are* we cheffing?"

"Ahem. *Sphagetti Nero*, fam. Whereby I abbreviate famulus, obviously. Involves squid, you see. Only, I've volunteered so many muses to stand these short watches, what with the new question mark over the alarums — what's *that* look for, my dear? You think I'm overreacting? Everyone will still get plenty revelry, never fear! They're assigned in twos and they'll be like those drunken Shakespearean guards you sometimes get, I daresay. Yes, it'll be like speed dating, where 'stand and unfold yourself!' must mean things are going well — and the veggie and vegan are all made up and just need to go in. Mainly, Myfanwy, you just need to watch me to ensure I'm actually *cooking* things, not just fretting with my index cards!"

"Index cards?"

"And probably losing them under all that ink, at that! State of the Chancel address, you see — I have butterflies in my tummy, can you believe it? Must find Eft now — hoping to hook up a live stream of the Address so the guards don't have to lose out. Veil have all the touchlesses so we'll have to rely on the wifi. Barbaric! Would you mind visiting the kitchen in about, let's say, two hours?"

*

An hour and fifty minutes later, Myfanwy was peering into a pot of ink and tentacles.

Better butterflies than this lot.

Blake rather agitatedly showed her how to peel the squids — the trick was locating a little translucent bone-like structure around which the various bags collected. Then they got shelling prawns, slicing squid, dicing tomatoes, cubing shallots and mincing garlic.

"Dissevering is so plural," commented Myfanwy.

"Fresh basil, tabasco sauce . . . we'll have everything lined up and ready to go. If you've got nothing on your plate, you could be zesting lemons."

"Lemons!" laughed Myfanwy. "We finally have lemons!"

"Don't neglect the hills of garlic! Is your heart at rest re the vampires yet?"

"Nope."

"Wise — oh, what a mess! — anything you zest, check first lest it be a stray little balloon — where's my spoon? — I rather rashly set that scarce-chested *Marinade* chap on inflation duty — limp balloons puffing away into the poor pilgarlick's still-limper chest out of pity, I daresay! — it's always them as have least who are the quickest to share it. But now where the blazes is that spoon —"

"Are there really to be yellow balloons, Blake? Aren't Chancelhouse's colours black and blue?"

"Black and blue? Black and blue? Oh dear! There again, the word 'brand' is pretty nasty itself. *Sizzle!* Yes, the tablecloths are lawns of azure, you're right. It wasn't deliberate. What colour is the night sky again? Oh dear! Black and blue, you're right! Marinade's gone off with Eft for wholesale helium. Pecorino, not parmesan, did I mention that rule? That's for authenticity! Ink procured separately, in these little baggies. Just as nice, half the price, as I believe Thoth implied to the king. '*Ink or sim, pom pom, ay-ee-ah! One thing is certain we'll never give in . . .*' Yes, yes! I simply get the stuff by the bucketload from the ink-well out back. I suppose they'll just be whatever colour balloons normally are. Aha! Found you! No, you are a false spoon."

"Is your speech going to be like this, Blake?"

"Sorry, am I being annoying? Just flick bits of squid at me if I am."

Myfanwy settled into a busy contentment, as delicious fragrance arose.

Vegetarians would be getting an ornate tartiflette, obviously inspired by stargazy pie, with astrally-inclined honeyglazed parsnips and gigantic GM carrots usurping Poseidon's customary yearners.

Vegans would be getting this gorgeously aromatic tofu-and-bean-thread-noodles tagine thing cooked in ginormous out-of-season pumpkins.

"Seuss and his sous!" cried Blake, as Myfanwy smugly flourished the sought-after slotted wooden spoon. "We're unstoppable!"

"I've been reading about muse mythology on the net," Myfanwy added chattily, handing Blake the spoon. "And I've been thinking about your callsong, Seuss. You used to be called *Zeus*, didn't you?"

"Aha! Very perceptive, my dear! Very clever little head. I'm quite sure anyone lucky enough to get cast by you will think himself quite mad. Zeus Hospites, Zeus Horkios, Zeus Astrapios, Zeus Brontios, yes, yes — I could never really get on with all that thunder and lightning stuff, for some reason! There's precedent for the pronunciation shift, of course, since 'Seuss' is a German surname, and would have originally sounded like 'Zeus' . . ."

"You know, it's funny all that stuff you were saying about Veil callsongs. Like Engrailed is a kind of butterfly, so *they* could go with Ladybird. Or they could be a cup like eggcup and go with Egg and Cracks."

"Or 'Zoice,' I suppose," added Blake. "Now, ve had better get ztarted ztirring zis zauce! How familiar are you with the good Dr Seuss's ouevre, Mnemosyne? *Because a Little Bug Went Ka-Choo!* is his finest, in my view."

"You know, there are these girls at my school, Blake. Guys as well, but girls more truly. They're called the Cool Kids but also called the Asians. But they're *not* Asian. I guess arguably they *are* cool. One had snails on her. I dunno. It reminded me of callsongs. I don't really know why."

"Eh? Ah, now there's but an insignificant leap," Blake began, "betwixt Dr Seuss and Dr de Saussure, and the latter's distinction between relatively motivated and relatively unmotivated signs —"

"Who was Dr Saucier? Some muse?"

"As it happens, yes. But that's another story."

"Hey," Myfanwy added casually, "is anyone at *Chancelhouse*, like, Asiatic or anything? Like, South East Asian?"

"Eh? Not that I know of . . . Meletē looks Sri Lankan but he ain't. A muse called Sequin, from Hong Kong, had a nasty accident in a Veil skirmish. And if you go back far enough, there did used to be an elder muse who — why do you ask?" said Blake, suddenly suspicious.

"Oh, nothing," said Myfanwy quickly. "That's just . . . what I thought."

Tonight's the night, she thought. *It's now or never.*

"Hmph!" brooded Blake. "*And* I've lost the spoon again."

"What was it you were saying?" Myfanwy added sweetly. "Something about distinctions?"

*

"—ew favourite pers—"

"—ldn't have to *as*—"

"—rst of all: *ew*."

Streaks of pink cloud and sprays of early stars stood out against the deepening blue sky. Across masses of chimneypots, satellite dishes and aerials, a darker band of cloud crested the flaky heathered peak of Arthur's Seat. Round her little maze of tables Myfanwy hustled to and fro in the fresh twilight air, setting down starters, pausing to compliment or hesitantly admire bare backs, bijouterie on breastbones, shaved jaws and aftershave. Blake met her at the top of the stairwell laden with steaming glowing trays and snatches of incomprehensible banter like, "I'm the Soup Dragon!"

Triffid and Kermitcrab looked ridiculous and skeevy in large dove-grey suits with huge shoulderpads, tails and cummerbunds, and top hats resting on their jiggling knees.

"Lads," Myfanwy said.

Kermit rumbled mega-appreciatively.

Myfanwy's occult governess looked particularly formidably stunning; Myfanwy could not approve of such heels unless you were already, as Aoide already was, almost seven foot tall. Then they became your ledges to tangle the twilight constellations with your cornrows (plus they were wedges not some silly stilettos).

"Babes," Simi told Myfanwy, with a look of severity Myfanwy had not seen since the incident with the scorpion, "you look lovely."

"Am I red in the face, Simi?"

"Rosy in the cheek, my love."

Grimalkin, the buff caster with the Bible tats, Myfanwy's taciturn neighbour, was doing sort of smart-casual in a fawn blazer but looked *totally disproportionately weird* . . . then Myfanwy realised it was because he wasn't wearing his normal red headphones. He flashed her a deranged grin as she set down his vegan.

"Ta," he said. "I'll enjoy that."

Another Brummie after all.

Bee wore a little wedding dress.

"Love dress," whispered Myfanwy, as she plonked down Bee's veggie.

"Kicking and spitting," intoned Bee flatly, "the unwilling bride suffered seven different perfumed baths. Blake's retinue of slaves, under the dispiteous instruction of the albino eunuch Aoide, massaged Bee's muscle tissue with their fragrant, boorish fingertips."

Bee ate some asparagus.

Soon Myfanwy was setting down Kitty's starter.

Kitty, leaning on her thin wrist, seemed so rapt in the ramblings of the patterner Triceratops as not even to notice the small pretty plate appear before her.

Trice looked distinguished in a cornflower blue military tunic with gold piping. He had waxed his moustaches to quite startling diameter.

And *Kitty* was — obv — more beautiful than all the other beautiful characteristics in the entire Chancelhouse complex, even had they been mixed with optimum emergent aesthetic excellence, and more *bold* in her look too (though the monocle was frankly a bit much). Myfanwy suppressed a smile.

As Myfanwy began to glide away Kitty — still nodding wide-eyed at Triceratops — extended her free arm and beckoned her back to her with brisk madam-ish strokes. She turned her face as Myfanwy slunk close. "Whenever anyone over the age of thirty talks to me," Kitty murmured semi-discreetly, "I notice they include *looong* periods where you can think complete, eloquent questions like, 'Why is this buffoon from a defunct oral society telling me of his Folk?' without even missing any content whatsoever."

"They should crossfade old people's comments," Myfanwy readily agreed as Kitty swiveled back to Triceratops — whom she had mesmerised in the meanwhile with a single uplifted index finger — and flashed him her sweetest smile.

Now Myfanwy made for the Valhalla stairwell for the final tray of starters.

Her legs were aching by the time she finally flopped into a chair at Kitty's table. Triceratops was shooing a pigeon. Tar, in an elaborately high-collared backless black dress, was showing everybody all the hand gestures they used in Italy, whilst insisting that nobody in Italy *actually* used them.

"This," she said, with her fingertips bunched together, yawing them to and fro, "this maybe like means, I'm having a drink and you all want to go but I don' wanna go yet, so I'm like, 'What, you gonna leave me all alone, all like a dog?'. But we don't do them, we don't do them."

"How is *that* different from *this* one?" said Triffid, wiggling his hands around.

"Twisty. *'An' don' do THA' innamaface!'*"

"I love it when people do their own accents!" cried Moth.

"'*Sticky di hands, I gotta sticky di hands now.*'"

Tar *did* have sticky di hands!

"What have I missed?" said Myfanwy. But she really was ignored now — Kitty was sharing some hilarity with Moth, Triffid was keenly hovering on the edge of the hilarity.

On a chimneypot on the rooftop across, the wind curled and uncurled a sort of snowy Luck Dragon cub of lost loo roll.

"—nd transferred to a weighted plastic bag," Triceratops told Tar with gusto, "for lake-side *faux* aircraft carrier sea-burial, the historical inaccuracies involved all being okay according to a painstakingly won consensus that certain concessions to (a) taste—"

"They *have* landed," murmured Myfanwy. "The Cool Kids. *Déjà vu.*"

"—nly humane if you remember to *check reg*—"

"—o buy pants and ended up with a be—"

"—is a mugging, a begging, a hugg—"

"— (d) involving *all* the bereaved guests, not just a few of them would all conform to what Hypnos probably would have wan—"

Sharp claps sounded from the dais. Myfanwy felt relief, though a new sort of nervousness was growing. The white tissue streamed from its nest, out of sight towards the street. "Everyone here should have their main courses!" Blake enquired loudly above the hubbub. "If not their just desserts. Everyone happy?"

Tired as she was, Myfanwy steeled herself.

"I have a few remarks to make," Blake continued, "as we tuck in — food for thought, and the much-maligned vice-versa — but lest we somehow lose our chance in the midst of all my claptrap, can we first have a round of clap-clap for our tireless sous chef Mnemos—"

"I *don't* think that will be necessary!" Myfanwy yelled loudly, over Blake and the rather resilient roof terrace chatter.

Myfanwy shoved back her chair.

A little dazed she rose to her feet, trotted across the terrace, and leapt lightly up onto the dais beside Blake. "I have something I wish to tell you all. *Everyone! Everyone shut up and listen!* Ever since I arrived, an atmosphere of distrust has pervaded Chancelhouse! Not long ago, the portrait of Genevieve Quaker was stolen. It's been the talk of the town. Well, *I* know who is responsible!"

Blake blinked and blinked.

Myfanwy took a deep breath.

All across the terrace, a swarm of gazes had swivellingly gathered. Gradually the hubbub subsided. Into the gap it left a soft new score swelled, of hushed traffic agitated with grace notes of half-suppressed giggles.

Okay. This is it.

"My dear Hercule Mnemo," murmured Blake, so that only she could hear. "This feels ill-timed. I hope you know what you're doing."

"There were Veil agents," Myfanwy announced, slowly and emphatically, "inside the Chancelhouse compound the night the portrait vanished. But could that have just been cover? An opportunity seized by whoever *really* took the portrait of Genevieve Quaker? Under the veil of, uh . . . you get it. There was no Veil, uh, hanging around, when the portrait *reappeared.* So it had to be . . . *an inside job!* So who was the thief? Which one of us paintingnapped Genevieve Quaker, and for what purpose?"

Don't milk the moment too much.

"*I did it!*" Myfanwy cried ecstatically.

Just as she had hoped, incredulous murmuring spread across the roof terrace.

"That's right! I, Mnemosyne, am the portrait thief! Ha, ha, ha! Nessus, do you remember the night you almost killed Merlin?"

"Can you narrow it down a bit?" Kitty called coldly.

There were nervous titters from the tables near Kitty.

"Nice one," Myfanwy acknowledged. "The night the portrait vanished, Merlin and I stayed up chatting while Kitty finished her patrol. But on the way back to our room, *I* went via the library. It was easy enough to conceal the portrait behind a bookshelf. The next night I took it with me to the Red Box restaurant, and later Finger's Piano Bar. My big annoying bag, that I refused to check? You all thought I was such a geek! Well, they have black lighting in the cubicles. There, by the black light, to the sound, I believe, of a dubstep remix of Zorba the Greek, the fluorescing pigments proved it beyond any doubt! That painting's no more than a few decades old at the most."

"Nobody cares," heckled Grimalkin.

"Didn't Ah kill you?" added Rook.

She easily ignored them — no Cool Kid could chip away at her shoulder now.

"Who's a geek now? I think we all deserve an explanation. But that can wait, because I have bigger fish to fry. Or should I say . . . bigger moles! Yes, the secrecy and evasiveness has made it all too easy a target for infiltration. Mole is on the menu, kids! For a time, *you* were my chief suspect, Simi. 'Pols, fam. It was because I overheard an exchange. 'At the moment they're up front with me,' you seemed to say. 'It can't continue. It's only a matter of time. It's got to be a *fait accompli*, or Blake will stop it from happening.' A few hours ago, it became clear to me. In the Clover briefing, we were flipping a memory around and I accidentally spoilt it. Merlin sweetly took the rap for me, but *I* was the sap who conflated that memory. Sentenced to hard sous in the kitchens, eh Blake? Incarceration as labour market failure?"

"Oh dear!" cried Blake, sounding mortified. "I didn't *at all* intend to —"

"Never mind, at least you thanked me. And you can thank me again in a moment. Because my point is, me and Kermitcrab also flipped my memory of eavesdropping to and fro. Now, I'm new at this muse stuff. Earlier I conflated Ladybird and Triffid. What if I *also* conflated Aoide's voice with the voice of the *real* mole?"

"Babes —"

"Eyes front, Aoide! Um, that's something she said to *me* earlier, BTW, if some of you aren't in on the joke? Okay. Sick. Anyway. Uh. A lot of things didn't add up. Someone was up to something. But vital pieces of the puzzle were missing. What was inside those west houses? Why were the elders so anxious to keep us out, when we're so crowded in here? That proved a red herring — as I think Blake's State of the Chancel address, and his consortium of Parisian haberdashers, will shortly reveal! But it led to something else.

The first time — the only time, sorry, that I went inside the west houses, after the playground fight with Veil, I heard a voice behind one of the walls. A woman's voice, I thought. It stopped pretty sharpish — had she *heard* us enter the Cache? I didn't realise what was so strange about it at the time. There was just *one* voice. Why would someone be babbling to herself like that? For a while my Northanger Abbey syndrome got the better of me. A secret, insane first wife! Then I thought — well, what if it's just someone on the phone or the net, wearing headphones? The mole, perhaps, debriefing in the dead of night, when no one is normally awake? At first I couldn't ID the language. Not Japanese, not Chinese, or at least not Putonghua dialect. Thai? Later I leafed through old images of Chancelhouse. One of the defector elders, Urania, looked of South East Asian heritage. Lucky for me, there was a head-shot good enough for a TinEye person search. I found his page from when he was a grad student studying Astrophysics — Umberto Souphanouvong. His last name's Laotian. It was Urania — Undine, to use his Veil callsong — and *not* Jasper, who was the handler! Under the cover of Blake's pet project, the mole was sneaking away to file reports to Undine, using Laotian for extra security! So far, so good. Who could she be though? Only the elder muses have keycards for getting into the west houses — right? And Aoide and Meletē were with us that night. So that only left Blake himself! I knew Blake was less than candid about the lineage of Chancelhouse, and enigmatic regarding our future. But what if his costumes project was secondary cover? What if Blake was disguising one secret as another? I thought I'd heard a woman's voice – oh sugar, that's a bit essentialist, isn't it? I mean, I wasn't completely sure anyway. So I didn't discount Blake right away. Pretty soon, however, someone flipped me a memory that *did* prove Blake's innocence. His keycard was accounted for at a time when this voice was once more heard in the west houses. *Who* then? Who could it be? I realised that the east houses are relatively recent. Perhaps in those less paranoid times, everyone lived in the west houses. Then everyone would have to have a keycard! Apart from Blake, Meletē and Aoide, there was one other person who featured in the images from six years ago. But I had missed her, because she wasn't technically an elder muse. *Why was that?* Why has she never been promoted, though she has served for so long? Did some of the elder muses have a question mark over her conduct and loyalties, though they were too polite to say so? Perhaps they asked the same question I asked myself — why did *only she* stay? Why did *all* the other young muses leave Chancelhouse, apart from *her*? For what purpose did she stay?"

She paused momentarily.

"Tar," Myfanwy then said softly. "*You* speak quite a few languages, *don't* you?"

Tar pushed back her chair and rose.

She seemed so *tall.*

Heels.

Light chat had broken out over the last part of Myfanwy's exposé. Now though there was sparse applause, and a vague bassy wooping from Kermitcrab. Myfanwy noticed the applause was really carried by two people — Yuri . . . and Tar.

*

"Brava!" said Tar. "Hurray!"

But Yuri was the very last to stop clapping. Then he hung his head. A little powered-down paranoid android.

The roof terrace was filled again with chatter. Myfanwy looked around in confusion.

Simi was by her side, pulling an "eek!" face. "Uh, babes," she explained quietly. "That *was* me, not Tar. But I was chatting about the five-a-side all-ball tournament, yeah?" She laughed, rather embarrassed. "Who's in defence, who's up front, yeah? Did I *really* say 'it's only a matter of time' in that . . . in that funny voice you just done . . ."

Tar was approaching them with an icy smile.

"Look babes, I'll leave you two to, uh . . ."

"Simi, don't go. You have to protect me."

"Best of luck, my love."

"*Simi!*"

Myfanwy hunted the tables for support. Some muses, bearded with tentacles and black pasta, swiftly averted their gaze as she caught it. Many muses seemed to be giggling about her. Kitty was distracted in an "I'm-over-it" kinda way. Blake, who had drifted to a discreet distance during her diatribe, fidgeted with his index cards.

Only Meletē and Grimalkin would hold her gaze steadily, grimacing at her with nasty ink-smeared grins. She shrugged expressively at Meletē and he shoved down a splashing forkful of squid and chomped voraciously.

Now Tar stood before her. "We have not really met?" Her chin dripped with ink. "'Nice to meet you,' you know, is a normal way to say? So you know, funny, I speak Maghrebi and Iraqi Arabic. I speak French, Spanish, Greek, Turkish, Persian, and even a little English. I speak Italian in Milan, Sicily, Naples. Oh no! I forgot Laotian! I'll go learn it now! But one thing, eh? Say again why would I wanna say 'they are up front with me' — if I don't even *know* you?"

"Well," admitted Myfanwy. "Aoide did just tell me that part was her. Still, that's not the —"

Tar interrupted her with a gesture. "Hon, just in case any *is* serious," she said, "I have really been leading Operation Terpsi, eh? If you wanna prove it, all it takes is to ask any of the guys. I've been annoying them all constantly, you know? No time to slip away."

"I thought Meletē led it," Myfanwy admitted.

"Ha! Not *this* time, honey! 'Aah, do this, do that. Hide in the tree with the knife! Paint my toe blue!' I've been a bitch. Also, I don't got a keycard. Why I wanna go in there? Okay, I'm gonna sit down. Nice to meet you. Have some wine, eh?"

"I guess I just assumed — aha! But you could have *flipped* them all those memories," said Myfanwy doubtfully, "to cover your tracks —"

Tar laughed. But not all that nicely. "Okay, I get it. It's still your joke. It's funny. I'm, uh, just gonna go report to my Veil superiors? So bye bye."

Could I really have been so wrong?

"Tar, you got some goop on your —"

"Some *more* dirt you got on me, eh?" Tar called halfway across the terrace, swiping her chin clean with elegant flickering fingers. Malicious laughter arose around her and waved her into her table's revelry like tentacles. Many more stars were glowing since last Myfanwy had raised her eyes.

Now Blake bustled up close to Myfanwy, looking rather worried and shamefaced. "Euh —"

He clutched a thickish stack of index cards, to which he instinctively glanced. Oh sugar. Even Blake didn't know what to say. Even he thought she'd totally humiliated herself.

Blake smiled weakly. "Tar seemed to take that well, eh? No hard feelings between you, are there? All my fault really! Three loose ends come to mind, Myfanwy. First, whilst of course we must be vigilant, I don't think we have cause to conduct a witch hunt. Marinade's hobby is fairly common knowledge. I'm not sure he *really* believes there's a Veil mole. Someone really should have warned you about him! In a way I'd rather he stick with the bananas-on-toast collages and the co-sleeping, but there you are."

"So who did I —"

"Well, I don't *know* whom you overheard, but I'd wager it was Mrs Phan. Her apartment backs on to the west houses, and we do take a friendly interest in the affairs of our neighbours. Giving her daughter Bella some bad advice again, no doubt — tends to Skype late because of the time-zone difference. She's a formidable woman. Addicted to chewing ice. Sometimes a sign of low iron levels but she does have quite a balanced — yes, second loose end, you were right about the paintings. Most of them *are* quite recent commissions. Rather expensive, so I'd prefer if they didn't leave the premises —"

"I'm sorry," said Myfanwy. "I don't know what to say."

"No, quite my fault for misleading you! Could have saved quite a lot of — the provenance of the paintings is fairly common knowledge too you see. I recall our chat about Genevieve Quaker was cut short, wasn't it?"

"If I wasn't so wrapped up in myself, I would have just *asked* someone!"

"I do scatter hints, but I forget with whom. I sort of assume everyone will just make friends and then — oh dear! In brief, Miss Quaker died twice — *truly* died in the Fifteenth Century, martyred, but died slightly more in the Nineteenth, when her last living memories were lost. It was a library fire, ironically enough, that claimed the life of the muse carrying them."

"Okay," said Myfanwy quietly. "So that's why she's in Tudor clothes and a Pre-Raphaelite style. To honour her death both times."

"Miss Quaker is a rather unusual martyr," Blake added with somewhat strained cheer. "Rather than expecting her reward in heaven, she left a part of herself here on earth. Her memories endured, cast down from muse to muse. Myfanwy, before Miss Quaker died, she gave all her . . . rather unpleasant recent memories, about a week's worth . . . to one of her interrogators. Feedback on her overall experience, we'd call it nowadays."

"Yeah," admitted Myfanwy, trying now to force some jollity into her voice. "I can see why they'd wanna pass that along —"

"Well! There *may* be more to it than that, actually. It's rather vague, but best as I can reconstruct it, when this interrogator experienced his acts from his victim's perspective, he instantly converted, *twice* in fact — once to the by-then unfashionable belief in the reality of witchery, and once to the cause of the witches themselves! Or the cause of the muses, as the mythos refined itself. Some trick, eh? Like inquisitors and qualifiers trooping out of Galileo Galilee's cell, each with his Level One NVQ in Copernican Astronomy! Yes, yes — proudly clutching their *papier-mâché* heliocentric orreries to their breasts, oh, Myfanwy, I can see it! Have you had some wine? Have I mentioned that rule? Dearie me, I hope this won't spoil our festivities. No, of course, it adds to them! Yes, our anonymous penitent took possession of Miss Quaker's talent. He made sure to pass it on one day, along with her final hours. That suffering was powerful enough to produce a change in any heart similar to the one it produced in his. And so was born a sort of early modern Amnesty International or Index on Censorship, only rather more secretive. Over the centuries, the organisation slowly grew into a more complex beast. Chancelhouse, I think they're called. Perhaps you've heard of them?"

"Rings a bell."

"A dinner gong, you mean! As I badly alluded to in the library, nobody knows quite what Genevieve Quaker *really* looked like. Chancelhouse has only ever looked *through* her eyes, not *upon* them."

"But Blake . . . I saw a photo of her! Cotching with you and Simi and some people I didn't recognise!"

"Did you indeed? Oh dear. My hunch is . . . let's see, shall I tell you? The person in the image was probably an old Chancelhouse muse named Sophie Black, and aptly callsonged . . . Melpomene . . . ha, no longer with us, alas! Yes, it was *she* who volunteered her image as the basis for Miss Quaker's, you see. Only time she ever sat still, I imagine, for more than a moment or two. Yes, yes. Well, I better ascend my pulpit, eh? The perils of staying on-message, eh Mnemosyne?"

The way he sometimes talks about that portrait! It's not Genevieve Quaker he lost. It's not her he misses. It's the sitter for the portrait. Sophie Black. Another casualty in the Veil war. Hypnos, Frog, Sequin, Geist, Lap, Melpomene . . . so many deaths, so much sorrow . . . he's trying so hard to survive, to create a community, even to celebrate . . . and all I do is open old wounds . . .

"I've been such a fool," she whispered. "And you're so kind. Oh, Blake."

"So there we are — from misapprehension comes true knowledge, and from tragedy, tragicomedy! You're about to be eclipsed, my dear. There was a lot more sense in your hypothesis than in the index cards in my top pocket! — now where on earth have they put the top pocket on this jacket — there she is, in the trousers, very aerodynamic of them —"

She blinked rapidly as the tears stung her eyes. "I'm a tough act to follow, Blake. Break a sweat."

"For goodness sake, my dear, *and* for your own, have some damn wine! Myself, I am already —"

"Um, I think that one's my glass —"

"— well on my way! Wish me luck! If I get any laughs, I'll know I've hiccupped a butterfly! Loose end number three, I should say, is re this memory which 'cleared' me of your most honourable and meticulous suspicions, Myfanwy! But *that* can wait! I have bigger fish to fry! Or should that be, butterflies to butter-fry? Here I go, my dear, here I go!"

He was so kind, but . . .

Oh no.

The memory which cleared him. Does he suspect Moth and Kitty broke his trust with the keycard? That they snuck into the west houses?

Sugar! This isn't over!

Blake returned to the dais and was tapping a glass. "Friends," he began.

He's kind, and he's trying to spare my feelings. Isn't that a bad sign? I've stolen from Chancelhouse, I've shown myself to be completely unreliable and weird . . . what if I don't get a second chance?

I could live with that. But what if I take Kitty down with me? I don't think she'd ever forgive me.

At least I was right about one thing.
That is definitely my wine glass.

*

There were two empty seats next to Yuri, and Myfanwy slid in next to him, grateful not to have to talk to anyone. She topped up her glass till it overspilled the brim.

"Friends," said Blake. "Muses."

The roof terrace hadn't really quietened all that much when Blake had tapped his glass, and now as he paused, the volume began again to swell, voices mingling one with another, and with birdsong and muffled traffic.

"—ever win anyth—"

"—n't normally do th—"

"—loody hope so. Do you know what I mean?"

Blake straightened his index cards. Sugar! Blake really was nervous! Had her stunt totes put him off?

"From the *heart*, Blake!" Kitty helpy-heckled him. "You don't *need* those notes!"

With her thumbs and fingers Kitty made a heart shape. Her face scrunchled up, she nodded compassionately. Again she mouthed, *From the heart!*

Myfanwy smiled despite herself. The chatter dipped slightly. Not much. But a start.

"Ah," said Blake, lowering his index cards hesitantly. "Nessus. Well, well. Not much in the old ticker but cholesterol these days, I'm afraid! I was saying only to my, uh, support act Mnemosyne, the other day, how an enigma, fried in breadcrumbs — let's see, I suppose you had to be there."

Oh, God, please *don't mention me! I just want to disappear!*

"I could pass the reminiscence round? I suppose not. Maybe I'm off to a bad start, with this 'heart' business. Ahem. Yes, yes. Well, I believe I've invented a new sort of preparation of egg! She wasn't poaching very well, this egg, and I drained her halfway done and fried her. Really quite a distinct experience, couldn't call it any other sort of egg! I thought Froached Eggs, from 'fried' and 'poached.' Or Pried Eggs, of course. And, uh, *pride*, ladies and gents, is precisely what we at Chancelhouse . . . uh . . . yes, yes . . ."

The babble of conversation on the roof terrace was again basically at its totally fully natural volume, as if no speech were in progress whatsoever.

"—ean in for a ki—"

"—ou forget, don't y—"

"—quid Lord."

Blake floundered, then dove headfirst into his first index card. "Friends! *Muses!* Consider mankind, suspended in his social space! Row upon row, each in his Excel brick crib. Can you picture him? Similar to a human pyramid — save no feet planted on shoulders, but only toes dangling in swirling mist. And of course no apex. Just mankind, as far as the eye can see."

"—ot going to sit there and rea—"

"—lake always goes on about the witches, but what about their *ca*—"

"—at's exactly the same as what's the same for me!"

Him, him, him, thought Myfanwy. *He, he, he. Ha, ha. Mankind, and mankindess. What does he mean, "social space"?*

"Mankind in his social space!" Blake orated. "Similar to paper dollies perhaps, silhouettes in open-armed salute, all proliferated and serried. See them? All lovingly sharing one long *shish kebab* limb — save *these* paper rows and ranks must spread apart . . . for *mist* to interpose . . . spritz but a wrist sample's worth of this mist, and all their mutual fists are perforated and torn . . . and the mists turn in-between. Got the picture yet? People, divided by mist! So what *is* this damn stuff, muses? That blurs the faces of our closest neighbours? Not perfumes and colognes. Nor quite lattice, my dear Chancelhouse. That is to say, this mist is irreducible to a system of merely *sensuous* refulgences and milky opacities, that supplement to obscure, and vice-versa."

"—orking hard on a peace pa—"

"—rutes were running on their hi—"

"—elicate in a way which disturbs most lawmen."

So Blake is talking about where one person finishes and the next one starts, thought Myfanwy. *And what brings us together or keeps us apart? He loves that taxonomy stuff. Muse classes, families, metaclasses or whevs. Always fiddling with the names for things . . .*

"There mankind squats," orated Blake, "like a dress print! And between every outstretched fingertip and the fingertip of whoso the first fingertip's owner most loves, interposes this milkiness. Operatively roseate, functionally ornate, it takes and holds ground, its every whorl's every detail in a way important, howsoever fungible."

Sugar, thought Myfanwy. *Give up. He's impossible to understand when he gets like this. Just let all this mist stuff flow over you. At least he sounds confident again.*

"—ony Bl—"

"—anted *me* to be called Cli—"

"—aw before him, capped with a fez."

"Are we . . . normal, friends? Is not the muse's cast the template for every human transaction? *You* get a little more like me, *I* a little more like you, and we go our ways? It is not so! If it were so, Darcy would grow more prejudiced, Elizabeth Bennett more proud, kiss, fade to credits! What then, is the difference? The difference is the mist, the mist betwixt persons! And what is the mist? This mist may be dust, muses. It may be . . . skin. It may be milk and eggs and butter and offal and phones and microwaves and luxury sportscars all ground up very fine. It may be wonga. I cannot define it, brave muses, I cannot deconstruct this mist. I admit defeat there. But I will attempt, if I may be so bold, to *demonstrate* it."

"—osing the plot past thirt—"

"—one of Tintin's painti—"

"—ullen inscrutable stares. I want him on my knee."

Maybe the mist, thought Myfanwy idly, *is shmist. Where's that wine got to? Oh sugar, I incriminated Kermitcrab too! We flipped against the rules! Now even Kermitcrab will hate me! Where's that wine bottle?*

"Say one day," Blake orated, "one figure of the suspension were to call upon his neighbour. A visit! What is the etiquette, when someone in social space wishes to abscond his coordinate? Say the weather today is . . . clement. Well, to start, he may peel his face off his face. He hesitates, but obliging mists make him a hook of thick haar on which to dangle it. There. Good. The peeled-off face puffs out its cheeks, waggles its tongue. Ooh, what is this? Are there Whiteness Wights, on the pattern of Wood Wights, Hindering Hands and other boggles of German fairytales? Or else is it wills of the wisps, as it were, that plump it? No time to wonder, mustn't be late! Now he pulls, finger-by-finger, a pair of living gloves, which the mists relieves him of most gracefully. Next he strips his belly's staves and hoops, confident of a fresh belly below. Before we know it, there stands his double, an ingeniously joined-up man, unfolded to his feet like a Jack-in-the-Jack. The duple smiles and sets out. A slap on the rump no doubt, and at the impact, a little mist escapes his seams."

"—eet them at first and you're like, 'Black shoes? *Really?*' and then yo—"

"—he diary bindery that actually meant for ten minutes no one wo—"

"—ll trying to explain it to me, but I wasn't really getting it."

Blake's confidence had peaked and plateaued. He now spoke with a sort of doggedness which reminded Myfanwy for some reason of *tennis*. Myfanwy really felt for Blake. She and Yuri were the only ones who still seemed to be listening. That was if Yuri even was listening, not just sulking.

Would Blake think listening was, like, *condescending?* Maybe the vibe *was* you talked through the background speech, and actually she was just making it awkward! Or, like, really obviously trying to make up for her massive *faux pas* with geeky raptness.

"*How* does he arrive, dear muses? In what state does he get there? It was, recall, only two steps to his neighbour! So he must be there already, hooray. Alas! What has befallen? The duple's face is twisted as if it were a safe's dial!

Ugh! His chin points to the two o' clock position, for instance. His hands are on backwards, his fine capillaries spritz hello, even as his fingers grope in his forearm for his heart. His testicles, like two cuckoo's eggs, share nests with his eyes."

"—mage may gradually diverge from the orig—"

"—gn *everything* 'HQ' and that wa—"

"—roofread with her eyes shut."

This is like a scarytale, thought Myfanwy.

"So Yuri," she said, leaning her chin in the well of her hands, "who do you think is the cutest girl or guy here that's single?"

Yuri was silent.

"Oh come on!"

"One iris," Blake ploughed on, "has gone missing — aha, suspended bobbing in the intrepid visitor's adam's apple. Spleen worn on his sleeve. You may extrapolate the rest. Nails out, back up, arse first, etc."

"I don't look around," Yuri told her airily. "I have lover in Kumanovo."

"*You* do! Oh Yuri, do you miss them?"

"Alas!" said Blake. "Inside the mess is far worse. Storeys of bone and offal swivelled in Rubick's cube fashion. To shift to a hip-hop idiom, he gets it twisted. Now consider this, muses!"

"I am afraid," Yuri said gloomily, "she is to be killed to make the next release of Windows. Command line, pointers, web integration, touchscreen integration. The people are bored!" Yuri cried emphatically. "*What* will satisfy them next? Only blood. Yes; we Skype."

Myfanwy smiled glassily. "So did your shrink headhunt you too?"

"Dear muses, if an entire figure of a man, with every resource and intelligence to draw upon, arrives a mere two steps away in such disarray . . . if drouthy neebors neebors meet organs all anagrammatised at best . . . what must happen to something so fragile as a *thought*? As a feeling, an intent, sent through this enwreathing milkiness? A good wish, a dream, a scheme, a plan?"

"For one time I had shrink," Yuri suddenly opened up. "I could not endure to be in a room where an apple was eaten. For you this sounds strange? To me as well. Preferred method: to assign intern to me, to eat apples beside me. Everywhere I go, *crunch, crunch, crunch*. Sitting next to me on a bus eating these various apples. Very soon, he is also spitting bites of apple into paper bag in lap. Overdose of apple. Sick to stomach of apple. Everywhere I go. One day I escape. No more shrinks. *Crunch, crunch, crunch.* Spit in bag."

"And can you eat apples now?"

"I could always *eat* apples," said Yuri scornfully.

"A plan, dear muses!" gasped Blake. "What happens to a plan? But my dear muses, we are an organisation of something else. Not merely men and women, not merely their wishes and dreams and plans. Oftentimes we are *not* those paper figures, but beings who populate the spaces between them! Some of you, dear muses, have questioned my . . . informal leadership, *primus inter pares*, of Chancelhouse, this past year. Oh yes, I'm quite aware. It is understandable. Yes, much has been achieved. Here a prisoner of conscience freed, there an energy contract awarded to the right bidder. Here a terror network infiltrated, there a fragile regime stabilised. New muses recruited, new funding streams secured, new research embarked upon! But too many unforeseen consequences, my friends. Too many tragic accidents. And far too many losses. Some are asking, 'What is Blake's grand plan?' Veil has outperformed us in the field, there's no question. That gap is looking increasingly challenging to close. Believe me, Chancelhouse, when I say I doubt any could question my leadership as searchingly or as seriously as I do."

"C-ringe," said Kitty's voice suddenly in Myfanwy's ear. "Can I scare you half to death? 'Needless to say, Mnemosyne had to leave town! She gathered her mittens on strings, and she and her dinosaur and rat and fished up in Peru, where she lived out her days, a wiser, sadder muse, under the assumed callsong *Waffler Mytty*.'"

"Ha," said Myfanwy wearily. "Don't be mean." Hanks of Kitty's blonde hair, and her vintage pendant with the carved ivory Nefertiti, drifted in the corner of Myfanwy's vision. She couldn't bear to look into her BFF's face.

"Everybody thinks you are *completely* insane," said Kitty. "You reflect badly on yourself and on me. I'm tired of defending you."

Kitty went back to her seat.

"Providence will reward you," Yuri muttered poisonously into Kitty's frou-frou as she passed. It was something he'd said to her once before, when he banged his knee and yelped and Kitty had laughed.

"Capitalism!" cried Blake. "Communism! Liberalism! Socialism! Social democracy! The grandest plans! The great ideologies! Are they all the same? Are they but anagrams? Ha! If *Tristan* was *Tantris*, the muse is the *artist* to the power of *n*! Yet even we, the ultimate anagrammatistés, cannot find such an equivalence, such a commensurability!"

"—at wine is the fountain of you—"

"—otally preposterous little gi—"

"—ick is to get *others* to actually drink it."

"So what's her *name*?" Myfanwy said to Yuri, with a forced brightness which was, rather oddly, more like a standard Kitty intonation — Kitty when channelling dappy.

Yuri just shrugged.

"Yet they are not mutually exclusive systems. Communism and capitalism, my dear muses, let's take that terrible twosome! In all their configurations they are but regions of a single great problematic, a space of possibilities tenfold larger than either. Muses, I vow to you by the crystal in my knee — graze 'em before you gaze 'em, ladies and gents — there exist systems of utopian social organisation, systems offering the good life to all affiliates, which lie across *either* of the terrible twosome, *neither* of them, and *both*! Were this gigantic problematic stated in a general form, just as a little aside, it might involve centrally the reproduction of ensembles of autonomous identities autopoietic from the furze of one-another's edges . . ."

"How long have you two been *going out*?"

Another little shrug.

"Can you pass that wine, Yuri?"

"Dear muses," Blake orated, "may I pre-empt my fellow elder Aoide a little, and congratulate the great strides taken by *you*, Rook and by *you*, Eft, in the doolittle and dryad specialisms respectively? Casting into inanimate complex objects is a tantalisingly close prospect! And yet, we have far to go!"

"The copy editor," Triceratops was loudly droning, "was the sweariest fellow ever! Like a fishwife! He would tell you, 'These FSC logos are pile of fuck but still you must proof Pantone on PDF.'"

God. God, God, God. I'm going to throw myself off the fricking roof. Convenient!

"How's the vegan option, Yuri?"

Fishspouse.

"For the world still listens to us in these isles," Blake orated. "Oh yes! For a few more decades yet. If we are ever to be great again, now is our last chance. And it will not be through some economic marvel. It will be by only one thing, muses — the exemplarity of our social justice! That we form our kingdom on better customs and laws, than they form their sundry kingdoms and republics. That we control our security, and when necessary, our military affairs, with the best possible kindness. That we muses never mistake what stalks us, or is waiting in the throats of other worlds. That we never forget our greatness of soul till it is meet we do, and that we then devote ourselves to our diaries and such other notes swiftly to rediscover that greatness, or its correct proxies. That we loyally obey our own edicts, when elegant strategy obliges us to forget the grounds whereon they have been devised. And that we demonstrate what it is to obey that edict, 'Know thyself!' Why have I brayed and bragged so re Rook and Eft's little miracles? Imagine this, dear friends. Take it away. Ponder it on the morn. What if every factory worker on every gizmo or doodad or component, in the moment they worked on it, cast the memory of that work into that component? What if every commodity bore in it every moment of labour that made it? And a part of its *cost of purchase*, were to *learn* that labour?"

"As well as all his actual swearing," Triceratops blared, "he was Polish, and whenever he said 'sheet' it sounded like extra swearing. Like proofing sheets, instruction sheets, spec sheets. I mean, that was our line of work. Of course it wasn't *Blake* in those days, the gaffer. None of us were. I mean, none of us were who we —"

"So," said Myfanwy with a sigh and a smile. "Tell me more about co-sleeping, Yuri. Like what about twins?"

The heavens sprang open and the rain poured down.

*

Routed to Valhalla with the rest, Myfanwy heard no more of Blake, nor of anyone really. Blake was speechifying all about the nature of grand plans, and executions and torture again, and war and famine, and economics and climate change and how Chancelhouse was supposed to fit in, but she didn't really get any of that stuff. No one seemed to. She got really drunk really quickly. At some point Simi and Meletē gave brief addresses or toasts or something, which were better received. Then it was just blurs and blanks. Shuttering postures.

Then, just as quickly, Myfanwy was sober again.

Now she stood alone in the dark kitchens, a little apart from the dregs of the party. Next door in the hall of Valhalla the light was low. People were *supposedly* having Eccles cakes and creamy Lancashire cheese and dessert wine by this point, but it wasn't really a feast any more. It was a rupture. People were having all kinds of things not on the menu. People were having it large, and having it off.

Wrapped in kitchen shadows, she peeked out at the stage. Kitty and Kermitcrab were still having appalling Freestyle Clashes, which had been alienating everyone except Triffid, in whom they produced unforeseen ecstasies and strange conductor-like gestures.

"'Yo! Nessus!" rapped Kermit. "Bless us. I will defeat you. First I'll meet you. I repeat. Lyrically and physically, I'll beat you.'"

For a few more minutes Myfanwy would stay in the shadows and watch fragments. Then maybe to bed. Or go wandering. It would be nice. It was nice to be less drunk now. Maybe she'd come across some sort of Veil security rupture again, which would gather her up with long hard arms. Everyone would realise they really missed her after all.

Or maybe just feel relieved she was gone.

"'Uh I didn't mean that, but I'm *obscene* when I *rap* — cuz I'm *lean*, like my *lap* does in my *dreams* —'"

Moth and Bee sat beside Blake, who was sad and apparently brooding on something, turning his long white locks round one another.

"'Only in yo' *dreams*, Kermitcrab, cuz your whacks blow, uh, like your blows are wack, and your 'erb is wack, yo, shiznat, shizzle, here're some hos I run: Eowyn, Shield-Maiden of Rohan's one —'"

There were Pad and Static. Static scrubbed up well too, and tonight she was in this sleek vampish three-quarter sleeve knee-length button-up silk dress, that Myfanwy knew was all graphicky interlocking rectangles up close, but just looked floral from a distance. She hadn't really noticed Static earlier. Hadn't said hi when she set down her starter, hadn't met her gaze during the whole oh-just-let-me-die-now spectacle she'd made of herself.

Merlin and Static were getting pretty cozy.

She had been completely alone since Yuri left, about twenty minutes ago. At first she'd hovered on the edges of groups of partygoers. Then just got up and walked towards the shadows.

Meletē and Tar were getting pretty cozy too. Meletē's toast had honoured fallen Chancelhouse agents. Hypnos, Frog, Sequin. Two of the dead she'd never met. The other, she realised, must have been Tamara Drago-Ferrante.

She didn't even know which one.

Kitty was doing emphatic hip-hoppy Karate chops now. When she happened to slice the air by her cheek, it looked a little like that gesture she did when she was trying not to cry.

When Blake's braids were fully woven, the light girl and the dark one left him seated alone, and looking silly and apparently still brooding upon It, whatever It was. Maybe It was Everything.

Then Paddy looked up and saw Myfanwy.

Her fingertips drummed the air by her chin and she gave him a weird smile that felt nothing like a smile. Actually it felt like something you might do trying to get a trace of lettuce out from between your teeth but without using your tongue, or something. Paddy waved back, then stared into his lap and said something that made Static laugh with shaking shoulders.

He got up and moseyed through the disintegrating revelry-transfigured Valhalla cafeteria, wearing a soft, stunned expression.

"Hey Myffed," he said, coming into the little room beside her.

"'Sup Pad," she said hoarsely.

He didn't put on the light. With the door fully open it wasn't so dark in here anymore. He breathed in the rich smells.

He waggled a finger at some plates. "Uh, these are actually 'plates'?" he said.

She smiled. "*Really?*"

He nodded like he was trying to look modest then shrugged in an "ain't no thang" kinda way. On the counter sat a solitary lemon that somehow had been spared the cheffery. He grabbed it. "I don't know if you, uh . . . but this a . . . a 'lemon'?"

"*Wow,*" said Myfanwy, with a big dollop of sarcasm. But then a sort of snort of laughter came. "Thanks for showing me around."

He tossed it up and caught it once and replaced it very precisely on the surfaces. "How are you?" he said, in a different kind of way.

"Oh, man."

"You were safe," he said gently. "It's safe."

He was looking at her in a funny way. She shook her head.

"No," he said. "You are. You are amazingly safe."

"Am I?"

Myfanwy thought she might know what that funny expression was now. Uh-oh.

At the same time, she suddenly felt a lot happier.

Weird!

"Hey," he said. "Shut your eyes?"

She laughed lightly. She considered it, pursed her lips, looked down at her hands. She shook her head. "Is that the best you can do?"

"Seriously. There's something about your eye shadow. I won't do anything to you."

She looked at him squarely. "My eyes *are* shut. This *is* them shut."

Paddy shrugged. "Okay, never mind."

She closed her eyes. It felt good anyway. She heard him laugh.

"What?" she said, in the darkness.

She could be anywhere. Anywhere where Pad was. "Keep them shut," he said. "There's, like, two smudges just in the centre of each eyelid. I saw you earlier when you looked down, after everything you said. It kinda really looks like your eyes are open."

"My eyes *are* open! This is them open."

A slight swishing sound, or even just a change in the air.

"Then you look like a freaky monster when the *bottom* set open," he murmured.

His voice was really close to her ear.

Hmmmmm.

She raised her chin just a little bit.

"Are your eyes really open?" he said.

After a moment, she bit her lip and nodded slightly. He kissed her cheek and she raised her face properly, and the edges of their mouths were kissing. His hand was holding her by her waist. She put her hands around the back of his neck. For a moment she felt like she was holding Genevieve again. She ran her hands in his hair. She tried to forget her face. She'd never kissed lips like Paddy's before. They were so big and soft. She grazed on them. Just having his bottom lip in her mouth was a lot like the tongue tip of boys she'd kissed before, at least like ones who kissed softly. Or like learning to kiss with Kitty. Paddy's hands ran down her sides and held her bottom. She giggled somewhere amid the snogging. This was so fun. But they were both being more, like, urgent now. Paddy's kisses tasted a little of red wine.

"Yum," she said.

Suddenly the kissing smiles disappeared and she was being levitated. He put her on the counter.

"Strong," she said dumbly.

"Grr," he said.

She wrapped one hand round Paddy's neck, spreading her knees apart and quickly drawing him close. They kissed hard and hungrily, his hands moving gently on her hips and legs.

Something changed about the rhythm of the kissing and they broke off. They looked around them and laughed at the same moment.

"Oh my God this is weird," she said.

"This is actually . . . 'kissing'?" Paddy explained.

They snogged again but it wasn't the same. He kissed her neck once then looked up, foolish and expectant.

"This is actually," said Myfanwy, "called a 'kitchen'?"

He laughed but looked like he didn't know what to say.

He kissed her throat again, close to her jaw.

"Hello," he said.

"Hi. Yeah. Hi." She made a kind of 'trying not to laugh' face. She knew she *could* have laughed if she'd wanted, and the laughing not felt fake. "In a way," she said, "it's weird we've never had a drunken snog before."

"Do you want to go somewhere else?" he said.

"No. I mean, Paddy, I think I should go." She nodded. "Yeah. I definitely need to go now. Sorry."

"That's okay," he said, with a cute little smile, and wide eyes.

But when she scooted down from her shelf there was some more kissing. She kind of started it by coming close to him and lingering her cheek on his shoulder. It was nice when he kissed her. They did it for a bit then she pulled away, studied his face for traces of hurt. Then she went off, with haunting, conflicted, backwards glances, leaving him with his little lemon, of which he had been randomly so proud.

Valhalla was almost entirely empty. Static shot her a gaze of unadulterated homicidal ice.

*

Moth was sobbing on the stairs, Kitty beside her, giving her a bit of a rub.

"Hon," said Kitty, "the key thing is expectations? When you're in a relationship, the same action can be kind or cruel, romantic or cold-hearted, depending on the *other* person's expectations. It wasn't that what *you* did was wrong. It wasn't that *his* expectations were wrong exactly. But in the long term, day-to-day, both of you need to create a context where just *following your heart* doesn't automatically make you a *criminal*! Then that's how you make space for all the *other* stuff, where you really show you care above and beyond your individual desires and interests. Yeah? I know that's hard to hear now."

Moth nodded and blew into a hanky. "You're so bang on about some stuff, Kizzy," she said, and hiccupped.

Kitty noticed Myfanwy and started sketching frantic grawlixes and jarns and mouthing words over Moth's head.

I am so sorry about this, Kitty mouthed. *I am so sorry.*

Myfanwy shrugged slightly.

"Like other people's relationships," Moth sniffed, unaware of Myfanwy. "Which is mad because you're so *mental* about most stuff."

"'We are all of us mentals,' hon."

A fresh theme of sobs shook Moth.

Kitty mouthed something frantically, but Myfanwy shrugged uncomprehendingly.

Kitty pointed to Myfanwy and then to herself and then made general boogying / throwing shapes mimes, then pointed in the direction of the world in general and, Myfanwy noted with a sinking heart, Finger's Piano Bar specifically, then made like an "eek" face and shrugged.

Then again mouthed, *Club?*

Myfanwy shrugged and nodded.

Make tonight stop, she thought.

But if Kitty wanted to go dancing, or wanted Myfanwy to chaperone her to some Cool Kids club then break away and not cramp her prodigious style . . . yeah, sure. She was like a flake of skin in the wind now.

Kitty held up a splayed hand and mouthed, *Five minutes?*

Myfanwy went back up to the terrace.

*

Rain filled the plates. In the wine glasses, rain mingled with dregs of red. Rain pattered steadily on the two figures on the rooftop.

Tar lay convulsing with laughter on the table, eyes shut, hands clattering among the crockery. She'd shoved ginormous balloons under her cardigan as comedy boobs, and now Meletē was quasi-erotically suckling helium from one of them.

"What even *was* the mission?" said Myfanwy as she wandered past, hardly caring if she got an answer.

Behind her, the chipmunk gurgled and cried, "*Don't you even know?!*"

Myfanwy turned back. Meletē had risen from his meal with blazing eyes. Tar was shaken by fresh convulsion. He smacked his chest emphatically.

"*Don't you even know?!*" he squeaked. "*We hit Terpsichore! It was your information that led us to him! We got Terpsichore! We finally got that son-of-a-bitch psychopath before he got us! We finally . . . killed . . . Jasper . . . Robin . . . !?*"

Book Five

"He started drawing a horse
then left off and blowing softly
made it waft into the air."

— Randolph Healy, *Hex*

"Myfanwy?"

"Mmph?"

"Can I scare you half to death?"

"Well of *course*, hon! Sugar, I had *no idea!*"

Ahead and to the left, buttery slivers of London streetlamp light shone through Kitty's two sets of curtains. Red digits shimmered from Kitty's lofty alarm clock, and a low green dot winked where Kitty's toothbrush charged down by the skirting board.

"Once there lived two little girls," Kitty began. "Only one of them was special. Only one of them was important. They were best friends. The other one was ordinary. There was nothing to distinguish her from millions of other pointless people. What was it, you wonder, that made the special little girl so special? It's hard to explain. It was like a kind of talent inside her. It was her secret. It was so secret, it was even secret from herself. But she told it to her friend. She shared it. She — *gave* it to her friend. And what did her friend do? Her friend told it back to her. From then on, that's what they did. Back and forth they told the secret, back and forth. They didn't know what they were doing. They didn't even know that the secret existed, exactly. They just obeyed their instincts and entwined their fingers. As they grew older, each took her turn at being the special little girl, and each took her turn at being the normal little girl — with nothing to distinguish her from millions of other pointless people. Needless to say, their secret got tattered, from so much toing and froing. Before long, a few fragments remained behind every time the secret was passed on. It was coming apart at the seams. Very soon, it wasn't at all like passing a stone or a sea-shell. No, it was more like the girls poured an amount of sand between their palms. And they both knew the grains were becoming fewer and fewer, and finer and finer, and slipping through their fingers. Soon neither girl would be special. Neither girl would be important. So one day, one of them made a decision. She would keep what few grains were left, all for herself, forever. And so she did. So was this girl the *same* little girl to whom the secret originally had belonged? Well, neither of them knew. It didn't matter. It didn't matter as much as the fact that one girl had been disloyal, and the other had not. Though perhaps it mattered a little. Anyway, at around that time, one little girl started to scare the other half to death, whenever she asked. She could always tell the little girl was about to ask her. There was something that shifted in her alchemy. A kind of hunger appeared. So she made sure to make up a story ahead of time. To set aside a few scraps of scarytale. It was as though now was the time to have childish things, and so to put behind them, *very* childish things. And learn instead to be just the right amount afraid. The end."

Silence.

"Do you —"

"Only it wasn't the end. As you know. Because then something even stranger started to occur. The grains within the special girl were not like sand but like seeds, and they began to flower. And there must have been one or two grains left behind in the ordinary girl after all, and *they* began to flower too. And so soon both girls were special after all. So then there were two secrets, two special girls. Two secret agents. Is the whole world big enough for even two special women? If so, can they ever be friends? Or must they forever resent . . . hate . . . each other?"

Silence.

"I don't remember that."

"I don't know what you're talking about."

"Do you think that's what happened?"

Silence.

"It's a *scarytale*," said Kitty.

"Blake says we often come in twos or threes. Says muses are just one letter shy of buses — you wait ages, then two come along at once. Says we tend to be drawn to one another. Blazons, obv, are the best at it. But all of us have a sense, an affinity. And Paddy — *he* says if his theory about the master taker is true, then maybe whoever is bestowing talents likes to do it by twos and threes. So you don't have to be alone. Because no one should have to do this alone. That's what they say. Blake and Paddy. That's what they say. No one should have to do it alone."

"I thought of a different explanation," said Kitty.

*

In an unruly tress of the edge of the spiral galaxy, where every star was young and rosy, a fine rain started to fall.

Surely such soft, sweet rainfall wouldn't douse any front-line stars they really needed? It would only extinguish the inefficient stars! Cut through all the unnecessary red giant!

But Blake sailed towards Myfanwy's spot on the waves, spinning his ship's big spoked wheel with his thumbs, and waved cheerily.

"Avast! Or should I say, ahoy!" said Blake.

She laughed. For some reason, it was a hilariously witty pun.

"I was just studying for Astrology," Myfanwy explained, feeling somewhat relieved. She pointed at the sky. "I realised I haven't revised my Spring Stars at all! I'm on my last chance, if I fail again —"

Kitty joined Blake on deck. She'd obviously just come from the ship Myometrium. "You are so hated by Natura," she chided, towelling off sweat, "that where your corpse falls, even songful birds will burrow the soil, and aid the worms in your decay."

Kitty was "joking" but also not really? Myfanwy would not let herself be baited. "You won't fail me, will you Kitty?"

Kitty laughed cruelly. The ship, Myfanwy marvelled, was put together from Edinburgh architecture. Of course — why else have so many silly monuments piled crinkle-crankle in one Citadel?

Pop! *Oh God, another star! There simply wasn't time to read up on this!*

Myfanwy looked about frantically for books. Obviously Muses had stolen them. She'd just have to take a wild guess . . .

"We'll simply have to grow the beards we wore when we were young!" Blake told Kitty. Myfanwy laughed. He had to be joking, right?

But no, actually they both meant it! Their beards grew and grew, lengthening, ramifying, looking like beautiful Chinese dragons, white and feathery.

Though the galaxy tried to cast their surging beards back down, their beards, sodden with steam, still rose and branched, snaking to and fro to the very heart of the galaxy. Beard flowed more swiftly from their chins than words from their lips.

Now was not the time to study! Now was time to fight!

Myfanwy concentrated on her own chin!

Blake and Kitty's beard lattice danced throughout the galaxy. Soon hairballs were everywhere aflame, and new life circled new suns. They had saved the universe!

Pop!

All Myfanwy had managed to grow was a huge Pancho Villa moustache!

"Time for a shave," laughed Kitty.

She woke up in London in Kitty's bed.

Kitty was beside her, wearing her glasses, checking emails on her oversized pink laptop and popping jumbo bubble wrap with turquoise oval fingernails.

"You know, I've stopped having those weird dreams," said Myfanwy. She yawned. "Everything's back to normal. And *instead* —"

"Mmm. Mmm. What?" *Pop.*

The alarm clock shone down 08:47. That meant it was 08:37.

The curtains were open but not tied. Their deep green, contrasted against the calm, bright grey morning flooding past them, made them seem almost black. *Pop.*

Myfanwy stretched and wriggled her toes. Study day. No school.

The reflection of Kitty's goldfish Eppy gracefully waved in a framed William Windus print, *Too Late*, leant against a wall.

The Citadel had haunted her, till she exorcised it. The Settlement was different. It was a place she could now enter . . . as a spook . . . whenever she liked . . .

"Nothing," said Myfanwy, sliding out of bed. "Can I feed your fishy?"

Pop. "Just a pinch. He's getting a waist."

*

Settlement. Exploring the crest, she half-exploded the cairn with her glorious comet.

Then she went down the hill a little to where Genevieve stood looking out over the valley, and cradled her in her arms. Was this Sophie Black? She didn't care. She remembered her as Genevieve. Even if Genevieve Quaker was a witch who went up in smoke centuries ago.

The day was blue and hot, barely any cloud to temper its intensity.

She kissed the shell of Genevieve's ear. Genevieve was preoccupied and slightly sticky and smelly in a totally tempting way.

"I added our pebble to the cairn," she told Genevieve. "Maybe we should go." She kissed the little sharp point above her lobe.

Far-off veils of dust floated up, up from the sun-drenched hillside into a sky too vivid to brook the role of background. Its vividness was difficult to bear, and so seemed to throb in waves, like a narc car's siren.

She inhaled the perfume of Genevieve's sweat mingled with sweet gorse, ticklish allergens.

The colour blue was throwing a tantrum, launching a coup. The sky was determined to be sovereign, to link in its flashing blue all the world's contending figures in one dazzling frame.

On the face of the far hill, pinpricks of dazzling sun tricked off vehicles' windshields and wing-mirrors.

Ah.

A line of bullyvans was trickling towards the camp.

Genevieve's hair, wisping out, glowed furnacelike. From the forest below, a wood pigeon flew up, and undulated along the line of the horizon as though sucked onto it.

"Mm-hmm?" said Genevieve huskily. "Rozzers, me love. This is it."

Genevieve leant back her heavy head for a kiss — and Genevieve opened her mouth, kissed her hard and impatiently, bit her lower lip lightly, and broke off abruptly. She cantered down the steep slope, laughing softly, as if teasing her to follow swiftly, to follow dangerously. She thought vividly of the downy wisps, wet with sweat, on Genevieve's neck under her hair.

She ran down, half hard with desire, and caught up her left hand, and together they helped each other pick through the steep shattered rock. Yellow flowering gorse, laced with red campion, escorted them ominously either side.

Would they be back in time?

They should never have come here.

*

While Eppy breakfasted on golden fish-flakes, Myfanwy tied up the curtains. That magpie, his wings a pale dynamo, was again barrelling right for her. He veered at the eleventh and vanished. Kitty thought he nested above the lintel. Alarming as always. *Pop.*

"I don't know if it's because Jasper's gone," said Myfanwy, "or because his memories are finally settling down inside me —"

Pop. Two storeys down and across the street, a dark-skinned man in a backwards baseball cap swished a column of water across a bloodstain in big lazy zig-zags. A slow jogger with poor posture left her path to skirt him.

"Focus on exams," said Kitty. "Jasper is *dead* to me."

"Yes," said Myfanwy dubiously. "To all of us, really. Well, whatever it is, my past mostly *obeys* me now. It doesn't try to do my head in with flashbacks and dreams. The Citadel, the Settlement, the Courts, the . . . other thing. Whether it's really what *happened*, I dunno — but it *is* really what I remember. You know what? It's more than that."

She left the window and sat cross-legged on the bed.

"It's me. I was there at the Settlement, at the Courts. I know it sounds weird, but it has to be *somebody's* past. And that person has to be me. What happened, I take responsibility. Whatever I did or didn't do, that's part of me now. Part of who I am."

Kitty groped distractedly, found her toes, and wiggled them around. "Great news, hon," she said, obviously not listening. Then, with excitement, "Oh, Aoide All-Ball All-Stars are in the finals! Oh, I'm such a hypocrite! '*Concentrate on your exams, Myfanwy, or you'll never amount to anything in this world.*' Meanwhile I'm literally chatting Moth now?"

Myfanwy smiled. Greedy for flakes, Eppy's reflection undulated from Windus's *Too Late* to Waterhouse's *St Eulalia.* There were little splashes and frantic taps.

"Okay, I just told Moth I might not go back," said Kitty.

"Kitty!" Myfanwy remonstrated.

Kitty whirled round with flashing eyes. "Myfanwy! Do I *really* want a career in the third sector? *However* smug it makes me feel? Do *you?*"

Myfanwy pursed her lips. "Chancelhouse is 'the third sector'? You'll feel smug *whatever* you do, hon. It's about justifying that smugness."

"Okay, okay," said Kitty, staring at her enormous pink laptop. "I'm up. I'm up. I'm up. I'm up."

Her enormous pink laptop started singing Shellsuit Massacre.

Myfanwy felt dazed. Was Kitty serious? It was too early for this. "*Kitty*, you have an amazing talent! You're way better than me! Fam, my Dwelling's *butters* next to yours —"

"What's a muse's starting salary?" Kitty demanded. "Do you *know*?" She swung her legs out of bed. "Room and board, that's all! With *Blake* anyway — now, with Veil, maybe a lot different —"

"*Nessus! Mammon!*"

"I'm just *saying*, fam, keep your options open. With the market these days, top marks are the bare minimum for getting into uni or getting jobs."

For one year at Bristol, Myfanwy had to get at least A, A, B, C. The better her exam results — the Student Loans Company bot had explained — the better her chances of doing two or even three years.

Kitty fished a Whistles top out of her floordrobe and gazed at it in despair. "Oh God, *this flat!*"

"The advantage of owning only beautiful stuff," soothed Myfanwy, "is even when it's messy it looks nice."

"Sark," muttered Kitty, kinda aggro. She crashed and clanged through the flat. "Do you think I'm over the line in here?" she called from the kitchen area. "Be honest!"

"Don't hype fam, your flat's like it always is," said Myfanwy.

"It's possible I'm now over the line."

In vengeance for Kitty's vibe, she leant over and switched her Shellsuit Massacre album for the BBC World Service.

Then she secretly fed Eppy a few extra flakes. "Dappy darling leviathan," she whispered, with great feeling. To and fro for the falling Fair Trade petals went Eppy.

There was flooding in the Paris Metro, remarked the BBC. Deaths. Huge inflatable plugs had been demoed. The correspondent, aghast, compared them to crenels of a bouncy castle for colossal children.

"I'm so two-faced and duplicitous!" cried Kitty. "My flat goes to pot, whereas I just keep *adding* to my damn Dwelling! I'm obsessed! *I'm* my own Person I Think About Too Much! My parents will think I'm a stoner!"

UN election observers accused of voter suppression.

Notorious Reddit troll Violentacrez unmasked. Not, as had been widely believed, Amy Rogers QC after all!

Bees taught to smell cancer.

Myfanwy went to the window. On the road below a wedding bendy bus twisted by decked with white ribbons.

"You *are* a stoner, darling," said Myfanwy mildly.

"Yes, but they'll solve the mystery using the red herrings instead of the proper clues! It would be mortifying! I have to stop pottering! And I just *can't!*"

Tens of thousands of email and social media users mourned their lost past, following coordinated terror attacks on physical storage media in Pashtunistan and California.

A blue-stripes Tesco bag swung in the nearby branches.

"'*Six British phishing emails feared among massive worldwide data haemorrhage,*'" murmured Myfanwy.

"What's that hon? Maybe if I had a smaller colander. This colander is of a plain design and takes up too much room."

"'*Plus Pinterest account closure warning*,'" said Myfanwy. She thought of gorse.

More self-immolations in Hong Kong.

*

Nearing the level of the tree-tops, they came upon a dilapidated, lipless birdwatcher, who wore a large brown wen upon his brow like a gem in a crown.

"Would you like one of you and the tit?" inquired Genevieve innocently.

"Eh? Oh!" he laughed. "Are you with the — eviction?"

"Yeah, we've been camping." Genevieve grinned. "I mean, blates. Look at us."

"Are you gypsies or bailiffs?" said the birdwatcher, with a twinkle in his binoculars. Obviously a roguish geezer. "Well, have a peek through these," he added more gravely. "Careful, I'm in negative equity with them —"

"Cheers, mate," said Genevieve. "But we should be offski."

"Can I have a go?" she said, intercepting the proffered binoculars — whereinto, she had noted, a camera was blent —

"There you are. See anything?"

Some of the barbed wire barricade she and Oscar had worked on in the night was already down.

"May I ask one thing?" said the birdwatcher. "Why the fancy dress down there?"

Between tree tops, she zoomed in on rozzers in riot gear, pensively ringing yellow JCB vehicles. Masses of yellow vests. So many more now. Like flowering gorse.

She couldn't work out how to access the binoculars' memory.

"Mate, tell me about it!" Genevieve said. "Yeah, some of us actually thought the carnivalesque felt dated for this action, seeing as it's people's domestic space, their homes . . . but," she laughed, "on the other hand, if people do want to party while the world is actually falling apart, like, can anyone be bothered to stop them?"

Activists were climbing into their bird's nests, entering their lock-ons like stone saints in their niches. She saw the Bride rising upon her tripod, and the ivory fabric flowing down over her stilts to the outstretched hands of fluorescent Legal Observer bridesmaids below.

"Jasper," said Genevieve. Gen always called her that. "Give the geezer his gizmo and let's go, yeah? We don't have leaders," she added to the birdwatcher. "So different groups do what they choose. But we do try to give ourselves loads of boring rules, such as no booze, and no rules. Sometimes I think we're as mental as you *lot. Jasper, mate —"*

A column of inky smoke rose from the site.

"Well, for what it's worth," said the birdwatcher. "I support you."

"Mate," said Genevieve. She gargled huskily. "You don't know how that makes me feel. Oh! Oh! Actually — can I just actually give you a hug?" She flung her arms delicately

around his neck and sighed. "Is that okay? If I just hug you?"

He chuckled, and raised a speckled hand to pat her freckled shoulder. "Do you think there's likely to be trouble?" he asked over the top of Gen's hair.

"Could be." She gestured with the fancy binoculars. "Swap you these for my girlfriend?"

The birdwatcher laughed. "Well, well . . . I don't know . . . *"*

Hand-in-hand with Genevieve, she descended the hill. At the edge of the trees Genevieve halted in a cloud of reddish dust, turning to yell up to the birdwatcher, "Mate, we support you *as well! You keep an* eye *on them!"*

The birdwatcher raised an arm in salute.

She kept glancing back as they ran through the woods. It seemed he trained his binoculars on them for as long as possible. Then the trees thickened, and he vanished.

*

Down below, a girl behind a pram angrily waved an arm at the guy hosing down the blood.

"Maybe it's the hopepipe ban —" said Myfanwy. "Ha ha! I called it a 'hopepipe.'"

Everyone was on edge these days.

A prisoner exchange with Somali pirates.

Those Somali pirates!

"Do you think the Fawcett Society would want this pineapple?" said Kitty.

It was an enormous terracotta one.

"I can't imagine inside of their offices," Kitty admitted, staring at the terracotta pineapple. "Thing is, I forgot to transfer my direct debit when I switched from HSBC to my local credit union, and I missed six months. I'm afraid they hate me there now!"

"The word 'grenade' comes from the Portuguese for 'pineapple,'" Myfanwy guessed plausibly.

"Mm, I see what you mean. They would be sure to interpret it as a threat. Do *you* want it?"

"Hon —"

"Would you mind dropping it off at Oxfam for me? I'm so embarrassed to go in there after last time. *Oh my God! Aaargh!* Sorry hon, it's not you. It's just, some of us actually have exams coming up, and can't afford to —"

The guy was swishing his water against the wheels of the pram. He gazed deadpan at the woman. The hosepipe ban, Myfanwy recalled, was caused by leakages, not low rainfall.

In fact the isle was beset by bogs and lagoons. It might go under any day.

Marzipan in Simnel cakes, Pancake Days and Lent. Was there any point in trying to stay slim? What was for breakfast today?

"Listen, Myfanwy, you know how you're, like, a massive Guardianista Leftie lunatic and everything?"

"Please don't sound like your dad."

"Heed, fam. *I'm* not the one who wants to change the world, *you* are. But there's one take-home point from all Blake's crapola re society and institutional continuity and mist and blah blah blah. It's that muses aren't gonna change jack."

"*That's* why you're thinking of quitting?"

"No, that's why maybe *you* should. Personally I think you should consider a career in private banking. None of you revolutionaries are gonna change jack, unless you infiltrate *every* major career path and type of institution, plus a good selection of the minor ones, and yet somehow work out how to stay on the same page. That's just the way society is organised nowadays, fam. It's complex. It reproduces itself in complex ways."

"Great. Thanks for musesplaining Capitalism to me, Kit."

"Young people shouldn't be encouraged to become *muses* any more than they should be encouraged to become *the masses*, that's all," said Kitty smugly. "Or to become poets or artists or workers."

"My Dwelling," Myfanwy said, only to herself. "It's —"

"OMG," Kitty added. "The packaging imagery on this Wind-Eze is so *provocative.* You can see her nipples! Check her out, Myffy."

Myfanwy said, "My Dwelling is a garden."

Down below, the girl gave the hosepipe guy a last aggro gesture and drove on. Myfanwy glimpsed her prawnlike infant. She filled with leaves.

"Hon? Have you been listening to a word I've been ranting?"

"My Dwelling," Myfanwy said, turning. "Oh, Kitty, it's a garden! It was never *meant* to be indoors! It's *always* been a garden! Oh, God!"

*

Bridge Croft. The Settlement.

Entering the site was no problem. Barricades and fences were everywhere felled, folded and splintered . . .

Activists and residents were weaving their living flesh with unprecedented ingenuity into the fabric of the traveller settlement, and the machines assembled there to tear it apart . . .

Yet many of the lock-ons — those various peaceful fortifications supposed to prevent police from just dragging away the activists — were still empty. Many activists weren't even in their damn costumes. The defence was in crisis . . .

Smoke and cries filled the air . . .

Sorcerers, beasts, clowns and monsters dealt with their randomly-generated encounters. Rozzers pursued them, cat-and-mouse . . .

She inhaled. The aroma was . . . opulent . . .

A high arc of sparks leapt up from a police angle-grinder . . .

"What's on fire?"

Genevieve didn't answer. A lion with tears in her facepaint, and her paw in a barrel-of-concrete-style lock-on, had caught Gen's eye.

They parted hands.

Her eye wandered farther. Up in their nests, on tripod and dipod stilts, giants gathered. The Bride. The Wicked Witch of NatWest. Eve. Athene Pallas. No Lilith yet.

Over the giant swung chopper blades. Cherry-pickers' baskets swung level with them.

"A heart! A home! The noive!" she sang.

Now Genevieve was talking to a second rozzer beside the locked-on lion. The rozzer held a supple cane with a little hooked blade on the end, and in his other hand, a little cordless pneumatic drill.

She caught snatches of the rozzer's speech. "If doesn't want . . . let go . . . his choice . . ."

*

"It's always been a garden! Oh, God!"

Now, Myfanwy was no stranger to landscapes gone pliant with surging CGI vegetation. But this was nothing like! No twee creak of time-lapse oak trunks gnarling here, no furnishings split by greenery pouring from their seeded hearts. She'd seen sidling Disney florals a-plenty, stepping from emptying curtains to rest their roots in freshly milled rug loam. None of that, no way! The Garden didn't need to burst the Dwelling's surface in hyper-animate splay, because the Garden had *been there all along!*

Instead, an atom bomb of order struck the centre of Myfanwy's Dwelling. Things were now seen as what they were, but without cinematic metamorphosis of botanics out of domestic camouflage. The tin of paint tubes did not become any mushroom-clotted stump in particular. Yes, her new shaded bowers took certain tributes from the shabby and dimly-lit nooks and cubby-holes of her vaguely Glass Room-esque ex-Dwelling, but without one-to-one correlations. The colourfully-spined little bookshelf had not become any one specific stand of slim straight oaks, nor had the shadow cast by one chairleg through a clutter of chairlegs and tablelegs, glimpsed through the wooden bars of the back of a chair, transitioned into precisely one path curving down through the ample orchards.

If there had been characteristic movements or gestures of the change, it wasn't outwards spilling and splay, *sproing!* and *floop!,* but a constellation of fractal signatures drilling subtle corrections through to the core of every objectified ingredient of her subjectivity. She was set free by a shock wave of precision calibration. Her equipage was not only intact, but for the first time plugged in correctly.

It was a big garden.

She looked . . . around, if that was the right word.

It was a biiiig garden.

Her Altar was now simply a large, mossy stone, near a wishing well roofed with higgledy-piggledy slate, not far away from a pond filled with fish and lilies. The Altar stone was the most comfortable thing in the Garden. Its shape wasn't worn smooth by her sitting. Rather, her sitting was worn smooth by its shape. Myfanwy's Dove was a small pavilion half a mile from the Altar, hidden from view just now by a wood of chestnut and beech. A hint of wings to its architecture. Her Radix was a set of ruined kennels in a myrtle alley way off in the southern reaches.

The Garden extended for many miles. Within its walls and ha-has the past existed in many forms, and the forms were fluid, flexible, pliable to the green thumb. Many aspects of the past could be poured one into another, grafted, bred, infested with one another, fed to one another, mossed over with one another, watered, flooded, replanted, hollowed out as one another's homes.

"Myfanwy? Are you okay?"

The most numerous traces of the past were more slight, more mysterious than memories as such. They were traces which might collectively be called *familiarities*. So many things had only brushed against Myfanwy's life. They left marks in the Garden, but such very light ones. If things that had touched her Garden were brought back within its convoluted walls, Myfanwy could say, *Yes — this was here once before*. A tree could take back a leaf or a blossom, no problemo. The prodigal badger sow could drift back into her sett, her paws fitting against the edges of her pawprints, and nurse her mewling cubs again, or else nose their skulls in sorrow. But for such traces Myfanwy would need the whole form which had once passed through, or near enough — a fragment would not do.

"Would you *like* one of these, hon? Maybe take a couple."

Next were those many vestiges Myfanwy felt would prove fertile in the presence of the right fragments. If a grain of the original pollen was brought from outside, the Garden could supply every other part to the blossom. She would not need the leaf itself brought back from beyond, but only the way the leaf shifted the sun in particular conditions — and from this the Garden itself could calculate and recreate that leaf flown away, build it down to the last detail of capillary wiggle, of dappled discoloured skin, of the Swiss Cheese constellatings of snacking caterpillars, yum. Like a demonologist or voodoo bokor, Myfanwy needed but a tuft of fur from that badger sow, and that badger could crawl from her sett again. Or even something less tangible! — a spark of scut in the grass and that rabbit could return, a writhe of worms and hey presto the lost thrush emerges in their midst, *persona grata* again. Lead but the *drinking* to the water, and Myfanwy could make the *horse.*

Then there were the actual *memories* . . . and that was when it got complicated . . .

There was also a pineapple plant. It was covered with red and lavender flowers and small hilarious pineapples. It looked a bit out of place in what was essentially the grounds of an English manor, gone ever so slightly to seed and with the manor sensibly removed. *Zwei Seelen wohnen, ach! in meiner Brost!* Was the pineapple plant a sign of Jasper, somehow? How much had he flipped her?

And how much of her was lost with him? A great deal, she felt.

"Hon?"

"Fine, hon. Something nice just happened. I think I'm going to stick with the muse thing."

"Suit yourself."

Myfanwy did last night's washing up. Kitty had made this Spanish rice type thingy. The plates were sunshine yellow with saffron. When they finally left Kitty's flat, old BBC events were cycling round remixed.

Shooting spree on a Welsh military base.

New species of endangered rabbit discovered. Gigantic, supposedly — but were they talking like a tiger or what? It wasn't clear.

Somali pirates swap hostages for more Somali pirates. Appalling exchange rate but zero commission.

More self-immolations in Hong Kong.

Cyborg ping-pong champ stripped of cup.

Floods in the Paris Metro had been controlled by huge inflatable plugs. Clip of Parisian mayor, speaking English.

There was a Garden inside Myfanwy. Perhaps later she would dig up that pineapple tree. That's how it worked, right? You're a muse, it's your Dwelling, you can do it up any way you like. Right?

Soon she was in still-wicked Starbucks, textbook stacks stockading her.

World War I was over again.

And there was a Garden.

*

The Settlement.

Snatches of the rozzer's speech floated up. "If doesn't want . . . let go . . . his choice . . ."

Where should she go?

The pointless half-giant, Klimt Kiss Puppet, swayed in the distance near the tents. It looked like a police kettle had boxed quite a few protestors in there — God squaddies, mainly.

She could just join them. No point getting arrested now.

Now one rozzer was off her grind, visor up and showing Gen some ID, while the other had lain down his cane and pneumatic drill and was fitting the lion with a transparent plastic face guard.

From elsewhere rozzers came walking briskly closer. A bullyvan reversed joltingly from behind a caravan. Be calm, be cool. She swivelled left started walking fixedly towards the kettle, where Klimt Kiss Puppet's face and a patchwork of placards bobbed over serried police backs and riot plastic.

In the corner of her eye she saw rozzers massing by the van, undoing one door to its belly.

A billow of dark smoke blew out between two caravans, and three rozzers dragged a wriggling pair of conjoined wizards from its midst, one on each arm.

She took her chance and darted right, then left, into a narrow corridor between two caravans owned by the same family.

A resident she vaguely recognised was there, jiggling his little girl in his arms.

"Hopeless," he said, with a disgusted smile. "Nothing in it."

*

Late at night, alone in the Glass Room, Myfanwy leafed the Revulsive pages.

World War I was over.

October 28, 1918. Czechoslovakia declared independence from, ahem, the Kingdoms and Lands Represented in the Imperial Council and the Lands of the Holy Hungarian Crown of Saint Stephen (more commonly known as the Austro-Hungarian Empire).

October 29, the South Slavs followed suit.

October 31, Hungary withdrew.

History was the day after tomorrow. Four days more, English. A week more, German, and *one* day more, Myfanwy would turn eighteen.

Eighteen! If she survived.

She turned another page.

If only, she thought, *I could "flip" them . . . ha ha ha . . .*

November 3, Trieste was taken by an Allied amphibious expedition. The already disintegrated Austro-Hungarian Empire, an empire which no longer even officially existed, signed its armistice with the Allies.

Chancelhouse doesn't Officially Exist either . . . ha ha . . .

"Days later," carped Secondary Source S, "in the Compiègne Forest, in a carriage of Marshal Foch's private train, the armistice between Germany and the Allies was signed. Very few details were up for negotiation. Foch complained that he could hardly decommission as many submarines as the armistice demanded — at least, not without building them first! Years later, swastika-swirled staff cars, filled with Fascist high command, would surround that very same *Wagon de l'Armistice* and use it as the venue of the French forced surrender."

Wow. Lame.

November 11, 1918. The eleventh hour, of the eleventh day, of the eleventh month.

Lame!

Guns fired from the Eiffel Tower and Fort Mont-Valérien signified the armistice. Wild elation in Berlin, London, Paris. Nowhere more than in the front lines. Song filled the trenches, spilled aloft from the trenches. Opposing armies played football in No Man's Land.

Did they keep score?

November 12, 1918. From the ashes of the defeated Austro-Hungarian empire, a new Austrian Republic was proclaimed. Its citizens had nothing to eat but ashes.

Rumours of Marxist uprisings in Budapest, Berlin and Vienna.

The Allied blockade of Germany remained in effect.

Hundreds of thousands of starving Austro-Hungarian troops abandoned the Venetian plain and trekked northward. As they went they bartered their artillery and horses for food and tickets. They pillaged, set fires, hijacked trains.

First World War Problems. Myfanwy was pretty sure that had been a meme once.

She clicked on the wrong link, but got in before it loaded and clicked on the *right* link.

Boom! This thing is sewn up! Da baws!

"Roofs, platforms, buffers, steps of carriages, even the engines themselves, swarmed with soldiers. Seen from a distance each train looked . . . rather like a madly rushing swarm of bees!" remarked Primary Source B plummily.

Aoide could have called All-Ball 'Bee-Ball' instead, thought Myfanwy. *Like basketball, but also allusive to our charming Chimeric colleague!*

Bit mean though.

"Like excess icing, hundreds of soldiers would be shorn from the sides of trains roaring into tunnels and cuttings. Men littered the tracks, dead or dying, their bones shattered by impacts with walls and bridges," frothed Secondary Source B.

Bit mean, thought Myfanwy.

The exodus of desperate soldiers flowed into Vienna, where food and fuel were scarce. Hungary, Czechoslovakia and Yugoslavia had all suspended exports.

Hmm. Interesting.

Primary Source D warned Myfanwy not to try to post him food, since it would only feed "ze postal vorkers!" Even Austria's own agricultural provinces were abandoning the capital.

Hmm!

"These rural provinces operated quasi-autonomously," Secondary Source C harped hammily, "running stop-and-search patrols to prevent *mouths to feed* from entering and *supplies* from escaping!"

Despite the influx, Vienna's starving populace shrunk. The crowds who had not succumbed were showing the classic signs of malnourishment. They grew dazed, apathetic, listless. They were seized by erratic bouts of irritation, obsession and manic hyperactivity.

"Compared to ze bitter enormity of zese months," Primary Source D added softly — he happened to be Sigmund Freud, author of *Jokes and their Relation to the Unconscious* — "ze four years of var vere a joke."

Myfanwy was pleased to see Franz Kafka was Primary Source K.

He wrote "The Hunger Artist."

*

She peered round the caravan.

No police in sight.

"Hiya," said the toddler shyly.

"Hi."

The toddler plunged her face in neck. The guy stroked her head and jiggled her.

A shadow swang across them. Above, arms from a JCB cherry-picker basket tore the Bride from her dress. Police were dragging the ivory white down off the wooden legs.

A lanky figure burst from a caravan door and bounded over its steps. Under a pear tree he was met by three police and clubbed to the ground. Two knelt on him.

She laughed without knowing why, slipped on her ski mask, gave the guy and his daughter a happy nod, and walked away briskly, making for a pillar of dark smoke.

What was once a shed or something was now up in flame, and before it, with the air shimmering round their shoulders and riot helmets, seven or eight rozzers with nothing to do.

Her side would lose this. She knew that.

Above, a second cherry-picker's basket swung towards Eve, extending arms full of tools to grind and drill her bonds.

It would take minutes, not hours.

Was there even a settled defence plan? The morning strategy meeting, interminable, going nowhere . . .

Damn. Why, why, why *had she and Gen climbed that hill?*

She followed the winding avenue of caravans. Two mounted police overtook her at a gallop and peeled off down different alleys.

A pearly king — for one confused moment, she remembered its glimpsed face as her own — that is, as Jasper's — but she was *Jasper! — wait — uh, this was confusing — anyway, the pearly king with the impossible face darted across the avenue from alley to alley. A second later a mounted rozzer reappeared, and vanished after him.*

But if it was Jasper dressed up as the pearly king . . .

Then whose memory was this?

Cinders from the shed, floating on the breeze, mixed with a plume of sparks spilling against it. Her gaze ran along the sparks to the yellow dipper arm of a Caterpillar digger. A rozzer was sawing — Christ! — through the D-locks which pinned a protestor, costumed as a goblin hussar, to the bowed arm of digger.

She hesitated.

Rozzers deftly disassembled giants. In the sky, only Eve and Athene Pallas still stood tall.

No, Lilith's tripod was still up too — and there was Molly Miller, shimmying along a tree bough to get back in her nest!

Where was Genevieve?

She had a sense of tremendous motion . . .

Like all the buildings and bodies and vehicles about her were shadows cast by a flame, stumbling on its last fragment of wick . . .

Now the Caterpillar digger was reversing . . .

With the goblin hussar still affixed by the neck . . .

Two rozzers were holding his legs and shuffling awkwardly backwards . . . Cursing, she broke cover and walked quickly closer, spreading her arms wide . . .

Another rozzer blossomed to block her way. "Sir," said the rozzer heatedly, "I'm asking you to remove that mask."

Bricks cracking and tumbling, screams close and loud . . .

"Jesus," she said, "at least let him walk it!"

"Sir, we're doing this for his safety, because if that fire spreads —"

"What's it going to spread on? *— it'll burn out —"*

"Sir, first you need to calm down, then you need remove that mask, turn around, and walk past that tape, or —"

She leapt onto tip-toes, shouting over the rozzer's shoulder, "Oi, stop *the vehicle!* Stop *the vehicle! Christ," she said to the rozzer again, "tell them to source bolt cutters. Man, we'll lend you 'em. Stop!"*

Very distinctly someone on the site was screaming for a doctor.

"That's enough," said the rozzer, moving forward, then balletically back, baton rising. "Get back! Move! *Get back!* Move!*"*

The baton fell — she stumbled back as it scraped her chest — bellowed with shock — already its second stroke came cudgelling — pounding her collarbone — pain ran down her spine and instinctively she raised her fist —

*

Reaching for her phone, Myfanwy knocked over some flowers in a jar.

"Flip."

She fetched a cloth to sponge the water off the table. Then she carried the cloth and jar to the sink, left the cloth hanging on a radiator and refilled the jar. She carried it back into the Glass Room and carefully arranged the flowers in it.

She scooped up some petals that had fallen loose and carried them downstairs to the little food waste bin, strewing them on shavings of potato and carrot skin. She went over the sink and shut off the kitchen light.

Jasper was at the window.

Dad —

Myfanwy suppressed the impulse to scream.

Jasper was wearing a red hoodie underneath a shiny black trackie top, which was zipped up just at the bottom. He had his hands thrust deep in the pockets, giving him the appearance of a very large important red pin on Google Maps.

"Well that's not very dead of you," Myfanwy said casually. Dad wasn't home. Working late. Maybe Jasper already knew.

But if she screamed — and no one answered — he'd know for sure. Her heart pounded. Without making eye contact, she lifted a tumbler from the drying rack and began to rinse it. Her hand only shook a little.

He just looked at her. She shivered.

"I'm almost happy to see you," she said. "I don't like the thought of people getting killed. Then again, you're one of the ones who kills them."

He came in very close to the glass. His face was a few feet from hers. For a weird moment she thought he was going to do that thing where you puff your cheeks up against the glass, bloating your face and making your mouth into a huge toothy pit.

"Why . . . you . . . the dark?"

"Speak louder, Jasper."

". . . op . . . the wind . . ."

"As if I'd open the window! I don't want to be able to touch each other."

Myfanwy pointlessly rinsed another teacup and put it dripping back where she'd found it. Jasper glared.

Stand-off.

She glanced upwards. A slightly bulging stain covered a quarter of the ceiling. One day the Glass Room would fall into the kitchen. Imagine that day.

Smash. "What broke?"

"Hold on," she said grimly. "Don't go anywhere."

She put out the light. He was masked by her reflection. Across the sink in the black window a normal looking girl with normal curly hair remonstrated her with fear-filled eyes.

So much for acting casual.

What a dumb face. How was she supposed to float into the world behind that? Like a sail, and her thoughts the fickle winds that filled it. Like a wax seal, and her thoughts the epistle undelivered. Sank to the sea floor, fallen in the Marinas rift.

Myfanwy tiptoed upstairs.

Faces were the fortifications mankind constructed behind which to manoeuvre their materiel. Women's faces were fortifications mankind erected in occupied territory.

But *hers* was not just *a face* and not just *a woman's face.*

At the top of the stairs, she considered quickly turning right to throw on a jumper, so she needn't face her nemesis in this scuzzy house hoodie. Then she shrugged, went left to the Glass Room and pulled open the window.

She leaned out.

Below in the garden shadows shifted and then suddenly Jasper's face appeared, bright and pale in the moonlight.

*

She walked into the dust cloud. Indistinct figures writhed in the sky. Columns of black smoke, and stilts, perhaps deliberately precarious, rose around her.

A pair of rozzers were rather brutally removing Nammond from her concrete lock-on. Nammond was obviously bricking it, whisker face-paint flowing down her cheeks, but showed no signs of letting go, bless her.

She felt so selfish and stupid for skiving when it kicked off. Even if she couldn't have done anything — especially then? Nah, but even *then — the whole point was to* be *there, to stand together with the residents! Solidarity was more effective at* short *range, she usually found . . .*

It was only because the General Assembly had dragged on forever, gathering unshakeable negative energy, that they'd skived and just climbed a bloody hill. It had been amazing up there and they'd lingered for bloody ages. People bang on about the sky being blue and the grass being green and that, but — mate! Mate! They'd had a decent view of the valley too, and while Jasper was away doing God-knows-what . . . 'I've added our pebble to the cairn," oh yeah . . . that'll help, Jasper . . . thanks . . . she'd seen stars cover the hill opposite, realised a rozzer convoy was a-comin'. Five-oh, yo! Obviously one million bullyvans weren't enough! The plan had to be to hang, draw and quarter each and every resident, activist and journo, four bullyvans per person! En route *down to the site a dodgy geezer had given Jasper a go on his binoculars. "Would you like one of you and the tit?" Ha, ha! Then when they arrived, people were still scrambling to get into lock-ons and on tripods and stuff like that. It didn't look good. The barricades were basically already down. Several structures on fire. No idea who started it. Well, some idea.*

Ha bloody ha.

What's the moral?

Stay in every *meeting,* ever, forever, *saying boring sensible things over and over and over and . . . twinkling your fists . . .*

Nammond still wasn't letting go.

Maybe she couldn't *let go.*

She helped Nammond and the rozzers to compose a serene and unruffled atmosphere in which to ply power tools. Cool.

Only then did she notice Jasper was gone.

Lotta clown meat out today. Smoke and cries filled the air. Beasts, wizards, fiends, faux suits, all zipping in and out among the caravans and buildings. Rozzers, cat-and-mouse, pursued them selectively.

The giantess glid magnanimously. Molly, masses of frizzy ginger hair glowing in the sun, ensconced in her Lilith nest. Hiya Molly!

Molly waved like a mad thing, looking like nobody owned her.

Now the Bride crossed in front of her.

The shouting swelled as a cherry-picker swung and officers swarmed up the enormous faux chiffon, a strange infestation intent on spoiling her big day. Some were saying the Bride *had been burning. Then everyone was chanting — "Let her go. Let her go."*

Eh?

Something was wrong. She wasn't meant to be here.

She joined the chant. "Let her go."

A police sergeant approached a bulldozer. Fletcher. She didn't know her name yet.

Then — blank.

Nothing.

The next thing she really remembered, Jasper in a mask, and just zillions of rozzers grasping him, almost as if he were crowd-surfing.

Only . . .

Only she knew *what happened next, because a thousand times she'd read the lies in the press, and a thousand times she'd read the reality in her diary.*

She knew how Molly Miller, peace activist, was plucked out of Lilith.

Knew how Sergeant Corina Fletcher gazed up as Molly, soon free of the arresting rozzers, clambered lithely up a cherry-picker and along a tree branch, back into Lilith's nest and started strapping herself in. Knew how Fletchers' hands spread in frustration.

Knew how, one second later, Molly, having trouble with the strap, looked down and saw Sergeant Fletcher.

Knew how Sergeant Fletcher and Molly looked at each other across the smoke and sky.

Knew Molly's mad little wave.

And wondered, always wondered, if Molly would have lived, if she hadn't waved then, waved her mad, yampee Little Kid wave. Maybe not smug, but would have seemed that way.

And Sergeant Fletcher gave the driver a quick thumb's up and turned around.

And Sergeant Fletcher saw her, saw Genevieve, met her gaze, and stopped, and fear filled her face as she started to turn back.

And the bulldozer was moving.

And she was moving.

And earth and brick were moving.

And Molly no more in the sky.

*

Cold air came into the Glass Room. Below shadows in the garden shifted and then suddenly Jasper's face appeared, bright and pale in the moonlight.

"There," she said down to him. "Now we can talk comfortably. What were you saying?"

"What? Oh. That was ages ago. 'Why are you washing up in the dark?'"

Myfanwy smiled. "Why would I wash up glasses up here?" It came out a bit weirdly babbly. "It's the Glass Room, where we've washed up. Stop it! You're trying to make me sound weird and unconventional! *You're* the one who's —"

"Well," he said very solemnly. "There's quite an established convention about me in the garden and you up on the balcony. Shall we stick with what's safe?"

"Spare me the viola, Jasper. Keep your voice down though, or you'll wake Dad."

"Peter, right? Does he know it's not actually compulsory to use honey every time he fries an onion?"

She hesitated. "You got that from me?"

The oval of moonlight skin swung slowly, nodding.

"Yeah," she admitted. "I think Dad actually thinks they're *dangerous* if left uncaramelised. Christ, I almost forgot to be freaked out that you know all this stuff about me. What else have you got? I've been so focused on mastering the freaky stuff you left in me."

Jasper smiled. "Like what?"

"God, Jasper! The Citadel, the Settlement, the Courts. And just random stuff. Wandering the big pet store with Gen? Pickle and Thumper and all the different rabbits people can adopt, all their stories written in the first person. Pickle, a white and brown dappled rabbit with a brown stripe right down her back, twitching in the wood chips and standing up. Yep. All the weird decor people could buy for fish tanks. Blue tetras and a tiny zebra danio floating through the spookily gutted TARDIS. Perfumed poop bags. Ringing any bells?"

"Nothing." He spoke in a deadpan.

She could barely see his lips move. His face was unearthly, faery, the shadows in it deep but the features obscure, and the expression meaningless. He seemed almost to be a statue again.

Remember this really happened, Myfanwy told herself.

"The strangely shabby Spongebob Squarepants fish tank set," she recited, "which Genevieve said cheapened the Spongebob Squarepants brand for her? Oh, God. Is that the right name? I remember her as Genevieve, the girl who looked like me."

Was that a hint of smile?

"I suppose you'll want to put me in a dove grey suit, and dye my hair blonde, and turn me into your lost silver screen starlet? No? Anyway, Genevieve said she really hadn't expected Spongebob Squarepants to *go there*, you know? She was like, 'Uh-uh, you *di'n't!*' Then the supposed corn snake we couldn't see anywhere in its tank, and kept assuming would pop up for days afterwards. Eek! Big bags of 'large straw' with a rabbit depicted on the packaging under a thought bubble. And the thought bubble read, 'Fields of gold!' They're clear, precious memories. I don't know how you can exist without them. I certainly couldn't."

The garden shadows shrugged. "I know the basic plot of what happened," he said. "Bad things, not good ones. Murder and more murder. My life taken away too, in a way. That's it. That's all they ever meant to me."

"No, you're wrong. They meant more than that. I almost don't want to let you have them again. Oh, Jasper," she fretted. "Why have you *done* this to us?"

"Why flip?"

"Is it really just because I remind you of her? What can that ever achieve?"

"At first," he said. "Yes, at first, that was it. You looked so much like Gen. Appearing suddenly, at a moment when I was thinking of nothing else but her. I mean, I think of her *always* anyway — but it was different. That day in the snow, I was punishing myself with my memories, making myself hate so I could do what I needed to do."

Ha! Here we go! Lean on him a little and he'll sing like a nightingale in a tree. Eerie, though. Later on, don't doubt it. This is really happening, okay, hon?

"You mean murder Mara," said Myfanwy softly.

"What?"

"Mara," she said more clearly. "She was trying to recruit us. You tailed her to the school."

"Then suddenly you appeared, Myfanwy. So much like . . . Genevieve. It was like . . . she was alive again. I wanted you so much, but it wasn't even you I wanted. How do you think that made me feel?"

Like any normal stupid boy, thought Myfanwy, but held her tongue.

"And you knew *nothing* about her," Jasper added. "Nothing. You'd never even met her. It hurt so much, Myfanwy. It was almost like I'd lost her all over again."

"No. You lost her again when you flipped me your memories."

"Don't be shallow. Loss and forgetting are only linked. They're not the same."

Myfanwy swallowed. "Were you trying," she whispered, "to make me into her?"

"No! It wasn't like that! I was just *angry*. At first, I wanted to punish you, to teach you. You were an affront, an insult. You know when, like, a man is mansplaining something, and it doesn't matter if he happens to be right, what's important is the form? It was like that at first. You were like a form, and your content didn't matter. You hurt."

"You wanted to *teach* me?"

"Later, on the bridge, it was different. I'm not apologising for that. I would do it again. I want to do it more, tonight. That's why I'm here. I'll just put a different interpretation on what it is I want."

Myfanwy sighed heavily. "I'm beginning to get a sense of why you're here and what you want. Which leads me to my next question. What happened on Operation Terpsichore? How come you aren't you dead yet, Jasper?" She bit her lips. "And *how much longer* do I gotta wait for that blessed day?"

He gave a cross little growl. "If it's left to Blake and his bungling minions, I may yet live forever. How*ever*," he added, with heavy emphasis. For some reason, Myfanwy's heart fell. "Wouldn't fancy my chances as an innocent bystander."

There was scarcely concealed wrath in his voice.

"Meletē said they'd killed you," breathed Myfanwy. "They *did* kill someone, didn't they? On Operation Terpsichore, they killed someone. But it wasn't you, Terpsichore — was it?"

*

Rozzers dragged Jasper twisting and bucking towards the bullyvan. They couldn't get the cuffs on him. Rozzer hands covered his ski mask. They'd got his chin out, but no further. Jasper's chin was their max. Their combined efforts? Chin. Even that was pretty grizzly at the mo to be honest.

She used to tell him this kind of important stuff: "Jasper, the beard is the Chains of the Chin. Be free, Jasper, and there will be extra kisses!"

Two more rozzers joined the fray — one of them was Police Constable Veitch, though she didn't know her name yet. Jasper was about two metres from the van's open back doors — hello! But his heels were dug in now. The rozzers weren't making progress.

Batons blurred down. Jasper buckled.

For a second he was bent double, rozzer hands on his ski mask.

Oh my beautiful boy.

Then a green arm flew free and he smacked some rozzer square in the mush. She gasped. Oh, that didn't just happen. He didn't just . . .

Simple battery? Idiot! Nine months! Assaulting a police officer? Nine months!

That was a punch, a lucid punch. Fingers all curly-wurly inside his fist. And Jasper was still *struggling! "Terpsichore!" she screamed, drowned by a rising roar. "Reel your neck in!"*

If you punched a police officer, then kicked a different *police officer, then punched the first one again, was that two counts of assault and battery or three?*

What could she do?

Be free, Jasper. And there will be extra kisses.

Could she do something with her talent? Something to make what had just happened un*happen . . .*

But there were so many police witnesses, plus journalists. God damn! Cameras everywhere. Two helicopters overhead, one of them so low she imagined she felt its wind.

Self-defense? Diminished responsibility? Entrapment? Duress? Insanity?

"Let him go!" she screamed, hopeless. "Let him go, let him go!"

Molly. Molly Miller was dead.

No, Molly wasn't quite dead. She was dying now in the ambulance on the crest of the hill. But in a moment . . .

There was nothing she could do. This was all over. The chant started up among the kettled. "Shame on you! Murderers! Shame on you! Murderers! Shame on you!"

And yet there was still that low, spinning muscle! They still *couldn't pin Jasper down! Jasper became the mighty battle-cat! Go, Jasper, go!*

Three horses trotted from behind the bullyvan, a piebald, a palamino and a black one. Their riders leaned down to beat him with their elongated batons. Police on foot swarmed among the whinnying creatures' sides, reaching with gloved hands and blurring batons. Black smoke rolled, shining bodies seethed upwards, zombic, a prolapsing mass grave, Jasper was momentarily lost, then Jasper's black ski mask and lithe green-sleeved arms came again flailing, appearing in fragments, among the smoke and horse flesh, among the high-vis yellow and flicking batons and gloved hands and fists, beating him and shoving him, inexorably, towards the bullyvan . . .

"Murderers! Murderers! Murderers! Murderers!"

Stop it, Jasper. Stop it. They'll kill you.

A sense of ritual bombardment was suggested by the most prominent mounted police officer now raising her baton. It wasn't slow motion, exactly — there wasn't really motion at all. More like a series of frozen images, each connected to its neighbours by a frenzy of every possible intermediate, plus overspilling frenetic chimerical energy besides . . .

What if she hadn't been up on the hill?

What if she'd stayed? Could it have changed things?

At the edge of the camp, the police line kettling the chanting protestors was wavering . . . stumbling under the mounting pressure . . .

*

Myfanwy leaned from the Glass Room over where Jasper stood in the garden with the moon on his face.

"Flip," she said. "Tell me! Who — who did Chancelhouse kill?"

"Yeah, poot! Oh well, accidents happen. His name was Oscar. Not even a muse. My mate from years back. Used to work the next station over in the bindery. He knew Genevieve. He was helping me out. Oscar never hurt nobody — never hurt anybody, his whole life. He's not coming back. She's not coming back. Nice one, Chancel."

"I'm sorry, Jasper."

"Pretty funny? Give you an idea of Chancer-house as an organisation? Jesus, even supposing they *is* the good guys, the sheer *incompetence* —"

"Jasper — I'm partly to blame. It was my information that led them to you."

"Did you *know* Operation Terpsichore was wetwork? Do you understand me?"

Myfanwy shook her head.

"Wetwork means assassination. Not your fault, Myfanwy. You didn't know they wanted me dead."

After a pause she said, "Have you, um — found anything else I left at yours?"

He laughed hollowly. "Your memories? Only what your dad wants for his birthday," he said.

"Geeze, that's coming up. Luckily it's the same every year."

"Plus Bee telling you about her wedding dress some time during the Spring Feast. '*I got it for six pounds? It was supposed to be like fifteen? I cried in Bethany Christian Trust? I said I couldn't afford twenty? No, wait, fifteen? Which is true.*

Twenty I mean?"

Myfanwy smiled. His Bee imitation was eerily similar.

"*'How boring is this story? Then when the little old lady put it in the bag, I was all like, 'It's gonna be so hot when my wife rips this off me tonight. We haven't done it in three days so it's like I'm saving it.' I invited her to the wedding?*'"

"I guess I won't miss that one," she admitted.

"I miss mine," Jasper mused. "I miss missing her like I did."

"Kissing her," said Myfanwy huskily. "Being naked with her — and — and — fighting side-by-side for something good, deciding things together, even against the wishes of everyone — Jasper — you never should have *done* this to us, Jasper! — you never should have done this to *Gen* —"

"You can't understand. I haven't explained it right. On the railway bridge, it became something else. I told myself I was just punishing you again. For daring to remind me of her, when you were so different to her, Myfanwy. When *you* never knew her."

"Talk more quietly."

"*Can* never know her. And *she* can never know anyone again. Only I was slightly wrong. For a moment, it was really you I wanted. You must have guessed it. It wasn't just her I was giving you — it was me, okay? It was the best part of me, the part that had loved her. And I wanted something in return. I wanted a part of you. I wanted to . . . get to know you better. It sounds so stupid! It sounded better in my head!"

"There are other ways to get to know someone."

"I wanted your *life inside me*."

"Calm down, okay? You're scaring me again."

"You don't *sound* scared, Myfanwy. You sound manipulative."

"Sugar. How can anyone 'sound' manipulative?"

"Please. Come downstairs and unlock the back door. Just a moment."

"No. You'll wake —"

"I won't even come in. I just want to see you on the threshold, Myfanwy. You've got a smudge on your cheek. Just let me brush it off."

"Hmm. I think it's time you left. It's been a blessing, *Jazz* —"

"Don't be such a cruel bitch! Okay, hold on. I'm coming up there."

His face disappeared and she heard heavy rustling. Shivers overwhelmed her as she slammed shut the window. Then the rustling was softer, but still getting closer. Her heart pounded. Her shaking fingers fumbled on the clasps.

Come on, come on . . .

The clasp turned and the window locked.

He'll smash it.

He's insane.

Myfanwy scanned the Glass Room for a weapon. Her gaze settled, stupidly, on the bunch of flowers.

In the corner of her vision Jasper's whole body sprang against the window. Ugh. Myfanwy's whole body sneezed with fright.

Grendel roadkill on a Renault Clio windshield. Jasper tilted his head with wordless expressiveness.

Okay. Okay. Okay — the paper shredder?

Myfanwy circled cautiously closer. His eyes were dark and bright.

The shredder was right by the wall. He couldn't see it.

She hooked the paper shredder with her foot. He drummed his fingers on the glass. She nudged the shredder along the wall. It was heavier than she expected. Good.

Can he tell I'm kicking something along the floor?

". . . lock . . . wind . . ."

Let's hope he thinks it's an M72 LAW.

"Go *away*," she said.

For all Myfanwy knew, Jasper had Dad's ginormous lawnmower or something just out of sight ready to brain *her* . . . was it better to brain him with the shredder, or pop it on and try to jam his face in it?

"Open the window, Myfanwy!"

Aha. Obv.

"Okay. But just to talk. You can't come in."

". . ."

"And keep your voice down."

Myfanwy undid the bolts slowly and jammed the edge of the window as hard as she could into Jasper's body.

His arms reached out for handholds that weren't there. He lay back on the air and fell.

Strangely familiar.

She heard a thump, but no cries.

"Oopsie," she whispered down into the darkness below. "That window opens both ways. I'd have thought you might have remembered."

No movement. No sound. No image.

"I also had a paper shredder!"

No cute line.

No cute line for Mara either that day on the bridge.

She shuddered, closed and locked the window and tilted the French blinds shut.

I hope Dad's home soon.

Another night in his bed.

*

What if she'd stayed? How would the course of events have changed?

At the edge of the camp, the line of police keeping the chanting protestors kettled away was wavering, stumbling under pressure.

Aggravated battery. How many months was —

Don't grab the baton, Jasper, don't grab the —

The baton was down and he'd grabbed it, swivelling lithely underneath, and now he was leaping high into the back of the bullyvan —

"Murderers!"

— and back out again. Bodies founted. The screams of a horse, the pretty palomino one, kneeling. Then she reared up, hooves thrusting, Jasper in her withers, his arms wrapping wildly around her neck.

For a moment the ranks of rozzers fell back, all the time he needed to set himself in the saddle. The original rozzer rider was dangling, still attached by some strap. Her colleagues swarmed below her, trying to lift her into the saddle.

"Murderers! Murderers!"

WikiSteed . . . the free, online steed, anybody can edit . . .

Kettled activists were steaming free. Just off from the bullyvan an agent provocateur was brutally clubbing her rozzer colleague with her placard. It looked personal.

The bulldozer's back tyres were alight. Bright flame burgeoned. A lasso went around a cherry-picker's basket and seconds later a chain was rattling into the sky. Jasper, mounted, broke free of the bludgeoning human mass, its placating batons and its battery-aggravating placards. The cherry-picker was lashed to a tree. The bridal chiffon was being arrayed over a digger. A delta of blue flames flew up it.

In front of that — Jasper — cantering towards her, ski mask squiffy, posture exultant, his reins in one hand, his long white polycarbonate baton in the other, his chestnut steed richly caparisoned in Perspex, a police officer bouncing against its flanks, attached by some strap, her arms flailing, her shrieking-whilst-still-professional head swinging to and fro among the horse's trotting hooves.

Then the rozzer dropped free and rolled away.

Other mounted police were lining up. What would they charge at, the punch-up, the tree, or Jasper?

Christ.

"Terpsichore! I call shotgun!" she bellowed.

He was helping her into the saddle. She was high. He'd passed her the baton lance.

She laced an arm across his chest and gripped its handle with both hands. "Hold tight," she told him. "I'm holding tight to you."

They cantered for a gap in the line of mounted police. The rank rearranged, the gap to freedom narrowing. With a quick movement of his rein, one police rider threw his snorting blond steed out in front.

The police line charged.

"Kya! Kya!" Jasper urged their steed into a gallop.

The rider on the blond led the enemy charge, bearing down on them with his baton outstretched. The thundering of hooves obliterated the chants.

At the last instant the rider on the blond shirked. Or misjudged. The tip of his baton ripped her sleeve harmlessly. Her own baton slapped him square across the chest. He flipped back in his saddle and the baton was torn from her grasp.

She didn't see what happened to him next. Thundering and yelling flesh surrounded them, then in an instant they had broken through.

She threw back a glance at riders, wheeling their mounts to make pursuit. Up ahead an officer was pulling shut the first half of a gate. Another dragged a length of barbed wire towards their path, one arm waving frantically.

They were going to make it.

Wow, her body was having a funny response to all that horse spine spilling all up between her legs. She let herself flow into the sensation. If not now, when? In a bath by a candle? Wooded hills lay ahead. The choppers were hovering louder.

"Were you seen?" gasped Jasper.

No, felt like she'd just missed it. Or maybe just had a little one, lost in the shudders. Difficult to tell with so many police attacking you all the time.

"I didn't put the ski mask on right away," he added, "but . . ."

As they crossed out of the site, both rozzers grappling with gate and barbed wire threw up their hands in an identical, oblique, impulsive gesture.

"You must be bloody joking," she laughed. She kissed his neck, more of a headbutt really. "They'll have us both on camera a million times over," she gasped. "Even if we get out of here, we're outlaws forever. We're on the run!" She squeezed him tighter. "We can never go back! We're bloody horse thieves, *babe!"*

*

"Wha gwaan, Myffed."

"Nah gwaan, Pad. Um, apart from Jasper Robin alive and well and in my garden?"

"Jesu! Not now?"

"No, last night. I hit him with the house itself. He didn't get to touch me this time."

"Oh my days. Who else knows?"

"You're the first. I haven't told Nessus yet because of something Jasper said. He has a memory of mine from the Spring Feast, right?"

"Yeah, and?"

"But the last time he touched me was in the rain by the taxi rank —"

"And the Spring Feast was *after.* So you've met Jasper since, and somehow lost the memory!"

"That's possibility A. The other possibility is that there's been an intermediary. Someone I've flipped with since the Spring Feast has been in contact with Jasper."

"Trust. That could be anyone you've touched."

"Yeah, but I dunno Pad. I'm getting better at perceiving when a cast takes place. If it was by stealth, my guess is only a really experienced muse could have done it. If not Jasper, then Blake, Simi, Meletē or Tar."

"Or Veil. Jostling you in a crowd."

"Maybe. Probably not Meletē, with his skiller specialism. Plus I have two other main suspects, okay? Kermitcrab, because I deliberately flipped with him once."

"Kermi— really?"

"That was before the Spring Feast, but only barely. Bee could have already shown me her dress, right? And the other person is someone I flip with all the time. It's . . ."

"Your training partner."

"Kitty."

*

Blake, Aoide, Tar, Germ, Vertical and Undine. The whole gang was already gathered by the time Gen arrived, wearing her enormous antler-esque spectacles.

Blake, in a winding white cloak of light woven wool, worn over a deep grey tunic, tapped the table with that weird thing he had with him these days — something between a slender sceptre and a thick, flanged wand.

"Brethren mousai!" *Blake cried. "Or kin, at any rate — welcome! We have quorum, or a full choir, I should say! Ahem. By virtue of the contrastive offices upon which this affair, in unfolding, inexorably touches, hitherto shall we name it with its lucky rubric,* viz. *the Matter of Blindness and Witness!"*

"Oh my God," muttered Genevieve, slipping into her seat. "I'm so sorry, everybody." She looked like she'd just woken up. Her hair was prickling with staticky wisps.

"Get going Zeus," Germ snarled. "Everyone's already bored half to tears."

Germ: late thirties, long unruly red hair, stud in her upper lip, tattooed fingers. Supposedly the same woman who one day would zoom down the zip-wire with a Go-Ball dancing in her fingers. The attitude sure matched.

"He's embarrassing for everyone, *babes," Aoide chuckled, smoothing a particularly flyaway wodge of curls on Gen's head. "Don't you worry, my love."*

Blake pursed his lips. If he had his ponytail yet, perhaps he patted it in reflective reflex. "Bored half to terse, *perhaps, Calliope? The executive summary, then!"*

In just two days' time, the murderous Sergeant Fletcher's trial would begin. Genevieve, for rather obvious reasons, would not be appearing as a witness. And so Blake laid out his plan. Tonight Genevieve would pattern her memory of the Bridge Croft affair onto her Altar. Then Tar — Euterpe, he called her — would cast some trivial memory into Gen in order to acquire this vital evidence.

Somehow it seemed a clunky, archaic way of working. But whevs, obv.

The muses would hightail it to London tomorrow morning. The day of the trial, Germ and Vertical would surveil the outside of the courthouse. Aoide would be nearby to take their place, just in case they got moved on. Meanwhile, Undine would go to the gallery, and try to feel out when PC Veitch — the rozzer who'd been closest to Sergeant Fletcher on the day, though Genevieve swore she was still nowhere near — might be called to testify.

"And Urania," added Blake, "I really do mean feel out. *I'm not tasking a taker for the hell of it. Cop a feel, or vice-versa."*

Undine nodded sagely. "Gotcha," he murmured. "My take on things." She recognised the man from the web site — the Astrophysics graduate, civvy name Umberto Souphanouvong. She'd suspected him of being Tar's handler.

God! She almost blushed to think of her humiliation on the roof terrace, even though it wouldn't happen for years, and arguably, happen to somebody else.

Urania / Undine / Umberto was soft-spoken, and wore a sweet little smile.

As soon as Police Constable Veitch was spotted going into the courthouse, Euterpe would slip in and cast her the Bridge Croft memory.

That was it. Veitch would be sworn in and give evidence. The evidence true, the witness trusted, the guilty convicted. Mission accomplished.

She stuck up her hand. "Really?" she said skeptically.

"I for one," said Blake, "have always admired the diverting surprises, and distributive subtleties, of the English Courts of Justice. Just give 'em a whiff of the right proof, and they'll deliver the right verdict! Now, any real questions?"

She hadn't bothered taking down her hand. "Yeah. You haven't even mentioned me and Gen."

"You'll be stationed . . . here! Ever seen what the English Courts of Justice do to cattle rustlers in these here parts? I've treated you to tickets to your own bedsheets! Yes, yes! Keep your fingers and toes and eyes crossed for us!"

"You're kidding," she said. "Why are we even at this meeting?"

"Holy father of lightning and thunder and stuff," Genevieve added gently, "We really want to be involved. We did start this thing."

"Why bring *us here," she fumed, "just to tell us we have absolutely nothing —"*

"Ah! Well, well," said Blake, with a soft, aloof smile, "perhaps it was a sort of test. I wanted to tell you explicitly, so there would be no mistakes, that we've got this one covered. And after this little outburst, Terpsichore . . . can anyone doubt I was correct to be so clear? Stand down, *Terpsichore. Leave this one to we muses who still have faces. For all our sakes. Stay away from the witness Police Constable Veitch. Stay away from the scoundrel Sergeant Fletcher. Stay the hell out of London. Can I be any clearer?"*

*

Myfanwy arrived, breathless, with two minutes to spare. Ha! Surely no historical events of import could form in those two minutes?

And, hmm, the invigilators hadn't even opened the building yet. Typical!

She homed in on Paddy.

"You *are* comforting, Patrick. Why is that? You're like a big group hug of Ruperts the Bear."

"Fully," said Paddy. He was dancing from foot to foot. "Can we not chat History, yeah?"

"Agreed," she said. "History Revulsion is officially over. We can't remember any more now."

Myfanwy's Garden was prone to soft vandalisms these days. She suspected zephyrs — probably high, like youthdems. Hopefully *somewhere* down there were some *massive* Facts About The Olden Days.

"What about . . . that other thing?" she said.

Paddy boggled his eyes and checked his blind spots. "I don't think Kitty's hiding anything," he told her quietly. "If she *was* scheming, yeah, why'd she be chatting like all about quitting Chancel?"

"You have no idea how devious she can be. That would be, like, the *least* of her bluffs. Then again, sometimes she's weirdly obvious." Myfanwy bit her lower lip.

Then, just for a change, she bit her upper.

Paddy laughed. She added some crossed eyes and was rewarded by another laugh.

She'd never noticed what a *lovely* laugh Paddy had!

"Come on, come on, I just want to go *in!*" she moaned.

She vaguely felt like it was about the gazillionth time she'd 'never before noticed what a lovely laugh Paddy had!'

"Have you noticed how hard it is to look sexy licking your *lower* lip?" Paddy enquired.

They passed a few pleasant moments in bold endeavour.

"Lol," she said. "Yeah. I think — never repeat any of this, okay? Kitty is realising Chancelhouse really wants to *change the world*. She can't deal with it! The world is already *on* Kitty's side, yeah? She's beautiful and rich etc. The other day, she told me off like I was some Sixties sassy terror cell with magnificent hair. She thinks I'm stupid for even caring what happened at the Bridge Croft protest."

"I've been thinking about that thing," Paddy admitted. "If they're Irish Travellers, why aren't they travelling around Ireland? Pardon me for asking."

"Why aren't Laplanders landing in laps all the time," Myfanwy retorted hotly. "Uh, why aren't people from *Belfast* tied to a *bell* —"

"Chax, fam," said Paddy mildly. "Lofl. You know?"

"Lofl?"

"Um, between lol and rofl, I guess."

"Laughing Out . . . Floor Loud. That's what you've decided to tell me now, Pad. Laughing Out . . . Floor."

"Big red carpet unspooling maybe. Bloop! It's the tongue thing again."

"Always you with the tongue thing."

Paddy looked embarrassed. Myfanwy felt a little colour sizzle in her face. "Yeah," she said primly. "Um. The travelling thing is complicated. One guy at Bridge Croft was saying the worst bigotry was often found *in* Ireland? You might get barred from certain pubs and shops, that kinda thing? Like the olden days in South Africa and America . . . hmm . . ."

Myfanwy gave her Garden a speculative rustle, the first of the day.

Oh, not again!

She saw, from the stone which now served as her Altar, that the scoops of moss and lichen had again been swept away, and lay scattered in a pattern in the grass, along with other tufts plucked from the slate roof of her nearby well.

*

"That's just what he's like, *" Genevieve said.*

"I know," she said. "I apologise. It just seems shambolic. I want maps of that courthouse. How many entrances? Where is the parking? We should have three times as many people helping. Why doesn't he bring in Christian and Mike and Sophie at least? Maybe even Oscar?"

"It don't gotta be Muses Only," Gen agreed, turning towards her shadow on the door. "He's acting like we're some sort of secret mystical agency or something."

"What if Veitch rocks up by bus," she complained. "What if she walks from the rail station —"

"What if she bounds in on a Gummi Bear?" said Gen. "They're so bouncy!"

They were in Gen's room, in what was not yet the west houses. The black curtains were tied up with one white and one green-and-lilac string. Gen, as she sometimes did, was using her sharp shadow cast against her door to help her put in her contact lens. When the light lay differently, Gen would instead reflect the curve of her eyeball in the glass of one of her many charity shop paintings.

She glanced around disconsolately. The dresser top, and the shelves Gen had created by attaching planks to step ladder, were swathed with clothing and underwear and books and elegant junk, such as Gen's half-finished ceramic bird Chess set, and Gen's writhen, quasi-Celtic love-spoons or whatever they were, one of which belonged to her *— or to* them, *that* *was how it worked — and which she'd watched Gen make, start to finish, first by rolling embers around in driftwood, then by whittling, tender and rapt.*

"Gen —"

"No, mate, I feel you."

She watched the back of her head a moment. "What kind of girl doesn't have a mirror in her room?" she muttered.

"Oi you," said Gen. She swirled round, eyes uncrossing, a tiny teardrop atop her cheek. "Maybe it would be cool," she added, "if we didn't have to wait three days either!"

As she was wont to do, Gen touched her cheek with her "Owl" contact lens case and smacked her lips.

"Yeah," she grunted.

Suddenly she laughed, to have been kissed by such a small, flat, saline-filled owl.

It had started with fingertips. Once or twice, during rush and confusion, she'd pinched Gen's shoulder and kissed the air — like the kiss was at the fingertips, like Gen was someone who could be kissed by fingertips, not just lips. She didn't know why.

But one day, Gen lifted a cushion, and batted her gently just as she parted her lips, mwa! *Now it was one of their games. All manner of creatures — ceramic birds, Celtic love-spoons, earthenware teapot spouts, rosy-cheeked organic apples, rattling medicine, glowing phones, candlesticks, books, cold kitchen knives — came twirling through the other's fingers with lips pursed.*

Kiss!

"Jasper," said Genevieve solemnly.

She realised she was wearing a stupid grin.

"We could be figuring out where PC Veitch works and lives," said Genevieve, "and trying to do the action there, *instead of —"*

"Exactly," she added. "Instead of leaving it till minutes before she —"

"Exactly, goes on stage or whatever. God!"

"You okay? I'm sorry, don't be vexed —"

"I'm not vexed, sexy man. It's just, aargh! I don't want to like hold that memory back from Euterpe tonight, or be like, 'Oh, it's not really working.' Like, I want her to feel positive about this?"

"Okay. You should let her have the memory. But — how do you feel about a city break? Just you and me? I was thinking, I dunno, like . . ."

"Ooh. Like London or something?"

"London? If you like."

"Sounds wicked. Hey wait a sec. Let there be kissing!"

And there was kissing. Kisses from owl-themed contact lens cases were all very well. But these were a bit better, really.

"Let there be," Gen eventually gasped, through kisses, "the taking off of the shirt!"

And there was that.

*

"Loads of pubs *here* look at you funny," Paddy was saying.

"Maybe because you're a nineteen-year-old who looks about twelve with ID that says you're seventeen, Paddy?"

Myfanwy made some swift repairs to her Garden. The rock's undulating dents were bare but for a patina of dark soil and a few straggly scraps. She was careful to transpose each vegetable mass perfectly. Sometimes she had to make herself very small within an individual injured clod of moss, grafting and pollarding, turning its boughs about one another like a tree surgeon.

She sniffily removed the sunflower sprouting over her well, and transplanted it to a shaded patch near the Garden's periphery, to sulk alongside its comrades. She returned the rest of the moss to her well's roof, methodically placing each patch, like a soft, papery battleship, on her higgledy-piggledy grid of slate.

Half-emerging from the shrubbery of her Garden, Myfanwy shrugged. "For years, European governments have been encouraging Irish Travellers to become less nomadic. I think some of it has to do with education too. When you've got little kids. *Integration*, innit?"

"Except when the government is like —"

"Yeah, clearing them off the land and everything. I get you, that's not exactly encouraging folk to stick around, is it?"

"So what was Kitty's beef with it all?"

"Hello you lot," Kitty said. "Plans for after?"

"Stealthy ninja!" cried Myfanwy, sproinging right out of her Garden.

"Fully," said Paddy.

"Ronin," said Kitty, as quietly as she had approached. "Masterless samurai. Sword for hire. Fragile speedster."

"Um," said Myfanwy. "No real plans. Thinking of taking a long lonely walk."

"Oh," said Kitty.

She sounded v. glum and Paddy burst out laughing. "What's *your* deal, fam? Aren't you normally all, '*OMG, OMG, I'm gonna fail, I don't know anything.*'"

"*Then* you get the top mark," Myfanwy added.

Kitty was strangely vacant. As if entranced by nothing in particular. Could she have been eavesdropping? She wasn't channelling any of the swarming nervous energy which animated the crowds around them among the elms, animating even the gaggle of Asians across the grass.

Not for the first time, Myfanwy wished she could inhabit the marbled and cloud-lit halls of Kitty's Dwelling.

"Hey," Myfanwy added, more quietly than before. "Are you, like, *nervous*? You're gonna be fine, hon."

Kitty tried to smile, but the smile didn't seem to work. She gazed at them vaguely, her expression inscrutable. "I'm not *nervous*," she said, with the same quiet tone. "God. It's only *History*."

Just then, across the grass, a gazelle-girl hyborg called Zulu or Lazurus or something removed her fashion popsicle in order to bray Kitty's name.

Kitty shrugged again and touched Myfanwy's arm. "Good luck sweetie."

"Good luck hon."

Although . . . *ha!*

Kitty had neglected to wish *Paddy* good luck, and he fully took that as invite to trot along behind her towards the Cool Kids.

When Kitty noticed Paddy was in tow — evidenced by an absurdly OTT falter in her step, as if sniped by an archer — then by her quickened pace towards her Cool gaggle — who spread out to admit her like a *very* expensive walk-in wardrobe, and elegantly closed ranks to leave Paddy hovering at their edge — Myfanwy giggled.

Social slapstick was like a drink of water to her.

Then she sighed. Alone again, she checked her sharp pencils and things and she checked her clock. The exam should have started in, like, thirty seconds.

Something else occurred to her. *Is Paddy being canny? Is he, like, surveilling Kitty? Kinda clumsy if so . . .*

Just then Myfanwy spotted a stray Cool Kid — Tallulah, sitting on the steps by herself. She was rocking the Sailor Moon hair with the two buns on top plus silky braids. Myfanwy felt a pang of envy over that hair. It had to be dyed, right? If she started growing hers now, maybe in a few years it would straighten as it reached her waist . . .

Myfanwy went over. Tallulah was sitting with her head bowed, her hands dangling limply from her knees. Myfanwy remembered that on the day of the Controlled Assessment, Tallulah had complained she hadn't even *started* revising History.

"Hey. Long time no see." She felt gawky as per normal. "Don't suppose you've been studying History?"

Tallulah looked up and smiled. "I did a wee bit on Saturday." Somehow Myfanwy knew Tallulah was about to say something strange and important. "*But* on Sunday my mum died."

Behind her, big doors slammed open. "Okay people, we're going to be *late starting*," said an unfamiliar voice. "So I need you all in here *now*."

"Oh, God." Myfanwy sat down.

Lines of people processed up the steps.

"So, you know," said Tallulah slowly. "And this is really the first time I've been *out.* So."

Are you okay? Myfanwy thought. Then: *How did she die?*

"Come on you two," yelled the same unfamiliar someone on the stairs. "*Move!*"

"Have you told *them* about it?" Myfanwy said quickly.

"Um, yeah. For the last week everything has been *it's what she would have wanted.* Which is completely pointless, but. This thing. *It's what she would have wanted.*" Tallulah stood up. "I guess."

Myfanwy stood too and grabbed her hand. "I guess you'll do your best," she said.

"Yeah. I guess you don't just mean History. Damn, I know you don't have a mum. When did that happen?"

"When I was thirteen. About four and a half years ago."

"Oh, okay. Let's go in."

They linked arms as they walked past the glowering invigilator.

"Less invigilance, you," Myfanwy softly scolded. "Hey Tallulah," she added. "Just let me know any small stuff I can do. I'll keep asking too. I'll keep bugging you."

Tallulah squeezed her arm, hard. "Thanks." They split up and found their desks.

"Ladies and gents, you may turn over your papers."

Hmm, thought Myfanwy. *Austria. They're the ones near Germany, right? I guess they were probably invaded?*

*

Survivors congregated on the grass.

Myfanwy asked Kitty how her exam went.

This raised Kitty's ire. "Oh God, darling, you know how I have *no life?* How like all I *do* is write model essays? Well, okay, my questions came up. So I was probably okay behind that." Kitty shrugged. "I probably got a massive 'A'. *You* left early."

"Yeah," said Myfanwy. "Probably because I didn't write anything."

Kitty blinked. "What? Are you fucking with me?"

"Uh-uh. Nope."

"You worked so *hard,* Myfanwy! Oh my God! You realise you've probably screwed up your chances of ever going to uni? You're taking the mick. You *are.*"

"For some reason," Myfanwy said gently, "by the time I'd got in there, I'd just gone blank. I'm going to look for Tallulah. Her mum's just died. Call me, yeah?"

Kitty, dazed, kissed her on the cheek.

She hoped that hadn't sounded like exploitative story-topping.

But actually, fuck it, so what? I don't care if you are a mole, Kitty, just stop being such a brat*!*

By the time Myfanwy figured out that Tallulah had already gone home, Pad had gone off to Brick Lane by himself, and Kitty was doing some glam X with any remaining Asians.

Myfanwy went seeking the Padster, obv.

She rose up Aldgate East. The evening was balmy. On a faintly pinkish wall Myfanwy saw the pale shadows of dog jaws snapping at scraps of graffiti, the beast invisible somewhere among the bright clutter of evening objects, and its barks muffled by an ambulance's maddening klaxon.

Restaurant workers touted the early crowds of suits, tourists and hipsters. Now a tout strode along Hermes-like with a brazen pigeon hopping at his heel. He traversed the street, folding his wings madly about his feet.

A mother and toddler, dressed almost identically.

Aha!

Who was *that* over hot minty cocktails but the notorious secret agent muses . . . Merlin . . . and *Nessus?*

Kitty was incredibly relieved and slightly cross when Myfanwy came through the tinkly rainbowy entrance. Paddy looked a bit blank. She remembered Kitty saying once how she felt like Paddy was really judgemental and she couldn't be herself around him at all.

Myfanwy squeezed her way round the crowded, buzzing tables and sofas. "Hon! I thought you were with el Asians?" She plonked down on a pretty tuffet.

"Paddy kindly texted me and told me you were here. Um, which you *weren't?*"

Kitty went to the loo.

"What do you think, Pad? Whose side is she on?"

"It's appalling how Kitty treats you," Paddy said.

"Pity you two don't get on better," Myfanwy said frostily. "Given you're my two best friends."

She glanced around. This was one of the newer generation of Brick Lane joints that flourished on social awkwardness and everyone being totally paranoid about everyone else's expectations. You could meet anyone here and nobody could be sure if it was, like, a date, a meal, just booze, coffee, business, all day, ten minutes . . . or what? All you knew for sure is that it would be overpriced and that, in a way, was comforting.

"Okay. Here's what I think." Paddy paused. "I think I'm not an objective person to talk to about Kitty, Myffed." He flashed her a shy grin.

"Oh my God," said Myfanwy. "You don't —"

He bit his lip. "Yeah, I do."

*

"Paddy! You're in love with Kitty! I kinda thought you and Static —"

"Static? Please, fam! Nah, it's Kitty all the way down."

"For real. For how long?"

"Gradual, yeah? She treats us both appallingly. Serious, Myffed. At best you're more like a hickey to her than a BFF. She's always trying to cover you up, like she's ashamed — even if secretly she's proud and wants to show you off." Paddy laughed. "Isn't *that* enough to make us trust her? At least, to trust she's not linked with Jasper? But, yeah." He glanced over his shoulder. "In ref to your question, I fancy the socks off her."

"Pad! No!"

"Seckle." He grinned wryly. "Not my choice. It's driving me crazy. Kitty is a wicked woman, fam. *Imagine* her and me on a date. She'd talk about herself the whole time. I wouldn't even mind. She's so *self*-centred. I'm so *Kitty*-centred. We're perfect for each other."

"I dunno. Chat just now looked *dry*, fam."

"Fam, some next chat is what you saw. Allow it, yeah?"

"Yeah?"

"Only *I* knew it was a date. I feel if she got the chance to know herself a bit better — she might have to proper fall in love with me! You get me?"

Kitty came back.

"Not really," said Myfanwy coolly.

"Um," said Paddy. "I'm just also going to go as well."

He left them.

Kitty opened her eyes really wide. "He's actually really freaking me out?" she said. "He texted me so persistently and . . . wait, I'll show you. I deleted them all. See? No texts! He made it all sound like *you* were desperate to see me. And then I arrive and you're not actually even here yet? *Then he asked me what bands I like.*"

"How long have you been here?"

"Ten minutes too long, hon. Can we leave?"

Brick Lane swarmed. There were restaurant touts, whom Kitty claimed she physically couldn't see.

"Free drinks, ladies?"

"I feel like there are vertical lines," said Kitty. She waved her purse around demonstratively. "Clustered between the bins and the stag night? But I can't process them into *planes* —"

"Ladies? Ten percent off?"

"I object to 'ladies,'" said Paddy.

"Not as much as we do, Pad."

"— let alone an *ensemble of objects*," continued Kitty, "let *alone* attribute it motives and thingies —"

"No thank you," Myfanwy told the restaurant tout politely, "we have already drunken," and she and Pad each grabbed one of Kitty's arms.

Many finance aristocrats came there too, their flushed faces studies in autistic hauteur, as though they mistook — how had Blake once put it? — each pinstripe for a serviceperson's hash mark, or a Napoleonic chevron. Hmm.

Napoleonic chevron.

There were Nathan Barley hipsters, braying in high mockney slang. Most were best left in their medieval bestiaries, but one, who was unusually mashed, Kitty approached in hope of picking up proper coke. Cool Kids® LLP — London, New York, Berlin, Singapore, Nappa, Oxbridge . . .

"What happened in the tournament?" Myfanwy quickly asked Paddy as they waited. She didn't want him to start going on about Kitty again.

"Fam, apparently Seuss All-Ball Unrepentant Rogues were two nil up at half-time till Blake proper demoralised them with this gruelling display of, like, rhetorical *discorso di incoraggiamento* of a completely different order of magnitude —"

"Discoteque de *wha'* . . ."

"— magnitude to any known peptalk, and very unbecoming of a captain manager. Ended up losing on penalties. Aoide can't stop laughing. Still can't, apparently."

"No!" Kitty called over her shoulder. "Myffy, I'm losing the image! The Barley boy is breaking up, Myfanwy! The Barley's breaking up! The vertical lines, Myfanwy! The vertical lines are coming!"

"Oh, *Kitty!*"

The three of them went down into the refurbished Aldgate East. It was even more futuristic than any hair salon. Paddy sauntered away to top up his Oyster Card.

Kitty pursed her lips and watched him with unreasonable irritation. "What would you do if it was your last day on earth, Myffed? What would you do today if you knew you died tonight?"

"I would plough my field," Myfanwy intoned. "But maybe have a nice big pizza for breakfast."

"Nice one. What if you had only three seconds to live?"

"Probably like, 'Aaah!' Or spin around. Or no, make like a mouth with my hand and kiss it."

"What is he *doing*?" said Kitty tightly.

"Like this. Mwa! *Mwmmwhwwmm. Oh, Hand-Mouth . . .*"

"What is he *doing?* Why is he *selecting* a machine? They're all the *same*. The *queues* are all the *same!*"

The night was turning out totally hilarious. Myfanwy felt a kind of comic synergy from all Paddy's and Kitty's little habits and rhythms surging into the same space. An elegant chaos for which she was the cosmos's only qualified audience. She thought she'd never be able to put it into words, but of course there was always . . .

"Fam," she said, "I have to flip you certain stuffs about Paddy one day. You need to understand how hilarious he is."

"Didn't even need it!" Paddy said cheerfully, strolling back and waving his Oyster Card as though it were, like, a raffle ticket he had this really good feeling about. "Bare credit!"

Kitty swang her head round towards Myfanwy with wide eyes. She moved this wide-eyed head forward, in a manoeuvre Myfanwy associated with Eppy the goldfish, then, very rapidly and stiffly turned and headed for the escalators.

Myfanwy had forgotten how much she missed civilisation — London, in other words — where people were not posed by enchanted moving stairways, but organised themselves organically into two lanes.

They were in the fast lane.

Well, *she and Kitty* were in the fast lane.

"Let's just go without him," said Kitty, giving her Humourless Face. "He's just going home. It's only for a few stops anyway. Look at him look at the adverts! He looks at each one — they're all for the same musical!"

"People just live at different paces. We've had such a nice evening. Besides, the chewing gum is on different places on each ad."

"I can't believe you fancy him."

"Oh, not this again. *Honestly!*"

*

Noon. Courthouse entrance.

With Gen she commanded a sniper-esque view of the steps. Four hours earlier Undine had ascended those steps.

For four hours they'd waited, fretful and tense. They tried to talk to break the tension, but only drew attention to it. Eventually they fell silent.

They kept careful watch — the steps, the courtyard, the street, the rooftops. No PC Veitch. And if Germ or Vert observed the scene, they did so in an attitude of invisibility.

Nothing at all.

Chopper blades got louder.

"What do you think?" said Genevieve.

Just a few more people on the streets now — the early lunch crowd.

Now an armoured bullyvan was nosing deep inside the courtyard. Its siren lights blinked, but silently.

"That couldn't be —"

"No way," murmured Genevieve. "Veitch doesn't need protection."

A cruiser screeched in, braking diagonally to the bullyvan. Blue lights strobed out of synch. Police uniforms spilled out.

"I mean," Genevieve added, "no one should know Veitch needs protection. This must be some unrelated thing."

Anxiously she scanned the chaos of faces. "Hope she doesn't turn up now."

More squaddies and a team of journalists approached along the side of the courthouse.

"Let's not assume she'll be in muftis, Gen."

Genevieve swore softly. "There. I'm sure that's Veitch. Just passed the lamppost. Where's Euterpe?"

"No — I see her." Out of nowhere, Tar was in the courtyard, weaving through police bodies. "She's clocked Veitch."

"She's going to make it!"

But PC Veitch was moving briskly, taking the steps two at a time.

Some rozzer laid a friendly hand of enquiry on Tar's forearm.

"Or maybe not," said Genevieve. "Let's get down there."

*

They chose their Tube carriage poorly — Pad's fault again, arguably? — and wound up standing.

They fell quiet. For a while Myfanwy felt suppressed giggles animate her body. She felt — even though she wasn't — as though she was between hiccups.

As Tube stops rocked gently by, gradually she felt less ebullient.

She tried to examine her feelings. How real and how recent was Paddy's crush on Kitty?

She'd not forgotten their kiss.

A kind of excess lingered from that kiss.

The label she'd put on everything — basically *"embarrassing drunken snog"* — was definitely inadequate, probably deliberately so. Like calling it a pixie or unicswarm or something. Perhaps she had just wanted to feel there was something else that was magical and full of promise in her life, something extra, and not yet named.

But really thinking about it, wasn't she just being shallow? — not "leading Paddy on" exactly, but — at least basking in the feeling of being fancied. At the back of her mind had been the knowledge Paddy wanted her, wanted her more than she would ever want him back.

Was that okay?

Um. Maybe for a while?

Myfanwy sighed and ran through her Garden.

The lofty arms, raised to grip the railings in the swaying Tube carriage, softly turned to tall trees.

She came upon one curiosity quite suddenly, after what seemed hours descending a heavily wooded hillside on slipshod pathways, strewn with fallen branches and laced by the limbo filigree of her Garden's infinitesimal spiders.

Crossing what felt like a slippery wooden bridge — though it was really only a railed wooden platform, running parallel to a creek down in a deep ravine — Myfanwy turned a corner and saw where the trees thinned and the ground levelled. She felt mild surprise, for she had come very close to this part of the hillside at a higher elevation, and had seen no clearing.

She felt vaguely exultant.

Her surprise soon changed into a sense that a suspicion she had been nursing about the topology of the Garden was now confirmed by a sharp and unmistakeable example of something which had been happening all along: space in the Garden was not a pure, unstructured volume, not something symmetrical no matter what angle you skewered it at.

Instead, the Garden's space was somehow more infolded, so that the distance between two points depended on whether you stood at one or the other, or at some other point. It was like something you read about in big physics books only much, much more interesting.

In the clearing was a kind of heap of branches and dried leaves and stuff. It looked like someone had assembled it for a bonfire, but abandoned or forgotten the fire long ago, because fresh moss and great floury crusts of bread-of-the-forest mushrooms now were sprouting in its recesses.

That wavy fungus, Myfanwy recognised, was her recollection of passages of Herman Melville's *Moby Dick*. Last summer she'd had a temp job, mostly composing rejection letters and proofreading children's books, at the publisher Simon & Schuster on Gray's Inn Road. She ostentatiously took *Moby Dick* to read during lunch breaks, even though she'd already precociously finished it the summer before. "I was eager to see the harpooner's face, but he kept it averted for some while, employed in unlacing the mouth of his bag." Memory wasn't often this condensed, this localised. It felt important when it was.

It would be good if, instead of a white ribbon to raise awareness of violence against women, everyone wore a white whale. That would raise so much awareness.

The sunset-lit grass was full of little shakes.

Myfanwy would trot nervously to work in those days — her first ever job! — imagining over and over the little snippets of chat she could have with her Colleagues, to try and seem Normal.

Whenever she finally blurted the words — a bit of news about her weekend, or whevs — the natural rhythms of her speech were completely destroyed, or at least, unavailable to her, just like sometimes really normal information is unavailable in dreams. Throughout the summer she carefully studied her co-workers' expressions, trying to infer if she'd bellowed, or freestyle-rapped, or miaowed and purred or anything.

She made billions of little pencil ticks. Her bosses didn't trust her to proof on PDF. *Tick!*

She rounded the pyre and pressed on into the trees. What was the morel of the story, lol?

Soon she found another resonant place. A path of white hay wound round a misshapen dome of moss-heaped tree-root, rose and vanished. Leaves from last year lay tatterdemalion on the hay.

She sat on the moss.

She started to become the moss.

It would be good, Myfanwy thought, if muses could proofread their thoughts and feelings before they felt them. That way if you were about to have, like, a racist thought about a cannibal harpooner, or about to fall in love with the wrong person, or something like that, then you could — what? Leave that thought tucked in the bonfire, like an undiscovered hedgehog cub? Or like a little witch or muse?

Tick! Tick! Tick!

I commit thee to the flames, inappropriate crushes, gollywog hedgehogs, chav owls, poofter puppies turned up proofreading my thoughts and feelings before I feel them . . . next, I will proofread the pain in my lips . . .

At Simon & Schuster the Arch-Editor blocked most social media, so whenever Myfanwy felt herself slipping off to sleep, she'd flip to a random page of *Moby Dick* and read a paragraph of Ahab pacing the Pequod's deck, or the cannibal Queequeg doing next level BFF shizzle on Ishmael's behalf, or something.

This was all very, very, very off-message, wasn't it?

Myfanwy supposed the English Canon counted as a primitive (but hard-to-block) social media site — like Friend-Space or http-My-Page or whevs.

Paddy!

There was the creaking of branches being bent back. Then Myfanwy *sproinged* back into the crowded Tube carriage.

The suit in the seat in front of her was staring at her. Perhaps the spectacle of a woman in thought affronted him?

Paddy and Kitty were both staring at Kitty's slightly Duck Face reflection.

Myfanwy tried another perspective on the Paddy Problem. Say Paddy *did* fancy her. Who was she to deny Paddy if — in order to help himself get over her — he chirpsed and flirted a little bit with Static?

Just for example.

Of course, if Paddy didn't draw the line at some point, Static would get hurt. And by analogy . . .

Where did Myfanwy draw the line with Paddy? Had she *cared* about any line? She half-supposed he fancied her. Had she really changed her attitude after that snog? If anything, she'd encouraged him! Teasing. Batting eyelashes. Hinting that Pad, not Kitty, was her BFF. How must that have felt to him?

She thought about Paddy's kindness. How he'd tried to stand tall for her at her first big Chancel briefing. How he could always carry her bags without it feeling like a boy coup. How he could be reasonable when she was in a rage and it made her feel more in control, not more impotent. How he always picked up right away and was never too busy to talk.

Down some Lemsips, come help me run this crew off this corner, Myffed.

Plural article, implying lemony lemony overdose in the snow. So it was clear it was just a joke, so Myfanwy wouldn't feel that tiny moment of pressure, to come out and play, that tiny moment of regret and increased distance when she decided to say *no.* So gentle.

And if her voice had been a little less husky? Would Paddy have had the nano-courage to suggest just one cuppa Lemsippa? She thought he would. To give her that little boost she needed, to rise from indecision, bring her out among the falling flakes.

She *knew* he would. She'd known Kitty all her life, Paddy only two years, and yet *he* was the one she could go to to find *herself.*

Was she in love with Paddy?

In *his* words, in his looks, there were these *contours* — invisible, except for the dappling of the nano-shadows they cast, except for the way, as it were, that the light lay on their surfaces — contours in which Myfanwy's true image was delineated. Those delicate touches, unthinking yet thoughtful, those details that could only come from constant attentive care. The objectivity of Myfanwy's being, the mask of her face, the person she was to the world, would never be hung in some resembling portrait, never pasted onto black glass to obscure where murderers lurked. Only a soul had the right reflective surface to reveal it.

But, thought Myfanwy, slightly anxious, *"soul" is completely the wrong word. And what,* she then thought, starting to panic, *what if I've been wrong, all wrong, wrong about Paddy's soul?*

What if she'd mistaken Pad's all-purpose kindness for specific care for her? It was just the kind of stupid self-aggrandising thing she might do! What if Paddy had already forgotten about their kiss? What if that kiss *really was* something closer to that false label Myfanwy had placed purposefully on it, so that she could gloat it was something indefinably better?

Just a drunken snog. Hormones and booze.

Or even something *worse* and more abased — what if it was Paddy *using* her, like trying to distract himself from Kitty, or even trying illogically to tangle himself with Kitty via some kinda voodoo association with Myfanwy? Kiss the lips that once her lips had kissed?

God.

She realised she'd been chewing her lips rather hard and broken the skin a little.

In a *way* though, wouldn't that be better? It would make her less culpable. It would mean she hadn't been careless with Paddy's feelings, because he never really cared about her — not in that way — in the first place.

Nonetheless, it left her feeling really empty, and like there was this tiny bud of irrational hatred and envy beginning to nose its way towards Kitty, a dark bud of dense creamy poison which would really need some kind of — or, wait a moment, was she just trying to talk herself out of the fact that actually when it came to Paddy, she really, really —

Abruptly, the suit who had been regarding Myfanwy for some minutes asked, "Would you like a seat?"

"No thank you," said Myfanwy, feeling herself blush.

"Oh, please," he said, rising. He picked his way down to the vestibule and stood there, chin on his shoulder, facing away.

Myfanwy, Paddy and Kitty regarded the vacant seat. So did everyone else in the carriage.

Eventually Kitty said, "Well shall I *spit* on it?"

"Is it wrong?" said Myfanwy. "I'm obviously not frail and feeble —"

"Hmm," said Paddy.

"— or pregnant —"

"Hmm," said Kitty.

"— so it *is* just because I'm a woman."

"Keep your voice down," said Kitty.

"Myffed," said Paddy. "Not every guy who offers you his seat is some fully rampaging sexist."

"Oh my God I was so *wrong* about you! That is such a strawman argument," said Myfanwy hotly. "You're strawmanning me."

"He's throwing straw on the flames," conceded Kitty. "But hon, men already have so many advantages. Why give up the one or two advantages we do have?"

The somewhat smudged zigzag-print seat cushion looked awkward and embarrassed.

"*Aargh,*" said Myfanwy. "I can't *believe* —"

"And hon, remember what we said about having to remember the reasons for what you think, not just *what* you think."

"Because those advantages only ever work on an individual level," said Myfanwy slowly, trying to will the blood out of her blush and into her brain. "But their consequences hurt everyone. Offering your seat. Holding doors open. Walking you home at night. Assuming you can cook. Not taking you seriously. Talking over you. Mansplaining you. Laughing at you and undermining you. Not paying you enough, not promoting you, not voting for you."

"Walking you *home?* Jesus, have you even *been* raped?" said Kitty.

"I didn't —"

"If you don't sit there, I will," said Kitty.

Paddy sat in the seat. "Hey," he said casually. "That woman we saw get killed? She just got on."

"Wow," said Myfanwy. "You should definitely offer *her* your seat."

"Definitely."

"Definitely."

*

"Stay on Veitch," said Genevieve. "I'll grab the testimony from Euterpe."

They split. She jogged up the steps, shouldering through squaddies and journos. Her phone was in her hand, dialling Undine.

She glanced back at Tar — who was shaking her head, eyes wide, hands clasped at her cheek — Genevieve was nowhere to be seen —

She was in the courthouse now. A bright, loftily vaulted foyer. Filled with breezes and clicking heels. A curved reception desk directly ahead. Three receptionists, blurred features and sharp stares. On the left a row of doors. An icon of a staircase.

No PC Veitch.

Lifts to her right. She looked at the LEDs. One blue light moved from "8" to "7" to "6." The other moved from "1" to "2" and dwelt there.

She walked briskly for the stairs. Lawyers and squaddies moved around her, murmuring and clicking. Maybe she was drawing glances.

Undine answered. "Terpsichore. You're here."

She pushed through the stairs door. "Euterpe missed the hand-off with Veitch. I'm in the courthouse, on the stairs."

"Put Euterpe on," said Undine.

"I'm by myself and I've lost our witness. Where do I go?"

"Second floor," said Undine. "Two above ground. Shall I stay in the gallery?"

"No. Move. Stall Veitch if you can."

"What's the point? We don't have the memory."

"Gen will bring it. I'm on the second floor."

"No. Abort, Terpsichore."

"Guide me, Urania."

Either she messed up or Undine did. She was soon lost, then back-tracking.

The corridors were empty. Her breath came fast. She passed an open door. A chamber full of faces looked up.

She smiled.

She passed it, broke into a light sprint, turned a corner.

Another corner. In her ear, Undine told her she was back on track. "But I have word from Blake to abort."

"Noted."

She turned another corner.

Veitch and another officer walked towards her.

PC Veitch was an androgynous woman, mostly bald, with a skin crack running across her jaw and through her lower lip like a bridle. She could be in her thirties or forties, but her face was lined with early wrinkles. The face of a guru or a hoodlum, as if painted on a grimoire's gilt fore-edge.

The other glanced up indifferently. Veitch stared and started.

"You!" she breathed.

"Run," called an echoey voice. Genevieve had appeared down a side corridor. "Terpsichore, just run. I have the testimony."

Genevieve strode close, breathing heavily but looking calm. Her craft knife was in her hand.

"This won't work," she said.

A distant door opened. Undine.

"What is this?" said Veitch.

"Hands against the wall, Veitch," Genevieve told her, swinging the blade level with her face. "No one wants to hurt you, I swear. You too, ma'am. Hands —"

Footsteps, drawing closer.

"Someone's coming, Gen."

"This will work. Turn around, Veitch!"

"You're barmy," said Veitch slowly. "Do you know how many police officers —"

"Veitchy —" said the other, very pale.

"Gen," she whispered. "Cast me the testimony. See who's coming."

Gen didn't hesitate. She placed the craft knife in her hand and with the same touch she cast the memory, clean and bright and smoking. Lotta clown meat out today. Molly's mad little wave. Earth and brick and sky were moving.

Gen was jogging round the corner. She heard her launch into a spiel.

"Get against the fucking wall or I'll cut you," she said.

"He will," said Undine mildly, drawing up next to her.

The pale other obliged. Then, disdainfully, so did Veitch.

She folded away Gen's craft knife and, digging in her Dwelling, touching Veitch on the back of her neck, she cast.

"Apologies for the inconvenience," said Undine. "Keep watching that wall."

"Done. Urania. Do them both quickly."

Now what was it she'd just been thinking of? Bridge Croft.

Undine placed a hand on each police officer's back. "Veitch is easy. This one's a mess. I can't tell what's what. Drat. I think she has —"

People were turning the corner. She turned her back to them. "What do we do?" she said.

"She has a condition." In the corner of her eye, Undine shook his head. "I can still handle it. Just leave."

She walked briskly away. Footfalls echoed.

As they approached the corner, she heard Undine. "Everything alright, ladies? Something I can help with?"

"No, we were just — uh —"

"I was looking for a room," said Veitch. "A room where I am supposed to be."

She laughed hollowly as she turned the corner.

In the foyer, someone fumbled for her elbow. It was Germ. "Terpsichore — what the hell is happening? Where are —"

"I think we did it," she said. "Have you seen—"

And there were Gen and Undine.

"Little late to the party," said Gen. "But what a party! Come on. Let's get the hell out of here."

*

Mara picked up a discarded newspaper. There was a fresh pinkish scar on her upper left cheek. It didn't look too bad, at least not from a distance. It hung from her big blue eye like the wake of a tear.

"Don't catch her eye," Paddy murmured. "Let's watch where she gets off."

"Maybe she has amnesia," Myfanwy whispered. "Doesn't know she's a muse!"

Kitty studied an ad for a certain nation's beaches. "Not convinced, hon. Is it definitely her?"

Mara didn't switch lines. They travelled northwards. The carriage gradually emptied. Soon Mara put aside her newspaper and stared fixedly ahead.

"She's bound to see us," whispered Kitty.

"Don't look up," Paddy said calmly. "Hide your faces. She don't know me. I'm on it."

At Seven Sisters Mara alighted.

Myfanwy hardly watched her as they tailed her. Paddy watched her. Myfanwy and Kitty just watched Paddy.

They slipped through unfamiliar neighbourhoods. The rain-slicked streets slowly emptied. Mara moved briskly, pausing now and then to check her phone.

"She's gonna spot us," murmured Kitty.

"I don't think so," said Myfanwy thoughtfully.

Grass soaked her socks through her shoes. The wet road glowed yellow lamp-light, while high atop tower-blocks blue light gleamed down.

A white woman marooned, by a recently fallen moat, from her green glass recycling bank, was lining up a Laroche Chablis at the edge of the shooting circle. As it deftly fell down the slot and smashed she swore with pleasure.

Two youfdems snaked past, stood tall on their bikes in caps and hoods.

Crossing a council estate, they came across a woman in pinstripes strewing rags around a row of bollards and photographing them. She glared.

They moved through a slightly busier area. A few figures congregated outside off-licences and cafés.

Then down wide, empty streets.

They passed a tall thin boy stalking a cat.

Rows of ill-kept mansions. White, peeling paint. Most of the "to let" signs were defaced.

Mara approached a tall, comparatively well-to-do block of flats. She started rummaging in her purse.

"Hang back," instructed Paddy. "Let me do this."

He sounded alarmed.

Mara stopped. So did Myfanwy and Kitty, beside a plane tree, partially hidden. Paddy put up his hood and strolled across the street.

Mara stopped rummaging and looked up at Paddy.

"Oh God," murmured Kitty. "Why did we send him? Can't he pretend to do his shoelace or something?"

Paddy walked past.

Then Mara was swiping a card and punching in a code. Myfanwy saw a little green light wink.

Mara was gone. Motion-sensitive corridor lighting came on as the thick glass door swung slowly shut.

Paddy darted forwards. He stumbled.

The door had — no, Paddy's skidding front foot had found the gap between the door and the frame.

Kitty breathed a sigh of relief. "We're in."

"Calm," murmured Myfanwy. "Don't rush. Careful."

They flowed around the plane tree and approached Paddy. He looked panicked, not proud.

Afraid and greedy.

"Inside!" he hissed softly. "I saw her go up the stairs! Inside! Inside!"

"Enough," said Myfanwy. She regarded coolly Paddy's glittering eyes. "You took a long time to top up your Oyster Card. Didn't you, Pad? That top up was long, fam."

"Not now, Myfanwy!"

"Myffy," said Kitty. "Allow it."

"Then you insisted we get on the last carriage, which was full. Even though we passed carriages with empty seats. Why *that* train? Why *that* carriage?"

"Come on, Myffed," Paddy urged. "We're losing her!"

"I don't think so," said Myfanwy. "No. I think she's waiting at the top of the stairs, pretending to check her phone again. Till she's certain we're behind her. I think you two arranged this whole thing. Well done. It nearly worked."

Paddy's eyes beseechingly sought Kitty.

"Paddy?" said Kitty, nervously.

"What I couldn't work out is why," said Myfanwy slowly. "Only I think I just did. Blake never mentioned Mara as our headhunter — only you, Merlin. That's because — Mara is Veil, isn't she? She was Chancelhouse once. That's all Blake ever said. He doesn't like to talk about it. Not because she died, but because she left. When Mara came to recruit us, it was for Veil. She's Veil." Myfanwy hesitated. "And so are you. Aren't you Paddy? That's why Vert was in your room that night — it was a drop-off. *You're* the one Yuri's been looking for. *You're* the mole."

*

Citadel . . .

City of dreadful dying. Betrayal. Terrible betrayal. Someone was dying . . .

Yes, this was it . . . this was how it happened . . . with a muffled roar . . . no, with a scream . . . a scream of . . .

No . . .

Genevieve . . . storming down a corridor of the west houses, before they were the west houses . . .

No . . . something was still missing . . .

Not yet . . .

Hidden, crouching . . . aching calves . . . wrong . . . did the wrong . . . waiting, gambling cowards in gardens . . . already too late . . . no atonement . . . no fixing . . . only something else . . . not yet . . .

The argument echoed up the corridor . . .

Gen and her in the kitchen, talking quietly. Flux miaowed and leapt, as was her wont, for the mop-head — hunting for buried tonsure? — and clung on for dear lives (nine, obv). Gen mopped the tiles, with judicious briskness, with Flux.

"Check the news again?" said Gen. Tense. Election day? No. The trial.

Flux stared wildly and yawned.

Now she was entering Blake's study. The old one, in the west houses, before they were the west houses . . .

Blake was exultant.

Genevieve was in tears.

Aoide was there, looking concerned.

Lain on the Blake's desk, among papers, grimoires and flowers, a tablet was playing Constable Veitch's testimony for the umpteenth time . . .

"You're gonna drive me out," Genevieve said. "This was our thing. All together. I can't do this."

"Hello Terpsichore," Aoide said briskly. "Nothing like a little family drama, eh?"

"What's happening, Gen?"

"Oh, Jasper. He thinks we'll be superheroes. He's banging on like we won."

"Paradigmatically," babbled Blake, obviously trying to check his cheerfulness. "Undine on spatchcock delenda duty, etc. I mean to say —"

"Look, I get *you! Swords at the back of their necks! Spells at the back of their skulls! Takers scrubbing all sign of our passing. We're, like, men in black. We can do anything, and we will. Jasper, it was monstrous and they want to do it all* again*."*

"No one is more distressed than I," murmured Blake, without any signs of distress, "that PC Veitch lied, that Sergeant Fletcher walked. 'Unqualified success' may have been unfortunately provocative phraseology. I've apologised already. But with what we have learned *from this episode —"*

"And that helps the families of Croft Farm how? *And that helps Molly Miller* how?*"*

"Babes," said Aoide. "Nothing could ever help Molly Miller."

Among the pagodas of papers and grimoires and beside the fresh azaleas in the red-figured hydria, PC Veitch's lying testimony was on a loop . . .

"But it helps Chancelhouse," Blake soothed. "It helps the world. It means Molly's sacrifice now has meaning. Now, I've said you two were out of line, mingling in the undertaking, putting yourselves at risk, directly in conflict to orders —"

"Orders?" cried Genevieve.

*"*Very *nearly ruining it —"*

"Come on*," she said.*

*

Myfanwy stood just where Paddy couldn't reach her without moving his foot from the door.

Kitty stood between them.

Myfanwy dropped in on her Dwelling.

Hello, you!

"Myffy's off on one again," Paddy said. "Looks like it's just you and me, Kitty."

His voice was so tense.

But his voice was elsewhere . . .

Into her orchard canopy, Myfanwy composed strange Dwindlings, shaped with the help of wood pigeon wings. Shuddering wings split sunbeams into suspicious searchlights, wriggling in the dark grass.

The memory she wanted to flip was proving difficult to find. Partly because she was panicking, because there wasn't much time. Partly because when the conversation happened, it hadn't felt important.

Myfanwy's Dwelling cooed and glimmered its complaint.

Hidden, crouching, aching calves . . .

The memory was more difficult to discover than any plant or beast. Star-nosed moles in the first spit of topsoil tilted blades of grass to strange glinting inspections of pigeon-slanted twilight. But the memory employed many hiding places at once. It was not like a very small ant. It was like a system of chequering shade, widely spread, soft and frail, and yet deeply implicated in the garden's most essential architecture and ecology.

"Leave Myffed behind," instructed Paddy. "Just come inside. Or I'll go alone. I'm not afraid of nothing."

She had to change strategy. These days Myfanwy's Hoard had become a large pond clad with lilies, its farthest edge indecipherable under masses of exotic flora . . .

Hidden, crouching, aching calves . . . wrong . . . did the wrong . . . waiting, gambling cowards in front gardens . . . already too late . . . low walls . . . dark like the entrails of statues . . . no atonement . . . no fixing . . . only something else . . . not yet . . . please, not yet . . .

I miss her so much . . .

"Go alone then," said Kitty.

Near to the Hoard there stood a tall ash tree ravelled in ivy. Now the veins of each leaf of ash flowed splicingly back down their stem. The proud ash bent like a weeping willow, panning the lily pond with its little blank palms.

Bark swelled, packed with root-hoovered wet earth. The tops of roots began to appear.

Elsewhere, cherry blossoms jealously unfastened to envelop shrinking thin brown pears for protection.

Red fruits disrobed.

Starting above the Altar, spreading throughout the Dwelling's orchards, fruits unpeelingly reared, skins of apples, satsuma, japonica. The wooden well bucket wandered out on its rope, brushing the heads of blades of grass. Fanning spirals and helices of orange, green and red peel wafted meticulously, formulating orders of zephyr which shared their shapes with typhoons.

"She's stalling," Paddy said. "Myfanwy, allow it!"

The linguistic ontology was maximally provisional. Myfanwy bred and transposed complex structure across every asset class. All phenomena were iterated across all properties and scales.

"Why does she want Mara to get away?" Paddy said. "What is she hiding?"

In her Dwelling, strange seasons lasted nanoseconds. Likkle neoclassicpunk seedpods interpenetrated with fine filaments of arching ermitage rock, lighter even than the mosses off their models, helicoptered crazily to and fro on quasi-autonomous pixie missions.

"Myfanwy?" said Kitty.

Come on . . .

In a way, Myfanwy thought, *I am insane right now.*

Does it count as insane, if you can go back?

Can I go back? Come on . . .

A marble folly, falling on the pattern of a small mist of plum juice cast up by rhythmic insect jaws, was laced by swifts and lapwings. Full-throated birdsong audits with bespoke multiple super-directionality required robin beaks fractured along shapes borrowed from excavated mycelium fibres.

"Myfanwy?" said Kitty. "What should I do?"

"Mmph," said a voice, that might have been her own.

Come on . . . mad muse skillz, Myfanwy . . .

There!

She snared the bundle-heart format as the aftermath of a massively multiple rep-shunt, mostly of dandelion dust. The rope creaked, taut in the air. There was a long golden-brown pear reflected waveringly in the well bucket. The reflection wavered and changed.

A little eye appeared. Then . . .

Boom!

A goldfish, more than a little like Eppy, flopped up from the lily pond into the well bucket.

Sploosh.

She ascended from the Dwelling. It rustled with relief.

She had the memory.

"Kitty," whispered Myfanwy. Kitty looked at Paddy as though hypnotised.

How much time had passed? Seconds.

"Hon," she urged quietly. "Remember the phone call in the Glass Room yesterday."

She took Kitty's hand and flipped.

Kitty gave her a weird, hard look.

Wow. Wonder what I just flipped her?

And why?

*

Citadel . . .

City of dreadful dying. Betrayal. Terrible betrayal. Someone was dying . . .

Yes, this was it . . . this was how it happened . . .

No . . .

"Babes, Molly is dead. Nothing on earth —"

"I wish you were all fucking dead!"

Genevieve . . . storming down a corridor in the west houses, before they were the west houses . . .

"You go to your room," Blake hollered.

"I'm not your fucking little girl!"

Faces . . . others . . . muses from the old days . . . Thalia, not yet Vertical, already bushy-bearded . . . Clio, worried, weak . . . Melpomene, wry . . . snow . . . Erato, enraged . . . a little Asian girl on crutches, caught in a spotlight at the foot of a high dark hill . . . "You are a member of Chancelhouse now, Genny. You'll stay in your quarters till you are civil."

"Leave me the fuck alone!"

Bee, sphinx-like . . . that would be much later . . .

Gorse and heather, ghastly grey behind her . . . noise of concrete folding in darkness . . . her bicycle shoved sideways into darkness . . . PC Veitch's face . . . like a face erected in the edges of a stack of faces . . . unstable . . . ready to shuffle, to fan out like cards . . . and Genevieve . . . and Sergeant Fletcher, facing the camera, happy and dignified . . . and Molly, waving madly in her nest . . . last thing she did . . . unless she woke up in the ambulance, who knows? . . . and Genevieve . . . and . . . not yet . . . not yet . . . please, not yet . . .

And . . . something was still missing . . . dead ends . . . darkness . . . dark hills never walked up . . . stone walls never crossed . . .

Not yet . . .

Hidden, crouching . . . aching calves . . . wrong . . . did the wrong . . . fell from a great height . . . didn't wake up, waiting, gambling cowards snoozing in gardens . . . already too late . . . no atonement . . . no fixing . . . only something else . . . not yet . . .

*

Paddy shook his head. "What's your game, Myfanwy?"

Then Paddy grabbed Kitty's other hand.

"Get *off* me! You *freak!*"

Kitty jerked her hand away and backed off. Paddy stood there desolately, his foot in the door. "It ain't *like* that," he said. "I swear to you. Listen, don't chat to me 'bout no mole. Myfanwy thought *Tar* was a mole. Kitty . . ."

Paddy stared at Myfanwy desolately.

"What?" she snapped.

'I'm sorry, I have to tell her . . . Kitty, yesterday, Myfanwy told me *you* were the mole! That you were working for Jasper!"

"That's a lie!" said Myfanwy hotly.

"Uh, actually, hon, it's not? You just flipped me the memory? You told him yesterday when he belled you?"

"Oh. Okay, sorry, hon."

"No, no, not your fault. I'll flip it back in a min. I think you did the right thing. First I'm just going to shoot Paddy with this. Then, if he persists in bringing arms to me, I'm going to cut his throat with this."

Kitty and Paddy were both producing objects.

"Um," said Myfanwy. Paddy appeared to be affixing a long silencer to a handgun's muzzle. "Jesus, Pad," she sighed.

She glanced around. Nobody in sight. Should she scream?

"I'm sorry," said Paddy. "In a minute you'll see how unnecessary this was. Now, inside —"

Paddy gestured with the gun. Myfanwy felt it very rude.

Faint blue lines of fire arced into his flesh.

There was a snick, a whirr and a buzz, and two snapping sounds as Paddy shot twice at the sunset. He fluttered around like an injured insect.

*

No way to go forward. *Too much missing.*

Earlier. Go back.

Before the Courts . . . before the death of Molly Miller . . .

The west houses, before they were the west houses. By the time she came to bed, Genevieve was already asleep.

She listened in the darkness to Gen's soft, deep breaths. Her stillness. Their contentment and secrecy.

She got undressed quietly but it was chilly, so she groped about for something to wear.

She found some things and slipped into them. They felt like they might be Gen's clothes.

She wriggled in as quietly as she could, trying not to wake Genevieve. For some reason she felt as though her heart might break.

At first she lay facing her.

As her eyes adjusted, a few features formed of Genevieve's face. Now and then, Genevieve's lips moved, or little jerks shook her arms or her entire body. Soon Genevieve's fingers found her chest, and brushed it erratically. And didn't stop . . .

Shuddered by the dreams of a still young sleep . . .

Her wrist joint, rolling at random . . .

Moving no more predictably than the droplets forming and falling on an untightened tap . . .

Eventually she rolled over, and Genevieve kept painting her back with her fingers, swishing the space between her shoulder blades with signs neither meaningful nor meaningless . . .

*

Kitty darted forwards.

She had Paddy leashed on taser wires. "Stomp to *me* yeah?" she growled.

Myfanwy's heart thudded skittishly. "'Step,' hon," she autocorrected. She considered it. "Or 'on'."

With her other hand Kitty brought a sword aloft, slanted down like she was ready to carve. "Boy a bring arms to *me*?" Now its tip played with Paddy's throat.

"Bare code switches," slurred Paddy weakly.

"Now where is that little line I drew earlier?" Kitty murmured, peering down her blade. "*Drop* the gun, snitches!"

"How does that sword fit in your bag?" said Myfanwy, picking up Paddy's handgun by its silencer.

"Honestly Myfanwy," Kitty said. "I had this puppy out slicing cantaloupe on Sunday, and you didn't even *notice*."

"It's a different context now," said Myfanwy tidily. "Well. Shall we make a move?"

"You fight with honour," Kitty told Paddy. "I leave you my barbs."

With two downward strokes she severed the taser wires.

"Joo teh roxor," Paddy slurred.

"That's just my *normal* reaction to him," Kitty expounded, as Myfanwy led her quickly away. "I'd actually momentarily *forgotten* he was the mole."

Once they turned a corner, then chose a new route to the Tube, looking constantly around them.

Paddy was nowhere in sight.

She been right about him — right? He'd pulled a handgun and everything. He never would have used it. Well, he already *had* used it — he'd used it to try to scare and manipulate them. That was bad enough.

"Let's get home," said Myfanwy. "We need to get home."

Now police tape diverted them slightly. High on a tower block balcony, a broad-shouldered woman in a floral bathrobe contemplated jumping. As they passed, she disappeared from the disk of light. Observers gasped, and the spotlight operator wavered optimistically *up* the side of the tower block, then swerved *down*, to discover her dangling two balconies lower than before.

"Progress," commented Kitty brightly.

"Nor am I loving all these feds about, and you with a vast shank," Myfanwy said quietly. "Where did you get that stuff? Stolen from armoury?"

"Shhh. Yeah. When Meletē skilled me, the admin came with the swordplay. I had to give it back, but I had *notes*. I just checked out the Bizen butterfly tantō on the Cache tablet. It's lovely and foldy."

"And the taser."

"Um, yeah. And there's a Korean tiger sword back at the flat. Won't go in the bag."

"Oh, hon!"

They were passing a half-open van. Mesh bags of enormous onions were visible within.

"It's weird," said Kitty. "I'm obsessed now with Paddy's throat. I really want to see if there's still a scratch from when I thought he was Veil. Oh yeah, he *is* Veil. You know what I mean. Paddy's throat is just really interesting. I really want to *slice* into it, you know? If he had an adam's apple as big as mine, I'd want to peel it so that the peel all stays as one piece."

A hot bitter aroma filled the air. Round the next corner a crew conducted roadworks quietly under blazing lights. A woman was busy bordering a missing band of road, carefully spilling her tarmac from a sort of roseless watering can.

A mustardy hotdog floated by being consumed by an obscure multiply-swathed figure.

They crossed the road by a cairn of chunks of broken tarmac.

"And just *one* neo-Edo ninja star," Kitty admitted. "You know me and shopping! But that's not armament, it's to go on a necklace for a look!"

"Hmm. Some looks can be militarised at short notice, Kitsy. I'm *worried* about you nowadays. You're a lot different!"

"Being obsessed with Paddy's throat, for instance," proposed Kitty helpfully.

"That's one thing."

They fell into a tense silence waiting at a pelican crossing, beside a tall, hollow-cheeked white guy who had two tiny sleeping infants strapped to him in a quilted, tecchy-looking papoose-like pack. The Rab brand was surely losing its top-of-the-mountain credibility, brooded Myfanwy. She looked at the whorls of baby hair on their heads and thought of Gen's snoozy fingers swirling on her chest — on *Jasper's* chest. Three women in burqas joined the party, then everyone crossed and scattered.

"I don't think Merlin wanted me," said Myfanwy.

"Agree."

"He wanted you, Kitty. Can you explain that?"

Kitty's eyes flashed fire. "Do I look like I care?"

Myfanwy cocked her head. So, she looked like she didn't give a flying frick. She was still glowing with her hype and lustrous post-fight aura.

"Listen," Kitty added. "I know you think Veil equals evil. I prefer a more nuanced view, okay?"

"They want us dead, Kitty."

"I consider Veil like a complicated moony-eyed suitor. Veil has, like, bad dress sense, and a habit of making the wrong subtext explicit. But Veil is kind and patient, and has good prospects in the IT sector, and would probably be really good for me, if I just *get over* myself one day. But luckily that's *not* going to happen — is it?"

"So basically . . . you just think Veil fancies you and not me?"

Kitty looked grim. "Story of our lives. I mean that in a good way."

"You think Veil just want you to jump ship? Does the memory I flipped you support that? Does it incriminate Paddy?"

"That? Uh, that was some next level shizzle. You suspected Paddy snitched about how you were accusing me behind my back. You wanted to tell me yourself, to get back my trust. But . . . yeah, it incriminates him a bit. While you're talking on the phone, Paddy basically begins his I-heart-Veil spiel. '*We need to get out of the paradigm of Veil as our foes.*' Hmm. A Reality Studio, eh?"

"A *what?*"

"Look, I can't be bothered. I'll flip you it back."

Kitty squeezed Myfanwy's arm. Her Garden rustled appreciatively and her phone rang.

Myfanwy had the number in her phone as MAYBE MARA? (9).

"Hello Mara," Myfanwy answered. "So sorry I couldn't make it tonight."

Silence.

Then a sort of pleasant purr. "Wotcha, girlfriend. Me *too.* 'Pols! We only wanted to talk."

"Um, there's this invention called the phone?"

"Won't you and Kitty stop by? I know you're somewhere in the neighbourhood. And Paddy doesn't have to be there," Mara added quickly, sounding pained. "He really showed himself up tonight. Little idiot."

"Golly. Why did you let everyone think you were dead, big M? Some people may have had girl crushes on you, and ting!"

"Ha! I didn't let *everyone* think it, mate. Just you lot. Got your voicemail in April, but wasn't too keen. Last time we met . . . you brought an unexpected friend . . ."

Myfanwy glanced at Kitty, who mouthed *What?*

Myfanwy shook her head. "OMG. You thought *we* led Jasper to you? No way! We only stumbled into him because he was stalking *you*."

"Well, I believe that *now*," Mara sighed. "But, blimey. You can understand me dragging my feet a little!"

"Yes," said Myfanwy. "Yes I can."

"Plus I had. . . I had scars to grow, Myfanwy. I hadn't meant to scare you. I'm sorry. It was wrong of me."

Kitty's hand was now doing a sort of frenzied duck-quacking / give-me-the-phone thing next to Myfanwy's ear, but Myfanwy shrugged her off.

"*I'll* meet you, Mara," Myfanwy quickly decided. "Some incredibly public place. No one else, and no Kitty. Expect to be *milked*, okay? I mean, I'm planning on bringing my little stool."

"Would be v. convenient if Kitty —"

"You *heard* me, Mara. You and me. Mano-a-Mara."

There was a little pause.

Mara snarled with frustration. "Jumped-up little madam. Don't you dare set terms! You haven't a *clue* what you're dealing with. Tell that bitch she has something that *belongs* to me. And I mean to *get it back*."

*

The Glass Room. Moon on face in the garden.

Gone. Blink. Daylight. Shiver.

"The other possibility," Myfanwy told Paddy. "is that there's been an intermediary. Someone I've flipped with since the Spring Feast has been in contact with Jasper!"

"Trust. That could be anyone you've touched!"

She switched her phone to the other ear. "I dunno, Pad. I'm getting better and better at perceiving when a cast takes place. Could someone still inspire me covertly? Maybe! But my guess is it would have to be someone really good. Maybe one of the original nine muses could do it."

"Not Meletē though. Too specialised in skills."

"Yeah, exactly. I also have two further suspects, okay? Kermitcrab, because I deliberately flipped with him once."

"Kermitcrab? That guy? You two flipped?"

"Yeah, off the books. Long story. It was before the Spring Feast, but only barely — Bee could have already shown me her bridal gizmos. And the other person is . . ."

"Your training partner."

"Kitty."

"Nuff flips. Still, no way, Myfanwy!"

"Paddy! Kitty has been really weird lately!"

"Yeah," he said tenderly.

"We had a wee row over the Settlement — Bridge Croft. She wanted me to stop thinking about it."

"The Bridge Croft thing is bare confusing, fam."

"I feel you. Yet it's coming together, bit by bit. Chancelhouse launched a mission, to try to influence the court case about what happened at Bridge Croft. It was kind of a pilot mission. Proof of principle, you get me? I guess it didn't work, though. As we all know, Sergeant Fletcher walked. You remember this?"

"Not really," said Paddy. "The travellers were being evicted from Bridge Croft. There was a protest. Then what?"

"There was this activist, Molly Miller, up on these kind of stilts. It was partly spectacle — she was portraying a titanic Lilith, supposedly the first woman before Eve. But it had a practical purpose too — to slow down the demolition. The feds grabbed her with a cherry-picker, but she was a real red squirrel, she slipped down the cherry-picker's arm, up a tree, and back onto the stilts . . ."

"Just as the structure she'd been guarding got bulldozed. And she died."

"Yeah. She fell and fractured her skull."

"And there were riots."

"So hard to remember which riot was which! I'm not being jaded, just practical."

"You can get an app apparently."

"Safe. Anyway, there was this enquiry, which cleared the bulldozer driver, but it led to a court case against Sergeant Fletcher. Fletcher had given the driver the all clear. Another officer, Veitch, gave the key testimony, obviously saying it wasn't Sergeant Fletcher's fault. It was really controversial. The prosecution claimed that Veitch's view of the accident was obstructed. In the end though, Sergeant Fletcher was cleared."

"Just a tragic accident."

"Except I have memories which say otherwise."

"Trust. You believe Fletcher let Molly Miller die. Why would Kitty want to cover that up? Like, 'Drop this case if you know what's good for you, Morris . . . or I'm gunna pull your ticket!' Why would Kitty do that?"

"Some things I'm still trying to remember. What I'm wondering is . . . could Jasper have been involved in Molly's death, Veitch's testimony, and Fletcher walking free? Could Kitty be helping Jasper . . . to cover up the truth?"

OMG. In retrospect, how embarrassing.

"Don't even joke about that," said Paddy.

"I'm not joking! There's more, fam. A while ago, Kitty flipped me a memory about the west houses. Seemed stuffed with stupid superhero costumes, right?"

"You think it wasn't?"

"That was only ever Kitty's *spin on it! Blake never* mentioned *them in his speech! I've been thinking. What if Blake doesn't* know *about them? Then I started thinking — what* other *function might they have?"*

"And?"

"Pretty quickly it hit me. Couldn't it be a costumes wardrobe? Couldn't it be part of a theatre? With props and sets stored elsewhere in the west houses? So the mole could be gearing up to, like, create artificial situations! Maybe the mole is a patterner muse, who could scrape away at those memories, slice them and recombine them and tweak them till they felt real!"

"Dastardly. It would be like a . . ."

"A Reality Studio! You could create any memory you wanted. Insert it into anybody you wanted."

"Sort of like verbatim theatre in reverse."

"Maybe it's already happening. You'd need a patterner for editing, plus a caster for inserting. And here's the worst part. Kitty really didn't want to flip me the memory of what she saw in the west houses. I basically had to force her. Then she was v. quick to say how hilarious it all was. She claimed she and Moth snarfed Blake's keycard to get in. But what if Kitty had access all along? What if Kitty was just using Moth as cover, because for some reason she had *to get in there quickly, rather than wait till dead of night? That could be the reason she was nervous — not because of what she might find, or anything like that."*

"Are you saying —"

"I don't have any hard evidence. But, yeah. Kitty's been recruited by the mole. She's been working for Jasper!"

C-ringe!

"Myffed . . ."

"What? You don't buy it?"

"Maybe you need to leave the mindset that all Veil are our foes, all Chancelhouse are our friends. Any *of the elders, even Blake, could have an ominous pet project. Or even Tar. Just because you've falsely accused her once —"*

"God, I hope not! I'll need the most amazing evidence ever *before I accuse Tar of anything ever again."*

"Even if Kitty isn't *everything she seems, she may have a good reason for that."*

"Please, please, please let it not be Tar. In fact, if it is Tar, I just give up. She can just win now. Some mysteries are just too embarrassing to solve."

"Myffed," Paddy laughed, "listen to me, yeah? The situation is complicated and, like, messy. It's not necessarily Veil. It could be some Chancel mandem controlling the Reality Studio, maybe with a cloned keycard or something."

"I guess it would be gutsy for Veil to run it right under our noses."

"Always with the 'us' and 'them', Paleface! I'm trying to say . . . think of the bigger picture, yeah? Is the Reality Studio necessarily some bad man ting?"

"I suppose it depends how it's used. To me, it's ominous because it's so secret. The Spring Feast would be the obvious time to unveil it, if it were legit. Right?"

"To be fair," pondered Paddy. "Blake's speech was pretty oblique. Maybe he does *know about it, and believes he's explained the whole programme to us from top to bottom. He's probably fretting that nobody shows up for casting call."*

"Maybe," said Myfanwy. "Dude. Things are so complicated!"

"Trust!"

"Trust is complicated, too. Well, whatever's going on, I'm pretty sure Fletcher was culpable for Molly Miller's death. Possibly Veitch too. I'm going to focus on those missing pieces. I have to go for a long walk soon. Maybe tomorrow."

"After the History exam?"

"If not during." Then she hesitated. "Paddy," she said in a small voice.

"What is it?"

"I can't believe she's gone," she whispered. "I keep thinking about her. I miss her so much."

"Kitty? Fam, please don't hype. It's all guesswork — oh, shit, I'm sorry — you mean your mum —"

"Genevieve, Paddy. I miss Genevieve."

*

Today Myfanwy had to go to the Post Office to do Three Things, including applying for her diplomatic passport (ooh!), then go to Stratford to do Four Things, the last of which was the infinitely absorptive "study," which would take her to midnight, and round the corner to Kitty's *pied-à-terre*.

Easy-peasy.

Some would go so far as to say, *lemon-squeezy*. Last night she'd put everything she needed in a little pile in the Glass Room, all ready to go. But actually, she'd absent-mindedly left many, many things out of her All Admin pile, so she looked for them until it was basically, OMG, the afternoon. But at the Post Office, she didn't have everything. She had no debit card! So she returned home and ransacked her room and the Glass Room and fumed and shouted at Dad, who must have hid it. She remembered she had it all along, stupidly tucked into her Tiny Planner which she'd taken to keeping for her Tiny Plans.

When she was back on the street, she turned round again and returned to get her keys which she'd absent-mindedly left in the lock. It was really only because she was thinking about the topic of her own absent-mindedness that she remembered them. Win!

In the Post Office, Myfanwy left her wallety thing on the little counter. Some Minimum-to-be-Expected Samaritan handed it in to the lady in the shoppy bit while Myfanwy was still storming around ransacking her handbag. Whew.

On the way to Stratford she tried to transfer some money to cover the passport application but ended up locking herself out of her account. So she was on the phone to Customer Support trying to remember the answers to her own security questions, because she hadn't put "first school attended" as the first school she'd really attended but as the *real* first school she'd attended, i.e. St Jerome's, whereas her first pet wasn't her first *real* pet but actually just *literally* her first pet, i.e. Doctor Cream.

She finally penetrated her security using her memorable date, which was actually a mash-up of her birthday and Mum's birthday, because they were both May and that's just how she'd accidentally mashed it up on the day she'd first given her memorable date, and since she'd felt so smug about guessing that that was how she'd mashed it, she'd always kept it as that, and in fact even though it didn't make any sense at all, and was in fact a date of zero significance, it was the one security answer she now never, ever forgot. She reset her First Pet and the First Educational Institute to be as crawlingly literal — literal in the literal sense — as humanly possible, against the next bout of forgetfulness, and transferred the necessary p, and things were now looking up.

At St Jerome's, she briefly tried to get into the main building by swiping her Vogue Video card, but that was really small potatoes on a day like this. She paid a random visit to the Womyn's Castle and found men in it again, this time reupholstering the pool table in sort of sugary pink florals. Plus she'd also forgotten her headphones which she needed for one of the Four Things she'd wanted to do, but such small potatoes, you'd need the Hubble Space Telescope merely to manufact *pomme de terre dauphinous*.

Kitty rang.

"Everyone has to fucking die!" said Myfanwy. "Fuck you! *I'm going to fucking kill you!*"

"Hype down, hon. You still sleeping at mine?"

"Fuck off! You crazy fucking bitch! Your *pied à terre* is shit!"

Myfanwy hung up, rang back. "I'm fine," she said. "I'm fine. Stop panicking. It's been a slightly annoying day."

"What time to expect you?"

"Ten minutes. Twenty, I go walk it off."

"Stress is not mentioned in the Bible. It could be a function of modernity. I'm thinking Brick Lane again for post-exam drink?"

"Safe. Pad as well again?"

"Veilbait? If you like. I'll have to nip back in-between for the swords and things, they won't let me have those in the exam. Toodles for twenty."

*

Wise pamphlets feinting to and fro on charnel stacks . . .

A rolled carpet fell and spilled out, dark patches on Persian arabesque . . .

No . . . can't go forwards . . . earlier . . .

Chancelhouse . . . angry voices . . . they're arguing*!*

Her and Gen!

OMG. One of their few ever rows. There wasn't time to have many, was there? And it had the silliest spark. Drowsing in each other's arms late at night, she had cuddled and squeezed Gen and then rolled away.

"When you're hugging me like that," Gen sobbed, the lamp on now, her fringes sort of dithered, "and I love you so much *in that moment, and in that very same moment, when you touch me like that, all you're thinking about is* letting go!*"*

"You're not properly —"

"I am*! I think it makes it like* every *hug can be fake."*

"— awake, I was gonna say, Genevieve! Try and use some bloody commonsense for a change. I mean, Christ."

"Commonsense is a feeling*, Jasper. I don't* feel *that feeling, okay?"*

"A feeling? News to me, mate. What do you feel?"

"I don't know. What do you feel?"

"Keep your voice down. I feel a bit hard done by, to be honest."

"I feel . . . exhausted . . . and like I want to trust you again . . . and don't *tell me to go back to sleep again, okay?"*

"Christ, Genevieve. I was going to say, you're taking on too much hippie work. That's what this is."

"Mate, it is what it is, yeah? I reckon I ain't taking on enough*. I'm not reaching the point where it nourishes me, Jasper. I'm all over the place . . . I feel as though I'm living, like, eight or nine different lives all at once . . ."*

"You're in Flux."

"What?"

"Sorry. Stupid joke."

"What a waste, to spend time arguing . . ."

Or maybe not a waste . . .

Can't go forwards . . .

Earlier . . .

She loafed on Gen's bed, observing between the black curtains as a certain beauteous lozenge-shaped gap in the clouds dwindled closed.

"Do black curtains send the right message, Gen?"

"I guess We Hippies don't wash after all," said Gen, mystified, peering into her mirror.

There was a little crescent of gooseflesh-ish rash on her brow.

She puffed out her ample cheeks. "I suppose this is it. I suppose I am turning into a lizard."

"Gen, let's make a list of all the things we know about the mysterious rash. One, it is on your forehead. Two, you are turning into a lizard."

"I am turning into a lizard. Three, it wasn't there last night. Will you love me when I am a lizard?"

"Possibly. Possibly I'll just want a bit of tail."

Earlier now . . . deeper . . . closer to the source, the fountainhead . . .

Strange, silent, kiss-like touches of lips with Gen, smiles and suppressed giggles instead of smacking lips, standing by the Rosebush Without Roses in Genevieve's garden in Quinton . . .

Genevieve had to go to the loo.

"Just wait for me."

She stayed beside the Rosebush Without Roses, hiding, really . . . listening to voices, watching through the leaves as a certain beauteous lozenge-shaped gap in the clouds dwindled shut . . .

Hmm . . . or maybe not . . .

*

Myfanwy put her stone on the cairn.

Then she began sifting the pile.

She'd wandered calmly round what had once been Bridge Croft . . . some of it now gutted wasteland, some of it being developed, foundations and cement mixers behind electrified fences — wasn't this supposed to be green belt land? . . . she'd wandered through the woods, climbed up that hill in the baking heat.

The day couldn't have been more similar, but the recollections weren't as clear as she'd hoped. The almond-scented gorse brought back memories . . . of almond scented gorse.

One thing she'd remembered was, as Jasper, dropping a total *beast* of a boulder onto this cairn, BOOM! — like a loose bit of masonry or something. She'd cut Gen's name — no, just the initials — into a facet of this outrageous meteorite. Kinda dumb. She didn't think she'd ever told Gen about it. Like, excess of Early Relationship style romantic creativity overflowing and going wonky.

Gen probably would have thought she'd *spoiled* the cairn, because the whole point of a cairn is all the touching anonymous solidarity the waves of hillwalkers express in dribbling their pebbles together.

She didn't really know why she'd done it.

Maybe because it was such an *effete* example of a cairn? Yeah, that was it! It wasn't a cairn diss. It was a critique of the direction it was taking.

C'mon, folks. Let's build *something!*

And in fact, there were quite a few bigger rocks there right now.

She found it!

"GQ," their rock still clearly said. She brushed the letters with her knuckle. The phrase "*Muse of the Year*" popped into her head.

She tilted the rock on one end. Cut into a nearby facet, more freshly — in a similar font, if you could call it that — were her own initials.

MM.

So Jasper had come back too.

She gazed down into the valley.

Maybe he was even there today.

*

Earlier . . . deeper . . .

Genevieve touring her round Colley Gate in Halesowen, the small town where Gen had grown up, just beyond the rutilant sprawl of Brum.

"That tree used to be a Tesco."

A rather splendid ash.

"I don't believe you. There should be them blue plaques up everywhere, wherever you done something Genevieve."

"Those two cats will one day be suns."

They came across two middle-aged nu ravers and a punk searching in the wet grass for an earring and a contact lens, lost by two of them at once, and stopped to help.

"Quite old school, looking for a contact. Everyone seems to have lasers or dailies."

The punk looked up expressively. One eye was a soft smoky grey, on the other there hovered a phantasmal Euro sign.

"Oh! What kind of earring?"

"Baroque pearl, pendant. Lilac lustre."

She studied the various studs and fleshtunnels which flanked the nu raver's stooped, intent face. She felt sceptical.

"I was carrying it in my hand," the punk explained.

They found the two lost things nestled together, like a subtle and badly-hurt bug.

When was this? They weren't yet lovers. She loved Gen already, but she knew it was impossible anything would ever happen between the two of them. Too different, blah blah blah. About easing the pain.

The day went by so fast . . .

Making stupid immature double entendre jokes for her, because that was the only reasonable way to try to be clever or funny in those days. Totally aching inside. Then when Gen casually made one too, afterward she thought about it over and over again, turning it over in her mind, running her own mind smooth against its contours, as if that cheeky dorky joke implied some grave, unfathomable sexuality, something unendurably large and sweet and dark, never meant for her . . .

*

On the train home, a mother and daughter sat across from Myfanwy. She observed them with a strange yearning.

"Three hundred dead?" said the daughter.

"Three *hunters*," said the mother.

"Oh. I thought you said three *hundred*."

They'd put out on the table a Keith Richards biography, an issue of *Killer Sudoku*, its cash prizes denominated in Aussie dollars — although they didn't sound Aussie — and a fawn-coloured glasses case, with its white Specsavers logo faded to sprinkles.

Had today been worth it?

For a nice view and some initials in a cairn?

Unless, of course, the initials on Jasper's meteorite had just been a lazy viral marketer starting a web address and wandering off.

WW . . . ah forget it!

She hadn't seen Jasper, though the Jasper Clone Army were out in abundance. Till the moment she boarded the train, she thought he'd jump out on her.

Across the table, the daughter picked a tin of Pret Pure Sparkling Ginger Beer from her bag, drank from it, and put it on top of the closed Keith Richards book. After a pause, she moved it next to the book instead. Being able to open Keith Richards biographies without spilling stuff everywhere, Myfanwy supposed, was actually a key part of literacy.

Myfanwy checked her phone. Four voicemails? What? She would wait till she got in. Not long till London now. She hated it when the signal cut out. Maybe they'd give her some clue about what to do with herself, while she stayed out late, so Dad would be asleep when she came home. No point in facing that dreaded question tonight.

How did your exam go?

Unless, of course, Dad already knew she'd skived. School could have already called him.

The train now pulled into a red brick station. The wall was patterned with flurries of whitened bricks, and regularly punctuated with porthole-style windows, full of cloud and sky and a few early stars.

God! Why had she done it? One exam already wasted on a stupid gesture, which probably didn't even help the person it was meant for, just sort of baffled her. Then she actually *skived* another. Something she'd never done in her life. How incredibly pathetic. Why?

Trying to burn her bridges. Be the toughest, realest muse there was. But why did she want that?

The train pulled out of the station.

Flooded country slipped past now. A little lake filled with shattered fencepost flotsam. Temporary bogs, mudflats, dim green grass grizzled with fresh fluorescent rape.

Kitty was the reason, wasn't she? Pretty much everyone at Chancelhouse either hated Myfanwy, or else was amused and bemused and just basically thought she was nuts. Myfanwy had Paddy and Kitty, that was all. Now Paddy had betrayed her, and Kitty was getting ready to quit. And to continue without *anyone* . . . well, there was just one way.

She'd have to make sure she had no choice. No other options. No other prospects in life. But where would she find herself, when her bridges were all burned and gone? Alone on a scab of concrete rising from Pacific foam. Nobody but weird muse seagulls for company.

Steep feldspar embankments rose either side. Then long deep green fields again, filled with stubby trees and telephone poles. Nearby poles seemed to scurry from one far-off pole to another. More flooding, much worse. Strange, expansive patterns of muddy water.

Would Kitty really leave Chancelhouse? So much more talented than Myfanwy was, and yet when Kitty thought of all the things that were, like, worth pursuing for a seventeen- or eighteen-year-old woman . . . the Chancelhouse arcana just weren't among them?

And even though whatever glam X Kitty *did* go on to do with her life, it would forever be understood that Kitty, had she deigned to develop her talent, would have been the greater muse?

And maybe that was true too.

Unless . . .

Unless that was *why* Kitty was going to quit. To give up being a muse — for Myfanwy's sake.

She remembered Kitty's scary story. Like, only one little girl got to be a ballerina, or whatever it was. The other one had to be sex-trafficked, or ground up for sausages, or just never be listened to. Or something. How do you decide something like that? Who to save and who to leave? When there is probably no God and no heaven, or if there was a heaven, it couldn't ever be for *you*, because the concepts of *person* and *heaven* are incompatible? It would be heaven just for blood, or something like that? Just a sea of self-pleasing blood pumping above the clouds . . .

My mind is going weird.

Myfanwy checked her phone again.

Four voicemails.

Hmm . . .

*

The further on you go, the more it hurts . . .

Got to go back, back even earlier . . .

The first time they actually met *was in town, in front of a giant ad commending the beaches of a specific nation state. Genevieve just came bounding up to her and said, "My God, Jabari, you look totally different!"*

The wittiest thing she could think to say was . . . just to look at Gen and smile.

Gradually it dawned on her. "Nice to meet you, Mr Someone-Who-Isn't-Jabari."

"I'm very —" she began.

"So you should be!" scolded Gen.

The next time was near work. Genevieve smiled and waved and adjusted her hippie headscarf. She looked away from Gen, because the headscarf fracas was obviously a way of politely breaking the fragile link.

No, she's bounded right over again!

Gen smiled companionably. That smile meant a particular mood. But she didn't know that about Gen yet — what the smile meant.

They were silent together for a bit.

"Still not that guy, huh?" said Genevieve.

"No. I feel like it's my fault now. I've had loads of time."

Genevieve laughed and made to go.

"There's another reason I maybe look familiar," she blurted. "I work in your father's bindery."

That word should have given the game away. Father. It implied innumerable tender pledges, lutes and lamentations. Every artifice of passion deniably declared, all in that one precious, archaic word.

She realised she was pointing towards the factory. What an idiot.

But no! She'd got away with it! — Genevieve wasn't listening, or better yet, she was listening with some strange part of herself . . . Genevieve glimpsed the sense of it, anagrammatised, systematically deranged . . . a semantic synaesthesia, or something . . . so difficult, so subtle to explain *it, but she could* recall *it perfectly . . .*

Genevieve gave a deep scowl then a screeching giggle. She looked breezily to the side. "I'm not drunk, by the way. I'm just like *this!"*

Genevieve wasn't like that. Not quite. She didn't know that yet, either . . .

"So what is pops like as a boss?"
"Best you don't know the answer to that."
"Oh, I've always *known . . . I'm just testing . . ."*
"I'm Jasper."
"Genevieve. Gen."

*

First voicemail. Unfamiliar voice. American accent, with an East Asian edge. "'Undine here again. We'd love to talk to you when you get a minute.' — message will be saved for — three days." Paddy's voice. "'Wha gwaan, Myffed. Sorry about, uh you know. I bet you didn't think I'd show up to the exam! It's weird at school how you can be mortal enemies and you all just show up and register. Um. Anyway. As it turns out, *you* didn't show up. Nobody expected *that.* You okay? They called out your name and everything. I also just wanted to say, um. Blud, I noticed Kitty had less make-up on than usual, and she actually has a really beautiful natural eyelid colour. So I don't know if there's a way, as her BFF, you can inform her of that. Because they're like these two natural beautiful rainbows? Anyway, um. She didn't tase me again. Do you think I've pulled? I mean, I dunno if it was just like an invigilator thing. Like you have to hand in your strap before the exam. Um, and she does make a point of referring to me as Padawanker, and ting. But she gives me these nice smiles. So. Yeah. Here's the point. I hope you haven't deleted me yet. Me and Kitty got talking after. We ended up going for a drink again. And. *Kitty is totally coming to work for Veil!* She agreed not to make, like, a mountain out of a mole-hill. Sorry. Supposed to be a joke. Like 'mole,' get it? Apparently there's *loads* of Chancel folk jumping ship. Like maybe Bee and Triffid and Moth and Static. It's just rumours, but. And Germ's gonna step me up, and ting, so soon Kitty's going to be totally into me. So that's where your two best friends are gonna be, Myfanwy. Veil. Um. You feel. Um. Anyway, I guess what I'm' — Message deleted." Next message. Same unfamiliar voice as earlier. "'Hi there, Myfanwy, this is Undine speaking. Earlier my colleagues Fisher King and Kitty contacted you about the possibility of a job interview. If you could give me a bell back to follow that up, that would be helpful. Thanks.' — message will be saved for — three days." Kitty's voice, rather echoey. "'So, English? I argued Robert Louis Stevenson's use of pirates was a bit risky but it *worked. Hello?* Where were *you?* Myffy, it's not like you! Out of character is serious business, okay? But listen carefully. After the exam at St Margaret's Paddy and I —'" Why would Kitty get the school's name wrong? Some kind of hagiography-based humour? "— 'talked things over. His Veil callsong is Fisher King. I know, right? I've gone with Veil, Myffed. You heard me, damn it! I'm there now. I want you to listen very closely. This is the purpose and provenance of this moist Veil. I mean voicemail. This is my official pitch. They've shown me the ropes. What they do is *tight*, blud. I've been given the most incredible *role* here. Like MacGyver. Best job since, like, Moth's nose job. Seriously, I'm like a kid in a candy factory! I'm Augustus *Gloop*. I'm a Lindt chocolate reindeer's reading of Goddard's *Detéctive*. It's like *feeding time at the zoo* down here. Behind the Veil. It's a piece of cake. It's a walk in the park. I've got my Vitalis on. You feel me? My *Vitalis Park*. Career's gonna fly by — only do two days behind the Veil, the day you go in and the day you go out. Fam, this needs some kinda *soundtrack*. Bare loud tunes, like we used to do in our room in Chancel. *Then* you'd know how I feel — no fronting. So maybe *you* should get *your* sorry ass down *here*. Because they wanna make *you too*, innit. They wanna make you like they made me. Get your sorry, sorry, sorry ass. Have you got a pen?" Myfanwy cursed as Kitty said a postcode very rapidly — she'd have to listen again — bare p, voicemail — "I really hope you do the right thing, Myffed. I can't tell you how much I hope you do the right thing. Okay. I've said what I think and then some. I've got a lot of stuff on right now. Bye, hon. Whatever happens. Love you.' . . . message will be saved . . . for three days."

What a totally bizarre message. Even for Kitty. Lindt chocolate reindeer? Vitalis Park? Myfanwy studied the mother and daughter across from her, then the guy emanating the music.

The hackles of her neck rose.

She looked at the phone again. Had Kitty *really* called and left a voicemail? She needed to dial it up again anyway, get the post code.

Myfanwy checked her call log. Three minute call to voicemail. Yep. She rang it again, jotted down the postcode this time. Kitty's voice was echoey, faint. What was that in the background? She couldn't be sure.

Try again when I'm off the train.

Soon she was approaching Kings Cross. Dusk had fallen. A red crane, with a silhouette poised inside its ladder, flicked by. Then a vast glowing sign, "The Emirates Stadium." High up behind glass, illuminated strangers silently gasped on treadmills and arctrainers. Their sweat-slicked skins flicked swiftly past.

Myfanwy's train overtook another, moving slowly in the same direction, all lit-up and empty inside. As perspective slid around in the parallel train's windows, the furnishings each wee room offered up were hastily rearranged, as if not yet ready, then snatched away, as if the whole idea had been stupid in the first place.

She rang Kitty. Straight to voicemail. The mother and daughter were gathering their bags. The beep came to start speaking and then she remembered and hung up.

Vitalis Park was where Kitty had been attacked. Two years ago. She'd been walking home alone after Sarah Cameron's sixteenth birthday party. There'd been three boys.

Myfanwy shuddered.

Something wasn't right.

Kitty gone to Veil? Moist Veil, she'd said, instead of voicemail. Moist with tears?

Vitalis Park?

And Moth's nose?

*

Earlier . . .

The first time she met Gen — no, the first time she saw *her. Gen was just the gaffer's daughter then, walking briskly through the bindery. Pretty dark curls and big eyes, but nothing too special. Like most strangers to the shop-floor, she took the instruction to stay between the painted lines literally. She made strange, Pacmanish progress.*

She'd heard it said the gaffer's daughter was spoilt and stuck up, but she didn't much look it. She just wore a look of . . . tolerance . . .

Yeah, she realised what it was. The girl was tolerating the gazes, wasn't she? Os was the worst, completely dumbfounded in the act of drawing down a set of plates from the racks.

For the scrappie. About bloody time. Your dad's stuck in the past, darling.

She'd acted nearly as badly as Oscar really. Just another statue, eyes raised, rapt in the act of greasing a perfector gripper.

She grinned, shook her head, got on with the job.

Fresh freckly skin she had. Call her a Pantone 109-7 C . . .

*

When she got home Dad was at the bottom of the stairs, still as a statue. He was doing his special wide-eyed stare at her. It meant he was struggling to remember something, or to articulate it. It didn't mean, *read my mind.* All he wanted was some comradeship, about how crap brains could be.

"*What* Dad?" said Myfanwy. She felt more grumpy than nervous.

It came to him. "Your friend," he said. "Jasper Robin."

"Oh," said Myfanwy.

"Is he an artist?"

"No."

"In a band?"

"No. I don't think so."

"Oh. Well." He shrugged. "You know strange people. He left you a letter. It's on your bed."

Myfanwy's heart quickened. "He was here?"

"I suppose young people don't understand about letters. They think you have to take them to the person's father."

Myfanwy took the stairs three at a time.

It was on her pillow. It looked like a birthday card. Inside was a hand-written note.

I'll be at the rose gardens in Peckham Rye, tomorrow at 9 a.m. OK? You can have back a memory of your mother. Just a little one. Talking to a man in a café. This is a bit dramatic, isn't it?

xJ.

P.S. Tomorrow would be Genevieve's birthday.

Until now, Myfanwy hadn't really associated nice barley white stationery with Jasper.

Dad appeared in her doorway. "Is he a boyfriend, this Mr Robin bloke? You know, for a time, I thought that you and Kitty . . ."

He trailed off.

Myfanwy shook her head. "He's not a boyfriend, and he's not a friend either. He's not someone I want anything to do with. If he comes round again, don't let him in, don't talk to him."

"Aye aye," said Dad. He leaned against the door frame, in a slightly Pin Uppy type pose, scratching his ear with his thumb.

"Sorry I grumped," Myfanwy said.

"Don't mean to snoop," said Dad. "Get a bit bored. Not hearing from you, weeks on end. Not really interested in much else. Bit sad, really."

"Oh, *daddy!* You're interested in *lots* of things! Why, when I called you that time from — from Kitty's *pied-à-terre* that one time, you didn't even want to *hear* from me!"

He shook his grizzled head, mystified.

"*Yes*," she chided, in one of her Family Time mollycoddling voices. "You were just having *too* much fun, weren't you?"

"Don't remember that, darling."

There was so much she wanted to tell him. She looked at his face and looked away. Her gaze settled on the kitschy aquamarine ashtray. Another gift from Kitty. Another density of lies. She'd persuaded Dad it was purely decorative, only ever useful in such innocent pastimes as the transport of fresh pencil shavings into the wicker bin.

"Dad," she said softly. "I'm making lots of plans for the summer. You know that, right? I may go visit Edinburgh for a few weeks."

"Not sure I want you going to Edinburgh."

"Oh, don't sound so troubled! You only know it from your crimey books, right?"

"Rebus is praised for realism," he pointed out.

"And there are *three* Christmas shops," said Myfanwy. "They do flourishing trade all year round. The townsfolk and tourists go about tinkling with freshly-bought ornaments."

"May be a gang thing," Dad warned gloomily. He entered the room, kissed her cheek twice, then made to leave. "I could ground you."

"I'd ground you back, daddy."

"I might like that. Do you want this door closed?"

"Yeah. Actually, no."

Alone, Myfanwy unfolded the note again.

This is a bit dramatic, isn't it?

xJ.

She hadn't told Dad she'd skipped the exam. How could she? It was weird how much she was locking him out. She felt like Genevieve would have taken her puzzles to her pops straightaway. But somehow she couldn't. She was afraid for Dad, and of him.

Jasper Robin. With no one to trust, no one to turn to, now there was *this* to contend with. Jasper Robin Requests the Pleasure of Your Company.

If she told Blake, he'd have Jasper killed. No mistakes this time.

So what? Who cared? She shivered lightly.

Veil? Veil wanted Jasper dead too. So Jasper could be her bargaining chip. Veil would have to let her see Kitty — on some totally neutral territory. Trafalgar Square or something.

"Let me know Kitty's okay, and I'll give you Jasper."

But Jasper would still die, probably. And part of Myfanwy would die too.

Or she could meet Jasper in the Rose Garden. What could he want from her? More memories? Jasper wanted *her*. He didn't seem to care if he possessed her or became her.

She felt like whatever she did would be wrong.

She pursed her lips and stared at her phone.

Okay. Okay.

Myfanwy rose and shut the door after all, scrolled through her icons, and dialled.

"Um, Tallulah? It's Myfanwy. This will sound weird, but . . . I really need your help."

*

She met Tallulah late that evening by the river outside Zapomnieć. "It's kinda expensive here, Myfanwy. Maybe we could just get some tinnies and sit on the pier?"

The night was warm. On the pier, sipping Becks Vier, Myfanwy told Tallulah pretty much everything.

"It sounds crazy," she said when she was done. "But I wouldn't have told you if I couldn't prove it. I'm not perfect at it yet, but I can flip you a memory."

"Nae chance, pal. I would lose one of mine, right?"

"Yeah, at random."

"Aye. Well, there's no memory I can afford to lose right now."

Myfanwy thought about it and felt a little guilty. Tallulah finished her beer with a long chug, then started crumpling the tin contemplatively.

"I think I completely understand what you mean," said Myfanwy.

"Whatever though," said Tallulah. "I trust you. It's no weirder than that race of giant rabbits. But — what can I do?"

"Advise me. Do I go to Jasper? To Veil? Or to Chancelhouse?"

"Well obviously —" said Tallulah. She paused. "Damn."

"See?"

"Aye. Explain Vitalis Park again?"

"Oh. When we were sixteen, Kitty got attacked there by some guys. Yeah. She was, like, sexually assaulted. So, uh —"

"I never knew."

"You'd only just arrived, I don't think you were friends yet. Plus she doesn't go around telling everyone."

"So 'Vitalis' was like a — a danger word?"

"Yeah. The whole thing's a trap. In Edinburgh we had a joke — *kind* of a joke — that our room was bugged, so we always had to pump up the tunes, to disguise our Secret Plans."

"Which were?"

"Well, our Secret Plans were always just dancing around. But in her voicemail, she also said, 'I need a soundtrack, like we did back at Chancelhouse.' Someone was with her, listening in. Probably Undine — maybe Mara too. I mean, I don't think she's in chains or anything. But I don't think she feels safe. I don't think she can speak freely."

Tallulah's bag furnished her a fresh tin of Vier. She tapped it but didn't pop the cap. "Any idea why these Veil guys want you? You said Paddy and Mara seemed more interested in Kitty than you."

"I dunno. Maybe they just want to collect the whole set."

"Lols. Well, c'mon then, I'll help you decide. Option A. Trade Jasper for Kitty."

"I don't really want to do that," said Myfanwy. "No. Not if there's any other way."

"Fair. Option B. Go to this interview with Undine. Upsides?"

"I don't totally know who I can trust at Chancelhouse anymore. Maybe my enemy's enemy is my friend? Also, no delay. No waiting for others to make up their minds. I can take my dad's car first thing. Be there before noon. If I wasn't drinking, I'd go now."

"Why exactly don't you trust Chancelhouse?"

"Partly some of the stuff Jasper and Paddy have been saying. I dunno. Their competence and ethics. I'm pretty sure the girl in my memories is Genevieve Quaker. Is she also Sophie Black? I don't know. Either way, why pretend she burned to death centuries ago?"

"Okay. And downsides?"

"I mean, I probably won't get the job. Undine will probably like tie me to a chair and wipe my memory and dump me wandering in the woods."

"Aye, naked." Tallulah popped open her tin. "On the other hand, it's important to get experience of interviews."

"Defo. Tough market out there."

"Brilliant." Tallulah took a meditative sip of Becks and waved at her bag. "Batter in any time, by the way. So, them's the bad options out the way. Option C — ask Blake to launch a rescue mission. Maybe Chancelhouse isn't all sweetness and light. Aye, the whole Saint Genevieve thing is creepy. But Chancelhouse *is* good for one thing — warring with Veil. If Veil have Kitty, that's the one thing you need. Upsides?"

"Hmm. Like you say. There's nobody better equipped to deal with Veil than Chancel."

"Downsides?"

"What if they escalate this? What if it really *does* turn into a war? Kitty's safety is what matters. Maybe a subtler approach is needed."

"Fair. There are implementation issues too — *would* you approach Blake? Or a different elder? Or recruit your own team?"

"Now that's interesting," said Myfanwy. "If I put together my own line-up —"

"Hold up. Wait till you hear Option D."

"Um. Feds?"

"Lols. Yeah, summon a gendarme. No, seriously — Option D is asking *Jasper* for help."

"Are you serious? Absolutely not. No way."

"Come on. Upsides?"

"I'm not doing it!"

"Just suppose!"

"Well," Myfanwy sighed.

She watched the lights on a boat go by. There *was* something strangely tempting about it.

"He might do it," Myfanwy admitted. "He hates Veil as much as he hates Chancelhouse. Plus the last time we met, before he went psycho, he acted like he owed me. Like I'd *saved* him or something, bearing his memories. But that's strange too. They aren't sad memories. They are beautiful."

"I can guess why," said Tallulah. "Jasper still carries the one memory that is the key for them all. The one where —"

"Genevieve dies. Yes." Myfanwy hesitated. "And no. There's never just one key to everything. The meaning of any memory depends on all the others. Among my memories, their meaning is beauty. Among his, it's sorrow. And hatred. And revenge."

"How did she die?" said Tallulah. There was the softest of extra emphasis on the "she." Like a canting of an ink cartridge, suggestive of italics at a lesser angle.

"I still don't know," Myfanwy admitted. "All I know is, he blames everyone from the original Chancelhouse. He blames himself too. For not being able to protect her."

"Okay, cool beans. *My* upside is that Jasper sounds really, really hard. Probably harder than Simi or Meletē. Downsides?"

"Similar downsides to whatever the Chancel option was, only more so — he's unpredictable, could escalate it. I don't really know his motives and desires. And I certainly can't trust him."

"On the other hand he's a solo operation. You'd go into it as partners. There'd be no worrying about power politics, chain of command, or double agents. One person to focus on."

"All my eggs in one basket case, you mean. Enough with the Jasper upsides already. What's Option E?"

Tallulah shook her head. "That's me, pal. So. What are you going to do?"

*

"I defo don't waltz over to Veil alone. I'm too proud to invite Jasper in on it. I'm prejudiced vis-à-vis the Chancelhouse elders."

"So have you come to a decision?"

"Yeah. The new generation — Moth, Triffid, Yuri, Bee and Kermitcrab. As many newbloods as still will trust me, after my Spring Feast debacle." She hesitated. "One hitch."

"Surveillance! Veil might be bugging phones. Can't you —"

"Um, it's worse than that, Tallulah. I was kinda a loner at Muse School. I don't . . . actually have any of their numbers."

Tallulah tittered. "And no emails, no Hexxus Nexus . . . no? Nae pals, eh? That's actually lols. So get up early and fetch them. That way you can flip 'em the necessary memories to trust you."

"What you're saying makes sense," admitted Myfanwy. "I know it does."

Tallulah regarded her carefully. She folded her hand on Myfanwy's arm. "So what's the problem, pal?"

"I have to see Jasper in the morning. Not to beg him for help. Just — just to see what he wants. I don't know how long it will take."

"Oof. All day and all night? Can you no maybe push it back in the week?"

"*No.*" She stared at the starlit water. "I don't trust him. I don't want to ask him for help. I don't know! I just feel, somehow, that he's the key to all this."

"Well," said Tallulah calmly. "You do what you need to with Jasper. I'll go get help from Chancelhouse."

"Damn!" Myfanwy turned to her excitedly. "Of course! You know the city. You even have a place to stay if you need one. And I can — I can make the muses trust you, Tallulah. All I need to do is flip you memories — Yuri is a taker, so he can receive them —"

"Myfanwy," said Tallulah, eyes suddenly flashing. "I told you before, *no!* I don't want you to *do* it to me! If it's really necessary, then you have to go to Chancelhouse, I'll meet Jasper. I'll tell him you're just not that into him, yeah?"

"No! Tallulah, it's *got* to be me," retorted Myfanwy. "I can't explain why. I just —"

"Well, I think I can explain it, Myfanwy."

"Forget the memories. Just go to Chancelhouse HQ. Tell them what I've told you. They'll believe you."

"Fine," said Tallulah. "First thing tomorrow. Give me the deets. How can I tell who're the right dudes? Where's HQ? How do I get in without the elders finding?"

"Okay," said Myfanwy. "There's this deli. You know the Meadows?"

"Aye, of course —"

And, Myfanwy thought, just for a moment, there was something immoderate about Tallulah's acquiescence.

Something a little too ready.

Something, in Tallulah's shadowed face, almost a little greedy.

"Myfanwy? You okay?"

Veil already knew about HQ. So giving away its location couldn't possibly harm Chancelhouse, right? Even if it *did* turn out Tallulah was working for —

"Myffo, pal?"

"Mmph? Yeah." Myfanwy exhaled. "Of course. Uh, the Meadows. So there's this deli pretty nearby. If we're lucky, Kermitcrab or Moth may be on shift. How shall I briefly portray the character of a Kermitcrab . . ."

Way too easily spooked nowadays.

I mean, Tallulah?

Book Six

"What wets your meat, if not my putrid body?"

— Sophie Robinson, *Souvenir*

"Yuri acted only after serious reflection."

— Julian May, *Intervention*

Myfanwy stood in Kings Cross St Pancras staring at Neck Tattoo.

He looked even more stunned than she was. He was sort of squinting.

"Um. Marcus, right?"

His pink hair, she noted, now sported some serious roots.

He gave her a weird look and laughed.

Marcus AKA Neck Tattoo was *not* looking his best today. One eye was watering and bloodshot. He sniffed. There was a rash or something on his cheek.

Now Myfanwy sighted Tallulah in the crowd. "Tallulah! Here!"

Marcus wagged a finger at her. "Blud, I'll do your legwork, yeah, but some point I gotta link you to give it *back*. Where exactly are you going?"

Damn! He knows I have his deck!

"Hon," she fibbed kindly. "I carted that dang thing around for weeks! Where *were* you?"

Wow, that day by the Thames she'd almost fancied this squirt. Maybe Gen was the reason he seemed so different now. A side-effect of some crushes, Myfanwy knew, was that hotness can kinda bleed out of its wonted hosts, and flood enchantingly into the figure of the Beloved . . .

Marcus groaned, "Wha' . . ."

"Myfanwy!" cried Tallulah, shocked. "Why are *you* —"

"Allow it," Marcus said quickly, turning. "Toodles, yeah." The revolving crowds consumed him.

Myfanwy giggled. Cameo over, now to business. She put on her Serious Face. "I came to find *you*, Looly. Things may have changed — may I see your ticket a sec?"

"Uh, sure — why? Who was *that* kid? I'd have liked to have said hi."

"Skater kid, Looly," said Myfanwy briskly. "I'm holding his deck for a couple weeks. That's what we skater kids call our skatedecks."

Tallulah handed over her ticket and reservation slips. "He totes vanished — um, like I'm some scary monster?"

"Mm-hmm," said Myfanwy primly. "You know why, Looly? I'll tell you why. I'm a detective, so basically I know everything. The skittish young skater assumed you were Kitty. He once spent fifteen minutes with Kitty. What's the moral of the story? Kitty's a Scary Monster." Myfanwy casually pocketed Tallulah's ticket, and tilted her chin up at the taller girl. "And *so am I*, Looly. I can't let you go to Edinburgh."

Tallulah stared. "Eh? You being here is pointless. Why aren't you with Jasper?"

"Oh, people may not *like* me and Kitty," Myfanwy continued pleasantly. "They may not *respect* us. They may not even be *scared* of us. But we're *weirdly disconcerting*, okay? And *we* have a quality that you and your little Cool Kids friends will never replicate —"

"Myfanwy, you're acting kinda erratic."

"Right! Whereas you're acting very helpful, aren't you Looly? You were a pretty cool cucumber on the pier last night. Weren't you?"

"I've heard about enough of this," Tallulah said frostily. "If you don't *want* my help —"

"Pretty cool about muses," Myfanwy continued emphatically. "Compared them to large rabbits, didn't you?"

"Those are epic rabbits! Listen, my train leaves in —"

"Pretty cool, and pretty *concerned* to stop me getting any of *your* memories."

"My mum is dead," Tallulah said flatly. "But it's fine."

Myfanwy regarded her for a moment, then looked away. "Yeah. So if I'm wrong, I'm sorry." She fixed her again with her steely gaze. "But I still can't take the risk! I had my first flicker of doubt last night, when you volunteered to enter Chancelhouse HQ. But I thought, 'Hey, Vertical's been in our yard. Jasper's been in our yard."

"I'm not saying this isn't fascinating, Myfanwy."

"I thought, 'Tallulah can't learn anything they don't already know.' But this morning, it hit me. How do I *know* Jasper was responsible for *any* of the break-ins? Did anyone actually *see* him Tallulah? *Did* they?"

"Uh, yes? No? Maybe just picture a baby owl, okay?"

"It's been *years* since Jasper was last a Chancelhouse agent! The east houses weren't yet developed. What if Jasper *doesn't* have that intel?"

"It's just that my train leaves in three —"

"*It's a Super Off-Peak Saver it's valid on the next service,*" snarled Myfanwy.

"Okay," said Tallulah, casting up her hands in surrender. "Okay. Nae bother. Nae bother."

"*I'll fuck up your owl!*" Myfanwy was squaring up to Tallulah now. She saw with satisfaction her skin paling beneath her make-up. Tallulah swayed slightly, though she didn't step back. "Is that some kind of Cool Kids in-joke, Tallulah? Owls? Is that what you guys all think? She's *mine*, Looly. Kitty belongs to *me*. She'll never, never be a Cool —"

"Did you go to the rose garden?" Tallulah asked quietly.

Myfanwy felt weirdly confused by these roses, challengingly whispered within kissing distance. She tried to gather herself up again. "So why are you so interested in me meeting Jasper, Looly? Yeah, I — I *went* to the rose garden. I even arrived early, I think. Yes, I must have. Totally exhausted. I only had two cans last night — *still* I feel hungover. Why? But I walked the labyrinth, or whatever, and recentred my chakras, and you know what? The mists cleared. And I remembered how, on the pier —"

Tallulah stepped back, and glanced up at the Departures Board. "It's only — I have a *seat* reserved and I feel totally *ming* if I don't face the direction of —"

"*On the pier,* you outlined my options, Tallulah. As though it were all the same to you if I chose A, B, C, D, or E."

"Never was an E," said Tallulah. "Sorry. Again, I've interrupted you. Three minutes. Continue."

"But there *was* one you preferred, wasn't there? Which was it? You pushed it a little hard, Looly. Just a little too hard, and *I noticed.* You sent me to meet Jasper. And *you* went to scout out Chancelhouse HQ for him, with me giving you the perfect cover."

Tallulah looked at her wide-eyed. "But it was *you*, Myfanwy, who chose Jasper. *'I can't explain why. I just know he's the key to all this.'* That's what you said! You're pure *mental* Myfanwy."

"Yes," said Myfanwy softly. Thousands of faces moved around them. "I am mental. We are all pure mental. And I really *couldn't* explain why. It was like there was this — compulsion in me. I fought against it. But it won that struggle. And *now* maybe, I *can* explain it, Tallulah. Because you touched me, didn't you? On the pier last night. You *touched* me."

*

One of the faces was Bee's.

"What's *she* doing here?" Myfanwy muttered.

Tallulah followed her gaze in vain. "Who? Quickly now, Myfanwy. You have to start trusting me."

She shook her head. Bee was scanning the crowd . . . or whatever phantasmagorical inner landscape she was currently inhabiting.

"Myfanwy," Tallulah insisted, "was Jasper with you this morning?"

"Him? No." Myfanwy refocused on Tallulah. "I worked everything out just in time. Then I came here."

"But it was nearly time to meet? Could he have followed you here?"

Myfanwy rubbed her face with her hands. Bee was bumbling towards them now, but still hadn't seen them.

She shrugged and gave Bee a wave. "Tallulah, it's not Jasper. It's just Bee."

"Don't trust her," said Tallulah rapidly. "She could have followed you from the rose garden. Trust *me*. Myfanwy, flip me. Do it."

"Bee doesn't do stuff like follow people. She's cool."

Tallulah seized her wrist.

"Hey!"

"Flip me, Myfanwy. I have nothing to hide. Test me."

"Hi," said Bee. "Mind if I join in on you guys? Your hair is very impressive and intimidating, ma'am. It's got two buns in it. I will refer to them as beehives, against all reason and morality. That's not what the history of hairdressing says. What are you doing here in London? I bet it's all trains-related."

Myfanwy sighed. She looked at Tallulah's fingers on her wrist. Tallulah wore yellow nail varnish.

"Well Bee," Myfanwy decided, narrowing her eyes. "We're *flipping.* Tallulah! February. St Jerome's Sixth Form Centre, also known as the Womyn's Castle. *Remember the first time you met Jasper Robin!*"

Hmm. Tricky little flip. She had to get seriously Gardener's Question Time on her Dwelling. Stars twinkled. A long brown pear dropped. Myriapods rose from leaves. Cabbage whites left their hiding places. Flusters of father fluff twisted soaking through little precipitating clouds.

There.

"What?" said Tallulah. "I didn't feel anything."

"How much is she charging?" Bee asked. "If you don't mind me asking. I've done some real rad activities which suit your brain, ma'am."

Myfanwy ignored her. "*Remember*, Tallulah."

"There *was* something," Tallulah admitted then. "Like a dream or something I saw on the net . . ."

"Tell me what happened."

"Jasper. She was really butch? She dressed terribly? She acted like a total bitch towards me?"

"Um," said Myfanwy. "Jasper's a guy. I must have flipped the wrong memory."

"What does hairstory of herdressing tell us?" said Bee. "Buzz, buzz, tase, tase, maze, maze, gays, gays."

"She was clearly so *into* me, you know?" Tallulah said thoughtfully. "I could have been into her, but she didn't even give me a chance. She said something like . . . oh yeah, like, '*Uh, put your clothes back on, you're pure minging.*' Then she shoved me into some ice? *Keeper.*"

"Damn. No. Guess it didn't work."

"Well," said Tallulah. "What happened the day *you* met Jasper in the Womyn's Castle?"

Myfanwy couldn't really remember.

A smile played lightly on Tallulah's lips. "Yeah, it's come back to me. Snuffling in my snotrag like a vestal virgin in her suffibulum, eh? I had never been so ill-used and insulted! I was totes bricking it and basically just weirdly horny!"

"No, no, *no*," moaned Myfanwy. "That *can't* be it. I'm pretty new at this muse business, so —"

"This train station," Bee commented, "was originally designed by Victorians from the Future."

"*Then* I think I've like slipped," Tallulah continued. "And there *she* was, Jasper, reaching out her hand. And me — in my instant of infinite disgrace — like, as flagrantly innocent and immobilised as a bridezilla, all in white — I'm reaching for Jasper's blurry fingers . . . then I can't remember. Aye. Brilliant. So what did *I* forget?"

Myfanwy shrugged. "I haven't spotted anything yet, Looly. I'll keep you in the loop. Nothing super-duper incriminating, anyway." She patted Tallulah's arm kindly. "It will pop up, I assure you. We're very different people, you and I."

Tallulah suppressed a sigh. "Okay. You trust me now, right? Give me my ticket back. I can still make that train."

Why was Tallulah still so desperate to go to Chancelhouse?

"Flipping with me was a good gesture, Tallulah. It could just have been a low-risk gamble. I haven't decided yet."

"Hey," said Bee. "Here's Jasper. Look what I can do."

And she touched Tallulah's face.

*

"It'll be okay," said Jasper. He took Myfanwy's hand. She was too tired to argue.

He was wearing a different stupid sports brand today.

Bee's fingers, strangely elongated for such a stubby girl, swirled across Tallulah's features. Her cheekbones, her patrician chin, her parted lips.

Bee was rapt, an artist. Tallulah was mesmerised, a portrait.

Tallulah's eyelashes flickered open and shut like teeth chattering. Bee's fingernails were each done their own colour, like paintbrushes.

"What are you doing?"

Jasper answered for her. "Just havering. Talent's on loan from Moth."

"*Moth?* Geeze. Does it hurt? Tallulah's had kinda a tough week."

"It doesn't hurt, exactly." He laughed. "It's like staying awake through nasty dreams."

Among the shuttering faces, Myfanwy glimpsed Paddy moving grimly towards them. "Damn. We need to leave."

"Isn't Moth weird?" said Bee, out of the side of her mouth. "Jasper, this tall girl was gonna see Blake."

Jasper hesitated. "Okay. Bring her along."

Bee led Tallulah from the station and the crazy blinking subsided. She still said nothing and from time to time her body shook with large, zoomed-in shivers.

Jasper's car was a purplish Hyundai station-wagon. There was rust on the bottoms of the doors. The cover of the fuel tank cap was partly shattered.

"Just shift stuff out the way," Jasper told Bee.

"I found lube," said Bee.

"Eh? Oh. Gel for replenishing of the silencers. Just shift stuff out the way."

Myfanwy buckled in beside Jasper and twisted round to check on Tallulah. "But she *still* can't say anything," she said worriedly. "She's just staring at me with this fixed expression!"

"Myfanwy," said Tallulah tartly, without shifting expression. "You just got us *abducted.* Can you *please* not speak to me for five minutes?"

"Sorry," said Myfanwy with relief. She sat back, adding in a small voice, "You might have got abducted *anyway.*"

"*Myfanwy!*"

"Sorry! . . . anyway," she added again, "*you're* the only one who's been abducted here."

As Jasper started the engine, he and Bee both laughed.

Not nice laughter.

*

"'I cried in Bethany Christian Trust,'" Myfanwy recited thoughtfully, as they idled by the lights. "Hey, Jazz! That night you tried to break into my house? You mentioned a really recent memory — Bee's slammin' dress at the Spring Feast. So I suspected you'd been in contact with Kitty or Kermitcrab. But it was *Bee's* memory, not mine! Ain't that funny?"

"Uh," he said, preoccupied, letting out the handbrake. All around Carmageddon revved and honked.

And Myfanwy reached for the dash.

"Whoa, whoa!" Jasper glanced sideways and seemed about to bat her hand away from the GPS. But his hand just hovered there. "What — what are you doing?"

"This is called a 'GPS,' Jazz. It's gonna take us to Veil HQ. Once we get out of London, the drive is about two-and-a-half hours. Um, can we have some tunes too?"

Jasper shook his head. His hands were back on the wheel. "There is a proper order to things. I'm taking you to our new safe house."

"Kitty's in danger, Jasper! Your last safe house wasn't exactly safe for Oscar, was it?"

"Shut *up*," Jasper grated. "You *don't* need to tell me that."

Myfanwy sighed crossly. "I'm sorry. Forget it then. If you won't help her, I'll go to Chancelhouse instead. I want that Mum memory. Then you can let me off here."

Jasper's knuckles grew pale. "No Chancelhouse," he growled.

"If *you're* not —"

"In a moment," said Jasper, "remember when you fell. And *remember what Chancelhouse did to Genevieve Quaker.*"

He fumbled for her wrist and flipped.

*

Wise pamphlets feinting to and fro on charnel stacks . . .

Please not yet . . .

In the air outside the west houses . . . ha . . .

A rolled carpet fell and spilled out, dark blood on Persian arabesque . . .

A pink van winding through Citadel darkness . . . lost . . . too much pain . . . go earlier . . .

Someone lifted a tea cup . . . and kissed her with it . . .

Walking along a row of stainless steel sinks, purplish-stained brushes scattered down in the basins . . .

Bees and rain . . .

Kisses and words . . .

Stone and bone . . .

*

"Safe house," grunted Jasper.

"Okay," Myfanwy admitted. "No Chancelhouse. I'm sure your den is really cool with pool tables and stealth-involving video games, and I'd *love* to see it someday. But we've wasted too much time already. By now, Veil know I know it's a trap. They may already have moved her!"

He laughed scornfully. "What's this to do with me?"

"Mara's still alive, Jasper. You know that, right?"

"Gaga. Yeah," he said grimly. "I heard. With mixed feelings."

"Plus don't you have some more scores to settle? Undine the taker, Germ the mesmer, Vertical the caster — all Parkour-pimped out with pinched beastware? They'll be defended by their many minions, you know. Oni, Ladybird, uh, Egg, Cracks, Crypt, Haeccacity, Scan —"

"Some of those muses are already dead."

"No thanks to *you!* What happened to the psychotic serial killer obsessed with vengeance? You've *changed* Jasper."

"I have a little actually," said Jasper briskly. "Still got it, though."

"Well, I *need* that psychotic serial killer in my *life* right now."

"Christ, Myfanwy, I have a million things I wanted to do today! What time is it?"

"Hush," said Myfanwy. "Don't stress. I'm sorry. You just concentrate on the driving."

She plugged the postcode into the GPS.

"Sorry I snapped," said Jasper. In a minute he growled. "*Why* are we doing what *you* want to do again?"

Tallulah piped up. "You guys seem to be doing Stockholm Syndrome sort of back-to-front," she observed.

"It depends who's kidnapped who," said Myfanwy.

"Whom," Jasper autocorrected.

Soon suburbia slid by.

"This is near where I live," said Myfanwy. "Hey, you should stop for petrol."

"I've got half a tank," Jasper complained.

"Yeah, but there's been some kind of panic buy. It might be tougher later on."

I knew he'd help, Myfanwy thought. *There was a time just like this, wasn't there? When he waited too long. He waited too long to help Genevieve. Or slept in, or something, or whatever. Must have turned off his alarm, but couldn't remember it. And she died.*

Jasper put on Duke Ellington. The pumps were dry at the first two garages they tried. At the third station they queued for twenty minutes, switching the Duke for Lady Leshur. Jasper was edgy. Myfanwy patted him.

Then they were on the open road, London dwindling behind them.

"What time is it on your phone?" said Jasper.

"Just gone twelve. It says right there."

"Just double-checking. Will you remind me about quarter to one? Just if I forget."

"I'll try to remember. Is this something to do with Gen's birthday?"

"Um, yeah," said Jasper. "We'll both try remember."

Bee was drawing.

"You have nebulous stuff back here," said Tallulah. "What's this?"

Jasper glanced in his rearview. "Two-player surgery game. You have to take the organs out with the tongs. Only if you touch the sides of the cavity, the guy's hands and feet flash blue."

"So it's also educational," said Myfanwy.

"No batteries though," said Tallulah.

"They should be back there somewhere, if you have a look. Frontal lobes too, rattling around."

"What's this?"

"Superdirectional shotgun mic. Can pick a voice out of a crowd or a sparrow's song out of —"

"No batteries though. Essentially it's the toy surgery again. This?"

"Part of a Sandia tacky incapacitant projector."

"You're telling me."

"I feel sick," said Bee. "Cool."

"No, 'tacky' as in — militarised foam party, basically."

"This?"

"I have no idea what that is," Jasper admitted.

"Some of this stuff shouldn't be back here," said Tallulah. "Not if you're going to be running people around. What's this?"

"Photo project I did. Careful, they're not all stuck in properly."

"Can I see?" said Myfanwy.

"It wasn't *meant* to be good," said Jasper, reddening slightly.

"This?"

"Be careful with that."

"Sure, Jasper! I won't break your toy submarine!"

"Fully submersible, radio-operated within a ten mile radius, with a periscope low-light camera transmitting encrypted signal in realtime."

"How did you afford all this stuff?" said Tallulah.

"Blackmail and extortion. In the old days, Zeus used to say all money comes from one place."

"Hell," replied Myfanwy.

"He still says that, huh?"

"'Am I to have all this,'" Tallulah murmured vaguely, "'and Hell besides?'"

"No Jasper," said Myfanwy. "He just said it a lot when *you* knew him. We're pretty mixed up by now, you and me. We've flipped in the snow, we've flipped in the rain, we've flipped in the sun. You even *sound* like me sometimes."

"I do *not*," said Jasper primly. "*Hey* everybody, you know Chekov's famous advice to playwrights? If you put an antique toy submarine on the wall in Act I, make darn sure it's fired an antique toy nuclear warhead by Act III. Well, I gotta admit most of that junk never gets any use. Um. Lol."

"It's *not* really the car I'd associate with you," Myfanwy admitted. "I expected something more kempt and succinct I guess. In a way I kind of prefer this."

Jasper shrugged, and took them into the middle lane to undertake a lorry. "When you decide to kill a long list of people," he said, "it's easy to fall into the trap of a spending spree, right? You think you're making progress, whereas in fact all you're doing is procrastinating. You start reading customer reviews, checking your emails, going on Pinterest and Snapchat and Hexxus Nexus. Much better to just knuckle down."

Myfanwy shivered.

"Your car is pointless," said Tallulah.

"Did you ever get inside Chancelhouse HQ? While I was there, I mean? Or did the alarms always stop you?"

"Never tried to get in," said Jasper. "Seems a stupid thing to do."

"Hmm."

"I staked it out a little though. And I'll tell you something. I saw Vertical come and go plenty, and no alarm ever went off till after he was safely away."

Myfanwy didn't answer but sunk again into her Garden. A lot to be done. She felt a kind of Seaside Holiday sleepiness. The pond near her Altar, supposed to be fringed with irises and forget-me-nots and iced with waterlilies, instead ran wild with exotica, dwarf mangroves, jacaranda trumpets, climbing jasmine and heaven-knows-what. Even worse, a lilyclad lychee tree had sprouted up in the middle of the pond. It could have lynched a koi carp. She was cross.

"What time is it now, by the way?"

"Oh my God, Jasper! Like, three minutes past noon?"

"Okay, okay. Sorry."

"I have another question," said Myfanwy. "You claimed Blake AKA Zeus was the first muse. Was Gen the second?"

"Yeah," said Jasper.

"How sure are you?"

"Huh? Why? What?"

"Nothing. Just thinking."

"Seriously, Myffy. What time is it?"

"Jasper!"

*

A little Asian girl on crutches, caught in a spotlight. A vast bulk behind her like a dead star.

Now Genevieve was storming down a long corridor in the west houses, before they were the west houses. Everything was flaking, peeling, hanging. The walls were covered in deep green millefleur wallpaper, a bit like a ragged medieval tapestry, with great grey tongues torn lollingly down.

Faces loomed, muses from the old days . . .

Everyone had something to say to Gen, everyone was reaching for her with compassionate fingertips . . .

Clio, worried, weak . . . Melpomene, wry . . . Undine, bored . . . Erato, enraged, blustering between English and Polish . . . Mara, Erato, Vert, Tar, Simi, all lurking at the back . . . Meletē standing just in front of them, arms rammed behind his back, looking martial and thoughtful . . .

Simi pushing forward, her lips pursed, her eyes cavernous. "Babes, that young girl is dead. Nothing on earth will bring her back."

"I wish you were all fucking dead!"

"You go to your room Genny!" hollered Blake, a distant purple face drifting round a corner. Was he crying?

"I'm not your fucking little girl!" Gen said.

She went into her room and closed the door.

Blake called along the corridor, "You are a member of Chancelhouse now, Genny! You'll stay in your quarters till you are civil!"

"Leave me the fuck alone!" Gen called, muffled by the door.

Now she was standing alone in front of Gen's door.

She tried the doorknob.

"Go away, Terpsichore!"

She sighed. Gen only used her callsong when she was really, really mad.

She knocked. Nothing but faint scraping and scurrying sounds. She hesitated, then called, "What have I *done?* I've *done nothing!"*

No answer.

She found Clio on the first floor. "Can you talk to her? I heard her moving stuff around. I'm worried she was, like, packing a bag. She won't talk to me."

"I dunno, Jasper. If she wants to go, nobody can stop her. Why would she talk to me?"

"You're slightly less her boyfriend than I am."

Clio smiled. "She never listens to me."

"She always listens to me, only I'm always wrong."

She went to the second floor. She realised she seldom came up here now.

The light no longer worked in the last section of corridor. Three canted slabs of whorled, late evening light illuminated the way, leant against three tall dusty sash windows. The carpet and walls were a state. The sprouts and twists of the millefleur had curlicued into the third dimension as the wallpaper peeled.

Terpsi, *she read, rummaging for keys.*

Her own gaff felt messy and unfamiliar. It was rapidly turning into storage space for, like, nebulous stuff. She paced round, pointlessly tidying stuff she really should have been chucking.

She gazed at her books. Her tablet was in Gen's room. Gen's clutter was at least always pretty.

She lay back on the bed, legs jiggling.

She jumped up. This was pointless. She'd go outside and just roam around like a loon. She swept up her maroon Lacoste hoodie.

She was struggling into the hoodie as she came around the corner, and the curtain fell on the strangest of scenes.

Genevieve was coming down the corridor, very pale now, and in company. Vertical and Mara each had a hand around Gen's elbow. Gen wore a little backpack, its gunmetal grey straps like the claw of a hammer. They'd just come up the stairs. Now Undine's head and shoulders appeared behind them.

"Terpsichore," Vertical greeted her uneasily. That high-pitched, mellifluous voice. Was he trying to disguise his surprise? Had everyone forgotten that, technically, she lived up here? In this shabby, quiet corner of the house . . .

She nodded levelly at Vert. "Thalia."

She looked at Gen's wide, shining and rather dashingly anime eyes.

Vertical wasn't wearing a belt today. She walked briskly forward and yanked his jeans down around his ankles. This brought her nose-to-bulge with today's — quite possibly this week's — warm Tartan undies, and also close enough to grip one of Mara's gleaming brown knee-high boots by the ankle.

Vertical hadn't finished his first yelp and she'd risen, yanking Mara's leg to chest height and forcing her onto the worn carpet on her back. Mara's face doubled its natural length with astonishment.

She began working on the boot zip, trying to stay calm. Was she being rash? From the look on Mara's face, she was just thinking, Why is Terpsichore frantically and incredibly violently trying to steal our clothes?

Had she misread the —

Genevieve struck Vertical as hard as she could in the throat.

It was a good solid blow and Vertical bodychecked the wall, wildly out of control. Mara wrenched her boot out of her grasp. Mara was loose again and getting to her feet.

Vertical gargled hideously, clutching at the wall as if it was a soft toy suddenly swollen huge and flat. Garlands of greenish millefleur wallpaper tore free, grey in his fists.

"Sexy lady," she panted to Gen. "I thought you were non-violent."

As Mara rose her half-pilfered boot furled before her like the hind limb of a huge puppy. She swooped again for the boot.

"Terpsichore!" Mara shrieked. "Quit it! What is this Achilles' heel bullshit?"

A flapping shape passed she dared not pause to examine. Mara's boot came free with a nasty zip-ripping sound, and Mara's eyes boggled. Undine snatched Gen's wrist. She didn't see what Gen did but she heard Undine's agonised squee.

"I am! I'm just, you know," Gen gasped, twisting free of Undine, "doing that 'couply' thing where you think the same —"

Gen punched, Undine dodged. She turned as Vertical threw a punch trawling a grey-greenish ribbon of wallpaper.

With both fists she drove the edge of Mara's heel into Vertical's gurgling face, feeling his cartilage crack. He howled like an engine igniting. She swirl-stepped in behind Vert. Blood droplets fluttered into the softly snapping scrap of wallflowers.

She pulled the boot round Vert's throat. Gen shoved an elbow in Mara's cheek. Mara *purred and grinned insincerely in agony. Obviously deeply-wired reflexes.*

Downstairs someone was listening to Nina Simone.

"Strange fruit . . ."

"Zeus!" Mara shrieked. Damn. "Polyhymnia! Meletē! Aoide! Ow! Meletē, dammit! Help!"

Garrotting Vertical with Mara's boot was going dandy. She struggled to impose the makeshift fell scarf without crushing the guy's larynx, or for that matter letting him scratch Mara's shimmering leather. It was so hard to please everybody. In a way you just wanted a trainer for this job. This felt a bit like throttling somebody with an elephant's ear.

Vertical's struggles softened and sagged. Strangling was never safe, not this trousers-down soft core asphyxia erotica, not the Fainting Game schoolchildren play . . . Gen was slamming clear of Mara and now headed for the top of the stairs. Mara flailed like a ballerina, grabbed Gen's backpack. Gen wriggled one arm free as Mara lunged for her hair.

She gave a last tug of Mara's boot and let Vert fall, turning to react to something in the corner of her vision.

Fractionally too late.

Every surface was briefly rinsed with darkness. In her right boiling ear the volume was zero.

She couldn't work out if Undine or Mara had clobbered her.

Undine stood near the top stair, smiling through a distorted circle of stars. Her heart was in a mad hurry to get somewhere. Something was terribly wrong.

She was clutching Gen's backpack. Gen and Mara had teleported halfway down staircase. Beside her, Vertical was gingerly waking onto his hands and knees.

Undine took a small step back, chewing his bottom lip coquettishly. He teetered on the top stair.

He smiled. "Terpsichore," he said mildly. "Are you enjoying my suckerpunch?"

She tensed, ready to run at him, ram the backpack in his chest. There was more blood and plaster and wallpaper than before. Vert spat blood and looked up bleary-eyed.

When Undine had pummelled her, he'd snatched away the last few seconds of skirmish. Just to confuse her. Or so she wouldn't realise that —

She started to turn just as Meletē fisted every organ in her belly simultaneously. Molten metallurgic upchuck flooded her lungs and her testicles. Blind and unable to breathe she crumpled onto the stretcher of Meletē's follow-through. Gen was shouting but she couldn't hear the contours of the words.

Now she was face-down on the floor, her head inside a black jellyfish, crawling towards where she thought the staircase probably was. Hands, maybe Meletē's, hooked roughly into her armpits. Her fingers drifted to the pocket zipper on Gen's backpack.

Would Gen perhaps have packed —

As they lifted her, she fished out the Celtic love spoon Gen had fashioned and struck it in two, driving one makeshift stake into Meletē's stomach and the other deep into Vertical's bare leg. One snort and one screech — now she was wobbling aloft, marshalling her frail moss and frass legs —

Four against two. And one of the four was Meletē.

Some furtive little critter who had figured amid the millefleur was now pinned into Vert's flesh. A ribbon of blood slipped across Vert's thigh. He gazed around aghast — at least he *was out of the ring for the moment —*

Gen and Mara grunted and cussed, wrestling down the staircase. Towards their fray Undine was unhurriedly descending. Meletē just seemed winded and incensed. His belly was too steely, or the second stake too blunt. She needed a new shard.

She stumbled for the sash window. From Gen's backpack came a tangle of little tops and a lacy black bra. She began winding herself a boxing glove with a red chilli print.

Meletē circled warily, wheezing. Vert moaned and plucked half a love spoon from his leg.

She lined up her chilli-chequered thump for the centre of the lower left-hand pane.

And her head broke the glass.

It was over.

It was done.

Maybe Meletē had thrown her by himself, or maybe Vert had helped. Either way, she exited the house with such force that, for one handsome instant, she felt almost as if she were rising.

She shut her eyes against the rinsing haze of razors. But she must have glimpsed the ground, because she knew roughly when she'd hit.

And she knew it might be gravel, or the plastic wheelie bins, or perhaps the spiked iron fence. She lay back in the scarce sky, wind whistling in her ears, bending her knees, and thought:

I should think a good thought.

Her feet smacked — must be gravel — and her legs snapped shut like a trap, and now she was folding and rolling — "rolling" a generous term, redolent of a ball running neatly down a grassy hill — this was insane motion in all directions at once— her bones jarred and she was somehow falling through the air again — *didn't make sense, the bounce was too much — her eyes opened and —*

a torture cabinet lid slotted shut.

She lay shivering in the gravel.

She'd blacked out.

The end.

Except it wasn't the real end, because muse talents change everything. There was some little obscure part of her Garden — no, sorry, of her Locomotive — where a story was still happening, where she still could work stuff out. She'd fallen on the wheelie bins, then bounced into the gravel.

In the story, she stood up, stared at her hand, with Gen's top wadded round it, and watched the blood start to well up. She inspected her other arm, crystallised with specks of glass.

This was like getting out of bed, but maybe just dreaming you had. It was fifty-fifty whether this really was happening.

In the story, she teetered slowly through the wrought iron gate, across the street.

She opened a second elegant wrought-iron gate. Some ivy, some straggly hedge. The door was green and white, painted in a pattern.

She thought to ring a doorbell, and stared at the column of buzzers. She was getting more and more certain that this wasn't really happening, that she was really lying unconscious in the gravel.

No one lived here anymore. Blake had bought up the last of these houses last month.

She licked her bloody lips, as you might when tears ran over them. She admired again the sparkling and darkening slivers in her palm and wrist.

She sat down heavily, and lay down.

If the story was really happening, she should try to drag herself somewhere less visible.

But no, the story was shutting down. This would have to do. Squished sea shells, filled with fags and ash.

She felt certain she was encased in an ice-cream spaceship, setting course for somewhere where they do things differently.

Darkness.

Very faintly — the faintest of any sound — Genevieve had begun to scream.

*

"Jasper, your Dwelling is, like, a big steam train?"

"Yeah, a bit. And?"

"You are *such* a little boy!"

At ten to one they were parked at a picnic area. Jasper shooed everyone from his stationwagon and rummaged in the nebulous stuff, eventually drawing forth two wands and a little tin whistle. He marched resolutely towards the picnic tables.

"Is this gonna take long?" said Myfanwy. "Hey, you're *blushing*! What is this about?"

"I'm not proud," said Jasper. "Me and Gen made this stupid band, just the two of us. It was like, um, a concept band? One of our songs was supposed to have the slowest Beats Per Minute of any track, ever. All the drum sounds are at least three months apart. Today's one of the days for these little bad boys."

He handed Myfanwy the whistle. She now recognised the wands were actually toy electric drumsticks, of the kind that made a crack when you swang them swiftly in the air.

"Um. So I'll count down, three, two, one. Then on the implied 'zero' blow the whistle. Do you mind?"

"*You* blow the whistle. I want to do the drumstick."

One o' clock came, Jasper blew the little tin whistle, Myfanwy went *dum-ch!* and Tallulah and Bee applauded politely.

"I'm interested in the effect of leap years on your BPM," said Tallulah.

They hit the road again. For a time they reminisced about mutual friends and acquaintances, and the deeds of years gone by.

"One time I remember Genevieve," said Myfanwy, "falling asleep during the day and grabbing that feathery belt thing that was lying on the bed. You know how her hands moved around when she slept? So she was just peacefully sleeping there, swishing this frolicking little dragon thing beside her. It was so cute. More than cute. You woke up in her clothes the next day, by the way. Skimpy, low-cut stripy top. My pecs, my little valley of velvet. Felt great."

"I remember your mum," said Jasper, "when she was in her phase of being bang on about turning off unnecessary lights? And one time you're just sitting there with Dad and this hand appears round the door and plunges you both into darkness. Then you both burst out laughing and the light goes on and she comes into the room, laughing and looking sheepish."

"Okay, I remember you horsing around with Gen. You had this fact about how bumblebees have to hide under leaves and things when it rains. They're too fluffy so if they get wet they can't fly. You said it to her in a really babyish voice, BTW. Then she comes back with the fact that everybody knows, about how according to computer models, bumblebees can't fly. But Gen looks really cute telling it and I kind of grab her and start telling her scientists have proved that Gen can't stand up without being cuddled, and we sort of play-fight. I'm all like, 'Scientists have proved she can't stand up,' and she's like, 'I *can* stand up! I *can* stand up!'"

"Yeah," said Jasper.

"What about the one in the café, Jasper?"

"Oh, yeesh! Don't let me forget to give that to you properly. Okay. Uh, your mum's chatting to this Greek guy on holiday. You're drinking this frappé. You don't like the taste, you're just trying to be grown up. You're willing yourself really hard not to slip another sugar cube in. Your mum's talking to the owner guy. 'Everywhere is more traditional than here,' he says. 'Windmills, threshing floors, shepherd's shelters, chapels. Here is very touristy. Well, not *even* touristy, but it's a long story.' He describes for her the route to Old Town. Then he's like, 'So, that's two frappes, one Coca-Cola, two moussakas and a salad.' He's joking about the food though, nobody ate anything. Your mum pays him. 'The moussaka was delicious.' Mum's playing along. He holds up the note. It's Euro at this stage. 'Of course, home-made.' He shakes his head sadly, joking that it's forged. Mum is like, 'That's home-made too.' Then we're all walking up towards the Old Town. It's hot but pretty empty. Mum tied my hair with a ribbon of pale dove grey colour and rubbed cream on my back and neck and nose. I did the rest. I smelled of coconut going down the road. There was a tabby crawling against a big fat palm tree, like a hamster on a treadmill. At this stage they were still Pineapple Trees. And Hampsters, in fact. There's this perfect little purse, made out of sea-shells and I let myself get mesmerised by for a bit, and for a moment I've panicked I've lost mum and dad. Then they pop around the corner again. The sunlight is very bright on a white wall. Some graffiti." Jasper spoke in tongues.

"Eh?"

"I'll write it down."

"Whoa! Not while you're driving!"

"I'm fine,"

"Seriously Jasper," Tallulah piped up. "Flip it to Bee, let her write it down."

"I'm very busy," said Bee. "I can't fit you in."

Jasper passed Myfanwy the scrap.

"There's a mountain in the distance. You know what? I think it's Olympus. I can't remember if you ever got to Old Town."

ΒΑΖΕΛΟΙ ΛΑΤΟΙ ΕΙΜΑΣΤΕ ΚΥΝΗΤΟΙ SNA4KES

"I don't think I'd remember that," said Myfanwy. "I don't think I'd remember the shapes of some letters. You know Greek, right?"

"A little."

"I think you've messed up my memory of mum, Jasper."

"I don't think so."

"I think you have. Jesus, Jasper!"

"Well, maybe just the graffiti part. I can remember it properly though. I promise."

"I'm cross with you. Really cross. I don't think I can forgive you for that."

Eventually only the GPS spoke.

When the album began again Myfanwy stopped it.

She let Jasper drive, and she let his driving's thrumming silence envelop her. She lost herself not in her thoughts, but in the abyssal landscapes of autonavigated England.

She felt a bit bad for talking about mums in front of Tallulah.

Bee was playing intently with the nebulous stuff.

Tallulah was looking out of the window, bored. "Jasper," she murmured. "I long to plunge my blade in your savage heart. Never have I been so ill-used and insulted."

"Tallulah. I'm just driving everyone. I'm not doing anything."

"In the Womyn's Castle," Tallulah explained, frowned.

"I've said I'm sorry."

"Not to me. Never to me."

Myfanwy shut her eyes and sleep took her.

*

Awaking in the pied-à-terre, *remembering the days when Kitty, still intent on being a soprano, would wake her up with a piercing cry of, "Habet acht! HABET AAAAAACHT!"*

Only today she was alone.

Hmm, it was late! She must have woken earlier and turned off her alarm, though she had no memory of that.

Wait, hadn't she already leapt out of bed? Or was that a dream? Where was Kitty . . . ?

She would go to her Garden and find her.

She couldn't quite find the Garden, though she was in nearby forests. It was raining, unseasonably . . .

Suddenly she realised exactly where she was!

This *was where they made bumblebees!*

A lot of things were falling into place. Bumblebees, obviously, were constructed the same way raindrops were. That's why they got so big— same way a fat globe of leaf-filtered rain would fall on your forehead and make for one moment a fountain play. That's why bumblebees thud into your window, in your pied-à-terre, *in the golden sinking sunlight, in the hazy summer evening, with approximately the heft of an obese kamikaze bald eagle.*

Elsewhere, the sun fell on her face.

Here she was in the forest where the bumblebees were made. Tragic. It must be just at the edge of the Garden. Tinkling little bee drops pattered onto the canopy, like the finest drizzles of honey possible, then ran down in hidden green rivulets, joining and sploshing and pooling into larger fuzzier organisms, which every now and then would chaotically bumble forth on one scale or another . . .

She experimented with different levels of honeybee mist flowing in at the top. She would see if she could make Bee . . .

Hmm.

Wait.

A scream.

Blisters. Blisters on her arms, blood sprinkling white concrete . . .

No . . . not that . . . something missing . . . or not yet . . .

Gently rocked side-to-side by something, Myfanwy was either dreaming or playing make-believe.

Please not yet . . .

No more screams.

The bees were gone.

It was earlier now.

Years earlier.

The ground was swatched with crunched up sea-shells. Up the long, curved street came a small pink van.

Its headlamps briefly swished through the garden where she lay. She touched Gen's strappy top, damp with blood, like a comfort blanket.

The van parked opposite. Mara was the driver. She entered the house.

Almost immediately, Undine and Meletē appeared and drove away in another car. She waited. Soon Blake, Mara and Tar appeared on the pavement. Others too, their faces were blocked. Who? Mara went to the back of the van and unlocked its doors.

The doors obscured what they put inside.

The doors to the van and the houses shut simultaneously. Mara and Tar pulled away in the van, leaving Blake alone on the pavement. She could not make out his expression.

Blake put his hands in his pockets.

Genevieve.

Soon she would pedal until her heart ached. Over the tangling dark hills and bridges of the Citadel.

But Genevieve was already gone.

She crept across gardens to her bike and undid its chain.

She would pedal till her legs were made of stone.

Genevieve.

The pink van was moving slowly. On the long unlit road at the edge of Holyrood park, it sped up. The tail-lights pulled away into the darkness.

Did it matter?

Change this memory. Change this past. Go to the dark lily loch and drown. Nothing matters.

Her hands were full of glass. She lay them lightly on the handlebars. Genevieve was already gone. She didn't know that yet. But it was impossible to remember the hope she must have felt . . .

A will o' the wisp — a phone light — kindled on the isle of the roundabout.

She put her bike light onto the face of a young girl on crutches. The girl was about nine or ten. She faced the rising ground of Arthur's Seat. Her leg was in a cast, striped like a bee, blanched to sepia in the diffusing beam.

"Go home," she said to the girl. "Or if you can't, go where there are houses and lights and cars. Don't go up there. There are murderers about."

Had she really said that? The girl wore a large backpack and a defiant expression.

"Ah willnae," she said. "Ah'm geyin hame."

"Have you seen a pink van?"

The girl shook her head and leaned more deeply on her crutches.

She pedalled on down the hill. She met a bright, wandering beam. An obese Asian woman rode a mobility scooter in the centre of the road.

"I'm looking for my granddaughter," she said. Her accent combined Bangladeshi with Scottish. "A wee girl on crutches. Oh, mister. The man and the women down there were carrying a body."

She pointed. "Your granddaughter's by the roundabout. She said she was going home."

"It was wrapped up but I could tell."

"Call the police," she said. "I'll try to stall them."

"My granddaughter's ran away," she said, her voice full of dread. "Do you think I've no already called them?"

Under the gloomy mass of Salisbury Crags she found the pink van. It was parked next to the building sites around Holyrood Parliament. The other car was there too, its headlamps glowing. Mara stood between them, smoking. The van's pink doors were open. Darkness filled its cave.

She dropped the bike on the grass and walked towards Mara.

Mara put out her cigarette. Then she reached into the car and put out all the light. It was hard to make anything out.

Her legs were stone. Her heart was stone. The world seemed to shake a little with each soft footfall.

*

Myfanwy awoke, much refreshed, to tall heads of wheat. A road sign read *Adverse Camber.* Jasper was turning off the lane. He parked the station-wagon among trees, hidden from the road. When she got out she heard the crackle of power lines overhead.

"Just over three miles," said Jasper. "We'll go by foot."

They walked through widely spread gnarled woodland and came out by yellow fields of rape.

Tallulah seemed lost in thought.

"Are you still pissed off at me?" said Myfanwy.

"Eh? No! I was just a bit —"

Jasper and Bee had walked out a little in front. Both had hold-alls slung on their shoulders.

"What did Bee do to you?" Myfanwy asked quietly. "Havering?"

"You snoozed through the scoop, eh? The idea is that, just before thoughts become thoughts, they're like this, uh, pre-cognitive goop? Supposedly called hoverware, but whevs. Bee kept flipping the goop I was about to shape into thought, and replaced it with inert slush, called neverware. There's more to havering than that, apparently — but that's one trick she can do now."

"So what was it like?"

"Like I was doing a task," said Tallulah, "and I'd just lost my place, over and over again."

"Wicked."

"I remember it was terrible at the time, but now I can't remember in what way it was terrible."

They met a German Hen Night coming the other way. Their eldest hen led them. Their bride wore L-plates and a cerise veil. The day was balmy, but several of their skins looked raw and sun-kissed. They all wore hot pink wigs, diamante Union Jack and German flag deely-boppers, sparkly pink fluff, sashes and boas, and seemed tired and cross. One or two of them had pink collection tins.

"Where is the main road?" asked the Hen Night.

Tallulah reassured the Hen Night.

Bee's gaze lingered on them, as though her loyalties were divided.

After that, they saw no other foot traffic. Every now and then everyone stood at attention at the roadside to let some vehicle pass.

At one point, Bee let out a long, terrible moan. She did not expand any further.

Turning off the road, they followed a footpath uphill through a kissing gate and among more tall trees. The woods really smelled of wild garlic.

"Did your friend Lucy wear some snails?" Myfanwy asked Tallulah shyly. "Really and truly?"

"Nah. Snails was *my* look, remember?"

"Sorry, random."

"Lucia was snogging some celeb — her loss —"

"Wow," said Myfanwy. "I think the two stories got snoggled together."

"Whoa, wait a moment! You were *there* that night, Myfanwy. That was Kitty's eighteenth!"

Myfanwy laughed. "Damn you, Jasper! So what else? Am I secretly a Cool Kid and don't remember?"

Tallulah shrugged. "Uh, no really pal. Sorry to break it to you."

Myfanwy shrugged right back. "I'm okay with that."

"Do you remember the pre-drinking at all? Kitty's entrance? OMG, I can tell this isn't ringing any bells, eh? Pervy wee Jaspo, keeping the girls' night in tae himsel'! Kitty insisted she come in doing all these masculine Flamenco-esque hand flourishes and got on the table and we all had to kinda bellow, 'Toreador, toreador, toreador.' No? Penny no dropping, eh?"

Myfanwy laughed thoughtfully. "All you guys are really close, aren't you? The — uh, the Cool Kids?"

"I dunno. Probably not much closer than any normal group of friends. They're a subtle palette, that lot. Usually you gotta learn to love the minute variation, you know? But it was kinda natural we all made a group, seeing as we all arrived at around the same time, and didn't know anybody. Plus St Jerome's was really cliquey back then. But I doubt if we'll stay in touch after school, to be totally honest. Kitty's different obv. She's a keeper. And us maybe."

"Me? You and me?"

"Who knows, eh?"

The woods were cool and pleasant to walk in. Presently they crossed an ivy-covered bridge high over a brook. They walked single file up along a sandy, stony path, the green gorge dropping steeply to the right.

A crow flapped in the air below her.

Myfanwy found her gaze drifting along Tallulah's waist. She shook her head clear.

OMG, has Jasper flipped me the Male Gaze?

Or maybe not. Who knew? As soon as the path was wide enough Myfanwy skipped up beside her.

"It's weird Looly," she marvelled. "How you can get people so wrong. You see someone as this distant, intimidating, and like infinitely judgemental presence, but *actually* that person may be just as vulnerable and —"

"Och no, I mean *that's* all true," interrupted Tallulah quickly. "We're very shallow and beautiful, and quite rich and incredibly bitchy, and we can more or less control any aspect of school habitus we turn our attention to. Um, why do you think we called ourselves the Cool Kids?"

Myfanwy narrowed her eyes. "Hmmph."

"Obv, eh?"

Myfanwy listened to the rushing water. The cigarette butts mashed into the footpath made her feel strangely sick.

"Halfway to Veil," said Jasper. "Which like guns would you guys like?"

*

The van's doors were open. Darkness in there. Genevieve gone now. How long too late?

She dropped the bike on the grass and walked towards Mara.

Genevieve gone now. Silly word for it. Dead. Tall hills around. Dark like cement. Set inside statues. Bones in foundations. Forget it.

Mara bent in the car. She made all the light go out.

Genevieve. Will not call on phone. Will not walk into room. Bones in foundations. Darkness. Not alive.

She thought a strange thought. A confusion, really, not a thought. That since she and Genevieve had kissed each other with dead things, when Genevieve was alive, now that she was dead, if she took a handful of grass . . .

No remedy. Gen had screamed. She had slept. No atonement. Hardly any shapes. Hardly any steps.

Small shapes came down the hill from Arthur's Seat, bringing a thin shaking beam and loud voices.

"Your email made no sense," the nan was scolding the girl who ran away from home. "You huv tae use them crutches whether you're hame or no."

"Ah ken," said a little girl's voice. "'Sno whit Ah meant."

Shapes arose from the building site with a rolled carpet across their shoulders.

The murderers had dumped their body. The girl and her nan were witnesses. They were in danger now.

Mara revved the engine. Now she was sightless in the brightness. As if a white sail unfurled.

The car approached her. She went away from its light. Turned her head. As if a black sail unfurled. Something at her foot. In the dark she lifted her wet bike from the grass.

No stars out. Genevieve in setting cement. No atonement. Only sacrifice. No, only revenge. No, only nameless.

The girl and her nan came close. Undine escorted them. She was very curious for their safety.

"Did you call them?" she asked the nan.

"Do we know you?" said the nan, squinting. "Did you meet this boy?" she demanded of her granddaughter.

"Nuh."

Undine waved.

The front corner of the carpet slipped and unrolled, hanging to Tar's hip. Enough to see the stain interrupt the arabesque pattern.

Tar and Meletē put the carpet in the van.

"These are all my friends," Undine said grandly. "We all ride around in our pink van."

She mounted the bike. She looked at Undine, the nan, the girl. "Did you call them?" she said. "The police?" She heard soft footsteps behind.

"Ah telt them Rachel's been found," said the nan.

"Except him," said Undine. "He prefers to cycle. I'll leave you now."

"Thanks ever so much, for taking the trouble," the nan said to him.

"Oh, forget it," said Undine.

She rode slowly, windingly by them.

"She should get a fat ear," said the nan. "She wilnae though. I can guarantee it." The nan was peering towards the van as she pedalled past them. "Busy the night, is it no?" she heard her say.

She could see no one now. "Goodnight, everyone," she called. "That man who took you back to your nan? And his friends in the pink van? One day, I'm going to kill them."

She rode away in the dark.

*

They refused Jasper's guns. When they rose from the gorge they saw a thin ribbon of sea.

The rough path they followed would flow gently uphill through fields, eventually pass some cottages, then turn along the cliff tops. They were perhaps a mile from the farm houses now.

"It might be wise to leave lanes and paths soon," said Myfanwy.

"This is already a roundabout approach," Jasper pointed out.

"Even so."

The strata of the landscape, layered by wannabe horizons, gradually shifted with the rising ground. The sea soon vanished from view and for ages would not return. There were freshly tilled fields either side of them, the broken earth dark as night, and beyond them more distant fields, some freshly broken, others of rape, sunflowers and wheat, and dimmer villages, hills and trees. Within each progressively more distant band of undulating landscape, the cloudiness of objects increased.

The final band blurred up into the encompassing firmament itself. Fluff mottled the soft mid-afternoon sky. The moon was also out, large and sickled, a Forrest Gump feather gummed to the skin of a bright lamp.

The static of power lines rustled overhead again. The neighbouring fields once more were full of rape. Bee spied slate rooves, covered with birds — black crows and white and grey gulls — poking over the next crest, and there they stopped.

"What next?" said Myfanwy and Jasper at once, and laughed.

At the side of the path where they had paused lay a small wood. Feeling exposed, they decided to enter it and recollect themselves. It was mostly of tall pines, mixed with a few small deciduous trees.

Myfanwy was glad to gather her composure and go on maps on her phone. She sat on a felled trunk, smooth and green. She counted the nests proffered by one of the middling-sized trees living under the high-crowned pines. Nineteen. She counted again. A different number.

Myfanwy started to remove her shoes. The blood of her skinned knee beaded through her dressing and black tights. She tipped so much sand from her first shoe, she wondered how any foot could have fit in there too.

A system of warrens, perhaps?

A wind whipped through the spinny. A dead leaf, which was transparent and brown, separated from the stem where it must have clung all winter in the pines' shelter, brushed against Myfanwy's arm, and turned crumbling through a rift in the pines, out onto the rough uphill path which carried on past the cottages and along the cliffs.

She heard a tractor's engine.

The path surely would be watched.

Myfanwy removed her second shoe — generating a second gleeful sand jin — put her shoes on top of the felled trunk, and barefoot wandered the spinny a little.

A little brook meandered through it.

She hopped across it. She was vaguely aware of the presence of the others. Not everyone was watching everyone every moment. A trust seemed to have sprung up among them.

Bare earth was irrigated by strong roots. She pressed them to the wells of her feet. Dry, straw-filled dung spread out here and there. The cigarette butts were all faded and flat. Pale grass blossomed in tufts.

She walked to the side furthest from the path. Beyond the spinny, over a drystone wall, there was a very dark squiggly tree on a distant golden hill face. She focused on the tree's twistings, pretending they were inverted, a set of cracks into the earth. For a moment she fooled herself — thought she had mistaken some cracks for a tree.

She turned back, and found the pipe whereout the brook spilt.

As she sat astraddle it, Tallulah came over.

"Aloha, Tallulah."

"Rofl," said Tallulah quietly. "So they're talking about doing two reccies of the farm houses. Me and Bee on the shore. You and Jasper avoid the cottages and come up parallel with the path. Regroup at the car. Depends obv what we find, but possibly we take doors just before dawn."

Myfanwy shrugged.

"Upsides?" said Tallulah.

"No," said Myfanwy. "Not keen. For instance. Sleeping arrangements."

"Seats fold down. Plus apparently the nebulous stuff includes a bivvy bag which *might* be big enough for two."

Myfanwy raised her eyes. Not far off, Jasper was pacing slowly along another fallen green tree trunk. It lay athwart a wider course of the brook. He was shoeless too.

Bee was nowhere to be seen.

"I don't trust him, Tallulah," she murmured.

"Don't mind sharing with you," said Tallulah. "I mean, I may just stay up."

"And I can't wait any longer," Myfanwy decided. "They could move Kitty any moment. I'm sneaking into the farm houses as soon as I can. I know just how to do it. I can walk along the beaches and climb up the cliff face. He's right that the path is likely to be watched."

"Geeze, Myfanwy," said Tallulah calmly. "I can't let you go by yourself."

"We'll go together. I'll tell those two I need a walk by myself. Clear my head. Then in like twenty minutes, say you're going to find me. Like —"

"Girl talk?"

"Hmm. Maybe —"

"As marketing," Tallulah added quickly. "We wouldn't *really* know how to do girl talk. And your head is already *exceptionally* clear."

"No — say we'll do the shore reccy. That will buy us more time. Then meet me where the rocks form an archway, about half a mile —"

"God, I'm so bored. Just create a Facebook event for it," Tallulah suggested.

"Safe. Remember birds and animals may be watching us."

"Geeze-o. What do we do, shoot everything that moves?"

"No. Just try to act natural to a squirrel, or a crab, as the case may be."

Tallulah spoke even more softly. "Should we try to get the guns anyway?"

Myfanwy shook her head. "Not for me. I worry when we finally find Kitty, I might put a bullet in her brain."

"You fit?"

"Fit?" said Myfanwy, bewildered. "Yes I am!"

"Sorry. Just what mum used to say. Proper Scottish I guess. You ready now?"

"Aye," said Myfanwy.

*

Myfanwy stood at the appointed place. There were no wee crabs nearby, and she felt unwilling to stray from her rock. Without even wee crabs to observe, how could she ever progress to the study of opossum shrimps? To the repatriation of Kitnapped BFFs?

Myfanwy was fed up seeking anything. She sought the moon.

There it was, counterfeiting a cloud.

The air was cool, but the beach was still quite crowded. Between her and the spot where she thought to scale the cliff there were, strangely tranquil and expectant, a line of surfers in wetsuits, strung across the sand between the black volcanic cliff face and the edge of the sea. Nearby, a yellow JCB digger was gouging another clawful of sand. The atmosphere was indefinably pregnant.

No one surfed, or really stirred much. A few of them picked slowly around the rocks of the rock pools, carrying their boards, as the surging breakers gradually narrowed the shore. It was good to have some innocent company, anyway. She hoped they would stay.

Atop the distant sea cliff, she thought she'd spotted the first grey corrugated steel roof. But she wasn't sure. Was Kitty still in there? What were they doing to her?

"Enemy compounds are pointless," Tallulah had commented.

Myfanwy checked her phone. It perturbed her a little that Tallulah, the only other person invited to her private event, had only checked "May Be Attending."

Myfanwy still found Tallulah's sense of humour a little mysterious. She wondered what Jasper thought about her. Then she wondered if him and Bee could be an item, or maybe already were, or had been. She'd be fine with it if they were, obviously. She wondered if Bee liked him, or if he liked Bee.

The JCB digger kept digging into the cliff. The surfers kept waiting for whatever they were waiting for. Her thoughts kept changing into confused ideas of Jasper, and then of Gen, and she felt her chest tighten, and tried to repress stupid stuff that rose up. It wanted someone to feel it. It had no right to choose her.

A huge arched kite held the sky.

Myfanwy sighed. She struggled to think only practical things, to feel only trivial things. If she got an A in German the following week, and an A in Art, maybe she could still get her second choice uni. Those waves didn't look nearly tall enough to surf on. Maybe that's why the surfers seemed so calm and enlightened.

A in Art. Unlikely.

Fidgeting, she updated her status,

FFS

and was about to delete it again when a girl from junior school she barely knew swooped in,

U ok hun??drinks soon, it's been sooo long..lets actually do it tho yehxx

Myfanwy blinked and put,

You! XOX

The backdrop cresting her phone screen grew flurried. She shifted focus to watch a crow flop off the sand as a wave hissed across, and come down again in foam.

Come *on*, Looly!

When Myfanwy next looked down the beach, Jasper was walking alone towards her. She knew perfectly well it was him, though he was little more than a dot.

Myfanwy lightly dismounted her rock and went along the beach away from Jasper, towards the surfers. Did she feel Zen like those surfers, or crackling with passion, like that dot? Myfanwy wasn't at all sure. Her chest felt very tight and small now. Like she could ball it up and pop it in her pocket.

Trains of dazzle gathered in the ribbed sea sand. She followed swathes of shattered shells. When Myfanwy glanced back over her shoulder, Jasper's dot had . . . dwindled?

He must have *stopped* walking as soon as she'd *started* walking. Hmm. Argh.

She turned and walked closer and he walked a little closer. She stopped and he stopped. She didn't have time for this. He took a few more steps then stopped.

I don't want to go out with a dot, she thought sensibly. She went him and he came to her, faster and faster. They'd wasted so much time. Foam flowed inland.

She met Jasper just as the foam touched their feet. "How did you find me?" she demanded, trying not to smile. "Did Tallulah tell you?"

"She just thought we needed alone time." He leaned down and kissed her shyly.

"She was *wrong*," she said. She kissed him back crossly. "I'm rescuing Kitty by myself. I don't need you."

"Really?" He stroked her hair and kissed her again. It was a timid, polite little kiss.

"Not for rescuing, anyway. Oh Tallulah, why have you sent me this boy? You must be Veil. Now I have to . . ."

She moved onto her toes and tipped her face up. His lips weren't like Paddy's.

He didn't kiss at all like she expected. He kissed softly and shyly. It was nothing like the time in the rain, when neither of them had really wanted to do it. And it was nothing like when they would kiss Genevieve together. It was just their own.

At first only their lips kissed, brushing to and fro. Then, as both their faces leant and drifted, their mouths opened, and his arms were around her. The tip of his tongue finally touched against hers for a moment, and as his lower lip lingered perfectly against her upper, a violent thrill ran through her body.

"Looly's not Veil," he murmured. "She's just a cool kid."

"*Shooosh*." She led him away from the water, to where the sand and grass rose to merge with volcanic cliff rock. She kissed him more, for much longer, and forgot what that sound was. *Mm.*

Oh yes. The sea.

I love you, she thought. *That's not true,* she thought. *I want you. I miss you. Thank you. Come here. Oh. I love you. I like you. Mm. Is it really you? We don't have time for this.*

She took hold of his jacket and pushed him against the steep sand bank. They kissed again and he put his hands in her hair. The ache tickled up inside her. Everything was okay.

"*Bist du's*?" she murmured.

"*Bisous*," he murmured.

"What?"

He drew back. "We're kissing," he said.

"No we're not," she said. She pushed up against him. He wrapped his arms around her.

Come here. Oh. You kiss like I do.

"Like what?"

Oh!

She must have murmured that one half-aloud. "You kiss like me," she clarified crossly. "Come *herer*," she murmured vaguely. "*Morer* here!"

She didn't have time for what she craved. They had wasted so much time already.

She opened her eyes. His were already wide.

"Christ," he murmured. She was wobbling in the air, no arms around her. The strength that had been all around her had vanished. Her shoulders hit the sandbank. Jasper was sprinting away across the sand towards the digger.

*

"Myfanwy," he yelled. "Come on!"

Another scoop of sand was lifted, and muddy water surged through a cutting in the cliffs, pouring from whatever unseen lagoon wherein it had till recently been locked, and surging incensed towards the sea. The surfers cheered and whooped appreciatively.

A river, Myfanwy realised, was swiftly forming across their path. She could be cut off from Veil, cut off from Kitty. Shame burned her cheeks and she ran.

One of the surfers, overly optimistic, already bellyflopped onto his board, lay wiggling in his pink and white wetsuit in a stormy puddle.

Now Jasper had reached the edge of the rising river. Muddy water foamed round his ankles. It grew deeper by the second. Someone was wobbling upright on her surfboard now. The surfer wasn't moving with the forming river, just hovering in one place, like some strange fish of prey.

Myfanwy waded in. A surge hit her hard, smacked her off balance. She steadied her footing. It felt not just fast but *accelerating*. It was more like cold, fast mud than water.

Myfanwy floundered. Was this river coming in on a permo or what? Should she go back and wait? What if it lasted for days?

She knew there were elated figures around her, but she couldn't focus on them. The current was getting stronger, the mud slid away under her shoes.

Now she was chest-deep in the surging water. Too late to go back.

The water sucked her under.

For a horrible moment she couldn't tell which way was up. In panic, surrounded by hushed, dim, rushing heaviness, she found her feet. The river was too heavy and she couldn't stand up. Then abruptly her head was in air, and she was gasping, wiping mud from her eyes, as freshwater draining from sinuses. The river rushed around her neck, and Jasper's splayed hand hovered inches from her face.

"Myfanwy!"

He was leaning, holding his hand out over the waves, his fingers striving. She was battling forward, spluttering.

"Take my hand, Myfanwy!"

She fucking *bit* it.

Boom!

Then she was struggling up out of the torrent, and Jasper's howls filled her ears, then he was grabbing her from behind, laughing. Maybe he forced her to the ground, or maybe she sort of collapsed and pulled him on top of her. Their arms and legs were tangling, rolling and wrestling, soaking in the sand. Of course, what with all the good-natured rough-and-tumble, he couldn't tell she was sobbing.

"I miss her," she gulped, grabbing his preposterous endless leg. "I miss her *so much.*" She twisted and he howled. "You don't care, Jasper. You never loved her. You come here and — and, you think you can *kiss* me — and you've just *forgotten* her! I want you, and I want you, and I still *love her so much*, Jasper."

Now she had him pinned down on the sand.

"Ha! I *love* her!"

His chest rose and fell. She dripped onto it. He was tense, but he wasn't struggling now. His expression mingled excitement, anger and something else. She felt if she so much as moved a muscle, she'd lose leverage and he'd spring out from under her.

She moaned and let her lips drop to his. Jasper's moved a little, but it wasn't a proper kiss, and she broke away.

"I don't know," she wailed. "I don't know how to *be!*"

Why couldn't it be like it was across the river? Something had changed. It was all spoiled now, all broken. Myfanwy bit her lips and stared emptily down at him. She couldn't tell what shook her — fear, passion, rage, grief.

"It's time," he said quietly. His chest rose and fell. "This is when you give her back to me."

"As if."

"Do it. Flip me everything I've ever flipped you. Everything that's — *mine*," he gasped. "Give me back my Genevieve."

"Your Genevieve? You never loved her like I do, Jasper. *Never.*"

She gave his shoulders a last shove and rolled off him.

She sat sullenly with her hands dangling on her knees.

Jasper sat up. He stared past her and she followed his gaze.

The beach river was in full flow. The surfers bowed to and fro on its contours. Some mysterious principle of fluid dynamics meant the swells never broke. Instead the waterscape stood steady between the rift and the surging sea line.

Or perhaps the waves moved very slowly, like sand dunes.

When she turned back Jasper was watching her. He wore a wan, dreamy look. "You see," he said. "I can't fight without my pain."

"Jasper," Myfanwy whispered. "I can't lose her again. It would destroy me."

"I'm not brave enough. I'm not hard enough. You've carried that pain for me. But it's never belonged to you."

"Then don't fight," she begged him softly. "Don't hurt anyone. Don't be someone who can. Climb those cliffs with me. Let's take Kitty home."

"You don't understand. It's not just about Kitty."

"Genevieve is dead. I'm the one who must live with that. I'm the one who let her down. You're not here because of her." She shut her eyes and felt two hot tears flow. "You're here because of me."

"You have to trust me," said Jasper's voice. "When this is all over, we'll make a spellsong. We'll change everything back."

Feeling him move she opened her eyes.

He knelt over her now, his lips parted, his eyes shining. "Every last scrap I ever begged," he said. "Now I need pain, I need hate, I need anger. I need Genevieve. I can't hate without her. I can't."

"This will never be 'all over.' This thing inside me — *I* will never, ever forget. Even when everything is repaid, I can *never forget.*"

She rose slowly to her feet.

He stayed kneeling. "Please," he said again simply.

Myfanwy's gut wrenched. Her lips formed the word, but her breath barely made any noise. "No."

The digger was leaving the scene. The surfers rode the unwavering waves. Across the beach river, Myfanwy saw Bee and Tallulah slowly drawing nearer.

Jasper thought it was all pain, hate, anger. He had no idea of what was inside Myfanwy. It was broken and it was ferocious but it was love. It was nothing but love.

"Then I will not help you," said Jasper.

"I don't want your help," she told him. "It's true, I never want to forget Genevieve. But that isn't the real reason, Jasper. Not really."

Jasper gazed up at her. He brushed back a lock of wet hair. "Then why?"

No, he had no idea.

"Here's the thing Jasper. I think maybe I love you. I know I want you. But I'm afraid. It is so hard to want anything, now that Genevieve gone. And I'm afraid —"

"You're afraid I won't want you. When you give me my memories, you think I'll forget about you."

For one moment Myfanwy stared, utterly frozen.

Then, mutely, she nodded.

"I promise you," Jasper said quietly, smiling just a little now. "It's *you*. It's you, Myfanwy. You must trust me. Because I can promise you that."

She turned and fled.

*

Myfanwy essayed a route up the sheer uninviting volcanic rock.

Slowly she worked herself aloft.

Damp petals and pieces of grass were pasted to her arms. They must have been in the beach river.

Her hands, creeping into cubby holes in the cliff face, disturbed wrack tucked there by former storms at sea. Her fingertips troubled faded picnic litter, estranged by long voyages, mingled and composited by the currents. A dry cigar shell. One of those flat, cloven sticks that fish and chips come with, with a crack in it. Ribbons of grocery bags — Sainsbury's, Tesco, basic corner shop blue — tangled with strings of pearls of parched bladderwrack seaweed. A swatch of fabric matching one she once had lost.

I'faith, now I might be mended, and attend the ball after all!

Newspaper with nothing printed on it at all. One of those transparent tubes that cigarette filters come in, crumpled in half, and filled with brown water.

A cool bead of sweat ran down the right side of Myfanwy's neck. Her arabesque ascent was drawing her inexorably nearer the roosting place of a monstrous gull. Those things were so *huge*, up close.

And she was getting closer.

She knew the gull would gouge out her eye on its huge, scimitar beak. Or tip her off the cliff face with slamming weighty wings.

Myfanwy didn't slow one bit, moving up steadily, listening to her own soft gasping breath muffled together with the surf.

The gull crooked a wing in vague threat.

Are you cooking up children under your chest? Roost assured. I shan't harm a hairline crack on their heads.

He settled back woozily. Myfanwy began to believe the skanky feathered wyrm would tolerate her passage.

Finally attaining the crest, Myfanwy found a diamond-mesh fence, not much taller than she was. Scribbles of barbed wire were snarled into it, in coiling spirals and twisting heart shapes, but she still shimmied up a post easily and without adding any new scratches. The fence rustled tinnily as she hopped down the other side.

She crouched breathlessly, well hidden by tall stacks of wooden pallets. They were half-rotted and swished with ancient indecipherable spraypaint. The ground by her knees was straggly pale green grass with lots of sand in it.

Yes, she would get revenge on Jasper one day, she decided lightly. She would break his heart right in half. Why? Revenge! There was a kind of distance to this thought. As when, on the edge of sleep, a part of you buds off and turns to face you with the pomposity and inscrutability of a fictional character and says, "The honour of the Womyn's Castle is still at stake."

Oh, she hadn't forgotten. She might have flipped Tallulah the deets of Jasper's impertinence, but the *sting* remained. What was it exactly he'd said? Something chivalric, she bet. *I want to protect you,* or whatever. *I can't be near you. It's too dangerous.*

And meanwhile, Jasper had taught her everything he knew about the value of vengeance.

When after some moments no security came, not even another seagull, Myfanwy got to her feet and slipped over to a second stack of pallets, a few paces farther from the cliff edge.

Before vengeance, Myfanwy decided, they would have to fall properly in love.

Peering round the stack, she saw a kind of agribusiness pagoda or band-stand straight ahead. There were obscure agricultural or construction vehicles beyond that, and further off, large warehouses with corrugated steel rooves.

She watched for ten seconds then walked briskly out. In the band-stand stood a rusted roller-topped conveyor table and a stack of empty perforated plastic trays.

She passed some tractors, parked at angles. One was burnt-out, gutted for its inner ash.

On the narrow wall of one of the larger warehouses was a low door. There was a hoop and a hasp for a padlock, but no padlock.

*

A system of vast crosses of soft, moted twilight filled the interior air. The warehouse — or old milking parlour, as Myfanwy now recognised it — was rooved with corrugated steel, regularly interspersed with windows.

Myfanwy shut the door and moved calmly down the length of the shed.

The floor was cement. There was no animal smell, no curds nor sourness, only a faint fragrance of citronella, mingled with pollen. Some paraphernalia Myfanwy would associate with a well-organised squat was gathered against the wall where she'd come in. There were whiteboards and chalkboards, portraying a rota and announcements, many tins of tomatoes, some cardboard boxes of beans, cabbages, cauliflowers and chard.

A low moan sounded. It sounded like an animal. She was pretty sure it was Kitty though.

She walked deeper into the milking parlour. The machinery looked like it hadn't been used in a long time. Milking bails, shaped like enormous wardrobe hangers, divided most of the space into many hundreds of pens.

At present just one pen was in use.

From the pipework of milking bails, a pair of manacles depended. Kitty's body lay in light shadow, her face in darkness. A metal bucket and a folded blanket sat nearby.

To Myfanwy's eye, the way in which Kitty's arms were lifted up into these manacles, and the way her body bent about on the white concrete below them, did not immediately suggest that Kitty was minimising the discomfort she felt in her constraints — rather, the angles gathered in those metal loops signalled a delicately achieved compromise, between comfort on the one hand, and on the other, the attitude in which a captive and histrionic damsel, one of historic courage and beauty, might long-sufferingly drape herself.

Looking anything less than fully the part, just to chafe her skin the less, would have chafed Kitty's soul the more. Even all alone in the milking parlour. Detainee snobbery — v. Kitty.

But then *again*, Myfanwy thought, as she drew swiftly and wordlessly closer, perhaps *any* pose would start to ache after a minute, or after ten hours? — and perhaps any prisoner might start to cycle among all possible poses, including the picturesque ones? The neck of any damsel, after all, to truly be made like a swan's, would have to be broken in *thousands* of places. So it might just be a coincidence, that she'd come upon Kitty looking so rescue-able.

Those were such slender things about her wrists. More like jewellery. Yet ringing blows to bust them apart would summon Veil from everywhere. Myfanwy could no more rescue Kitty from them than she could free her image from a photograph.

Or, Myfanwy's conjectures continued, what *might* turn Kitty's pose just so were *cigarette burns* — horrible agonising injuries, which even if left to heal properly, would heal only to fall apart again, flesh collapsing like the swamps of tallow around stuttering wicks, over and over for many weeks — fresh burns such as these, hundreds of them, perhaps, upon every side of Kitty's legs. Those burns, atop livid bruises, soaking her insides, and filthy slashes, filled with grains of the glass which had cut them, and more, worse burns, where scalding cherries were smothered in already open skin, drilling deep into her limbs to douse them in blood and pus and raw muscle — injuries Myfanwy had not yet seen, but felt, with swelling sickness and love and fear, that she would soon see — horrible injuries such as these might bump Kitty's silhouette into some seemingly simulated pose, perhaps this one, coincidentally suggestive, though not markedly so, of sighs and the wimple.

"Darling," said Myfanwy. "I love you. Was it Paddy? Did he know they'd do this? What have they done?"

Kitty's face tilted only slightly. Still it lay in shadow. When she spoke her voice was thick and indistinct. There was a fear in it which Myfanwy somehow sensed was brand new. "God, my love. You said that last night. How much have you forgotten?"

Tallulah?

"How long since I was here?" said Myfanwy dreamily.

Jasper? Who —

Doors were opening and shutting in many corners of the milking parlour, the softest catastrophes, influencing the light and atmosphere not one bit.

"You came around three or four, I think. No, I don't think Paddy knew they'd do it. They're all in on it, Myffy. But not him, not really." Kitty lifted her two black eyes and bloody lips into the light. "Oh, Myfanwy. It's good to see you again, but I hope you know what you're doing this time."

"No," said Myfanwy quietly. She bent to kiss Kitty's wrist where one thin band of skin, perhaps protected by the manacle, wore no burns at all. "No idea."

*

There were perhaps four Veil agents stalking about her in the darkness and shadows and twilight shafts. She moved rapidly along the pens without much hope. She felt she would have no more say in what would happen now than milk.

They drew in with the inexorability of murderers who also happened to be very clear on where exits lay.

Mara Drago-Ferrante held her handgun in one hand, her arm fully extended. The angle of her approach was such that her face toggled to and fro rhythmically from light to shade. In the light, she used one of the smiles the Asians used. Angelic composure. Then masked with shadow.

Myfanwy crossed a row of milking bails. Another figure she recognised as Germ. Germ once had floated down a zip-wire and engaged Kitty's intelligence with a Go-Ball, or glo stick wand, or whatever it was. Germ now held her handgun close, in both hands, the silencer tucked on her shoulder where a baby's head might be.

"No, Myfanwy," came Kitty's voice, ghostly and soft, from where she had left her manacled to the bails. "Don't, hon. Germ shot at you last night. You were nearly killed."

After the pier. Option E. Come immediately. Come alone. That's what I must have done. In dad's car? Why have I forgotten?

Two more gunsels crept in at angles Myfanwy did not see at all well. They were tall men with beards.

"That was when it was just her," called Kitty. "There's no way out, this time."

Perhaps she could duck under the machinery. What if it was a dead end?

"Hello, Myfanwy Morris," said Germ. "Remember us?"

Myfanwy took two more steps and faltered.

Germ's face was always in shadow as she drew in, yet Myfanwy's eyes registered its gradually growing detail. Mid-forties, sun-bronzed, with the collected air of a morning telly presenter. She wore her red hair in a scruffy eyrie.

This was it.

Myfanwy raised her hands to shoulder height, and walked slowly back to Kitty. She stopped right beside her, her left wrist level with Kitty's right. Kitty's fingers curlingly fidgeted in the air.

Myfanwy stayed very still as the four Veil agents gathered round.

This isn't the worst it has ever been, she thought. *This isn't the most frightened.*

As three of them, relaxing, holstered their handguns inside their jackets, Germ lifted hers from her shoulder and trained it meticulously between Myfanwy's eyes.

*

Germ spoke first, her tone mild. "Sounds like I may have to introduce myself *ah*-gen! I'm *Germ.*" She wore navy jeans, a diamond stud in her upper lip, and a plastic red poppy pinned to a slate grey tank top. Her bronzed, catlike face creased with deep lines when she smiled — as now she smiled — and her size 90 Garamond dimples curved from the corners of her nose to the corners of her mouth. "Do you remember Oni?"

The guy from the playground. "Hello, Germ. Hello, Oni," said Myfanwy. "Nice to see you again."

So. No summary execution. Always a start. Oni's eyes were very bloodshot. Like a fiend's eyes, really.

And maybe, just maybe, Tallulah and Jasper and Bee would come busting through those four doors at any moment.

"And Gaga, of course," said Germ.

Myfanwy mentally projected where she would step, what parts of the gun she would try to grab.

"Hello Mara," she said. "Polyhymnia was nicer."

"Wotcha," growled Mara/Gaga/Polyhymnia. "That callsong has bad memories, girlfriend." She glanced at Germ and gave a kind of Cool Kids leer. "Got some leverage *now*, Germ?"

"And *this* is Undine," Germ said, ignoring her.

Myfanwy had never met this person, but she remembered him. Umberto Souphanouvong, AKA Urania, AKA Undine.

He placed a hand on each police officer's back. "Veitch is easy. This one's a mess. I can't tell what's what. Drat. I think she has —"

He had scarring around the eyes she hadn't noticed before — or else it was newish. He wore a little beard now too.

"Of course you met last night," Germ continued. "Only I'm not sure you remember. Undine, *you* remember Mnemosyne — colleague of our other guest?"

Undine nodded sadly.

"Of course I remember meeting Undies," Myfanwy fibbed. "What *is* it with all you guys and beards? Which reminds me, how's Vertical? Are we not honoured by his presence tonight? How's his arm? I mean, other than badly wounded?"

This probably wasn't the way to play it *at all.* If she lived, she'd probably be really bad at job interviews one day.

"Well," Germ laughed. "It was Vert spotted you scaling his cliff again."

"Strange you came in just the same way," said Undine. "After running off so sharpish last night. A double bluff?"

Undine trailed with him an aura of sullen frailty when he stood in his idle loop. The aura was dispelled when he spoke, by a smile which seemed to play behind the surface of every syllable. Myfanwy guessed that the smile was a habit of his lips and not of his heart.

"To be fair," clucked Germ, "I see her point. Nessus hasn't thought much of our hospitality, have you mate?"

Kitty smiled. "One star!"

"You're welcome to leave."

Mara snarled softly. "Soon as I have —"

"Yep, yep," said Germ, sounding rather irritated. "I think she *knows* by now, Gaga, mate."

"Your talent!" Myfanwy guessed. "That's what you want, right? Guys, listen to me. This is important. Kitty doesn't even want to *be* a muse anymore. She told me just the other day."

"And I told them," Kitty murmured. "A million times."

"She never *was* a damn muse," said Mara.

"No," said Myfanwy, pensively. "I think I see. Merlin wasn't sure about Kitty's talent, was he? Mara — um, Gaga — you were out to recruit *me*, right? Kitty had nothing to do with it, at first. Yet by the time we met Seuss at Chancelhouse, both our talents were strong."

Mara's eyes flicked to Germ. The villainous carrottop now wore a look of detached tolerance.

"Yeah," Mara nodded. "Because she pinched my talent."

"Because you *gave* it to her," corrected Myfanwy. "You touched her on the bridge, didn't you? When Jasper grabbed you, you stashed your talent in Kitty. Why did you do that?"

"None of your bloody business," said Mara. "She needs to return it, is all!"

"It's just instinct," muttered Kitty. "Stashing ish like that. The number of perfectly good little coke foldies I've wasted on fire engines driving by. Honestly, they're like nature's feds! They *get inside your head!*"

Germ laughed pleasantly. "More to the point, Gaga was afraid, weren't you mate?"

"Not exactly," said Mara. "Though I should have been."

"Mara thought it was a kidnap, not a hit. Thought Terpsichore might torture her. Dig out her muse talent. Put it up on Gumtree or something."

Try not to bring up torture as a topic, thought Myfanwy. *It's the sort of thing that could really break up the band.*

"What? *Sell* it? Why?" Myfanwy said. "Why would Jasper do that?"

"Sort of thing Gaga does," Kitty said.

"Shut it," said Mara, briefly flashing that Cool Kids smile.

"I think that's fair," Undine sniffed. "Though maybe more Craig's List, or various Chinese sovereign agencies."

Mara looked stoically on.

"To be fair to old Gaga," Germ added mildly, "we didn't really know what Terpsichore was about at that stage. There were indications he wasn't going for kills. Not clean front-loaded kills anyway."

"On at least one prior," Mara said, "Terpsichore had a target in his sights who managed to slip away."

"Kitty hardly cares for the talent," said Myfanwy. "Like I say. So I think she must have a different reason for not returning it. Like maybe she's not sure how she'll get treated, once you've got what you want."

Undine frowned. "Can her treatment get any worse?"

"Slightly," Kitty pointed out.

"*Listen*," said Myfanwy passionately. "I think things have changed, now that I'm here. And I think . . . if you just *listen* to me for a little while, you won't want to scare us and hurt us anymore! I know we've all done wrong. And I don't know if we'll ever be able to forgive each other. But if anyone can do it, *we* can! We are masters of our past! I understand a lot of things now. I understand about Blake and Chancelhouse, and why you war with them. It's not rivalry, it's not vengeance. It's atonement, isn't it? It's . . . accountability. Germ, Undine . . . Gaga . . . I was there among you that night, six years ago in the west houses. As Jasper, I was there. I know you probably could have stopped Blake, but you stood by. I watched you help to hide the body, in the foundations of the expanding SPL building by Holyrood Parliament. Jasper doesn't remember loving her. *I* do. Jasper doesn't remember the screams. *I* do. It was me now, who saw you that night. It was me now, who believed no atonement could ever be possible. Who vowed something more, who vowed vengeance, who vowed to make you all pay. As far as you are concerned . . . *I* am the muse Jasper Robin! As Jasper, I vowed vengeance! And as Mnemosyne, I *know* I can forgive!"

*

"Yes," added Kitty, "as for me, I would as lief *die* on the morrow, as marry thee, Gaga!"

"I wish you wouldn't always joke," murmured Myfanwy. "It can be really undermining."

"'As Mnemosyne'?" said Germ incredulously. "Who gave you the right to speak for Syn? You're very full of yourself."

If only.

"Sorry hon," Kitty said wearily. "I assumed you were joking. I mean, 'I am the muse Jasper Robin!'?"

"The Chancel war has become more *best practice*," Undine commented dryly, "than *atonement*. Our sovereign sponsors like to see we keep busy."

Undine's earpiece came to life. He took a few steps and leant on a milking bail.

Well stirring oratory didn't work, thought Myfanwy. *Now what? What's good hostage practice? Make myself into a Person. Not a Disposable Asset.*

If only I wasn't so annoying!

She waggled her head at the blurry poppy behind Germ's silencer. "When I went past the burnt-down playground, I *saw* a poppy."

"Oh yeah," said Germ. With her free hand she fidgeted with it. She had sparkly green fingernails and flowers and dots tattooed on her hands. "I did lose one that night. Some punch-up, eh?"

"Sure was!" said Myfanwy. "Pretty even Stevens!"

Form a bond, she thought. *Even a band!*

"Do you like *always* wear a poppy?" asked Kitty scathingly. "Is that like your Thing?"

"Not just mine," Germ added tightly. "I wear it to honour the sacrifice. To remind us that you can't put a monetary value on everything."

"Safe!" said Myfanwy. "How true that is! Do you play any musical instruments, Germ?"

"In *April,* though?" said Kitty.

Undine drew close again, having a stressful conference call experience on his earpiece. "Something on the beach, Germ. Achelois investigating."

Germ looked at the girls. "Friends of yours?" she said softly. "Oni, Gaga. Go give Ache a hand."

Oni and Mara slipped out a side door.

*

"I'll go too," said Kitty brightly.

Voices rustled at Undine's ear. "Egg going too," he said. "Vert and Pest moving to perimeters." He paused. "Someone halfway up the cliffs too." Pause. "It's the muse Bee. Ache on her."

Myfanwy's throat closed up.

Come on, Bee.

"Egg on her," said Undine. "Back-up coming. Oni coming. Gaga coming. I can't —" Pause. "I don't know what's happening."

"Let's go," said Germ quietly. She produced some sort of ultra-convenient saffron yellow zipcuffs and a big bunch of keys. The key fob was a sort of cutesy leather dove thing you could get at a pop-up Christmas boutique.

"Two more on the beach," said Undine. "Egg has Bee. Ache was temporarily incapacitated. Ache's back in the field." Pause. "Shit! Two on the beach have side arms," he said rapidly. "Shots fired. Ache on them. Gaga on them. Oni on them. Returning fire. Back-up coming." Pause. "Correction, seems like only one armed. Handgun."

As Undine said "handgun" he casually produced a long handgun from a belt holster, as though pedagogically, and gestured to Myfanwy with it. Germ had been leafing through her keys. Now she undid Kitty's manacles, twisted her arms together behind her back, looped her wrists in the yellow zipcuffs and yanked on something.

There was a sound like the scales on ice skates ratcheting.

"Up," she said.

They were led out into the twilight.

"Second is Tallulah Gordon," said Undine. "Maybe unarmed. Vert and Pest coming. Ghoul coming. Fisher and Engrailed coming up from the cottages." Pause.

Myfanwy gasped as if winded. She hadn't been breathing properly.

"Gaga on them," said Undine. "Ache on them. Pest on them." Pause. "Pest hurt. Self-evacuated." Pause. "They're in the rocks. Lots of back-up coming. Session coming. Bigwig coming. Aoide coming."

Myfanwy hung her head.

They were led a way Myfanwy did not know, tending towards the sea. Undine's commentary was unceasing. "Cracks coming. Fisher and Engrailed coming. Session on them. Ache on them. Gaga on them. Egg coming bringing Bee." Pause. "Session hurt."

Of course. How had she missed it?

Simi.

"Christ," said Germ, quickening their pace.

"Gaga says she thinks she knows no ID but still no ID. Egg on them. Bigwig on them. Aoide on them. Gaga on them."

"What does that mean?" snapped Germ. "Knows no ID but still no ID?"

"Session self-evacuating." Pause. "Ache hurt. Gaga has Gordon." Pause. "No ID has surrendered!" Pause. "They've been searched and disarmed. Pest, Session and Achelois are getting medical on the beach. All lower leg small arms injuries."

Myfanwy exhaled.

"Bring them inside if they can be moved," said Germ. "Keep patrolling, tight perimeters."

Undine greatly elaborated these instructions through his earpiece. While Germ was preoccupied with overseeing him, Myfanwy was able to come close to Kitty and talk without risk of being overheard. "Moth lent Bee her havering," she said quietly. "She can paralyse them if she can touch them. Bee's been working for Jasper. I think they're with us."

"'Kay," said Kitty.

"So I guess the Veil mole was Simi. Didn't I tell you there was something wrong with the muses who stayed behind, when everyone went on Operation Terpsichore? There were doubts about their security. Bee and Moth . . . and Simi too!"

"A little worse than that," Kitty said. Her voice was completely flat. Myfanwy found it a little bit annoying, the way Kitty always found reserves of energy to be bright and comical in a group sitch, pretty much no matter what — but didn't make the effort when it was just the two of them.

What was it about the visage of a BFF's loving face that let Kitty just deflate? But she'd been through a lot, Myfanwy reminded herself. Still, she was sounding like Depression Kitty!

"Hon, I think you should just flip me last night," whispered Myfanwy. "I'll take it from here, okay?"

Kitty shook her head. "Need it. Using it. Making— Womyn's Castle."

Germ looked sharply towards them.

"So, Germ," Myfanwy blurted brightly. "I hear you can clone your mirror talent? That's amazing!"

Germ nodded warily. "The quality deteroriates though. And it sort of accumulates random noise."

Myfanwy nodded back, at a loss what to say next. She chirped, "How about a tour, Germ?"

Germ laughed. "We call it the Distillery. Why? No idea. That's practically the one thing it's never been. It was once farm houses. There was a dairy herd. Later it became a vegetable growing and packaging plant, and later part of it was used to warehouse whiskey barrels. It was derelict for the good bit of a decade though."

They moved along the chain link fence. The sea looked calm. The tide had narrowed the beach somewhat. No figures were visible.

"We've got about eighty acres," said Germ, "and we're gradually restoring it to working order, inasmuch as that's compatible with a low profile. We livery some horses, but we won't be letting any cottages. The neighbours think we're a hippie commune. I'm not sure what a hippie commune is. I thought I knew once. We're closer to farmers than hippies. Veil is, I mean. We're Britain's undervalued backbone. We're always busy, no time for hobbies or holidays, but we love our work. Some people think we have too much power, influencing governments, swaying multilateral international treatises, manipulating transnational actors. But mostly we're just trying to survive, assaulted from every corner. We are unsentimental. Ready to get our hands dirty. We won't prolong an animal's life past its usefulness. We're farmers. We do try and achieve consensus though."

"It's too late to stop me now," said Kitty. "I destroyed New York thirty five minutes ago!"

"What? I don't get you."

"You sounded 'gloaty,'" explained Myfanwy kindly.

"I was just giving you the run-down of the farm," huffed Germ. "*Fine* then."

"Love watch," said Kitty.

"Ten pounds from Argos," said Germ. "Online."

"You're joking."

“What it is,” said Germ, “is that you want something that’s going to get knocked around —”

“You are joking,” Kitty repeated.

“But at the same time you want something that’s ‘me’, do you know what I mean?”

“If I escape,” said Kitty firmly, “I’m going online.”

Germ laughed lightly. They came to a gate in the fence. Germ leafed through her keys. Myfanwy thought of locked-up tennis courts.

The cliff was not so sheer here. They took a rough path down onto the sand. Undine was still on the line, reporting curtly on their progress every now and then.

“Don’t you think Undine,” said Kitty merrily, “is just like one of those messengers you get in Sophocles and Aeschylus, where all the battle happens off-stage because the CGI is still basically limited to *dei ex machina*? ‘A messenger ran into the room! “There have been two *coups d’etat*! *Status quo* is restored! Carry on!”’”

“Enough,” said Germ. “Shut up. I don’t understand half of what you children say.”

In the distance, a few dots appeared, walking towards them. It looked like the two groups would meet by a small isolated set of rockpools.

“When you’re chatting someone on the phone and then you start chatting them in real life?” said Myfanwy. “I *hate* that.”

As they approached the figures, their captors were suitably distracted so that Myfanwy could draw up beside Kitty and whisper, “What did you mean, *worse* than that? Who else besides Simi?”

“I think ‘Ghoul’ is Triffo. ‘Egg’ is definitely Blake. And ‘Cracks,’” Kitty concluded quietly, “is Yuri.”

*

On the rock the five prisoners sat — Myfanwy, Kitty, Tallulah, Bee, Jasper, Myfanwy, and so on — back-to-back. Nine Veil muses — could you really still call them Veil? — ringed the cinquefoil captives round — Blake, Germ, Mara, Simi, Vertical, Oni, Triffid, Undine, Yuri, Blake, and so on.

Their captors stood all on different levels — some were on the sand, so from time to time sea water flowed over their feet, and seawrack climbed against their ankles, whereas others balanced up on the sharp barnacled rocks, spritzed by the wash. The tide crept relentlessly ashore, clearing off old curds of foam. Whitecaps kneaded among the gathered rocks, bearing forward, and partially withdrawing, bands of fine black grains.

Farther off, a pair of dark, skinny figures were picking their way along the beach, coming ever closer, feet sometimes splashing in the wavering edge of waves.

Their captors had noted the newcomers, and did not seem unduly perturbed.

Stars were out — a few. But now that dusk had well and truly fallen, the moon had given up the ghost.

Five prisoners, six guns at their heads.

Kitty broke the ice. "Daffoflid!" she cried, in one of her fakest *ever* voices. "You're *evil!*"

Triffid laughed. "I'll put it on my CV, Ness. Thanks."

"Can I go?" said Tallulah. "I'm not a muse. I don't even have a callsong. See? 'Tallulah.'"

"Tallulah isn't a callsong?" Mara said skeptically.

"Daffoflid," continued Kitty lightly. "Being evil does *not* affect your likeability either way, you know. You are not *less* unattractive. You are not *more* unattractive."

"Yeah," said Triffid. "Whereas you're all rocking that 'guns on my face' look?"

"Ooh," Kitty said, mildly impressed. "Bitchy."

Jasper apparently merited an extra captor. Fair enough, really. Yuri's silencer was firm against Jasper's forehead, and Blake was moving his restlessly in Jasper's hair, as if combing it.

Mara's silencer was leant lightly against Kitty's head, Simi's against Tallulah's, Undine's against Bee's — and Germ's horrid silencer, meltingly evading focus, still swam before Myfanwy's gaze.

"He's *the same* unattractive?" Tallulah enquired. "I find that hard to believe."

"Swearsies," said Kitty. "Simi, I'm surprised at you. I realise Blake has been banging on about bridges with Veil for *ages*. Bit of a stonking clue there."

"Yes, yes," Blake chuckled, "from espionage and sabotage, to cabotage and arbitrage, all in a few easy casts and conference calls! The third sector these days is all about clusters, so I'm told. Really, ladies, it was Mnemosyne's remark about five-a-side all-ball against Veil —"

"I draw the line," said Germ sharply.

"— that suddenly made me think, 'We're in a new era here! We're all in this together! So few muses could give a fig about what happened in deep history. Why not bring my Veil links back into the light a little?'"

"Don't look so *frightened*, my loves!" chuckled Simi.

"It's the guns," explained Tallulah.

"And Yuri's a troubled teenager," said Kitty. "Bless him. Bless him. But *you*, Simi?"

"When I come to Chancel," Yuri blurted nervously, without lifting his gaze, "I have brought to Blake my idea about cutter patterners. 'Please sir, I am humble shrouder. Please let us think Cubist thoughts, let us think Fauvist thoughts, let us understand concepts shaken gently inside an envelope. Let us have season of spellsongs, so we may think what does not arise from our circumstances, but directly from combinatorial possibilities of thought itself!' Blake becomes very impressed by my vision and ambition. 'I am impressed,' he says. 'Marinade you are like me,' he says. 'You can transcend personal network of relationships, and care in your heart for all human life, all human suffering, all human history. But hush. The time is not ripe,' he says. 'Too many Chancelhouse want to keep only nose clean. Too many think small. Too many imperative talents tied up in petty minds and petty alliances. But I have a contact elsewhere, young Marinade.' 'I am called Yuri now,' I say. 'Someone who thinks as we do, young Marinade. And me and this contact, we have an arrangement. And the time for bold visions will come soon enough.' And so Blake appointed me . . . his PA!"

"There, there," said Blake tenderly. "Let it all out, young Marinade."

"And soon I discover, this contact elsewhere, who thinks as we do, is the disgraced muse Germ, who co-founds Veil. This frightens me, but Blake consoles me. And moreover, Blake says to me, 'You are more than my PA now. You are someone I can really talk to. Someone I may share my troubles with.'"

"Maybe don't let it *all* out, Marinade," said Blake thoughtfully. "Not yet, at any rate."

"But *you*?" Kitty urged. "Simidelay Bullock, oh my days!"

Simi shook her head smilingly. "To be honest, my loves, this has all been news to me too! This lot all being bloody double agents! Blake only recently brought me up to speed. I couldn't stop laughing for days! I'm the lastest buy-in, my loves. So you see, there's even hope for you!"

Germ and Blake shared a skeptical glance. A breeze stirred up, and a wisp of foam that must have blown into Simi's corn rows now blew free.

Not far off the sand was coloured with peculiar patterns. Dark blood fallen in bespattered constellations and banded contours here and there was softly disarrayed into scatters and splays, where feet had scuffed up bloodsoaked grains and sods.

Something wasn't right.

A *lot* wasn't right.

But something in particular.

Something to do with Jasper and Bee.

Blurring breezes changed the bloody sand's shapes.

*

"Or big wipes?" suggested Triffid slash Ghoul. "Scrub 'em clean and set 'em loose?"

"Very costly, at this stage," Germ replied gravely.

"*I* haven't been running around with a secret second callsong," Simi rattled on, "like old Egg and Cracks here! I'm just plain old Aoide! Nobody told *me* I had to have a Veil one too! Still playing catch up — shall I get me one? What do you reckon, girls?"

"Oh, Aoide!" cried Kitty sweetly. "Let's see. How about DOA? Or AIDS?"

"So who *is* in charge?" said Myfanwy carefully, studying their expressions. "Blake or Germ?"

"We're partners, at present," said Blake. "Calliope and I —"

"Please don't call me that," said Germ mildly. "As per our original agreement of three years ago, Egg works for me. I'm his handler. But as for 'being in charge,' Veil doesn't have leaders, not the same way Chancel does."

Simi roared with laughter. "Germ, babes, never you mind! Chancel governance is a proper mess too! Chancellor, Executive Director, Praetor! Who's in charge? Who knows!"

"Me," said Blake mildly. "*De facto.* You know that, Aoide."

"Veil governance is *not* 'a proper mess,'" said Germ icily. "We do things differently. We try to achieve consensus."

Simi grinned. "Well babes," she babbled happily, "just wait till you bung us lot into the equation. We've got a consensus at Chancel too, and it goes like this. '*I'm* in charge here!' Blake believes he is, *I* believe I am, Meletē *knows* he is! Nessie, soon Meletē's going to need a Veil callsong too! What would you call him? Syphilis or something?"

"Not my Meletē!" cried Kitty. "Oh, you are *kidding!*"

"Oh *yeah*, babes!" Simi cackled. "Oh, we do laugh. We do laugh."

"What about you, sir?" Tallulah asked Undine. "You're regarded as an equal so long as you're looking slightly down and to the side, right?"

Undine heaved a sigh.

"I mean, Melee is sore at the moment," said Simi thoughtfully, "being the last to know what these bastards have been up to." She nodded at Blake. "All your mucking about with his alarums, eh? He does love secure compounds, our Meletē. It's sad really."

"And I," sighed Blake, "love the tinkling of tocsins! Why should anything be locked away? The tangling of fingers, and the trade in talents in the dead of night!"

"Not on the *same* night preferably," said Vertical.

"You'd disarm the alarm," guessed Myfanwy. "To let Vert in. Sometimes, when he was long gone, you'd set off the alarm yourself, so we all kept believing it was working."

"You've got it exactly, my dear," frowned Blake, "and that's why your painting theft was temporarily rather frustrating! Undermined my system and so on. Nor am I fond of whatever tipsy muse tripped the alarm bang in the middle of a certain Vertical visit! Never did find out who was responsible —"

"Kermitcrab," interjected Kitty.

"Aha! My chief suspect, Nessus! That ninny would roach the toes off his own reflection, wouldn't he? He may have to go."

"I mean, prolly," said Kitty. "Just guessing. I'm sorry. I'm woozy. It's been a . . . detailed night."

"And Yuri is a shrouder, not a taker," added Myfanwy. "He's been encrypting your incriminating memories. That's why he's so reluctant to use his taker talent. He doesn't even have one."

"I am reluctant," said Yuri dully, "about many things."

"Give Cracks more credit," Blake chortled. "On numerous occasions, to the oohs and aahs of his captivated Chancel chums, Cracks has wielded the taker talent. Yes, yes! Our friends Undine and Leech have been kind enough to loan me their talents from time to time — as indeed have Ladybird, Clone, Scan, Season and many others. A friend in need is a friend indeed — or should that be, in the dead of night?"

Deid, thought Myfanwy.

"There's more, isn't there?" said Myfanwy softly.

Hypnos, Frog, Sequin, Lap, Geist, Bit, Dribble, Caddy, Turturle, Cricetid . . . What does Germ get out of their arrangement? Scan, Season . . .

"How much has he told you, Simi?" Myfanwy said. "There's more to Blake's links with Veil than a talent swap-shop. Was part of the deal to conduct each other's purges? Am I right, Germ? Is that why you're in charge here, even though Veil is supposedly governed by consensus? Because Chancel takes care of your troublemakers for her? Scan, Season, Foreigner . . ."

The gun was blurred into Germ's face like a beak. At its base, a hideous frown was forming.

"Piffle," said Blake cheerfully. "Working with Veil is a way of *preventing* any more bloodshed!"

"And is that," Myfanwy continued, "why Blake *de facto* rules Chancel, even though all three elders are supposedly equals? Because whenever Hypnos or Frog, or Lap or Bit — any those muses who died even before I arrived — showed a little too much loyalty to Aoide, or to Meletē, the next time that muse was on a mission, somehow, mysteriously Veil knew *just* where to find them? Knew where to find Caddy, Turturle, Cricetid . . ."

"Hush, my love," Simi intervened sharply. "Jasper Robin murdered all those muses. Don't speak ill of the dead."

"Now why would *he* do a thing like that?" snapped Jasper.

It was the first thing Jasper had said in ages, and he looked like he regretted it.

What was going on? Myfanwy's tactic was to drive a wedge. Were Jasper and the Cool Kids on the same page?

Had she messed up? Simi, just before she'd told her to hush, had looked very thoughtful indeed.

"I'm not speaking ill of them, Simi. I want the truth to be known."

"You lot are jokers, you are. I'll have to keep an eye on you."

"*Aw*-kward!" said Kitty. "Let me tell you all something," she added conspiratorially. "I saw Meletē walking in the Chancelhouse gardens once. Dragging a stick with him. You'd think he was a million miles away, but then I noticed the stick lifted a little over every daisy? Part of him was clocking where each one was! I dunno, I kinda *liked* that!"

"'My friend fancies your friend,' I believe is the *modus operandi*, eh Nessus?" said Blake. "'Yes, sir,' you say now."

Or were the Cool Kids just prattling to buy them time? Time to do *what?* Myfanwy had heard the terror in Kitty's voice. Others might not notice. There was another quality too — as though Kitty was packed with billions of the boiling scarytales, the least of which would scare Myfanwy half to death, or burst Kitty's body if she didn't rid herself of it quick. Why were Jasper and Bee so *quiet?*

Who were coming up the beach?

Dei ex machina?

*

The waves' advance had reached the foremost edge of the blood-streaked sand and begun to rearrange it in frightening dark frills.

"Ghoul," said Germ. "Have a wee wander down, make sure it's them."

Triffid wordlessly hopped from his perch and slouched away down the beach. Myfanwy thought she could make out the afro on one approaching figure now.

"Can I jump in with an observation?" said Kitty. "I just want to say, Simi, in this context you still seem so nice and *friendly!*"

Simi laughed merrily. "Thank you, my love."

"Even your gloating feels, like, really validating and supportive, with a playful teasing edge."

"Does she *know* she's a bad guy?" Myfanwy concurred frostily.

"Ooh, yeah," said Simi. "The number of times in class when I could have done with shoving a shooter at you lot! Do you know what I mean?"

"Like the gun she's pointing at me," Tallulah blurted. "Sorry. I know. That was your guys's whole point. She's actually bad."

"Simi, classroom behaviour is a complex issue," Myfanwy objected. "Often it has something to do with what's going on at home."

Simi wiped her face and chuckled. "Anyway, Nessie's beloved Meletē will come round eventually," she said. "Don't you reckon, babes?"

"He's making the strongest arguments," Blake agreed.

Simi nodded thoughtfully. "Controlled skirmishes, to alert various funding streams to all the exciting security opportunities, *blah blah blah* . . . if he'd just *listen* to himself."

"Chancelhouse and Veil would be hard to *join*," said Blake. "Like trying to write two equals signs in cursive. But *teamwork* . . ."

"There you go!" cried Simi. "From *our* perspective, it's *fewer* bodies piling up, it's more shared best practice, more shared talents, less bloody stress! And you lot will come round to it too, my loves. Then I'll bet you'll be a bit red in the face, from all your wild accusations! Master Mystagogue didn't tutor no fool muses. *Teamwork*, that's what's important, my loves!"

"Ah," said Blake awkwardly.

"Right," said Vertical gruffly. "If we're all caught up now?"

"Aoide, my dear," said Blake. "I think we're a little more committed."

Simi's face crumpled a little. "No. Oh, no. You ain't just blowing their bonces off."

"A *lot* red in the face, I think we're thinking."

"Babes, you *ain't!* I've worked bloody hard with these ladies. I've only just got them up and casting!"

"No one is suggesting we be wasteful," Germ told Aoide gently. "I feel we finally have the appropriate shoehorn we need to retrieve that talent from Nessus. Mnemosyne's talent too, *mutatis mutandis*."

"Oh, agreed!" Blake prattled. "We'll stir up *ciel et terre* for those talents, as the French have it! Clouds and clods! Whereas the English content ourselves with turning stones, eh? Stones! But then they're a funny lot, idiomatically. Surprise the French and their arms fall off, but you can't knock 'em down with a feather, let me tell you! You'll need a pillowcase at least!"

"Sir, I'm the only one who's following you," said Tallulah. "Spare my life?"

"You see Simi," said Kitty kindly, "torture opens a drawer in the mind which can *never* be shut again!"

"I dunno," brooded Simi. "I dunno. I suppose. I suppose."

"Plus when Fisher gets here," said Germ, "he can tell us who else has anything worth salvaging."

Why wouldn't Jasper's talent be worth salvaging?

Unless they're not sure he's got it?

Blake looked suddenly agitated. "Yes," he pondered. "Perhaps Leech should give him a once-over too. Find out who this damn chap is! Who the blue blazes — or blazons, I should say!"

Find out who he is?

He's Jasper Robin!

Isn't he?

*

"Just a precaution, Mnemosyne," Blake was saying, with a kindly twinkle in his eye. "A confiscation of your caster talent, till we've cleaned up this whole mess! Did I mention that rule? Keep it under your hat! Did I mention that rule? This whole mess, I mean, under your hat! Yes, yes! At least till we've lain down some newspapers — talk about a big splash! — keep up! Did I mention that rule?"

"Where are we going?" said Myfanwy.

"*I mean keep up with my festering mind.*"

"You're a bit unhinged. It's odd I didn't notice that before. You're manufacturing memory in the west houses, aren't you? Verbatim theatre in reverse. Reality Studio."

"Reality Studio!" Blake wiggled his booty gleefully. "And is that *all* the west houses held, eh, Mnemosyne? No mad first wife after all? Yes, yes! Reality Studio is a very apt title — just the right fusty and sort of *anachronistic* aura. Personally I called it Chancelhouse People's Theatre, but then, no one ever lets me name things. Do they, Nessus? Kick-ass Nessus and her acquiescent nequient side-kick, lulz! You centaur brute, ha ha! How is Hell treating you, my dear? But to come directly to a point, like a pyramid — speaking of which — but no, where was I? Yes, yes! Chancelhouse People's Theatre! That was all prior to formalisation of relations with Veil. Prior to putting Simi and soon Meletē in the loop and so forth. Now that we have reliable access to mirrors, we'll have to move with the times. I expect we'll shut up shop!"

Tallulah had a suggestion. "Maybe just put on shows during the Festival."

Kitty squirmed strangely.

Had Kitty's toe just touched Vertical's? Something light and intangible passed between them — nothing like static electricity.

Vertical looked sick.

"So your Reality Studio was a big flop?" Myfanwy demanded quickly. "It never worked?"

Vertical stroked his beard.

"Mnemosyne!" cried Blake. "It *would* have worked fine, my dear. Back end just a bit labour-intensive, that's all. Fourth wall turns out to be nine metres thick. But we have already trialled a false memory — such an unsatisfactory term! — constructed by more modern methods."

"Yeah babes," said Simi. "We're probably gonna wind up the whole thespy workstream now. Bloody hard staging a provoked massacre in a town square, let me tell you. All that sewing! We're dandy for mirror muses now. So we'll concentrate on doppling, spalling and sculpting memory."

"Vidding existing footage," said Tallulah. "Obv."

"If you like, babes. Cut out the middle man, eh?"

"The 'middle man,'" Myfanwy mused, "being *the material universe* . . ."

"Alas," said Blake. "To have such a damning review of our opening night, and from the star of the show herself! Our trial subject, my dear Mnemosyne, was you! Always *flip*, never *flop!* Can you guess which memory?"

"Seeing Jasper at the station," said Myfanwy. Then she tried something a little cunning. "Jasper was already dead by then, wasn't he?"

"Close! No, my dear, Jasper was not yet dead. Your encounter with him was real enough, and indeed, staking out Kings Cross was what eventually led Meletē to Jasper's so-called safe house —"

They all still think Jasper's dead!

Can they see him?

Y-e-es, prolly — they're pointing the guns at him.

"The false memory, Mnemosyne, was up on that stone balcony, overlooking the courtyard!"

"The conversation with Dad," gasped Myfanwy, trying to sound appreciatively aghast.

For some reason, they just didn't recognise Jasper.

"A Blue Peter Morris special," chuckled Simi.

"Do you recall?" said Blake smugly. "Our fingers touched during the nonsense with brollies and the bikes."

"All that never happened?"

"Pastoral fibbage, Mnemosyne. Yes, yes! When I found you — not that I'd ever *lost* you, mind — you were obviously still in two minds about remaining at Chancelhouse. But I had just the thing! With the help of Aoide, Triffid and Trice, and a mirror talent out on loan, I'd prepared a little propaganda . . . a real tearjerker, your beloved father rather *lukewarm* about the prospect of your return . . . and a feeling, perhaps, of joining a *new* family . . ."

Triffid, returning from his peek down the beach, gave Germ a little thumbs up. It was pathetic little thumb, barely peeping over the knuckly battlements, as if it might get its nail blown off by beautician artillery.

Actually, it was that peculiar gesture politicians get coached into making, like a fist but a bit less fascist and more pointy. Triffid, Myfanwy thought, was stressed. Was Triffid about to jump ship?

"What's the matter, Ghoul?" said Germ. "You look —"

"Sorry Germ," muttered Triffid. "Thought someone had taken my rock. Actually it's *this* rock."

Triffid mounted his correct rock. He looked much less stressed.

Blake cleared his throat. "A little *propaganda* we cooked up," he resumed. "Against the contingency of a cold foot or four! Such generic memories were child's play — easy-peasy, lemon-squeezy, yes, yes! — for the Chancelhouse People's Theatre in our heyday! '*Alas! No one cares! I can't tell anyone my feelings! Even my pony doesn't believe me! Daddy doesn't love me!*' It's the actual daddy I allude to, although the pony is probably called 'Daddy' as well — keep up! Here they come trotting now, our blazon and his boy. How *do* I sleep at night, eh, Yuri? More like a log of wood than a log of deeds, is all I'll say!"

"Maybe the noob should toddle back to the cottages," said Vertical, looking pale and awkward. "Do you know what I mean?"

Blake nodded. "No need to radio for squeamish, horrified reinforcements who make one feel bad about oneself, eh? Something is troubling Vertical, everyone. Can everyone hear it in his voice?"

"No, Blake," said Vertical.

"Well, well! We shall find out!"

Myfanwy saw now that it was Paddy and Marcus trudging up the beach towards them.

Foam lapped at their heels.

"Next I think the trick is," said Blake, "speak loudly and viciously but carry a big stick. A log, more or less! Which is to say, now we may *demonstrate* to poor stoic Nessus, with Tallulah Gordon and this gentleman here as our display models, what may well befall her BFF Mnemosyne, should she remain so admirably and pointlessly recalcitrant!"

Germ waved a hand. "Fine. But let's check in with the noob first. Him and Fisher were covering Mnemosyne's gaff, after she scarpered last night."

Paddy and Marcus were close now. Close enough to read the expressions on their faces. If only there had been any expressions there to read.

"She parked her vehicle there," Germ continued. "Then their story becomes vague."

"By all means," beamed Blake. "I rather think it's an indoors sort of thing anyway. Bit chilly anyway."

"I'd quite like to go in," admitted Undine.

"Does it look much like tsunamis to you?" said Blake. "Me either, but it's been a funny sort of day. 'Oh I don't like to bleed beside the sea-side!' Yes, yes. I jest. You know, Calliope —"

"Don't *call* me that," said Germ.

Drive a wedge, Myfanwy thought. *Pull a wedgie among them.*

Vert moved awkwardly — like he was trying to pass a note he hadn't written yet.

Mara looked up sharply. "What did you just cast, Vert? Oni, what did he just cast you?"

"I forget," said Vertical thinly.

"I can't tell," Oni admitted, slightly cross-eyed.

"What's going on?" Germ demanded.

"I'm sure my reasons will become clear," said Vertical thoughtfully.

"Speaking of pillowcases," Blake continued, "and getting knocked down with feathers, and dreams which were so vivid but now you can't remember, and so forth — I believe our girl has forgotten the whole of last night. Is that right, Mnemosyne?"

"You shouldn't have that name," said Undine. "It's such a sad name."

"It's true," said Myfanwy. She shrugged. "I've forgotten everything. I don't ever remember coming here before."

"Now why is that?" Blake pondered, jiggling his pistol. "Why is that?"

"Fisher?" Germ called out down the beach. "What happened? You were s'posed to be on 'em, then they showed up here and shot Achelois, Pest and Session in the three arses!"

A pause, then a distant, flat cry: "Christ!"

It had been Marcus.

Was he wearing *make-up?*

"I'm just saying!" Germ called. "They're alive and everything!"

Jasper frowned deeply. "Technically," he said. "*I* shot them, and I shot them in the leg."

Myfanwy noticed that some principle of drift and fatigue had slightly skewed all the firearms. Like a school of snoozing goldfish.

If Germ pulled the trigger *now*, Myfanwy guessed, she might merely lose a scrap of ear. Mara's silencer pointed down into Kitty's spine now, Simi's pressed against Tallulah's shoulder now, and Undine was actually *resting* his gun on Bee's head, like she was a little stand. Well, functionally, she *was* a little stand.

She remembered a Bonfire Night years ago, when the Council's firework display had all gone off simultaneously.

Blake and Yuri's handguns were still right there on Jasper's head.

"Who the hell is this guy?" Germ sighed. "Gaga was saying he looks uncanny. And Egg, you seem —"

"Yes," brooded Blake. "He's familiar. From a long time ago. Now isn't that interesting?"

Kitty and Bee's hands were bound behind their backs. Myfanwy reached behind her, found Kitty's hand and squeezed it.

Kitty squeezed back.

Myfanwy groped for Bee's hands.

"Quit squeezing my hands already," drawled Bee.

"My name," revealed Jasper proudly, "is Martin Forjacks. I am a teaching assistant who fired in self-defence. And I demand you release us at once!"

"I am with Papa Seuss on this," said Undine. "Best for all if Leech and I . . . clarify for Mr Forjacks who he is."

"Do," said Germ. "Get Fisher to blaze him up too. Make sure it's totally thorough. It doesn't take a taker to tell this fellah's a liar. Afterwards, perhaps Vert's due for a check-up himself. Ain't ya, hon?"

Vertical sneered.

Germ nodded to Oni. "You too."

He nodded back. "Yes ma'am."

Blake's obliviousness, Myfanwy realised with a falling heart, was a pretence. There had been a subtle shift in his stance. He knew something was changing. He was on it, even more so than Germ. But what? What was about to —

Paddy and Marcus both had black eyes. Paddy's was worse. The skin was broken and puffy, the eye almost swollen shut. She thought briefly of her and Paddy's silly kiss in the shadowy kitchen, and then, earlier, of skate wheels spinning and her ribs pummelled on the train tracks.

Had Paddy and Marcus been *fighting?* Why? Why were they working together now? She needed to *think!*

Somebody is about to die.

Or some of us, or all of us. And there are no such things as good guys and bad guys.

"Forjacks!" cried Blake. "Well, we'll call that your honorary callsong, sirrah! Yes, yes! Put down some newspapers, of course. A sort of Kitty litter, eh Nessus? Might even have to brew a cuppa first — I'm not finished with today's papers, and they won't be much use afterwards! Forjacks, I recognise you now, young man. You used to work in my bindery."

A large breaker showered them. Oni moved back a little, bumping lightly against Triffid.

Something altered in their auras. Like the spout of water you expected to pour from your empty kettle.

Paddy and Marcus were drawing long handguns from jacket pockets.

*

"And I remember your gaffe," said Blake. "A very young man you were then. A friend of Jasper's perhaps? Even of Genevieve? You were active in my union, weren't you? But *quiet* about it. I didn't like that combo. Very busy, very quiet. The sort of thing you want to nip in the bud, when you're running a business. And you're quite quiet now. Aren't you, my boy?"

Triffid, half-overbalancing, grabbed Undine in anger or fear, then gently released him. Undine shrugged. He teetered atop his rock, regaining his own balance with a soft hand on Yuri's shoulder.

A heaviness agitated the air between them, as if someone had stepped roughly onto a landing, expecting a final stair that wasn't there.

Germ greeted the two newcomers. "Fisher, Engrailed. Cheers for checking in."

Their expressions were flat.

Marcus studied Myfanwy and nodded coldly. "Followed her from the roses at Peckham Rye. She goes Kings Cross. Fisher lurks by the roses, in case her contacts showed up. Which they did. We all linked up at the station." He shrugged. "Then I lost 'em. That's my day, Germ. How's yours been?"

"Those newspapers won't be much use *before* either," Blake prattled, "though arguably there's a veneer of verisimilitude *during* the actual splatter."

"Not now, Egg," said Germ irritably. "And lads, no need for the shooters."

Paddy and Marcus did not put away their guns.

"Yes, yes," Blake rattled on. "Whenever Germ has guests, the walls end up freshly painted. Ain't that right? Sequin, Frog, Hypnos, Moirai, Kratos . . . the list *is* endless! You're quite correct, Mnemosyne. Assembling the right talent mix, with the right loyalties, that's been our first priority. Aoide, my dear, you'll forgive us, won't you? Really, you *knew*, didn't you? It was just finding the right moment to admit it to yourself."

"Lads," said Germ. "It's under control this time."

"Ghoul stroke Triffid, *you* don't mind, do you? You *didn't* know, did you? Dim boy!"

Triffid was unreadable.

"Yes, yes! I've always thought Kermitcrab was the brains of your particular operation! Never mind, we are where we are, eh? Germ is rather like a strange inverse monarch. Wherever the *king* goes, of course, everything smells of fresh paint, wherever *she* goes it smells of fresh —"

Yuri howled. He span as he howled, so the sound whipped past Myfanwy swift and red-shifted.

Yuri was grinding the end of his silencer into Blake's cheekbone under his right eye.

Blake gave a little grunt of pain, and raised the relevant eyebrow.

Yuri's face, even without a gun ground in it, was the more smooshed and contorted of the two.

"Is that," said Kitty thickly, "just because he drifts off the topic?"

Mara's handgun traced a wavering arabesque. Many confused gazes sought each other in a circle. Mara sighed and lightly struck the back of Kitty's head with it, as if ticking a box, then swung it past Simi and levelled it at Yuri.

"I can't be sure," she muttered, eyeing Undine, "but —"

Paddy nodded and calmly put his gun to Mara's head. She shut then opened her eyes. She smiled her Cool Kids smile. She swore softly, twice.

"Fisher King," Germ said calmly. "Think carefully."

"I'm trying," muttered Paddy.

The tip of Germ's gun drilled harder into Myfanwy's cheek, against her teeth. Sweat dribbled in a crescent around it.

"Engrailed," Germ said. "It's alright. Stand down, lad."

"She's *done* something to him," said Mara. "It's gone right round us, hasn't it? The little bitch in the cuffs — Christ, she's somehow — Germ, watch out for Fisher —"

Marcus stood beside Germ now, his gun tickling her ear. Myfanwy's heart leapt.

"She's somehow done something to Cracks," Germ said serenely.

Jasper started laughing softly.

A wave came and went.

Germ exhaled. "Fisher King, I don't know what Engrailed told you, but this isn't your battle. Never was. You've my permission to skive."

"Don't listen," blurted Myfanwy.

"Slowly, Gaga," said Paddy. "Hold it by the silencer and put it in my hand."

"I have dreams," said Undine, looking down his barrel to Bee's head, "where they run after me, calling me that sad name."

Vertical said, "I think maybe —"

He stopped, lifted a hand jerkily to his mouth.

Undine's face turned. He was staring at Yuri.

"Nessie, I'm with you lot," Triffid said loftily. "I don't remember what you flipped me, but at the time I knew to pass it on. I sided with you. Whatever was reasonable then is reasonable now. It's logical."

"Make cause with whoever you want, Ghoul," snapped Mara. "You ain't strapped."

"Simi," said Myfanwy. "Undine. Please."

"Fisher," said Germ.

"Aoide," said Blake.

"Bugger this for a game of soldiers," Simi said. She pulled her gun back from Tallulah, and let her arm drop. "One move and the crab gets it!" she chuckled.

"Fisher King," said Germ gently. "All you have to do is pop it away, and walk down the beach. No one will hurt you. No one will blame you."

Germ couldn't see it, but Marcus seemed to be trying to suppress a smile. "You as well Germ," he said. "Hold it by the silencer and pop it in my hand."

Blake's gun still pointed at Jasper's head. Yuri's still pointed at Blake's.

Undine turned his face back slowly, looking to where his silencer touched Bee's head. His posture was awkward, his arm held out stiffly, almost as if the gun were some little railing he leant on for support.

Now he pointed it at the evening sky, and opened his other palm appeasingly. "I don't know what's happening," he murmured. "I can't remember what's happening."

Bee gave a little shudder.

*

The next time a big spray showered them, the thing against Myfanwy's cheek relaxed its pressure and drifted away.

Paddy was slipping Mara's handgun into his jacket. Marcus was pocketing Germ's.

"Uh, maybe *drop* it, Simi," Myfanwy said. Simi's gun, she noted, was not exactly *not* still pointed at Tallulah. "We know what a joker you are. We have to keep an eye on you."

"You too Blake," said Myfanwy.

"Simi," said Blake. "Pal."

Simi shrugged. There was a soft thump, and her hand was empty.

"Undine," said Blake, his gaze shifting. "Old friend. Urania. Alas. Orient your shooter at *one* of these thugs, surely? Umberto! Whaddayasay? Nobody's actually opening fire, of course. But re best bargaining practice —"

"Now would be a good time to turn into a lizard," said Undine dreamily.

"Fine," said Blake placidly. He handed Jasper his handgun. "There you go my boy, hold it by that end, and that end goes in your gob, one hopes! Now, *who* the devil are you?"

"I'm Jasper," said Jasper, inspecting the gun. He hesitated, and looked up and around the circle of faces. Some shook in confusion. "I'm what's left of him anyway. When I started tailing Mara — I mean, I knew the risks."

"It *is* him," hissed Mara. "It's his bleeding *voice*, Germ! And . . . it was him on the bridge!"

"Golly," said Blake mildly. "Pity you couldn't have spotted that one a bit earlier, Polyhymnia! Never the sharpest stool in the slop bucket, were you?"

There was hardly any malice or irritation in Blake's voice at all. He seemed unperturbed that he and his allies were disarmed, guns at their heads and not in their hands. He accepted it with his usual air of domestic jolliness, as though everyone had just tried their cuppas, found out the wrong people had been given Earl Greys — or teacups with green-capped milk or whevs — and all just whirled their cups around.

Mara shrugged. "It was a bleeding statue smacking me about with a tripod. It could have been my bleeding dad, for all I know."

"You're a troubled lady," said Tallulah compassionately.

Myfanwy exploded. "Are you Jasper or not?"

He spread a bitter smile. "Yeah, I believe so. We just invented the perfect disguise, or so we thought. We flipped . . . *everything*, me and Oscar. It took us months to figure out. Everything. Do you get it?"

Two waves came and went.

"It was hell to do," Jasper added.

Blake laughed hollowly.

"In short," said Tallulah softly, "you swapped souls?"

"Everything?" said Oni, obviously playing catch-up.

"In a way," pontificated Triffid, "like they swapped bodies. Wow. Has anyone seen *Freaky Friday*?"

"I've seen *The Parent Trap*," said Kitty. "Is it like that?"

"Couple months later," said Jasper, "Oscar was dead."

"Never mind," said Kitty. "Tell me later."

Myfanwy ran panicked through her Garden.

Jasper studied her wryly. "I didn't know if you knew. I didn't know what you'd think."

Once long ago, at Bridge Croft, she'd glimpsed a pearly king as he fled the police. She'd thought it was Jasper. But it was *this* face, *this* body . . . it was Jasper's friend, tall and beautiful, seen through Jasper's eyes.

Before he and Jasper . . . changed places.

A column of inky smoke rose from the site.

"Well, for what it's worth, I support you."

"Oscar?" she said hesitantly.

"*Jasper*," he said. "Myfanwy, don't be afraid. Inside, I'm Jasper. And this . . . form . . . I mean, I'm all you've ever known, right?"

"Mate," said Genevieve. She gargled huskily. "You don't know how that makes me feel. Oh! Oh! Can I just actually give you a hug?" She flung her arms delicately around the birdwatcher's neck and sighed.

Myfanwy shook her head. "Yeah," she said. "I had no idea. I've been inside you, looking out. I remember you at Bridge Croft, but you wore a mask. When we rode the horse, I held onto you but couldn't see your face."

She tried to peer discreetly at his chin.

Blake snorted. "I'd say your trick merits a new muse class," he muttered. "How does 'possessor,' shall we say, *grab* you?"

Jasper bit his lip. "OMFG. What's the point?" he sighed. "It's *over*, Blake! Can't you see you've lost? Naming things doesn't mean you control them. Nor can you pardon yourself with your hundreds of new names. What you've done follows you. It hunts you down."

"Scarcely hundreds," said Blake. "Yes, yes. 'My name is Legion' — my italics — obscure one, that — look, it's perfectly transparent, Jasper. *Was* Zeus re Chancel, relaunched *that* brand as Seuss. *Always* been Scotch Egg vis-à-vis Veil, shortened to Egg. Sort of faint aura of egghead, I like to flatter myself. Civvy street, always Haduken or Duke. Nothing to hide, and I don't see that —"

"Well, except you weren't Haduken Blake when we knew you," Germ cheerfully contradicted him. "You were Haduken —"

"Black," Myfanwy blurted. "You're Sophie Black's father, aren't you? One of the missing muses. I can even see a little resemblance."

Blake seemed tongue-tied. "Well," he said.

"Not quite," murmured Jasper.

Germ shrugged. "Don't know what you're on about, Mnemosyne. He was Haduken Quaker when I met him."

Jasper laughed hollowly. "Haduken Quaker. 'Glad it's you and not me, mate' — that's what you said to me when Gen introduced me. Odd thing to say to your daughter's boyfriend. Always thought that. We was standing by your rosebush that never had any roses."

"Genevieve," said Blake. "Yes, yes. She always had terrible taste in boys. *Were* standing, Jasper."

"Gen, who disobeyed her daddy," said Jasper. "And whose daddy murdered her in his turn."

"Piffle," said Blake coldly. He seemed to swell in stature.

"Your own little girl," Jasper said. He wasn't looking at Blake. He was looking right at Myfanwy. She shook her head. "Your valiant sacrifice," Jasper added softly. "And then you canonised her, like you were doing her a favour. I can't ever —"

"I don't care whose daughter she is," blurted Myfanwy. "She was *Gen*."

Jasper nodded. "I can't ever understand you, Blake. But I think I understand how you understand yourself. You think you're Abraham, don't you? Bible bloke. Shows how great he is because he's all set to kill his child."

Blake tsked scornfully. He was a frightening presence now, as though the focus of a slow dolly-zoom. The darkening sky and beach seemed to steady themselves for his sake. "You *really* —" he began.

"*Abraham*," said Jasper, "and no God. You do it all yourself. Even the admin."

"You really ought to do your homework," Blake said. "None of us killed Gen. She just *disappeared*. The funny thing is, the only ungracious brat is *you*, Mr Robin. Impudently repaying life with life's defilement, rudely requiting milk with ink. Honestly, my boy, neat trick, the body swap. Pity Static zotzed Oscar, eh? Yes, yes! Still, rather inevitable! Rather inevitable, when a man with a contract on his head swaps that head for somebody else's!"

"No. No, Blake. Don't you dare try to —"

"Do you think what *you've* done will follow you, my dear boy? *Hunt* you down? Pity too I'll probably never know the ins and outs of it, the *swap*, that is to say! *In* the arse and *out* the nose, I expect! Yes, yes! Has anyone really been paying attention to what's *happening* here? You don't have the slightest clue, do you? Look at his little face, for God's sake! No, I'm afraid I'm not in the least afraid of you, Jasper Robin. Doubt you've got it in you any more, frankly. Either way, you won't kill me. And you know why? Because Marinade will first. Won't you, lad? Won't you?"

And once more Yuri howled.

*

"Does anyone have any *snacks?*" said Kitty. "I haven't eaten in over a day, and *not* like in a good way! Also we're getting wet. Also I'm incredibly *thirsty*. Does anyone know what the deal is with not drinking sea water? Yuri, do you know? I mean, that sounds like an urban myth, right?"

"Yuri?" enquired Myfanwy softly.

Bee stepped between Myfanwy and Yuri. "Hey," she said. "I have a freebie for you. Get it? Free . . . Bee!"

"Not now, Bee," snapped Myfanwy sharply.

"Zzub zzub zzub! Flip!" Bee turned around and started groping for Myfanwy's hand. She found it, grabbed it, squeezed it. Myfanwy felt the flip slip in.

"*Basically* Yuri," continued Kitty brightly, "*and* everybody — I just think we should start thinking a bit more in terms of medical attention."

Yuri's handgun drew back a little from Blake's skin. He was breathing heavily.

"And Moth too," added Myfanwy. "We need to make sure she's okay."

It wavered.

Yuri lowered it.

"I think what Yuri has remembered," said Blake, "is the sound Lockean principle, that someone who cannot remember their crimes cannot be held responsible for —"

"*No*," Yuri said. He sounded calm though. "It is just that I am my own man."

"Yuri," Myfanwy said. "Maybe could I have the gun?"

"No," he said. "Even though I am my own man, I am also okay."

Myfanwy's gaze flicked to Jasper. He was chewing his bottom lip. He gave a prim little sniff. He didn't look about to kill anybody either. He looked adorable.

She was right to keep Jasper's memories. Even if it had been for all the wrong reasons.

Could she risk plunging into her Garden? Try to discover what was different, what Bee had flipped her?

*

She was sitting in her room, surrounded by horses and fairy lights.

"When you see the Bee," she drawled, "leave a message."

She stared at Moth.

Moth stared back. "Oh! Hello, Myfanwy! I am here with uh, Bee. Well I guess now I'm here with you. Anyway. Helloo!" She waved. "This is me in your past! Hiya! I am now waving for the camera!"

"I'm not a camera," she said.

"Maybe we can cut these bits out."

"Sure," she told Moth. "I'll leave these bits out when I flip, so you don't have to look dumb to Mnemosyne, who is a really cool girl. I wouldn't want to look dumb to Mnemosyne if I were you," she chided. "Mnemosyne means so much business."

"Me and Yuri are gonna run away," said Moth conspiratorially. "Oh, hello, this is Moth by the way."

"I can see you," she said. It was fun being Bee.

Moth put her hands together in silent applause, then suddenly looked crestfallen and frustrated. "Can't you just tell her?"

"No, I'll forget."

"Yuri isn't really a taker, Myfanwy! He's something called a shrouder! There's something bad in Chancelhouse! We think it goes to the top! Me and Yuri and maybe Bee and Terpsichore — ooh, bugger, he's alive by the way — are going to break away from Chancel and Veil and do our own research! Um. What else?"

"Tell her about that thing you and Yuri made up."

"Oh yeah. Research programme. Memory's gonna get mirrored, cast, caught and split, again and again. Myriad fragments will be cast, caught and joined. Retagged as a thought.

Sculpted, recombined. We could have ideas outside the main sequence of intellectual history."

"Why should such a cool girl endorse such dangerous utopianism?" she said.

"We could think thoughts," said Moth, "that don't follow from anything ever thought before. Thoughts . . . that don't arise from our circumstances, but directly from combinatorial possibilities of thought itself. It's going to be amazing, Mnemo! You should join us. Please come with us, Mnemo! Everything's going to be amazing from now on! That's it. End of — oh, yeah, and we think Yuri's sad about killing lots of people, even though he never really killed them. Um, Gid, Erinaceine, I don't know how to say that, Cui and Squab. Can you remember the others Bee? Ooh, I suppose you're busy remembering these ones! Um, Struct, Frog, Sequin, Asphyxia, um, Nora, Aglet, um, Anemone . . . no, Ameonna . . . Enenra, Te-No-Me, Caddy, Turturle, Foreigner. It's quite a lot in my opinion. We're going to look after him. He really likes you. Cricetid, Metis, I think I said that one, Tax, Cithara. Scan. Oh, and another muse called — but he says he really never killed her, whatever that means — called Mnemosyne."

*

"That will be seventy pounds," said Bee.

"Blake has memorised his many acts," said Yuri hoarsely. "Their outlines. Strategic forms. Often he studies these to refresh. It is really only the *shame* of his acts he gives to me."

"It is the *shame* which deserves itself," snapped Blake. "*Honestly*, to pursue the good life is nowadays quite impossible without outsourcing sanity somewhat. And even so, I feel a little lopsided! Ever noticed, girls, with what agonies I mount even the littlest flight of stairs? As though it were a flight of stars! No, you probably don't notice, lallygaggling in some distant corridor, lords and ladies of that corridor, no doubt! Can you really expect someone with *my* responsibilities to cope with the ravages of age and the ravages of conscience at the same time? That's age for you! That's decay for you! And I do mean *for you*. One day, ladies! Day by day, I attend more raptly to the insensible easeful motion of the young. As raptly as I attend to the location of every loo and every bench, every railing to cling to. One day you'll know it too. Yes, yes! That pain, the stiffness in your hands and knees! You can never adapt to it, because it's a little different every moment. I'll wager there's no global capitalism so cunning as the average aged kneecap, pouting on its bed of gout!"

"OMG," said Tallulah. "Please stop villainsplaining everything to us?"

"We're not judging you," said Myfanwy.

"You can email Myfanwy about this stuff later," said Kitty.

"We've all done similar stuff," said Jasper.

A large wave soaked Triffid, who yelped. Simi tittered affectionately.

"Leave now Blake," said Kitty quietly. "You too Aoide, Gaga, Germ. All of you. It's over. Yuri, I won't let him hurt you again."

"I think Yuri freed *himself*," said Myfanwy firmly. "And before they go, we want Blake and Aoide's keycards for the west houses."

"Whoa!" cried Paddy. "No sense fishing in pockets, fam. How about everyone frisks their bad guy?"

"Good idea," agreed Myfanwy. "Plus Blake can't go just yet. He still has to tell us things. About Yuri, and about — my namesake. About what happened to Genevieve."

"You're well bossy," sniffed Kitty. "Germ, you give Myffy the key to my cuffs then scram. We must have drinks some time soon."

"There *aren't* any keys," Germ sighed. "They're not those kind of restraints. You'll need a wire cutter. Or a tough pair of scissors and some patience."

"*'Pols*," hissed Gaga.

Kitty looked sad. "I wish there *was* a key."

Tallulah sort of pursed her lips sideways, and gave Simi a conspiratorial stare, as if acknowledging both of them had better things to be doing.

Then she started patting her down. She was impressed though, when she found the big sword.

Simi winked.

"Yes, yes," Blake prattled. "Could we cast the total experience of age, I wonder? The flesh hung on aging bones is the *more* changeable, I'll warrant, than that flesh borne in the four winds!"

Myfanwy started gingerly and ineptly patting down Blake, but Yuri interposed. "Please. Allow me."

"Whatever little brave motion one made," said Blake, "whatever 110% one gave, the last time one succeeded in climbing a stair, or zesting a lemon — the next time one tries it, maybe now it's not brave enough, or brave in the wrong direction, as it were!"

As Yuri's small neat fingers moved in and out of Blake's pockets, something imperceptible was included in their transactions. As though a cup of a shell game were lifted, and nothing at all was underneath — perhaps not even the print of the tablecloth.

"And that's just the legs and fingers, my dears! It's the same with the *heart!* And the heart — oh! — Marinade! — Yuri — please don't — please! . . . not *everything*, Yuri . . . not everything . . . right now . . ."

Yuri was returning Blake his conscience. His deceit, his torture, his murders, were coming home. The Chancelhouse muses he'd sent to their deaths, the Veil muses he executed on Germ's behalf. Hypnos, Frog, Sequin, Lap, Geist, Bit, Dribble, Kaiou, Struct, Asphyxia Noir, Aglet, Turturle,

Ameonna, Enenra, Caddy, Cricetid, Moirai, Kratos, Season, Scan, Foreigner, Tax, Swat, Cria, Te-No-Me . . . how many others? And Gen?

"Ah," gurgled Blake. A soft borborygmus of a Granny Smith decomposing. For a moment his eyes flipped shut. "You'll also need the codes," Blake said stoically.

Blake opened his eyes. Tears welled and hovered. Kitty recited the codes to the west houses and the armoury.

"Besides," said Myfanwy, "we're basically taking Simi's keycard just to annoy her."

"You're a troublemaker, you are," said Simi. "I'm going to have to keep an eye on you."

"I thought," Myfanwy told Simi, "that when you smugly fed someone's catch-phrase back to them in changed circumstances, they stopped using that catch-phrase."

"Do I say that a lot?" said Simi, mystified. "Do I really, babes?"

"I'm as baffled as you," said Myfanwy primly.

"Um," said Vertical. "I might bust a move too. If you don't mind? Sides have broken down a bit, haven't they?"

"No hard feelings, eh?" said Oni.

Kitty's gaze moved over their faces. "Anyone who wants to, go now. But Blake lingers a moment longer."

"Well, well," said Blake. "Yes, yes."

Blake looked quite changed.

"I am unafraid," said Kitty. "As befits a BFF of Myfanwy."

Simi, Germ and Gaga filed away down the shore. After a few moments, Undine also hopped from his rock. Then he hesitated. "I love you too," he said. The little smile played behind each syllable. Like Beatrix Potter bookmarks left in *Mein Kampf.*

"Go," said Kitty. "We're not going to shoot you in the back."

Undine shrugged ever so slightly. "Wait till you see it, before you decide that. It's very . . . infuriating."

He strolled away down the beach, but seemed to make no effort to catch up with the others.

A moment later, Vertical followed slowly.

"Cards on the table," said Oni. "I'm off my face."

He went with Vertical.

"Safe," said Marcus. "Almost too easy."

"Not for Kitty," said Myfanwy quietly. She looked at Blake. "Nor for him."

"All I'm *saying,*" trilled Kitty, "is that *certain people* who seem to be very much sticking around, just in my opinion, have got *quite a sinister thing going on.*"

Gradually everyone was glaring at Triffid.

He folded his arms.

"Ghoul," said Paddy eventually. "How long have you known Blake and Aoide were working with Veil?"

Triffid leaned back and shrugged. "Aoide was telling the truth. She didn't know about Blake and Germ's arrangement till a few days ago. Well, okay. Next we meet, guys, remember I helped you today."

"Did you?" said Myfanwy.

"That's not exactly what I asked," said Paddy.

There was a small moat around the rock where Triffid stood. He cleared it with a clumsy cabriole. The soft muddy sand where his feet landed did not fly up. "Bye guys. Bye, Paddy. My real name's Jamie, by the way. We'll all — link up later, yeah?"

And he walked away down the beach.

*

"Don't give *me* no evils!" laughed Paddy nervously. "I ain't going! Me and Marcus stood tall for you."

Paddy wore the same diffident smile he'd shown in the kitchen, when she had kissed him then pushed him away.

Myfanwy glared hard at Paddy.

Next at Marcus. Marcus's neck tattoo, she now noticed, comprised English letters, pinched and interwoven to vibe tribal. She could just about make out the words *believe* and *bed*.

When she looked at Blake he shrugged his shoulders convulsively, as if trying to shake something loose. He was ashen-faced. Crushed. Not so much from his present situation, Myfanwy guessed, but still suffering under the influence of all those unwanted feelings he'd dumped in his poor wee PA, returned to him all at once.

She would try to be gentle with them. With the Veil muses gone — hmm, she was still thinking of them as 'Veil muses' — and despite everything, Myfanwy felt a kind of cosiness enter the ambience.

"I want to get it straight," she said. "Starting at the beginning. *My* beginning, okay? The world was covered with snow. Paddy, you were ready to recruit me for a secret society of muses, known as Veil."

"Trust," said Paddy. "Maybe Kitty too."

"What a privilege," Kitty commented dryly.

Paddy looked at her, bit his lip, then exhaled loudly. "I didn't know what Veil could be like! Swear down, Myffy!"

"Let's not run ahead of ourselves," said Myfanwy. "Hey Marcus, what does your neck tattoo say, BTW?"

"I Believe I Will Eat My Bed," said Marcus. "It's just this thing."

"O-*kay*," said Kitty.

"And I thought we were the *good* guys!" wailed Paddy. "Veil, I mean."

"Yes, yes," muttered Blake.

"Paddy," continued Myfanwy calmly. "You were also working undercover at a rival agency, Chancelhouse. What other double agents were you aware of?"

"Only Ghoul stroke Triffid," Paddy said sullenly.

"Not Blake," Myfanwy agreed meditatively. "No. I think I believe that."

Blake remonstrated her with rheumy, tear-filled eyes. He looked so different now. His frolicking energy was transformed into the tremulousness of age. He kept patting his ponytail and licking his lips in a half-controlled manner. She wanted to tell him everything would be okay.

She was a little angry at Yuri. Maybe that was unreasonable.

"I used to debrief to a muse called Scan," Paddy added. He gave a wry smile. "I gave her some intelligence on Chancelhouse, but I didn't take any risks. My main job was out in the field — I flagged up quality talent for Veil to recruit. Now and then I'd let Chancel recruit some butters patterner or lame-ass caster I came across, just to preserve my cover. But when Scan went, Vertical took over. He made me shift my focus to spying on Chancelhouse."

"What happened to Scan?"

"Killed on a mission. It was bad, fam. That whole Veil clique were killed, over time. Season, Swat, Te-No-Me, Cria, Foreigner."

"Casualties of the Chancel war," said Myfanwy.

Paddy shrugged. "Nah. Casualties of Germ's purge, as subcontracted to Blake. Other Veil muses have vanished too. Supposedly they just left, but no one's heard from them at all. Surfeit, Gid, Erinaceine, Cui, Snow, Squab. I don't know who's really dead and who's alive. You know what, I *did* know Blake wasn't what he seemed. He was deceitful — sadistic —"

"'*Blake was straight fronting,*'" said Kitty, in a stupid deep voice. "'*All the more reason to stay loyal to Veil.*' Paddy, you are such a *tube.*"

"Are you meant to be me?" said Paddy, sounding genuinely interested.

"We're all meant to be ourselves," said Tallulah briskly. "Even though that too is pointless."

"Now, now," Blake chuckled weakly, waggling his finger.

"Don't waggle that," said Jasper.

Myfanwy looked at Yuri, who still wore a solemn, bewildered air as he stood sentinel over Blake. Then she focused on the trigger guard. "Yuri," she added kindly. "Don't wiggle yours."

"Sadistic, my dear Fisher King?" said Blake. "A little mutual purge outsourcing — all for the greater good, when one drills down into the details — and of course loan of the mirror and shrouder talents, as and when. How can that possibly be called 'sadistic'? One does what one must, but one takes no *delight* in these difficult decisions. Difficult decisions, or shall I say *impossible* decisions? Knowing the difference between 'right' and 'wrong' is the bee's knees, I completely agree — present rather skinned company excepted, obviously! — but when everything which confronts you belongs to *neither* category — well, I've had a bit of a winge re me own knees, innit, but *it's the same with the heart!* Yes my darlings, the same with the heart. At least *you* can develop a repertoire of limps. How many limps have your young chests developed so far, eh?"

Bee tilted her head. "One feels no pain in taking these impossible decisions," she drawled in her customary deadpan. "As one disposes of it in one's little Yuri."

"Pragmatism, Bee! Just my little Caledonian Antisy-zygy!" Blake's voice seeming to leap up now, only to stumble a little on the *zygy*. "Have your young hearts yet learned the complex dance — every step, a new limp, the tottling, the toddling, the Trendelenburg, the eggshell, the kangaroo, the magnetic — the complicated gimped rhythm necessary to murder — aha! the right word, for a change! — yes, to murder people who truly must be murdered? Must be murdered, *must* be murdered. So that others may *not* be murdered. And may live *life*, and not merely live some defiled atrocity proxy of life, some pestilential and disfigured cousin of life? Speaking of which, the horrorshow political economist *Hayek* might shed some rather interesting light on our Jekyll and Mr Hide —"

Someone had to do something. "Hush now Blake," Myfanwy instructed. "We want to hear it, but not now. Not like this. Your turn will come." Her gaze flicked to Paddy's uncertain smile. "I am interrogating Paddy. I'm giving him one last chance."

"Yes, yes!" cried Blake. "The whole is goutier than the sum of its parts! Antisyzygy, meaning *duality*, more or less —"

"Here we go again," said Jasper gloomily. "I think the shame is wearing off, guys. 'Tigger Tigger burning bright.'"

"Si, Zi and Li'l' G are the three members of Vop Rush," Tallulah added helpfully. "They're pointless though."

"*Are* they?" marvelled Blake. "PhD in that! Alas —"

"Your turn," repeated Myfanwy, "will *come*."

"Yuri," said Kitty pleasantly, "do you know what a 'cold-cock' is?"

Yuri looked puzzled but Blake fell silent.

"They're a band," Tallulah added, half to herself. "Vop Rush are. Well, would you call them a band?"

*

"Paddy," said Myfanwy. "You didn't know Blake was working with Veil. Did Triffid?"

"I don't know," said Paddy carefully. "Just now he dodged the question. Didn't he seem proper sketchy?"

"*I* will ask the questions," growled Myfanwy. Paddy grinned and she scowled, trying not to grin back.

Blake silently tugged his ponytail with trembling fingers. He gazed intently at Paddy. Then a hand shot up.

Myfanwy sighed. "What now, Blake? Triffid *did* know about you? Make it fleeting."

"Indeed!" cried Blake. "You see, Merlin, you'd always been Scan's boy. Never really clicked with Vert."

"Funny that," said Paddy.

"Germ and I took the view that your loyalties had lain with Scan, rather than with Veil or Chancelhouse *per se*. With Scan's dissolution, you were rendered ambivalent. We brought in Triffid stroke Ghoul to keep an eye on *you*."

"Thank you Blake," said Myfanwy. "Providence will reward you. Okay Paddy, what about Yuri and Bee? Did you suspect they weren't just normal Chancel agents?"

Paddy shrugged. "Bee, I had no idea Jasper had got to *you* —"

"I have certain ideas," drawled Bee.

"As for you, Yuri — you weren't a taker like you pretended. I sensed that. I just didn't know why yet. I still don't, really."

"Blake was bullying Yuri," said Myfanwy. "Weren't you, Blake? That was a rhetorical question. Stay shushed. Blake pretended Chancelhouse was fresh outta shrouder patterners. He kept Yuri close. Flattered him, coerced him, made him dependent."

Yuri nodded. "Blake was assigned Aoide under Partnering Rule."

"She might have stumbled on something incriminating. So Blake had you encrypt all his memories of dealings with Veil."

"And God knows what else!" said Kitty brightly. "Or Yuri knows what else, anyway."

"Also God," said Yuri, sounding bewildered. "Now Aoide is on-board, perhaps Blake no longer requires me?"

"Dear boy," murmured Blake. "Quite the contrary. You've still something quite important to do for me."

Yuri was looking now like Milhouse had wandered out of *The Simpsons* into the contraband smuggler's camp in *Carmen.* Myfanwy giggled a tad wildly, then wheeled her gaze to Jasper. "So Paddy flagged us for Mara to recruit for Veil. And *you* were hunting Mara."

"Yuri's on our side now, right?" said Tallulah uneasily.

"You wanted revenge for Gen," said Myfanwy. "Mara was out in the field a lot. I guess that's why she was first on your list. One day you followed her to St Jerome's Senior School. You intended bloodshed. Every, um, claw has its silver lining. Because that's when you met me!"

"You have been a reforming presence in my life," said Jasper.

"There's a gendered aspect to that remark which you and I will discuss later in a lively fashion. Anyway, Mara got spooked, made her getaway. Her next attempt to link up with us was by the Thames. You snitch again, Pad?"

"Yeah, I texted her," confirmed Paddy. "About you. But Kitty — why were *you* there?"

"She'll ask the questions!" growled Kitty.

"Serious," said Myfanwy. "Why were you there?"

"It really was coincidence," said Kitty. "Except I guess for the fact that you and I had vaguely talked about seeing Reverie and Stanchion some time. Dude, I *told* you I had tutorials and MacAonghas and stuff, which to be fair *were* all cancelled at the last minute. Then I was wandering in town, I texted those guys to meet up. I didn't really think that you and Gandalf would be —"

"*Nuff* confusion," said Paddy, "without you calling me Gandalf all the time."

"Really? I've been thinking you'd suit Alf?" said Kitty. "Or Gandhi? You *do* know about Fisher King's *wound*, don't you?"

"This is all very cozy," muttered Jasper. "But maybe we should move on." He was looking down along the beach. Myfanwy followed his gaze, counting out the seven figures moving slowly away.

"Fisher King is like . . . fisher of mandem, innit?" said Paddy. He looked puzzled. "I never actually did much depth research into the brand."

Myfanwy giggled. "*Anyway*," she said. "On message, Kitsy. Sorry, Jasper. Only this is really interesting? It's just — what really puzzles me about that day is *you*, Marcus. Were you working for Veil, or Jasper, or what?"

"Can we walk and talk?" said Jasper. He sounded exhausted.

Marcus shook his head. "Nah, nah. I realised a few years ago I had a special way of teaching mates of mine tricks and things — but I'd have to re-learn them myself afterwards. That was the price." He motioned to Jasper. "When I met this geezer, that's when I realised I wasn't alone. You flipped me some next Jedi mind trick, yeah?"

Jasper looked awkward. "It was a bit budget, yeah."

"Me supposedly remembered offering you fealty?" Marcus laughed.

"Actually you standing on the sinks in lavs saying, like, 'My liege! My liege!' to your own reflection? Bare unconvincing, bruv! I could *feel* the memory go in!"

"Only he looks a bit malnourished and crazed," said Tallulah — who had evidently been following her own replacement rail service of thought — to no one in particular.

"It was Oscar's idea," Jasper brooded. "Fake fealty vow. Supposed to do the job of a Go-Ball. Sorry. Bit patronising. Quite funny if you knew him."

"Wait," said Myfanwy. "Marcus, you're saying that —"

"I told you all this in Kings Cross," said Marcus. His brow furrowed. "But I guess —"

"Mind like a sieve, this girl," said Paddy. "Marcus wasn't working for anyone, Myfanwy. He was just skating around bothering nobody."

"We weren't bothering anybody."

"Then who —"

"This mandem's something special. He's a *self-taught muse.* Veil called him a skiller, but that don't really sum him up."

"I let Jasper borrow my board anyway. It wasn't the specific memory he flipped me. It was the fact that I recognised him as a brother — you get me? As a *muse*, even though I've never called myself that. Till that day, I thought I was one of a kind." Marcus grinned sweetly at Myfanwy. "Then when I saw you were chasing him . . . I was like, 'Damn, maybe I've done the wrong thing!' Um, I know this might not be a good time, by the way — but you still have something of mine?"

Myfanwy blinked. "Your *skateboard!* I'm so sorry. Of course. Sand is a tricky surface anyway, hon. It's just, you were gone, and all the other skaters took Kitty's phone number and promised to get in touch with us, and they *did* only —"

Marcus shook his head. "Nah, the board ain't the main thing. Years of skinned knees? A fractured ankle? Grinding, getting hassled? C'mon mate. Game's up. Hand it over."

"Oh. You gave me the skill to skate, didn't you?"

"Damn right. I can't even *stay* on them things anymore."

"Ooh. Can I have *one* more go with it, before I do? It was so fun."

"I can teach you for real, if you like."

"Or *I* can teach *you*," she teased.

"So, yeah," Marcus continued, with colour in his cheeks. Jasper looked faintly cross. Myfanwy liked that. "You're chasing *this* geezer away down the embankment. Meanwhile this bloke with the sopping afro and skinny little chest comes up to me, and is all like, 'Aah, I've done spells on you, you are the Chosen One,' and tells me all about this secret society he belongs to. So secret, I can't even know its name yet."

"What did he say *his* name was?" said Myfanwy thoughtfully. "Merlin, or Fisher King?"

Paddy looked quietly on.

"*That* day?" Marcus was meditative.

"Remember," urged Myfanwy. "Merlin, or Fisher King?"

"Mate . . . I think it was just 'Paddy'."

"It *was* Paddy," blurted Paddy. "Mate, I never even *considered* you for Chancelhouse. But I also trusted Vert and Germ less and less. That day I was thinking . . . maybe you and me, we could start our *own* agency."

"Trust," said Marcus doubtfully.

Paddy turned to Myfanwy. "That's why at first I kept Marcus to myself. I thought you, me, him, maybe Kitty, we could be like a gang. But you were too good. You were already on the trail to Blake. I didn't know what to do. In the end I told Vertical everything. So Veil started training up Marcus. Not here — in London. He got his callsong, Engrailed."

"Okay. Were you worried we'd blow your Chancelhouse cover?"

"Yeah. On Vertical's advice, I told Blake that a Veil recruiter had gone after two girls at St Jerome's. Said that Veil's solicitations were what led me to blazon you two and realise you were muses. I didn't think he'd buy it, but he did."

Blake's hand shot up again.

"Yes," said Myfanwy. "The, uh, evil genius hostage at the back?"

"Well," said Blake mildly. "Germ told me that the cover story was coming. I had time to compose my features into blissful — ah, now there's a Scots word for the expression I used . . ."

"Safe, I guess," said Paddy. "Anyway, it was *mad* after that! Myfanwy, you showed up at Chancelhouse. Static killed Oscar, thinking he was Jasper —"

"Static," murmured Jasper. "Yes. Someone said that."

"Oopsie," said Paddy. "Yeah. Operation Terpsichore."

Blake chirped up again. "Happened to be Static's team that did it — her, Rook, Tase and Kermitcrab. *Everyone* was primed for it though, Jasper me lad. It could have been *anyone*."

"But Static pulled the trigger," said Jasper.

"Tugged the garrotte, but in principle yes," said Blake cheerfully. "A sort of big sharp trigger around the throat."

Jasper shook his head in disgust. "You can't get to me anymore Blake. I'm not who I used to be."

"By that time," Paddy continued, "I was putting in so many hours at Chancelhouse that I hardly saw Marcus — Engrailed, as he now was — not really till last night."

"And you still didn't know about Blake?"

Paddy shook his head. "Nah. I gave Vert the goss on you girls though. Said you were progressing in your studies and that."

"What about that night he was in your room?" said Kitty.

"We were taking a consign—"

"I stabbed him," Kitty interrupted, rather blankly.

"Um, yeah. Triffid was supposed to come to my room and take a talent consignment from Vert. He's a cloister, they're the best at stacking talents without wear and tear. But there is a limit to how many talents any muse can stack. Supposedly that's all it was — a storage issue. We'd done similar things loads of times. Thinking about it now, yeah, I suspect Triffid was Blake's, like, talent cubby-hole. Vert left Blake what he needed with Triffid. Right guys?"

Yuri nodded, and Blake smiled feebly.

"Okay," said Myfanwy. "When did you finally find out him and Germ were bezzy-bezzy?"

"Like yesterday, blud. Day before yesterday, you weren't at the English exam. I chatted at Kitty, she agreed to meet with Gaga to discuss coming over. We went to a Veil safe house in Kensington. There was a big welcoming party, Germ, Gaga, Vertical, Achelois, Surd, Down. It was all like, 'Thank you, Fisher King. That will be all.' Didn't feel so good, yeah? The plan supposedly was to induct Kitty here — *in*-duct, yeah — so I came up yesterday to check up on her."

He gazed uneasily at Kitty, searching for confirmation. "What?" she said. "From the *heart*, Gandalf! From the *heart*."

"Yeah. So I arrived here. Everyone was, like, vague about where Kitty was. Then I'm like, 'Whoa, that's *Blake* and *Simi* and Germ and Undine all chatting and cotching!' So they're like, 'Yeah, Blake and Germ have been co-operating, and now we're all going to roll together, and this is great news for *you* young Merlin stroke Fisher King, whose loyalties have been somewhat confused.' And I'm like, 'Safe, whatever, sounds boring, so anyway where's Kitty?' And they're all like, 'What, do you fancy her or something?' And I'm like, 'Uh, yeah, is that wrong or something?' And Gaga is like, 'You might not fancy her now,' but Germ tells her to shut up. And I'm like, 'Hmm.' Then they're all giving me air. Like, No Further Questions, yeah? This is mad. I stay over that night, and about, like, I dunno, three AM, there's a commotion, and I go towards the Assembly Space — the milking parlour, yeah — and Myffed, you've stolen in like a fox, fam, but you've come out like a raging bull, trust! They're mad shooting at you, brap! brap! except all with silencers, so it's more like tick! tock! tick! tock! and because of where I'm standing, man, my weave is like cheese with holes in it, yeah, so I duck down, and then you're coming right past me, and I know I'll have to face them in a minute, so I plan to make, like, a fake grab at you, and just let you past — because you are obviously in somewhat of a hurry, yeah — but then you sort of bellow and lift your leg admirably high and gracefully and kick me in the eye."

"I did that?" said Myfanwy. "Good."

"In a way it was. Afterwards, Gaga said they weren't aiming at you, just trying to scare you to stop, but I wasn't sure. Everyone looking proper booky and shifty and that. Germ is looking vexed. Germ says, like, maybe you were ready to come over to Veil, that's why you came here, but you got shook, and we didn't exactly help by shooting at you. So then I'm like, 'Safe, well, I guess I'll hit the hay.' Germ's like, 'Nuh-uh.' So they have me pick up Marcus and stake out your house. I used the time to reconnect with my boy, seen? I still hadn't heard anything from Kitty. By now everything was proper weird. After you parked your daddy's whip, me and Marcus followed you to the rose garden in Peckham Rye. You were behaving strangely even for you."

"Yeah," said Marcus. "Obviously you meant to meet someone. Except suddenly you were like, 'Ohhhh!' and you ran off. I followed. Fisher stayed to see if your contact ever turned up."

"Yeah," said Myfanwy. "I'm missing these memories. Early this morning, I suspected Tallulah was working with Jasper — maybe even Veil?" She turned to Tallulah. "My bad, hon."

"Nae bother," Tallulah replied. "Paranoid before a date. Been there."

"I don't remember the exact moment I turned on you. I guess in the rose garden. Maybe earlier."

"A rose is a rose is arousing," murmured Blake. "Foolish passions and foolish suspicions both."

"Or maybe even earlier," said Myfanwy. "After the milking parlour. During Veil Ambush, Take One. Like, 'How did they know I was coming? Gasp! Looly!' kind of thing?"

"I wanted to trail you to Kings Cross myself," Paddy continued, "but Engrailed thought you'd be less likely to spot him."

"Marcus," said Myfanwy, as another puzzle piece fell serendipitously in place. "You saw me about to jump on the Edinburgh train. You came up to me. We talked, maybe we argued —"

"Worse than that," said Marcus sheepishly. "I kind of stepped to you. Grabbed you and that. In the nicest possible way. Fisher had said you were solid, but by then I didn't have much conviction in him —"

"You're an excellent judge of character," sniffed Myfanwy. She was still cross with Paddy. No, 'cross' didn't cover it. "So Marcus, are you one of those guys who can hold both my hands with just one of yours?"

"Nah," said Marcus. "I'd need four hands for that."

"So I told you what Veil were doing to Kitty."

"Actually," Marcus laughed, "you proper banged me."

"I did? I really don't remember *that.* To be perfectly frank, I think you're having me on."

"Um, I mean you punched me. Yeah? Gave me —"

"I gave you your black eye too? Ooh, God, sorry! Sorry! Is there anyone I didn't —"

"Don't worry hon," said Kitty. "*My* black eyes are from my torturers."

"It's fine," said Marcus. "After you flipped me, I understood why you punched me. I would have punched me. I mean," he said, looking endearingly confused, "I feel like I did punch me."

"That wasn't all I flipped you, was it?"

"I didn't really trust you, so —"

"So I just flipped you the entire night!"

"You got it. One big chunk. From driving up here, right up until that moment."

"Why not just a glimpse? Wait, I get that too. Because at that stage, I still trusted Blake more than I did Tallulah."

"An excellent judge of character!" cried Blake. "But a terrible handover."

"What happened to quiet times?" snapped Kitty.

"I was going to Chancelhouse to find Blake. Ha! He wouldn't even have been in. But in the meanwhile —"

Marcus nodded and grinned. "While you did that, *I* needed the intelligence you'd gathered on your first raid."

"And so I had to trust you too, Marcus. That you were a new muse, blah blah blah. That really you didn't yet know what Veil were like."

"Yeah. You made me *promise*, blud, that if you could prove to me what Veil had done, I had to go rescue your friend."

"Wow. Do you think I maybe slightly overdid that flip?" said Myfanwy. "In the rush?"

"There was so little time. Meanwhile, you'd go for back-up —"

"And meanwhile also," said Paddy, "back at the rose ranch, I'd spotted Bee with some dude in tow. I had no idea you were the real Jasper, but I thought you looked vaguely familiar. I guess I'd seen you on the bridge at least. I tailed them. Turns out *they* were tailing *you*, Myffed. We arrived in Kings Cross just after you and Engrailed did."

"A muse by any other name," said Kitty, "would smell as sw—"

Blake lunged for Yuri's gun.

Their fists locked. The barrel swivelled to the sky.

"Geeze," said Myfanwy. "No."

Paddy and Marcus had their guns trained on Blake's head. "Drop it." The fist pivoted. Tallulah stepped forward, afraid, raising Simi's sword.

Yuri shot Blake in the head.

*

Blood swept Blake's chin. His eyes rolled and he collapsed.

Marcus went deathly white. He retched.

"So you see everyone," said Paddy softly. "This is quite serious."

Yuri stepped athwart Blake's body. A receding wave swept blood into a long streak.

Blake's cheek twitched. His fingers curled.

"I think he's still alive," said Myfanwy. "Please don't shoot him again, Yuri. Please let us call the ambulance. Just in case. Yuri, I will do anything. Please."

Tallulah was kneeling in the dark water, laying herself carefully across Blake's body. She was holding his head, trembling violently. There was blood on her fingertips.

But there was a small struggle, and Yuri moved aside Tallulah's fingers, and shot him in the head twice more, and then Blake lay dead.

Yuri's grasp disintegrated. The gun fell with a small splash. Jasper lifted it from the bloodying water.

Yuri's eyes shone with tears which wouldn't drop.

"You did what you had to," Jasper said hollowly. He could have tried to sound a bit more convinced.

"Let's go," said Myfanwy. "Come on, Yuri. Let's go."

"Quite serious," said Paddy quietly. "There's just one thing wrong with your story, Myfanwy."

"What about him?" said Kitty. "If we leave him here, the tide will take him."

Some of them could look at him and some couldn't.

The voice which broke the silence was almost unfamiliar. It was Yuri — utterly blank. "I can only see six," he intoned.

It took a moment for Myfanwy to work out Yuri was not talking about six things wrong with her story, but about the six distant muses dwindling down the shoreline.

"*Vertical*," said Kitty softly. "He's gone up the cliffs to the farm houses."

"How many more Veil up on the cliffs?" said Jasper huskily.

Jasper also looked like he might be sick.

Marcus and Paddy both shrugged.

"Veil have touchlesses, don't they?" Kitty shuddered. "They just need to *see* you, to flip you."

Jasper nodded slowly. "Yeah. Heptapora, Achelois."

Was that movement, up on the cliffs?

"I love you," Paddy told Myfanwy unexpectedly. "I don't ever want to lose you. Um, no homo, yeah?"

"They also have guns," said Jasper.

"Okay," Myfanwy decided. "Let's leave him."

*

They walked along the shore. Myfanwy led.

Myfanwy was lost in thought.

When she was not lost in thought, she was lost in conversation. Behind her scampered Jasper, Bee, Kitty — still cuffed, and limping — Tallulah, Paddy, Marcus and Yuri. From time to time, some pair or trio of them came, or one came alone, a little way out of the pack, walked beside her and spoke with her.

Jasper and Marcus and Paddy were near to her now.

"Paddy, I can't believe it."

"Myffed, we're in shock." He dropped his voice. "Yuri's the worst. Man on *suicide watch*, yeah."

Myfanwy shook her head. "Sugar. As if he didn't have enough problems. We're strong though, aren't we? We come intact through what destroys others. Kitty did. We've all been doing it, a little. Is it because we're muses? Or just good liars?"

"Maybe it's because we're young," said Jasper.

Myfanwy ignored him. "What's wrong with my story, Merlin? Or do I mean Fisher King?"

Paddy looked thoughtfully at her hand, slipped into Jasper's. "Neither, fam. Just Paddy will do. And the only thing you got wrong," he said, his voice swollen with stifled anger, "is the *way you look at me when you talk*. Like you don't care *nothing* about me anymore! Please, Myffed — I'm sorry about setting up the meets with Gaga, yeah? I didn't *know*. I'm sorry I had that shooter out on you and Kitty. I have the barbs from my chest in a memory box, yeah? I've started one just for them. You know I could never — I only wanted you to come over to Veil because I didn't trust Blake, Simi, Meletē. You can see why *now*, yeah? I thought you were in danger. I had no idea Germ and Blake were rolling together, or that Simi and Meletē would come over so easily. It was for your protection, Myffed. I messed up. I done wrong. I'll never forgive myself. Ain't that enough?"

"Can I speak to Paddy alone a moment?"

Jasper squeezed her hand and he and Marcus melted away.

"Hi," Myfanwy overheard Tallulah said to Marcus. "How come 'Engrailed'? I'm callname Grande Latté, by the way, eh?"

Myfanwy smiled. She remembered how quickly Kitty had picked the name Nessus. Cool Kids knew how to brand.

Myfanwy felt the frozen smile on her lips, and frowned. "Paddy," she said quietly. "Even though I think you meant right —"

"Allow it!"

"Geezer suggested an Arthurian theme," Marcus was telling Tallulah now. "I've got all these skate trophies. I'm not saying, 'Come back and see my skate trophies,' so."

Tallulah laughed. "I'm gay, so."

"And even after everything we've just been through ," Myfanwy whispered fiercely, "I don't think I can *ever* forgive you for what happened to Kitty."

"You're right *here*," said Paddy. "And *I'm* right here. And yet I miss you so much."

"I'm going to *try* though," said Myfanwy. "I can promise you that much. I'll try as hard as I can. As hard as anyone like me ever could try."

*

Tallulah wanted to be near to her now.

"You okay?" said Myfanwy.

"It's like I'm thinking about her every second," Tallulah said quietly. "Like, it hasn't been really distracting me or slowing me down, or anything. Maybe it is a bit now. But not back there. Still though, every second, I just think, *mum's gone, mum's dead, I can't see her, I can't talk to her, I can't touch her, she can't touch me, she's gone, I won't tell her I came here, I won't not tell her, she'll never know I just called myself Grande Latté, she'll never see me again, I can't see her, mum is dead, mum is gone.* You know, *blah blah blah.* I kind of want it to stop. I want to do it another way."

Myfanwy nodded. "Yeah." She ran through her Garden.

And a nagging paranoid part of her wondered if, in the outside world, she might mix up the land with the sea. So when she eventually turned "inland," and walked up to the spinny, perhaps she would really walk into the sea and drown. Or at least lose the world forever, and spend her life idling, lost, inside herself with figments of friends. Like she'd been lost in one of Kitty's scarytales once, straitjacketed and exultant, partying on a bridge. The last scarytale Kitty had told before Paddy came to St Jerome's and the whole thing began.

She ran through her Garden.

"It's like — I've never know *anyone* who's died. And this is *her*, it's mum. It's like in my brain — I – *gone!* – am – *gone!* – walking – *gone!* – down – *gone!* – the – *gone!* – beach – *gone!* – talking – *gone!* – to – *gone!* – Myfanwy – *gone! Gone.*

Gone. Like that. Folded into everything else. Goes to show how much space there is, eh, just in *being* . . . just space in the world or your heid, all folded up that usually you don't use. All the space. All like *fucking crinkled in* —"

Tallulah sobbed violently three times. She tried to talk but couldn't. When she stopped trying to talk, her sobs turned into soft, semi-controllable crying.

Certainly the spinny they were headed for was more similar to a corner of her Garden panorama than anywhere she'd ever roamed.

Yes. Here she was. A sort of half-path surrounded by tall plants and corseted by tree roots. This spot here, it was *great!* Once on her head there fell a quince! Tall trees cast down full-bleed shade, encompassing this space down to its last crystal of reality. Yet now and then a glitter off the river glowed up among the greenery.

A path of white hay wound round her misshapen dome of moss-heaped tree-root, rose and vanished. It occurred to Myfanwy that it might not be obvious to everyone else that she was a fleck of moss. What would a visitor see? Could there be such a thing as a visitor?

What to tell Tallulah? That it would get easier? Tallulah was so smart. She already knew that it would get easier. And right now it was impossible, completely impossible to feel that it would ever get easier.

Leaves from last year lay tatterdemalion on the hay.

Hmm. The Garden didn't exist last year.

Well done me.

No doubt every young mouse had her navel too.

This was the spot in Myfanwy's Garden where she stashed all her memories of The Powerpuff Girls – an unusually coherent bloc of thematic remembrance. Perhaps, Myfanwy speculated, it was so solid as a sort of side-effect or leakage of the level-headed and enterprising leadership of Blossom Utonium, leader of The Powerpuff Girls.

"So, now how do we get the money to afford the destructoray? Think, girls, think. Except you, Bubbles."

"Just because you're a genius doesn't mean you're so smart."

Myfanwy knew she was only being paranoid about mixing up the Garden and the world. She knew where her Garden really ended and the world began. She *knew*. She knew what was real, knew that Blake was really dead, that Tallulah's mum, whoever she had been, was really dead. Like you know when you're awake. You just know.

Okay, sometimes you dream that you "know" you're awake. But that's different somehow.

Maybe that's what it was like to be mad. You would know they weren't "really" out to get you, but the "really" itself would be wrong.

Hmm.

Myfanwy ran through her Garden towards Tallulah.

"I once saw," Myfanwy said, "a picture of like the first walrus they ever stuffed. They'd just found the skin, no one had ever even seen a walrus, so they just kept stuffing it till it was completely taut and smooth, by which time it was ginormous. And they were like, we made a walrus."

Myfanwy wondered if she had really filled her words with all the soft cadences she'd wanted to. Something a bit like music or the feelings of music, but cadences that said something, something she couldn't ever say with stupid old collages of meaning. She thought maybe she had, a little. But then maybe it was just a massive projection.

Sometimes you think you're being kind, and you're actually being paranoid?

"Aye," said Tallulah. She wiped her nose. "And some things are so shite, you can just say any old shite about them, eh?"

Myfanwy struck up the pose of the stretched walrus.

"*Gone*," said Tallulah, "walrus, *gone*, smooth."

*

Kitty limped and stumbled by her side. "Did you notice Bee was *doodling* back there? I thought she was doing like spy-type escape stuff, but she actually was just awkwardly secretly manoeuvring pen and notebook from her pocket."

Myfanwy smiled. "Geeze, I didn't notice. Bee gets bored easily. It's kind of cute."

"Did Bee flip you, BTW?"

"Yeah. A kind of message, re Moth and Yuri leaving Chancelhouse. Deets later, okay? First, hon, how do you feel?"

"I'm okay," Kitty said. "A bit Chimerical, I think, plus a bit epi. I've skipped my meds. Paddy just watered me though. He spilled it on my top on purpose."

The beach river had run dry. They wandered down into its muddy bed. Up ahead was something dark and indistinct. Not rocks. It seemed to ripple. There were white flecks in it.

"Kit, gosh darn, sister! What just *happened?* When we were in the rockpools, what did you flip round the circle? Everyone who got it just passed it on. Was it what made Yuri . . . uh, turn his gun on Blake?"

Kitty shrugged. "As soon as Blake and Germ banged me up and started knocking me around, I started saving it up. You know? I was going to do what Genevieve Quaker was supposed to have done in the legend. I was going to show them how it felt. But in the end . . . exactly what it was . . . I honestly don't know. It's gone."

Myfanwy hadn't asked Kitty her real question. Did whatever Kitty flipped cause Yuri, minutes later, to pull that trigger? If so, who was really responsible for Blake's death? Yuri, or Kitty? Or everyone who passed it along the circle?

"Can one of us retrieve it from Yuri?" Myfanwy asked.

"No. He flipped it to Blake when he was patting him down."

"Geeze," said Myfanwy. "So it's dead."

"I guess it's best. Blake would have just offloaded it into some innocent mixed-up kid again."

In the distance ahead of them, the indistinct dark band resolved itself. A large company of crows had gathered. A few intrepid seagulls interloped.

"Whatever it was," said Myfanwy thoughtfully, "it could probably have gone round the circle either way. You could have passed it through the three women — Aoide, Gaga and Germ. But you chose to go the long way — Vert, Oni, Triffid, Undine, Cracks. Why?"

"Like I said, I don't know! I mean, I have a vague idea what it was — it was like my version of a Go-Ball. A Hegemony Dog, we may term it. I *really* don't think you'd understand."

"You're using one of your Cool Kid voices, Kitsy. How was it different to a Go-Ball? Just try me, okay?"

"The difference to a Go-Ball being, it was bigger and cruder, and with a higher density of affective memories and information, compared with impulses. Hon, I think I have a bit of patterner in me! I was, like, *archiving* everything they did to me through the night and in the morning. Blake, Gaga, Germ, Undine. But I was *structuring* it too. I was taking all that raw affect, weaving it together in a particular order, with a particular pattern of priorities and associations and, like, logic gates, if/then statements, stuff like that. I'm sort of working this out — it's like a vanishing dream or a variable in calculus or something. I'm still struggling with all the associations and coefficients that got left behind."

"Mathy lady."

"Trust. Maybe too many have been lost. Maybe there aren't enough to know, to ever work it out."

"Perhaps our greatest powers are necessarily opaque to ourselves," said Myfanwy.

"Okay, thanks for being randomly wise Myfanwy."

"Wait, I think I mean transparent. I'm confused. Earlier you called it a Womyn's Castle, you know."

"Did I? I was stressed. TBH, hon, my Hegemony Dog kind of only makes sense *inside my Dwelling*. Your Garden always seems a bit CGI to me, Myfanwy."

"God. Your Dwelling is always how Pizza Express *thinks* of itself."

"Let's not snipe. The weird thing was . . . dude, it never even worked!"

"What are you talking about, hon? Your Ideology Dog was incredible! She saved us!"

"*Hegemony*, hon, and *it* — not '*she*,' hon — was no Hegemony Lassie. Nobody acted, when it entered them! I thought, okay, when they actually *felt* what they'd done to me . . . only, all anyone did was pass the buck. Anyone who got it just passed it on. Then again —"

"Yeah, but wait, they dashed it to someone with a gun, standing next to Blake. That *is* acting."

"Uh-huh. Think about it. Yuri had it in him to kill Blake even *after* he *let go* of what I flipped him! Right? That means he also had it in him *before*."

"Oh. Relieving, in a way. For you."

Kitty shrugged. "I don't really care. But yeah, I think Yuri was just about to crack anyway. Then who knows what Germ and Gaga might have done, if they'd still been strapped? Paddy and Marcus arrived just in time, so it wasn't a total bloodbath. I don't think it was me and my Hegemony Dog that made the difference."

"I'm just not so sure."

Myfanwy thought on Moth's message. Yes. Yuri *was* ready to flee Chancelhouse. Maybe he was also ready to betray Blake.

The company of crows took to the air.

But ready to *kill* him?

"Maybe that's why Blake called him Cracks," Kitty said. "He knew one day he'd crack."

"Ha. More like nobody could crack his codes, I think. But I guess Blake always liked things to mean different things all at once. Wait — so Yuri was a shrouder posing as a taker, but now he can *flip* too?"

"No, that was a temporary thing. Sorry, I missed out one of my best bits! I knew that the thing I flipped might have to pass through Triffid, who's a cloister, and Oni, who I think is a decrypt. So I passed on my talent too. Sort of like a freebie covermount. Yuri's holding onto it."

"Hmm. So you did suspect they might pass the buck."

"Where is Cracks, Myffed?"

"I'll talk to him, hon. One-on-one, okay? Then you get your talent back from him. He needs a clear head right now."

Kitty nuzzled against her forehead against Myfanwy's shoulder, and fell back, and in a moment, Yuri took her place.

*

"You don't remember what Kitty flipped?"

Yuri seemed no higher than her knee. "No," he said. "And perhaps it wasn't the same, by the time it got to me. Perhaps I think it grew."

They were silent a while. She just didn't know what to say to him.

"I wonder," he volunteered eventually, "what shapes the sand so."

He pointed. He meant the sand where the waves still worked it back and forth, where sinuous rills imperfectly spooned one another, filled with shattered shell and deep shadow.

"I bet if all this sand were flat," said Myfanwy, "and you drew a line gently with your fingertip and let the sea come back and forth it would deepen whatever you'd drawn. And crabs and other sons and daughters of Poseidon and Belona would have your finger's whim for their trenches and fortresses."

This seemed to cheer Yuri. No surprises there! For a while more they were silent.

Myfanwy ran through her Garden.

Myfanwy shook her head. "Yuri," she said. "You told us the whole story, didn't you? On our very first night in Chancel. Two moles. Not necessarily Veil. You might be one of them. And we should never talk to you about it again."

Yuri nodded. "He . . . Blake . . . flipped me things very often. So I lost much to him. The more I colluded, the more danger he would discover."

"You've still got Kitty's talent?"

"I have it."

"Blake says — said — it was risky to stack talents unless you're a cloister. I guess he meant the talents might degrade, but I bet it's not exactly helpful to the muse either. So I want you to flip it back, okay?"

Yuri was a picture of indifference. "I don't mind," he said. "For me, two talents is easy-peasy."

"*I* mind, Yuri. Do as I say."

He nodded and half-turned.

A dull crack sounded from somewhere above them. Heads nodded down. Something had altered among their feet. Myfanwy stared dumbly where a little veil of sand had flown up.

Oh.

Someone is shooting at us. Can I hide in my Garden?

The air around her body filled with crows.

*

Cawing and beating surrounded her. Wings smacked into her head and uplifted arms. Little blades scrabbled and nipped at her skin and hair.

"Forget them!" Myfanwy yelled. "They're a decoy! Someone's shooting!" She shrieked as a crow pecked hard at her cheek. "Ow, ow! The shooting's a decoy! *Run! Kitty! Yuri!*" She lashed out into feathers.

Four more little veils of sand flew up around her.

Bee was gently prising crows from off the air and discarding them, like apples into a bucket, on the sand.

Myfanwy glimsped through black thrashing blurs as Kitty's blonde hair slipped over her bound and butchered forearms, Kitty stumbling forward, her head bowing.

A dull loud *crunk* came as Jasper fired at a cluster of rocks atop the cliff.

Kitty fell with a moan to her knees. A fledgling crow swooped at her sporting an aura of kamikaze. With a bijous flying kick and follow-up swat Myfanwy shooed it off Kitty's head. She grasped Kitty's forearms near the cuffs.

"Looly, grab her legs!"

Tallulah had loped off ahead. She turned back uncertainly.

"I'm *fine!*" said Kitty.

"Got her," said Marcus.

Somehow Yuri had seized a large crow by its legs. He whirled this way and that, eyes tightly shut, wielding his cawing, wildly flapping club against the other members of its murder with great violence.

"*I'll* grab my legs!" said Kitty.

Myfanwy and Marcus raised Kitty from the sand and scurried onward through the diving and swirling murder. Any bird Bee touched slipped unconscious to the strand. Gradually their numbers were thinning.

"Such old little horses," Bee explained, "love a low and geostationary orbit."

"Yuri!" cried Myfanwy. "*This* way!"

"Put me down!" barked Kitty. "Save yourselves!"

Myfanwy ran, as best she could, backwards along the beach. Behind the griping Kitty Hammock she and Marcus cherished between them, a sable pathway was strewn to the spot where the birds first had swooped. A few tiles stirred or fluttered softly.

She could tell now that their attackers were mostly crows, but not only: jackdaws, thrushes, a few gulls and even moorhens speckled the fallen flock.

Tallulah was way ahead now, zigzagging elegantly across the dunes in a zealous, put-upon manner. A few crows energetically mobbed her as a side project.

Myfanwy saw blood flow in a bird's breastfeathers. Its small chest was burst apart by a bullet from the cliffs.

Bee kept building her road from scraps of the sky.

Jasper fired again and again. He dropped a flotsam spear that had kept birds at bay, and loaded a fresh cartridge.

"I didn't know you could do that," Myfanwy remarked to Bee.

"Me either," said Bee. "I am a muse. I wonder if it could be connected."

Jasper's figure was dwindling now down the road of birds. Now he knelt down among them, sighting at the gloomy clifftops.

"Jasper!" Myfanwy cried. "Come *on! Jasper!*"

*

They only really slowed when they spotted the path up from the shore.

"I still can't get over you and those crows," Tallulah told Bee. "I know I should."

Kitty craned her neck and planted her chin on Yuri's head. "Nothing to report from the crow's nest!"

Kitty had accepted a piggyback with very bad grace, and a sort of garbled diatribe about how making *Yuri* do it would prove how light she was.

The last few birds had soon flown into the twilight sky. Whoever had attacked from atop the cliffs seemed not to have followed. On the beach, the dark pathway of dark fallen flock had dwindled. Myfanwy pictured the path, the cottages, the spinny. "We're not through the woods yet," she murmured.

"Just a sending to us off," Yuri said, slightly out of puff. "Maybe they is not serious in their meaning."

"Shush, piglet," Kitty chided, with a dim, delirious grin. "Your grammar is *far* worse than usual tonight! Bee, can you haver piglets too?"

"How long will the crow coma last?" Myfanwy asked her.

"You know what?" said Bee thoughtfully. "I just don't know. I have never havered a birdbrain before this very evening. I'd never havered a Tallulah before this very morning. Observe how the infinitely charming Tallulah awakes as soon as you break contact! Whereas here comes the tide, and I believe the snoozing birds will drown. I think it's cruel."

"BTW Jasper," said Kitty, "remember dress-down Fridays? When everyone changed their look for Friday? And remember that film *Freaky Friday*?"

Jasper shook his head bemusedly. Kitty was laughing all the way to the blood bank. They were climbing up the dune now. Knee deep in cold, pale, tall grass flickering in the breeze.

"And remember hashtag FF on Twitter?" Kitty continued. "Well, mash it all up, we can have 'hashtag Flipping Fridays,' where everyone has someone else's body for a day . . ."

"Look at who I drew," Bee said to Myfanwy, "even though my captor Undine intimately monitored my every move." Bee opened a little fluorescent Letts notebook. "No, not that one . . ."

"I know some people find that doodling helps them focus," said Kitty crisply.

"Not me though!" said Bee. "Here, it's this one."

Equus redux.

"So *these* tall horses," hazarded Myfanwy, "are floating around on the backs of bees? Like skate-bees?"

"You've got it all wrong, Mnemo. Those aren't tall dark horses, but the shadows of zebras. The thin stripy things are the backs of zebras."

"Oh, I see the POV is directly overhead. Wow, good cartoon, Bee. Under *any* circumstances!"

"Crow's eye view," murmured Tallulah, dazed.

They mounted the red earth path. It felt good to leave the shore. Myfanwy was growing happier and happier. The spinny was close.

"Can *you* fly, Yuri?" said Kitty. "Hey Myffy, did you get it when I left the voicemail and said, 'I've got the most incredible *roll*, like MacGyver'? It was a roll of duct tape!"

"Ooh!" said Myfanwy with a small smile. "Missed that, Kitsy."

"Aww! You *must* have got Lindt chocolate reindeer's reading of Goddard's *Detéctive*? Oh, Myffy!"

Myfanwy grinned thoughtfully but shook her head. "I got Vitalis Park," she explained. "And Moth's nose, but only because she never had a nose job. That's all."

"Vitalis Park?"

"But I still can't get over Bee and those crows," said Tallulah.

"But mainly, Kitsy, you just sounded weird and freaked out, you know? No codes necessary."

"But reindeer was —"

"I always would have come."

"But reindeer was my *favourite bit!*"

Myfanwy was mystified. "This is supposed to be some private joke you and me have, Kitsy?"

"Film night in my *pied-à-terre*? When we invited the chocolate reindeer to our film night over Christmas, but it was actually a trap? *No?* You don't remember this *at all?*"

"Sorry, hon."

Jasper started to laugh.

"And the chocolate reindeer," said Kitty, glancing to and fro between Jasper and Myfanwy, "is all chuffed that we've invited him . . . and trying to make a good impression . . . and babbling slightly . . . and you and me are just eyeing each other up over his little head . . ."

"OMG," said Jasper, "*that was hilarious!* 'Film Studies Lindt reindeer, I *believe* you! I *believe* you now! Wake *up* Film Studies Lindt reindeer!'"

"Is that supposed to be *me*?" Kitty had giggly, hiccuppy conniptions, disorienting Yuri and introducing a slight zigzag to their progress. "And there was just only a hoof left over . . ."

Jasper lifted a hooked hand and mimed, apparently, remonstrating with a chocolate hoof: "'Film Studies Lindt reindeer, you *weren't* just trying to save yourself! Explain postmodern cinema to me, Film Studies Lindt reindeer!'"

"OK, whevs guys," sighed Myfanwy.

"It's a private joke," Jasper told her primly.

"You had to be there," said Kitty. "Giddyup, Yuri!"

"I is giddying," he grumbled.

Myfanwy rolled her eyes. "Whevs," she grinned. "Things don't end well for Augustus Gloop either, right? Basically you left me an overkill of coded 'save me!' messages, Kitty." She thought about it and beamed again. "Which is maybe why I had to come rescue you *twice!*" she said, and a bunch of them all laughed.

"So is this our happy ending," said Marcus, "till next we face Veil and/or Chancelhouse?"

"Still one remains surrounded by enemies," Yuri panted.

"All the loose ends tied up for you, Myfanwy?" said Jasper.

"Do you want a break, mate?" Paddy asked Yuri.

"Allow it Gandalf," said Kitty. "Yuri's scrawny neck is the perfect fit for my massive thighs."

"As if."

Myfanwy frowned thoughtfully. "I doubt *all* the loose ends are tied up. I mean, I *think* I know how we got where we are. But even if I understand everything, I can't really hold it all in my head all at once! But I think . . . I'm learning new ways of embracing my confusion. You know, kids, there are *many* kinds of embraces. Recently when I go to embrace my confusion, it keeps giving me these, like, lingering squeeze, smell-my-hair kinda hugs? Like my confusion thinks we can be *more* than just friends?"

"Yuri," said Kitty, with a very strict tone. "Doesn't Myfanwy look amazing, given the day she's had? A piff ting, we say idiomatically. Don't you think she makes Xena look like Bella?"

For some reason all the boys sighed in unison. Then all the girls laughed.

"Do you know about Xena, Yuri?" said Tallulah. "You should. I kind of want those birds back. Does anyone else feel like that?"

"Still," Myfanwy added thoughtfully, "there are just one or two things I want to run by Kitty. Is that okay, everybody? I think it might be important. Really important. Can we be alone for a bit?"

"I'm often bang on about certain stuffs," Kitty explained. "Yuri, I'm coming down. There will be extra truffles in your nosebag tonight."

"Stay in sight," said Jasper.

"We'll go ahead a little. Yuri, don't forget to flip Kitty's talent."

"Uh, hon, I'm not sure I even *want* that back. My Dwelling is still intact. It's very clear to me now. Much simpler, but better. More beautiful. More me."

"Flip it to Tallulah then," said Myfanwy. "For now. Oh God, Looly, sorry. You don't want it. Or do you?"

"Maybe," said Tallulah shyly. "I think so. Just a temporary thing?"

"Yeah? You guys talk it out amongst yourselves. And Yuri, you take good care of any memories you get flipped back. Tallulah needs them some day."

"It'll be like a glimpse," said Tallulah. "Of when my *gone* gong has, like, a slower beat. God, those birds!"

"We're going ahead," said Myfanwy. "And you watch over us, okay? Just don't listen in."

*

They went walking, up from the shore, down to the spinny, talking quietly for a time. There they sat on a fallen green trunk.

"Listen hon," said Myfanwy. "This is weird. I don't know how to put it. Even though what you flipped round the circle was empty, it wasn't . . . *empty*. I mean, maybe your pain, or whatever was in the — in the —"

"In the Hegemony Dog," said Kitty primly. "Answers to 'Hegemony Dog'."

"Uh, okay. The experience of last night, anyway. Whatever was in it didn't work directly on Vert, Oni, Ghoul, Undine. Not when it was inside them. But it worked *in*directly on them when it *wasn't* inside them, you know? When they saw Yuri turn his gun on Blake . . . they trusted him. They all remembered that they'd passed something on, and they all trust themselves. They believe in *themselves*, so they believed in *him*. He was their trustee, their representative. Do you see?"

"I get you. They endorsed his act as their own heroism. They assumed they would have done the same in his place. Do you think I could have made that happen on purpose? Am I that clever? I am, aren't I?"

"Who would really have fired the bullet, in Yuri's place? Who knows? But listen, hon. That's not all. Do you remember when we first came to Chancelhouse, and Blake talked about witch-hunts . . . about torture?"

Myfanwy and Kitty kept talking.

Myfanwy talked mostly and Kitty stopped her when she got something a little wrong.

Jasper interrupted them briefly, bringing things from his car. "Yuri finally flipped Kitty's talent. He was really reluctant. I think it's starting to sink in — what he's done. He's not himself at all. It's going to take a long time for him to be okay again."

Myfanwy used the opportunity to probe Jasper a little more. "Is there any memory of that night that you've withheld? The last night you were with Genevieve?"

He shook his head. "Not really." He gave her a hard look. "The truth is, I hardly remember what happened. Something about seeing them . . . bury Gen."

"Gen quarrelled with . . . with her father. She tried to run away from Chancelhouse. You and her got into a punch-up with a few of the others. Meletē threw you through a window."

"Sounds like us," said Jasper, sounding oddly disinterested.

"Just before you blacked out, you heard Gen scream. You might even have dreamed it. You woke up in a garden. Do remember that? Paved in crushed sea-shells? You followed them to the foot of Arthur's Seat."

"Like I say, not really," said Jasper. "Can I just show you something quickly? I know it's a weird time. I only just found it."

Using a tool Jasper had brought, Myfanwy cut through Kitty's zipcuffs. Jasper led them to a huge tree at the edge of the spinny.

"Look," he said proudly.

A bicycle was immured in the trunk. Only its front wheel and handlebars, and a little smile of its back wheel, protruded from the engulfing wood.

"I guess someone leaned it up against it and forgot about it," Jasper said. "The tree kind of ate it, and lifted it."

"You can tell we're not in London," said Kitty. "That front wheel would be *gone*."

"I once found a single slice of bread with a crust running through the middle of it," said Myfanwy. "Like a seam. In the middle of the loaf."

"From what I know of baking," said Kitty, "that's impossible."

Myfanwy was troubled.

"Unless someone shuffled the loaf, hon," said Kitty soothingly.

Myfanwy looked again at the bicycle. "This is *cool*. Have you shown the other guys?"

"It's only Yuri who's still here," said Jasper. "Marcus and Paddy have their ride parked by the cottages. Bee and Tallulah caught a lift. Sugar, maybe I *do* have a funny association with broken sea-shells! Back on the beach. Their edges were, like, totally fascinating!"

"Jasper, keep Yuri company, okay? Don't leave him alone again."

Jasper bit his lip, ducked his head once in apology, and walked away through the trees.

They returned to their fallen green tree trunk. Myfanwy cleaned some of Kitty's burns with soap and bottled water. She daubed her with a salve called Silvadene which rocked all the right stuff on the side of the tube. To a few burns she applied cool compresses and loose bandages.

"I don't really want to mess with these ones though," she admitted.

Some had turned waxy and white.

"On the plus side," said Kitty, "I'll never have to feel guilty about mocking disfigured people!"

"Only mildly disfigured ones hon," said Myfanwy.

"Isn't it relative? I start from a really high level. It's *this* bit here that worries me," said Kitty, indicating where skin was charred. "Because it *doesn't* hurt. Something else for me to miss."

And they talked.

And talked.

Eventually Myfanwy had it all figured out. "Go back to the car, hon. Hang out with Yuri. Charm him with your ways. And send me Jasper. We won't be long."

*

"You wanted to see me, ma'am?"

"Back there by the sea. Why did Undine say, 'I still love you'?"

Jasper shrugged. "Sometimes that just slips out."

"That's true."

"He's the strangest of them all, Undine. And the scariest. I just can't figure him out."

"Sit by me," she said, her heart starting a mad thud.

They sat side-by-side on the same fallen tree where she'd sat with Kitty. The spinny had grown quite dark. She breathed in the mulchy scents.

They weren't quite touching.

"Jasper," said Myfanwy. Nervously she twirled a fresh little leaf in her fingertips. She couldn't remember picking it. "You told me something once. I want to know whether you still believe it. You told me . . . that there were no muses before Blake."

"No muses before Blake. Who knows? But yeah, Meletē, Aoide, Polyhymnia, all the elders — they all knew Blake *before* they were muses. He's known Aoide since she was six, apparently. The earliest muses were mostly Blake's bezzie mates. A few he just stumbled upon and took a shine to. So yes, I don't know how — but I think Blake was always the fountainhead. The inspiration of inspirations."

"You believe Blake gave us all the muse talent?"

"I think he gave it to me. When he realised Gen and me weren't . . . just some summer thing, he tried to make a muse out of me. Like he'd made a muse out of her. You know. *Prospects*. I think I even know the moment he cast me the talent."

"I think you're wrong."

"We had this long, weirdly intense handshake. It's the sort of thing you expect from your bird's da, so. Now maybe there will be no new muses. I still can't believe he's gone, Myfanwy." Jasper shook his head. "What? What am I wrong about?"

"Blake wasn't the first. Genevieve was before him."

"I find that hard to — no. Why? Why should Gen keep something like that from me?"

"She didn't like lying, did she? But did she ever tell you that she *wasn't* the fountainhead?"

Jasper scrunched up his lips contemplatively. Then he broke into a small, sly smile. "No," he admitted. "I mean, not that we remember."

Impulsively she reached up and kissed him with the leaf.

"I'd forgotten we used to do that!" He smiled more broadly but stopped when he saw her face. "Why so sad? Why are you asking this stuff, Myfanwy?"

"I want to go back to the car."

"No. You want to ask me something. I can tell you do."

"Are you sure?"

"Completely."

"What did Blake want from Gen that night? I don't think he ever meant to kill her."

Jasper searched her face carefully. "What did he *want?* To break her. To possess her."

"He wanted something else too," said Myfanwy. "They all did that night. Something . . . *specific*. What was it?"

"What are you saying? How should I know?" Jasper shrugged slowly. "So, so sad. You're smiling but you're so *sad*, Myfanwy."

"Time confused me, Jasper. Paintings, photographs, all the changing names, all the new recruits. The timescale of Chancelhouse seemed impossible. Not any more. There were nine muses, named for the nine muses of Olympus. Terpsichore. You were Terpsichore."

"Yes."

"And Tar was Euterpe. And Undine was called Urania. Mara was Polyhymnia — she became Gaga and helped to found Veil with Calliope and Thalia."

"Yeah. They became Germ and Vertical."

"Calliope, Thalia, Urania, Terpsichore, Euterpe, Polyhymnia. Count them."

"Six."

"Only six muses. *Nine* were spoken of. At first I assumed the others were Mnemosyne, Aoide and Meletē. Blake above them all, as Zeus. That's not right though, is it?"

"No, it's not right," said Jasper. "Those three took their callsongs from an older tradition. The three Boetian muses, Mnemosyne, Aoide and Meletē. Before the nine Olympian muses. Some say Zeus and Mnemosyne were mother and father to the nine."

"The three and the nine," Myfanwy said with a gentle nod. "Plus Zeus above them all. Chancelhouse's first incarnation. The nine never included Mnemosyne, Aoide or Meletē, did they? The nine were Terpsichore, Euterpe, Polyhymnia, Calliope, Thalia, Urania . . . and Erato, Clio and Melpomene. Three muses I've never met."

"Not surprising."

"And seldom heard spoken of, and only very dimly recall. But they lived with you in Edinburgh, long before the Veil split. In those early days of Chancelhouse. They were there — the day Gen tried to run."

Jasper nodded. He looked slightly away, then met her gaze levelly.

"Jasper?" Myfanwy didn't want to go on. "What became of them? Erato, Clio, Melpomene? They didn't go over to Veil, did they?"

"No," Jasper said eventually. "They were like me. They fled. They wouldn't pledge either to Chancelhouse or to Veil. After everything that happened, after what they *let* happen to Gen — they tried to flee from what they'd done. Erato, Clio and Melpomene. They were every bit as guilty. I've always known that. I've always believed it."

"They ran. Then what? Tell me the whole truth, Jasper. It matters."

"They split up, got as far as they could. They laid low. Erato — Toby — I tracked him to Bytom, in Poland. Then I lost him for a bit. He popped up again in Tibet. I lost him again. Could be anywhere in the world. Can't get a trace on him."

"Melpomene?" she urged. "Did you find her?"

"Sophie was in Texas. Yeah. That's where."

"Oh, Jasper! What aren't you telling me?"

He shook his head angrily. "You should know. It's who I am. And Clio, her whereabouts I never learned. Clio's betrayal was the hardest to take. But not a trace of her since the night they murdered Gen. I searched hard for Clio. I so wanted her to be the next to pay for what she'd done. Clio was her — *friend.* She should have *protected* her. Instead —"

"Oh, Jasper." Myfanwy shifted closer to him. Their arms and legs touched. She spoke softly, flatly. "How do you *know* Genevieve died, the night you heard her screaming? You know so little, Jasper. You assume so much. How do you know it was her that Tar and Meletē buried that night?"

"Because," said Jasper, leaning away. He was silent a moment. "Because she's dead, Myfanwy. Because she's never coming back. Her bones are down there. They used to be in my dreams. We can find her now. In the cement. Gen's bones prove Gen's gone. We can take them up. Make sure she is buried. It's time, I think. A grave. You're right, it's time. A grave." He hesitated, barely daring to hope. "Unless —"

"Jasper," Myfanwy said quickly. "Make no mistake. Genevieve is *gone*. She's never coming back. But where is Clio? The memories you flipped me, the ones you told me would clear everything up — everything about them feels wrong. You let your fear and guilt fill in so much, Jasper. You just said Clio should have protected Gen. But what if she *tried* to? You never saw Clio after that night. What if Clio — gave her life, that night, trying to protect Gen? Standing where you would have stood?"

"I can barely remember anything. *You* were there now, not me. I need my diaries —"

"Forget your diaries. You have me. I think it's Clio's bones that lie buried, Jasper. Not Genevieve's. You heard about a body. You never saw a face."

"I have you. We'll go there — we'll dig —"

"It's Chancelhouse we have to go to. There is a room in the west houses we must visit. I remember, as you, Jasper, the bedrooms which were once where the Cache now stands. I remember Gen's room. Black curtains tied up with one white and one green-and-lilac string."

Myfanwy's voice broke. She paused for a moment, then, when Jasper seemed about to speak, she forced herself on.

"The west houses . . . have transformed, Jasper. But I also remember, as Kitty, seeing one door that was left *untouched* — although its sign was ripped away. One untouched room, still tucked in beside the Cache."

"I can't remember," said Jasper. "I don't understand. She can't be there. She can't be."

"And I can't be sure. No, I can't be sure. We just have to go there, okay? I don't remember if we'll need a code. Maybe we'll have to break it down. We'll go together, okay? You can hold my hand and —"

"*What room is it?* I can't remember. What are you saying about her? What happened to Genevieve?"

Myfanwy could not speak. She blinked against the tears, but they flowed anyway. "I can't be sure," she said finally. "I feel so sure, but I can't trust myself. I'm sorry. No, I'm *not* sorry — the little room was Genevieve's room,

Jasper. The room where you and I and she — oh, *why* was it kept, Jasper? Blake's sentimentality, his grief? Over a murdered delinquent daughter? How easy is it to change a dead child's room? But perhaps there was a different reason. Perhaps Blake never intended Genevieve to die. She was only being naughty, after all. She wanted to run away. She was only being wilful. He wanted what was best for her. He *knew* what was best for her. 'You can leave if you like, Genny, but you leave your talent with me. Not until you've proved you can use it responsibly.' That's what he would have said, isn't it? And here's my guess. It wasn't just any talent Gen had inside her. It was the inspiration of inspirations. Would Blake have destroyed the very source of the muse talents? Never."

"Yet I would always remember hearing her die."

"I remember that scream. You carried it with you, but you never understood it. In me, it means something different. It wasn't a body's scream. It was a spirit's scream. Not a scream of pain. A scream of *disorder*, Jasper. Of a spirit coming apart."

"I don't remember much," said Jasper quietly. "I don't know so much about that scream, any more."

"I do. And maybe even now, the form of Genevieve Quaker lives alone in that room. The face we remember. That we loved. The *living* face, though that's a silly word, living. Because her spirit was scattered abroad, Jasper. I saw her in her father. But I see her in the others too. In Undine, in Aoide, in Tar, in Vertical, in Meletē, in Gaga. In every muse who questioned her that night. You were sleeping then, my love. In a way, you've been sleeping ever since. Why did you never see it, Jasper? See our Gen? See her alive in the nine muses who ransacked her? Gen would have run from Blake that night. She would have taken her talent with her. Take it where he couldn't control it, couldn't control her. So he told them. Told them that *she* was the fountainhead. That it was she who had made him a muse, made all of them muses. Come to her father with a gift, and then chosen to remain demurely in the shadows. Smiling, sarky, watchful. But now they sought to steal it from her once and for all. Rummaged in her almost at random. The taker, Urania, he must have looted her the most. 'Confess! Confess!' Gen never did. Clio didn't join in. Clio tried to stop it, and she paid with her life. Calliope didn't join in. She was a mirror muse, she couldn't. Perhaps that's why she led the Veil exodus, eventually. Convinced herself she was horrified. That she was innocent. But she's not innocent. She didn't stop them. Undine taking, and the casters and skillers throwing themselves into Gen. Anything they didn't want or could spare, every pain and guilt, every lapse and trauma and regret. Casting more and more into her, filling her up, filling her up so more and more of her poured out into them. Each wanted to be the one to find it, to have the fountainhead talent. Gen hid it so deep. They contended, but no one won. Everything low and sorrowful they sacrificed. And they sifted whatever the debris came flying the other way, and just kept pouring. But one by one, and all far too late, they gave up. Perhaps it was the appetite, the competition, that had made them go so far. Perhaps it was her screams. Into her body flowed a spirit made of nine others. Mostly the poorest shares. Whatever share of themselves the muses least loved. And even now I think someone still lies there, Jasper. A strange being, shaped from those poorest shares, locked up in her room in the houses in the west, trying to make sense of her world. A living face. And everything Mnemosyne ever was before that night has been scattered among those nine. Now Blake is gone, and Jasper — with Blake, something of Gen dies. Truly dies, I think for the first time. I hope, Jasper, for the first time. Though no matter what else happens, all these years she has been fading, lost in their lives. She fades still."

"Seven."

Catastrophe dulled Jasper's voice. Myfanwy bowed her head.

"If Erato hadn't fled me," he said, "if Polyhymnia hadn't survived me, it could have been five. But it is *seven*, Myfanwy. *Seven*."

"I had hoped," she whispered, "you weren't going to say that."

"Seven."

"Seven then. Yuri murdered Blake, and with him, a part of Gen. But before today, you murdered Melpomene. Mara wasn't the first on your list. Before you came to murder Mara, you murdered Melpomene."

"Melpomene. Sophie Black. Yes. She fled the country. It was me she was fleeing, I suppose. She was living on a farm in Texas. I tracked her there. I . . . later, in Tibet, when I confronted Erato, he just *ran*. I never found him again. He ran. Vanished. Knew why I was there. But Melpomene never ran. Told me she'd changed. She knew why I was there. Why I was there. She knew but she didn't run. She *begged*. Oh, God. It was Gen who was begging. *It was Gen*."

"Hush, Jasper. Kiss me on the lips. You murdered the one I love. Oh, now kiss me."

They kissed, their faces wet and hot with tears.

"No," he said. "No."

"Yes. The day you killed Melpomene," Myfanwy said, slipping into his frail embrace, "you killed whatever part of Genevieve she kept alive within her. You said Genevieve had nine murderers. You were so wrong. The only murderers she has ever had are time, which murders us all, and little Yuri, who is so troubled, and you."

*

Kitty entered the spinny, ghostly pale. "Hon," she said. "Can I scare you half to death?"

Yuri appeared behind her with a gun in his small hampster-esque hand. His eyes blazed. "At least! Yes, yes," he said with grim rapidity, "one last thing — quite like my keycard back. Really I ought to change the Chancelhouse codes more often, oughtn't I? Do you see, my dears? I wasn't grabbing the poor boy's *gun* back there on the beach! I was grabbing his fingers! Well, every story has its little moral, yes, yes! Hadn't planned on taking up residence *chez* Cracks for another few weeks. But then, what with the poor little fellow spontaneously combusting . . . waving that wretched thing around . . . well, that said, *was* it *spontaneous* combustion, eh? The nuance of 'spontaneous' vis-à-vis 'extemporaneous' is quite fascinating! A *spontaneous* combustion would have to come from *within*, whereas Nessus meddling with Crack's noggin suggests something else . . . mm, let's see . . . *impromptu* combustion would be exploding on the spur-of-the-moment . . . whereas an *extemporaneous* combustion, you'd have a pretty good *idea* you'd be called on to explode, but you wouldn't plan it all, you'd sort of 'explode as you went along' . . . gauging the mood of the room, and all that . . . maybe with one or two keywords to guide you . . . well, anyway, *smash!* Ha ha! No more Cracks. If you want to make a *homlette*, as they say, you must break some . . . though of course, it was the Egg preserved in this instance . . . I mean really, you need to chop some onions and grate some courgette too, mustn't you? No one ever sheds tears over the courgette! Onion's another matter. Oh, keep up, you two! Did I mention that rule? Well, I think I may become quite insane! Which *surely* would warrant a new callsong! 'Haduken Cracked'? Ha, ha, ha! Shall I splatter you all over the trees, my dears? What do you think of 'Haduken-is-Back'? Ha, ha! I don't mind saying, I don't feel quite *right* in here, you know! Yuri's Dwelling is a quite terrible place. Quite awful. I had no idea such places existed! You feel your *skin* is already *dust* while it's still *on* you. I thought I'd feel young again! Is that sad? I feel so much *older*. Lol, eh? It feels . . . haunted. Ha! Yes, that's just the word. I feel there are others in here with me. Hell, I'm in Hell, but I'm still *here* too. Did you feel that way, Terpsichore? When you traded with Oscar? Just at first? Did you get that sense that you were . . . no? You're just saying that! You're just being kind to be cruel, aren't you, ha ha ha! Dear boy, did it *really* take you months for you and Oscar to swap over? I slipped in Cracks in half a second. Is that unfair? — I suppose it's all about prep! Months of prepping poor little Cracks for it, and I think he suspected it too! Like those veggie options, eh Mnemosyne? "Marinading," yes, yes! Prep thoroughly beforehand, then it's just a matter of *shoving* it all in! And the vegan options, obviously. My apologies, it's been a stressful day. Yuri chose *Marinade* for Chancelhouse — I might reboot as *Marienbad*, I believe, for this new era!

Well, can't stay all day. Looks like rain. With a constant supply of fresh blood, we're *immortals*, you and I, Terpsichore. Yes, yes. In a way, I suppose, we're *vampires* after all. Vampires after all. The keys to your car would be handy. Come on! Most kind. Pity it's such a hunk of rust. And that junk you keep in there! Took me ages to find this little shooter. Thought I might have to menace you with a submarine! That would have been memorable, eh? Can't say I think much of Yuri as vehicle either. Pigeon chest, skinny little arms like soggy baguettes. I *was* trying to train him up, you know. All-ball, health and wellness, all that. Make a man of him. That man being me. Just my rotten luck he was a melancholic. I'll miss you, my dears! I'll miss you so much! And the *junk* he kept in here. Well, adieu, my dears. I'll be seeing you anon — hold your blasted tongue, Mnemosyne, I *am* being grammatically correct, I mean 'anonymously' of course! *Au revoir,* until we meet again . . ."

EPILOGUE

Epilogue goss — Paddy and Kitty totally got together.

I know, right? Everyone assumed she would eat him up and spit him out! Leaving yours truly as piece-picker-upper in chief, as per usual.

But it actually seems like it's going okay!

Do I mind?

I don't mind. I'm so into Jasper. And he's so into me.

Plus Bee and Tallulah (callsong Tall Order) are on and off, incredibly riotous and tumultuous and romantic. You only live once, right?

I don't mean that literally, obv.

So, like, I'm not sure I can totes 100% endorse everything you've been reading. All those asterisks and italics and long dashes — give me a break!

Plus, I really don't think of myself as that bookish and prim and temperamental!

Plus, what kind of person doesn't know a four-litre hand-held propane blowlamp when she loses her eyelashes to one, or even the proper names and specs for the P226 SIG Sauer side-arm, the Heckler & Koch HK417 7.52mm calibre sharpshooter rifle, the FN Minimi L110A1 belt-fed LMG, the Bullpup SA80, grenade launcher accessoriseable, or the L129A1 7.62x51mm calibre long range semi-automatic rifle — am I right?

And that bombastic Auld Reekie Citadel, built out of black honey! Mein Gott!

I guess that's the risk you take, when you go get your ghost-writer almost at random, at the end of the Foule Series Poetry Open Mic night, as all the poetasters bustle with their brollies, down the pub back-stair, when you go brushing your hand against the small of her back, because you thought you quite liked the poem she read, although you weren't really listening too hard . . .

Then what?

Suddenly the poet is writing a novel, something she's never done before. In two months, it's done. So fast. Awake late. Flowing onto the page. As though possessed . . .

What a prang.

There are nine of us now, in the new organisation. Me, Jasper, Kitty, Paddy, Marcus, Triffid (semi-forgiven), Moth, Bee and Tallulah.

Tallulah ended up keeping the caster talent which Mara stashed in Kitty, and then Kitty stashed in Blake, when everybody thought Blake was Yuri. She likes it. We're all really glad she's agreed to keep it.

And Paddy AKA Merlin was right about Kitty — she did *have her own talent, right from the start! Which kind of explains why her Dwelling was always so nuts and OTT — two talents were struggling for dominance!*

She's nurturing her new talent and she's not sure yet exactly what it is. She's some kind of patterner. Maybe a cloister, or a mirror, or a shrouder . . . or even something new entirely.

What else can I tell you?

Our organisation is new. So new we haven't even got a name yet.

But we already have our first mission. Actually, I've had enough of missions. Let's call it a quest.

We found the real Mnemosyne, just where I said she'd be.

Chancelhouse was in total disarray. Nobody had seen Blake since the day in the spinny. We got in and out as quickly as we could, and we took Mnemosyne with us. A few who were left tried to stop us. At one point Kitty had to kick Grimalkin where it would count. Triffid helped us do it — that's why we figure he's okay, for now anyway.

Mnemosyne is terrifying! OMG, she makes Bee look like, you know, the total paragon of the patriarchal stereotype of sanity and got-it-togetherness. She talks like Twitter or a prophetess.

Kitty is kind of in awe of her. Kitty's kind of regressing to her shortlived Roman *Catholic / Liberation Theology phase, except with Mnemosyne in the place of La Santa María de la Inmaculada Concepció. Kitty's a bit strange these days. I think it's not just because of what she went through. She also put a whole lot of herself into that thing she cast. A lot of what it's like to be her, I think.*

Maybe too much.

Though Kitty vs. Grimalkin was a joy to behold, I gotta say. Maybe she'll get back to her old self yet.

Anyway, her and Pad reckon Mnemosyne is defo still the fountainhead of all muse talents. They reckon that's the reason there were so many new muses recently. Locked up in that room, it was Mnemosyne's only way of calling to the world. And it did lead us to her, in the end. Almost like she chose *us . . .*

Superstitious nonsense, obvs.

Though I often wonder nowadays just how much Blake foresaw, in giving us all callsongs. They always seemed a bit pointless. Not anymore. Because now that we've found "Mnemosyne" . . .

. . . we've promised to find "Genevieve."

To gather what was stolen that night in the west houses and strewn all round the world, sown in nine different places.

We've promised to undertake this quest. It means finding eight elder muses —Meletē, Simi, Tar, Gaga, Vertical, Undine, Erato and Blake — who may not want to be found! Bit of an ask! Then suturing her together, or what's left of her, or what's become of her.

How do I feel about this, you ask?

Is it really our place to put Genevieve and Mnemosyne back together? Do the parts want to be put back together? Are they happier where they are? Or more sorrowful and yet somehow, like, better?

Anyway, that's supposing we can even find the eight elder muses.

Or maybe . . . just maybe . . . find nine.

Because, we've had messages. We also think they're from Toby, callsong Erato, the muse who disappeared. Trying to set up a meet in Cairo. Well, whoever it is, they say they have something they need to tell Jasper. Something to do with what happened the day this person flipped into the mind of someone they loved, the very moment that person died.

So that might be interesting . . .

Okay, clearly I have somewhat conflicted feelings about all this! Jasper swears he's all about me now, that him and Genevieve — Jaspervieve, as Kitty calls them obvs — are history.

But Kitty says history is a tricky area and ex-girlfriends is a really tricky area and I should watch out. You know, like what if she starts getting him to schlep around and do all this stuff for her, like enter the Underworld to bring back the last lost ninth of her soul . . .

As you maybe can tell, I've got stuff on. I better go.

I've been calling myself Melpomene, BTW, since we found the first Mnemosyne. It just seemed right. I thought "Mel" might be a nice and innocuous nick name. Mel and Ness — people would think you're just a Melissa and a Vanessa! Ha ha!

Failing that, "Mene" sounds like it could viral.

But everyone just calls me "Poem."

Bye for now. Take care with yourselves. We are alive in amusing times.

Acknowledgements

Special thanks to: Alison Croggon (DPS), jUStin!katKO (DPSPS), Mike Wallace-Hadrill (healer), Samantha Walton (tank). Thank you also: PiP (esp. nick-e melville, Colin Herd, Iain Morrison, Lila Matsumoto, & Greg Thomas), Robert Kiely, the Goat, Edinbrother Sophie Robinson, Charlie Boz, Alexandra Beal, Gwydion Benyon (who told me stories), Chloe Mona Ivy Head (who told me facts), Sean Bonney (who wrote Marcus's neck), Magda Boreysza (who drew the dogs), Ryan van Winkle (who told me so), Ian Heames, Spring Decoys, Christopher Doyle, Tony Daly, Ciara Reagan, Lara Buckerton, Helen True, Caitlin Doherty, Frances Kruk, Jenny Ready, Lorqel Blanks, Sylvia Villa, Francesca Lisette, Jeremy Prynne, Josh Stanley, Fabian MacPherson, Jane Austen, Mary Findlater, Jane Findlater, Dr Button, Sarah MacDiarmid, Georgie M'Glug, Gladys Mitchell, Harkheimer Keat, Pickle, FL Carsten, Connie Scozzaro, Crime Scotland, Keith Tuma, Fluxes x2 of Cork and of Cam, Mr Prickles, Paul Trembath, Kayleigh Bohan, James Cummins, Rachel Warriner, David Strong, Norbert Schausberger, Peter Gay, Melinda Churches, Christopher Churches-Lindsay, James Lindsay & Claire CC Lindsay, & the Aunties. And of course anyone I may have . . . *forgotten* . . .

Contact

Twitter: @jolwalton
Justin Katko's Critical Documents: www.plantarchy.us

Invocation is the first of The Poet Boiler Trilogy, or Quartet, completed by *Interlude*, and/or perhaps by *Integration*, and *Interpellation, or, Mrs. Knowles-Carter, His Tragedie* – all working titles – & also obviously it *should* be the first novel in the Myfanwy Morris: Intergalactic Muse of Mystery series. But you may have to write the others yourself. ISBN of first edition (1.X) was 978-1-4811052-9-3.

Dramatis Personae

NB: Contains spoilers. Queries and suggested amendations are very welcome. Since muse talents can be handed from muse to muse, the ascriptions given here should be understood as provisional and based in reputation and operational categorisation within the now largely defunct organisations Chancelhouse and Veil. The muse talents are moreover proving themselves increasingly unamenable to the traditional taxonomy devised by Haduken Blake, as implied, for instance, by Vertical's animality, Germ's Go-Ball, Kitty's Hegemony Dog, Bee's stunning of crows and other fowl, Paddy's characterisation of Marcus's talent, and the totalising flips practiced by Jasper and Oscar and by Blake and Yuri.

Abbas. See Macleod, Abbas.

Achelois. AKA Ache. Veil touchless muse. Wounded by Jasper Robin during the raid on Veil HQ.

Adika. Pupil at St Jerome's Senior School.

Aglet. Chancelhouse muse. Killed in the Chancelhouse-Veil purges.

Akifemwe, Patrick. AKA Paddy. Close friend of Myfanwy. Blazon muse. Chancelhouse callsong Merlin, Veil callsong Fisher King.

Ameonna. Chancelhouse muse. Killed in the Chancelhouse-Veil purges.

Anu. Pupil at St Jerome's Senior School.

Asphyxia Noir. Chancelhouse muse. Killed in the Chancelhouse-Veil purges.

Atë. Chancelhouse caster muse.

Bee. Chancelhouse caster muse, loyal to Jasper Robin. Borrowed Moth's havering talent for the raid on Veil HQ.

Bigwig. Veil muse.

Bit. Chancelhouse muse. Killed in the Chancelhouse-Veil purges.

Black, Sophie. Chancelhouse callsong Melpomene. One of the nine Apollonian elder muses in the first era of Chancelhouse. Sophie Black fled Scotland to Texas following the Chancelhouse-Veil split, and was hunted down and killed by Jasper Robin. Blake claimed, untruthfully, that Sophie was the sitter for the portrait in the Chancelhouse library.

Blake. See Quaker, Haduken.

Brocken. Veil muse. Non-canon. Although you have read about Brocken, this is a muse who always manages to remove your memory of doing so.

Buckerton, Simon. Pupil at St Jerome's Senior School. Currently the first boy Myfanwy ever kissed.

Bullock, Simedelay. AKA Simi. Callsong Aoide. Arch-Chancellor, Master Mystagogue, Head of Development, Chair of Senatus Academicus, and High Balneator of Chancelhouse. Co-convener, with Blake, of the Chancelhouse All-Ball

Tournament. Before the Chancelhouse-Veil split, Aoide was one of the three Boeotian elder muses, along with Meletē and the first Mnemosyne. A lifelong friend of Blake.

Caddy. Chancelhouse muse. Killed in the Chancelhouse-Veil purges.

Calliope. One of the nine Apollonian elder muses in the first era of Chancelhouse. She left Chancelhouse and founded Veil, adopting the callsong Germ. She remains the closest Veil comes to having a leader. Originally a mirror muse, she has collected many muse talents.

Cameron, Sarah. Pupil at St Jerome's Senior School.

Cithara. Veil muse. Killed in the Chancelhouse-Veil purges.

Clio. AKA Chloe. Close friend to Genevieve Blake. One of the nine Apollonian elder muses in the first era of Chancelhouse. Killed shortly before Chancelhouse-Veil split.

Clone. Veil mirror muse.

Copycat. Veil mirror muse.

Cracks. See Yuri.

Cria. Veil muse. A close friend of Scan. Killed in the Chancelhouse-Veil purges.

Cricetid. Chancelhouse muse. Killed in the Chancelhouse-Veil purges.

Cricket. Veil doolittle muse. It is likely that Cricket and/or Not Cricket convened the flock which attacked Kitty's rescue party on the beach near Veil HQ.

Croque, Francis. Celebrated Edinburgh-based author.

Crypt. Veil shrouder muse.

Cui. Veil muse. Killed in the Chancelhouse-Veil purges.

Dopple. Veil mirror muse.

Dora JayJay. Pupil at St Jerome's Senior School.

Dorothy. See Farmer, Dorothy.

Down. Veil muse. Suspected to be doolittle or doolittle-taker class.

Drago-Ferrante, Tamara. AKA Mara. Before the founding of Chancelhouse she was a friend of Blake. She was one of the nine Apollinian elder muses in the first era of Chancelhouse, under the callsong Polyhymnia. Following the Chancelhouse-Veil split she joined Veil, adopting the callsong Gaga. She lost her caster talent to Kitty. It was later passed through several muses, embedded in Kitty's Hegemony Dog, finally winding up with Tallulah. It is unknown whether she has acquired a replacement caster talent, although one of Myfanwy's comments seems to assume that she has.

Dribble. Chancelhouse muse. Killed in the Chancelhouse-Veil purges.

Eft. Chancelhouse dryad muse. Shared a corridor with Myfanwy and Kitty.

Egg. See Quaker, Haduken.

Enenra. Chancelhouse muse. Killed in the Chancelhouse-Veil purges.

Erato. AKA Toby. Caster muse. One of the nine Apollonian elder muses in the first era of Chancelhouse. Fled after the Chancelhouse-Veil split. Whereabouts unknown.

Erinaceine. Veil muse. Killed in the Chancelhouse-Veil purges.

Esi. Pupil at St Jerome's Senior School.

Esterhase, Catherine. AKA Kitty. BFF of Myfanwy Morris. Chancelhouse callsong Nessus. Also briefly went by Anastasia von Enigmengera. Before learning to develop her patterner talent, she acquired a caster talent from Tamara Drago-Ferrante. Used both talents in creating a Go-Ball-like effect which she described as her Hegemony Dog.

Euterpe. See Tar.

Fairfax, Sid. Pupil at St Jerome's Senior School. In Myfanwy's A-Level art class. Friend of Kevin Thomas.

Farmer, Dorothy. Veil muse, callsong Foreigner. A close friend of Scan. Killed in the Chancelhouse-Veil purges.

Fisher King. See Akifemwe, Patrick.

Fletcher, Corina. Police officer. Responsible for the death of the activist Molly Miller during the eviction of Bridge Croft.

Flux. Cat. Friend of Rook.

Fontleroy, Detective Inspector. Police officer who tried to interview Myfanwy about Jasper Robin's attempted murder of Mara Drago-Ferrante.

Foreigner. See Farmer, Dorothy.

Frances. Friend of Kitty Esterhase.

Frog. Chancelhouse muse. Killed in the Chancelhouse-Veil purges.

Gaga. See Drago-Ferrante, Tamara.

Geist. Chancelhouse muse. Killed in the Chancelhouse-Veil purges.

Genevieve. See Quaker, Genevieve.

Gid. Veil muse. Killed in the Chancelhouse-Veil purges.

Glass. Veil mirror muse.

Golem. Chancelhouse driver muse.

Gordon, Tallulah. AKA Looly. Pupil at St Jerome's Senior School. Member of a clique dubbed the Cool Kids or the Asians. In Myfanwy's art class. Wore snails at Kitty's eighteenth birthday party. Acquired a muse talent and adopted the callsong Tall Order.

Grimalkin. Chancelhouse cloister muse. Shared a corridor with Myfanwy and Kitty. Previously worked in Haduken Blake's bindery.

Haduken. See Quaker, Haduken.

Haecceity. Veil muse. Killed in the Chancelhouse-Veil purges.

Heptapora. Veil touchless muse.

Hick. Veil muse.

Horae. Chancelhouse cutter muse.

Hypnos. Chancelhouse muse. Killed in the Chancelhouse-Veil purges.

Jamie. Cloister muse. Chancelhouse callsong Triffid, Veil callsong Ghoul. Arrived at Chancelhouse not long before Myfanwy and Kitty. Besides Yuri, he was the only Chancelhouse muse known to have known that a conspiracy existed between Blake and Germ.

Jasper. See Robin, Jasper.

Jemima. Pupil at St Jerome's Senior School. Member of a clique called the Cool Kids AKA the Asians.

Kaiou. Chancelhouse muse. Killed in the Chancelhouse-Veil purges.

Kenneth. AKA Passenger for Norfolk. Useless man whose help Myfanwy enlists in a confrontation with Jasper Robin.

Kermitcrab. Chancelhouse caster muse.

Kevin. See Thomas, Kevin.

Kojo. Pupil at St Jerome's Senior School.

Kratos. Muse, presumably Chancelhouse, killed by Germ.

Ladybird. Veil mirror muse.

Lake, Stacy. Pupil at St Jerome's Senior School. In Myfanwy's A-Level art class.

Lap. Chancelhouse muse. Killed in the Chancelhouse-Veil purges.

Leech. Veil taker muse.

Lego. Chancelhouse cloister muse.

Lewis. See Porteous, Lewis.

Lucia. Pupil at St Jerome's Senior School. Member of a clique dubbed the Cool Kids or the Asians. Myfanwy has semi-deliberate difficulty remembering her name, thinking of her as Lucinda, Lala, Logan, Cecil, Samphire and Lucy.

MacAonghas, Professor. Kitty's therapist.

Macleod, Abbas. Veil callsong Vertical. As Thalia, he was one of the nine Apollonian elder muses in the first era of Chancelhouse. Originally a skiller muse. It is possible he has now acquired a doolittle talent: Meletē theorised that he has absorbed significant beast skills.

Mara. See Drago-Ferrante, Tamara.

Marcus. Veil callsong Engrailed. Self-taught muse with skiller and other capabilities. Lent his skateboard to Jasper Robin and his ability to skate to Myfanwy.

Marienbad, Duke. See Quaker, Haduken.

Marinade. See Yuri.

Meletē. Skiller muse. Praetor and Chief Arms Officer at Chancelhouse. Before the Chancelhouse-Veil split, Meletē was one of the three Boeotian elder muses, along with Aoide and the first Mnemosyne.

Melpomeme. Callsong used by approximately two different muses. See Morris, Myfanwy and Black, Sophie.

Merely-Pointy, Valerie. AKA Madame Merely-Pointy, AKA MP. Art teacher at St Jerome's Senior School.

Merlin. See Akifemwe, Patrick.

Metis. Veil muse. Killed in the Chancelhouse-Veil purges.

Miller, Molly. Activist, killed during an action at Bridge Croft to resist the eviction of a community of travelers.

Mimesis. Veil mirror muse.

Mnemosyne. Callsong used by approximately two different muses. See Morris, Myfanwy and Quaker, Genevieve.

Moirai. Muse, presumably Chancelhouse, killed by Germ.

Moo. Pupil at St Jerome's Senior School.

Morris, Myfanwy. Caster muse. AKA Myffy, Myffed, Mnemosyne, Mnemo, Melpomeme, Poem.

Morris, Peter. Myfanwy's father.

Moth. Chancelhouse haverer muse. Arrived at Chancelhouse not long before Myfanwy and Kitty. Lent her talent to Bee during the raid on Veil HQ.

Namond. Pupil at St Jerome's Senior School.

Neilo. Chancelhouse caster muse.

Not Cricket. Veil doolittle-caster muse. It is likely that she and/or Cricket convened the flock which attacked Kitty's rescue party on the beach near Veil HQ.

Nova. Chancelhouse caster muse.

Oni. Veil decrypt muse.

Oscar. Activist who resisted Bridge Croft eviction. Also a worker in Haduken Quaker's bindery. Close friend of Jasper Robin and Genevieve Quaker. Following the disappearance of Genevieve, Oscar swapped bodies with Jasper Robin. Killed by Static during Operation Terpsichore.

Ouzo. Chancelhouse skiller-taker muse.

Paddy. See Akifemwe, Patrick.

Pest. Veil muse. Wounded by Jasper Robin during the raid on Veil HQ.

Phan, Bella. A person invented by Haduken Blake. Supposedly the daughter of Mrs Phan.

Phan, Mrs. A person invented by Haduken Blake. Supposedly a neighbour of Chancelhouse.

Polyhymnia. See Drago-Ferrante, Tamara.

Porteous, Lewis. Pupil at St Jerome's Senior School. Briefly the boyfriend of Kitty.

Puck. Chancelhouse dryad muse.

Quaker, Genevieve. Fountainhead muse. Chancelhouse callsong Mnemosyne. Daughter of Haduken Quaker. In the first era of Chancelhouse, she was one of the three Boeotian elder muses, along with Aoide and Meletē. Static and Paddy theorised that the first muse in this world may have been the accidental recipient of a hypothetical master taker talent, soon complemented by a master caster talent.

Quaker, Haduken. AKA Blake AKA Duke Marienbad. Founder of Chancelhouse. Father of Genevieve Quaker. Adopted the name Haduken Blake and the callsong Zeus during the first era of Chancelhouse. Following the Chancelhouse-Veil split he changed his Chancelhouse callsong to Seuss. Later he adopted the Veil callsong Egg.

Currently occupying the body that was once Yuri's. Whereabouts unknown.

Robin, Jasper. Worker in Haduken Quaker's bindery. Lover of Genevieve Quaker and Myfanwy Morris. As Terpsichore, he was one of the nine Apollonian elder muses in the first era of Chancelhouse. Also adopted the name Martin Forjacks as a brief and unsuccessful disguise.

Romanoff, Susan. Veil muse, callsong Season. Close friend of Scan. May have been a decrypt muse. Killed in the Chancelhouse-Veil purges.

Rook. Chancelhouse doolittle-caster muse. Several times champion of the Chancelhouse Annual Murder Game.

Rune. Veil muse. Killed in the Chancelhouse-Veil purges.

Scan. Veil blazon muse. Scan was Paddy's main point of contact within Veil. Killed in the Chancelhouse-Veil purges.

Sean. Friend of Kitty Esterhase.

Sequin. Chancelhouse muse. Killed in the Chancelhouse-Veil purges.

Session. Veil skiller muse. Wounded by Jasper Robin during the raid on Veil HQ.

Seuss. See Quaker, Haduken.

Sid. See Fairfax, Sid.

Simon. See Buckerton, Simon.

Snow. Veil muse. Whereabouts unknown, perhaps killed in the Chancelhouse-Veil purges.

Souphanouvong, Umberto. Taker muse. Chancelhouse callsong Urania. Friend of Blake before the founding of Chancelhouse. One of the nine Apollonian elder muses in the first era of Chancelhouse. Together with Calliope, he founded Veil, adopting the callsong Undine.

Squab. Veil muse. Killed in the Chancelhouse-Veil purges.

Stacy. See Lake, Stacy.

Static. Chancelhouse caster muse. Close friend of Paddy.

Struct. Chancelhouse muse. Killed in the Chancelhouse-Veil purges.

Surd. Veil muse.

Surfeit. Veil muse. Whereabouts unknown, perhaps killed in the Chancelhouse-Veil purges.

Susan. See Romanoff, Susan.

Swat. Veil muse. A close friend of Scan. Killed in the Chancelhouse-Veil purges.

Sylph. Chancelhouse caster muse.

Tallulah. See Gordon, Tallulah.

Tamara. See Drago-Ferrante, Tamara.

Tar. Chancelhouse callsong Euterpe. Tar is a shortening and corruption of Euterpe. She was a friend of Blake before the founding of Chancelhouse. In the first era of Chancelhouse, as Euterpe, she was one of the nine Apollonian elder muses.

Following the Chancelhouse-Veil split, she was less centrally involved in Chancelhouse affairs than Blake, Aoide, and Meletē, and gradually became regarded as only an honorary elder. Co-convener, with Blake, of the Chancelhouse Annual Murder Game.

Tase. Chancelhouse haverer muse.

Tax. Veil muse. Killed in the Chancelhouse-Veil purges.

Tea. Veil muse.

Te-No-Me. Veil muse. Close friend of Scan. Killed in the Chancelhouse-Veil purges.

Thomas, Kevin. Pupil at St Jerome's Senior School.

Thorn. Chancelhouse driver muse.

Tiffin. A dog.

Toal. Friend of Kitty Esterhase.

Triceratops. AKA Trice. Chancelhouse cutter muse. In pre-Chancelhouse days he worked in Blake's bindery.

Triffid. See Jamie.

Turturle. Chancelhouse muse. Killed in the Chancelhouse-Veil purges.

Umberto. See Souphanouvong, Umberto.

Undine. See Souphanouvong, Umberto.

Vaguerat. Veil muse. Killed in the Chancelhouse-Veil purges.

Veitch. Police officer. Constable at the time of the Bridge Croft eviction, risen to Inspector when encountered by Myfanwy. Veitch testified in the trial of Sergeant Corina Fletcher. Despite absorbing Genevieve's eye-witness memory of the event, Veitch refused to implicate Sergeant Fletcher in Molly Miller's death.

Yuri. Shrouder muse, posing as a taker muse as per Blake's instruction. Chancelhouse callsong Marinade. Veil callsong Cracks. Secret Personal Assistant to Haduken Blake. His body was inhabited by Blake during the raid on Veil HQ. It is likely that Yuri died moments later along with Blake's body, although Blake, while making his getaway from the spinny, did admit to feeling somewhat haunted.

Zeus. See Quaker, Haduken.

29903017R00257

Made in the USA
Charleston, SC
28 May 2014